THE DAY

CW01460605

JAMES RAMSEY ULLMAN was born in
tion from Princeton in 1929, he worked as a reporter for a Brooklyn news
paper and then turned to the theater, first as a playwright, and from 1933
to 1939 as producer or co-producer of a dozen Broadway plays. Beginning
in 1939, aside from a stint with the American Field Service in Africa during
World War II, Ullman was "a full-time writer—and roughly half-time
traveler."

Two trips to the Amazon jungle resulted in the writing and publication
of *The Other Side of the Mountain* (1938), and the later novel, *River of the Sun*
(1951), a Book-of-the-Month Club choice. *Windom's Way*, a Literary Guild
selection in 1952, is the story of an American doctor in Southeast Asia, and
The Sands of Karakorum (1953) tells of a missionary's disappearance in the
interior of Communist China. Four of Ullman's books were adapted as
major motion pictures.

Travel, and particularly mountaineering, provided the physical background and spiritual core of most of Ullman's books. He climbed in the
Rockies, the Andes, the Alps, the Himalayas, and in Africa, where he
reached the top of Kilimanjaro. Two of his novels, *The White Tower* (1945)
and *Banner in the Sky* (1954), a novel for young readers, are set in the Alps,
and *Tiger of the Snows* (1955) took him to India and Nepal to work with
Tenzing Norgay, the Sherpa who, with Sir Edmund Hillary, made the first
ascent of Mount Everest.

In 1957, Ullman traveled in Europe and Africa, retracing the steps of
Arthur Rimbaud and gathering material for his great biographical novel,
The Day on Fire (1958), which took him eighteen months to write.

Ullman died in 1971.

JAMES RAMSEY ULLMAN

THE DAY ON FIRE

A NOVEL SUGGESTED BY THE LIFE OF

ARTHUR RIMBAUD

VALANCOURT BOOKS

FOREWORD

Jean-Nicolas-Arthur Rimbaud was born in 1854 in Charleville, in the Ardennes country of northern France, and died in 1891 in Marseilles. For the first fifteen years of his life he was child and schoolboy in his native provincial town. For the next four—and four only—he was, simultaneously, a poet of genius, a visionary idealist, and a deliberate wallower in the gutters of depravity perhaps unmatched in all human experience. For the next six, now through forever with both writing and debauch, he was a vagabond wanderer through Europe and Asia. And for the last twelve, until a few months preceding his death, he was a trader, explorer, gunrunner (and also, probably, slaver), along the Red Sea coasts and in the section of northeast Africa known then as Abyssinia and today as Ethiopia.

As stated on the title page, this story has been *suggested* by his life. In broad outline it follows the known pattern of Rimbaud's career, but in most of its details it is fictional, and I have therefore given fictional names to all characters, with the exception of a few historical personages—of whom the only one to play an important role is the Emperor Menelik of Abyssinia. Some, in conception and presentation, are very close to their real-life counterparts: e.g., Claude Morel to Arthur Rimbaud himself, the Widow Morel to Rimbaud's mother, Maurice Druard to Paul Verlaine. Others, including most of the secondary characters, derive more indirectly from actual persons. And a few are wholly invented. Most important among these last is Germaine Lautier, whom I have used to personify "the girl with the violet eyes," whom Rimbaud knew in his dreams, forever sought, and never found.

So, too, do the scenes, incidents, and situations of my story range from the largely factual to the entirely imagined: the factual predominating in the earlier part, for which Rimbaud's life is well documented—though even here there is much rearrangement of time, place, and event—and the imagined in the later part, when he had all but vanished from the Western world. As for Claude Morel's writings, they are in part actually Rimbaud's in translation (for which I make grateful acknowledgment to Louise Varese and J. Norman Cameron), and in part my own paraphrase. And Morel's thoughts, conversations, and correspondence are a composite of the factual and fictional—but with the imagined here, again, predominating. Indeed, the blend exists in almost every page and paragraph of the book.

Arthur Rimbaud existed. Claude Morel did not. In my own mind, however, now that my story is written, I can scarcely tell where the one ends and the other begins. And my hope is that this does not matter and is as it should be; that though I have fictionized I have not falsified; that though I have manipulated outward fact to my purpose I have held tight to inward truth.

For the truth, the inward core, of Rimbaud's life is not something to be held lightly, but a thing as bright and precious as, in another way, it is appalling . . . a truth, I believe, that holds meaning and value for our time no less than for his own . . . indeed, for all times, as long as men are men; as long as the rest of us, too, each of us, all of us—if in less spectacular degree—have our nights alone and our days on fire, our seasons in hell and our hope of heaven.

J. R. U.

New York
February 1958

AND A NOTE

An ugly word is used in this book: the word *nigger*. And it is used only after much reflection and substitute-seeking, in the conviction that, for the purpose required, it is the only right word. Rimbaud, in his writings and conversations, used the French word *nègre*, which today is usually translated—and properly so—as *Negro*. But it must be remembered that he used it at a time, almost a century ago, when the Western world's concept of a black man was very different from what it is today. And the word *Negro* has a formality and propriety to it which seem to me to vitiate completely the symbolic strength and intensity of Rimbaud's meaning.

So I have used the ugly word: not as a man among my fellow men, but as a writer trying to render a true meaning in its proper time and context. To say that I intend no offense is too mild a statement. Let me say, rather, that I hope with all my heart that no offense is taken.

My eternal soul,   Mon âme éternelle,
Redeem your promise,   Observe ton voeu,
In spite of the night alone   Malgré la nuit seule
And the day on fire.   Et le jour en feu.

Rimbaud

PART I
THE POSSESSED

"I had been damned by the rainbow."

I

Today they were all wearing blue serge suits.

Usually it was only Claude. Day after day, year after year, it had been only Claude; the others in old smocks, vests, work shirts, whatever they laid their hands on when they got up in the morning; he alone in serge and starched collar, black stockings and black shoes. *"Le beau gosse,"* they had once called him. "Pretty boy. Mama's darling." But that was before they had learned that his small fists could hit and his shined shoes could kick. Or that his help with homework made the difference between honors and failure.

And now, today, they were all mamas' darlings. All in serge and starch, with scrubbed faces and slicked hair. Even Pierre Berthoud, who loomed over the tallest teacher and was sprouting whiskers; even Henri Clauson, who, rumor had it, bathed only in cow dung and assembled his clothes from the town dump. In the rear of the room were the mamas themselves, with a scattering of fathers and brothers, sisters and aunts. The females looked proud. The males looked bored. All looked hot. The only one who would not have looked hot was the mama of the original mama's darling, who had no time for such trivia as physical discomforts. But the Widow Morel had also not had the time to be there.

It was the final day of the term—prize day—for the next-to-last form of the Lycée de Cambon. Monsieur Izard, the headmaster, and Monsieur Chariol, the class teacher, were on the platform, and the headmaster was speaking. He had, indeed, been speaking for some twenty minutes, and for each of them the temperature had seemed to increase by one degree centigrade. Sweat trickled into the starched collars. Eyes glazed. When at last the speech ended the applause was limp and damp.

"And now—" Monsieur Izard nodded to Monsieur Chariol, and Monsieur Chariol took from a table a pile of silvered paper wreaths. "Now," said the headmaster, "it is time to make the term awards for achievement." He produced a slip of paper and adjusted his pince-nez. "For excellence in mathematics"—a brief pause for effect—"Louis Carnot."

A boy rose, went to the platform, and received a handshake and wreath. In the rear, a few pairs of hands applauded, less limply.

"For excellence in theoretical and applied science—Georges Vuiton."

The procedure was repeated.

Monsieur Izard put away the slip of paper. There were five wreaths left. "For excellence in French literature," he announced, "—for excellence in English, excellence in Latin, excellence in Greek, excellence in medieval and modern history—" He smiled. "As time goes by, this has become rather a habit. . . . It is my pleasure to award these classic laurels to Claude Morel."

Claude rose and went forward. At fifteen, he was the youngest in the class. And the smallest. Most of the others, in their middle and late teens, were already far along in adolescence; big-boned, raw, and awkward; half boys and half men. But there was no man in Claude yet. There seemed less boy than child. His face was soft, oval, fine-featured; his hair light and silken; and his eyes were wide and unshadowed, the whites very white, the blue very blue. A most immature fifteen, one would have judged—until he moved—and then, strangely, the impression changed. For his bearing was wholly composed. His movements were poised and sure. As he passed between his classmates, mounted the platform and stood before them, it was suddenly he who seemed the adult, and they the children.

Monsieur Izard shook his hand and put a wreath on his head. "Ho, ho, there are so many they would not all balance," he said, chuckling. Then, addressing the room; "We shall now hear the class oration from our honor student."

Claude faced the room. He bowed gravely. He began to speak: "*Salvete, O magistri honorati, hospites augusti, amici lectissimi. Insigne honoris mihi datis quod permittitis est ego in vestram praesentiam hoc die felici veniam. Pro vestro summo beneficio, gratus sum . . .*"

He stood erect but at ease. His face, under the leaves, was blandly calm, and the Latin flowed from his lips as if it had been his daily language. Looking down at his audience, in their sweat and boredom, his eyes glinted with mockery.

The boys shuffled out. Monsieur Izard greeted parents. Monsieur Chariol, the class teacher, put a hand on Claude's shoulder. "My little monster of erudition," he said affectionately.

Monsieur Chariol was young—a mere twenty-four—with a slender figure and dark sensitive face. And he was not greatly given to smiling. Indeed, after three years in this backwater school, he had often thought grimly, he would probably have ceased altogether—had it not been for this one pupil fate had granted him. For Claude Morel was that rare and precious bird of which all teachers dream but seldom encounter: the true student: the one among the hundreds who almost compensated for the drudgery, the frustration, the gawking cretins, the starvation salary, the loneliness and hopelessness of a profession that led to nowhere on a grinding treadmill. Try to give to the others, and they took nothing. They yawned. They dozed. But give to this one, and he took it all; took it and gave it back, brighter, fresher, fuller than it had been before. Albert

Chariol pressed his fingers into Claude's shoulder. "I am proud of you, boy," he said.

"Thank you, *mon maître*."

"You have made it a happy year for me."

Claude looked up at him, and there was no longer mockery in his eyes. "And you have made it happy for me," he answered.

Outside there was a confusion of boys, families, hellos, goodbyes. Henri Clauson ripped off his jacket with a whoop. Two others pounded each other in a delirium of liberation.

"*S'il vous plaît! S'il vous plaît!*" shrilled Monsieur Izard.

Michel Favre came up to Claude. He too was a small boy, but broad and sturdy, with a freckled stub of a nose and black imp's eyes, and he was Claude's closest friend in the class, if he could be said to have had one.

"No mother?" he asked.

Claude shook his head. "She wouldn't leave the store."

"Mine's not here either. Let's go."

"Go where?"

"Anywhere. But away from here—fast."

Then the crowd and the school were gone. They walked down the dusty summer street, kicking stones.

"Where are your wreaths?" Michel asked.

"I found a wastebasket."

"Won't your mother want to see them?"

"She'd just say, 'Why isn't the silver real?' "

Michel picked up a stone and threw it at a tree. "The hell with wreaths," he said. "The hell with school and the hell with mothers. It's vacation. Let's celebrate!"

"How?"

"Let's—let's—" Michel thought it over. "I've got it: girls!"

"What do you mean, girls?"

"We get two—for tonight." Michel became excited. "Yes, look, listen —There's one of those traveling carnivals playing now over in Antimes. It's just an hour's walk, so after supper we get the girls and—"

"What girls?" said Claude.

"Louise Croz for me. Mimi Rouger for you. They'll come: I know they will. Their parents let them do anything. . . . Look, Louise lives right near here. Let's go now and talk to her, and she'll talk to Mimi, and we'll meet them out on the road about seven, and. . . . What's the matter, you don't want to?"

"I—I don't know them."

"Sure you know them. You've seen them all over town. Just last week out in the park, when Jacques Brun and I were with them—remember? —and then you came by and—"

"—said hello."

"All right: they said hello back, didn't they? They smiled."

"But—"

"And when you'd gone do you know what they said? Louise said, 'What's the matter with that one? He's scared of girls.' And Mimi said, 'Yes; he's cute, though.'"

"Cute," said Claude.

"That's the way girls talk. She likes you."

"How can she like me if she doesn't know me?"

"Well then, she'd like to like you. Give her a chance.... Look, I'm telling you: these aren't the prissy kind, with their mamas all over them. They're live ones, wild ones, wait and see. We'll go to the carnival. There're all sorts of games and rides, and we can have fun with them there, and then later on the way home—"

"I can't go to the carnival," Claude said. "I've no money."

"Nothing?"

"When did I ever?"

"All right—I've got four francs still from my birthday, and that's enough for us both." Michel paused and waited. "Well?" he asked.

Claude shook his head.

"You won't?"

"I can't."

"What do you mean, you can't?"

"I just—can't."

"You mean you're afraid. Louise was right. You're afraid."

Claude said nothing.

"You want to be a baby all your life, is that it? My God, you're fifteen —nearer sixteen. You're supposed to be a *man* when you're sixteen, and you're scared of two silly brats." Michel got angry. His black eyes snapped. "You're scared as a puppydog. All right, be a puppydog. You're the one with your mama all over you. Mama's darling. *Le beau gosse.* Pfui!"

"I just can't go," Claude said quietly. "I've other plans."

"Plans? To do your homework for September? To stick your snoot in a book?... Aaah!" Michel kicked a stone hard. "Go on then. I'll get Jacques or Georges or someone that's not a puppydog. Pfui! Go home to mama. The hell with you!"

They had come to a corner and he veered suddenly off. Claude did not try to stop him, but walked on alone, slowly, along the dusty street. School and crowd were out of sight behind; only a few passers-by and idlers were about, and the houses were all shuttered against the summer heat. A distant cock crowed; a dog barked; an old woman hobbled by, prodding a pig with a stick. When she was gone, the only sound was the scrape of his own shoes on the cobbles. He passed the church, whitewashed and still; then a row of houses with cracked plaster fronts. He knew every line of every crack, as if they had been weathered into his own brain. The one that looked like a river. The one that looked like a railway track. The one that looked like the coast of Brittany. . . .

Oh God, thought Claude. Cambon.

He walked on. There was no sound. Nothing moved. The town was fixed in torpor, in stasis, devoid of breath, blood, bone, life itself. It was a town of the desert, parched and crumbled; a town of the sea bottom, lost and drowned. The boy's eyes went down to the dust on the cobbles. They went up to the dust on the leaves of the plane trees. The leaves were brittle and silvered, like the paper leaves of his laurel wreaths. They gave no shade, no coolness. They simply hung there. Beyond them the sky glared, empty and inane.

Claude sat in the dust against a blank wall.

"You're afraid," Michel had said. And it had been the truth. He was afraid. Whether with no francs to his name—or with ten or ten thousand —he was still afraid. Of Louise Croz, of Mimi Rouger; of all girls; of their faces, their smiles, their giggles, their clothes. Of their bodies beneath the clothes. . . .

"I've other plans," he had answered. And this too was the truth. Now at last he knew it was the truth, and of this he was not afraid.

Other boys carried francs in their pocket. They carried knives, keys, matches, girls' brooches and lockets. . . . He carried a pencil. . . . Now from his pocket he took his pencil and the folded paper on which was written his class oration, and on the blank side of the paper he wrote:

> *I shall not speak, I shall not show my heart,*
> *but still, within that heart, a fire will burn.*
> *Far, far I'll go, alone, a wanderer,*
> *and life, the wide earth itself, will be my love.*

The Widow Morel sold dry goods and notions. Her store was not the biggest in Cambon, but it was not the smallest either, and in recent years it had prospered. Madame, however, was not prodigal with her francs. Though she could long since have afforded to move herself and her children to better living quarters, she had chosen to remain in the cramped quarters above the shop; and though her trade was enough to have warranted at least one paid clerk, she refused even to consider such extravagance. Claude helped out after school hours. So did his sister Yvette, but she was four years younger and could manage only simple transactions. The one full-time assistant was his brother Felix, now seventeen; and though "simple transactions" were his maximum, too, he at least possessed the virtue, in his mother's eyes, of costing her only bed and board. Starting school two years ahead of Claude, he had dropped back until for a while they had been in the same form, and then still farther back, and finally out. He had long since done his adolescent sprouting and was tall, big-boned, powerful, with thick dark hair and heavy features; and his mind was heavy too—slow, dull-edged, covered over (in Claude's metaphor) with whatever dust missed the Cambon streets. He seemed admirably designed (also Claude's appraisal) for a truckman or a railway porter, but his heft was at no premium in a dry-goods store, and he was no more a salesman than an astronomer. Wrapped in lethargy, he was barely able to emerge sufficiently, on occasion, to add up the cost of a button-hook, three clothes hangers, and a darning egg.

Felix was behind the counter when Claude came in. There were no customers in the shop, but they ignored each other.

Then Madame Morel came quickly down the stairs. "Ha, so it's you at last," she said. "What's taken you so long? School was to be out at three."

"There was—"

"And what have you been doing to yourself?" His mother came closer. "Your clothes are filthy. Look, those trousers—like you'd been rolling in the street." She slapped dust from his blue serge with a bony hand. "And your shoes. You've been kicking stones again, haven't you? I sweat and slave in this store—ten, twelve, fourteen hours a day. I work myself to the grave to dress you decently, educate you, make you into a gentleman, and what are you instead? A pig. *Un sale cochon!*"

It was not only her hands that were bony. Her face was, too, and her body, under her long black dress. Often that was all Claude saw in the face —the bones beneath the taut white flesh; or at least until she got angry (which was often) and then he saw the eyes too, black and harsh. They were harsh now, as she stared at him, and her voice was shrill.

"Do you hear me? *Cochon!*"

Claude said nothing. His face showed nothing. It was neither cowed nor defiant. It was blank.

Madame Morel turned abruptly away. She was a woman given, conversationally, to either torrents or silence, and now came a silence, as she rearranged merchandise on one of the shelves. Felix yawned and kept carefully out of her way. Then Yvette came down the stairs, saw Claude, and ran to him.

"Hello, princess," he said, and smiled. For this was the one girl he was not afraid of.

"More!" she demanded. "More names."

"Hello, Cinderella, Rapunzel, Red Ridinghood, Goldilocks."

Unlike Felix, she bore him a strong family resemblance. (By way of their father, he had surmised, though he could scarcely remember what their father looked like.) She had the same lightness of hair, of complexion, of body and feature; the same blue-white eyes—though softer, gentler; and now those eyes looked at him with adoration.

"How many wreaths did you win?" she asked.

"Five," he said.

"Ooh—let me see them."

"I—I left them at school."

"Five?" The mother had turned back to him. "Why only five? There are seven subjects. Why not all of them?"

Claude shrugged.

"Which did you not get?"

"Mathematics and science."

"So—mathematics and science. The two subjects out of all of them that are of some practical use. In those you do nothing: no work, no results. It's with the others, the useless ones, you spend all your days and half the nights. Trashy novels, verses, Latin, Greek. Maybe one day we will have a Greek in Cambon and you can make him a sale of some spools and buttons."

A customer entered the shop and she gave him her attention. Claude waited.

"What are you standing around for?" she snapped, when the man had left. "I told you this morning there's new stock to be checked and sorted."

"I want to speak to you, Mother," he said quietly.

"Speak to me? What about?"

"About money. I would like some money."

She simply stared at him.

"I would like ten francs," he said.

"*Ten francs?* Are you out of your head?"

"Most of the boys get a franc a week. I haven't had anything all spring. I've done well in my work and won five wreaths, and I think I'm entitled to two francs for each of them."

"Entitled? You mean you should be paid for going to school? For learning how to talk to Greeks? For running around in the street, moping in your room, reading crazy books, while I work ten, twelve, fourteen hours—" She broke off, fixing him with her sharp eyes. "What *is* this?" she demanded. "This new craziness? Ten francs. And what will a child like you do with ten francs?"

"I'm not a child. I'm fifteen; nearer sixteen. And now school is over—"

"So now school is over, and what? You want to buy yourself some nonsense maybe? Or to go hang around a café?. . . I know. It's that carnival at Antimes. With its games and dances and godless goings-on. You want to sneak over there with some of your hoodlum friends."

"No," said Claude, "I'm not going to the carnival. I've been asked, but I'm not going."

"Oh? So then where is it? What is it?"

"I have other plans."

"What plans?"

"I cannot tell you."

There was a silence. Yvette looked, almost in terror, from her brother to her mother, and Felix gawked unbelievingly. Not even Claude had ever before defied their mother so openly.

Madame Morel found no words.

"You will not, Mother?" said Claude.

"Give you ten francs? You are mad, raving."

There was a certain change in the boy's eyes: a slight widening, a slight hardening. But his voice remained quiet. "Then I am sorry—" he said. "And perhaps you will be sorry."

"Sorry? Are you threatening me, boy?"

"No, not threatening, Mother. Just telling you—"

"I've had enough of this insolence. There's the new stock. Get to work on it."

Claude stood still for a moment. Then he moved—but it was toward the door.

"Where are you going?" his mother shouted.

But he didn't answer. He went out. Circling the counter, she started after him, but as she reached the door a woman customer came in. "I hear you have received a new shipment of cretonne yard goods," the woman said. "May I see what you have, please?"

The Widow Morel breathed in once, deeply. "But of course, madame," she answered. "And I am sure you will find the prices most reasonable."

Claude walked through the streets of Cambon. He went down the Rue de Lille, across the Place du Sépulcre, into the Rue Gauchet. This was the center of town, the district of shops, offices, inns, cafés, and there were more people than on his route from school to home. Some of them knew and greeted him, and he said hello in return; but he did not stop, he kept walking steadily, until he reached the Place de la Gare. He was conscious of his heart's beating, but it was not the bad sort of beating. Not quick and jumpy, but slow, even, strong.

"No," he thought, "I am not afraid."

Crossing the square, he entered the station and went to the ticket window. "When is the next train for Paris?" he asked.

"At five thirty," the clerk said. *"Deuxième ou troisième?"*

"Neither, thank you. I'm finding out for a friend."

There was about a half-hour to wait, and a public place was no good. Finding the W.C., he went in and locked the door, and though at intervals there were knocks and handle-turnings, he paid no attention. He was still wearing his blue serge, black shoes, and starched collar. There was nothing he could do about suit and shoes, but he took off the collar and dropped it on the floor. He waited. Having no watch, he waited for what seemed like hours. Then he heard the train and, moving quickly, left the W.C. and went to the far end of the station platform. The train was already coming in, and when it stopped he was beside the last coach. The *chef de gare* was at the center of the platform, a safe distance away, and there was no ticket taker in sight. He looked around once, briefly, and climbed aboard. A whistle screeched, the train shuddered, the wheels turned.

2

Other boys had francs, knives, girl's brooches and lockets. He had a pencil. And the pencil wrote:

> *. . . and so the mother, holding the Book of Law,*
> *stands proud and righteous, proud and tall and blind,*
> *blind to the other eyes—her child's—proud, too,*
> *and blue and cold;*
> *cold with a fire she cannot know, she cannot dream. . . .*

The pencil moved on. The train rolled on. The woman beside him was asleep.

He had not made his boarding haphazardly. The last coach, he knew, was composed of second-class compartments (in which—he had guessed correctly—no other Cambonards would be riding); and once in, he had selected a seat beside an elderly well-dressed lady. Thus placed, he hoped, he might be taken for her traveling companion, or at least appear solidly respectable during the journey. And for journey's end, and the collection of tickets in the Gare de l'Est, he had already made his plans.

The lady and a few of the other passengers had glanced at him briefly as he came in. But now they ignored him, taking his presence for granted, and soon most of them had closed their eyes and were nodding in sleep. Taking out pencil and paper, he had begun writing. And when, now and then, he paused, he looked out the window.

Beyond the sooty glass the countryside of northern France flowed by. First the dark green forests, the Ardennes, the world surrounding Cambon that he knew so well. Then fields with only groves of trees, fields without trees at all, open, light green, with bands of yellow and amber, spreading soft and gleaming in the late afternoon sun. . . . Color! He could not merely see color, but feel, smell, taste, almost hear it; he could drink it, as others drank wine. . . . What color would Paris be, he wondered? Not green, surely—except in its parks. Not the amber and yellow of grain. It would be gray, of course, the gray of stone, but within the ancient stone there would be the glow of pink, of lavender. At night it would be black, but of a blackness pricked by a million fireflies.

He was writing again.

Fragments. Words. Words that leaped and gleamed in his mind like the gleam of the sun:

. . . *tumult of cities, in the evening, and in the sun, and always.*

. . . *official acropolis, apotheosis of modern barbarity. Opaque light from immutably gray skies and the glitter of imperial buildings.*

. . . *and, from the indigo straits to Ossian's seas, on pink and orange sands washed by the vinous sky, crystal boulevards arise and cross, inhabited by poor young families who get their food at the greengrocers.*

. . . *a white ray falling from the sky destroys this comedy.*

Then he too must have slept; for when he looked up again the train was slowing, the light was fading, and beyond the window the flat twin towers of a cathedral stood up against the summer dusk. The train pulled into Reims. He had been in Reims before. Once, long ago, his mother had brought him here to visit an aunt, and it was the farthest from home he had ever been. When the train stopped, more people got in. Outside, a man was saying, *"Vos billets, s'il vous plaît."* But he did not come in. The train began moving again, and now Claude was farther from home than ever before. In terra incognita.

Again he felt the beating of his heart.

The window was sooty. As the leaves of Cambon were dusty. Both filtered the light, but they could not shut it out, and now the sky beyond was wide and deep. The sky arched over the land, over forests and fields, over towns and cities, over Reims, over Paris. It arched beyond Paris over more land, over all land, over the sea. He had never seen the sea, but he knew it well. The sea of the north, of the longboats, the Vikings: gray, sullen, surging, under its pall of cloud. And the sea of the south, of the triremes, the galleons: blue, pure and glittering in golden sunlight. He knew the lands beyond. The walls of Rome, the pillars of Greece, the twilight of Carthage, the white dazzle of Arabia. He knew Persia, Peru, India, Africa. Best of all, Africa. The Africa of rivers and forests, of jet idols, silken jungles, verdigris moss, and hidden jewels.

It was like drunkenness to think of. There were no words for his images. He would have to invent new ones, stretch the dry withered skin of language until it could hold the flesh and blood of life—and the white breath of vision. For was that not what vision was: a whiteness? The whiteness that encompassed all else; all color, all sound, all sense, all waking, all dream; that was the infinite and ultimate, the oneness beyond the multiple.... *Life, like a dome of many-colored glass*. That was an Englishman: Shelley.... Life, like a rainbow. With white radiance at its core.

Wheels clicked. The land flowed. Then he slept again and dreamed —or dreamed without sleeping—and when he opened his eyes the land was gone and in the window was only the reflection of lighted lamps. Presently he was aware that something else was different. The train was slowing. Some of the passengers rose, reaching for hats and bags, and the old lady beside him opened her pocketbook and took out her ticket.

"*C'est bien Paris?*" he asked.

"*Oui.*" She nodded. "*C'est Paris.*"

In a few minutes they would be in the Gare de l'Est. There would be a man in uniform. And the man would say, "*Vos billets, s'il vous plaît.*"

Claude rose too. He moved to the compartment door. He grasped the handle. But he did not turn it at once, standing, instead, with his face pressed against the window, and beyond it, now, he could see the lights of the city. The train was moving at half speed between low stone walls.

Then he turned the handle, and the door was open. Someone spoke sharply behind him, but he paid no attention. Outside, on one side of the door, was an iron bar, and he reached for it, held it, swung himself out and forward. Then he jumped. He landed. Gravel and cinders jerked away beneath his feet, and rose and hit him in the chest. Then he was sliding, and they were grating into his face. His knee struck something hard, and he felt a sharp pain. When he looked up the train was gone.

The city roared. The city blazed. They were not fireflies that lit the night, but great gas lamps like yellow moons, by the thousand, the ten thousand, burning on the streets, the boulevards, the squares, the towers, the rooftops. Here was the City of Light. And of Life. A city of the past: of the Valois, the Bourbons, two republics, and two empires. A city of the present: of power, politics, science, art, literature. Here, in the full of the year 1870, was the end result of all the centuries of history, the distillation of man's culture, of what he had achieved in his long climb from savagery. Here was the heart of France, and of civilization.

In the Palace of the Tuileries, in a hall of crystal and gold, stood the emperor, the third Napoleon. Greeting his court at that evening's reception, he was tall, medaled, imperial; but the stones in his bladder were hurting him, and in his thoughts was the even more rankling hurt of the insolent note he had received that day from the Prussian Bismarck. Radiant at his side, his empress suffered no such inner discomforts. Her husband had showed her the note, but what of it? Were they not Bona-partes and Catholics, born to rule and conquer, supported by the Pope, the Holy Church, and the armies of France? The sooner war came, the better, Eugénie had assured the emperor. The barbarous upstarts in Berlin would be shown their place once and for all, and France's Second Empire would shine as brightly as the First.

In an office in the Palais Bourbon, nearby, a minister of the government (currently not high in favor) paced the floor restlessly while three subordi-nates watched him. "Church, aristocracy, landowners!" he snapped. "Why not bring back the Bourbons and have done with it? It is as if there had never been a revolution."

In a white-walled cubicle in an old building of the university a chemist named Louis Pasteur sat alone, perched on a stool, peering at the contents of a tube suspended in the blue flame of a Bunsen burner. He had assured his wife that this one evening he would be home promptly for dinner, but he was unaware that it was any later than midafternoon.

In another obscure room, crowded and disheveled, on the Butte de Montmartre, a painter named Pierre Renoir stood brush in hand, scowling at a canvas in the wavering light of an oil lamp. He made a stroke, stepped back and swore; made another stroke, stepped back, swore louder. Then he threw the brush into a corner and went down to the corner café, where he would find Manet, Monet, Pissarro, and the rest, and tell them his troubles.

In another café, not far distant, two other men named Leconte de Lisle and Sully Prudhomme were deep in argument about the verse of the late Charles Baudelaire. "You are wrong, all wrong, he was the greatest!" declared Leconte de Lisle warmly. "Look—there's Zola going by. Call him over. Ask him what *he* thinks." . . . "Zola?" Sully Prudhomme snorted. "*Mon Dieu*, what does Emile know about poetry?—And besides, he won't drink."

In a hundred other cafés, from Montmartre to Passy, sat the manufac-turers and businessmen and salesmen of the city, postponing, like Pasteur (though for other reasons) the return to hearth and spouse. They talked of the day's fluctuations on the Bourse, the races at Longchamps, the rising price of wine and cigars. They watched the *grisettes* go by.

In a thousand more (but here there were no tables, no waiters; only a zinc bar and standing room) stood the small tradesmen and laborers, the butchers, bakers, masons, carpenters, factory hands. They talked of the rising price of shoes and cabbage, of the threatened strike at the Schneider ironworks, of the variegated bosoms and rumps of the passing whores. Voices rose: "War will come." "It will not come." . . . "We will fight." "We will not fight." . . . "We will sing the *Marseillaise* again." "Maybe. But sitting down."

City of light, of sound, of voices. Capital of the world. . . . And through the city, now, a boy walking; a small-town boy, a yokel, a country *mioche*, who seemed, alone among the millions, not to be talking, because there was no one for him to talk to.

Indeed, at first there had been no one even in sight. He had come up off the railway tracks into a district of factories and warehouses; instead of light and sound there were darkness and stillness, and he groped along blank walls, through black alleys. He was still shaken from his grinding plunge from the train, and his right leg throbbed painfully. Coming at last to a street lamp, he stopped and looked down, and saw that the blue serge of his trouser leg was dangling in tatters. He smiled. That was all right. But the knee under the tatters was bloody, and that was not so good. Opening his jacket, he pulled out his shirttail, ripped off a piece, and made a bandage. Then he went on. He went slowly, gropingly, but not aimlessly. For he was not lost; he knew where he was heading. He might be a *mioche*, a bumpkin from the provinces, but for years he had read of Paris—in the books of Balzac, Hugo, Dumas, a hundred others—and he was sure he knew it better than most of the millions who had lived their lives there.

This, too, made him smile.

And then presently, surely enough, the city began to change. The darkness thinned and receded; the streets grew wider, the gas lamps more frequent. Where there had been blank walls there were now lighted windows. There were shops, stalls, kiosks, bars, cafés, restaurants. There were light and sound—and people. Everywhere, people. Always more and more people. Then ahead there was still another corner—the twentieth he had come to, or the fortieth—and he knew as he approached it that it would be different from all the others. He turned it, and it was. For now he was on the Grands Boulevards. The lights, streaming away before him, were like the torches of an emperor's triumph. And under the torches moved the multitudes. Curb to curb, marched the fiacres and landaus in vast jumbled procession; curb to house front, flowed two rivers of walkers. Above them, lights, awnings, chestnut trees; beside them, more lights, shopwindows, the serried tables of cafés; within them, the faces, figures, clothing, and color of cosmopolis. Claude plunged into the stream, flowed with it, merged with it. Paris took him, enveloped him.

How long he moved down the enchanted way he could not have said; for he moved in a dream. He forgot his scrapes and tatters. He forgot the pain in his knee. He forgot everything. The old Claude Morel, the boy in blue serge, the *mioche* from Cambon, was gone and lost, and he was without identity, without memory, without past; a being newly created, whose only functions were to walk, to watch, to listen, to feel. And to walk on. There were the boulevards: the Bonne Nouvelle, the Poissonnière, the Italiens, the Capucines. There was the Opéra, like a temple of Jupiter, and

beyond it, blazing, the Grand Hôtel. There was the Rue de la Paix, the
Place Vendôme, the Tuileries, the Rue de Rivoli, the Place de la Concorde,
the Rue Royale, the Madeleine . . . and again the boulevards, on and on,
through the magic night.

And it was not until much later, long hours later, that he realized the
night had changed. It was still magical, but the magic was different. For
the crowds were thinning, dissolving, the light and sound withdrawing,
and now at last a hush was falling on the city, until even Paris itself, the light
of the world, was quiet and dark. True, there were still lights behind walls,
lights underground and high under the rooftops, glinting on undimmed
in a thousand bins and boxes in the night. But these were not the lights
for the multitude, nor for a stranger walking the streets. The streets were
now in silence and stone shadow. The corners had moved farther apart,
and above them the gas lamps burned like lonely flares. A single fiacre
rolled by with a hollow clopping of hoofs. Two gendarmes, in capes and
tricorn hats, came down the pavement, glanced speculatively at Claude,
and moved on.

He moved on too. It was time to sleep. Even for him to sleep. And,
again, he knew where he was going, for a hundred stories of Paris had
not left him ignorant of its traditional dormitory for the homeless and
moneyless. Once more he came to the Rue Royale; to the Concorde, vast
and empty. And beyond it was the Seine. He heard the lapping of water,
saw the outline of a bridge. Detouring, he clambered down a bank to the
underside of the bridge, where it met the shore, and crept beneath its
sheltering arch. In the gloom he could see dim figures sprawled around
him, and he moved carefully, lest he step on one. Finding a bare space,
he lay down on the stone. A figure beside him stirred, cursed, and raised
his head, and he had a quick image of a bearded face and small bloodshot
eyes. Then the face fell away. Claude had come, he well knew, to the city's
lodging of last resort, the caravansary of tramps and beggars, thieves and
vagabonds. But he was not afraid. He belonged here. For was he not a
vagabond himself?

Again he smiled—and fell asleep.

There was gray light, hard stone, an aching knee. The bleared bearded
face was bent close to his and a hand was shaking him.

"Hey you—snotface. Get up. Get going."

Claude rose.

"The *flics* always come at six."

"The *flics?*"

"The police. If they find you they'll run you in."

The tramp turned and vanished. All the others had gone. Claude
shook himself awake and moved off too: out from under the bridge, up

the bank, back again into the streets. He was walking again ... walking
... at first slowly and painfully, because his knee was stiff and swollen,
then a little more easily, as the movement loosened it. Looking down at
himself, he saw that his trousers were not only torn but filthy. His jacket
too. His hands were grime-streaked, almost black, and he supposed his
face was the same. But it didn't matter. What mattered now was that he
was hungry, and for this he had made his plans.

A half-hour brought him to Les Halles, the city's great central food
market. Even at this hour, sunrise, the rush of the day's trade was already
over; but that was the way he wanted it, for there were no longer many
people about. Circling the long glass-and-iron walls, he searched for edibles
that might have been dropped on their way from the stalls to truck or cart.
Here and there he found something: a cabbage leaf, three beans, a lone
turnip. But the prizes were few; French tradesmen were no more prodigal
of their droppings than of their bank accounts. And when at last he did
strike a windfall—two apples and a pear that had rolled unnoticed into the
gutter—a white apron and red face loomed instantly beside him. *"Fous le
camp!* Get going!" the man yelled. The fruit moved back toward its stall,
for resale, and Claude moved on. Around the whole market: once—twice.
But the pickings were still lean. Leaving Les Halles, he walked down a side
street, and another and another, and at last came to a *boulangerie* with a dis-
play of cakes and rolls in a tray at the entrance. He had made no plan about
it. He simply lunged, snatched, ran. No one shouted, no one followed, and
after another corner or two he walked leisurely, eating his breakfast.

"Now I am not only a vagabond," he thought, "I am also a thief. . . . Do
you hear, *chère Maman?* Do you hear, all you Cambonards? Your monster
of erudition, your *beau gosse* in blue serge, is now a thief!"

He walked. He walked. The thief became a tourist. And the monster
of erudition was again in the ascendant, for almost everything he saw
found its place in his awareness beside what he had read and studied. The
ages met and mingled at every step. On the Ile de la Cité, the statue of
Charlemagne, a tall memory of the ancient days. Nearby, Notre Dame,
of medieval Paris, the Paris of Abélard, Villon, and Rabelais. There were
the Tuileries of the Bourbons, the Place Bastille of the Revolution, the
Arc and Invalides of the first Bonaparte and streets by the dozen named
for his victories. And among them all, crowding them all, was the new
Paris. The Paris of the gas lamps, the cafés, the shop fronts, the crowds,
the traffic, the billboards, the telegraph wires. The Paris of, reputedly, the
finest sewer system known to man. The Paris of *pissoirs*. . . .

He stopped and used one. "To the glories of France!" he thought. You
were supposed to drink with a toast, but this was a reasonable substitute.

He walked. *Rive Droite. Rive Gauche.* Back and forth across the bridges,
to the Etoile, to the Luxembourg, from one end of the city to another.

And in spite of his bad knee he did not grow tired, for all his life long he had walked, by the hour, the day, the tens and scores of miles, along the roads and through the forests of the Ardennes. When occasionally he stopped it was not from weariness, but to sit on a curb or against a wall and jot down the words, phrases and images that filled his mind.

> *boulevards of raised platforms—*
> *pastures of emerald and steel—*
> *elegance, science, violence—*
> *and Hôtel Splendide in the chaos of ice and the polar night—*

His black hands smudged the paper, and walking a mile, he returned to the Seine and washed them. A barge went by, moving downstream toward the distant sea. His eyes and thoughts followed it; then he wrenched them away. For now, Paris was enough. And he plunged back into Paris.

Morning passed into afternoon. Afternoon into evening. Again he filched something to eat—this time a chicken leg and roll from a table at an outdoor restaurant which the diners had left but the waiter had not yet cleared. He moved on, through the crowds, under the gas lamps. And now at last he came to his real goal—Montmartre—the goal he had been saving and treasuring all day against the coming of night. Here was the heart of the world of enchantment; the streets, the lights, the crowds, the very air and stone, all shed an aura of special excitement. He climbed the hill, the famous *Butte*, and looked out across the city; then climbed down again into the Place de Clichy. He moved past the cafés, the music halls, the cabarets, the pleasure palaces, among the tourists, the gawkers, the hawkers, the pitchmen, the pimps, the whores. He saw faces white as candle drippings that could never, in all their years, have known the sky or the sun. He saw the sharp faces of spreeing clerks, the broad red faces of spreeing countrymen, the brown faces of Arabs from Morocco and Algeria, the blue-black glistening faces of Negroes from Dahomey and Senegal. And he put them all away among his memories and his images.

But these were only incidental, only background, and not truly what he was seeking. What he was seeking were still different faces: faces with beards, with gaunt cheeks, with wild hair, with flashing eyes: the poets, painters, philosophers, men of art, of song, of vision, who, he knew, had also, among all the others, made this world of Montmartre their own. What he would do when he found them he did not know. Nor did it matter. It would be enough, now, simply to find; to watch them, be near them, and by that nearness to become, in a fashion, one with them. Passing the long sweep of the cafés, he moved slowly. Often he stopped, his eyes searching. But the crowds were too great; it was like searching for minnows in an ocean.

Then he had an idea. The streets were thronged with what the Parisians called *chansonniers*: minstrels who moved from café to café, singing their songs among the sidewalk tables in the hope that a few sous might be thrown to them. To be sure, *he* could not sing. Father Lacaze, back in Cambon, had once warned him, with a clerical chuckle, that his voice might someday crack the church bell. . . . But he had his poems; the lines he had been writing all that day and the day before on the back of his class oration. And he would read them. . . . He was not afraid. Not ashamed. Perhaps the world still looked on him as a mere boy, an adolescent; but this was no adolescent trash he had written, fit only for moonlight drooling and the ears of a simpering girl. It was the stuff of his mind and soul, the stuff of creation. And any true poet who heard it would feel it. He did not care about the rest; did not want their sous or their attention. But if there were poets among them, they would recognize him as one of their own. He knew that. *He knew it.* They would listen. They would come forward, call to him. Mallarmé, perhaps—Leconte de Lisle—Villiers—Sully Prud-homme—

He stopped before a café. He began reading. He read all he had written, and looked up, but no one looked back at him. No one had listened. Moving to another place, he began again, but this time, before he had read six lines, a *chansonnier* appeared and gave him a shove. *"Fous le camp, salaud!* Get going! We allow only professionals here." Claude moved on. He tried again. *"Fous le camp! Fous le camp!"* He tried a small place in a side street and was not interrupted, but again no one listened. Another side street . . . another . . . up and down, down and up. Another boy might have been beaten, in tears; but not he. Instead, at the last place, he stood very straight and stared at the blank drinking drunken faces with mocking eyes. "Messieurs," he announced, "a little rhetoric for your entertainment." And turning his paper, he read his Latin oration.

Then again darkness—even in Montmartre. Again the empty streets, the stone shadows, the lonely flares. . . . And the bridge. . . . Crawling under the arch and past the sprawled figures, he found his resting place of the previous night, lay down, and prepared for sleep. But before sleep came there was again a stirring beside him, and a moment later a low voice.

"Well, it's little snotface again."

Claude said nothing.

"Sort of moving in here, *hein?*"

"Sort of."

There was a silence. But the man had raised his head. Claude could see the beard and small bloodshot eyes.

"Say, kid—"

Claude looked away.

"Say—you know what?" The voice was a gravelly whisper. "I was thinking about you today. After I left here this morning I was thinking: now why did I wake that kid up? Why was I so nice to him, saving him from getting caught by the *flics*? For a while I couldn't figure it—and then I had an idea. Know what the idea was? I said to myself, maybe it wasn't a him at all. Maybe it was a her."

Another silence. Claude heard the lapping of the river.

"Know what I mean?" the voice said. "A boy outside, maybe, but sort of a girl inside. Sort of good-looking under that snotface. Sort of soft and cozy—"

Claude tried to move away, but there was nowhere to move to. He lay still. Something touched his leg.

"And then I thought: yeah, I been nice to him. So maybe now he'll be nice to me—"

Claude leaped up. Half running, half jumping, he dodged past the still figures around them, came out from under the bridge, climbed the bank, reached the streets. When he could run no longer, he walked. When he could walk no longer, he lay down in a doorway.

And at first light he was walking again.

This time he did not bother with Les Halles, but stole his breakfast in two courses from a baker and a fruit stand. He had decided he must find work, and first, on perverse impulse, he went back to the bakery. *"Fous le camp.* Get out," they told him. He tried a grocer, a butcher, two laundries, several restaurants, and perhaps a dozen dry-goods and notions stores of the sort owned by his mother. *"Fous le camp,"* they all told him. One look at his grimed face and torn clothes, and that was the end of it. *"Fous le camp!"*

He came to a great library and stood looking up at stone giants. There were Molière, Voltaire, Corneille, Racine; Rousseau, Chateaubriand, La Rochefoucauld, Diderot. And he knew them all. He had read them all. The building was fifty, a hundred times the size of the library at Cambon, but still it was a place of books, and in a place of books he would be at home. He mounted long steps, entered a vestibule, and the attendant said, *"Fous le camp!"*

His steps led him back to Montmartre: no longer a realm of mystery and dark magic, but bleak and frowzy under the summer sun. His knee was stiff. And he was hungry again. But this time he did not have to steal, for at the back entrance of a restaurant he came upon a freshly filled garbage bin and extracted the best meal he had had since leaving home. He tried again to find a job: here, there, at ten places, ten more. But there was nothing doing. . . . And now he walked again; simply walked; no longer seeking, no longer with a purpose, but just walking, walking on, on, endlessly through the streets; watching, listening, feeling, feeling the city around him, within him; looking at it, beyond it, through it, into its very heart, while the tide of images surged up into his brain.... He was sitting on a curb in an empty alley, his feet in the gutter, in the gutter filth, before him a crumbling brick wall on which was chalked the word MERDE.... He was reaching into his pocket, bringing out his paper and stub of pencil.

I shall travel, he wrote. *I shall hunt in the deserts. I shall sleep on the pavements of unknown cities, uncared for and without a care....*

He was looking down at the gutter. At his feet. He had not noticed before, but his shoes were not merely scuffed; they were torn, broken, with loose soles. Raising his feet he flapped the soles. He smiled. He wrote:

> *... where, rhyming in these shadowy fantastic places,*
> *as if I played a lyre, I'd gently pluck the laces*
> *of my burst boots, one foot pressed tight against my heart...*

The pencil cracked. It was no longer even a stub, but two severed shreds, without lead. Claude got up. Leaving the alley, he walked on through the streets until he found what he was looking for. He stopped at the door of the small stationer's shop and saw the pencils in a tray on the counter, just inside. A woman, presumably the proprietress, was busy with a customer in the rear, and there was no one else to be seen. Claude darted in, snatched, turned—and a man who had been stooping behind the counter rose up and shouted. Claude bolted from the store, and there in front of him was a policeman. He tried to dodge past, but his bad knee buckled and he couldn't make it. The policeman threw him to the pavement.

"What is your name?"

He didn't answer.

"Where is your home?"

He didn't answer.

"Who are your parents?"

He didn't answer.

And at last the desk sergeant gave up. The jailer led him along a narrow passageway, opened an iron door, and pushed him in.

"Well if it isn't snotface," a voice said. "The little girl-boy."

There was nowhere else to sit, so Claude sat on the stone floor, in a corner. The cell was small, there was no one else in it, and from the other side the tramp could almost have reached out and touched him. But he didn't. He didn't even speak again. He was busy picking lice from beneath his clothes and cracking them between his fingernails.

When he had finished he stretched out and seemed to sleep. And at last Claude fell asleep. When he awoke it was to find the bleared bearded face bent over him, and the tramp was holding something in his hand.

Claude pulled himself up quickly. The man returned to his own side of the cell and sat down. What he was holding was the grimed paper with the class oration and verses.

"Give it back to me," said Claude.

The man ignored him.

"Give it to me. It's not worth anything."

"If it's not worth anything, why do you want it?"

He held the paper up in the dim light and turned it over. Obviously he could not read, but he examined it closely, all but sniffed at it.

"If you don't give it to me," said Claude, "I'll call for help."

"Try it," the man said, "and see what happens."

There was a silence.

"What can you want with it?" said Claude. "It's only some writing."

"I'm going to tear it up."

"No."

"All right, I won't tear it. I'll do my business and wipe my behind with it."

"Give it back. Please give it back."

"Please?"

"Yes, *please.*"

"Well, now, that's better. How about a pretty please?" The man smiled crookedly, showing the black stumps of teeth. "How about a nice pretty please and maybe some tears? That little snotface would look real sweet with some tears on it. Like a little girl's—"

He folded the paper carefully and put it in a pocket. Then, without rising, he moved toward Claude, pushing himself slowly along with his hands.

"Like a little boy-girl's," he said. "Yes, a little girl-boy's. . . ."

3

In the black-walnut and horsehair parlor of her home above the store, the Widow Morel was speaking with Father Lacaze.

"I have done everything, Father," she said. "In the name of *le bon Dieu*, I have done everything. Since he was the smallest boy, no more than an infant, I have taken him every Sunday to Mass. Often on weekdays too, and he has never missed a Communion. All my life I have worked, slaved, thought only of my children, so that they might grow up decent and godly; and now see how I am rewarded."

Father Lacaze pursed his lips and looked down at his paunch. "Yes, it is a sorrow, madame, and I know your feelings. A sorrow, and also a mystery.

He has always been so good, so fine a boy. It is hard to explain."

"I am afraid I can explain it. All too well. It is the bad blood coming out—the blood of his father. My own parents warned me before I married him. 'You are making a mistake,' they said. 'He is no good; it will come to no good end.' And they were right. First—well, you have seen what happened. And now this. This shame and disgrace. It is retribution; the sins of the father—"

The priest looked uncomfortable. He was accustomed to distressed women; indeed half his life had been spent in soothing and comforting them. But most women were soft in their distress. They wept. They dabbed at their eyes. But he could no more imagine the Widow Morel dabbing at her eyes than—well—dancing at a carnival. Her face was set like iron; and her hair was like iron too, pulled back hard and black from her high forehead. Her nose was sharp: sharp as a dagger. Her lips were tight over her long teeth.

"At least he is coming home now," Father Lacaze said gently. "Perhaps when you have talked—"

"Yes, coming home. And how? With a policeman, a special officer." Madame Morel looked at the watch that hung on a ribbon down her black dress. "By now the train is already in. They are walking through the station, across the square, along the streets: my son a jailbird, with a policeman, for all Cambon to see our shame."

"My daughter, the good Lord works mysteriously. The boy is still young. We must try to have charity, to understand—"

"Understand? Such a thing as this? To run away; to become a tramp, a thief; to be put in prison.... And then after he is in prison—who can understand that? For a week, they say, he will not talk, will not answer a word, nothing. And when finally he gives a name it is not mine, not his own mother's, but this Monsieur Chariol's. It is from this teacher, this outsider, that I must learn what has happened to my son."

Father Lacaze began to speak, but she forestalled him abruptly. "Why is it the teacher he has them notify, will you tell me that?—No, I will tell *you*: it is because this Chariol is involved in it. He has been a bad influence. All year I have suspected it. All year the boy has been coming home late. 'Where have you been?' I ask him. 'To Monsieur Chariol's,' he says. And from there he brings back crazy ideas and godless books. Do you know what I caught him with last month? With a book called *Les Misérables*, by that Victor Hugo. The one with the twenty mistresses; the one so evil he has been exiled from France. Yes, that is what he brings home. And so I take it from him and look at it, and do you know what it is about? It is about tramps and thieves and harlots, that is what, and is it expected that a mere boy can read such filth and not be corrupted?—He is a bad one, this Chariol, I tell you. I am going to go to Monsieur Izard, the headmaster, and complain. And you should too, Father. Yes, the church should investigate, take action—"

Again the priest tried to speak, but again he was interrupted. This time it was by quick footsteps on the stairs, and the girl Yvette ran into the room. "They're coming, *Maman!*" she cried. "They're just down the street."

Father Lacaze rose quickly. "Ah, he is home then; that is good. So I shall go now. It is best that the first meeting be only with the family. But I shall talk to him later, I promise you. I shall talk to him from the heart."

He made a sign of blessing, took his hat and went out. Yvette ran to the window and looked down. "There are four of them," she said. "Claude and Felix and Monsieur Chariol and a policeman. They're all coming in. . . . No, Monsieur Chariol is leaving. . . . Oh, *Maman*, how Claude looks!"

Again there were footsteps on the stairs. Madame Morel stood facing the door.

Then Claude appeared, and behind him his brother and a man in uniform. Claude's face and hands were now clean, or at least fairly clean, and some of the dirt had been brushed from his suit; but his collarless shirt was black, his trousers were still torn, and his shoes barely clung to his feet. His light hair was long and matted. His cheeks were thin, almost sunken; his eyes like blue stones, hard and opaque.

Mother and son stood without speaking. Then she nodded to Felix and Yvette. "You may go now," she told them.

They hesitated.

"You will go down," she said sharply, "and take care of the store."

They went out. The policeman stepped forward and cleared his throat. "You are Madame Natalie Morel?" he asked.

"Yes."

"This is your son?"

"Yes."

"I am a special officer attached to the Préfecture of the Ninth Arrondissement of Paris. My instructions are to turn this boy over to your custody." The policeman was tired and bored, and showed it. Barely stifling a yawn, he produced two documents. "This is the record of arrest and sentence," he said, "of which you have already been sent a summary." He put down the first paper and held out the second. "And this is an acknowledgment of transfer of custody, which you will please sign."

Madame Morel took it from him and read it slowly and carefully. "There is an error," she said. "It gives the effective date as August fifth, and today is the eighth."

"The form was made out several days ago. Then there were delays."

"Why were there delays?"

"There is, as Madame may have heard, a war on. Most of the trains are being requisitioned. Our troops are moving on Berlin."

"I shall change the date."

"You may if you wish."

Madame Morel took a pen from a drawer, changed the date, and signed her name.

"A copy of this," said the policeman, "will be filed with the Chef de Préfecture of Cambon. You will be responsible to him for the boy's conduct."

She inclined her head very slightly.

"Then there is one final item."

"Yes?"

"There is a charge of twenty-five francs for transportation."

"Twenty-five francs?"

"Nine for the boy one way. Sixteen for myself round trip."

"Those are second-class fares."

"Representatives of the Préfecture de Police, madame, travel in the best available accommodations."

Madame Morel eyed him stonily. Then she turned, went to another drawer, and took out a sheaf of bills. Counting them over twice, she handed him twenty-five francs. "A receipt, if you please," she said.

The policeman made out a receipt.

"If you have now completed your duties, you may go," she told him. "And may I suggest that, since you are used to such fine accommodations, you learn, when in a lady's parlor, to remove your hat?"

The policeman started to answer, thought better of it, and went to the door. Following him, Madame Morel called down the stairs: "Felix, you will show the man the way out."

Then she came back into the room. She looked at Claude. Claude looked at the window.

"I have only this to say," she said. "That I have always done my duty as I see it, and that I shall continue to do so."

The boy was silent.

"And you—what do you have to say?"

He was still silent.

"You have nothing to say?"

Claude looked at her. "No, nothing," he said.

He walked past her, out the door and down the hall. She watched him as he opened the door of his own room, went in, and closed it. She waited. For several minutes she stood exactly where she was, erect and motionless in her black dress; then she went down the hall to his room and entered it. It was empty, and the window was open. Again she stood still, but this time for only a moment. Turning, she went down the stairs, through the back of the shop, and into the yard. On the far side of the yard was the privy house, and crossing to it, she rapped on the door.

There was no reply.

"Claude! Answer me. Claude!"

"What, Mother?"

"Come out of there. Come up to your room."

"There's no lock on my room."

"Come out at once, do you hear me?"

"I'll come out later, Mother," he said. "I'm busy writing."

He sat with Albert Chariol in the young teacher's lodgings, where he had been so often before. For the past year this had been his refuge, his one oasis in the arid desert of Cambon: a place of talk that was not merely empty sound: a place of thoughts, theories, dreams, horizons. The walls were lined with books, and he had read every one.

"You don't understand?" he asked.

"Yes, I think I understand," said Chariol.

"But you don't approve."

"How can I approve, you crazy boy?—Vagabonding, thieving, arrest, jail. Shaming your family and friends. Driving your mother frantic."

"Let's leave my mother out of it."

"No, we will not leave her out of it. That's the whole point." Chariol's face was serious and earnest; leaning forward he put a hand on Claude's knee. "You are a bright boy. No, more than bright—you are brilliant. But you are also still *only* a boy. You are sometimes wild, thoughtless, unstable. Let me tell you something: you may think you want to, but you cannot leave your mother 'out of it.' You can never leave others 'out of it.' If you do, you'll lose everything you hope to gain. You won't end up free, but just defeated and alone."

Claude was silent. Chariol stood up and smiled. "With the school term over, I suppose you hoped you'd heard the last of my lectures. . . . Well, behave yourself and you won't hear any more."

Outside, on the street, there was the approaching thump of a drum and the scraping of feet on the cobbles. The man and the boy looked out the window as a platoon of troops went by.

"How do you think it will go?" asked Claude.

Chariol shrugged. "It's hard to say. Everyone keeps shouting 'A *Berlin*, à *Berlin!*' as if it were no more than a few days' walk. But I'm afraid the Prussians are tough soldiers—and that Bismarck is perhaps not quite the imbecile our emperor thinks him."

"It's the emperor who's the imbecile. It's not the Germans we should be fighting, but him, with his aristocrats and plutocrats."

"You're quite the revolutionary, *hein*, my young one?"

"What else should one be, in the sort of world we live in?" The troops had vanished, and Claude looked at his teacher. "And you?" he asked. "Do you want to fight in such a war? Will you volunteer?"

"No, I don't think so."

"Will you be called up then?"

"If it goes on long, I suppose so."

"And meanwhile?"

"Meanwhile I'll stay around." Claude smiled, and the teacher smiled back at him. "You'll like that, *hein?*" he said. "You'll still have someone to argue with."

"What will you be doing mostly during the holiday? Writing?"

"Yes. I'm planning a few short stories; in fact, I'm already at work. I'm trying a detailed naturalistic style—rather in the manner of Flaubert."

"Oh."

"You have something against Monsieur Flaubert?"

Chariol regarded him quizzically, and Claude considered a moment before answering. "He has great talent," he said, "but also great limitations. He's a master of psychology and motivation, but it's all too precise, too disciplined. There's no real freedom—and no magic."

Chariol nodded, with a slight bow. "I shall bear that in mind, *monsieur le professeur*. . . . And now what about you? With all this wild craziness you've been in, have you done any writing?"

"Yes, I've done some verses and fragments."

"You'll let me see them?"

"Of course. But I must copy them out first. Now they're just scribble and dirt."

"You're lucky they didn't take them away from you in that jail of yours."

Claude didn't answer at once. His eyes seemed to move past Chariol and fix on something behind him. "Someone did for a while," he said. "But I got them back."

"Well, I hope they're as good as the last ones you showed me. The alexandrines, I mean. They were excellent—exquisite."

"No, those were awful."

"Awful?"

"Yes. Pretty-pretty. Tinkle-winkle. The sort of stuff the Parnassians do."

"And what, may I ask, is wrong with the Parnassians?"

"Everything's wrong with them."

"Nonsense."

. . . And for the next hour they were off on one of the literary battles which they had been waging so happily for a year past. Over Poet A and Poet B—Group X and Subgroup Y—romanticism versus classicism—

prose versus poetry . . . until at last they were back where they started, and
Chariol was asking:

"So what about these new verses of yours? In what revolutionary non-
Parnassian style are they?"

"In my own," said Claude, as he went to the door.

When the boy had left, Chariol sat down at his desk. He read through
the half of a short story he had already written, made a few erasures and
additions, and went on with it. But the going was slow. The right words
did not come. His thought drifted from his work to himself. . . . He was
only twenty-four years old. He was a university graduate. He was ambitious, industrious, and literarily talented, and one day, God willing, he
would break away from the drudgery of teaching and become a full-time
professional author. . . . So far, so good. But beyond that—well, life was
strange. And its strangeness was sometimes harsh. For in his heart he
knew that he could write every hour of every day, year after year, all his life
through, and yet never become the writer that Claude Morel already was,
still a schoolboy, aged fifteen and nine months.

"Never mind the geography," said his friend, Michel Favre. "What
about the girls?"

"There weren't any girls," Claude told him.

"No girls? Rats! Who're you kidding? What does a fellow run away for
if it isn't girls?"

"It's not what I ran away for."

"No? What then?"

"Oh, lots of things."

"Such as?"

"Such as to sit in a gutter. To sleep under a bridge."

Michel studied him and shook his head. "You're really crazy, aren't you?"

"Yes, maybe I am."

They were walking along the streets, kicking loose stones. The dust
rose from under their feet and hung in the hot air.

"All right," Michel said, "be as crazy as you want. If you haven't the
sense to get a girl for yourself—I *have*. And I've done all right, too." He
waited for Claude to question him, but Claude failed to cooperate.
"That same night you chased off—remember?—when I said let's go over
to Antimes with Louise Croz and Mimi Rouger. Well, we went. I got
Georges Vuiton, and we took them over and had fun at the carnival, and
then we walked them back, real late, and had more fun. Not just kid stuff,
I don't mean; the real thing. Almost the—you know—"

Michel's eyes danced. His round snub-nosed face was beatific. "You've
never felt a girl, have you? No, of course you haven't. Really felt her, I
mean—not just her hand or something, but all over, and underneath—

Wow! And this Louise—that's the one I had—she didn't mind a bit. She kept snuggling up and sort of twisting around and giggling. Boy, I'm telling you she was good. And the other one, Mimi—the one you were going to have—Georges said she was good too. You sure missed out on—" He glanced at Claude. "Hey, what are you doing?"

Claude had a slip of paper in one hand and a pencil in the other.

"Writing," he said.

"Writing what?"

"Words."

"Words?" Michel looked baffled, then disgusted. "Oh, those damn poems again. You're still at that."

Claude kept on writing. "Yes, I'm still at that."

"About the birdies and the flowers?"

"No, this poem's about Paris."

"Paris? Well, that's an improvement, anyhow. If you didn't *do* anything, at least you must have *seen* something. . . . What did you see, *hein?* Don't be such a clam. Did you see whores? Lots of fancy whores, all over the place? Did you see naked women dancing?"

"I saw boulevards of raised platforms. I saw pastures of emerald and steel."

"What?"

"I saw stone, stars, filth. I saw men with eyes full of pilgrimages, and men with eyes full of death. I saw little red eyes and black teeth, bending over me—"

"You're a loony! My God, yes, a real loony. That's what you are."

"Maybe. I'm just telling you what I saw."

"In Paris?"

"Yes, in Paris."

Claude smiled, but his eyes were like blue polished stones.

Father Lacaze chose his words carefully. With most of his flock, a few platitudes, a judicious mixture of sternness and gentleness, were sufficient to any situation; but for this boy, he knew, rather more was needed. "It is not simply a matter of outward actions, of right and wrong, my son," he said quietly. "It is a matter of inwardness, a question of grace."

He paused.

"Our Lord is merciful. He is understanding. He understands that His children are weak; that they will err and sin; and He will always forgive them if they truly seek forgiveness. If they truly repent of their sins and wish in their hearts to regain the state of grace."

He paused again. Thus far the boy had said nothing.

"Come with me now," the priest said. "We will go into the confessional and you will bare your heart to God."

Claude did not move.

"You will not come?"

Claude shook his head.

"Why not?"

"Because I can't."

"You have sinned, have you not?"

"I suppose so."

"Suppose? No, you know it. You are still young. In your heart, I am sure, you are good. But you have sinned. You are a sinner."

"Perhaps that's what man is supposed to be—a sinner. Perhaps God made him a sinner, and it's best to leave it that way."

Father Lacaze looked down at him for a long moment. His plump face showed puzzlement and pain. Then he said softly: "I have known you all your life, Claude. With my own hands, in this very church, I baptized you. With my own hands I gave you the wafer of your first Communion. Since you were a little child six or seven years old your mother has seen to it that you have never missed a Mass, and I have been confident that you would always be a true son of our Father and His Church."

"Yes, of course," said Claude. "Hurrah for the Jesuits!"

"The Jesuits?"

"The Jesuits say, 'Give us the child before he is seven, and we will never lose him.'"

There was another silence. Father Lacaze stood up. "We have talked enough," he said. "Come."

"No, Father."

"You will not confess?"

"No."

"You will defy your church? You no longer believe in God?"

"Yes, I believe in God. At least I *think* I believe in Him. But I no longer believe in any cult."

It was no longer pain in the priest's face. It was sudden red anger. "Cult? You dare to call the Holy Church a cult?"

"I will go now, Father," said Claude quietly.

"Yes, go! Leave this place before you desecrate it any further. Now! At once!" The old man almost trembled with emotion. "That I should live to see a thing like this! A boy I have known so long—of good family, of the best upbringing—now a thief, an unrepentant thief—and a blasphemer. . . . Yes, go! Go home to your mother, whom you have caused so much grief, and beg her forgiveness. Go home and look into your heart and ask God for *His* forgiveness. And when you have done that—no sooner—then you may come back here to this holy church."

The boy had started to go, and now he followed him, struggling to control his feelings. "Claude, Claude," he said, again gently, "think what you have said. What you are doing. Only stop and think and go home and pray, and I know you will see—"

He stopped. They had reached the church steps; the boy had turned and was looking at him; and he could scarcely look back at what he saw in his eyes.

"Goodbye, Father," said Claude, and went down the steps.

Behind him, the priest made the sign of the cross.

Madame Morel was out, and Felix drowsed behind the counter in the empty store. Upstairs in the living room Yvette was hopping methodically about on one foot, but she stopped as Claude came in.

"You went to see Father Lacaze?" she asked.

Claude nodded.

"Was it fun?"

"Not exactly."

"I always have fun with Father Lacaze. He's so nice and jolly. When he smiles he wrinkles up his eyes so he looks just like Père Noël."

"And he's just as much of a humbug."

"Humbug? What does that mean?"

"It means a fake."

"Father Lacaze a fake? Why what a terrible thing to say! You know something, Claude Morel? You'll be punished if you say things like that."

"Who'll punish me?"

"God."

"He's too busy."

"And Mother."

She began hopping again.

"What are you doing that for?" he asked.

"Because there's nothing else to do."

"You could go out and play ball."

"I don't have a ball."

"Yes, you do."

"I do not. I never have."

"You have now." He dug into his pocket, closed his fist over something, and held the fist out toward his sister. "What do you think's in there?"

Again she stopped jumping. She seemed almost to have stopped breathing, as she stared with wide hypnotized eyes. "Let me seeee—"

"Say abracadabra."

"Abracadabra. Pleeease—"

He opened his hand and showed a small red rubber ball. Yvette's stare grew wider.

"It's for *me?*" she whispered.

"Yes, for you."

He gave it to her, and she held it. She turned it over. She squeezed it. She bounced it. "Oh Claude—" she said. She bounced it again, then looked up at him. "Where did you get it?"

"In Paris."

"Paris? In Paris—for me. Oh—" She stared at it. "And it's *new!*"

"Of course it's new."

"It comes from a store. It cost money."

"That's right."

"But you don't have any money."

"I—I found some."

"You found money—on the street—in Paris. And you took it to a store and bought me—" She leaped at him and threw her arms around his neck. "Oh, Claude, I love you!"

"Just be careful Mother doesn't see it."

"Yes, I will."

"If she sees it she'll take it away."

"Oh, I'll be very careful. I'll only play with it when she's out. I'll keep it hidden in my drawer, way deep down, like it was—jewelry." Still holding him, she jumped up and down. "I love you, I love you, I love you!"

Claude smiled and pulled her pigtails. "You know something," he said. "You're getting sort of pretty."

Felix thumped up the stairs and came into the room that he and Claude shared. Sprawling out on his cot, he yawned and said, "The old woman's back."

"Yes, I heard her," said Claude.

"Some chance of not hearing her. Yammer yammer yammer. Jesus!"

"What about, this time?"

"I don't know. I don't listen."

Felix yawned again. He closed his eyes, his heavy face grew heavier, and he seemed to fall asleep. Claude got out pencil and paper and sat at the table by the window, his head bent in concentration. After perhaps ten minutes his brother opened his eyes. "Christ," he said, "are you at *that* again?"

"Uh-huh."

"Don't you ever get tired of it?"

"No."

"I get tired just watching you. Or even not watching. I get so tired and bored around this dump I could puke."

"Why don't you get out then?"

"Get out? Sure—like you did, I suppose. Off to Paris and into jail."

"You're older. You could get a job."

"Sure, a job. Pfui! I got all the job I want right here." Felix sat up slowly, picked his nose with his forefinger, and examined his findings. "Know what I been thinking?" he said. "I been thinking maybe I'd join the army. They don't call you up till you're twenty, but they'd take me if I enlisted."

"Since when have you been so patriotic?"

"Who's patriotic? I just want to get away from the old woman and that yammer yammer yammer. . . . Look, here's how I figure. The war will be over soon. I was talking with Jacques Durand this morning and he said we'd take Berlin in a month. That means by the time I'm really in—you know, after training and all that—the fighting'll be finished. Just peacetime stuff again. A snappy uniform, some good buddies, drinks, girls—and out from under the old woman. The only bad part is the goddam drilling and marching; I don't go much for that. But if I play it smart and tell them I have pains in the feet or something—"

He was interrupted by their mother's voice from below. "Felix!" she called. "Felix!"

"Oh Jesus—"

"Felix, come down at once!"

He groaned and heaved himself to his feet. "Yammer yammer yammer." He went wearily to the door and thumped down the stairs. Claude went on with his writing.

And he was still writing when, a while later, his mother came in. "Will you please have the manners to stand when I enter a room," she said.

"I'm just finishing a line," said Claude.

"You can finish it later."

Claude wrote another two words and got to his feet. Madame Morel took a chair. "Now you may sit again," she said. "I want to speak to you."

Claude put away his paper and pencil.

"You have been to see Father Lacaze?" she said.

"Yes."

"He spoke to you?"

"Yes."

"And you listened to what he said?"

"Yes."

His mother nodded. "I am going to wait until I hear the Father's advice before I decide what to do. I am only a woman—a poor widow. I need the help of those stronger and wiser than myself to deal with so monstrous an affair."

She paused. Her lips were a white line.

"Monstrous," she repeated.

Her emotion seemed physically to jerk her to her feet. She stood straight and stiff in her black bombazine. "I wonder if you are even aware," she said, "of the consequences of what you have done. Of the disgrace you have brought on us all."

Claude said nothing.

"Answer me."

"Yes," said Claude.

"Of the shame you have caused me?"

"Yes."

"And your brother and sister?"

"Yes."

"And your school? And your church?"

"Yes."

"Today I was ashamed to go into the streets; to show my face. I was ashamed when customers came into the store. Do you know how they look at me? With pity. Yes, pity! At me, who has never asked even for God's pity, who has never been beholden to anyone, who has worked year after year, ten, twelve, fourteen hours a day, to support my children, to bring you up decently, to give you education and manners and godliness, so that we might all hold up our heads in pride. And now—now. . . . Shall I tell you what I have thought of doing? I have thought of leaving this town. Yes, of leaving Cambon, where I have lived all my life, because I cannot bear the disgrace. And I would, too, if I could afford it. If we were not so poor. I would take us all and go and hide somewhere, and they would never see us or our shame again."

She paused. Her thin chest rose and fell. "What has brought us to this?" she demanded. "What has happened to you? Is there a devil in you? . . . You have not done such things before. You were a good child. With your brother I have always had trouble—yes—he is an ox, a fool, a good-for-nothing—but with you, no. You were quiet, neat, obedient. You were a prize student. Your teachers were proud of you; Father Lacaze was proud; I was proud. Proud—hah! And now look what you have done. To all of us. To me. The reward you have given me for all I have done. I cannot believe it—no. I cannot understand—" As she spoke, Madame Morel had undergone a subtle change. Her voice remained charged, but it was deeper, less harsh. Her black-sheathed body was no longer stiff as iron, but swaying slightly, and she grasped the back of a chair with white-knuckled hands. For a long moment she looked down at her son. Her lips moved wordlessly, seemed almost to tremble, and it was no longer only anger that filled her eyes. Then she said: "Have you done this on purpose, boy? To hurt me? Because you hate me?" She leaned tensely forward. "Is that it? Answer me. You hate me—is that it?"

For the first time, Claude's eyes met hers, and there was neither anger in them nor any other emotion, but only a remote cold blueness, as of a winter sky. "I've hated you, Mother," he said quietly, "since I was six years old."

She raised a hand to hit him, but something held it back. Instead, she straightened slowly. Her face and body went rigid. The iron returned to them. "Very well," she said, and her voice, too, was iron. "Very well—I shall speak to Father Lacaze, and then we shall see what will be done. Meanwhile, you are forbidden to leave this house. Do you understand? You will stay in this house, in this room, until I tell you that you may leave it."

Abruptly she turned, walked out and closed the door.

Claude waited until he heard her footsteps on the stairs. Then he got up, clambered through the window, and let himself down by way of the sill and a projecting shingle below. This time, however, he did not go into the privy, but climbed the wall behind it, came out into a back street, and walked away.

4

He walked. He walked. That day, and the next, and the next. Every day for a month, and often on into the night. He walked in the town and in the country; along the roads, beside the river, through the fields and the forest. He loved walking—as he loved the sun and the sky—and the only problem was that he had not the right shoes for it. A dozen times, over the years, he had asked his mother for a pair of stout hobnailed boots, but she had informed him that such things were for farmers and road builders, and not for a boy from a good bourgeois family.

She still tried to keep him from leaving the house. What her conversation with Father Lacaze had been, or what decisions had been arrived at, he did not know; but it made no difference, for he was now too big to be held back physically and was no longer afraid of her tongue and her anger. Sometimes, when she stormed at him, he too got angry and shouted back; but more often he ignored her. Sometimes, when she had been quiet and not bothered him, he worked for a while in the store, but never when she ordered him to. He did not go back to the church to see Father Lacaze, nor even to Mass. Occasionally he joined up with Michel Favre or some of the other boys for a day or evening, and, rather more often, visited Monsieur Chariol. But, increasingly, he spent his time alone.

Tardily, but now quite suddenly, he had begun to grow. His face was still that of a boy, fresh-skinned and small-featured, but his frame was becoming long and angular, his feet swelled out of their old shoes, and his hands hung, big and awkward, from the too-short sleeves of his shirts. Walking through the miles and hours, he moved with long gangling strides.

He read voraciously—as he had since he was scarcely more than a baby. Already he was familiar with all the classics of French literature, plus many from the German and English (not to mention the Latin and Greek), and now he read them a second and third time, as well as such new books as he could get from Chariol or elsewhere. He read novels, dramas, essays, history, biography, philosophy, sociology. He read Hugo, Balzac, Byron, Heine, Schopenhauer, Darwin, Marx. He read the poetry of the currently popular group of writers who called themselves the Parnassians, for the enjoyment he derived from his violent dislike of them; and he read the verse of Charles Baudelaire, whom he had just discovered, and who filled him with an almost magical excitement. When he could find books nowhere else, he went to the public library, prowling the stacks and shelves like a hunter in a forest; but the attendants were stuffy and pompous civil servants who, more often than not, would refuse him what he wanted, because he was "too young for it." Great as was his love for books, and for the life and wonder that he found in them, he yet grew to hate the dust-dry bloodless boredom of the reading rooms and the creaking pedants who haunted them. *Les Assis*, he called them. The Sitdowners . . .

> . . . *who've grafted in long epileptic love-embrace*
> *their weird bone-structures to the big black skeleton*
> *of every chair; their feet endlessly interlaced*
> *with the rachitic bars, while days go on and on . . .*

He got out. He walked. And walked. Across the Place du Sépulcre (well named), through the Place de la Gare (escape—but to where?), on to the town's public park that was called the Bois d'Amour. This was a lovely place of green grass and tall trees, the one beauty spot of Cambon. But it had not acquired its name for no reason. It was full of lovers strolling, sitting on the benches, lying entwined on the grass in bosky shadow—and no place for a lone wanderer. He walked on.

In a field beyond the park a squad of home-guard volunteers was drilling. There was still a war on. Or was there? At the moment no one seemed quite certain. A few days before there had apparently been some sort of great debacle over at Sedan. The report was that a whole army had been captured, the emperor taken prisoner; but at the same time the newspapers kept talking of "successful realignments" and "triumphant withdrawals." No one was heard saying *"A Berlin!"* any more, but otherwise nothing seemed to have changed, and although Sedan was a mere thirty miles distant across the countryside, the only sign of war in Cambon were the decrepit home guards with their shouldered broomsticks in the field. For the rest, the town drowsed on—as it had for centuries, as it would for eternity. *"Plus ça change,"* a wise man had once said of the world, *"plus c'est la même chose."* And it would always be *la même chose* in Cambon. Claude walked on and left it behind him.

He walked beside the River Meuse, his thoughts lost in its coiled yellow flow. He sat on its bank and wrote a few lines; then rising, skirted a pasture, crossed a road, and entered the woods. Again the trees were tall above him, as in the Bois d'Amour, but there all resemblance ended, for the Bois was a park and this was untouched timberland: the dark forest of the Ardennes, the wildest region in northern France. *Le Pays des Loups*, it was called. The Wolf Country. And cautious people avoided it. But for Claude it had been refuge and sanctuary for many years, the nearest to a true home he had ever had. He had been no more than seven or eight when he had first come there, running away from his mother, moving deeper and deeper into the shadows, expecting at any moment to see the wolves around him, their teeth glinting, their eyes like yellow lanterns in the gloom. And later he had come many times, dozens and scores of times over the years: running away again, running from Cambon, running from school, church, home, mother, searching for his father who was gone and lost. . . .

He had only dim recollections of his father. He remembered that he was tall, that his voice was deep, that he was blond and fair-skinned like himself. And he remembered his uniforms, for his father was a soldier —an officer. Piecing together the fragments he had heard (from his brother, an uncle, older townspeople, but not his mother—never so much as a word from his mother), he knew that his parents had met while his father's company was stationed in Cambon on garrison duty; that they had been married against the wishes of his mother's parents, who had had a prosperous grain merchant picked out for her; and that their actual time together as husband and wife had been very brief. For his father's soldiering had not kept him long in Cambon. He had been sent to the south of France, then to Morocco and Algeria, to which, Claude gathered, his mother refused to accompany him, and from which he returned only on long-spaced leaves. From the last leave, when Claude was six, the boy could recall just two things. One was the three stripes on his father's blue sleeves, which showed that he had been made a captain. And the other was a terrible fight. He had had no idea, of course, of what the fight was about, but every detail was vivid in his memory: Felix and himself crouching by the open door (Yvette, too young, was asleep in her crib); the voices rising to shouts, the rage blazing from eyes, his father's face growing redder, his mother's whiter and whiter; finally his spitting a curse at her (it was the first time he, Claude, had heard the word *merde*), and her seizing a pewter bowl from the table and throwing it at him, and the bowl missing and crashing against the wall. The next day he had thought he must have dreamed it all, until he went alone into the parlor and, examining the bowl, found a great dent in its side. And now the bowl was still there, dent and all.

After that leave his father had never returned. He vanished. It was as if he had never been. Soon after, his mother had taken to wearing only black, and she began to be known in Cambon as the Widow Morel. But whether she ever really became a widow or not, no one could be sure. For all any of them knew—and Claude often mused about it—Pierre Morel might still be very much alive. He might be a major or colonel, or even a lesser general, still campaigning in Africa; or more likely, serving in France, in the war that was now all around them; a prisoner at Sedan, perhaps; with the troops marching through the countryside, even nearer. . . . It was a strange thought.

He moved at random through the dim wilderness. His feet sank deep in moss, brambles plucked at his sleeves, and the trees rose above him like the columns of a temple. Ahead, now, was a tree taller and darker than the rest. As tall, straight, and black as the image of his mother. . . .

His mother marching them to church. (Yes, it was a march, not a walk.) In single file: Yvette first, himself second, Felix third, mother fourth. Himself and Felix in their blue serge. All of them with umbrellas. ("But, Mother, it isn't raining." . . . "It may rain on the way home, and then your good clothes would be ruined.") At first he had liked church; more than liked it—loved it, thrilled to it. The panoply of the Mass, the color, music, and solemn ritual had sent his child's mind soaring off on its first voyages of imagination. But as time passed there had been a slow change. The "march of the damned," as he came to call the family procession, grew progressively more humiliating and unbearable; and in the church itself, the prayers and liturgies, the endlessly repeated round of Masses, confessionals, and Communions seemed to him less and less a communication with a living God and more and more the playing out of an empty pageant. Increasing knowledge only hastened his apostasy. In the early days the droning of the priests had at least held the attraction of mysterious unintelligibility. But once he learned Latin and could understand, the boredom was unrelieved and encompassing.

At school it had been much the same: at first the excitement of new horizons; later dullness and routine. And for years he had had to carry the two-ply cross of his small size and his blue serge suit—of *le beau gosse* and Mama's darling. But he did not reject learning as he rejected religiosity. He consumed it, gorged on it. Except for mathematics and the sciences, everything came easily to him, and soon he was skipping classes. In languages he was particularly adept. At ten he could speak fluent English, at twelve fluent German and fair Italian as well. He could not only read Latin and Greek; he could talk them, write them; and when he was thirteen, and in the fourth form, a two-hundred-line poem he had composed

in Latin hexameters, in the style of Horace, was entered in a national
scholastic competition and won second prize (the first prize winner
having been a university student of twenty-one). His mother, whose inner
iron comprised ambition no less than discipline, brought herself painfully to the point of dipping into her cash drawer to pay for after-hour
private tutoring—which pushed him still further along. And for himself
he earned the only pocket money he had ever had by, in turn, tutoring
his classmates. His title now became "the monster of erudition." But he
much preferred monsterhood to being a *beau gosse* or a darling.

Learning and books he loved. But routine and pedantry he hated. He
loathed most of his teachers: the droning ones, the dry dead ones, *les assis*.
Sometimes he played truant from the dullest classes. Sometimes he slept
in them. And once, in study hall, he ostentatiously began tearing the pages
from a book and stuffing them into his mouth.

"What are you doing, Morel?" the teacher in charge asked sharply.
"You are supposed to be preparing for your rhetoric examination."

"Oh, but I am, sir," Claude replied through his mouthful. "I am eating
a dictionary."

Mostly, though, he behaved himself. He won his laurel wreaths. He
wore the mask that was expected of him. And in the past three years, at
least, school had become brighter through the coming of Albert Chariol.
For Chariol was no creaking pedagogue come to grind out his dotage
in the backwater of a provincial school, but a young man, a man still
reaching out, growing, with his life ahead of him, for whom teaching
was—or could be—a challenge and an adventure. In Claude, and Claude
alone, the "could be" had been realized, and each had found in the other
something that he profoundly needed. From master and pupil they had
gone on to become friends. Soon, outside the classroom, they were on a
first-name basis, and the long hours they spent together in the teacher's
room, reading, talking, exploring the world of ideas and of each others'
minds, were the fullest and richest the boy had known.

He was miserable when it came time to leave and go home. He had
always hated to go home: to the prim, arid, dismal rooms above the store.
They had moved there when he was seven, about a year after his father
had vanished, when his mother, with money advanced by her parents,
decided to go into business. And in all the years since, Claude could recall
no single day or night there that had been truly happy. Within the family,
companionship and communication scarcely existed. His brother had at
first been too old for him, and more recently, in full reversal, too childish
and stupid. And his sister, though he was very fond of her, was too young
and innocent to share his thoughts. As for sharing thoughts with his
mother—the very notion was preposterous. He might as well have tried
to share them with a tree or a stone. Sometimes he tried to imagine what

she had been like when she was younger: a girl among other girls, going
to school and parties, meeting boys and men, meeting his father, defying
her own parents (as he was now defying her), and getting married. Most
especially, he tried to imagine her being made love to by his father. But it
was hopeless—an impossible fantasy. If she had ever been anything other
than what she was now, it was forever lost, crushed and withered behind
walls of iron.

He lived alone. He had never had a room to himself, nor a day's or
night's privacy, yet he had still, all his life, lived alone. While Felix, a bare
arm's length from him, slept, grunted, scratched, belched, and picked
his nose, he would wrap himself into his own world, into his books and
writing, his thoughts and dreams, with Felix, mother, home, store, street,
town, all of them and everything, gone and forgotten. Once, when he
had been much younger, he had found a strip of canvas in a dump and,
bringing it home, used it as a spread when he was reading on his cot.
The canvas was a sail. Stroking it with his fingers, he could almost feel
the encrusted salt of distant seas. He could almost see it bellying out
above him, sun-gleaming, wind-struck, as it carried him outward toward
unknown shores.

His mother interrupted. She nagged and scolded. But he slowly
trained himself to ignore her, rather than waste his time by fighting back.
He developed the stratagem of locking himself in the privy and became
adept at leaving and re-entering the house when her attention was occupied elsewhere. Only occasionally were there major fracases, and the
worst of these had been when he was only ten. It had been about a piano.
In church he had been deeply impressed by the organ music and chanting;
its sound had filled him, become part of him, excited him as he had never
been excited before; and he had decided that he himself must become a
musician. So he had asked his mother for a piano. And she had refused. He
begged, pleaded, cajoled. And she said, "Are you crazy, boy? Do you think I
am a millionairess?" Then he got mad. Anger and wildness rose up in him
—not hot and shouting, but cold, silent, vindictive—and when his mother
went out he took a knife from the kitchen and carved a complete keyboard
into the dining-room table. On her return she had found him sitting at it,
his fingers thumping while he sang *Malbrouck s'en va-t-en Guerre*—and the
explosion had frightened the sparrows off half the roofs in Cambon.

"All parents are dogs," his schoolmates assured him. "You're the lucky
one; at least you don't have an old man."

But it was just talk, boys' gabble, with no meaning, no reference to the
life he lived within. With his schoolmates, as with his family, there was a
wall, a barrier, and through that barrier could pass only trivialities, jokes,
gripes, swearwords, never the inward reality of what was truly themselves. The nearest he had had to a close friend, among boys of his own

age, was Michel Favre, but in the past year even they had been drifting apart. Michel was no Felix. He was quick, alive, aware. But he could not accompany Claude—as could Albert Chariol—on the ever-widening journeys of his mind. He was absorbed in facts, things, actions, people: the events of day to day. Above all, he was now absorbed in girls. That seemed all that he thought about—girls. "Come on, let's get Louise and Mimi." (Or Jeanne and Hélène; or Odette and Marie.) "We'll take them out to the Bois d'Amour."

So he and his girls walked off to the Bois. And Claude walked his own way, alone. He walked out of the town onto the country roads; along the Meuse, across the fields, into the woods. He walked on and on, as he was walking now, ever deeper into the dark forest of the Ardennes.

He was alone. He was alone because he was different. He knew that, and he knew *how* he was different, but what was harder to understand was *why*. He and his brother, for instance: they had the same parents, the same upbringing, everything the same, and yet were utterly unalike. In varying ways, it was similar with Michel. With girls. With everyone.... But most of all with girls. With women.... Men and women were supposed to be different; nature had made them so. The difference was designed to attract, but for him it had only repelled. For him it had raised the highest of all barriers, through which no act of mind or will could carry him.

In the beginning there had been, not many women, but only one: his mother. His mother tall above him. His mother in black, in church, murmuring her prayers, counting her beads. Then, as he became conscious of others, he had seen that they too were the same. Women in black, women in church: they were the devout ones, the pure and righteous ones, the ones who were free of sin and would go to heaven to stand beside the Virgin Mary. Through his early childhood he had not questioned this. It was simply so—the way God had ordained. But then, as he grew older, he had begun to watch, to notice, and to doubt; to see that this was not all of it—that women were something else besides—that, like the church, they were a fraud and a deception. On the streets, in the shops, during Mass itself, he had begun to look at them—at the women and the girls and the girls turning into women: not merely at their outwardness, at what they wished to be seen, but at what lay beneath, at what they really were. And what they were was, above all else, a lie. For beneath the devoutness was coquetry and lust; beneath their pious black was their nakedness, their animal flesh, the flesh of sex that yearned for rutting, like a cow's or a pig's. And the blackness, the virtue, the purity were only lies.

"I don't know her," he had said of Mimi Rouger. But he knew her all right. He knew Louise and Mimi and Jeanne and Marie. He knew them all. Time and again, in his sleeping and waking dreams, he had taken them, held them, and ripped through their disguises to the flesh. He had seen, smelled, and touched the flesh. Alone in the night he had lain with their flesh, with their nakedness, until his own flesh convulsed and he possessed them. . . . Except that, in the end, he possessed nothing; he had *been* possessed. He was alone, spent, shaken, filled with shame and self-disgust; and he who renounced God had prayed to God—to cleanse him of woman, free him of woman, of the blasphemous lie that was her piety and the blasphemous truth that was her flesh.

To a degree at least, his prayer had been answered. For though the dreams sometimes recurred he was no longer their slave and their captive; and though he had now reached an age when others not only dreamed of girls, but began doing something about it, he was able to renounce them without envy or misery. If he was different—all right, he was different, and he could live with it. And not only that, but be proud of it, glory in it. As, in the end, he had gloried in the childish voices calling him *beau gosse* and Mama's darling, for he had learned that within him he had tenfold the strength and power and self-sufficiency of those who mocked him.

Now, alone in the forest, he heard another voice. "Little boy-girl," it said. "Little girl-boy—"

He had heard it for weeks. For weeks, in his dreams, he had seen the bloodshot eyes, the beard, the stumps of teeth. And he had recoiled in horror; tried not to hear or see; to wake, to wrench his mind away. . . . But he had not succeeded. The voice, the image had remained with him. And now at last he accepted them, with all the rest, as a mark—the secret ultimate mark—of his apartness. . . . All right, he was different. He would go on being different. And the voices were only voices, knowing nothing of the truth, of how and why. He himself, and he alone, was at last beginning to have an understanding of the *why*, and it had nothing to do with *gosses* or darlings or girl-boys, but with something as opposite to these as midnight to noon, with dark shadows and echoes from a distant past. . . . A few days before he had taken pencil and paper and tried to describe himself, and he had written: *I have the blue-white eye of my Gallic ancestors, their narrow skull, and their clumsiness in fighting.* And perhaps that was it, or part of it. That he was a throwback, a sort of genealogical sport: not a nineteenth-century Frenchman at all, but a Gaul, a Teuton, a Viking, a wanderer from an older freer age, born out of his time into a world he was not made for.

Into a world of churches. Of women. Of lie piled upon lie in the name of civilization.

All right, he was different. He was the queer one. The outcast, the vagabond, the voyager on strange seas. He saw things that others did not see; thought and felt things that were beyond their imaginings. Most of all he was different because the others—whatever was within them, whatever the truth beneath the lies and pretenses—kept it locked away and hidden, whereas he could not rest, could scarcely live and breathe, unless he poured them out in words. They were words, he already knew, to which few would listen—or, listening, understand. For every Chariol, there were a hundred Mothers, Felixes, Michels, Mimis, priests, and teachers, with minds held tight in the bonds of their stupidity or hypocrisy. There was one thing that would listen, though—that he could make listen—and that was paper. Pencil would speak, and paper would listen, and he held them as naturally as others held a knife for whittling or a stone for throwing—or held a girl in their arms in the Bois d'Amour.

He held them now. He held and loved them and commanded them. He was sitting at the foot of an ancient tree in the forest of the Gauls and the Teutons, and his mind ranged back over the sea of the centuries. *I am I,* he wrote, *and the prisoner of my flesh. But I have also been others, elsewhere. A villein, I have made the journey to the Holy Land; my head is full of roads through the Swabian plains, views of Byzantium, ramparts of Jerusalem. From these a thousand memories stir. A leper, I am seated among potsherds and nettles at the foot of a sun-eaten wall. Later, a knight, I have bivouacked under German stars. I have danced the witches' sabbath in a red clearing with old hags and the children of werewolves....*

The images flowed into him. In a tide, a flood—wildly. His head almost burst with them; and though he did not know where they came from, he knew that they would keep flowing, that they were there within him, inexhaustible and illimitable. The trick was to fashion words for them, to find a tongue for what had never before been said. "Dear God," he thought, "—not the God of church, of priests, of dogma and droning litanies, but the living God, God who *is*—dear God, give me that tongue. Let me pour out what is in me: the flood—and the fire. Let me be a thief of your fire, as was Prometheus, so that I may give it back, brighter and purer."

He moved up out of the past. He moved over the present, across the earth, across the oceans. He sailed again over the horizon on his canvas bedspread, on the old journey, the journey after his father. He came again to Morocco and Algeria, the coasts of the sun. He went on farther, into the desert, across the burning Sahara, on and on, deeper and deeper, until he came to the end of the desert, and now the sun was gone and he had reached the borders of Cimmeria, land of whirlwinds and darkness. But still he kept on, and beyond the whirlwinds he could hear the beat of wild music; beyond the darkness gleamed the glory of a rainbow. And now, suddenly, green jungles lay before him, filled with orchids, emeralds, tawny lions, scarlet birds. And among the jungles, black nations, white cities on yellow rivers; on the rivers, canoes; on the riverbanks, dancers; dancers in files, by the thousand and ten thousand, naked, bodies glistening, their hair laced with threads of gold. Only two among all the thousands were not dancing. They stood apart from the others, above the others: high, silent, motionless: two idols above the multitudes. One was the king—the Black King—and Claude knew him well. All his life he had known him, watched him: watched the white of his teeth and the white of his eyeballs, watched him standing there—waiting. And the other he knew too. The one beside him: the Black Queen. He knew her curved lips, her flanks of ebony, the nipples like two moons on her swelling breasts. And he knew, also, that he was afraid of her, as all his life he had been afraid, deeply and terribly, in his blood and his bone. But he could do nothing about it; he still watched her, still came closer, and she too waited; and then it happened as he knew it would happen, as it always happened; he was close beside her, reaching out to her—and she changed. The lips were gone. The breasts were gone. Her flanks were no longer the black of ebony but the black of iron. . . .

For the Queen was his mother.

Claude looked around him. The sun was low, and it had grown darker. Rising, he walked on through the jungle of the north.

5

He walked. He read.

He wrote:

> . . . on the black gallows, one-armed, bland,
> they dance and dance, the paladins,
> thin paladins, the devil's band,
> the skeletons of Saladins. . . .

The images swelled, multiplied, thronged in on his brain: glowing, gleaming. Then they faded, and he pushed his paper away. Cambon returned. The world returned. Out in the world, beyond the town, France struggled and seethed. Napoleon the Little was gone, and with him his empress and his empire; but the war went on, and in Paris was a new Government of National Defense. There were battles, skirmishes, marches, countermarches, advances, retreats. But mostly, for the French, retreats. Now the Germans were moving quickly toward Paris; they swarmed over northern France, and it seemed that only the Ardennes was free of them. Half the time Claude wished they would come there too. A few Krupp shells in the Place du Sépulcre might jolt the Cambonards from their depths of lethargy—or at the very least stir up the dust.

No Germans came. Cambon, apparently, was not worth the bother.

But finally, as summer passed into autumn, there were some signs of the war. Food began running short, troops shuttled in and out, and in October it was announced that the lycée would not reopen because the building was to be used as a military hospital. No school was fine with Claude; educationally he had gone far beyond anything it could give him. But its closing cut down his day-to-day outward life to even drearier limits than before: to home and store, mother and sister. His brother Felix was in the army—it having resolved his hesitations by reducing the age limit and conscripting him. Monsieur Chariol, though he had not been conscripted (thanks to a slight heart murmur), was also away, living with his married sister in St. Quentin. Michel was working on the farm of one of his many uncles and rarely came into town.

"And you will work too," said Madame Morel. "You will stay in the store every day. All day."

Sometimes he did, because there was nothing better to do. Sometimes, ignoring her, he went out: wandering, walking. And one day in late October he walked down the road, along the Meuse, past the forest, and did not stop until he came to Antimes. Here was a small army post, and, standing outside it, he thought, "Well, at least there's no more emperor." And he went in and presented himself to a recruiting sergeant.

"I want to enlist," he said.

The sergeant looked him over and grinned. "In what?" he inquired.

"In the army."

"In this army, it so happens, we do not have a nursery school."

"I am eighteen," said Claude.

"If you are eighteen, *mon brave*, I am a hundred and three and fought in the Battle of Wagram."

"I am eighteen, I tell you. I am as big as many soldiers. And strong—"

"And your diapers show through your pants. Get going!"

"But—"

"Fous le camp!"

Then he was walking again. Through Antimes. Out of Antimes. Along the road. But it was not the road that led back to Cambon. It led in the opposite direction, to the west, and all the rest of the day he followed it, moving steadily on through the autumn countryside. When night came he slept in a hayrick. And the next day he kept on. By noon hunger was gnawing at him, but he could find little to satisfy it; though all around him were the farms that fed a nation, the pickings were poorer than on the stone streets of Paris. In an orchard he came upon some fallen half-rotted apples and ate what he could of them. Later, in an empty barnyard, he cornered and caught a chicken, but he could think of no way of cooking it and let it go. Toward evening he knocked at the doors of several farmhouses, and at one of them was given a few scraps. But at the others he was turned away, and twice dogs were set after him. He spent the second night, too, in a hayrick.

He forked from one road to another. They bent, twisted, rose, and fell. Some were deserted; on others there were passers-by, on foot and in farm wagons. Now and then he passed a tramp ("—and what am *I*?" he thought), but they were busy with their own affairs. And once there was a cloud of dust ahead and a troop of hussars came riding toward him. For an instant he was seized by a wild notion. "It will be my father," he told himself. "He will be riding at their head, and he will see me and know me and take me with him." Then the troop reached him and rode past, and all that was left behind was dust.

He was alone again. The fields lay brown and still, and beyond them were the woods. At night it had been cold, and there was still a tang in the air, but the sun was warm on his face and body. He sat down beside a fence and mused, and, as always when he mused, there came enchantment. There came from his pocket pencil and wad of paper.

. . . In the woods there is a bird, he wrote, *his song stops you and makes you blush.*

There is a clock that never strikes.

There is a swamp with a nest of white beasts.

There is a cathedral that goes down and a lake that comes up.

There is a little carriage abandoned in the copse, or that goes running down the road beribboned.

There is a troupe of strolling players in costume, glimpsed on the road through the borders of the woods.

He paused, licked his pencil, and added:

And then, when you are hungry and thirsty, there is someone to chase you away.

When he looked up, the sky was darker. Evening was coming on, and, with it, clouds, and as he walked on again it began to rain. At first there was only a drizzle, but then it poured. Soon his face was streaming with water, his clothes were soaked, and the road under his feet was a river of mud. He was cold, tired, and hungry. Coming to a farmhouse, he knocked —and was chased away. After a while there was another—and the same reception. He walked on. It was full night now, and he moved through watery blackness, and then at last, beyond the others, he came to still another house, standing dim and alone.

"It will be the Witch of Endor," he thought, as he approached, "and she'll do the chasing with a broomstick."

But it was not a witch. It was a young woman who answered his knock, holding an oil lamp, and she looked him up and down, much as the sergeant had done in Antimes. "What do you want?" she asked.

"I've lost my way," Claude said. "I'm cold and hungry, and if you'd give me some food I'd be glad to work for it."

She continued studying him, her eyes narrowed on his face. Then she stepped back and let him in, and he found himself in a dingy low-ceilinged room. There were a table, a few chairs, a cot, a cold fireplace. Playing on the floor were two small children of perhaps four and three.

"I've been wanting to make a fire," said the woman. "But all the wood's out in the shed, and it's raining too hard."

"I'll get it for you," Claude said.

He made three trips to the woodshed, bringing in logs and kindling, and then laid them in the hearth and started a fire. While she prepared a meal, he stood by, warming and drying himself, and waiting for her to say something. But she didn't.

"Are you alone here?" he asked at last.

"There are these two." She indicated the children.

"I mean—you have no husband?"

"My husband's in the army. He's been gone four months now."

"It must be hard on a farm without a man."

"I manage," the woman said.

She went on with her cooking, chopping up pieces of meat and cabbage and putting them to boil in an iron pot. She was a big woman, with a broad high-colored face, and her hands looked strong and competent. As she moved about, her hips and breasts bulged under the cheap cotton of her dress.

"This is kind of you, madame," Claude said.

She didn't answer. When the stew was ready, she ladled two small helpings onto tin plates and fed the children, squatting beside them on the floor. Then she divided what was left into two portions, set them on the table, and motioned to Claude to sit down.

"It's good," he said, eating.

"It's garbage," she said. "But it's all there is."

They ate in silence for a few moments. Then the woman rose suddenly, went to a cupboard in the corner, and came back with a bottle of wine. "Maybe this will make the garbage taste better," she said.

Claude looked at the bottle in astonishment. It had not been opened, and she gave him a knife and told him to pry up the cork. Meanwhile she brought two glasses, and when the bottle was open she filled them. "It's been standing there four months," she said. "That's long enough."

It was the first wine Claude had ever tasted. Many children in Cambon were all but weaned on it, but his mother would have roasted in hell before allowing a drop in the house, and he had never had any luck trying to cadge a sip at the town's cafés. Now at last he had it—and he liked it— first sipping with the caution of unfamiliarity, then drinking it down in full swallows. It was red wine. It was warm and glowing and better than the fire, as it spread slowly, deliciously, through his chilled body. Soon he felt wonderful—like laughing, like singing—but he controlled himself carefully. Perhaps the wine would make the woman begin talking, he thought, and then he could let himself go a little too.

But she still didn't talk. She emptied her glass and refilled it, and then his, and they sat silently at the table until both wine and food were gone. Then she got up, again abruptly, and took the two children into another room; and while she was gone Claude cleaned the plates and glasses in a pail of water. He almost dropped one glass, but not quite, and by the time she returned he had finished.

"Thank you, madame," he said.

She didn't seem to hear him.

"And now I guess I'll be going."

He was halfway to the door before she spoke. "It's still raining," she said. "You can sleep here if you like."

"Oh. Thank you. That's very kind. But—"

"It's no trouble." She nodded at the cot. "Use it, if you want to."

She went out again and closed the door. Claude sat for a while before the dying fire, and he could feel the wine in his head, and within the wine a host of gleaming images. But when he brought out paper and pencil the images began at once to spin and fade. Rising, he went to the cot, sat down on it, and took off his shoes. Then he stretched out. The images spun and flickered and mingled with the sound of rain on the roof, and soon he too was spinning, softly, darkly, into sleep.

When he awoke he was no longer alone. There was someone beside him. A hand was touching him.

"I'm cold," said the woman's voice.

She lay down beside him. In the darkness he could see her only dimly, but could tell she was wearing some sort of shift or nightdress. Her big breasts pressed against him. Her body had a heavy pungent odor.

"We'll keep each other warm," she said.

He lay motionless and rigid. Her hand touched his hair and moved through it, and then down his cheek. It was big and rough, but it moved gently.

"It's been so long," she said. "So long. One can't be alone and cold forever."

There was a silence. The hand kept moving. And now the other hand was moving too. After a while she said softly:

"You're young, aren't you? You haven't been much with women? . . . That's all right; don't be afraid. I'll help you."

Then what seemed like a long time passed. The hands grew less gentle, and the woman's body, like his own, became tense and rigid.

"What's the matter with you, *hein?*" she asked. Her voice was no longer soft. And suddenly she jerked up. "You're not a man at all, *hein?* You're only a baby, is that it? A baby that can't take a woman, but can only play with itself. *Petit emmerdé—*"

The words rasped out. She got to her feet. And now Claude moved too. In one quick trembling leap he was up off the cot. He was groping for his shoes, pulling them on, clumping across the floor with dangling laces. He bumped into the table, skirted it, reached the door. He opened the door, ran out, slipped in the mud, fell, and picked himself up again. He ran on, blindly, through the night and the rain.

Three days later, in his sister's house in St. Quentin, Albert Chariol sat in an upstairs room revising one of his short stories. He heard the bell ring downstairs, and his sister answering it, but paid no attention until, a few moments later, she called up to him. Then he got up, went down the stairs, and stopped abruptly at the bottom. *"Mon Dieu!"* he said.

His sister looked at him nervously. "This—er—person says—"

Chariol came closer. He stared at the boy. He looked at the broken shoes, the torn clothes, the wild hair, the mud-caked face. *"Mon Dieu,"* he said again, "what is this?"

"I knew you were in St. Quentin," said Claude.

"But what are *you* doing here? When did you leave home?"

"A few days ago."

"A few days? You mean you walked?"

"Yes."

"Why? For what reason?"

"Because I—I—"

Claude hesitated. Chariol glanced from him to his sister and made a slight gesture, and after another nervous and uncomprehending look she turned and left them. "You've run away again," Chariol said.

"Yes," said Claude.

"Why?"

"You know why."

"When did you leave?"

"Last—Wednesday."

"It doesn't take that long to get here—even walking. Where have you been meanwhile?"

"Around."

"Around where? Did you try to go back to Paris?"

"No."

"Have you been in jail again?"

"No."

"Where, then?"

"Just—walking."

"And why did you finally come here?"

"Because you're my friend."

Chariol bit his lip. He studied the boy's face; then walked away a few paces and came back again. "Claude, Claude!" he said. "What's the matter with you?"

The boy didn't answer.

"First Paris and prison. And now this. What's got into you anyhow? You're too intelligent for this sort of thing."

There was another pause. Then Claude said: "I can't go on living in Cambon, that's all."

"Why not?"

"Because I'd die there."

"Die? What sort of child's talk is that?... You're not yet even sixteen. After school reopens you'll still have another full year of it, and then you'll be ready for a university and there'll be plenty of time to talk of going away." Claude seemed scarcely to be listening, and he added in exasperation, "Right now there's only one thing to talk about, and that's getting you home."

"No," said Claude.

"We won't argue about it. I'll make the arrangements. But first"—he was looking the boy over again—"we'll see what can be done to make you resemble a human being. . . . How much have you eaten since you left home?"

"A little."

"How many real meals?"

"One."

"My sister will take care of that. Meanwhile, get yourself upstairs and take a bath. The bathroom's the first door on the left. I'll be up in a while and see if I can find you something clean to wear."

Claude hesitated, turned, and went up the steps. Chariol went into another room, spoke for a few minutes with his sister, and then went up too. The bathroom door was open, and there was no one inside. Going on to his own room, he found Claude, still in his rags and mud, bent concentratedly over the manuscript of the story he had left on his table. "This is better, Albert—much better than before," the boy said, without raising his head. "But why do you go on trying to write like Flaubert?"

Chariol himself took him back to Cambon. When they entered the store Madame Morel was waiting on a customer, and she merely glanced at them and said coldly, "You will please wait a minute."

They waited; and when the customer had left she spoke not to Claude but to Chariol. "So you are involved in this," she said.

"I have only brought him home," replied Chariol.

"Brought him home from where?"

The teacher told what he knew, and she listened impassively. "Still it is you who are largely responsible," she said when he had finished. "Before you came here he was a good and obedient boy. It is you who have given him his wild and evil ideas."

"Madame, I assure you I have had nothing to do with—"

"If you have nothing to do with it, why is it you to whom he goes?"

"He came to me only yesterday, and I have brought him home as soon as possible. I have told him that he has done wrong; that here is where he belongs."

"Where he belongs is in an institution. And that is where I would put him, if it were not for the shame—and the cost. While he was away I went to the police; I spoke to *Monsieur le Préfet*, and he said, 'Yes, there are institutions for such cases.' But when I inquire further he tells me something fantastic: that there would be a charge. Yes, it is hard to believe, but that is what he says: that for families who can afford it there is a monthly charge. 'Afford it!' I say. 'And what makes you think *I* am such a one as can afford it?' 'Because you have the store,' he says. 'Because you are a businesswoman.' . . . Hah!" The widow's voice rasped with her outrage. "To me he says this. To me, who has nothing, who works ten, twelve, fourteen hours a day, slaves like a dog, pays unjust taxes—"

"Madame, I am sure an institution is no place for Claude," said Chariol mildly. "He is far better off—"

"I will thank you to let *me* decide where he is better off."

"I only wish to point out—"

"No pointing is necessary. You have caused enough trouble already, and I am quite competent to handle my own affairs. So now, if you please, monsieur. I am a working woman. I am very busy."

"May I say simply that—"

"You will please leave, monsieur."

She eyed him stonily. Chariol hesitated, shrugged slightly, and patted Claude on the arm. Then he went out.

Claude went upstairs.

. . . And upstairs was where he stayed for the better part of the next several weeks. With Felix gone, he at last had a room to himself; and though he still had no key, he devised a way of jamming a chair against the door so that his mother could not come in unless he moved it. School remained closed, his classmates scattered and at work. Sometimes, when his eyes were bleared from reading or writing, he would go downstairs and work himself, in the store. Sometimes he let himself out the window and went off on walks or to the library. But, mostly, his world was bounded by the four walls of his room. And the only visitor to that world was his sister Yvette.

Yvette was concerned about him. With all her eleven-year-old powers she strove to right the mysterious wrongs that she knew existed but could not understand. She begged Claude to "be nice to *Maman*." She begged him to go to church. "You've been bad, Claude. *Maman* says you've been very bad. But if you go to church it won't matter; it will be all right. If you talk to Father Lacaze, and then he talks to God and Our Lady—"

"Sure, *ora pro nobis*. . . . Thanks, I'll speak for myself."

She looked at him uncomprehendingly. "And even if you don't *want* to go, still you *ought* to," she persisted. "Think what Father Lacaze must be thinking. And what everybody's saying."

"The hell with everybody."

"Oh, Claude, such awful language!"

"I know a lot worse," he said. Then he pulled her yellow pigtails. "All right, go get your soul saved—quick. I've got reading to do."

He read. He thought. He wrote. He wrote slowly and carefully, in his small fine hand; then scratched out and discarded and revised and rewrote, striving always to "find a tongue," searching endlessly for the exact word, the exact color and tone and vibration of word, that could alone bring outward life to inward vision. For years, already, he had worked at the technique of writing. He had written prose and verse, narrative and lyric. He had tried all manner of verse forms: ode and sonnet, triolet and rondeau, rondel and villanelle, alexandrine and sestina. He had experimented with meter, rhyme, nonrhyme, alliteration, onomatopoeia; with all the tricks and skills and traditions of the poet's craft, until he was able to use them as he pleased. Now, however, he was no longer interested in forms and techniques, and least of all in tradition. They were prison walls, and he scaled them. They were rubble, and he threw them away. All his concentration, his dedication was to the expression of the inward; of what lay within himself—and himself alone.

For hours he sat at his window staring at the drab nothingness of the back yard, struggling to master the ideas and images that thronged his brain. He thought of women. Of his sister, his mother. Of their goodness and primness and piety, and of their bondage to the church. He thought of the church itself, of priests and Masses and mumbled Latin. And he wrote:

> . . . *when coming from the naves through which no sunlight files,*
> *banal in silk, the ladies of the town's best quarter*
> *—oh Christ—the ones with liver trouble and green smiles,*
> *offer bleached fingers to the kiss of holy water.* . . .

But he thought of God, too. And that was a different matter. So different that in a thousand centuries he could not have explained it to his mother or sister, or to Father Lacaze. . . . Could he explain it even to himself? . . . He tried.

From the same desert, in the same night, he wrote, *always my tired eyes awake to the silver star, always; but the Kings of Life are not moved, the three Magi, mind and heart and soul. When shall we go beyond the mountains and the shores, to greet the birth of new toil, of new wisdom, the flight of tyrants, of demons, the end of superstition, to adore—the first to adore—Christmas on the earth?*

He thought often of Christmas. Of the Mass of Christ, the birth of Christ, the birth of hope and love. And then he thought of the other Christmas, the holidays in Cambon, the cold, the grayness, the pinched pious faces, his mother leading the march to church in their panoply of serge and umbrellas. He, Felix, and Yvette had never had a celebration or a gift for the holidays. "Those are for rich people," his mother had said. "And for godless people. For the poor and decent, Christmas is praying in church—not heathen fripperies and red ribbons."

His birthday—the sixteenth—came and went, and there were no gifts then either. But at sixteen he was no longer concerned with such things. And besides he had found, for himself, something far better. This was a slim volume of verse by a poet named Maurice Druard, which by unlikely chance had made its appearance on the musty shelves of the Cambon library, and which Claude's eyes had spotted as if it had been an ingot of gold. Having no money for deposits, he was not allowed to take books home from the library, but this one he had taken anyhow, smuggling it out under his jacket, and in a few days he had read and reread its contents until he knew them, word for word, by heart. The poems reminded him of Baudelaire's, but of a younger, fresher, even more daring Baudelaire who had gone on from *Les Fleurs du Mal* to still more exquisite renderings of cadence and imagery. The book told nothing of the author; but he was young, Claude was sure of that—perhaps not a great deal older than himself—for in every page, almost every line, he found vibrations and echoes that were his own, no less than Druard's. "This man is my brother," he thought. "More than a brother: almost a part of me. Someday I must meet him, know him, share my heart with him."

Meanwhile he read and reread—bewitched. His mind moved on from Druard's fantasies to his own, and they welled up out of him, richer and more fecund than ever. Working with a concentration he had never before attained, he wrote a half dozen new pieces: some in verse, some in prose; some of the world of Cambon which he knew and hated, some of the world of his imaginings which he knew and loved. And when he had finished, another new thing happened to him, for he found that he was no longer content simply to push his work into a table drawer. He had to *do* something with it, make someone aware of it—someone beyond the dead

world of Cambon who might understand and appreciate. He thought
first, of course, of Chariol, but Chariol could wait. He would see it in due
time, anyhow. What he wanted now was something more than that: a true
professional opinion. So, selecting his favorite among the Parisian literary
magazines he had seen at the library, he put his new pieces in an envelope,
filched postage money from his mother's cash drawer, and sent them off.
I am only a young writer, he added in a note to the editor, *but I think the
enclosed will show I am a true writer. I beg you to hold out your hand to me. . . .*

The next day the envelope came back. Paris had been cut off by the
Germans, and no mail was going through. Seeing the stamp on the envelope, his mother stormed.

Though the invaders had not yet bothered with Cambon and the
Ardennes, they now seemed to be all over the rest of the country. Paris was
not only cut off, but surrounded and besieged, and the siege dragged on
through the fall and early winter. The Government of National Defense
had withdrawn to Tours, from which it was directing its scattered armies
and sounding trumpet calls for *la patrie;* but the defense of the capital,
one gathered, was less and less in the hands of the regulars and more and
more the work of the Garde Nationale, the civilian auxiliaries, the people
themselves. Again, for the first time in many years, the political left was up
and stirring, and one heard the words "Commune" and "Communard."
There were demands for peace, marches on the Hôtel de Ville, demands
and demonstrations by factory workers, who were banding together into
an organization called *les blouses blanches.* All reports from the city indicated that, behind the defense against the Germans, an even more bitter
internal struggle was brewing. A struggle of workers against employers,
poor against rich, ruled against rulers. A struggle that might soon be revolution.

As the weeks wore on, Claude became increasingly aware of all this.
Slowly he surfaced from his pool of dreams, and, putting away his paper
and pencils, devoured all the news he could find about the changing pattern
of events. For this, unlike the war itself, was a thing that fired his sympathy
and imagination: not a clash of state against state, power against power,
in another of Europe's endless wars of unreason, but a true upsurging of
right against wrong, of oppressed against oppressor. He had long since
read deeply of the great romantics: Rousseau, Lamartine, Chateaubriand,
de Vigny, Hugo. Of Voltaire, Montesquieu, Diderot, the *philosophes* of the
Enlightenment. Of Shelley, Heine, Michelet, Marx, all of them prophets
and proclaimers of a new order. And he believed with them in their sort
of future: in *liberté, égalité, fraternité,* in the rights and brotherhood of
man. Most of all, with the vehemence of his sixteen years, he believed in
anything that was against the bourgeoisie, against the gods of his mother
and of Cambon, against authority and hierarchy and orthodoxy and the

status quo. When there was nothing left to read or hear of present events he would go back to what, for him, were the greatest days of French history: the days of 1789, of 1830, of 1848, when the vision of freedom gleamed bright in the land and the barricades went up in the streets of Paris. In 'thirty and 'forty-eight the risings had been crushed; liberty had drooped, reaction risen again. But this time, if the rising-up came, perhaps the end would be different. As the *sans-culottes* of the old revolution had destroyed the tyranny of Bourbon and aristocracy, so might the *blouses blanches* of a new one end forever the choking death grip of the bourgeoisie. At any rate, if the issue was joined, he, Claude Morel, wanted to be part of it. He *would* be part of it. Not as he had tried to be part of the army fighting the Germans—that had been only childish adventure, a running away—but as a fighter in a cause that was *his* cause, with the dedication of the three Magi that were mind, heart, and soul.

The days and weeks passed. It grew colder, and a film of snow coated the back yard and the roof of the privy. And in his room it grew colder too, until he had to take to wearing coat and gloves as he sat reading or writing.

"Claude!"

No answer.

"Claude!"

No answer.

His mother rattled the doorknob; but the chair was tilted tight against it, and she could not get in. Claude smiled as he heard her footsteps recede. He was secure behind the barricades of his own revolution.

At night he lay on his cot in the darkness. He thought, planned, waited, and waiting, plunged back into the pool of dreams. He was again—as he had done so often in reality—letting himself out the window, crossing the yard, scaling the wall, moving quickly through the streets. He was walking beside the river, along the roads, into the forest; but this time the forest was not the end, it was the beginning, and he was moving on past it, between the fields, through the countryside; and even here there was no turning back, no detour to St. Quentin, no retreat to Cambon, but only the road stretching on ahead, and himself following it, until at last he was again in Paris. He was in the capital, the metropolis, among the lights and crowds, in the squares and boulevards, but he was no longer a country *mioche* sleeping under a bridge, stealing his food, wandering hungry and alone through the streets. He was not alone at all, but one of many, one of a great throng, a battalion, an army of the people, marching the streets, shouting, singing, moving on toward the palaces, the stone towers, the seats of power, while a flag flapped above them like a golden flame. He was in the councils of the people, in the place of liberty, equality, brotherhood, with victory won, the night behind them, the sun of freedom shining. . . .

And there the dream should have ended. There he willed it to end.

But it did not happen that way. It went on.

He went on.

It was for others to stay, for him to move on; and he was moving far and high, far and deep; no longer in the city, nor in a countryside, no longer marching or walking, but in a ship on the sea, with a tall mast above him and the wind of freedom in the sail. He was reaching the lost shores, the magic shores, crossing them, passing them, passing beyond the world of men, through desert, through waste, until again, as always, he came to the land beyond. He came to the green forests, the yellow rivers, the black nations, the black savages; to the place he had known all his life, the place he had come from and to which he must return, the place of dreams, of wild music, of beating feet, dancing files; and there, as always, beyond the files and above them, were the two who waited for him—the Black King—the Black Queen—

Again he came closer, closer. And again the Queen began to change. As always—

Except that now, for the first time, it was *not* as always. She changed, but it was differently. She did not become his mother. She became Mimi Rouger, laughing, beckoning, and the jungle behind her was the Bois d'Amour. She became a farmer's wife, and she reached out and touched him; she pulled him to her, roughly, savagely, and he could feel her breath on his face, see the whites of her eyes. She became a shadow in the darkness, and the eyes were no longer white but small and bloodshot, the lips were hidden by a beard, the stumps of teeth showed in a twisted grin—

"Give me my poems!" Claude cried. "Give me my poems!"

And his own voice wakened him, cold and trembling in the night.

6

Christmas. Christmas on earth. The silver star burned brightly, and the Magi walked the night.

At four in the morning Claude left his room and went softly downstairs into the store. Going to the cash drawer, he opened it (his mother had of course hidden the key, but he had found it) and by the light of a candle counted the contents. It was about eighty francs. He did not take it all; he took twenty francs—one fourth of it—for he was one fourth of the family, and this was his Christmas gift. Stuffing the bills in his pocket, he went out the back door, over the familiar wall, into the streets. A few minutes later he was out of town, on a country road.

It was about a two hours' walk to the farm where Michel Favre worked for his uncle, and dawn was just breaking when he reached it. Hearing sounds in the barn, he looked in, and there was Michel, milking cows.

"You're up early for a holiday," said Claude.

Michel grunted. "The damn cows don't know it's a holiday." Then he eyed his friend curiously. "What's going on?" he asked.

"I'm taking a trip."

"A trip? Where?"

"To Paris."

"Again?"

"Yes, again. It's my Christmas present. Want to come?"

"Come? You mean now?"

"That's right."

"And walk all the way?"

"There's no other way to go. The Germans have Paris cut off."

"Then they'll catch you. They'll stop you."

"No they won't. They're too dumb. I'll get by them."

"And when you get there—what will you do then?"

"I'm going to sell my poems."

"That's all? Just sell your poems?"

"No. Then I'm going to join the revolution."

"The revolution?"

"There's going to be one. Wait and see. . . . And I'm going to be in it. . . . I'm going to join the *blouses blanches*, the Communards, the army of the people. And we're going to fight and win and make France free at last."

Michel stared at him for another moment. Then, finishing with a cow, he moved stool and pail to the next.

"Well," said Claude, "are you coming?"

"I—I can't."

"Why not?"

"Because I can't. Because I've got work to do."

"You always said you wanted to come. That you'd go with me next time."

"I know, but—"

"—but you're afraid."

Michel went on with his milking.

"All right, you're afraid." Squatting beside the pail, Claude scooped up some milk in the dipper and drank it. "A man needs some breakfast for a long walk," he said. Then he went to the door. "I'll bring you a souvenir from Paris. What do you want? . . . No, never mind, I know. I'll bring you a whore in lace panties."

He waved, left the barn, and headed down the road. An icy wind had risen, blowing from the gray dawn sky, and he hunched his shoulders against it and turned up his collar.

"Well . . . Merry Christmas," he thought. "Merry Christmas to all!"

In Reims he was picked up as a vagrant and spent three days in jail (with no view of the cathedral). Near a small village, farther on, he spent a week, more profitably, helping a farmer repair his barn. But mostly he kept going—going: west and south, south and west. It was, they said, one of the coldest winters in men's memory. Day after day the wind blew, the sky was leaden, and snow mounted higher on the frozen earth. But he was now a veteran vagabond; he had learned some tricks of the trade, and fared, on the whole, less badly than on his earlier ventures when the earth had been green, the sun warm and kind. Often he was cold, but never freezing. Usually he was hungry, but always, somewhere, somehow, found enough food to keep him going.

Very soon he had come to occupied France, and there were German troops everywhere. But there were civilians everywhere, too, and no attention was paid to him. It was toward the end of his journey, when he approached the front lines and the defenses of Paris, that he had thought it most likely he would have trouble, but even there the going was clear. He simply left the road, cut cautiously through woods and brushlands, and when he came out of them he was in the eastern suburbs of the capital. Late at night, finding a street door carelessly unlocked, he sneaked in, found himself in a billiard parlor, and fell asleep on one of the tables. And in the morning, the proprietor, discovering him, was so pleased with his story (though he obviously didn't believe it) that he gave him a fine breakfast of eggs and cheese. Then he went on again. For almost the first time since he had left Cambon, the wind dropped and the sun glittered. As he marched into the city proper, through the squares, down the boulevards, he felt it was he, and not the Germans, who was the invading conqueror.

But he was not long in discovering that Paris was not the same as before. Winter and siege together had taken their toll, and he moved through streets that were the mere ghosts of what they had been six months before. Half the cafés were closed, and the rest had receded from the bleak pavements into small dismal cubicles behind grimed walls. The crowds were no longer promenading, but hurrying intent and pinch-faced about their business. The shop windows were almost bare of merchandise and food.

It was not of food or cafés or crowds, however, that Claude was thinking. For he too had business to attend to. Checking the address he had written on a slip of paper, he walked on to the Seine, crossed a bridge to the Left Bank, and followed the Boulevard St. Michel into the heart of the university district that was known as the *Quartier Latin*. In a side street off the boulevard he found the building he was looking for—a decrepit pile of small shops and offices—and entering, climbed a flight of stairs and tried a door. But the door was locked, and when he knocked there was no answer. Hearing him, the concierge appeared and asked gruffly what he wanted.

"*La Nouvelle Revue*," said Claude.

"It's closed."

"Closed?"

"For the duration, yes. Most of the offices here are now closed."

Claude went slowly downstairs. *La Nouvelle Revue* was the magazine to which he had tried to send his writings a few weeks before. He did not know the addresses of any other magazines, and even if he found them, they would probably be closed too. For a few moments he stood irresolutely in the foyer of the building, holding his sheaf of manuscript in his hand, while the concierge, who had followed him down, watched him suspiciously. Then he stuffed the papers in his pocket and went out. . . . All right, poetry could wait. That wasn't primarily why he had come to Paris, anyhow. As he again walked the streets, his step was firm, his head high, and in his thoughts were the lines of another poet, and a great one —Heinrich Heine. . . . *Whether my songs are praised or blamed*, he had said, *matters little to me; but on my grave lay a sword, for I was a soldier in the war for the liberation of man.*

But exactly where and how humanity was being liberated was, on that dreary winter day in Paris, not easy to discover. The city lay cold and petrified, sheathed in grime and stone. As evening closed in, the crowds hurried by, shut their doors, and were gone. The branches of the chestnut trees rose black and bare against gray walls, and when the gas lamps came on they were no longer bright flares but mere flickering glints in the darkness. From old habit he turned his steps back toward the Seine, and the bridges, but now the vaults under the arches were deserted, and he knew that if he tried to spend the night there he would freeze to death. Going on toward the center of town, he followed his vagabond's instincts, searching for the haunts of other vagabonds, and presently found them in a tangle of squalid streets behind Les Halles. Here, block after block, was an array of decrepit establishments that, for a minimal fee, provided shelter and food of sorts to the city's flotsam; and having still a few francs left from his raid on the cash drawer, he selected one called the Hôtel de Babylone and went in. For twenty centimes he was given a bowl of soup and a piece of black bread, and for another twenty the use of a burlap pallet on a stone floor. As the bridge lodgings had been during the summer, so was this winter refuge crowded to the last square inch. But here this was by way of blessing, for the old building had no heating, and the only warmth came from the close-packed bodies of its occupants. Lice immediately invaded Claude's clothing, and for a while he picked at them indolently. Then he fell asleep amid the snores and stenches.

No one molested him. In the morning no one seemed even to see him. At first light a man appeared in the room banging a pan, and in five minutes the night's guests were out on the street and headed in their various directions—wherever they might lead. Claude's led all over. He walked. He walked. For, though he knew the *what* of his search, he still did not know the *where*. Signs of the war and the siege, of ferment and crisis, were everywhere: in the littered streets, the uncared-for buildings, the grim-faced crowds, the very tension in the gray winter air. And soldiers were everywhere—more soldiers than he had ever seen: infantry and artillery, hussars and lancers, guardsmen in horsetail helmets, Zouaves in kepis and baggy pants, soldiers singly and in pairs and in squads and in troops, standing guard, marching, riding, deploying, scouring the streets in *moblots*, or flying patrols. But these were not the ones he was seeking. These were the regular army, the tools of the rulers, the servants of reaction: no better than the *flics* in their patent-leather tricornes, whom he already knew well as the enemy. What he was looking for were *the others*, the enemies of the enemy, the revolutionary *blouses blanches*, the detachments of the Garde Nationale, the people's army, who he had heard were on the point of deserting from the established government to the Commune. But the only white shirts he saw were under bourgeois jackets and waistcoats. And the men of the Guard, if he actually saw any, were so ill-uniformed and equipped that he could not tell them from mere civilians.

He walked on. He still searched.

Finding, at last, what seemed to be a sort of National Guard headquarters, he tried to present himself for enlistment, but was turned away at the gate. He hunted for another headquarters, but without success. Then, quitting the center of the city, he walked out to the workingmen's districts, in the eastern faubourgs, which were known to be the home grounds of *les blouses blanches*. And in time his long search bore fruit. In a small dingy square flanked by tenements and warehouses, a speaker on a box was addressing a crowd of perhaps a hundred men; and while his shirt was not white but dirty blue, his message was good Communard gospel. *"A bas la guerre!"* he cried. *"A bas les bourgeois! . . . Vive la paix! Vive la Commune!"*

His listeners cheered. Claude cheered with them. Pressing his way forward, he was soon at the very center: standing close beside the speaker, with the crowd around him: drinking in the words, drinking in the closeness, touching it, feeling it, feeling with a great surge of elation that he had found at last what he had been seeking—the common people of France, together and united. . . . But then suddenly, in the next moment, not united. Suddenly wavering, weaving, turning their heads. Suddenly without center, without speaker or leader, but now a milling mob, as shouts flew, whistles shrilled, and a uniformed *moblot* swept into the square. Claude was caught in a tide of lurching bodies and trampling feet. There were yells, curses, groans, and above them, sharp and dry, the crack of a few shots, but whether anyone was hit he could not tell. The crowd was carrying him along with it, out of the square, into a side street; and then it was breaking up and disappearing; there were only a few left, then none left; he was running through the streets alone, and the noise faded behind him.

When, a while later, he returned, the square was quiet and empty. But in a small *estaminet* nearby was a group of workingmen, and several he recognized as having been part of the crowd. He went in and bought a beer—the first of his life. He stood at the zinc bar while angry voices told how the speaker had been shot and several others beaten and arrested. His indignation swelled with theirs. But when at last he found the courage to say something himself, the response was a general stone-eyed stare.

"Fous le camp!" someone said sharply. *"File!"*

And he went slowly back toward Les Halles.

Again and again he returned to the suburbs. He was in more street gatherings, more raids, more flights and post-mortems. But never was he able to become anything more than a spectator. In whatever neighborhood he entered, everyone seemed to know everyone else. Only he was the unknown, the outsider; and as such—the others being all good Frenchmen—he was an object of suspicion. He came and went, came and went, alone.

Meanwhile he was running out of money. Even at twenty centimes per meal and per night his few francs could not last long, and he was soon faced with the necessity of action. Food-snatching on the streets was no longer possible, for the little that was now on sale was not displayed on sidewalk stalls but carefully hoarded within the shops. And even if food had been no problem, there was still that of night shelter against the cold. Fortunately the fraternity of bums at the Hôtel de Babylone was less exclusive than that of the workingmen in the faubourgs. Most of them at least answered when he spoke to them; presently he had a few who rated, if not as friends, at least as acquaintances; and with them he managed, on and off, to scratch out an existence. The most respectable of the available occupations was ratcatching. For almost all the city's population of expendable horses, stray dogs and cats, and even the animals at the zoo in the Jardin des Plantes, had already made their appearance in the butcher shops of the hungry city, and rats were in great and ever-growing demand. The work, deep in cellars and sewers, could scarcely have been described as pleasant, but Claude soon became an adept, both as hunter and seller. And also, his companions were, for the most part, perversely happy and cheerful. "It's the only goddamn honest work I ever enjoyed," one of them told him. "Now all the fancy bastards are eating the same as us."

There were other guests of the Hôtel de Babylone, however, who were not so easily convertible to labor—the professional beggars, panhandlers, pickpockets, and housebreakers—and with these too, in time, Claude became involved. One early morning he helped pilfer a wagon carrying food from Les Halles to the Grand Hôtel. Another time he stood guard while an even bigger job was done on a *grand magasin*. And his reward, in addition to pocket money, was a growing reputation for toughness and daring. To himself he justified his actions out of his most deeply held convictions: that any blow against the established order was a good blow; that the poor, the lowly, and the outcast were the just inheritors of the earth. But when once he rashly tried to express such ideas to his companions he quickly found it was a waste of time. At the rock-bottom level of society, the concept of revolution—indeed, any concept, anything that could not be eaten or drunk, spent or stolen—was as meaningless as a cipher.

Time passed. The winter wore on. He didn't read. He didn't write. He scarcely lived, but simply existed—and waited. And he knew with increasing certainty that he would not have to wait much longer. "Let them stew in their own juice," Bismarck had said, back in the autumn, when the Parisians had defied him and the siege had begun. And now the siege had gone on for more than four months, and it was obvious that the city could not stew much longer. The Germans took Versailles and there proclaimed their empire. Then they drew the ring tighter. Von Moltke's Krupp cannons lobbed shells into the streets and buildings. Paris shook. Paris starved. And finally the National Government, from outside the capital, recognized the inevitable and asked for armistice. It was granted. The war ended. Stillness descended on the guns and on the city, broken only by the thump of boots as the conquerors marched through: in from the west, across the Etoile, down the Champs Elysées, across the Place de la Concorde, in long arrogant files, and then on out of the city, on back to the east and the Rhine. Paris watched with stone faces. Paris watched in silence. And when the Germans were gone, the silence remained: growing, swelling . . .

Until it exploded.

Out of the suburbs they came at last; out of the warrens, the tenements, the factories, the alleys, the slums. The people of Paris, marching. The *blouses blanches*. The Communards. Red posters appeared everywhere. Red flags flew—and beside them the tricolor—while trumpet and drum rolled out the *Marseillaise*. And down the streets they came, by the ten and the hundred thousand; down the boulevards, across the squares, through the parks; to the center of the city, to the halls of power. The National Guard joined them—by the company, the troop, the regiment —and when the government ordered them to disband and lay down their arms, they roared their defiance. Arsenals were raided. Barricades went up. Gunfire sounded and fires blazed through the streets. The regular troops resisted, and they had the better arms and organization; but now they were hopelessly outnumbered and forced slowly to retreat. Behind their lines the bourgeoisie was in panic. All who could were fleeing the city—by train, river boat, charabanc, van, and on foot—and into it, in their place, flowed crowds of the poor from the countryside, deserters from the scattered armies, radicals and liberals from all corners of France, hurrying to be in at the death of the old regime and the birth of the new. Almost overnight Paris was changing not only its temper but its very population. And now the new population swept in a great tide through the city to form the Government of the Commune.

In the squalid cells of the Hôtel de Babylone the derelicts blinked and scratched the lice from their hair. But Claude was not blinking. He was no longer even there. He was out in the great squares and boulevards, a part of the crowd, running, shouting, singing, his eyes shining, his heart all but bursting with excitement and joy. For here and now, at last, was what he had come for, what all France had been waiting for—the rising of the people, the march of the people—the days of old glory rekindled and reborn. . . . Except that this time, he told himself fiercely, it would be better than before. Victory would be won—and held. Today was history. And he, Claude Morel, the *beau gosse* of Cambon, the *mioche* from the Ardennes, was part of the birth of a new France that would last through the centuries.

There was no loneliness now; no suspicion and rejection such as had been his lot in the suburbs. The crowd welcomed him, enveloped him. All men were brothers. As brothers they marched shoulder to shoulder into the Place de la Bastille and stood in close-packed ranks of thousands while the new leaders hurled defiance at the old. Gun barrels glistened. Torches flared. Clenched fists shot upward. And when the speakers had finished (there were no *moblots* now to stop them) a roar rose that seemed to shake earth and heaven.

"*Vive la liberté! Vive la Commune!*"

Then the crowd was moving again: flowing, dividing, spreading out in a hundred streams through the streets of the city. There was work yet to do, battles yet to be fought, for the Regular Army still held the western arrondissements, the rich part of the city, and behind them were the hated bourgeois plutocrats who had to be driven out once and for all, if victory was truly to be won.

"*En avant! A la victoire!*" roared the thousands.

Claude found himself attached to a group of boys about his own age, a shouting, racing gang from the factory suburb of Belleville. All were typical slum brats—pale, pinch-faced, rachitic—except one, a boy called

Hervé, who was big, broad, muscular, and their natural leader; and it was he who gave Claude the accolade of membership. "All right, *beau gosse*, come on!" he shouted. And off they went in search of glory. Of the lot of them, perhaps twenty in number, only Hervé was really armed; from somewhere he had got a detached bayonet which he brandished in a massive fist. The others carried sticks, stones, lengths of lead and iron pipe, and Claude had snatched a discarded torch from the gutter. But it was no longer burning, he had neither matches nor fuel, and as they ran through the streets he kept his eyes sharp for a place he might find them. Suddenly he saw it: a small housewares shop, closed like all other stores, but on which the proprietor had apparently not had time to put up the shutters. He found a brick. He threw it. The window glass crashed. In a moment he was through, in another moment out again, with matches and a tin of benzine. He ran faster, to catch up with the others, and deep inside him was a proud smile. "Now I am *really* a thief of fire," he thought.

They came to a street on which there was fighting. A detachment of Regulars, at the far end, was trying to advance, and the Communards were quickly throwing up a barricade. Claude and his companions helped, dragging chairs, tables, chests, anything they could lay hands on from the neighboring houses. One of the boys was nicked by a bullet, but it was only a flesh wound in the upper arm, and they tied a rag around it, like a badge of honor. Then they all helped man the barricades, shouting, ducking, and throwing rocks, until a troop of National Guards, bigger than the enemy's, arrived and cleared the street.

Soon after, they came to a house that was held by snipers; the best sharpshooters of the Guard could not dislodge them. And now came Claude's moment. Racing zigzag across the street with his torch and can, he reached the shelter of the house wall, found the cellar door and plunged into it. In a few seconds he had done his work. In five minutes the house was ablaze. "*Ah, c'est un vrai pétroleur!*" said the Guard officer, clapping his back.

Pétroleur. Franc-tireur. Partisan. Revolutionary.... He was a child of words, and the words reeled in his brain.... *Vive la Commune! Vive la liberté! Princes, lords, tyrants, perish! Cry freedom! Cry blood! Blood and the golden flame....* And the flames glared; the rifles cracked. They ran on. They came to another street, another fight, another barricade in the making. They raced into a house, seized furniture, began heaving it out; and within him the reeling grew wilder, it was itself like flame, like music, and exultation of doing, of fighting, of being. It swelled, brightened, blazed....

And stopped.

Everything stopped. Everything was suddenly gone, except the man and the woman across the room. Hervé and a few others had lunged toward an old, elaborately wrought cabinet that stood in a corner, but the man had moved in front of them. "No, not that!" he pleaded. He had a brown drooping mustache and his face was whiter than the wall.

"Out of the way!" shouted Hervé.

"Not that, please. I beg you. It is an heirloom—"

"Out of the way, *vieux con!*"

"I beg—"

Hervé struck. The bayonet went home, and he jerked it free as the man fell. The woman screamed. An iron bar rose and fell, and the screaming stopped. Hervé dragged the cabinet out. Others stripped the rest of the room, and still others ran upstairs. Claude stood at the door. Suddenly he was conscious of something falling outside, close beside him. It landed, and he looked, and it was a child, a girl, of perhaps three years. The blood ran out of her mouth and reddened the litter on the pavement.

He sat on the cobbles of an alley in a quiet part of the city. It was much like the alley in which he had sat the previous summer, contemplating his broken shoes, writing his verses. But his shoes did not interest him now. He did not write now. A while before, he had been sick—retchingly, chokingly sick, his head pressed against a wall, his body racked by convulsions—and he was still weak from it. His head throbbed; tremors passed through his arms and legs; his mouth was sour with the taste of vomit. For a long time he sat looking at the stones of the alley, while his mind struggled back to clearness—and to what he would do.

He was not a baby. He was not going to run away, to run home. He still believed in the Commune, in the revolution, in the new world, the freer better world, of which all his life he had read and dreamed. He had made a mistake, that was all: a stupid terrible mistake, but still one that could be rectified. He had cast in his lot, not with revolutionaries, but with hooligans, and he had learned his lesson. From now on it would be different. True, he had already tried three times to become a member of a real organization, and three times he had been rebuffed. At Antimes, the recruiting sergeant had laughed at him; at the Garde Nationale head-quarters, he had been turned away at the gate; in the suburbs, the *blouses blanches* had said to him, *"Fous le camp!"* But that was before. This time it would be different. He knew more. He had done more. He would *make* it different.

He stood up. He steadied himself and started off. After a few blocks he came to a horses' drinking trough and washed what was left of the vomit from his face and clothes. Then, making his plans as he went, he walked back toward the center of the city. In one hand he still carried his torch, and in the other his now half-full can of benzine. The best thing, the perfect thing, of course, would have been to find the Guard officer, the one who had slapped his back and said *"un vrai pétroleur"*; but in the hugeness of Paris there was not a chance in a million. He would have to do it on his own, start over again, convince someone else that he could be of use to the cause. Walking on, he came out of empty streets into crowded ones. Again there was milling, shouting, the tramp of feet, the crack of gunfire. But he kept straight on, unstopped and undistracted, until he came to the Garde Nationale headquarters that he had found on his earlier wanderings.

It had changed. It had grown. Before, it had been a single building, housing a few offices and billets, but now it had swelled prodigiously; it was a whole row of buildings, then courtyards and more buildings; it was a barracks, a cantonment. And the whole vast establishment swarmed with troops. In the past days of turmoil the Guard had expanded to the point where it was no longer a mere auxilliary to the army, but an army itself —or, perhaps better, a horde—a huge ragtag-and-bobtail agglomeration of any and all arms-bearing men who were minded to fight for the Commune. There were the original guardsmen: those of the Paris units in their regular companies and battalions, those who had entered the city since the German withdrawal in all manner of makeshift squads and detachments. There were deserters from the Regular Army—singly, in small groups, in large ones—in the uniforms of infantrymen, artillerymen, Zouaves, lancers, hussars. There were Arabs and Negroes from the African regiments, and sailors who had left their ships in Nantes and Toulouse. There were men from no recognizable unit, in half uniforms, shreds of uniforms, a tunic or a coat or a cap or a bandolier. There were the *blouses blanches*, with only their shirts to show they were soldiers of the revolution. And there were those like Claude who had not even that; merely a torch or a stick or a stone; and the burning desire to join, to *belong*. . . .

If there was such a thing as a recruiting post, it was lost in bedlam. Claude wandered up and down the street, through the courtyards, into the buildings. Voices shouted, drums rolled, bugles blared, troops marched past. Now and then, finding a man who seemed approachable, he tried to ask a question, but the answers were either negative or unintelligible. He wandered on. The buildings were enormous. As far as he could gather, they were a series of lofts and factories which the Guard had simply seized and occupied, without installations or furnishings of any kind: a great sprawling bivouac between stone walls and a roof. Some of the rooms and lofts were empty; the troops who camped in them were obviously out on the streets. Others, housing off-duty units, were a welter of life, with men sleeping, eating, drinking, shouting, swearing, swarming, and shouldering one another over every available square inch. Trying one such room, Claude could not even squeeze in. Trying another, he could get no one's attention. Doggedly he moved on from building to building, floor to floor, threading the dingy labyrinth.

Then he was at the door of still another loft, a long low bare room seething with men . . . and suddenly a hand reached out and seized him. "Hey, look what I got!" the soldier yelled. He snatched Claude's benzine can and held it high. "What we been looking for!"

There was a yell of approval, and he shoved his way quickly through the crowd to where a circle of men was squatting on the stone floor around a pile of damp kindling. "Here," he said, "this'll get the frigging thing going."

Eager hands grabbed the can and poured. Matches spurted. A small blaze leaped up. There were more yells from the men, they pressed closer to warm themselves, and some time passed before anyone noticed that Claude was among them.

"What are *you* doing here?" a soldier finally asked.

"It's my benzine," said Claude.

"It *was* your benzine. *Fous le camp!*"

"I'd like to stay," said Claude.

"Stay?"

"I want to join you. Be one of you."

The man hooked a thumb toward the door. Another man laughed.

"I could be of help," Claude pleaded. "Give me a chance—I'll show you."

There was more laughter. Someone shoved him. Then a voice said, louder than the rest: "Hey, yes, by God—he *can* help!"

The others looked at the speaker.

"He can clean up the perfume factory."

"By God, yes!"

"Sure!"

"That's it!"

"You're a genius!"

Claude was being shoved again; this time, however, not toward the exit, but to the far end of the room. Here there was another door and someone kicked it open.

"All right, *monsieur le volontaire*—get going!"

Behind the door was a closet. Not a water closet. Just a cubicle with a stone floor.

"Latrine detail, forward march!"

Claude hesitated. The hands behind him were still pushing. "What—what do I use?" he asked.

"A master craftsman supplies his own tools, *mon brave.*"

The men liked that one. There was another hoot of laughter. Then they returned to the fire—but not without keeping an eye on Claude to make sure he made no break to escape.

"And keep that damn door closed!" someone yelled.

Claude did the job. After all, he was a veteran of privies, he thought grimly—although this one, unlike that at home, was nonconvertible into a refuge. Stripping his torch down, he made it into a rough spade. In a corner he found some old paper and burlap. When the closet was clean, he took his load down to the courtyard, found a sewage pit, and dumped it. He was now free to make off, but he didn't. He went back upstairs again. "Now you can start over," one of the men told him, grinning. "We got nice regular bowels in this outfit."

When he came back a second time, however, they were easier on him. They let him warm himself by the fire. They gave him scraps from their rations. And—best of all, and what he had been hoping for—when it came time for them to go down into the streets, they let him go with them. "Our goddamn drummer boy, that's what you'll be," one of them said to him. "Only we got no drum."

For hours, then, they were out in the city. Up this street, down that one, across squares, through parks, in and out of buildings; knifing through the crowds, leading the crowds, deploying, maneuvering, charging; a spearhead, quick and darting, in the wild rampage that was Paris. As far as Claude could tell, they were in no way a regular unit, either of the Guard or anything else, but simply a group that had been thrown together helter-skelter during the turmoil of the past few days. Most wore uniforms, or parts of uniforms, and most were armed; but their discipline was rudimentary, and the two or three officers who had assumed command when they left the barracks were all but lost in the confusion. Yet they managed somehow to hang together and move on. They came to areas of gunfire; to snipers, barricades, explosions, burning buildings. And still they moved on: from street to street, fight to fight. Claude had no gun. He had no weapon at all. But he picked up rocks, as often as he could, and hurled them. He kept up with the men, racing and shouting. He carried messages, passed cartridges, reloaded guns. At one intersection, blocked by a tangle of wire, he was the first to wriggle through and point a way to the others. A while later, to his joy, he again found a torch and fuel and once more became a *pétroleur*. Faster and faster, wilder and wilder, the streets and the city flowed past them. Sound and image, din and flame grew louder, brighter, until again, as when he had been with the gang from Belleville, his head spun with the delirium of excitement. Except that this time the delirium was even sweeter, even better, for now he was fighting not with a mere crowd of hoodlums but as part of the true Army of the Commune.

"*Vive la Commune! Vive le peuple!*" he shouted in his ecstasy.

Cry blood! Blood and the golden flame....

Dusk fell. Then night. And with night, gradually, the fighting slackened. The Government troops had retreated everywhere; they held only parts of the westernmost faubourgs, and even these were now being evacuated. Paris was won. It belonged to the Commune, to the people. A mere handful of fresh Guard units were still needed for mopping up, as the rest of the city turned with a roar from revolution to celebration. And Claude's troop roared with it. On the march back toward the town's center, they yelled and sang, waved their guns like flags, fired their unused cartridges into the air. Stores and cafés were reopening, crowds thronging them, lights going on everywhere. Swarming into a liquor shop, the troop rushed the proprietor, dumped him happily into a wine barrel, and swept the bottles from the shelves. Back in the street again, the bottles went from hand to hand, from rank to rank, and, when empty, sailed crashing against the walls of buildings.

They reached the barracks. They poured in. They rebuilt the fire, lighted it, danced around it, singing and yelling. There were still bottles: dozens and scores of bottles: bottles of wine, marc, cognac, calvados, absinthe. They went the rounds, and then went crashing to the floor. Soon everyone in the room was drunk. Everyone but Claude. A soldier grabbed him, tilted a bottle into his mouth and poured, and the brandy sloshed half over his face and half down into his throat. He choked. He tried to get away. But the man held him and poured again. Others crowded around, cheering, laughing. The brandy flowed and the bottle went crashing.

Several of the men became sick, and the floor was slippery with their vomit. Others subsided gradually into coma, propped against the walls or lying sprawled in the corners. But some were still drinking, still shouting, hoarse, disheveled, wild-eyed, as they swayed about the fire. "Women!" someone yelled. "That's what we need—women!"

"Yes, women!"

"Let's get women!"

"Get them where? . . . Anywhere. . . . Like hell. . . . Sure we can. . . . Whores. Lots of whores. . . . And use what for money? . . . The hell with money. We just take 'em. . . . Just like that, *hein?* . . . Yeah, just like that . . ."

The room was a garble of shouting. Some of the men ran out. More followed. Soon less than a quarter were left: the too-drunken ones on the floor and against the wall, and another group of perhaps a dozen standing sullenly, still drinking, in the center of the room.

"It's a hell of a time to be on guard duty," said one of them.

"*Merde* with guard duty!" said another. "I'm goin' too."

"And get yourself a jail term?"

"Who'll put me in jail?"

"The officers. They're all over the place, God damn 'em. Swarmin' like lice."

Other voices rose. Two more men ran out. The others shouted, argued—and stayed—and Claude watched them from a corner. One tipped a bottle to his mouth, leaned back and fell, joining the sprawled figures on the floor. Another pulled a crayon from his pocket, lurched to the wall, and drew an enormous obscene figure. "There's your woman, boys!" he announced. "Step right up, messieurs, and have a piece." He made a second drawing—of a male. "See, *une petite illustration*. Step right up, messieurs. It's free. All for free—"

Some of the others laughed. Some scowled and swore. One man began singing a dirty song at the top of his voice, while still another bottle sailed through the air and shattered against the drawing. A little apart from the rest, a soldier was looking at Claude with drunken thoughtfulness.

"If we can't have a woman," he said, "let's have the next best thing."

There was a sudden silence, a turning of eyes.

"Well, by God—" someone said.

Claude's head was spinning. He tried to stop it, but couldn't. He felt the brandy in his throat, in his stomach. He felt it coiling in his brain.

The man who had been watching him moved forward. He was a small man, thin and sharp-faced, and the others called him *La Belette*—the Weasel. "You're a real cutie, you know that?" he said.

He seemed to be grinning. And then not grinning. As he stood before Claude he swayed unsteadily—or perhaps it was not he who was swaying, but Claude himself. The brandy was coiling, weaving; he couldn't tell.

Several of the other men had moved closer too. They all seemed to be grinning and swaying. A hand reached out and jerked at him.

"Ah, leave him alone," someone said. "The brat's scared."

"What's there to be scared of?" There was a laugh.

"He's had it before," said *La Belette*. "I know the kind. You can tell by looking at 'em."

The swaying increased. It became a spinning. Faces and forms blurred, and there was only a spinning, and at its center, at its heart, a pair of eyes. The eyes were small. They were weasel's eyes. They were bleared and bloodshot. Claude had seen them before. . . .

7

The Germans had come late to Cambon. And they stayed late. Long after most of the occupation troops had been withdrawn beyond the Rhine, a small garrison remained in the town, and Feldwebel Gunst, first sergeant of the Third Brandenburg Fusiliers was consumed by boredom and aggravation. The boredom was brought on by inactivity and the very fact of Cambon itself; the aggravation by the presence therein of a young hoodlum named Morel.

The sergeant was billeted a few doors down the block from the Morel store, and it seemed impossible for him to enter the street without encountering the boy. Sometimes he would be lounging at the door and leap to attention with a stiff salute. Sometimes he would be walking in the opposite direction and break into a burlesque goose step. Usually Gunst ignored the performance, but at least once it annoyed him to the point where he stopped and spoke.

"You think you are a soldier," he said. "Is that it, *hein?*"

"*Ja*, Herr Feldwebel." Claude stood at attention. "A veteran."

"So, a veteran? Of what reform school?"

"Of a march to Paris, Herr Feldwebel. My own march. It was right through the German Army; but, if you will pardon me, it is not a very good army—so it was easy."

"You are an insolent French pig!"

"No, Herr Feldwebel. I am a pig, perhaps—yes. But French—no. I am a Hun, like you."

"What?"

"I say that, like yourself, I am a Hun. You see my eyes, do you not? You see my hair? And how military I am? I too grew up in a forest, eating acorns, and it is my destiny to conquer the world. There is only one slight difference, Herr Feldwebel, and that is that I am an educated Hun."

"Watch your tongue, boy—"

"Ah, you disagree. You mean you are educated too. Good. Let us talk then. Let us sit comfortably in the gutter and discuss German literature. Are you an admirer of Heine, Herr Feldwebel? What is your opinion of Lessing, of Storm, of Hoffmann von Fallersleben? Do you agree with Haushofer that Schiller's imagery is superior to that of Lessing, or do you feel with Rittmeister that—"

"Silence!" roared the sergeant.

"I am only—"

"Silence!"

Claude saluted. "*Jawohl*, Herr Feldwebel."

"You will remember your place!"

"*Küss die Hand*, Herr Feldwebel. *Küss mein Arsch.*"

The sergeant knocked him down with his revolver butt; then had him taken to German headquarters, where he was locked up for two days. When they let him out he saluted smartly and said, "Automaton Number 28,374 departing with full indoctrination, *meine Herren*. May I wish you good luck in all your future wars?"

He went home. He went upstairs to his room. He closed the door and jammed a chair against the knob, and his mother shook and pounded until the panels almost split. But he sat down and began writing, as if there was no sound at all. He wrote until suppertime, and then joined his mother and Yvette at the table, and by this time she was no longer wild and raging but icily controlled. They sat for most of the meal in silence; then she cleared her throat and said:

"I have been about to go to the police again and have them send you away. But I have changed my mind."

Claude said nothing.

"The lycée reopens for the spring term next week. I have decided it is best that you return there."

"No," said Claude.

"What do you mean, no?"

"I'm not going back to school. There's nothing more I can learn there."

"You will do what I say, or—"

"No, Mother, I will not do what you say. You should know that by now."

The fire rose into Madame Morel's eyes. She almost burst through her control, but not quite. "If you do not go back to school you will be unable to go to the university—you know that."

"Yes, I know it," said Claude.

"And you do not care? You no longer want an education?"

"I'm getting an education."

"Living the life you are living? Doing the things you are doing?"

"Yes, exactly."

There was another silence. His mother's lips were as white as her face, but when she spoke again her voice was still quiet. "And this," she said, "is what you propose to go on doing?"

"That's right."

"You will not go to school?"

"No."

"You will not even work?"

"I am already working."

"Working? You call—"

"I am working at my writing. At my poetry. And you may as well get used to it, because it's what I'll be doing all my life."

This last was too much for his mother. She got to her feet and her eyes blazed at him. "All your life, *hein?* So that's how you have it figured out? All your life you will do nothing, you will lie around your room, sit and scribble, while I work ten, twelve, fourteen hours—"

Yvette's face had gone pale and frightened. "*Maman*, Claude— please—" she began.

But her mother paid no attention. "Do you know what you are?" she shouted at her son. "You are a no-good. You are a loafer, a tramp, a thief!"

"That's right," said Claude placidly. "And I'll tell you what made me that way. . . . You did."

"I? You dare say that to me? I who have—"

"And I'll tell you something else," he went on. "Something rather interesting. It's been you too, I think, who have made me a poet."

For a moment she was beyond words. Then they poured out in a torrent. "You are all the things I have said, and more," she screamed at him. "You are mad—you are a lunatic. You are the son of your father, the son of the devil. You are mad, evil, a devil yourself, and I pray God to protect us all from you." She stopped, panting. She struggled to regain control. Her lips again went tight and white in the gaunt whiteness of her face, and her body, which had been trembling, was now as rigid as black iron.

"Bravo! Bravo, Mother!" said Claude. "Now you're really the Queen of the Cannibals—"

He got up and went out.

Not one but two Claude Morels had returned from Paris to Cambon, and the outward one was not prepossessing. During the months past he had kept growing, until he was now almost of normal man's height; but he seemed even taller, because of his thinness and gawkiness, and half the time seemed a creature composed solely of elbows and knees. His features were still fine-cut and boyish—whatever had happened to him otherwise had not touched him there—but there was the beginning of a beard on his cheeks, and he had let his hair grow until it hung wild and disheveled over his ears and forehead. Once erect in his posture, he now walked—except when saluting Germans—with an indolent slouch. And though his mother, reluctantly, had bought him a new jacket, he never wore it, preferring the oldest clothes he could lay his hands on, and, most especially, the remains of the old serge suit, out of which his arms and legs protruded like a scarecrow's. "I am a *beau gosse* fallen upon evil days," he would explain to anyone who commented. From under the brim of a discarded hat he had picked up in the street, his blue-white eyes surveyed the world of Cambon: seeing everything, telling nothing.

He wandered the streets. He sat on the curbs. He walked out to the Bois d'Amour. But the Bois had changed; before the Germans had come all the trees had been chopped down to make barricades for the town's futile defense, and there were only black stumps—and no lovers. "They've swung the ax on me too," he thought sardonically. "But they forgot I'm not a tree: I can swing back."

He walked on: into the fields, into the forest. And here no ax had fallen. It was the same as it had been a year, and ten years, and twenty centuries before. Again he moved down the dark aisles and sat on the moss beneath the great trees; and again his mind went back to how he had come as a small boy, alone, to this *pays des loups;* how he had sat under these same trees, watching for wolves, waiting for them, waiting for their eyes, like yellow lanterns, to close in around him through the shadows. He had not been afraid of them then. When they came, he had been sure, they would not hurt him; they would accept him, know him for one of themselves. Perhaps, he had used to think, he had been suckled by a wolf, like Romulus and Remus. (It seemed no less implausible than by his mother.) Or perhaps he was himself of their own blood: a werewolf, a lycanthrope, a creature of forest and night, destined only outwardly, in face and form, to wear the guise of a man. Even then he had felt himself close to the beasts. And now—now who knew beasts better than he? The wolves of the Ardennes. The wolves of Paris. The wolves of street, jail, flophouse, barracks. . . .

"Yes, the wolves," he thought. "And I am one of them."

Or if not a wolf, the nearest human counterpart. A Hun. (A faint smile touched him, cold and inward.) Not a Hun *manqué*, like Herr Feldwebel Gunst, not a fat imbecilic sausage-eating goose-stepping hog of a Prussian sergeant; but a real Hun, an ancient Hun, one of the dark hordes from the wastes of Asia. Yes, it was not from the Gauls that he had come, nor the Teutons nor the Vikings. It was from the Huns, the Scourges of God. It had been only a few miles away, at Châlons-on-the-Marne, that the great wave of Attila's horde had broken at last on the parapets of Europe; and from the remnants of that invasion, strangers and outcasts, barbarians among the civilized, had come his ancestors—and himself.

"There is only one slight difference," he had said to the sergeant, "and that is that I am an educated Hun."

But there was another difference too; and he knew it, though he did not understand it.

He was a Hun who kept returning to his *maman*.

That night he called on Albert Chariol.

The teacher had come back to Cambon at about the same time he had returned from Paris, but they had seen each other infrequently. And for this there were two reasons. The first was that Claude had told him of his intention not to return to school and that Chariol had strongly disapproved; and the second was that Claude had, some two weeks before, given him a new poem to read. It was a poem such as he had never written before—indeed, he was sure, such as *no one* had ever written before, at any time, in any language—and he had composed it during his long miserable walk home from Paris. In the beginning it had seemed to him that he had not composed it at all; that it had simply been ripped full-born from his flesh and spirit. But later he had worked on it, struggled with it, lavished on it his last measure of talent and energy, until he felt it was exactly right in every cadence and image and nuance of meaning. And its meaning was terrible. Its meaning was that which had happened to him in the jail in

Paris and later in the barracks of the Garde Nationale. Not only to his body, but to his mind and soul; not only to himself, Claude Morel, but to all youth, all hope, all ideals, all love. *The Ravaged Heart*, he had called it. And what was left of that heart lay now in penciled words on two sheets of school copy paper.

Chariol was of course the only person in Cambon to whom he could possibly have shown the poem, and even with him Claude had had misgivings. He had not handed it to him himself, for he did not want him to read it then and there, while he, Claude, stood by, but had instead left it under the door of his lodgings, along with a brief note. *This does not mean nothing,* he had written. *And I beg you not to be too harsh with your pencil or with your mind.* He had expected to hear from Chariol. He had waited for days, for over a week. But no word had come, and now he could wait no longer. *The Ravaged Heart* was, for him, more than a poem. It *was* his heart, his mind, his soul—his three Magi—and he had to have the verdict of the one man who might understand.

Chariol's lights were on. Claude knocked at the door and the teacher let him in. "I'm glad you've come, boy," he said. "I've been wanting to talk with you."

He sat Claude down in a comfortable chair and brought a glass of apple juice for each of them. "In another year or so we can make it beer," he said, smiling.

Claude sipped his drink nervously. Chariol's smile faded and he assumed an earnest expression. "Yes, I'm glad you've come," he repeated. "It's time we settled this nonsense."

"Nonsense?"

"This business about not returning to school. You've done some thinking it over since I last saw you, I hope."

Claude didn't answer.

"Have you?" said Chariol.

"No."

"No? What do you mean, no?"

"There's nothing to think about. I've made up my mind."

The teacher bit his lip. "Claude, I'm amazed at you," he said. "Amazed and disappointed. What can you possibly hope to gain by this sort of headstrong foolishness?"

Again Claude said nothing.

"I'm your friend, you know that. I think I understand you better than —well—say your mother, and some of the other teachers. I know your intelligence and your talent, and they're tremendous. And I know your restlessness too, and your ambition—the thing that makes you hate Cambon, that drives you off on these wild runaways. That's all right; I'm not blaming you. A little wildness is good. A little craziness. I'm not asking you to grow up like a vegetable. But there's a thing you must remember, boy: that you *are* still growing up. That you're only sixteen. *Mon Dieu*, at sixteen I was still so scared of my parents and teachers I wouldn't have dared miss even a day of school."

He smiled a little but got no response. Then he raised a hand quickly. "Don't misunderstand me, boy: I'm not saying you should be scared of anyone. I'm only telling you to use your brains, to stop and think. To think of your future, of the university, of what you want to do."

"What I want to do," said Claude, "is write."

"Yes, of course—write. And you'll go on writing; why should school stop that? You write beautifully—like an angel. Some of your recent things have been superb."

"And my *most* recent—thing?" asked Claude.

"Your most—?"

"The poem I left here about a week ago."

"Oh."

"You've read it, Albert?"

"Yes, I've read it."

"And what did you think?"

Chariol considered a moment. The boy was obviously trying to get off *the* subject, and he didn't want to; but then perhaps it would be good tactics for a few minutes. Rising, he smiled, made a little bow, and said, "It was a masterpiece, *mon vieux*. Do you need me to tell you that?"

Claude looked at him without speaking.

"So great a masterpiece, indeed, that, when school reopens, I shall recommend its publication in the lycée magazine."

"The lycée magazine?"

"Yes, of course." Chariol chuckled. "Monsieur Izard has been complaining for years that it is very weak in pornography, and your verse, I think, will fill the deficiency quite nicely."

His chuckle became a laugh. He waited for Claude to laugh with him. But Claude sat motionless and rigid.

"I am asking you seriously, Albert—" he said at last.

"But of course, seriously. And I am answering seriously. It was a work of genius. Villon and Rabelais put together couldn't touch it. The only pity is that it is not set to music so it could be sung at Mass every Sunday."

There was a silence. Claude's stomach felt suddenly empty, and his hands were cold.

"That is all you have to say about it?" he asked.

"It is enough, don't you think?" said Chariol.

"Then may I have it, please?"

"Have it?"

"My poem—please give it to me."

"I'm afraid I can't, *mon vieux*. You see, the basket gets emptied every day."

"You mean you threw it away?"

"Of course I threw it away." The teacher chuckled again. "Monsieur Izard is one thing—*un homme du monde*. But it wouldn't be so good for either you or me if the cleaning woman or some visitor found it. No, let's get famous some other way and keep your little joke private."

"Joke—?" said Claude, rising. His arm knocked over the glass of apple juice, from which he had taken only one sip; but he paid no attention. "So that's what you thought of my poem—that it was a joke."

Chariol looked at him in astonishment.

"That it was something to throw away, to make fun of, to laugh at? All right, go ahead, laugh your head off."

"Claude—what is this? What's the matter with you?"

"There's nothing the matter with me, except that I don't feel like laughing. . . . That's for you, damn you. Go on, laugh! Ha ha ha. Laugh—"

"Claude!"

"—like you'd laugh at the crucifixion of Christ—"

Chariol lost his temper. "Stop that!" he commanded. "Stop it, do you hear me? You'll behave yourself when you come here. You'll have some manners."

"The hell with manners!"

"Oh, that's the way you feel? The hell with them. All right, I'll do it your way too. I'll tell you what I think of those verses of yours, and that's that they're nasty dirty drivel. I can see now I should have told you in the first place; but no—I think of my *manners*. It's just a boy's joke, I tell myself; he's trying to shock me; I'll joke back at him. And now this happens. You have a tantrum. You turn on me like an animal."

"I *am* an animal. I'm a wolf. I'm a weasel—"

"You're a willful insolent brat, that's what you are, and I'm beginning to sympathize with your mother." Chariol was not basically a choleric man, and he began gradually to gain control of himself. "Claude, Claude," he said more quietly, "what gets into you anyhow? Carrying on like this. Or even writing such a thing in the first place. . . . It was dirty. Yes, I repeat: it was dirty and disgusting. I found myself wondering how a boy of your age could imagine such things."

"I—"

"Yes, I know, your imagination is great. And sometimes it's for the good and sometimes for the bad. All right—let's forget the bad. You had your joke and that's the end of it. Let's not take a little *bêtise* so seriously."

He stopped and waited. The anger was gone from his face and the earnestness had returned. Claude looked at him and then away, and his own wild rush of anger was gone too. He started to speak, but stopped.

He stood for what seemed a long while without speaking, and then he said quietly:

"Is that all, Monsieur Chariol?"

"My name is Albert."

"Is that all?" Claude said.

"About the *bêtise*, yes, that's more than enough. Now let's get back to important things—to this business of school—"

Chariol stooped and picked up the glass that the boy had knocked over. Then he got a rag and mopped up the spilled juice. Claude did not help, but simply stood watching, his face frozen and white.

"There now," said Chariol, and stood up.

Claude turned and ran.

His whole life was a running. From home and mother, school and church, from Cambon, from Paris, from everyone and everything. And now even from Chariol. Chariol, too, had turned on him, become the enemy; and there was no one left.

He ran into his room. He barricaded the door. And for a week he did not come out, except to sit silently at meals or to climb out the window to the back-yard privy. He rewrote *The Ravaged Heart*, word for word as it had been before and at the bottom he signed it *Morel-sans-coeur*. "When a heart is ravaged," he thought, "it is no longer a heart. And that will be my strength: that I have no heart."

He put the poem away. He went on to other poems. He worked through the days and the nights ("oh yes, *chère Maman*, for ten, twelve, fourteen hours"), forging thought into image, image into word, writing, rewriting, destroying, beginning again, until his pencils were stumps and his paper was gone. He asked his mother for more, and when she refused him simply took them from her desk. He went on writing. He wrote like one possessed. If his heart was dead, his mind was alive and aflame.

His mother pounded on the door. One night she pounded longer than usual, and at last he opened it. "School begins tomorrow, and you will go," she told him.

"No, I won't," he said.

And he didn't.

But a few days later, he did. He went there in the afternoon and sat on the curb at the main entrance as his old classmates came out. "What are you up to?" they asked him. "I'm taking a postgraduate course," he told them, "—in how to be the town tramp."

Even a tramp, however, needed money occasionally, and, his mother's cash drawer being now under double lock—and general thieving overly hazardous—he fell back on his old part-time profession of tutoring, GUARANTEED PASSING GRADES—ONE FRANC PER SEMINAR; GUARANTEED HONORS—TWO FRANCS, he announced on hand-printed cards that he passed around. And it gave him a sardonic satisfaction that, with no preparation at all, he was still far ahead of the struggling class. With the money he earned he bought the stout walking boots he had craved for so long; a supply of good quality paper and pencils for his writing; and, best of all, a pipe and tobacco. His favorite place for smoking was at the school entrance at coming and going time, and he took care to exhale large clouds whenever Monsieur Izard, the headmaster, went by.

The only person for whom he did not put on his show was Albert Chariol. Chariol, to be sure, was now an enemy too; indeed, he had hurt him as he had never been hurt in his life. But still he was an enemy to be avoided, not taunted.

He sat on the curbs. He wandered the streets. He was the town tramp and vagabond. But if he was a vagabond he was also a prisoner, and in his prison, inwardly, he raged. Revolt seethed in him like a deep fire, but in a place like Cambon what was there for the fire to burn? Who was there in the whole town who could comprehend what he was doing; who could recognize that his actions were not merely those of a wild hooligan, but a conscious, passionately felt protest against a whole way of living? In the streets he could taunt, he could shock, but he could not communicate. His only communication was through pencil to paper, behind the door of his room; his only communicants those men of his imagination he had never met who would someday read and understand what he was saying.

He wrote the testament of his vagabondage—and his aloneness:

". . . Forward: the march, the burden and the desert, weariness and anger.

To whom shall I sell myself? What beast should I adore? What holy image is attacked? What hearts shall I break? What lies shall I uphold? In what blood tread?

Still but a child, I admired the rebel convict on whom prison doors are always closing. With his eyes I saw the blue sky of the country; in cities I sensed his fatality. He had more strength than a saint, more common sense than a traveler —and he, he alone, the witness of his glory and his reason.

On highroads on winter nights, without roof, without clothes, without bread, a voice gripped my frozen heart: "Weakness or strength: for you it is strength. You do not know where you are going, nor why you are going. Enter anywhere, reply to anything. They will no more kill you than if you were a corpse." In the morning I had a look so lost, a face so dead, that perhaps those whom I met DID NOT SEE ME.

And then he turned on the enemy; on the lawmakers and imprisoners:

Priests, professors, masters, you are making a mistake in judging me. I have never belonged to this people; I am not a Christian; I am of the race that sang

under torture; laws I have never understood; I have no moral sense, I am a brute;
you are making a mistake.

Yes, my eyes are closed to your light. I am a beast, a savage, a nigger. But I can
be saved. You are sham niggers, you—maniacs, fiends, misers. Merchant, you are
a nigger; Judge, you are a nigger; General, you are a nigger; Emperor, you old itch,
you are a nigger: you have drunk of the untaxed liquor of Satan's still. . . .

The time of the Assassins is here.

He sat at his table, alone. For the time being, at least, his mother had
stopped knocking. He saw her only at meals, which they ate in stony
silence; and now even Yvette seldom came to him, or spoke at table, but
said only "Good morning, Claude—Good evening, Claude," and went
to school and returned, and lived a life of her own. Like him, she had
grown greatly in recent months. Her pigtails were gone; her rubber ball
was gone; she no longer hopped about on one foot and demanded to be
called the names of fairy-tale princesses. For she was twelve now—no
longer a child but a *jeune fille*—and her walk was different, her face and
body different, and beneath the blouse of her school uniform rose the
small mounds of her breasts. When their eyes met he looked away. She
looked away. She went into her room and did her lessons and prayed on
her rosary, and he went to his and sat at his table and lay on his cot.

He lay on the cot in the night, and his aloneness was vast around him.
Then through it once, very late, very soft, there came a sound, and he
knew his mother was moving about in her room. What she was doing he
could not tell, nor even imagine, but she was not asleep, not resting. She,
too, was awake—and alone.

"As alone as I am," he thought.

A fantastic notion struck him. He would get up and go in to her. He
would enter her room and sit on the side of her bed and say: "You are
alone, and I am alone, but if we sit together for a while now neither of
us will be alone." And his mother would answer. . . . But that was where
it grew *too* fantastic. His mother would answer what? . . . "Your nails are
dirty. Go to school tomorrow. I shall speak to Father Lacaze. I work ten,
twelve, fourteen hours. . . ." Together they would be more alone than
when apart.

The sounds faded. He slept and dreamed. He dreamed of his mother,
tall and black, tall and rigid, and she was going to church with an umbrella
to dip her bony hands in holy water, and of all the tall black ones she was
tallest and blackest, she was the Black Queen—the Nigger Queen. He was
walking beside her, in his serge suit and with his own umbrella. He was
close to her, very close, becoming ever closer, and she was looking down
at him; and then the change came, and it was not only her clothes that

were black, but her face; her body and face, all but white eyes and red lips, and where her clothes had been were black thighs and swelling breasts. He tried to pull away, but couldn't. He tried to cry out, but couldn't. He tried to beat at her with his umbrella, but it was no longer an umbrella, it was something else, a part of him; and she was drawing him still closer, closer and tighter, until she too was part of him, or he of her; until she had him, possessed him, was devouring him, and now at last he did cry out, once, wildly, in the moment of fulfillment and extinction. . . and awoke, spent and voided, back in the aloneness of night.

The dream was not a one-time thing. It was recurrent. And during the daylight hours, too, he was now increasingly tormented by a new hunger; to the three Magi he had known—the kings of mind, heart, and soul— he had added a fourth, and the fourth was flesh. Waking or sleeping, his dreams followed the same pattern. Though the backgrounds and details varied, there were always the two constants—or one?—of his mother and the Black Queen, alternating, blending, merging, and re-emerging, as they asserted their possession. Sometimes other images intruded: the farm woman, girls he had seen around Cambon, once, even, Yvette—with the body of Mimi Rouger. And sometimes, darkly, there were *the others*, too: the bearded face, the weasel face, the hunched shoulders, the teeth, the little eyes. There were stone walls and stone floor, the swaying, the spinning, nausea—but always, in the end, the same two again. Always women. Always Woman.

He looked deeply into himself. He searched for answers. For as long as he could remember he had felt himself to be different from others: not only in his mind and thoughts, but in the very chemistry of his body. When, a few years back, Michel Favre and his other friends had begun to think of girls, he had shared no part of their interest. And his own even- tual introduction to sex had been a far different thing: so different that there seemed not the slightest connection. Therefore he *himself* must be different, he had thought. True, he had not sought the experiences he had had—in fact he had previously not even surmised their possibility; but there had been something within himself, unknown to himself, that invited them and made them possible. What had happened to him could not have happened indiscriminately to anyone; no more than anyone, by a mere act of will, could have summoned up such thoughts and images as thronged his brain. If his mind and soul were different, so perhaps was his flesh—and he had paid the price. This is what he had tried to express in the wild and bitter obscenities of *The Ravaged Heart:* that he was sexually now truly ravaged and destroyed, that he was inwardly dead, and would never be capable of feeling and desiring as did other men.

Now, however, he was no longer sure. The memory of what had happened was still strong within him: of the Paris prison cell and the barracks and, even more strongly, more painfully, of the lonely farmhouse and the woman and his flight in the rain. All these added up to abnormality, to *difference*. But at the same time there were his dreams, opposed and contradictory: the dreams that were always of women, and the hunger that was that of a man. He had read, in stories of ancient Greece and Rome, of men who had had homosexual experiences but still retained their basic maleness. And from his reading, too, he had gathered that young men's first attempts at lovemaking were not always spectacularly successful. As time went on he knew that, one way or another, he would have to find out. He could not live with his hunger forever, in darkness and alone.

There were only two known professional prostitutes in Cambon, and they were beyond his reach. It would have taken weeks of tutoring to earn the francs to pay their fee; and even if he had had the money he would have had no idea how to make the arrangements.... So his thoughts turned to Mimi Rouger. There was only one possibility: Mimi Rouger.... Michel had said she was wild. He had said she liked him. What was the hideous word she had used? "Cute." All right: cute. He had no idea of how to make arrangements with Mimi either; but he would take his chances. One evening after supper he went out and walked toward her house.

Halfway there he stopped. His legs were weak. His hands were clammy. "She won't be there," he thought. "Her father or mother will open the door, and what will I say?—Or worse yet, she *will* be there, and what will I say to *her?*" He turned to go back; stopped, waited. He drew in a deep breath and went on.

Mimi herself came to the door. He had thought of several possible things to say first, but what he said was "Hello."

The girl peered at him in the dim light. Standing close to him, she was shorter than Claude had expected—though that was probably because he himself had recently grown so much. Like all the girls and women of Cambon, she was dressed in prim black. But there was nothing prim about the eyes that looked at him, or about the figure under the black, ripe and full for its age, with breasts high against the tight bodice; and suddenly he was seeing her again as he had seen her so often before—in his dreams, in his arms, in her nakedness.

In the dreams she never spoke. But now she did. "Oh, it's you. What do you want?" she said.

He swallowed. He was sweating. "I—I came to ask if you'd like to go for a walk."

"A walk?"

"Yes. It's a nice night. We could walk out to the Bois d'Amour and—"

He stopped. Mimi was looking him up and down. "Oh," she said, "I thought maybe you'd come to borrow some soap."

"Soap?"

"Or some clean clothes."

Claude didn't say anything. Mimi looked at him for another moment, then suddenly laughed and called over her shoulder. "Georges! Georges, come out here. There's something you've got to see."

The figure of Georges Vuiton appeared behind her: big, clumsy, and staring.

"Look, you've got a rival," Mimi said. "Aren't you jealous? This fine well-dressed wealthy monsieur has asked me to go for a walk."

Georges sniggered. *"Ah, c'est le beau gosse!"* he said.

"—to the Bois d'Amour, no less," said Mimi.

She was laughing again. Georges laughed. Then Claude was running again. The sound of their laughter followed him down the empty street.

8

"Achtung! Vorwärts! Hoch der Kaiser! Küss mein Arsch!"

Feldwebel Gunst's red face grew redder as he heard the jeering voice from among the onlookers, but, discipline being discipline, there was nothing he could do about it. On a mid-May morning the Third Brandenburg Fusiliers goose-stepped down the Rue Gauchet, across the Place de la Gare, and onto an eastbound train, and by afternoon Cambon had sunk back into its millennial torpor. All was the same as it ever had been, except for the fallen trees in the Bois d'Amour and a somewhat higher-than-usual incidence of extramarital pregnancies. . . . And except for a phenomenon (though this was not attributable to the Germans) the like of which the town had not seen in all its centuries, and whose name was Claude Morel.

Le Voyou, the Cambonards called him. The loafer. The hoodlum. And he did his best to live up to the title.

His clothes got still older and dirtier. His hair grew still longer and wilder. "If it's a *voyou* they want," he thought, "I'll give them the real thing." He wore an old German helmet which he had topped with a chicken feather, and from a dump he had salvaged a cracked meerschaum pipe the size of a trumpet. Blowing clouds of smoke, he sat on the curbs and street corners of the town, surveying the bourgeois world around him like a derelict king.

One day, after school, Michel Favre came by, and they walked for a way together. The two had seen little of each other lately, and to Claude his old friend now seemed little more than a child.

"And how are things, *mon vieux?*" he inquired. "How goes it with Lower Patagonian history and the lesser poems of Tertius Quadrilaterus?"

"I'm having trouble with my Greek," Michel said gloomily.

"There's always the Morel Tutoring Service. Here, take a card. And for you, *mon vieux*, it will be only half price."

"Thanks, I can use some help."

They walked on a bit. "And for the summer?" Claude asked cheerfully. "What are your summer plans? You'll return to your uncle's farm, perhaps? For a course in advanced cow-milking?"

"I suppose so," said Michel.

"Ah, that should be stimulating."

Michel said nothing. He was increasingly ill at ease, but Claude was cheerful and animated. "And—yes—your sex life," he said. "That's the main thing, of course. How goes it with your sex life?"

"Oh, all right," said Michel.

"You're still making progress on all fronts? With Mesdemoiselles Louise and Mimi?"

"I don't see much of Mimi any more. She's going mostly with Georges Vuiton."

"Ah, with Georges. How elegant. . . . And Louise?"

"Well, her parents are getting stricter, but—"

"Meaning things aren't really so good?"

"No, not so good," Michel conceded.

They walked on a little farther. Claude watched his friend's boyish snub-nosed face and a sardonic glint touched his eyes. "If I may say so, *mon vieux*," he said earnestly, "I think you yourself are mostly responsible for your troubles."

Michel looked at him questioningly.

"I'm afraid you're old-fashioned in your approach—a provincial stick-in-the-mud. We live in a modern world, boy, and fashions change in love, as in everything else. But I'm afraid you've been too involved in Tertius Quadrilaterus and cow-milking to notice it."

"What are you talking about?"

"I'm talking about the new love—*l'amour chic et récherché*—as practiced in Paris by the best social, intellectual, and military circles." Claude looked at his friend condescendingly. "Good God, where have you been? Haven't you heard anything? Girls are out now. Absolutely out. A good patriotic Frenchman wouldn't be caught dead with a girl."

Michel looked back at him. His eyes grew wider. "Girls are—"

"Yes, out. Finished. *Passé.* It's boys now—only boys. Handsome upstanding ones, like you and myself." Claude was warming to his subject. "Just think, *mon vieux*, how much more sensible it is; how much less trouble. There's no nonsense about it. No wooing, no pleading, no sighing, no tears, no tantrums. Above all, no pregnancy. It's not only chic and patriotic, I tell you. It's practical and scientifically sound."

Not only Michel's eyes were now round, but his mouth too. Words seemed to be trying to force their way out, but nothing came.

"Look." Claude pointed with happy inspiration. "There's a nice little outhouse, through the yard there. I bet it's empty. Come on and I'll show you. I'll help you in all phases of your education."

He took Michel's arm, but the latter jerked away. "No, no. I can't. I mean I—" He had begun to tremble.

"You mean you want to be a *mioche* all your life? Never advance yourself? Never learn anything."

"Yes—no—I mean—"

Michel stared at him for another wild-eyed moment, then turned and bolted; and Claude looked after him, grinning. It was pleasant to see someone running, besides himself.

Mimi Rouger went by, and he looked up from the curb and tipped his helmet. "Why if it isn't Mademoiselle la Princesse des Jambes-ouvertes," he said, "—the favorite concubine of the late Manchu emperor."

The girl's nose went up. Her eyes looked through him.

"Mademoiselle is looking most elegant today. Most regal. Her figure, particularly, is extra regal. *Mais dis donc*, she carries her pregnancy well!"

Mimi kept walking.

"Well, good for old Georges; I didn't know he had it in him. . . . Or maybe it wasn't Georges. It was one of the Prusscos. Of course. How hospitable, Mademoiselle. *Comme c'est gentil.* . . . And what will you call him? Hans, perhaps? Or Heinz or Fritz or Schmutz? Schmutz is especially nice, don't you think—?"

His eyes followed her down the street. Now it was he who laughed.

But at home, in his room, he didn't laugh. He put the clown's mask aside. He sat alone through the hours and thought of women and love.

> *O mes petites amoureuses*, he wrote,
> *que je vous hais! . . .*

For his hatred was now stronger than ever: of all that women were and all they pretended to be. From birth to death they were creatures of lies; of appearance, adornment, concealment, falsity; of black dresses, rosaries, pious words, girlish simpers—and beneath them of nakedness and lusting flesh. Nature itself had twisted them, made them false. But . . . and here always came the blank unanswerable *but* . . . if nature had made it so, *how* could it be false? Unless it too were a lie, a monstrous hoax. . . .

His dreams returned to plague him. Dreams of Mimi Rouger. Of his mother. Of the Nigger Queen. Of women without face or form or identity, but only flesh. And in the sleepless tortured night he rose with his hate and wrote his ode to women:

> *The star has wept down rose into your ears' deep nests,*
> *the infinite rolled white along your nape and back;*
> *the sea pearled russet at your crimson-nippled breasts,*
> *and on your sovereign flank has Man himself bled black.*

Albert Chariol came to see him, and reluctantly he opened the door.

"Monsieur Izard has asked me to speak to you," the teacher said. "We can no longer have this business of your tutoring the students."

"No?" said Claude.

"No. It's demoralizing for the boys and unfair to those who can't afford it. We've issued an announcement that anyone found to have had help from you will receive an automatic failure."

"I see. Well, maybe I'll have to start a school of my own."

He shrugged and returned to the papers on his table. But Chariol didn't leave.

"That isn't the only reason I came, Claude," he said.

"You have another edict?"

"No, no edict. I want to talk with you."

Claude looked up at him with blank eyes. "What's there to talk about?" he asked.

"About you. And what you're doing." Chariol came closer and stood beside the table. "What *is* this, boy?" he said. "What sort of madness and stupidity?"

Claude nodded at his papers. "My work, you mean?"

"No, not your work. Yourself. Your life."

"I've changed my life, haven't you heard? I'm now a *voyou*. The town no-good."

"What nonsense—"

"No, it's not nonsense. It's the simple truth. And now if you'll excuse me, monsieur—"

He bent over the table. Chariol watched him, biting his lips; then his face relaxed and he leaned earnestly forward. "Claude, listen to me," he said. "You must listen. We are friends—"

"*Were* friends," said Claude.

"Were?"

"Yes, were. Before you rejected me."

"*I* rejected *you?* What are you talking about?" The teacher stared at him. "Oh, Lord, you mean that night at my place a few months ago. And those silly verses—"

He tried to go on, but Claude leaped to his feet. "Yes, those silly verses," he said. "And shall I tell you something, monsieur?" He slammed the table with his hand. "I'm still writing silly verses. I'll spend the rest of my life writing silly verses. How do you like that, *hein?*"

"Claude, Claude! I'm only trying to say—"

"That they're silly; that they're rubbish. All right, you've said it."

"I'm only trying to say," said Chariol patiently, "that, whatever you think, I'm still your friend. What's happened to you, or what you're about, I don't know, but I can see you're unhappy and miserable, and if there's anything I can do—"

"What you can do, God damn it, is get out!"

There was a silence. The former friends faced each other: the one quiet and sad, the other blazing with cold fire. Then Chariol sighed and went to the door.

"Well, I'm glad that at least you are still writing," he said. "But I'll tell you this, boy, and from my heart. It will have to be wonderfully good to make up for what you are doing to yourself."

Then, on the street, Father Lacaze stopped him and looked at him carefully with his old bright eyes.

"So, my son?" he said.

"No psalms please, Father."

"No, no psalms," said the priest. "But perhaps a prayer or two would be in order?"

"No prayers either, thanks."

"You do not need prayers, is that it?"

"That's it."

"Nor grace nor light nor the way of truth?"

"I have my own ways of finding the truth."

Father Lacaze shook his head slowly. "I do not understand, my son," he said. "I do not understand at all what has happened. Once you were a fine boy, a pious boy, the best and brightest in Cambon; and we had the greatest hopes for you. Once I had even thought you might someday be a priest. And now—" He shook his head again. His mind groped for a way to reach the sinner who stood before him. "If you care nothing about yourself," he said, "at least think of your mother and what you are doing to her."

"I prefer to think," said Claude, "of what she has done to me."

"Your mother is a good woman. She is devout, decent, respectable, God-fearing."

"My mother is a nigger. She is mean, stupid, frustrated, avaricious, bigoted, superstitious, and hypocritical. And I wish she was dead."

The priest took a step back and crossed himself. "God have mercy on her," he murmured, "and on all of us who have you among us."

"Yes, I hope He does, Father," Claude agreed. "You all need it more than I do."

He walked on. He went home. He sat at the table in his room and thought about God—as he often did. And then he wrote:

> He is a God who sees it all and laughs aloud
> at damask altar-cloths, incense and chalices,
> who falls asleep, lulled by adoring liturgies
> —and wakens when some mother, in her anguish bowed
> and weeping till her old black bonnet shakes with grief,
> offers him a big sou wrapped in her handkerchief.

But that was one God. The God of the church and the priests and his own mother (no sous from her) was another matter. That night he went to the square in front of the church with a piece of chalk and wrote in fine big letters on the paving:

MERDE AUX PRETRES

MERDE A DIEU

"I am going to turn you over to the police," said his mother.

"Fine," he answered. "Let me know when they're coming and I'll wear my blue serge."

Actually, a policeman did appear one day—about the chalking in the square—but it was only for a brief dressing-down and a behind-doors conference with Madame Morel. And when he had left she was back on another tack. "The police are right," she said. "There is only one thing to be done with you. You will go to work at once."

"That's fine too; in fact, just what I was planning," he told her. And closing himself in his room, he sat down at the table. She called out and rattled the knob, but he scarcely heard her. Later, when he came out, he scarcely saw her.

Indeed, increasingly now, he saw nothing but what he wished and willed to see: the images and visions of his inward eye. The world knew him as a *voyou*, a ne'er-do-well, and that was that; but he himself was aware that he was also in the process of becoming something else—something that, ironically, sounded like it, and was in a strange way related to it—and this was a *voyant*—a seer. It was not a thing he imagined. It was a thing he knew. And it was not an accident, nor a spontaneous development, but the result of deliberate and conscious effort: a determination to turn his thoughts, his mind, his very soul, into the path that he had chosen for them. Slowly and painstakingly, struggling with each word and phrase, ransacking the depths of being, he set down his creed: . . . *I say that one must be a seer, make oneself a seer. The poet makes himself a seer by a long, immense and reasoned derangement of all the senses. He seeks in himself every kind of love, of suffering, of madness; he exhausts all the poisons in himself in order to keep only their quintessences. Unspeakable torment, in which he has need of all faith, all superhuman power, in which he becomes, of all men, the great Sufferer, the great Criminal, the great Damned—the supreme Scholar! For he comes to the unknown. . . .*

Derangement—*reasoned* derangement: that was the key. To break the mold, the chains, the bars that held the flesh and the spirit; to throw off the blinds, the slings, the splints, and trusses with which life binds us; to derange and twist and destroy the whole fabric of the prison, and to emerge whole and free. He was not afraid to be free—nor to find his own way to freedom. He was not afraid of "queerness" and "difference," of apartness and aloneness, of ranging beyond the bounds which men set for themselves—into fantasy and hallucination, rapture, and ecstasy. As a *voyou* (for this was part of it—the seen, the outward) he must pledge himself to the rejection of all forms, all rules and customs, all mindless conformity and acquiescence. And as a *voyant* he must push on forever outward, forever expanding his experience and consciousness; seeing clearly, with fresh eyes; seeing beyond the veils, beyond the shams and effigies, beyond illusion and lie, to the truth. *"Yea, verily, verily, I say unto you—"* (sayeth God) *"—ye shall know the truth, and the truth shall make you free."*

The truth was not always pleasant. It did not always have good manners and clean its fingernails. Sometimes it was in the eyes of a child or in a bird on a treetop, sometimes in a gutter, on a gallows, in a barracks latrine; and it was no less the truth in one place than in another. The dedication was to find it in all places—everywhere. To face it, know it, and be unafraid. Without evil, there could be no good; without filth, no purity; without hell, no heaven; without Satan, no God.

Derangement of the senses. Disorientation of the mind. Disorientation from the glib, the hollow, the banal, the accepted; from the vapid charade men have made of the act of living. . . . There was a price for this, amounting almost to self-crucifixion, but it could buy a depth of perception and freedom of spirit that passed the world's imagining. To be saved you must sin; to be blessed you must be damned; to be healed you must be sick; to live you must die. And most surely of all was this true for the poet—the seer. Only if he were crippled could he know the swift ecstasy of the racer; only with a ravaged heart could he know the heartbeat that was sound and strong. "Very well," he thought: "I have been ravaged, I have been maimed. Once the church itself maimed its choirboys so that they could sing more purely to its God. Now perhaps, like theirs, my own manhood is gone before I have had it, but thereby my own song, to my own God, will also be more pure and clear."

It was not an issue of good and evil; but of the truth. Of seeking it, seeing it, knowing it, being in and of oneself true to it—to make it doubly true—and then transmitting it to others through the medium of art. As for himself: . . . *Je est un autre*, he wrote. *I is another.* . . . Not *I am*, but *I is;* the "I" who is someone and something else; who is the medium, the vessel, the catalyst. *If brass wakens to life as a trumpet, it is no merit of its own. That is obvious to me. I am present at the hatching of my thought; I watch it, I listen to it; I make a sweep of the bow. The symphony stirs in the depths.* . . .

He wrote. He slept and dreamed. He rose and wrote and dreamed again—and went on writing. The trumpet wakened. The symphony stirred. The *voyant*, who was *another*, looked out from his back-yard window across a world of muck and rainbows.

The *voyant* lived in solitude. When Claude left his room—the moment he was in contact with another human being—he was transformed into the *voyou*. But his *voyou* habits were now changing. The pleasure of idling around the school to mock his ex-classmates had worn thin, and the ban on tutoring had removed the profit motive. Indiscriminate curb-sitting and corner-lounging had grown boring. He had come to the point where he needed a new field of action; and he found it in the cafés.

There were, of course, problems involved, for without his tutoring income he was again penniless, and the proprietors expected an outlay of at least a few centimes for the privilege of sitting at their tables. But his ingenuity was well up to the challenge. Recalling his efforts as a non-singing *chansonnier* at the cafés of Montmartre the year before, he adopted the same technique—but with a difference. He left his serious poems at home. For his public appearances he composed *vers impromptus:* a stream of ditties, jingles, and limericks, all of them bawdy, many whole-hog obscene. And once he had perfected his technique of delivery he was a thumping success. Cambon being scarcely a spendthrift town, few coins were thrown to him; but there was no lack of applause, laughter, and return repartee. And from there it was a short step to sitting at the tables and cadging drinks.

He became known as a "character"—*un type*—and at one place in particular, the Café du Printemps, he was soon established as a fixture. The Printemps' clientele, in terms of social level, was a mixed one, consisting of roughly equal numbers of workingmen, tradesmen, and civil servants, but in general it comprised what might have been called the "free souls" of the town. There was a minimum of bourgeois stuffiness about it, no women patrons whatever, and a few regulars who, after six in the evening, seemed not to have anywhere else to go. The beer, wine, and marc flowed freely. The arguments were lively, the jokes raw, the laughter loud. And the *voyou fou*, with the baby face and the outsized meerschaum, was accepted as an added attraction.

Claude played his role conscientiously. He came at six and stayed until closing. He dressed like a tramp and wore his Prussian helmet askew on his long uncombed hair. He declaimed, argued, clowned, hurled insults. And soon drinks were coming his way without his having to ask for them, on the theory of many in his audience that he put on an even better show when drunk. Indeed, few nights now passed on which he was not drunk —and he gloried in it. For it was fitting not only to a *voyou* but to a *voyant*, another form of liberation of the mind and the senses. "I shall be the first sixteen-year-old drunkard in the history of Cambon," he told himself. "And I shall write greater drunken poetry than Poe or Baudelaire."

He saved his "great" poetry for his room, however; at the Printemps his contributions were confined to what he called his "swill for the hogs." And for the most part the hogs liked it. Their guffaws and jibes were good-natured, and they treasured the half-grown lunatic as their special *enfant terrible*. Occasionally, though, there was trouble. Claude went too far in his exhibitionism, or someone was not in the mood for it, or had had a drink too many, and suddenly the storm clouds would gather. And these were the times he enjoyed the best of all.

"Here you!" A man threw a franc at him. "I'm tired of looking at that mop of yours. For Christ's sake go get yourself a haircut."

"*Mais oui, monsieur. Certainement, monsieur.*" Claude bowed and disappeared—but only to return a moment later with a double-sized glass of marc.

The man glowered. "You fresh brat, I told you to—"

"Yes, of course, monsieur, to have my hair cut. But this will have the same effect—truly. If you drink enough, the doctors say, it's sure to make your hair fall out."

Another night. Another heckler. . . .

"Hey squirt—don't you go to school? Don't you have a job? Don't you do *anything*?"

"I am retired, monsieur."

"Retired?"

"Yes, monsieur, I have had a full career. I have been a storekeeper, a farmworker, a ratcatcher, a thief, an arsonist, a sodomist, a soldier of the Republic, and an instructor in classical languages and literature. In short, a squirt, monsieur, who has had considerably more experience than you."

"Why you snotty—"

Claude laughed. The man pushed back his chair. "I'm going to teach you some manners right now," he snarled. "What do you say to that?"

"I say *va te faire foutre*."

"*What?*"

"I believe you understood me, monsieur. If not, I can say it in other languages. Would you care for it in English, perhaps? Or German or Italian or Latin or Greek? You see, I am quite a philologist. . . ."

Many fists were raised, but none ever quite struck. All that flew was the talk—sometimes in threats and curses, sometimes in jokes and laughter—and usually working around in due time to the *topiques majeurs* of politics and sex. Of the two, politics was a slight favorite among the older men, sex among the younger, and rare indeed was the evening at the Printemps without long discourse, among the juniors, on amours factual and fictional. As the hour grew later, invariably the described adventures became more colorful, the feats of prowess more wondrous, the women more ravishing and co-operative. "And you, *voyou*"—someone told Claude one night, grinning, "—you've contributed nothing. Now we'll hear your adventures, *hein?* How it feels to be a virgin."

Claude waited for the laughter to subside. Then he said politely: "Oh, but I am not a virgin, monsieur."

"No? . . . Well, cheers for our baby boy. You're a man of the world, *hein?* You have a little *amie* hidden away somewhere?"

"Yes, monsieur."

"Fine—tell us about her. Is she nice? Is she pretty?"

"She's very pretty, yes. But to be honest, she's—well—a bit of a bitch."

"Ah, now. But that makes the dish all the spicier, doesn't it? Come on, tell us. What does she do? What's she like in bed?"

"We don't use a bed, monsieur. We use the floor; it's easier for her."

"Easier—?"

"Yes. Less complicated, you know. And besides, it's what she's accustomed to."

"Accustomed to? What are you talking about? What kind of an *amie* is this anyhow?"

"She is a poodle, monsieur."

Politics. . . .

The Commune had controlled Paris for less than three months. The hoped-for uprisings in the rest of the country had not taken place; the National Government had rallied its scattered armies, and at the end of May they had retaken the capital. The violence and bloodshed had been terrible. When the fighting was over, the victors had lined up the Communards and *blouses blanches* and massacred them by the thousand. Once again, the bourgeoisie and reaction rode high, and left-wing revolt lay prostrate and broken.

At the Printemps, as elsewhere, sentiment varied largely with economic status. The workingmen had been largely pro-Commune, the

tradesmen anti, the others somewhere in between, and the arguments
continued long after the issue had been settled.

"It was the one hope of France."

"Hope for what? Extermination?"

"It would have made us powerful."

"We would have been attacked by every other government in Europe."

"Ah well, *plus ça change—*"

"There has to be change. Without change there's death."

"Better death than this rule by moneybags."

"The Communards were anarchists, scum—"

"They were men of the people. The people can do no wrong."

"Of course not," said Claude. "They're all patriots, idealists, heroes."

"Keep out of this, brat. We're discussing serious matters."

"Your pardon, monsieur."

A fist pounded the table. "The people will rise again."

"And be shot again."

"No, not the next time. The next time they will conquer. It will be the
time of decision, of victory."

"Of liberty and enlightenment."

"The time of—"

"Of the Assassins," said Claude.

He returned to his room. He sat at his desk. It was raining now;
thunder rolled; beyond the window lightning split the darkness of night
and towered clouds.

He wrote:

> *We stand on earth, among our rages and our boredoms.*
> *We raise our heads;*
> *see passing in the stormy skies the banners of ecstasy.*
> *Is it God or Satan who paints such skies,*
> *so fabulous—and false?*

Among the regulars at the Printemps was the fattest man in Cambon.
His name was Fernand Archambault; he was a clerk in the railway offices
and the possessor of a wife and seven children; but neither job nor family
seemed to require great attention. Every evening of the week, plus many
afternoons, he was to be found enthroned on two chairs (for one could
not hold him) at the best corner table: smoking endless cigars, draining
endless beer glasses, holding discourse by the hour on all topics under
sun and moon. He was rarely serious. His small fat-padded eyes were
usually twinkling, his great jowls quivering with laughter. He knew as
many stories as Scheherazade, and told them better, with a rich scato-

logical overlay of which Claude himself would have been proud. Like the younger *voyou*—though on a far more authoritative level—he was an eccentric, a "character," *un type formidable*. But his clown's mask, the boy presently discovered, was like his own, too—a mask and no more. For, beneath it, the immense Monsieur Archambault was a remarkable man.

This revelation came to Claude through (of all things) a sleight-of-hand demonstration. Archambault, among his sundry other roles, was an amateur magician; he often amused himself by bringing cards, balls, rings, and other paraphernalia to the café for the mystification of his fellow drinkers; and one night, after an exhibition, he left the place with Claude. "They are *salauds*, these friends of mine," he announced suddenly. "And they have the brains of hamsters. Not that they can't understand my little tricks; that means nothing. But that they can't even understand what a trick *is*—what magic *is*; that is depressing. Would you like me to tell you what it is? No? Well, I'll tell you anyhow. Magic is life. And do you know why? Because life is magic. Life itself is legerdemain, prestidigitation, fakery, illusion, hallucination. Only there it's God's abracadabra, not Archambault's."

Claude looked at him curiously. This was not the way people talked in Cambon.

"You, of course, are a *salaud*, too," said the fat man. "A brat, a hoodlum, and a disgrace to your parents—whoever they are. But I don't think you're a hamster. I think you're a smart one, a deep one, the most dangerous kind of hoodlum." He eyed Claude sharply. "You write, don't you?"

"How do you—"

"I can tell. The disease is all over you—like pockmarks. . . . Very well, you write. If you write you deal in magic. You deal in the goddamnedest most magical abracadabra ever devised by man or God: the abracadabra of words." Archambault patted his vast paunch and belched. "I was a writer once, God help me. A very bad writer, but still I had the disease. . . . I suppose you think you're a good writer?"

"Yes," said Claude.

"Well, that's part of the magic, you know. Illusion, hallucination. . . . No, don't try any of your foul talk on me; I'll slap you right down into the sidewalk. . . . You're mad at the world, aren't you, boy? Yes, I've watched you. You want to attack it, choke it, kill it. All right, more power to you; the world can use plenty of that—and magic can help you. That's the nice thing about magic, you see: it works both ways. One way for you and one way for me, and for me it's the opposite. I wanted to be a poet, and I'm a clerk. I wanted to be a genius, and I'm a sideshow for drunks. With me it's life, not Fernand Archambault, that's done the choking and killing, and all I want is to keep it away from me. . . . Magic helps there too."

They had stopped at the door of a small house on one of the town's nondescript side streets. "Come on in and I'll show you my magician's lair," he said. "But watch out where you step; there're lots of children lying around."

What Claude expected to find he could not have said. Some sort of laboratory, perhaps. Or a collection of props and gadgets such as the fat man brought to the café. But what he did find was something very different. What he found were books. Books by the scores and hundreds, lining the walls and crowding the tables of the tiny room that Archambault had made his study; old books and new books, French books and foreign books, strange and rare and exotic books, such as he would never have dreamed existed in Cambon; and all of them (for his host had not lied, but merely laid a false trail), all without exception, dealing with the magical, the mystical, the occult, the arcane. There were the tomes of the ancient Hebrew cabala, and many commentaries on the cabala. There were the sacred writings of India: the *Rig-Veda*, the *Ramayana*, the *Bhagavad-Gita*, the *Bhagavata Purana*. There were histories of Hinduism, Buddhism, Lamaism, Taoism, Zoroastrianism; studies of yoga and karma; works on deism, theism, transcendentalism, Rosicrucianism; on alchemy, demonology, satanism, the Black Mass. Indeed, in that little room there seemed to Claude to be contained the distillation of all the mystic adventurers, the seers and visionaries, of history, and he stood among them as another might have stood in the inner chamber of a temple.

"If you want magic, boy," said Archambault, "here it is. Help yourself." Claude did.

During the weeks that followed he spent almost all his time with the new-found treasure: partly at Archambault's and partly in his own room, to which the fat man let him take whatever he wanted. For the time being he gave up his writing. He gave up the Printemps. He turned from every phase of active outward life, and lowering himself, as if in a diving bell, into the ocean of the mystic, moved entranced through its ambiguous depths. Always adept at languages, he now added to his repertory a smattering of many new ones, among them Hebrew and Arabic, Sanskrit and Hindustani. And to his knowledge of literature and philosophy, confined theretofore to the writings of the Western world, he added roots that spread out across the whole subsoil of human history. To Cambon he might seem merely an eccentric, a *voyou*, an *espèce de fou*, but he knew now, once and for all, that in his revolt against the accepted he was not alone; that in his striving to become a seer and a mystic he was part of great and holy tradition. Buddha and the Hindu sages were his true ancestors. The swamis and anchorite monks were of the same bone and blood. St. Augustine and Dante, Paracelsus and Swedenborg had all struggled, as he was now struggling, for the purity of vision, the "derangement of the senses," that would let them see beyond the shifting prisms of the here-and-now into the white changeless blaze of truth. From this wealth of new discovery he came back to the men he had already known and revered—the seers and mystics of more recent times: de Maistre and Ballanche, Leroux and Enfantin, Poe and Baudelaire. He came back to Maurice Druard, the unknown whose poems he had found in the dreary library of *les assis*, and now, more than ever, he was his brother—his twin, his *Doppelgänger*, a very part of his own being.

Yes, here was magic. . . .

And he made it his own.

Spring passed into summer. Cambon lay in heat and dust. In mid-July his brother Felix returned from his army service.

"Where did you go?" Claude asked.

"Oh, places."

"What did you do?"

"Marched."

That was the sum of their conversation. Felix went back behind the counter of the shop. He yawned and dozed. He clumped on the stairs. He moved again into their joint room that Claude had come to think of as his own, and lay on the bed, scratching and passing wind. In a few days Claude was desperate; but then relief came when his sister Yvette went off to spend a month with their aunt in Reims. He moved into her room —over his mother's protests.

His relationship with his mother was of the same pattern as always: a compressed Hundred Years' War of attrition spaced by occasional violent, but always indecisive, pitched battles. "If you're not at work by next week, I'll put you out!" she announced regularly. But she didn't. "I can't stand it any longer. I'm going!" he kept telling himself. But he didn't. Twice he made a start: once getting as far as the station, where he planned again to hitch a free ride, once following his old route through the Ardennes to Antimes. But each time he turned back. . . . Why? . . . Partly, perhaps— though he did not like to admit it—it was because he was afraid; because he could not bring himself to face a possible repetition of the defeat and humiliation in which his previous escapes had ended. But there was also, he knew, another reason—a deeper, more subtle and more powerful reason—and this had to do not with fears and consequences but with his mother herself. He often thought about it. He tried to analyze it. But it eluded him. It was simply *there:* a fact, a climate, a condition of existence that somehow held them together, a perverse compulsion between two opposites, two enemies, that was stronger than the will to break apart.

One day a strange thing happened. It was at supper, and she had been berating him in the usual fashion, and he had been giving the usual answers.

"Yes, I know," he said. "I'm hopeless, worthless. Just like my father—"

"No," she said, "not like your father. Your father was a fool and a weakling. You are a devil all right, but those two things you are not."

When he left the table she followed him to his room. "This reading —this writing," she said. "You will keep at them no matter what, hein?"

"No matter what," he answered.

"You are stubborn, aren't you? You are proud?" For a few moments she was silent, thinking her own thoughts; then her black eyes flashed at him. "If you are proud," she said, "why don't you make something of yourself. If what you write is any good, why can't you sell it?"

He was too surprised to speak.

"I am told that some literary men make a good living. The editor of the *Journal des Ardennes*, in Antimes, is said to make five thousand francs a year. Why don't you make money with this stuff of yours? Send it to the *Journal* or some other paper."

"Newspapers don't print the sort of thing—"

"Then write what they do print. . . . Look, boy—" Her voice was becoming harsh again. "I am patient with you. I put up with a lot from you. Now I am even willing to put up with this writing of yours; but you must earn a living, you must make it pay. . . ."

The discussion ended, as all did, in anger, shouting, and slammed doors. But at least it had had a new turn to it. That night Claude dreamed again of the Nigger King and the Nigger Queen, and the Queen, in the black hand that was beckoning him, held a pencil and a sheaf of francs.

The notion crossed his mind of showing his poems to his mother. But it was too wild, too fantastic. Instead, one night, on impulse, he took several of them to the Café du Printemps and gave them to Archambault, and the fat man stuffed them in his pocket and took them home. Through the next day Claude waited impatiently. "It's ridiculous," he told himself. "What does his opinion matter?" But still he was impatient—and nervous. He would not be able to bear another wound such as had been inflicted by Albert Chariol.

Back in the café in the evening, Archambault was in an expansive mood with several cronies, and hours passed before Claude could catch him alone. Even then, he seemed not disposed to speak of the poems, but instead kept Claude in misery with another of his disquisitions on magic. "Do you know what I'd have liked best of all to be in my life?" he said. "An alchemist! There's the royalty of all magic, *voyou*—alchemy! If I'd been lucky enough to live in the Middle Ages instead of this damned Age of the Bourgeois, by God, I'd have been a second Faust!"

Claude squirmed in his impatience. Then it happened. Archambault looked at him with a curious expression, stroked a jowl, and added: "Of course your sort's lucky. You don't need the Middle Ages."

"Don't need—"

"You're an alchemist in any age. An alchemist of words."

Claude's heart leaped. "You mean you liked—"

"I don't know about 'liked.' It would be pretty hard to *like* the sort of stuff you write. But it's alchemy, boy—yes. It's got magic."

"Then you think—"

"I think what you think. That you're a poet." He looked Claude up and down with slow insolence and shook his head. "Meaning you never can tell."

"Monsieur, I—"

"Never mind the speech. What do you do with these things of yours?"

"Do with them?"

"Who's seen them? Whom have you sent them to?"

"No one. That is—once I tried, with a magazine—but I wasn't successful."

"Hmm— Well, I have a suggestion. I'd like to send them to someone in Paris."

"In Paris?"

"Yes. A chap I used to know there when I was trying to write myself. Only I didn't make it, and he did. He was just a youngster then, and I guess not so old even now. But he's a poet and a damn good one. Name of Maurice Druard."

The leaping heart all but stopped.

"*Druard?*"

"Yes, do you know him?"

Claude could scarcely speak. "I've never met him, of course—no. But I've read his poems—some of them—all I could find. I know them by heart. He's a genius!"

"So? I'm sure he'll be glad to hear that." Archambault chuckled. "As a matter of fact, you *would* like his things," he said. "When Maurice gets going, he's almost as crazy as you are."

He was not just talking. Later, at his house, he put Claude's poems in an envelope and addressed it. Then he wrote a covering note, and Claude, with shaking hand, wrote another. The closing words were not new to him . . . *I am only a young writer, but I think the enclosed will show I am a true writer. I beg you to hold out your hand to me. Claude Morel.*

He went home. The night gleamed. The stars sang.

Druard . . . Druard. . . .

The next morning he was at his table at dawn. And again he stayed there through the days and the nights. He worked as he had never worked before, fired twofold by the insights of his recent reading and the thought that, even as he worked, Druard, the great Druard, might be sitting over his poems and thinking of him. With all his intensity, all his mind and heart, he gave himself to the act of creation. He wrote with a passion, a frenzy, that was more demonic than human, and a dedication that was absolute. His goal was not merely to write poetry—even great poetry— as it had been written before, but to cast off every vestige of the literal and traditional, to follow his mystic masters into the unknown, to go on beyond them, into new, farther unknowns, into which he, of all men, would be the first to enter. The potential was there: that he knew. The visions and images were there, burning within him. The struggle, now fiercer than ever, was to find a tongue, a language, that could express them: a tool of art that would match the tools of science and technology —ever more powerful, more delicate, more controlled, and yet more free —a mighty living force in the expansion of man's consciousness. To this end he took language apart and put it together again. He waged grim unceasing battle with words, phrases, grammar, syntax, and verse forms, striving to rebuild the whole fabric of expression to his desire and will. If he was to be what he dreamed of being—a thief of fire, the greatest of all thieves, all visionaries—he must first forge himself the perfect instrument in which that fire might burn.

"God, fill me with your light!" he prayed. "Hell, fill me with your flames!"

And both God and hell seemed to answer.

He became as one possessed. His blood boiled. His brain reeled. He was no longer Claude Morel, no longer the *I* of self, but *another*—a *voyant*, a seer—his perceptions heightened to a supernatural pitch, his senses deranged to catch the whispers of eternity. *"J'ai vu quelquefois ce que l'homme a cru voir,"* he thought. *"I have sometimes seen what Man thinks he has seen."* And out of this vision, this clairvoyance, he now wrote a poem which, before, he would not have dared to try: a poem of his soul and his soul's voyage.

For now, as always, it could be only a voyage that expressed it. Now, as always, his soul was a ship and its milieu the sea. Of all the memories of his early childhood, the clearest, the most magical, was that of a toy ship and a puddle . . .

> *the cold black puddle where, under an evening sky,*
> *a crouching child, full of sorrow, launches*
> *a boat as frail as a May butterfly . . .*

And in the years since, it had not changed. It had only grown; the puddle into a sea, an ocean; the butterfly into a gull, an eagle, a fabulous frigate bird of the ocean sky. He himself was the bird, he himself the boat. And his poem was the story of that boat's voyage: out from the ports of home, from the parapets of Europe: out across unknown seas: through the poem

of the sea: *past glaciers, silver suns, pearl waves and fiery skies*
and turbid maelstroms,
rutting behemoths,
electric moons

. . . down to the depths of the sea,

to dark gulfs,
dark blooms with yellow mouths,
flowers and eyes of panthers . . . and rainbows, like bridles,
stretched through stillness: spinning a motionless and blue eternity

. . . and up at last from depths of sea to depths of sky, where

I have seen star-archipelagoes and islands
in skies that call the wanderer, fierce, forlorn.
Is it within these ancient nights you sleep in exile,
O hosts of golden birds, O day as yet unborn?

It was a voyage without passport, without compass, without boundary or limitation; a hurricane of the spirit: an ecstasy, a madness, a wild celestial drunkenness of the lone craft that was his soul. And it was for this that he named his voyage: *Le Bateau Ivre—The Drunken Boat.*

The pitch of fever held. It sustained him, kindled him, until he had finished. But by then it had consumed him. He was written out, burned out, gutted. For two days and two nights he slept the sleep of the drugged, and even when he at last got up and left his room he felt as weak and hollow as a ghost. He walked. He walked out from the town and sat beside the River Meuse. He sat alone for hours deep in the forest of the Ardennes. When he came back and entered the store he asked his brother if there had been a letter from Paris, and Felix said, "Who in hell would be writing you from Paris?" Then he went upstairs, and his mother said, "What is all this mooning around, *hein?* I give you permission to write, so you stop writing. Get into your room at once and do something for the newspapers."

He put on his Prussian helmet and lit his meerschaum. He went to the Café du Printemps. Perhaps Archambault had had a letter. . . . But he hadn't. . . . And Claude cadged drinks that night as he had never cadged before. He got drunk; not celestially drunk; blind, staggering drunk. He vomited. The proprietor put him out. He fell across the curb, and his helmet clattered on the cobbles. Archambault and a friend took him home, and his mother roared.

The next day: "Any mail . . . ?"

The next week: "Any mail . . . ?"

The summer days dragged on. Yvette returned from Reims, and he had to move back to his room and his brother's scratchings and belchings. But it didn't greatly matter, because he could not have worked anyhow. A few times he tried, but nothing came. Nothing came from Druard. Nothing would ever come. His poems were lying on some shelf in Paris, discarded and forgotten—just as *The Drunken Boat* was lying in the drawer of his table. Opening the drawer, he looked down at it: his testament, his vision, the blood of his heart and the cells of his brain. No one would ever read it. No one would ever know it existed. He picked it up, held it, almost tore it. . . . But not quite.

He stopped going to the Printemps, because he could not bear to see Archambault. He stopped playing the *voyou* in public, because he no longer had the spirit for it. But inwardly he was now more the *voyou*—more the tramp and outcast—than ever. He shambled along the empty back streets. He sat in the stillness of alleyways. He did nothing. That was his life now: nothingness—*le néant*. Cambon drowsed under the sun. The dust rose from the cobbles. The dust coated the leaves. He walked through the dust aimlessly, going nowhere, doing nothing—himself nothing—a dusty ghost, a sleepwalker, caught in an evil dream.

And it was still as if in a dream that one day, in late summer, he entered the store and picked up the letter that lay on the counter. For a long time he simply held it, without moving. Then he climbed the stairs, went to his room, closed the door, and sat down at his table. He opened the envelope and a fifty-franc note fell out. He extracted a sheet of note paper, unfolded it, and began to read.

He read: . . . *brilliant, magnificent* . . .

He read: . . . *have been away; I am sorry . . . we must meet as soon as possible . . . we have room and would be honored . . . enclosed is a little something. . . .*

He read: . . . *Come, dear great spirit. We call you, we await you! Yours in homage and admiration, Maurice Druard.*

9

"Vos billets, s'il vous plaît. Vos billets!"

The guard at the gate extended his hand, and Claude gave him his ticket. ("No jump today," he thought. "No ties or gravel or bloody knee.") And he passed through the gate and into the concourse of the Gare de l'Est. Public fiacres were lined up at the main entrance of the station, but though he had the money to take one he had decided to walk. Walking had always been his medicine for a fast-beating heart. And it was beating fast now: fast and hard, like a flailing hammer, against the cage of his ribs.

Two weeks had passed since the first letter from Druard. Immediately upon receiving it he had run to Archambault—who had received one too —and then he had written back. Again Druard had replied. The invitation had not been a hollow one; a firm date was set; and through the days that followed Claude had lived in a fever of anticipation. In fact, so great had been his excitement that he had made a tactical error: he had told his mother. And she had not only forbidden him to go, but had stormed and shouted about it until she was hoarse. Not that it had made any ultimate difference, to be sure, for on the appointed day he had simply climbed from his window, scaled the back-yard wall, and gone down to the station to catch the midday train. His only regret was he had not been able to say goodbye to his sister. In all his goings, all his leave-takings, he had yet to say goodbye to anyone in the family.

"But the hell with that," he thought. That was all in the past, and he was now in the future—a future so bright and beckoning that his imagination could only grope at it. Once again Paris enveloped him. Again he moved down the great boulevards, past the shops and cafés, through the evening crowds, through the life and stir, and this time it was even better and more thrilling than before, because he was no longer a stranger and outsider, wandering aimlessly, but a part of it, one with it, a creature with a purpose and a destination. "I have been called," he thought. "I am awaited." And the words held a magic as potent as any in Archambault's books.

His mind raced ahead as far as it could go: to Druard's home, his arrival there, his welcome. The address was in Montmartre, on a street he did not know, but he had long since visualized it: an old history-encrusted building on a steep hill, with a bistro on the ground floor and studio flats above. Druard would live on the top floor, up long mysterious steps, and his rooms would be an eyrie looking out over the rooftops of Paris. They would be full of books, manuscripts, and paintings, all in wonderful confusion: casual, free, womanless. Indeed, there would be no woman in the whole building—except for an ancient concierge and assorted visiting *grisettes*—and the tenants, to a man, would be young writers, painters, and composers. Soon after he arrived they would troop up to Druard's, and they would all eat sausage and drink beer, sitting on the floor; and then later they would go down to the café (the most famous in literary and artistic Paris) to continue drinking and talking for the rest of the night. The painters would show their new sketches, the poets would read their new verses. Claude's hand went to the sheaf of papers in his inside pocket, and he felt the thumping heart beneath. Perhaps—perhaps he himself would read *The Drunken Boat*. . . .

He stopped and looked around him in the gathering dusk. Lost in his daydream, he had apparently also lost his way. But when he reached the next street sign he was still more confused, for he had *not* lost it. He was in Montmartre all right, and on the right street—the Rue Nicolet; but it looked like nothing he had ever seen in that *quartier*. It looked, rather like some of the streets he remembered from the western faubourgs, in the solid, stolid domain of the bourgeoisie. Puzzled, he pulled Druard's last letter from his pocket. *176 Rue Nicolet*, it said. And he went on. He came to a solid, stolid house of three stories and stood looking at the neat steps, the potted flowers, the curtained windows, the brass doorknob.... Well, he would find out what was wrong soon enough.... Mounting the steps, he pulled the bell.

A woman in a white apron and cap opened the door. "The delivery entrance is in the rear," she said.

"I—I'm not—"

She looked down and saw that his hands were empty. "And we have nothing for tramps or beggars."

The door started to close.

"Doesn't Monsieur Druard live here?" asked Claude.

"Monsieur Druard?" The maid seemed surprised that he knew the name. "Yes, Monsieur Druard lives here, but he is not at home."

She again made as if to close the door, but was interrupted by a woman's voice behind her.

"Is there some trouble, Jeanne?"

"No, madame, it is only a—"

Claude pushed forward. "I want to see Monsieur Druard," he said. Behind the maid he could now see the woman who had spoken. And there was another woman besides. The first was middle-aged and plump, with a broad bosom, high-piled hair, and strong, almost manlike features. The other was much younger—twenty or so at the most, Claude judged—with a soft round face and simple coiffure; and though she too was plump of body, it was obviously with the plumpness of pregnancy. Both were fashionably dressed in gowns such as Claude had only glimpsed before through Parisian windows and doorways. And both looked at him as if he were something that had blown in off the street in a gust of wind.

"The maid told you Monsieur Druard is not here," the older one said.

"Then I'll wait."

"What do you want of him?"

"I'm a friend. He's expecting me."

"Expecting—?" The two women looked at each other, then back at Claude. Neither had lorgnettes to raise, but they should have had.

"*Mon Dieu!*" said the older.

"I may come in, please?" said Claude.

"You are Monsieur—I mean, you are—"

"I am Claude Morel."

Both women's lips had parted to form an O, but no sound came out. Again they looked at each other and then back at Claude. The maid looked at Claude. She had moved aside a little, and he stepped into a large well-furnished foyer.

The older woman swallowed. "Well," she murmured. She was obviously trying to stop staring, but couldn't. "Come in—er—young man—"

Claude advanced a few steps farther, and there was a pause.

"Jeanne, bring in the—er—gentleman's bags," said the woman.

"I don't have any bags," Claude said.

"You don't have—" She decided not to pursue it. She swallowed again. "Maurice—that is, Monsieur Druard—went out. He went to the station to meet you."

"He must have missed me. He doesn't know what I look like."

"No, he doesn't know—" There was another pause; then she got hold of herself. "I am Madame de Bercy," she said. "Monsieur Druard is my son-in-law." She indicated the young pregnant woman. "This is my daughter, Monsieur Druard's wife."

"Oh," said Claude.

"How do you do?" said the young woman.

Now Claude was staring as well as they, and his eyes moved around the foyer. On the right, double doors opened into a large, richly furnished parlor. To the left was a smaller reception room. Ahead, a graceful staircase curved upward to the next floor, and behind it he could glimpse a dining room, bright with linen, silver, and lighted candles.

"This is Monsieur Druard's house?" he said slowly.

"It is my house," said Madame de Bercy. "Mine and my husband's. My daughter and son-in-law are living with us."

The maid looked at her inquiringly, and she nodded, and the maid went out. "Won't you come in and make yourself comfortable?" she said. And the three of them went into the parlor and sat down.

"*Eh bien—*" she murmured. Her daughter smiled vaguely. There was still another silence. Claude looked at the Turkish carpet, the gilt Empire furniture, the white marble fireplace, the huge ormolu clock. The women, as far as he could gather, were looking at his feet, though what could interest them in an old torn pair of walking boots he could not imagine.

Madame de Bercy cleared her throat.

Her daughter said, "The weather was lovely today."

Then the front door opened and a young man came in from the foyer. "Well—" he said. "Well, well!" Hurrying across the room, he grasped Claude's hand and held it. "I missed you, eh? I'm so sorry. But you got here all right—that's the main thing. You're here. Welcome, my friend. Welcome!" He looked at Claude closely, and his face, like the women's, showed his surprise; but what followed was a quick smile and a warm hand on the boy's shoulder. *"Mon Dieu,"* he said, *"comme il est enfant, ce génie!"*

Druard himself was about thirty. He was of medium height and slightly built, with a small, fine-featured face to which high cheekbones and slightly slanting eyes gave a certain oriental cast. One remarkably unpoetlike aspect was a hairline that had already receded almost to the point of baldness, but this was well counterbalanced by a soft reddish beard, long delicate hands, and an extreme sensitivity of gesture and expression. And though he was dressed in a conservative black suit, like a bourgeois businessman, this too was offset by a striped waistcoat and a drooping string tie.

"My boy, my boy!" he said, holding Claude close to him. "It's good to have you here. Good for me, for Paris, for all of us!"

He went on talking animatedly. He asked questions, told stories, brought in apéritifs and glasses. As he was pouring the drinks the doorbell rang, and a moment later the maid appeared. "Monsieur, it is the coachman of your fiacre," she announced, "and he says that—"

"Oh, yes." Druard's face clouded. He seemed to hesitate briefly and then turned to his mother-in-law. "I—I happened not to have the change for the cab, and—"

"You will find it in my dressing table. In the same drawer as usual."

"Ah yes. Yes—thanks."

He went out quickly. Claude sipped his yellowish drink, and although he didn't know what it was he liked it.

"May I ask how old you are, young man?" said Madame de Bercy.

"Nineteen," said Claude.

"Ah, that is very young."

"Yes," said Claude.

When Druard returned he was again in fine spirits. "Well, I hope we won't be disturbed again," he said. "We have so much to talk about. So very much!" He drank down his apéritif and poured another. "I had thought of asking some friends in tonight; they're all dying to meet you. But then I thought, no, that can wait. This first night we will just dine *en famille*. The four of us here, and my wife's young cousin who's staying with us." He glanced toward the foyer. "She'll be down any moment."

"My husband is away in the country." Madame de Bercy put in. "He is a keen huntsman, and this of course is the season. He rides with the Bourgeville Hounds."

"For two years he was Master of the Hunt," her daughter added.

"You are from—where is it?—the Vosges," said Madame de Bercy. "That is unspoiled country. There should be good hunting there too."

"It is the Ardennes," Claude said. "And we have wolves and weasels."

"I was referring rather to—"

"I doubt if Monsieur Morel is a hunter, *Belle-maman*," Druard interrupted. "He is a poet—remember? A poet's function is to create life, not destroy it."

"Because you are not able to ride to hounds yourself, Maurice, is no excuse for being snide about it. I simply asked—"

"And I simply said—"

"My husband is so tremendously impressed by your poems," young Madame Druard interposed tactfully. "And I too, I thought them lovely—" She smiled self-deprecatingly. "—What I could understand of them, that is. I'm afraid that perhaps I'm not very bright, for often I can't understand even my own husband's verses."

Druard smiled at Claude. "The women are always the conservatives, boy. Have you found that out yet? They don't want any part of poetry if it isn't birds and flowers and kisses in the moonlight."

"You don't believe in beauty, Monsieur Morel?" Madame Druard's brown eyes were as earnest as a child's.

Claude did not answer at once. Then he said quietly, "I believe in truth. I believe with the Englishman Keats: that beauty is truth, truth beauty. If a thing is true, true in its essence—even though ugly, even though evil —then it is also, because of its truth—"

"I beg your pardon," Madame de Bercy said, "but that is a rather fine chair. I would appreciate it if you would not tip back on it, please."

Druard jumped to his feet. "Damn it!" he said.

"What is that, Maurice?"

"I said—"

"*Maman*, Maurice—please!" Madame Druard looked at them beseechingly. Her husband drew a long breath and said more quietly: "Monsieur Morel was trying to tell us his creed as a poet, and I for one should like to hear it."

"Yes, yes, we shall all hear it," said Madame de Bercy. She glanced again at Claude to make sure his chair was down. "You may proceed, my young man."

Claude said nothing.

"You were saying something about truth, I believe."

Claude still said nothing, and Druard coughed nervously. "We can go on with it later," he suggested. "It's almost dinnertime, and I'm sure Monsieur Morel would like to wash and change."

"He has nothing to change into."

"Nothing to—" Druard laughed off his surprise. "You *are* traveling light, aren't you? We'll have to take care of that.... Well, have a wash anyhow."

He was about to lead Claude off, when there was the sound of steps from the foyer and a young girl came in. "Am I holding things up?" she said. "I'm so sorry. Sometimes I think I still need a nanny to get me dressed."

She went quickly to Madame Druard, turned her back, and pointed over her shoulder; and Madame Druard fastened two of the buttons on her bodice. Looking at Claude, the girl smiled. "Excuse my bad manners —and how do you do," she said.

She was a tall girl—almost as tall as Claude and Druard—and her body was midway through the change from a child's to a woman's. Her uncorseted waist was as slim as a boy's, but her bosom was high under the molded bodice, and her bare shoulders were full and firmly fleshed. She had a fresh-skinned, oval-shaped face, delicate of line in chin and cheeks but broadening to a full high forehead under light chestnut hair. Her mouth was soft and pliable, as if it smiled a lot. Her eyes were a deep and gleaming, almost violet, blue.

"This is my wife's cousin, Mademoiselle Lautier," said Druard. "She's spending a few weeks with us while her parents are away."

Mademoiselle Lautier, the buttoning-up finished, moved forward and extended a hand. "We have been hearing a lot about you," she said.

Claude mumbled something. The hand in his was as soft and fragile as a small bird, and he had a sudden wild impulse to close his grip and crush it. His own hand, he noticed for the first time, was streaked with soot. He hoped some of it would rub off on hers.

"And I am happy to be here for your visit," she told him.

The maid appeared and announced dinner. The matter of washing up seemed to have been forgotten, and they went into the gleaming dining room. "Here, if you please," said Madame de Bercy, indicating a place; and Claude sat down. She herself sat at the head of the table, on one side of him, and her daughter on the other. Druard and Mademoiselle Lautier took the seats opposite.

There were some strange-looking white lumps on the plate before him, and he began to eat them.

"There will be sauce for the crabmeat in just a moment," said Madame de Bercy.

Claude waited while the maid passed the sauce, and then began again. But he seemed suddenly to have a mouthful of hot pepper and spat it out into his napkin. Druard, watching, smiled at him from across the table; but the women didn't seem to notice. A light sweat broke out and glazed his forehead.

Because of her condition Madame Druard sat back a bit from the table. Presently she began patting the front of her dress and looking pertly at her husband. "Well, no comment?" she asked him.

"Comment?"

"On my new dress. Don't tell me you haven't noticed."

"It's very nice, my dear."

Mademoiselle Lautier leaned forward quickly. "Oh—and I didn't notice either. How awful of me! . . . It's lovely, Isabelle—just lovely."

"We had it made at Gauchon et Rollet," said Madame de Bercy. "They're doing such interesting things this season; even for—er—special requirements like Isabelle's. See—the way they handle the lines from the shoulders; and the pleats there, with a little ruching. And then of course, the skirt—stand up a moment, dear—you see how they do it—with a flare, almost bouffant—"

"Lovely!" Mademoiselle Lautier repeated.

"Of course I usually much prefer to get my things at Maison Dominique," said Madame Druard.

"Dominique is quite all right for casual things," her mother stated categorically, "but for *haute couture* there is no comparison with Gauchon."

"Before she went away, *Maman* got some of her fall things at Worth's," said Mademoiselle Lautier. "They're terribly expensive, of course, but she said—"

"Worth—*mon Dieu!*"

Madame de Bercy proffered her opinion of Worth. She gave her condensed analysis of several other *couturieres*, switched in midstream to the impossibility of any longer getting good house servants (thanks to the recent war and the hateful influence of the Commune), and moved on to a newly opened shop on the Rue de la Paix which featured rather extraordinary costume jewelry imported from Italy. "I happened to pass by yesterday with the Comtesse de Barville," she said, "and—where are you going, Maurice?"

"I'm getting the wine," said Druard.

"Jeanne will bring it."

"She always brings it too late."

He brought a bottle from a cabinet. The maid served soup and then a roast. Druard ate little, but kept draining and refilling his glass, and he refilled Claude's, too, whenever it was low.

Suddenly Madame de Bercy turned to Claude. "Do, please forgive these little interruptions." She smiled graciously. "You are our guest of honor, you know, and you must tell us *all* about yourself."

There was a silence.

Druard chuckled nervously. "Starting as far back before birth as possible," he said.

His mother-in-law ignored him. "You come from—er—Charbon, I believe Maurice said? In the Vosges? That interests me, you know. To be truthful, I had never associated the Vosges with an active cultural life."

"Oh, *Maman!*" Madame Druard protested. "Paris isn't the *whole* world, after all. I'm sure there are good schools—perhaps literary societies—"

"You are a member of a coterie?" Madame de Bercy asked. "A group of young poets, perhaps? I think that such organizations are an excellent idea. I remember one summer my husband and I were in a little town near Vichy—he had been taking the waters there—and a group of the local ladies asked me to tea. I had assumed of course that the conversation would be about local matters: their gardens, perhaps, or sewing or recipes. But no, it was on a remarkably high level. They had formed a poetry circle for weekly readings, and they were studying the Parnassians.... You are acquainted with the Parnassians, Monsieur Morel? They are today's leading poets, you know. Truly a group of geniuses."

"Oh yes!" exclaimed Madame Druard. "Their things are exquisite. I've never known such loveliness and sensitivity.... Leconte de Lisle, for instance. Have you read Leconte de Lisle? And Yves Balmer? There's a new volume by Monsieur Balmer just out, bound in the most exquisite green morocco—"

Druard had risen again. He went to the cabinet and returned with another bottle of wine.

Madame de Bercy eyed him coldly. "Don't you think—"

"No, I don't," he said.

The women's glasses were still full, but he replenished Claude's and his own. "Here's to the Parnassians!" he toasted. "May they drown in their own syrup."

His mother-in-law bit her lip. Madame Druard smiled apologetically. "Maurice has such strong opinions—"

"They're not opinions," said Madame de Bercy. "They're prejudices, pure and simple. Just because he himself has not had the success of—"

Druard's hand was tightening around his glass. "Of course I always say everyone is entitled to his opinion," his wife put in quickly. "But it does seem strange to me how anyone could dislike the Parnassians." She turned brightly to Claude. "And how do you feel, Monsieur Morel? You wouldn't call their poems syrup, would you?"

"No, madame," said Claude. "I'd call them garbage."

Druard laughed. His wife and mother-in-law were silent. Across the table, Mademoiselle Lautier was silent too—indeed, she had said nothing since almost the beginning of the meal—but her eyes rested on Claude with a curious measuring fixity.

Claude drank his wine. His hand shook a little, and the sweat was thicker on his forehead. Druard drank too, and refilled their glasses. The maid brought dessert and then coffee.

"Another glass, boy?"

"Thank you, monsieur—"

"My name is Maurice."

"Thank you, Maurice."

This time he spilled the wine. He dabbed at the tablecloth with his hands and some of the soot rubbed off. Putting his hands in his pockets, he felt his meerschaum pipe and some shreds of tobacco. He took them out, inserted the tobacco, found a match, and lighted up. The thick smoke drifted out and hung in a haze over the table.

Behind the smoke, Madame de Bercy's face was like a stone image. "Young man," she said, "I must really ask—"

Druard jerked his head up at her. "Oh, stop being such a—"

"I will not stop. And I will not countenance such things at my table." She drew in a breath and tried to control herself. "I don't wish to be ungracious, young man," she said quietly, "but there is something I should explain to you. How things are done back in the Vosges I do not know, but here in Paris a gentleman does not smoke a pipe at table when there are ladies present."

Claude said nothing.

"You wish to be a gentleman, don't you?"

"No," said Claude.

Madame de Bercy drew in another breath. "I know very little about you, of course; but my son-in-law says you are a poet, and if you are a poet you must have some education. Some sort of family and bringing-up. May I ask you, please: does your own mother permit smoking at her table—by anyone, let alone a boy of your age?"

"No," said Claude.

"Your mother is a lady, then?"

"My mother is a Nigger Queen."

"I beg your pardon?"

"My mother is a black bitch from hell."

Madame Druard made a sound like a frightened bird. Madame de Bercy stood up. "I think we have had enough of this," she announced. "Come, Isabelle. Come, Germaine." But her daughter seemed too stunned to move by herself, and she had to help her up from her chair and out of the room. On the way the bird cries began to turn into muffled sobs.

Mademoiselle Lautier looked after them but she did not rise. Druard seemed about to follow, but changed his mind and, instead, drank down another glass of wine. When he had finished he sat staring at the empty glass and shaking his head. Claude wanted to say something to him, but didn't know what. He glanced at the girl, who was watching him, and then away again.

After a few minutes Madame de Bercy called from outside. "Maurice, you will come here please!"

"Oh, Christ!" said Druard.

"Isabelle has been made ill. You will come at once!"

Druard mumbled something under his breath; then got up slowly and went out. Claude's first impulse was to follow, but he didn't. He didn't know where to go or what to do. Defiantly he drew in deep from his pipe and blew the smoke out across the table.

"I suppose you're quite proud of yourself," said Mademoiselle Lautier.

Again he looked at her, and again away. But he could feel the blue-violet eyes fixed on him, watching him.

"What are you afraid of?" the girl asked.

His glance flashed back at her. "I'm not afraid."

"If you're not afraid, why do you act this way? Showing off and using bad words like a nasty child."

He didn't answer her.

"How old are you?" she asked.

"What business is it of yours?"

"None. I'm just asking."

"I'm nineteen," he said.

"No you're not. I think you're"—she studied him—"sixteen. That's what I am," she added. "Only I'm more mature for my age."

Claude reached for his wineglass, but it was empty. He pulled at his pipe, but it had gone out.

"Why aren't you at school?" the girl asked.

"Why aren't you?"

"I am. I go to one in Passy, where I live. But my parents are away now, so I'm staying here with my aunt and cousin."

"That should be fun."

"Sometimes it is, and sometimes it isn't. . . . But you didn't answer me. Why aren't you at school?"

"I left more than a year ago."

"You don't approve of it?"

"No."

"Or of your mother?"

"No."

"Or of us here?"

"No."

"That must be an interesting life: disapproving of everyone. Hating everyone. Spending all your time going around trying to shock people."

"Most people need shocking," said Claude. "To make them know they're alive."

"And you've appointed yourself to the job?"

"That's right."

The girl was silent a moment. She sat very straight in her chair, her shoulders gleaming in the candlelight; and her eyes gleamed too, deep and tranquil, with perhaps the hint of a smile far within them.

"I think I know what you disapprove of most," she said. "And what you're most afraid of too."

"I'm not afraid of anything," Claude said defiantly.

"Yes you are. You're afraid of women."

Their eyes met somewhere in the candlelight.

"You hate women," she said. "Why?"

"Because—because—"

"You don't know."

"Yes I do. Because they *are* women."

"And that's wrong?"

"Because they crush. They imprison. Because they hate the truth and worship lies. My mother is a woman, and I know what she has done to me. Druard lives with women, and I can see already—"

"What can you see?"

"How miserable they make him."

"Maurice makes himself miserable. He has an unhappy soul." The girl paused and seemed to lean forward a little. "So do *you* make yourself unhappy," she said. "Why? Must you be unhappy and full of hate to write your poetry?"

"What do you know about my poetry?" Claude said harshly.

"Maurice has let me see the things you sent him."

"And you couldn't understand them?" He mimicked Madame Druard's voice. "Or the syrup content wasn't right?"

"No. You see, my taste is somewhat different from my cousin's and aunt's."

"Oh. And so for *your* taste—"

"—they were the most wonderful and exciting things I have ever read."

For a long moment Claude looked at her, and the violet eyes looked steadily back at him. He raised one hand a little and then lowered it. Words formed on his bps but remained unsaid.

"Claude—" said the girl.

"What?"

"Have you written anything since those you sent?"

He hesitated. "No," he said.

"If you have, I'd like to see it. I'd like to see all you've written. Truly—"

There was a sound in the doorway, and Druard came in. His expression was tense, and he was passing a hand distractedly over the dome of his forehead. "Come on, boy," he said to Claude. His voice was higher pitched than before—almost shrill.

Claude rose. The girl was watching him.

"I'm going out," said Druard. "Come on. For Christ's sake let's get out of here."

He seized Claude's arm and all but propelled him through the door.

In the foyer Claude could hear female voices from the second floor, one sobbing, the other calling down the stairs. Then the door slammed and they were in the street.

For a few blocks they walked in silence; or almost in silence, for at intervals Druard would murmur, "Jesus—oh Jesus—" He kept passing a hand nervously across his forehead, and his eyes darted from side to side as if he expected momentarily to be ambushed. Then gradually he grew calmer, and at last began to talk.

"There's only one piece of advice I can give you, boy," he said. "Don't marry money."

They walked on a little.

"For that matter"—his voice grated—"don't marry."

"I'm sorry if I—"

"Don't be; you gave them what was coming to them. By God, I wish I had your guts. For months I've been putting up with them—with their gabble and their insolence and their emptiness and their imbecility—and all the while asking myself, 'Why do I put up with this? What am I doing here?'" They passed a corner kiosk, and on its wall was a large poster of a music hall dancing girl. Druard spat at it viciously. *"Merde!"* he said. *"Merde* to all women. And double *merde* to women with money."

"I hadn't thought you'd be married," said Claude.

"No?" Druard made a sound that might have been a laugh. "Well, I hadn't thought so either—once. But I am, boy. I am. Look at me. Do you know who you're looking at? Judas, that's who. Judas Iscariot, who sold out for thirty pieces of silver."

He paused, then went on. "A poet doesn't make much money, boy; you'll find that out soon enough. And I'm no exception. Before I married I was a clerk. I worked in a government office, like our friend Archambault, and we were both trying to be poets. Only there was one difference between us: that he wasn't a poet, and I was. I am. I have talent. No, I'll go farther than that—I have genius. To you I can say that simply, and you will understand. It's not boasting or fantasy. It's a fact. One knows."

"Yes," said Claude, "one knows."

"Anyhow, there I was: by day a clerk, by night a poet. I had friends, good dear friends, but only men. No women at all; no damned entanglements with women. I was happy, but unfortunately I didn't know it. I thought I wanted more: money, position, all the rest of it. So—my family knew another family, and that family had a daughter—" He shrugged. "And here I am. Something bought by a woman; fed and kept by a woman; without freedom, without self-respect, without even a home I can call my own."

"Haven't you ever tried to get out?"

"Tried? My God, yes. In my mind, every day, every hour. And a few times I've even done something: packed up, gone, disappeared. But—"

Druard shrugged again. "But it isn't that easy, boy. No—it's hard, hard. I don't mean the money part of it; Christ, I'd rather sleep in the streets than under that harridan's roof. I mean—well—all kinds of things. Obligation, convention, what's expected of you— And sentiment. God damn sentiment! Six months ago I had the battle won. I was through, I was getting out, I was free. And then what happened? My wife got pregnant. She sniveled and moaned and fainted. She got bigger and bigger. . . . And I stayed in my prison."

Their steps had taken them from the Rue Nicolet into the brighter side of Montmartre. Here, in every block, there were a half dozen cafés, and suddenly Druard took Claude's arm and pulled him into one. "Here's a man's world, boy," he said. "It's like living again just to see and smell it."

They sat at a corner table, and a waiter came.

"Absinthe," said Druard. Then he looked at Claude. "You like absinthe? Or perhaps you don't know it? . . . Ah, you must try it then. It's magic, green magic. The drink for poets—and prisoners. . . . *Oui, garçon, deux absinthes.*"

The waiter left. Druard's eyes rested broodingly on the table. "Of course only one of us is a prisoner," he said. "Chained, weak, helpless." He looked up suddenly. "You are free. You are strong."

Claude smiled a little. "I've had my own prison days too."

"Yes, I'm sure you have. All men have had them. But you've had the strength and power to break out. It was plain to me at that horrible meal just now. It was plain to me, even before, from the poems you sent me— those wonderful free singing poems. I wonder if you realize how few men have been able to do what you have: break out, throw it all over, sign their own Declaration of Independence and make it stick. And to do it at your age—as a boy. That takes not just genius in art, but in living."

The waiter brought two glasses in saucers and set them down. "Well, here's to art," Druard said. "And to living. And to absinthe." He watched as Claude drank. "You like it, eh? I knew you would: the drink of poets. . . . *Psst, garçon.*" He beckoned. "These are small ones. Two more."

He went on talking. But now the talk was different. Sipping the drink of poets, he became the poet, with all else forgotten, banished, lost in limbo. He spoke of Claude's verses. He remembered each one of them, line for line, phrase for phrase, word for word, even as Claude remembered those of his which he had read with rapture back in the dreariness of Cambon. His comments were sure, subtle, brilliant. They were by no means all praise. Some of the poems he found inferior, and said so, but even in his sharpest criticism there was a clarity, a perception and sensitivity, that gave light and not shadow—that did not offend or wound Claude, but rather deepened and illumined his understanding. Of *The Ravaged Heart:* "Its greatness is that it is a heart speaking. Not a voice, not a man, but a heart itself." Of a poem on poverty and suffering: "No, you went wrong there. Your hatred reads black and you wanted it white. The white hatred of love. . . ."

Two more drinks came. And two more. And still he talked, and Claude sat entranced. How much was the green magic of absinthe, and how much Druard's own magic, he didn't know; but it was such magic as Archambault, with all his alchemists, had never dreamed of. Again he felt as he had the first time—and every time—he had read Druard's poems: that here was a man to whom he was mystically bound, who was his brother, his twin, a part of him. "With such a man beside me, I can do anything," he thought exultantly. "I can think and feel and create like God himself."

He looked up, and Druard was staring at him silently. Somehow a thread had broken. His eyes, brown before, seemed now themselves to have taken on a greenish tinge, and his face was pale and pinched.

"God in heaven," he said quietly, "what I'd give for your strength and your power. Instead of my weakness, my self-disgust—" His glance went to the saucers piled before them, with the price of their drinks stamped on the china; and a smile twisted his mouth as he counted the figures. "Five ones are five," he said. "Times two is ten. . . . And do you know where the ten francs come from, my friend? From my mother-in-law's dressing table, like my fiacre fare. Only this time I didn't ask—" With a sudden jerk of an arm he swept one of the saucer piles from the table, and the china clattered on the floor.

The waiter came running. "*Monsieur! S'il vous plaît, monsieur—*"

Druard waved him off. "We'll pay for it, don't worry. My rich *belle-maman* will pay."

He crossed his arms on the table and laid his head on them. Whether he was just drunk or weeping, or both, Claude didn't know. But when after a few minutes he looked up again he seemed the same as before.

"*Garçon, deux absinthes!*" he called. Then to Claude he said quietly: "You see what kind of man I am. How weak; how beaten. I've been through the hell of women, and it's burned me to cinders."

He relapsed into silence, staring out past the café tables into the darkness of the street, and his eyes in their slanted sockets, were themselves like smoldering ash. The waiter had picked up the smashed saucers. Now he brought two more drinks. "I must request the gentlemen—" he began.

"Yes—yes," said Druard, scarcely hearing him.

He drank. He turned his glass slowly in his hand and again looked at Claude. "I've told you what I think of your poems," he said. "Now tell me what you think of mine."

"I've already written you—"

"And you meant what you said?"

"With all my heart."

Druard's eyes were no longer like ash. They were deep pools that seemed about to overflow into tears; and when he spoke again his voice shook with emotion. "God bless you, boy. God love you for that," he said. "Because that's all I have left. My belief in myself—as a poet."

"You stand with the greatest," said Claude. "With Shelley, Heine, Baudelaire."

"Baudelaire. Dirty damned divine Baudelaire—" Druard underwent another of his sudden changes. Now his eyes kindled and his hands closed into fists. "Yes, I will," he said. "I will. I *will*. I'm fit to stand beside Baudelaire; beside any of them. I'm fit to sit at this table with you, boy—who, as God is my witness, will be the greatest of them all."

He drained his glass.

"As a poet, yes. But as a man. . . . I'm strangling, suffocating. With my Judas money. With my bitches. . . . You don't know what your coming means to me: with your youth, your strength, your courage. . . . Oh, God, I'm so weak, so sick at heart. Give me some of that courage. Hold out your hand to me."

There were no more words. There was only echo. Claude put his hand on the table, and Druard took it and held it tight.

10

He sat at the window of his room in the de Bercy house and looked out at the quiet primness of the Rue Nicolet.

He wrote:

General, if on your ruined ramparts an old cannon remains, bombard us with lumps of dried mud. . . . On the mirrors of chic shops. In salons. . . . Make the city wallow in its dust. Oxidize the gargoyles.

Turning, he looked at his room: at the soft mauve rug, the flowered wallpaper, the taffeta bedspread, the gilt-framed mirror.

Fill boudoirs, he wrote, *with the burning powder of rubies. . . .*

Druard was out. The women were off shopping. Rising in sudden restlessness, he left the room, went downstairs, and sat on the front steps of the house in the late September afternoon. He waited for Druard. His anger was gone and he smiled. In the warm sunlight he was now wearing only trousers and soiled undershirt; and though he was fully conscious of the stares of passers-by, this only increased his enjoyment. "*Monsieur et madame*," he announced to a genteel and suddenly startled couple, "you are gazing upon a *voyou* in the flesh. Not to mention a seer at his seeing."

Bowing to them ceremoniously as they moved quickly away, he turned his attention to the itching beneath his shirt, and was still so occupied when a fiacre pulled up at the curb and a gentleman got out. He was an important-looking gentleman, solid, florid, and well dressed, and was followed by important-looking luggage, carried by the coachman.

Turning to the stoop, he saw Claude and stopped. "Who are you?" he demanded.

"I am a holy man from the East," said Claude.

"What? What's that? What are you doing here?"

"I am looking for lice."

"Lice?"

"I collect them to throw at priests. But I'd be glad to throw one at you, as soon as I find one."

The gentleman's eyes bulged, and he made an inarticulate sound in his throat. Then he went into the house, with the coachman following him. And that was Claude's first meeting with Monsieur de Bercy.

The second, at dinner that evening, was scarcely more successful. An icy silence hung over the table until Druard, after his fifth glass of wine, wormed the story out of Claude and promptly burst into hoots of laughter, whereupon Monsieur de Bercy snapped at his son-in-law, Druard snapped back, and in five minutes he and Claude were out of the house, slamming the door behind them. Again they walked and went to a café—as they had every night since Claude's arrival. And again they sat over their drinks and mounting saucer piles until far in the morning. "Ah, you're wonderful, boy—a master, a genius," said Druard, his eyes shining. "Lice, no less. Lice! I'd have given a week of absinthes just to see the old bastard's face!"

Claude smiled. He was pleased that Druard was pleased. For he was now playing his role of *voyou* less for its own sake than as part of a planned campaign for the liberation of his friend.

The very word haunted his thoughts and dreams.... Friend—*friend* —FRIEND.... For he had never had a true friend before. Not Michel Favre, not Chariol, not Archambault, not anyone: the others had been merely people he knew, companions of an hour, a day, an evening, but at bottom aliens, strangers. Whereas Druard, through some magic of affinity, was already closer to him than he would have believed any human being could be. It had been so even before they met, through each other's writings, and now it was doubly so, tenfold, a hundredfold, in their companionship. "*Tu es mon maître*," said Claude. "I wasn't alive, I didn't dream what I could do, until I read your poems and felt your heartbeat." And Druard answered, smiling: "You didn't write *The Drunken Boat*, you know. I wrote it. The stronger, freer *I*—the *I* who is you." They held out their hands to each other: across a café table, across a gulf of loneliness. And they walked home, arm in arm, through the quiet gaslit streets.

On the upstairs landing, one night, Druard stopped before he reached his wife's door and leaned his head against the wall. "I can't," he murmured. "Oh Christ, I can't share that room and bed—not any longer—"

"All right," said Claude. "Come with me. Share mine."

Soon, he knew, the hateful house would no longer be "home." They would have a place of their own. . . .

But first there was another departure: that of Mademoiselle Lautier, whose parents returned from the country.

Claude had seen little of her since the first evening. During the day she was off at school, and though she was present each night at dinner, he and Druard were usually there only long enough to bolt their food and hurry off to a café. A few times she had tried to speak to him; especially once on a Sunday when she had found him alone in the library and again tried to talk of his writing. But he had managed to duck away with a few mumbled words.

On the day of her leaving, however, he happened to be going up the stairs as she came down, and suddenly there they were face to face.

"Oh—I'm glad," she said. "I wanted to say goodbye."

"Goodbye," said Claude.

He made as if to pass her, but there was no room; and he stopped, hesitant. "And I've been wanting to talk with you," she added. "So much, really. But you've never given me the chance."

"Talk to me?" Claude's eyes were wary. "What about?"

"About your last poem. *The Drunken Boat.*"

"Did Maurice show you—"

"No, not this one. But he left it on a table one day, and I—well—I looked. I hope you don't mind."

Claude shrugged, and there was a pause.

"Would you like me to tell you what I thought of it?" the girl asked.

"Not very much."

"Oh, you're going to be that way again. . . . Well, I'll tell you anyhow. I thought it was your best. I thought it was magnificent."

"Thank you, mademoiselle."

"My name is Germaine."

There was another pause.

"And do you know what else I thought," she said. "I thought, what a shame it is that such a great poet can be such a foolish person; that a boy with a mind and soul like that can also be so weak and so afraid."

She was standing two steps above him, very straight and tall—as straight and tall, he suddenly thought, as the Nigger Queen. Except that the Queen was black and she was light and gleaming. And her eyes were not white but deep violet-blue.

"You have so much, Claude. Don't spoil it all," she said. "It's not for me I ask; not for anyone; just for yourself. Don't spoil it."

"Germaine! Germaine!" Isabelle Druard's voice came up from the drawing room. "I think they're here. I see the coach."

"Coming," called Mademoiselle Lautier, and went on past Claude down the stairs.

It was three days later that he made his own exit; and, appropriate to his perverseness, it was the result of an attempt at civility by Monsieur de Bercy. For once, dinner had gone through to the end without open clash or precipitate withdrawal, and in the drawing room, afterward, that gentleman suddenly cleared his throat and addressed him directly, for the first time since the affair of the stoop. "My wife and I are having a small soirée tomorrow evening," he said. "Several of our guests, particularly the ladies, are quite literary, and we think it might entertain them, along with the music, to have a reading of poetry. My son-in-law"—he cleared his throat again—"is unfortunately not co-operative about such matters, although it would of course help him greatly professionally. But my wife and daughter have said complimentary things about some of your verses, and thought perhaps you might like to take advantage of the opportunity."

Claude glanced at Druard, then back at de Bercy. "I am deeply honored, monsieur," he said.

"You think you have something suitable for the occasion?"

"Oh, yes, monsieur." Claude thought it over. "Something about—say, love, perhaps."

"That would be fine," said Madame de Bercy.

"Love poems are always the nicest," said Madame Druard.

"I've something I've just been working on. About Venus—"

"Ah, Venus!" De Bercy nodded. "Very nice. The classical approach. Something, perhaps, about her rising from the ocean foam?"

"Well, not exactly, monsieur. This is a somewhat more modern Venus."

"Oh?"

"A strictly up-to-date Venus. *Chic, soignée, à la mode.* A true Parisienne. Instead of from the foam, she is rising from an examination table."

"An examination table?"

"Yes. Unfortunately she has not taken care of herself, and she is suffering from gonorrhea."

De Bercy's face went crimson. His lips moved convulsively as he rose to his feet. But Claude didn't wait for the explosion. Before his host could say a word he was out of the room, out of the house, and on the street, and his residence at 176 Rue Nicolet was over.

He spat over his shoulder as he moved away. But down the block, sitting alone on the curb, he came as close as was possible for him to suffering a change of heart. It was not that he was sorry for what he had done, in terms of the de Bercys or himself: by now such actions were as natural to him as breathing—an automatic response to attack by "the enemy." But he was concerned with the effect on Druard and their relationship and afraid that he might have gone too far, too quickly, in his War of Liberation.

He need not have worried, however. Presently there were steps on the pavement, and his friend appeared, and his first word was "*Bravo!*" They walked on together. They went to a café. They stayed until closing. And the crisis, far from alienating them, had brought them closer together than ever.

"We'll work it out," Druard kept saying. "Don't worry, we'll work it out."

And they did. Druard did. . . .

That same night—meaning at dawn the next morning—he found Claude an attic room in the nearby Rue Fontard, and later in the day returned with the money for both a month's rent and a supply of food. "With the compliments of Monsieur and Madame de Bercy, staunch patrons of the arts," he announced.

Actually he had been able to filch only a few francs, and Claude's prospective living standard was little higher than that of the old days at the Hôtel de Babylone. The Rue Fontard, though close to the Rue Nicolet, was also a world's breadth away—neither a part of bourgeois Montmartre, nor yet of night-life Montmartre, but of a frowsy slum world in between; and the house with the attic room looked as if it had been already old and decrepit in the days of Villon. The room's single window looked out into a dark squalid court. The smell of refuse and urine flowed up the crumbling stairs. The furnishings consisted of a cot, a table, a three-legged chair, and an army of cockroaches. But Claude was not complaining. This was *his* room, *his* home—the first of his own he had ever had—and it was better than a mansion or a palace that was someone else's. Surveying his domain, he smiled and thought: "Yes, it is in the great tradition. The poet in the attic; the muse in the garbage pail." Removing a shoe, he swatted twelve cockroaches. He laid out the pencils and paper which Druard had appropriated from his in-laws. And he went to work.

He had written little since leaving Cambon. Poetry was damned up in him. It flowed out. Since the unhappy termination of his friendship with Chariol he had worked in total solitude: the *voyant* alone with his visions, the dreamer closed in by his dreams. But now there was more than just himself, than the "I-who-am-I" and the "I-who-is-another." There was *still another*. There was Druard. And from Druard, in writing as in living, he drew deeply, thirstily, like a drinker at a well. "I need your strength, your power," his friend had told him. But it had not been asking without giving, for whatever he received in these he gave back, in full measure, in sensitivity and understanding. He came to the attic room every day. He stayed for hours. Often the two would write there together, sharing the table, one sitting on the cot, the other on the three-legged chair, each working on his own verse, until the day's stint was finished, and then they would show each other what they had done. Druard's comments, to Claude's joy and wonder, were always perceptive, always helpful, always *right*. Never once did they have the effect of twisting or adulterating what he had written, but only of brightening, purifying, refining; and from the alchemy of his own art, rare and exquisite, he passed on to Claude's qualities it had never before possessed. No less than Claude, he detested the traditional, the conventional, the empty forms and formulas to which French poetry had for centuries been bound. "Take rhetoric, boy," he said, "and wring its neck." . . . "Take fact, take statement," he said, "and wring theirs too. The core of poetry isn't statement. It's music—nuance—" And in a poem he wrote:

> . . . *seek the nuance,*
> *not color, just nuance.*
> *Oh, the nuance alone*
> *joins dream with dream*
> *and flute with horn.*

Through him, to Claude's sledge-hammer strength, were now added new depths of subtlety and inwardness. And again, as when he had written *The Drunken Boat*, his very brain and heart seemed ready to burst with the passion of creation. *All is flame and flood*, he wrote. *I have stretched ropes from steeple to steeple, garlands from window to window, golden chains from star to star; and I dance.*

They wrote. They read. They talked. They dreaded the hour of separation. And Druard loved the frowzy garret no less than Claude. "It's what I needed most all this time," he said. "Simplicity. Poverty. It is how God intended poets should live." Often he almost reached the point of moving in altogether, of making the final break with his wife and family. But never quite. Without his daily return to the Rue Nicolet there would have been no rent money, no food money, no drink money, nothing. "To be a poet," he rationalized, "one doesn't necessarily have to be an imbecile."

Of their few expenses, that for drinks was by far the largest. For every night when their writing was over, and after Druard had gone home for a quick-as-possible dinner, they went out to the cafés and stayed out until they closed.

Good pilgrims, let us seek
absinthe's green-pillared hall, Claude wrote. . . .

And they sought it. They found it. Almost all of their time together, when they were not writing, they spent at small round tables behind rising piles of saucers, talking and drinking; but even this, strangely, was not release from writing, not mere escape and debauchery, but a part of their enterprise and their communion; for from the talk came the thoughts and feelings that nourished them, and from the green magic came fresh dreams and visions.

They wrote. They talked. They drank.

They were friends, inseparable.

And they were lovers.

"Yes, lovers," Claude thought. "We are what the world calls homosexuals—perverts." He thought it coolly, clearly, explicitly. And then he thought: "But I disagree, if you please. It is not I, but the world, that is perverted. It was not I who chose my mother, lost my father, created the *beau gosse*; who made me alien to women, a prize for tramps and drunken soldiers, and gave me as my only mistress a Nigger Queen of dreams. Very well: now I have something at last that is not a dream—nor a nightmare. I have a human whom I care for, and who cares for me, and that means more to me than the mouthings of a thousand judges and priests. You call me, evil, World. All right: so be it. In my evilness I hold up my head. I spit in your face. I tell you, *'Va te faire foutre!'* "

He wrote a poem about himself and Druard—a poem as wild and strange and deeply felt as *The Ravaged Heart*, of a half year before. And he called it *The Heart Restored*. "It is our testament," he told his friend. "Our freedom song. Our *Marseillaise*."

But Druard, as he read it, was somehow not the same as when he had read Claude's other poems. He did not look up at intervals, as he usually did, with a warm approving glance. He did not read aloud lines which he especially admired. And when he had finished he sat motionless and silent, holding the sheets of paper in his hand.

"You don't like it," said Claude.

Druard didn't answer.

"What is it? Tell me."

His friend seemed to be thinking deeply. His eyes were troubled. At last he said, "There are fine things in it, of course. Beautiful, marvelous things."

"But—"

"But I think it would be better if—well—if we kept it to ourselves. If you didn't show it to anyone."

"I haven't shown anything to anyone except you."

"No, not yet. But—but later—when the time comes—" Druard was silent again: his head bowed, brooding. Then suddenly he leaped to his feet. "Damn it, boy, there have to be *some* reticences!" he cried. Tense and distraught, he paced back and forth across the tiny room; then, without warning, made for the door and went quickly down the stairs.

This was the first time there had been so much as a shadow between them. Claude was puzzled. And he was hurt and angry. At the height of his anger he tore up the poem and hurled the scraps from the window, but later in the day he sat down at the table and wrote it word for word as it had been before. The afternoon passed, and Druard didn't return. "That's all right with me. The hell with him," he thought in cold defiance; and he set to work on another poem. But by the time dusk came his mood had changed and he felt lonely and lost. For supper he ate a few bits of bread and cheese, while the slanted walls of the garret seemed to close in on him. Then he went down the stairs into the street—and found Druard just arriving.

"I'm sorry," his friend said. "I was nervous and upset. . . . Come on." He smiled saturninely. "I drew a double allowance. We'll have a big evening—"

They had it. They had dozens of them. One after another, night after night: prowling the sheets, sitting in the cafés, going from the first to the second, from the seventh to the eighth, talking and talking, drinking and drinking, watching the saucers rise, watching the piles revolve, the table revolve, the walls and streets and gas lamps revolve and spin, as they groped their way through the green-pillared halls. Now and then they met friends of Druard's—presumably those he had spoken of on the first night. But Claude remembered neither their names nor their faces; he did not even know if they were writers and poets—nor, for the moment, did he care; for he and Druard were sufficient to themselves. And, far from seeking others, they were soon going only to places where they were sure to meet no one at all.

Each night was bigger than the night before: more frenetic, more feverish. And each morning—or noon—when Claude awakened, it was was harder to recall what had happened. But that didn't matter. A few broken glasses, a fight with a waiter, a stumble on a street, a sudden sagging in an alley—what were they? They were nothing. All that mattered was the residue, the inward not the outward consequences; and these, strangely, were not sickness and torpor but a heightening of his perceptions and powers. The poison of the absinthe drained away. What was left was its dreams and images, a derangement of the senses more profound and subtle than he had imagined possible, and out of them he fashioned poems of depth and splendor. As with his fabulous boat, drunkenness did not swamp or sink him. It filled the sails of his soul with the wild wind of freedom.

Druard, too, was lifted, driven. He dreamed dreams, saw visions, evoked beauty and passion from his heart and brain as if with a sorcerer's wand. But he had neither Claude's extreme youth nor strength. He could not fly so long, work so long. A poem finished, or sometimes only a stanza or a few lines, he would be drained, exhausted. He would slump forward over the table, his head on his arms, and remain for a long time motionless, or throw himself onto the cot and be almost instantly asleep. Claude knew that he slept very little at home, that he spent his mornings as well as his dinners wrangling with his wife and the de Bercys; and again and again he urged Druard to move in with him. But this Druard would not do. Each evening at seven, and each morning, however near dawn, he would make his way back to the Rue Nicolet and the world he despised and hated. And although he claimed this was purely for the purpose of insuring their continued "allowance," Claude surmised that the reasons were not quite so simple.

Then the morning came when surmise became knowledge. They had been out late as usual, drunk as usual, with the memory of night's end lost in the mists of absinthe; but when he awoke in the morning it was not as usual, for Druard was on the cot beside him. He was not asleep. He was sitting on the edge of the cot, hunched over, chin in hands, staring at the wild disorder of the room—at the clothes strewn everywhere, the broken glass of a bottle, the puddle of absinthe on the floor—and his face, when he turned it to Claude was hollowed and ravaged, as if by disease.

"Oh God, boy," he murmured. "What are we doing? What are we doing?"

"I know what I'm doing," said Claude. "I'm halfway through a poem, and today I'm finishing it."

Jumping up, he quickly pulled on his clothes. Going downstairs to the bistro, he bought a tin of coffee and two brioches. When he returned Druard was still sitting on the cot: naked, skeletal, and forlorn.

"Come on, eat," Claude said. "You'll feel better."

But Druard didn't move. He looked past Claude at the window. He seemed to be listening.

"Do you hear them?" he said presently.

"Hear what?"

"The bells."

"Of course I hear them. What of it?"

"They're church bells. Today is Sunday."

"Oh for Christ's sake—"

"Yes, Christ. Christ in heaven. Christ forgive us. At least on Sunday—every Sunday—ever since we were married—"

Druard bent his head into his hands. Claude ate his breakfast. When he had finished he saw that his friend had raised his eyes again and was staring at him.

"What are you looking at?" he asked.

"At you," said Druard.

"Why at me?"

"Because you are young," said Druard, "and strong and beautiful. Your body, your face, your hair, your eyes. Most of all, your eyes.... Look at me, boy. Yes, like that.... How can they be so blue, so clear and pure—pure as the eyes of an angel?"

"Because I wash them every day in a sewer," Claude said.

He crossed the room through the green puddle, and the broken glass cracked under his soles. Then, taking his pencils and paper, he sat down at the table and began to write.

It was the morning of his seventeenth birthday.

By afternoon Druard was at his writing. That night they went out again. Every night for the next few weeks they went out, every day they wrote, and there was no repetition of the incident; but Claude noticed that his friend's moods were intensifying—at one moment more nervous and febrile than before, at another more brooding and remote.

Then the day came when he didn't appear. Instead, toward evening, as Claude went downstairs, he was handed a note by the proprietor of the bistro; and it read:

Dear boy—

This morning my wife had her baby, a little boy. She has had a hard time of it, poor thing, and I am standing by to be of what help I can. I have not been a good husband to her; I am conscious of my guilt and must try to make it up to her in such ways as I can. Today I went to church—to confession—and asked forgiveness for my sins. For what we have done is sin, let us face it—mortal sin in the eyes of God. I think it better, dear Claude, if we do not see each other again. This does not mean that I reject or turn against you; far from it. I salute your strength, your courage, your rare and shining genius, and know that you will soon stand among the great poets of our time. But for ourselves, in our sin and weakness, the time has come for parting. Adieu and my blessings.

Maurice.

Enclosed, as in the first letter to Cambon, was a fifty-franc note.

Claude went back upstairs. He did not go out that night, or the next day, or the next. As always when he had been struck a blow, he closed himself in behind the armor of his solitude. He wrote. When he could write no longer, he slept. And when he could sleep no longer, he rose in the night and stood at the window, looking down into the black pit of the courtyard and up at the patch of sky sewn with stars. The stars he had bound together with golden chains. . . .

The days went by; then the weeks, and a month. Knowing Druard's volatility of mood, he had at first expected his imminent return; but Druard did not appear. And he, for his part, often played with the notion of going to the Rue Nicolet and ringing the bell, just to see what would happen, but each time, in the end, decided against it. What would happen, he told himself, was that the door would be opened either by de Bercy with a shotgun or Druard with a diaper, and it was a toss-up which would be worse.

October passed into November, and the days grew colder. From a dump (and it was easy, for he was an old hand at dumps) he scavenged a benzine tin which he made into a stove, and enough coal scraps and kindling to heat his freezing room; and from a used-clothes dealer he bought an old army overcoat. ("If I still had my Prussian helmet," he thought, "I'd cut a really fine figure.") There were parts of Paris where fifty francs would not go very far, but for him they could be made to stretch through weeks, for food, shelter, all he needed—provided only he didn't drink. . . . And for the first few weeks he felt no need of drink. Heavily as he had drunk with Druard, and before that back at the Café du Printemps, it had been for only short periods; there were not, as with Druard, the long years of habit behind him that could make him a slave and an addict; he could take his liquor or do without it. Or so he thought. So he was convinced. . . . Until, as always happened to him, he reached a peak in his writing, passed it, and entered a valley of sterility. And then gradually, sitting alone in his room, his blank paper before him, and his mind blank too—dull, drained, and powerless—he became aware of a need for drink, for absinthe, for the potent green magic that would restore his strength and his vision. For days he resisted. He all but chained himself to the table: grim, determined, struggling—and accomplishing nothing. And then the time came when he could stand it no longer, and, bursting from his prison, ran downstairs to the bistro and drank six absinthes in half an hour. He groped his way back to his room, sat at his table, tried to write. But still nothing came. Nothing but a spinning, a retching, and then nausea. And in the morning, instead of a residue of dreams, there was only heaviness, dullness, and apathy. He had spent as much as it took him to live for two weeks, and the result was—*le néant*. Absinthe alone, it seemed, was not the Key to the Kingdom; but only absinthe plus Druard.

More days passed. He had lived so long within himself that he had come to believe he was immune to loneliness. But he was lonely now. He was so lonely that there were times when he considered beating still another retreat to Cambon: even fighting with his mother and listening to his brother's grunts and belches seemed preferable to this nothingness of four walls and blank paper. But he never reached the ultimate. He stayed where he was. The only contact he made with home was to go, one day, into a shop and send a small bright-colored scarf to his sister Yvette. *From an admirer*, he wrote on the accompanying card. And though he gave no address and would receive no answer, it made him, for a few hours, feel better.

He would go crazy in his prison. He took to walking again. As in his earlier Paris days, he roamed endlessly through the streets, along the boulevards, across the squares and parks, up the hills, beside the river, into the faubourgs. He passed the one-time barracks of the Garde National, now again a bleak warren of factories and lofts. He revisited the suburban square where once—a century past, it seemed—he had joined the crowd around the *blouse blanche* speaker, before the *moblot* came with its guns and clubs. He ranged out into the western suburbs, where he had never been before, into the new bourgeois neighborhoods near the Bois de Boulogne. In his old army coat and with his *voyou's* sneer, he walked the clean prim avenues of Philistia—and late one afternoon found himself, with sardonic satisfaction, sitting on the curb before the entrance of a school. It was like the old days in front of the lycée, he thought, with the hapless time-servers inside and himself outside and free. Soon school would break and he would watch them mockingly. "Guaranteed passing grades: one franc, gentlemen. Guaranteed honors: two francs. . . ."

When the students came out, however, they were not boys but girls. They were *jeunes filles* in their teens, dozens and scores of them, in white shirtwaists and blue skirts, swarming down the steps and along the pavement and chattering like flocks of birds. Most of them did not notice Claude. A few stared and moved on quickly. Then one stared and stopped, while her companions went on, and as he stared back incredulously, came directly toward him.

"Why, Claude—" she said. "What a surprise!"

He got to his feet. "Hello, Mademoi—"

"Germaine," she said. "Remember? Germaine." She smiled warmly. "How nice of you—"

"Nice?"

"To come here. To call for me."

"I—I didn't—" Claude floundered.

"Oh, you didn't?" The smile became quizzical. "You mean you just happened to be here? You usually spend your afternoons sitting on a sidewalk in Passy?" Claude was silent and she laughed. "Anyhow, I'm glad you're here. It's nice to see you. . . . How have you been?"

"All right, I guess."

"I went to my cousin's last week, to see the baby; and I asked about you. But they didn't say much."

"I left—"

"Yes, I know—soon after I did. It wasn't right for you there; the de Bercys can be difficult. . . . And so can you," she added. "You were rude to them, you know. You were awful."

Her voice was stern, but deep in her eyes there was still a smile. Claude tried to meet them with his own, but couldn't. They were the only eyes he had ever seen which he couldn't stare down with ease. "What are you looking at?" she asked, after a moment.

He realized he had glanced down, and he still did. "At your skirt," he said.

"My skirt?"

"Its serge," he said. "Blue serge."

"Of course. It's our school uniform. What of it?"

"Nothing."

She looked puzzled. Then she laughed. "I don't just think you're rude," she said, "I think you're crazy. . . . But that's all right—at least with me. A lot of people think I'm crazy too."

The other girls had scattered. But now suddenly there was the sound of footsteps and a middle-aged woman came quickly from the school entrance. "Germaine! Germaine, are you all right?" she demanded sharply. "Is this—er—person bothering you?"

"Bothering me?" Germaine's eyes went wide. "Of course not, Mademoiselle Barraud."

The teacher looked Claude up and down. "Anyhow, you had better be going, young man."

"Why should he go?" Germaine demanded. "This is my cousin, and my parents asked him to call for me."

"Your cousin?" Mademoiselle Barraud looked skeptical. "You have never made any mention of—"

"My cousin is from the country, and *Maman* has asked him for tea." Germaine took Claude's hand. "Come," she said, "or we'll be late and she'll be furious." She hurried him off, leaving the teacher staring after them; and over her shoulder she called, "Good night, Mademoiselle Barraud."

When they had turned a corner she released his hand and moved more slowly, but still stayed close beside him. "The old pest," she said. "That took care of her. Now we can walk and talk a little."

Claude was looking at her curiously. "You're a funny girl," he said.

"Not funny," she answered. "Just crazy. Like you."

"Aren't you ashamed?"

"Of telling a little lie? Of course not."

"I don't mean that. I mean of—being with me. Being seen with me."

"Why should I?"

"Look at me, and look at you."

"And what do *you* see?"

"A nice little schoolgirl in a blue serge skirt. A sweet bourgeois *jeune fille* of the finest family."

"All right, now I'll tell you what I see. I see a very boorish, very dirty, very nasty young man, who needs a soap bath on his face and in his mouth. But also, it so happens a young man I'm not ashamed, but proud, to be with."

"Proud?" Claude repeated.

Germaine turned her head and looked squarely at him. Her eyes were no longer light with laughter but a deep and glowing violet-blue. "How often," she said, "do you think a girl like me has a chance to walk and talk with a great poet?"

They moved along the quiet tree-lined street.

"Have you been working hard, Claude?" she asked.

He shrugged. "Sometimes."

"No, I'm sure all the time. You're an all-the-time sort of person. It must be wonderful to be that way; to *care* so much about something." She glanced up at him. "But you mustn't overdo it, you know. You look thin and tired. You must take care of yourself."

They walked on a way.

"What have you been writing?" she asked. "What new poems? Tell me about them. . . . No, that's stupid of me. A poet can't *tell* about his poetry. . . . But could I see it some time—your new work? I'd love to."

"It—it isn't—"

"Oh I know how you feel: that I'm just a silly girl, prying. And you're angry that Maurice showed me those earlier poems. . . . But you shouldn't be, Claude. I may be a girl, yes: just a—how did you put it?—a bourgeois *jeune fille* in a blue serge skirt. But I'm not silly—truly. And I may not be a poet myself, but I've read poetry and studied it—as much, perhaps, as you have—and I understand it. I know what is bad and what is good. And what is better than good," she added softly.

Claude looked at her, and then off down the street. They turned another corner.

"Please hold my arm," Germaine said.

"Hold your—"

"Arm." She smiled. "You know what an arm is? This." She took his hand and put it under her elbow. "There, that's fine. I'm a very frail *jeune fille*, you see, and need a gentleman's support."

He held the hand rigid.

"You don't go often with girls, do you?" she asked.

He shook his head.

"They're not so terrible, you know. I'm not so terrible. Really, I won't eat you up." Her eyes sought his, but again he looked away nervously. "It's strange how things are," she said after a few moments. "I know a lot of boys and young men. They're all well brought up and have nice manners, and some of them pay a lot of attention to me; but that's all there is—there's nothing inside of them. Inside of you there's so much —so wonderfully much—and nothing comes out at all—except in your writing. If you could only give to other people the littlest bit of what you give to your writing. . . . You're so lonely, Claude, aren't you? So hurt and angry and afraid. . . . And you shouldn't be. You mustn't be. Most of all, you mustn't be afraid of me. *Truly.* I think so much of you. I want so much to help you—"

She broke off abruptly. They walked on. Around more corners.

"You live a long way from school," Claude said.

"It depends which way you go," she said, smiling. "Sometimes it's nice to walk a little farther—on a nice day. A nice evening. With your cousin—"

And looking up, he saw that it was indeed already evening, with the early autumn dusk closing in on the streets and a half-moon brightening in the western sky.

Germaine looked at the moon. Then at him. She sang softly:

> *Au clair de la lu-ne,*
> *Mon—cousin—Pierrot.* . . .

Then she laughed. They went on in silence. And a little later she stopped and turned to him. "But now our walk is over," she said. "I'd better leave you here."

"Leave—?"

"We've arrived at last. The next house is mine. And—and, well, my parents can be difficult too. They've heard about you from the de Bercys, and it's better, for now at least—"

Claude realized that he was still holding her elbow. He dropped his hand awkwardly.

"But I want to see you, Claude," she said. "Won't you come to school again? I'm out every day at four, and we could take more walks—longer ones—and talk, really talk, and maybe you'd bring your poems. . . . Oh, please do. Please. I'd love it so."

"I—I'll—"

A window was thrown open in the next house down the street, and a woman's voice called, "Germaine!"

She turned. "Yes, *Maman?*"

"Who is that? What are you doing there?"

"Nothing, *Maman.* I'm coming, *Maman.*"

For an instant her eyes returned to Claude, and they were violet and gleaming. "Please," she said again. The eyes smiled. "Please—cousin—"

And she was gone.

It was well after dark when he reached the Rue Fontard and climbed the long stairways to his attic. The door was open, the oil lamp was burning, a valise lay on the cot. And on the three-legged chair sat Druard.

"Dear boy, dear boy, I've been waiting for hours," he said. "Come on!" He jumped up. "We're going to have a night to remember!"

II

He had tried. Dear God, how he had tried! He had carried medicines, changed diapers, run errands, climbed the stairs a hundred times a day. He had put up with the pomposity of his father-in-law, the autocracy of his mother-in-law, the endless malaises and vapors and megrims of his wife. He had gone to bed every night by eleven. He had not had a drink in weeks. He had been the very model of a good bourgeois family man, and if it had gone on another day, God help him, he would have been ready for an asylum. . . .

And besides (it came out a bit later) there had been another development. His father had died. His father, a widower, had lived in Lyon; he had not seen him in years; he had almost forgotten he existed. But now the old man had died—and, incredibly, left a trust fund. It was no fortune, to be sure, but no pittance either. He, Maurice, would receive between seven and eight thousand francs a year. . . .

In the telling, it seemed to Claude, there was some cart-and-horse trouble. But he took it as it came.

Druard was full of plans. Notice the valise, please. There would be no more ridiculous double life for him, shuttling back and forth between the Rue Nicolet and the Rue Fontard, but only one life, the life he was made for. His wife could get a separation, a divorce, anything she wanted. He would never see her again—or her damned parents. He and Claude would set up a proper ménage, with no women, no in-laws, no babies, no diapers, but only the two of them, living as poets should live. And it would not be in this miserable garret, of course. Now at last he had some means of his own, they would take a decent place in a decent quarter, and as remote from the Rue Nicolet as possible.

"The Left Bank, that's where we'll go," he declared. "Le *Quartier Latin.* . . . Montmartre is finished now. It's for farmers, ribbon clerks, and

British tourists. All the writing crowd has moved over; all my friends; we'll be at home there. . . . Yes, the Left Bank—and freedom!"

It was not just talk. In three days it had happened. They found a two-room, semifurnished apartment in the Rue de Lacque, near the Boulevard St. Michel; Druard bought what other furnishings were needed; and they moved in. As the door closed behind them, Druard threw his arms around Claude and led him in a dance around the premises. "The dance of freedom, boy!" he cried. "The dance of the poets! . . . Down with babies, bottles, Bercys, and bourgeoisie. . . . Come on! Out! For a celebration!"

He was starved for talk. "In all these weeks," he said, "I neither heard nor spoke one sensible, sensitive, intelligent word." And he was bursting to write, for he had been able to do nothing in his Rue Nicolet bondage. "It was slow death," he said. "Like drowning in a dark thick lightless ocean—and now at last coming up to the surface, into the air and sun." He wrote by the hour, with concentration and passion. And Claude wrote too. For it was the same with him as with Druard: in their companionship he found a stimulation that he profoundly needed. The dullness and emptiness of the lone days were gone, and in their place were all the old fire and vigor.

They worked. They talked. They clung to each other. And as before, when evening came, they went out. Now the focus of their nights was the "Boul' Mich" and its radiating side streets, and in its cafés and bistros they drank their absinthes and watched the saucer piles rise. Sometimes, as in their Montmartre days, they drank alone. But increasingly they found themselves in company with others; for, as a couple, they were now ready to expand their horizons, and, as Druard had said, most of his writer friends had preceded them in migration to the *Quartier Latin*. The Parisian literary world was small, compact, and intense. Almost everyone in it knew everyone else—from the central core of the fashionable Parnassians to the outer fringes of the struggling *arrivistes*—and many of the cafés were run more like clubs, with their regulars, their special tables, and conversation that rolled on like rivers from night to night and week to week. In this society within a society, Claude soon discovered, Druard was far from a stranger. Though not yet read by the general public (for he had been published only in limited editions, financed by the de Bercys), he was much admired by many of the "insiders" and, even by those—such as the Parnassians, who withheld admiration—considered a poet to be reckoned with.

Furthermore, Claude made a discovery far more startling and exciting, and this was that *he himself* was not unknown. And for this, he learned too, thanks were due to Druard. Even before his arrival his friend had circulated his poems, beaten the drum for him, hailed him to one and all as a certified genius; and now that they discovered he was no more than a boy, he became in short order a personality, a celebrity. "Aha, Druard's prodigy!"

he was greeted. "The marvelous brat. The bard of the Ardennes." And though the reception varied from warm to skeptical, from cordial to facetious, there was no one who ignored or was unaware of him. The poets and artists and intellectuals of Paris—who, before, had seemed as remote and inaccessible as men on Mars—shook his hand, asked him to join them, plied him with questions, bought him drinks. They talked of *The Ravaged Heart* and *The Drunken Boat*. They looked incredulously across the tables at his gangling figure in its army greatcoat; at his outsized pipe; at his dirty cherub's face, his wild yellow hair. And their eyes widened.

Claude soon widened them further. The graduate *voyou* of Cambon's Café du Printemps was no less in his element in the cafés of the Boul' Mich, and he played the part with new relish. He drank drink for drink with the grown men around him. He matched them word for word, opinion for opinion, argument for argument, and was not long in discovering that, with most of them, his were the sharper, deadlier weapons. Age and reputation fazed him not at all. Indeed, as back home, he particularly delighted in deflating the self-important, the pompous, the prestigious, the authoritarian, and the satisfaction was all the greater in that these were no dusty provincials he was pitted against but the very intellectual cream of *la ville lumière*. In literary discussions he gave his pronouncements with the serene assurance of an Academy member. When patronized or challenged he dug casually into his scatological vocabulary and emerged with comments that left his listeners stiff with shock.

In general it was the younger, more Bohemian writers who gave him the warmer welcome, the older and more conservative who were more annoyed than amused. But young or old, Bohemian or conservative, all were aware of him; all talked about him. And he knew it.

"*Il est formidable*," they said.

"*Incroyable*."

"*Impossible*."

"*Dégoûtant*."

"He has the manners of a pig."

"And the eyes of an angel."

"No, the eyes of a devil."

"Eyes like stone."

"Like steel."

"Like smoke."

"Like the sky."

"He is a hoodlum. A loafer."

"A poet."

"—and a sewer rat."

"He has glory in his head."

"—and garbage in his mouth."

"He is only seventeen and a great writer."

"Only seventeen and a drunkard."

"A pervert."

"What do you mean, a pervert?"

"What did you think—that's he's Druard's son?"

"Oh, I didn't know."

"Well, you know now. . . ."

They talked. They speculated. They watched with fascination as he and Druard walked past on the Boul' Mich or sat at a table behind their rising saucers. And they listened with fascination, however reluctant, when now and then, at a café, Claude pulled a new poem from his pocket and read it aloud in his clear boyish voice. For Claude himself these were the best moments. He thought of the country *mioches*, in their countless thousands, over the centuries, who had come to Paris as he had, full of hope and dream, and made not so much as a ripple on the vast sea of its indifference. He thought of himself two summers before; a would-be *chansonnier* of the Montmartre cafés, to whom no one would listen. Whereas, now, everyone listened. When he rose there was silence. There were turned faces, listening faces; even the hostile faces of those he had antagonized turned and listened intently, because they could not help it, because they were *compelled* to listen by the power that was in him. As time went on he became more and more conscious of this power, and the consciousness filled him with a glow more potent and magical than the glow of absinthe. He had power, he knew now, not only to create but to impose his will; not only over words on a page but over his fellow men.

Above all, he had power over Druard. And this, he realized, was not merely a matter of influence on his writing, but of his own self, his person-ality—and Druard's need of him. He was a youth of seventeen, his friend a man of thirty; yet their relationship, increasingly, was inverse to their ages, with himself the leader, the dominant partner, and the other the willing follower and colleague. In their rounds of the cafés, for example, it was he, once he had learned his way about, who decided which one they would go to, at what table they would sit, who was worthy of respect and who not, and, for the nots, what the treatment would be. Sometimes, when he overplayed the *voyou* and tempers grew short, Druard would try to restrain him. But this was usually early in the evenings when they were still fairly sober; once the absinthe was really at work, Claude's dominance was so strong that he was no more than a complaisant second. Druard, for all his talent, was one of many: a Parisian among Parisians, a poet among poets. Claude was an "original," a phenomenon, the incredible *petit sauvage des Ardennes*—and he humbly yielded him center stage.

The core of their relationship, Claude further knew, was its sexuality —particularly insofar as Druard was concerned. For his friend, it was obvious, was a true, and precariously balanced, bisexual. That he was, on occasion at least, susceptible to women was self-evident, for he was a husband and father; but when the change came upon him, his need for another man was imperious and irresistible, and over the years, Claude gathered, he had had several such associations. All of them, however, had apparently been brief, and in none had there been even a fraction of the intensity of emotion which he now felt for Claude. In the beginning, their relationship had been split into two separate, almost hermetic parts; one of the day and one of the night, one of intellectual sharing and mutual respect as artists, the other of drunkenness and animal instinct. But now the two had merged and fused, until, for Druard at least, there was only a oneness of desire and need. "This man is a part of me," Claude had thought when he first read Druard's poetry; and now those same words were repeated back to him, day after day, night after night. "You are part of me, boy. Of my mind, of my heart, of my flesh." And on him Druard lavished all the fierce devotion that another would have given to a beloved mistress.

With Claude himself it was different, and he was profoundly aware of it. If his friend was bisexual, he, for his part, he was now convinced, was essentially nonsexual, a creature without deep need, in the flesh, for either woman or man. His few fumbling hopeless experiences with women had been the most painful and humiliating of his life; the very sight and sound of them had become repulsive to him. But, in counterbalance, the boy of "the ravaged heart" had neither sought nor enjoyed its ravaging, and the need for homosexual love was no integral part of his nature. What he needed—the one and only thing he needed and craved from life—was freedom. Freedom from both women *and* men. Freedom from his mother. Freedom from home and family, priests and teachers, restraints and conventions; from everyone and everything that could bind and imprison him. And this freedom, strangely, he was finding with Druard. For what, to the other, was emotional bondage was for him a liberation of the senses and spirit such as he had never known or even dared hope for. From their talk he drew breadth of knowledge and enrichment of vision; from their drunkenness and debauchery new strength to break all bonds; from Druard's very dependence an ever-growing consciousness of his own power and dominance.

I am not a prisoner of my reason, he wrote. *O my God, O my beautiful! Atrocious fanfare where I never falter. Rack of enchantment. . . . They have promised us to bury in darkness the tree of good and evil, so that we may bring hither our very pure love. . . . Little drunken vigil: holy—if only because of the mask you have given us. We have faith in the poison. We know how to give our whole life every day.*

To give one's whole life: that was it—all of it. To give it in its entirety, without fear or restraint—alike to art and drunkenness, beauty and filth, reason and unreason, heaven and hell—for these were all part of the whole that was reality and truth. To give to the utmost measure. To be oneself whole, to be free. . . .

Our very pure love. . . . Druard took the phrase and made it his own; for it was more necessary to him than to Claude to rationalize his actions, and his revolt against convention and the concepts of bourgeois Catholic morality had not yet been wholly won. It was Claude's way to make his decision, to set his course consciously, and then abide by it, whatever the consequence. But Druard would act first and think afterward, struggling to fit theory to fact, what-should-be to what-is. In his eyes they got drunk, not as other men got drunk, but as a form of purification—as other mystics before them had fasted or mortified the flesh in their quest of purer perception. And their sexual relationship was simply that advocated by Plato and practiced by the greatest of the ancients: a purging spiritual love of like for like. It was not vice or sin in which they were involved, but in their very opposite—enlightenment. In an opening of windows, a breaking of barriers, an affirmation flung defiantly against the negations of the world. For what was society, what was Christianity, if they were not negation: a denial, a rejection, a casting out; a deliberate curbing and binding of life to its minimal limits? Sin was an invention of man and his fear. Beyond fear, there was no sin. There was no good or evil. There was only beauty and truth. And in truth, fulfillment.

A few months before, he himself had been a creature of fear. It had been fear, and no more, that had impelled him, upon reading *The Heart Restored*, to ask Claude not to show it to others. But now fear was gone. He was pleased not only for Claude to show it, but to read it aloud, to publish it abroad, as the manifesto of their creed and their freedom. Indeed, he too was now writing a poem on their relationship, and on his own emergence from "ocean darkness into the sun." And it had been Claude, Claude only —he told him again and again—who had made that emergence possible, who had brought him up into light and freedom. He called him "child of the sun." He called him "my magnificent pagan." In his poem Claude became a new Apollo: not a mere boy or man but "a god of light, music, healing, poetry, prophecy." Above all, prophecy. Prophecy of a new and freer and better world to come.

Claude smiled as he read. "Apollo?" he said. "I have another name, you know."

"Another?"

"Yes—Attila."

"The Hun—"

"The Huns were pagans too," said Claude. "But of a different kind."

He too was writing, writing hard and well. For of all the aspects of their relationship, this was the most remarkable: that, for all its demands on them, all its excesses and aberrations, it nevertheless brought out in them their fullest power as poets. At night they were wild men. They were drunkards and perverts. But each day, for hours on end, they sat in their room at their adjoining worktables, as industrious as two bourgeois wage slaves, and out of their labors, their experience, their companionship, came poetry of depth and purity, beauty and splendor. What they had willed to happen *did* happen. In what they wrote was neither virtue nor sin, neither good nor evil. There was only art.

Claude was working on a series of short poems in verse and prose to which he had given the over-all name *Illuminations*. And the name was right. For they were not poems in the conventional sense, singing a song or telling a story, but rather fragments, snatches, the glint of sunlight or the beam of a candle, touching emptiness with color, piercing darkness with light. He wrote again of his childhood: of the frail butterfly boat in its puddle, the dark aisles of the Ardennes, *the thousand rapid ruts of the dark roads* of his wanderings. He wrote of his mother, of his home, and of *the cool latrine, the place of peace and dream.* He wrote of another latrine; of barracks, of streets, streets aflame, streets empty, streets long and gaslit, with a boy asleep on a doorstep. He wrote of alleys, prisons, a tramp dead in a garbage dump, a sparrow pecking at a crumb of bread between the tramp's blackened teeth. He wrote of other sparrows, other birds, huge golden birds. He wrote of the sky, the sea, the ocean, the shore. He wrote of flowers; he wrote of lice; he wrote of dreams. He wrote the dream of werewolves and the dream of the weasel. He wrote the dream of the jungle and the jungle river and the Nigger King and Nigger Queen. . . . *And the Queen, the witch who lights her embers in the earthen pot*, he wrote in ending, *will never tell us what she knows: the thing we do not know.*

Sometimes he wrote with hatred, sometimes with love. But always he wrote with passion, out of the pure flame in his heart. More than ever now he was struggling with the recalcitrance of words, striving "to find a tongue" that could express the inexpressible, and his experiments with language became bolder and wilder. He tried literally to take it apart and put it together again, hunched like a watchmaker over its wheels and springs and coils of meaning. He tried to give it more than its original dimension; to add suggestion, vibration, echo. He tried to break down the barriers of the senses, the walls that divided them, so that experience might be recorded clear and true, in its totality, as the meld and fusion it really was.

He wrote a sonnet of the vowels, attempting a synthesis of their sounds with colors, their music with imagery. . . . *A* was black: the glitter of flies, a gulf of dark shadow. *E* was white: steam, tents, kings, glaciers. *I* was the crimson of blood and of laughing lips; *U* the green of seas, of fields, of a scholar's quiet contemplation. Last came O—for O should come last. The old O—Ω. And he wrote . . .

> O, the last trumpet, loud with strangely strident brass,
> the silences through which the worlds and angels pass:
> O is omega—Ω—His eyes' deep violet glow.

That night he slept. He dreamed, as always; he dreamed the dreams of absinthe. But the dreams were different from before. There were not many, but one; not a wild flickering pageantry of color and movement, vision and illusion, but a single continuing image: the Omega eyes—Ω— deep and violet. They did not move. They did not change. They watched him quietly all night until the instant of his awakening.

"I have seen the Eyes of God," he thought.

But was God a woman?

Winter came. Paris lay in mist and gray slush, and a thin wind blew over the hills and under the bridges across the Seine. But in the rooms on the Rue de Lacque it was snug and warm. Druard had installed a big stove and the newest type of kerosene lamps; other furnishings had been added as needed; and the place was the most comfortable that Claude had ever lived in. He was also clothed better than ever—or at least since the days of the blue serge suits. One night, during their round of the cafés, he had lost his old army coat, and the next day Druard had bought him a fine new one. He had also bought him a suit, a hat, shoes, gloves, all he needed; and it was he too, of course, who supplied the money for their rent, food, and drink. Claude had not earned a sou since he had been in Paris, and Druard had only what he received from his trust fund. But his openhandedness was without limit. "What's mine is yours, dear boy," he said, not once but many times. "My mind, my heart, my soul—and my wallet." He took his support of Claude as much for granted as if they had been a married couple. Which indeed in most ways they were.

The cafés had of course moved indoors. They too were snug and warm; the lights brighter, the voices louder; the voices of poets and novelists, critics and editors, expounding, arguing, boasting, pontificating. After the hours of solitude, of dedication, they fell upon Claude's ears like the blatting of sheep, the cawing of crows. And he took increasingly few pains to conceal his contempt.

To a group of Parnassians arguing a theory of versification: "I am sorry, messieurs, but our professions are different. I write poetry, you see, and you write doggerel."

To the sedate and professorial Mallarmé, who delighted in presiding over intellectual discussions: "If I may make a suggestion, *mon maître*, you

are wasting your time in this cultural desert. You should be teaching literature at the Lycée de Cambon."

And to Yves Balmer, beloved of Madame Druard: "With my compliments, sir"—presenting a strip of toilet paper—"to wipe your green
morocco bindings."

Even with those few whom he respected he was little more restrained
—as on the night he at last met "God in person," the great Victor Hugo.
The old man, sitting in state at his favorite café, Le Procope, nodded as
Claude was presented and rumbled, "Ah yes, I have been hearing much
of you—the boy Shakespeare." To which Claude replied, "If you please,
sir, I am not the boy anything. I am Claude Morel, and I think that will be
enough."

The Olympian chuckled. The story spread. Claude's reputation as an
enfant terrible was now secure, and for every one of the café crowd who
resented and snubbed him there were a dozen who crowded around
delightedly, waiting to see what he would say or do next. Soon, in perverse
fashion, he, no less than Hugo, was holding court among the tables and
saucer piles of the *Quartier Latin*.

But, perversely too, this had another, and unforeseen, effect; for
Druard, who in the beginning had so proudly exhibited him, now began
to resent the impingement of outsiders. Again like one half of a married
couple, he expected the other half's full-time devotion, and during their
public appearances he became increasingly possessive and proprietary.
Claude was his protegé, his *génie magnifique:* he wanted that clearly understood. And when others paid what he considered too much attention to
him, he would sit in sulking silence or turn suddenly on the outsiders in
waspish anger. The later the hour and the more he had drunk, of course,
the greater was the likelihood of trouble. Several times he repeated his
Montmartre performance of sweeping his saucers from the table; and
once, when he wished to leave a café and Claude didn't, he made such
a scene that they were both ejected. On the days after such outbreaks he
was always contrite. ("I was wrong, boy. I'm sorry. It was ridiculous. It
won't happen again.") But inevitably it *did* happen, and each time it was
a little worse than the time before. Such a relationship as theirs was too
highly geared to follow a smooth course—particularly in the late hours of
their nightly drinking bouts.

"It's the damned absinthe," said Druard. "I'm going to switch from
absinthe." And for a week or two, instead, he drank cognac. But the cognac
was worse. It made him drunk too quickly. It made him sick. It gave him
headaches. Soon he returned to absinthe—and the fights continued.

Late one night on their way home they had an especially bitter argument—over what, neither could subsequently remember—and when
they reached the flat Claude locked the door of his room and would not

let Druard in. The next morning, for the first time, the latter was not contrite, but still angry and recriminating.

"So you turned on me," he said. "Turned and rejected me."

"Oh for God's sake," said Claude.

"You're tired of me, is that it? You want to push me aside?"

"I'm just tired of your damned tantrums."

"Tantrums? You ignore me, you insult me, you act as if I were dirt under your feet; and then you dare to say that—"

Claude didn't wait for the rest. Suddenly he felt as if he were strangling, suffocating. Leaping to his feet, he ran from the flat and down the stairs, and for the rest of the day he walked alone through the city streets.... When, toward evening, he came back, Druard was busy at the stove preparing his favorite dish of veal strips and white wine sauce. "For the prodigal's return," he said smiling. And then, later: "I'm sorry, dear boy. I get upset, I guess. I need you so. I love you so...."

A few days later, however, they had another fight, and a week later another. Each time Claude fled and roamed the streets, and each time when he returned Druard was gentle and conciliatory, calling him with a smile "the boy who took a walk."

But when still the next one came it was the worst yet. They had, as usual, spent most of the night at the cafés, and when the last of them closed a young poet with whom they been drinking asked Claude, but not Druard, to his rooms. Claude accepted. Druard protested. They shouted insults at each other then and there, and later, on their way home (the young poet having vanished) they went on with it. Suddenly, with a cry, Druard struck at Claude; Claude struck back; Druard reeled against a wall and slumped to the pavement, where he lay softly moaning. And in the end Claude had almost to carry him home.

In the morning he had an ugly welt on his cheek, and it was Claude's turn for apologies. But this time Druard did not recriminate. Indeed, through the whole day he said almost nothing, but sat brooding in his room, his thoughts turned inward; and when at long intervals he did speak it was softly and sadly. "We must learn control, boy," he kept repeating. "We have so much to give each other. We could be so happy. But we must learn control—control—"

Then he wept.

For a week thereafter there were no scenes; even when most drunk Druard was restrained and quiet. But it was the quietness, Claude knew, not of peace but of inner turmoil. His work was going badly. He could not concentrate. At the cafés he would sit silently, staring into his glass, and on the way home walk blindly, like a somnambulist. Only when they were at last together in their rooms, in the depths of night, would he break, suddenly and wildly, out of his caul and lose himself briefly in emotional abandon. Then for hours he would pace the floor, sleepless, and in the morning be again silent and withdrawn.

Still another crisis was sure to come. And it did. But it took a different form from those that preceded it.

They had had their latest of late nights; going, after the cafés closed, to the rooms of a friend where they drank until dawn, and it was full daylight when at last they made their way home. Or at least it seemed to be daylight—it was hard to tell—for the sky was not blue but green, the green of absinthe, and the sun was not the sun but a violet eye. The eye revolved slowly, and the sky around it, and then the streets too were revolving, they were spinning and tilting, and the pavement jerked up and hit Claude in the knees. Druard bent over him and fell too, and there was a crowd around them staring, and they stared back, and Druard's face was as green as the sky, and he smelled of vomit. They got up and went on and fell down again and got up, and then they were almost home; they were turning from the Boul' Mich (or some other boulevard) into the Rue de Lacque (or a street like it); and the street was spinning again, Claude was about to fall again—but he didn't fall—because something was holding his arm. Druard was holding it, grasping it, and with his other hand he was pointing, and then he cried out in a voice that was almost a shriek: "Look! O my God, my God! Look!"

Before them was the stoop of a small house, and on the stoop sat a young woman with a baby. It was a winter morning, but the sun was warm, and she had opened her blouse and was nursing the baby. Her breast was white; the baby's face was pink; the sunlight flooding them was no longer green or violet, but golden. Druard released Claude's arm and moved slowly toward them. His steps were wavering, his whole body seemed to be trembling, but he kept on until he reached the stoop. Then he stopped and for a long moment stood looking down at them. Then a sudden sob shook him and he dropped to his knees. "Madonna," he murmured. "Madonna, forgive me, a sinner—"

The woman stared at him in fear. With a quick movement she pulled the baby from her breast, got to her feet, and ran up the stairs into the house. Claude jerked Druard to his feet. He dragged him, still sobbing, down the street, found their own stairs and pulled him up. And a minute later he was sprawled out on his bed.

When he awoke, hours later, it was to the consciousness of a soft mumbling sound; and opening his eyes, he found Druard sitting beside him. His friend's face was yellowish, his cheeks hollow, and with his slanted eyes, high cheekbones, and wispy chin beard he looked less like a European than an old mandarin. His thin fragile fingers should have ended in a mandarin's long nails—except that a mandarin would not have been holding a crucifix.

Claude sat up.

"Quiet, boy. Quiet," said Druard gently.

"What are you doing?"

"I am praying."

"Not for me, damn it."

"For us both. For our sins and their forgiveness."

Claude rose quickly and moved away from him. "Where have you been?" he demanded. "You haven't been to bed. What have you been doing?"

"I have been to church," said Druard. "To confession."

"Oh God—"

"Yes, that is exactly what I have been saying. 'Oh God. God forgive us.' And I went back to Him."

"Again."

"That's right—again. But this time forever."

Claude made a noise with his lips and went into the other room; but Druard followed him. He stood watching for a few moments while Claude lighted the stove and got a pot for coffee. Then he said, "Do you remember this morning, boy? And what happened?"

"Of course I remember. We were drunk. We fell down."

"Yes, we fell down." Druard's voice was still soft; he spoke almost as if in a chant. "We fell and wallowed in the street. But then we got up—and I saw a vision. I saw it in golden sunlight: mother and child, the Christ child. . . ." He paused. . . . "And another child, too. Yes another: pure and innocent. I saw my own child, my own baby, in his mother's arms."

Claude rattled the pot. "You need some coffee too," he said.

"No, boy, I don't need coffee. I don't need food or drink or flesh or anything of this world, but only grace—the grace of God." Druard came closer. He put his hand on Claude's arm. "And you too," he said. "You and I, the two of us, dear Claude: that is what we need—all we need: to find grace again, to become clean again. . . ."

His voice trembled. His eyes brimmed with tears. With a sudden movement Claude knocked his hand away. "Damn it to hell," he shouted. "Stop the whining and drooling!"

It had not been a hard blow, but Druard reeled from it. He took a few steps back, then stopped and stood motionless. His eyes were closed, and his arms hung at his sides with the palms turned forward.

"Now what are you doing? Showing your stigmata?" Claude's voice was thick with contempt. "Yes, of course," he said. "Excuse it please; I didn't recognize you. The martyred Christ himself, that's whom I've been living with. The Lord Jesus Christ Almighty, pickled in absinthe!"

Druard's thin body swayed. He seemed about to fall to the floor. But instead, after a moment, he opened his eyes. Fumbling in his pocket, he brought out his crucifix and held it toward Claude. "Boy, dear boy," he said, "I forgive you. God will forgive you; He will forgive us both. Only hear me. Pray with me. I told the priest I would come back with you. We will go together, pray together, cleanse ourselves for Communion. . . ."

As once before, Claude didn't wait for the end. He didn't even wait for the coffee. Again the feeling of suffocation rose in him, gripping and choking, and he turned and rushed to the door. There was a moment when he heard Druard's voice calling after him but then it was lost in the thumping of his feet on the stairs.

For the rest of the day he walked the streets. But this time, when night came, he did not return to the Rue de Lacque. He crossed the Seine to the Right Bank, walked more streets, walked the boulevards, walked at last down the Rue de Rivoli to Les Halles, and past Les Halles into the slum beyond and the door of the Hôtel de Babylone. From the two francs (from Druard) in his pocket he paid the twenty centimes for soup and bread and the other twenty for a pallet, and when the lights went out he lay stretched on the thin burlap, breathing in the stench, listening to the snores, feeling with pleasure the cold stone of the floor beneath him. No one spoke to him. No one disturbed his sleep. No one was sitting over him when he awoke in the morning.

He became a vagrant again. Again he eked out a vagrant's living. With siege and revolution now well in the past, ratcatching was no longer an open profession, and thieving seemed to him to offer more in risk than in reward; but there were still plenty of ways to keep body, if not soul, together. For a while he hawked shoelaces on the Rue de Rivoli. Then he got a more lucrative job selling pornographic pictures, and this in turn led to a term of pimping for a small brothel—the inside of which, however, he never saw. Between times, he walked—and walked. Along the boulevards, through the squares and parks, along the river, into the faubourgs . . . and one day, at last, into the faubourg of Passy, through the tree-lined streets, to a corner, a curb . . . and again he sat on the curb beside the entrance of a school. He waited for the girls to come out, the *jeunes filles* in white blouses and blue serge skirts. And then they came—the first of them—out the doorway, down the steps. But now he waited no longer. He rose. He moved off. Quickly, almost running, he moved off down the street alone —as he had come.

All right, he was alone. He was free. He belonged to himself. He needed no one.

He didn't drink. He didn't fight. He didn't waste himself in fever, tension, and debauchery.

And he didn't write.

He couldn't write. He tried; he more than tried; he strove, struggled, drove himself with all his power of mind and will. But he couldn't. With his meager savings he had bought himself pencil and paper, and he carried them everywhere he went. He sat with them in the parks. He sat in alleyways. He sat by the hour on the cold floors of the Hôtel de Babylone. He tried and tried to set one to the other. And couldn't.

"It will come," he thought. And the days passed.

"It will come," he thought. And the weeks passed.

Then winter was gone; spring had come; and he thought: "O God, my God, what have You done to me? Have You taken from me my one function, my one reason for being?" ... He was walking again, walking as always; only not as always, not as he had walked in many weeks, across the Seine to the farther bank, along the quais to the Boulevard St. Michel, up the boulevard between the long files of the cafés. He walked past one café and another, and a dozen others, and it was evening now, and the lights were on, and the faces of the drinkers glowed in the lights, flowing by him; flowing, flowing. . . . And then no longer flowing, but stopped and frozen. No longer many faces, but one face. . . . And the face staring, the face rising, moving toward him, the face yellow and hollow-cheeked, with slanting eyes, and the eyes bright with joy and absinthe.

"Boy, dear boy!" Druard said, with his arms around him. "I've searched for you everywhere. This time you took a long walk, didn't you? But now you've come home—come home—"

12

Claude Morel, aged seventeen and a half years, took stock of himself.

"I am a poet," he thought. "That is the root of the tree, the foundation of the building, the heart of it all: that I am a poet. At an age when most boys are wondering where to put a comma in a school essay, I have written poetry that will transform literature. In a world where most men see only what they wish to see—what society tells them they may see—I have seen beyond the veils and blinders into worlds they have not dreamed of. I am a poet and a seer. If the word must be used, I am a genius.

"These are facts that I am speaking. Not wishes. Not dreams. The world of the next century will be my witness.

"I look about me at my own world, and I do not like it. I do not like its rules, its shams, its lies, its hypocrisies. I see differently, think differently, speak differently from other men. I am opposed to them, in revolt against them, and in revolt there can be no half measures. Therefore I must *live* differently. I must have the courage of my difference, and of my convictions; the courage even of my depravity, if you will, for this is no less important than the courage of my virtue. I will embrace what the world rejects—what it calls sin and evil—not because I am weak, but because I am strong.

"World, I salute you. I put my thumb to my nose, with the fingers well spread, and I say to you, *'Baise mon cul.'* You may do as you like. You may strike back at me. You may condemn me, mock me, insult me, imprison me, torture me. But you will never defeat me."

Druard would come up behind him and pass a hand through his hair. "Dear boy," he would murmur, "never leave me again. I need you. I love you."

"Yes, yes," he would answer, "I love you too."

Then they would go out: down the stairs, along the Rue de Lacque, into the Boul' Mich. They would walk arm in arm, or with arm around shoulder, and the crowds stared; and Claude stared back at them with his pure blue eyes. "You, not we, are the spectacle," the eyes said. "You are the charade, the circus; you the jugglers and wire walkers and clowns and freaks, absorbed in the performance in your own little tent, while God stages his own elsewhere."

The eyes smiled in their arrogance. "I alone," they said, "have the key to this savage sideshow."

At the cafés there were the lights, the drinks, the voices. Always the voices—and Claude was sick of them. At first he had been hostile only to such of his fellow writers as he actively despised: the Parnassians and their imitators, the snobs and the aesthetes, pedants and prudes. But now he could scarcely abide even the more talented and intelligent ones. The oh-so-French rationality and intellectualism on which they all prided themselves had become anathema to him: the neat, tidy, sterile little minds that had the answer to everything, put the universe in its place, reduced the whole of chaos, mortal and celestial, to rank and category, rule and reason. And, more than ever, he himself became the apostle of unreason. He made statements and comments less because he believed them than because he knew they would shock or irritate, and when the absinthe was really at work on him he would go to almost any length to goad his listeners to unreason of their own.

"You are discussing democracy, messieurs? ... Ah yes, hooray for democracy! Hooray for you democrats! Swilling your liquor; flapping your wings; dropping tears in your saucers for poor dear humanity. Do you know what you really think about humanity, you lying sots? You think: Let it croak."

"You speak of colonialism. The plight of the black man.... I do not get your points, messieurs. Are you perhaps color-blind when you look at yourselves?" (Then, improvising new words to an old tune and pointing around the table): "*Monsieur le Grand Editeur*, you yourself are a nigger. Little poet, you are a nigger. Journalist, you are a nigger. Critic, you are a nigger. We are all niggers, prowlers in a jungle—only ours is a jungle we have made for ourselves."

"Catholicism? . . . A witches' sabbath for cretins."

"French literature? . . . The muse with golden hair and an ulcer in her anus."

And so on—and on. More wildly. More bitterly.

One night, when he and Druard were alone at a table, his friend's face turned as green as the absinthe.

"I'm going to be sick," he said.

"All right, be sick."

Druard stumbled off, and a moment later a stranger approached. He was a small man, obviously a Jew, his eyes large and dark behind thick-lensed spectacles. "My name is Herz," he introduced himself quietly.

"And you'd like to buy me a drink."

"No, no drink. But I would like to speak to you for a moment."

"I speak only Gaelic, Basque, and Urdu."

Monsieur Herz smiled a little. "You speak many languages, I know that. In your poetry. I am a great admirer of your poetry, you see."

"So?"

"So I would like to help you, if I can."

"Help me?"

"You do not know me, Monsieur Morel, but I know you, in a fashion. I have seen you around the cafés, in the streets. I have watched you. And I know you are confused and unhappy."

"And you are Père Noel with a sack of happiness on your back?"

"I am an editor. An editor who, as I say, has great admiration for your work. And who hates to see you following your present course."

"Why, damn your nerve—"

"I am not trying to be insolent—truly." Monsieur Herz spoke softly and with deep earnestness. "I am the editor of a small magazine, and someday I hope to have the pleasure of publishing your verses. Unfortunately that time is not quite yet. It will come soon, I am sure, but for the moment your work is too advanced, too unusual, even for a magazine such as ours. However, I have a suggestion, and that is why I came over to speak to you. It so happens that there is a vacancy right now in my small organization. I need an assistant; a sort of—well—junior editor. And it has occurred to me that you might fit into the place. That your freshness, your great talent, might be vastly helpful to the magazine; and that, in turn, such employment might help you to independence—to finding yourself. If you think you might be interested—"

He took out a card and laid it on the table. But Claude did not look at it. He finished his absinthe and looked over his still-raised empty glass at Monsieur Herz. "I think I would be interested," he said clearly, "if you disappeared."

"I beg your pardon?"

"I said fill your own inkwells. *Va te faire foutre.*"

The little man stood looking at him for another moment with his dark magnified eyes. The eyes were not angry, as were those of most men Claude had taunted or insulted, but soft and sad. Then, without speaking again, he turned away.

Claude ordered another drink, and it was not until he had finished it that he idly noticed the card on the table, CAMILLE HERZ, it read. EDITEUR, LA NOUVELLE REVUE. His laughter caused the drinkers nearby to turn and stare at him. And he was still laughing when Druard came back from the washroom.

More and more now the two sat alone at their tables. Many of the café crowd began openly to avoid him, and when he approached would pay their chits, rise and move away. Others treated him as a freak, *un type insupportable*, calling him The Drunken Boatman and The Hun of the Ardennes; and he would call them names in return—but with a richer vocabulary. A few resented him so intensely that they could scarcely keep their hands off him. And the time came, inevitably, when one of them didn't.

It was on a night when a group of writers met in the back room of a café to read their latest work aloud, and well on in the proceedings the floor was held by a young quasi-Parnassian poet for whom Claude had a particular distaste. As the reading went on—and it was a long one—he stretched himself out across three chairs, in an elaborate facsimile of sleep, and diligently produced a snore at every pause. Heads were turned in annoyance, and he was hushed a few times; but still the reading continued, and finally, deciding that stronger measures were needed, he abandoned the snores for more articulate comment. There was a pause. *"Merde,"* he said. Another pause—*"Merde."* The third time the poet not only paused but stopped. His face was white and his hands trembling. "What did you say?" he demanded; and Claude raising his head slightly, answered, "You heard me. Do you want me to spell it?" The poet gave a sharp cry. Dropping his manuscript, he rushed at him, fists flailing. Claude, bigger and stronger, got up and pushed him away. The man charged again, and Claude knocked him down. There was a general fracas of shouts, curses, swinging arms, and crashing glassware—and then Claude and Druard were out on the street, moving on to the next café and the next absinthe. "Boy, dear boy," his friend said to him in agitation, "You shouldn't do such

things. You mustn't." To which Claude answered, "Why? It damn well
WAS *merde* and you know it."

After that there were many fights. The chip on his shoulder grew
larger and larger; his restraint grew less and less. And the latter was by no
means only a matter of drunkenness, for the rejection of restraint was a
matter of principle to him, the key tenet of his creed. He would only say
what he thought, he would do as he wished, and if the world didn't like
it, it could kiss his rump. At first Druard made certain efforts to control
him. But they were feeble and feckless. For one thing, with his penchant
for scenes and plate-smashing, he was no hand at controlling even himself;
and beyond that, Claude was wholly unmanageable. He was the stronger
of the two, and he knew it. The power that Druard had felt in him from
the day of their first meeting had grown and intensified until it was now
wholly dominant. He knew no fear, no qualms, no inhibitions. Above
all, he knew no remorse—which Druard knew all too well. And increasingly he seemed to his friend scarcely a man at all—much less a boy—but
rather a creature beyond humanness, a sort of genie or godling. Where
he led, Druard followed; at all he did, Druard marveled. He had called
him Apollo. Now he saw him as Lucifer as well. Not the old Lucifer—not
Satan, the ancient incarnate evil of a theological hell—but the young
Lucifer, the Light-bringer, the rebel angel: Lucifer defiant, Lucifer singing,
marching to battle. Lucifer, god of the possessed and dispossessed. . . .

Others, however, used less Miltonic imagery. The word *voyou* was
often heard. The words *salaud* and *crapule* and *fils de putain*. Even the
most tolerant among the café crowd tired of Claude's insolence, of his
exhibitionism, of his and Druard's ever more pointed flaunting of their
relationship. More and more their appearance was greeted by silence and
turned heads. More and more they were snubbed and avoided, until there
was scarcely anyone left even to fight with. Their war against Philistia had
carried them so far that now Bohemia too had ostracized them.

But they didn't mind. *"Fous le camp!"* was their answer. For they were
sufficient unto themselves. Leaving their old haunts, they found new
cafés, with new groups to taunt and scandalize, and as they went they
perfected their techniques; staging their performance for whomever
they thought it would shock, reciting scatological verses *à la chansonnier*,
delivering a *Proclamation d'Emancipation—Edition Française* on the evils of
coeducational love. When trouble threatened—which it did increasingly
—Druard usually sobered up sufficiently to suggest a tactical withdrawal.
But Claude rose to every challenge, every protest and counteroffensive,
liking nothing better than to turn a quiet, dull, genteel establishment into
a chaos of shouts and curses and swinging fists. In time, inevitably, he was
arrested. But Druard paid his fine. And sometimes they were arrested
together, when they ran afoul of gendarmes on their weaving way home

at night; but each time they were released the next morning. They were mad. They were berserk. They wallowed in depravity. But they loved it, gloried in it, and to himself Claude repeated his old litany: "Without evil, there can be no good; without filth, no purity; without hell, no heaven." . . . *On se fait coucher dans la merde.* . . . And then, only then, could one soar into sunlight.

One night:

They were in a café where they were not known, and a group of men and women at the next table were observing them. "Well, I got her at last," said Claude, in a whisper loud enough to be heard. "Ah, you got her," said Druard. "Good. Was it easy?" "No, not easy. She fought, she scratched and bit; she almost got away. But I caught her and pulled her back and then I let her have it." "Right in the heart?" "Heart, hell. What fun would that be? No, not in the heart, not in the belly. Down you-know-where. Right in as neat as you please; then up with a big rip, clear to the chin. Oh, it was quite a sight, I tell you: all the guts and things—like an open book." "But messy?" "Yes, messy, of course. I never saw so much blood; so red and thick. Look—" Claude took from his pocket a red-painted knife. The women screamed. The waiter came running.

Another night:

Wandering aimlessly, they found themselves at the Etoile, and before them rose the tall bulk of the Arc de Triomphe. "Come on," said Claude, "let's go up and see Bonaparte's ghost." And forcing the door to the stairway, they climbed to the platform at the arch's summit. "*L'Empereur* must be out," Claude said. "But there's Paris," said Druard. "Ah, Paris. Beautiful Paris!" Claude murmured, and standing at the edge of the platform, he opened the buttons of his trousers. "What are you doing?" Druard asked. "I'm preparing to salute beautiful Paris." "From here?" "But of course from here. From the imperial *pissoir* of the City of Light." Druard hesitated; then he joined him. "I hope we hit a general," said Claude. "Or a judge." "Or a Parnassian." "Or my father-in-law." They made their salute and looked down dreamily. "It droppeth," said Claude, "As the gentle rain from heaven."

Then they met Dar Misheram.

Just who or what Dar Misheram had been originally, they never discovered (though they leaned toward the theory that he was an unfrocked priest); but by his own story he was a Zoroastrian from Persia who, before coming to Paris, had spent twenty years in a hermit's cave in the holy mountains of northern Kurdistan. In his current incarnation he was a small dark man with a black beard, a long crimson cloak, and an income, from invisible sources, that enabled him to sit in the cafés all night and all day behind even higher saucer piles than Claude's and Druard's. When asked point-blank about himself, he replied, "I am a Satanist." He was given to mumbling incantations in obscure languages, and to sudden trances and seizures during which he claimed to see apocalyptic visions. By general consensus he was considered the most *outré* of all the strange and fantastic denizens of the *Quartier Latin*.

But if he was *un type*, he was *un type formidable*. His *outrance* was genuine. Besides his private gibberish, Claude soon discovered, he actually did speak several of the Eastern languages: among them Arabic and Urdu. He was a mystic, a cabalist, an occultist, with a knowledge of alchemy and thaumaturgy that made the fat Archambault's magical researches seem, in comparison, like the dabblings of a schoolboy. He claimed that he was an appointed representative of the Antichrist. Beelzebub and the hosts of hell were his intimates, and he was a practiced celebrant of the Black Mass, to whose mysteries he introduced Claude and Druard. For the latter, with his deeply inbred Catholicism, this was the ultimate in willful degradation; he almost literally believed that God would, at any moment, strike him dead. But for "the young Lucifer," already a master of blasphemy, it was another triumphant step on his path of revolt. In the hidden candlelit cellar where they held their rituals he saw himself as, at last, a true high priest of corruption. In the phallic Christs and rutting harlot-Virgins he found the unsurpassable expression of his contempt for the faith of his fathers—and of his mother.

With Dar Misheram, too, they went on to another experience: the smoking of hashish. And soon this became as much a part of their lives as the drinking of absinthe. Here, too, Druard had his difficulties; after a night with the pipe he was often queasy, ill, too weak to work or even stir from bed. But Claude found only satisfaction: not merely in the drug itself but for the part it played in his conception of himself.... Hashish —the word was Arabic. The user of hashish was a *hashashin*. An *assassin*. Almost a thousand years ago the name had come into being, in Egypt, to designate the members of a secret sect who with the help of the drug reached a point beyond ordinary human capability. They were bound to total and unconditional devotion; they performed acts of incredible violence and courage; they were indifferent to suffering, to good and evil, even to life and death, caring only for the mission that had been set for them. To disregard all consequences; to give of them themselves utterly, without fear or restraint: that had been their creed—as it was now Claude Morel's.... And from the magic of the pipe, as he now smoked it, came dreams of fierce joy and fulfillment. For now, truly, the Day of the Assassins had returned.

Or had it—quite yet?

"I've been thinking," he said to Druard one night as they smoked, "of that woman I killed."

"Woman you killed?"

"At the café, remember? With the knife. All nice and bloody."

"Oh, that."

"Yes, that. I've been thinking a lot about it, and it could be done, you know. Not just in talk, but really done."

"For God's sake, boy—"

"No, not for God's sake. For Satan's. And our own. If we've given ourselves to him, we should give to the ultimate. If we're Assassins, we must be true ones."

There was a silence. There was blue smoke. Then Claude set down his pipe and leaped up. "Come on!" he said.

"Come on where? What are you talking about?"

"I'm talking about the ultimate. About murder. Come on—now, tonight—it'll be easy. We'll find a woman, a man, a child, anyone; it doesn't matter. Don't you see?—it'll be easy. We'll never be caught. There'll be no clues, no reason, no motive—or at least no motive that fools can understand. It will be our great blow for Satan—our ultimate blow—the last absolute step beyond good and evil."

He seized Druard's arm to pull him up. But Druard drew back. His drug-shrouded eyes stared at Claude in horror, and his body began to tremble.

And then, suddenly, Claude laughed. He released Druard and pushed him back, and then picked up his pipe again and sat laughing as he smoked it.

But, beneath the laughter, he too was trembling.

A week passed—or perhaps a month. They could not tell.

Then, through the blue haze, Claude saw Druard on his bed and heard him calling weakly.

"What?" he said.

"I'm sick, boy."

"You're drunk. You've smoked too much."

"No, I'm sick. Terribly. Come to me, boy. Sit by me. Hold my hand."

"Go to sleep. You'll be all right in the morning."

"I can't sleep. I can't breathe. Claude—Oh God! Claude—Claude—"

Then Druard slept. Claude went into the other room and closed the door. But other doors opened, windows opened, and he sat through the night with his pipe, gazing through them. . . . "Hashish," the great Baudelaire had written, "makes of discords a rhapsody. It plumbs the glittering abyss. It bares to the eyes the immortal rhythm of the cosmos." . . . And this, now, Claude saw—he knew—with eyes and mind preternaturally clear. It was a dark night, and moonless, but through his windows he saw the moon, he saw a galaxy of moons, and they were black, and the sky was yellow. It was late April, and warm, but the city lay deep in snow. And against the snow, faintly at first, then more and more clearly—brightly, dazzlingly—there was a form, a figure. It was not a human figure, yet it glowed with humanity. It was not a man nor a woman, yet womanly; a radiance rather than an image; an essence—a *being*. It was no longer his pipe in his hand. It was his pencil. And he wrote. *Etre de beauté. . . . Against the snow a* BEING OF BEAUTY, *tall of form. . . .*

He waited. He watched. And then . . . *Whistlings of death and circles of muted music make the beloved body, like a specter, rise, expand and quiver; scarlet and black wounds burst in the superb flesh. The very colors of life darken, dance and re-form themselves around the vision. Shudders rise and spin, and their wild mad savor mingles with the deathly whistling and the hoarse music that the world, far behind us, hurls at our mother of beauty. She recoils. She straightens. Oh, our bones are covered with a new and loving flesh. . . .*

His was a frenzy of vision. Of debauch—and of creation. Abandoning the cafés where once he had all but lived, he now scarcely left the rooms on the Rue de Lacque. Hours and days meant nothing. He was as likely as not to get up at midafternoon, work through the night, and have dinner while Paris woke up the next morning. Or he would keep going for as much as forty-eight hours, and then sleep twenty-four. Bottles of absinthe and packets of hashish were always at hand, and there were periods of days at a time when he was never wholly out from under the influence of one or both. Probably no man alive, he thought, had abused his body more thoroughly and mercilessly. And he thought it proudly; for he didn't falter, he didn't flag. In the wild disorder of his life he achieved prodigiously. Out of drunkenness and narcosis came the pure radiance of art.

At intervals a change came, and he swung to the opposite pole. He touched neither bottle nor pipe; he scarcely even touched food, mortifying his body now by abnegation, fasting and purging himself like an Indian sadhu in quest of "enlightenment." He went almost without sleep. He trained himself to sit absolutely still, without moving a muscle, for hours on end. Sometimes he held a lighted match to his hand until the flesh smoked and turned black—and still he did not move or cry out. And this would go on for days, for a week or more, until again the change came, the poles turned, and he plunged back into debauchery. . . . Except that, for him, it was not debauchery. Absinthe and hashish, no less than fasting and vigil, were for him a means to an end—the end of self-liberation and illumination—and the pursuit of that, far from being debauch, was the one sacred and austere objective of his life. Beside it, good and evil, virtue and vice, were no more than mumbled shibboleths for weaklings and fools.

Indeed, the time had now come when he truly believed he had broken all bars and shackles. One by one he had encountered the Seven Deadly Sins; he had not feared them but embraced them; and, in embracing, he had destroyed them. He had, by his own efforts, of his will and vision, cut down the Tree of Good and Evil, until it was no more than rotted wood under his feet. He had succeeded in his "reasoned derangement of the senses," until they were free of the bonds that held the senses of others. He had found a tongue with which to speak. He became a thief of the fire from heaven. And if the fire at times burned so brightly that it almost consumed him, it was a thousand times worth the while, for the fire was the fire of truth.

"I will be a poet," he had said. And he was.

"I will be a seer," he had said. And he was.

And he was an alchemist too. Above all, an alchemist; for his apprenticeship to Archambault and Dar Misheram had convinced him that that word, better than any other, described his essence and his function. Through his vast reading he had absorbed the lore of alchemy and incorporated it into the very fabric of his thinking. Its form and symbols had become an integral part of his writing, and its processes of transmutation, of refining the impure into the pure, dross into gold, were those that he himself used consciously in his alchemy of the word. Not only the method was the same, but, at bottom, the end as well, for it had not been actual palpable gold that the true alchemists had sought; it had been philosopher's gold, the gold of purity and salvation, the vision of the absolute. And that was what he was seeking too. The absolute. The Key to the Kingdom. Like Faust, he had sold his soul to the devil, but only that he might beat the devil at his own game—and not by weakness or repentance, but by his own greater strength. For who, between heaven and hell, was stronger than the alchemist? Who more dedicated and more pure? The alchemist was the true priest, the true holy man; not a mindless subservient lackey of dogma and ritual, but a seeker, a seer, a communicant with the infinite; and as such, as the greatest of all alchemists, he, Claude Morel, had found his own communion—and epiphany. In his heightening of perception, his expansion of consciousness, he was approaching oneness with God. In his will and power to create, he was sharing the very function of God.

He closed his door. But other doors and windows opened, and he looked through them. He looked through the green glow of absinthe and the blue smoke of hashish, through the veils, through the darkness, to what lay beyond darkness. He saw the snow, the shape against the snow: the shape of beauty, the shape of truth, pure and absolute. He saw the violet eyes of truth, and the eyes looked back at him, deep and gleaming.

Druard lived with him, beside him. He drank his absinthe, smoked his hashish, looked out through his own windows in search of his own truth. Claude knew that often, beyond those windows, there loomed a crucifix. There loomed a bloody Christ and a pink-and-white baby. But Druard didn't speak of them. Instead, he seized his bottle and lit his pipe. He sat for hours staring blankly at the white paper on his desk, and then plunged into his writing. What he wrote was masterful, exquisite: a fusion of nuance and vision, passion and pain.

But he could not write for long at a time. His shoulders would droop, his eyes grow blank again, and he would return to pipe or bottle. Or he would come into Claude's room and sit disconsolately beside him, holding his hand, and say: "Boy, dear boy, be kind to me; be gentle. I am tired, I am old, I am sick." His long high-boned face had grown more skeletal than ever. His flesh was yellow as parchment. Sometimes his depressions would last for days on end, and he was sunk, as at the bottom of a pit, in a stupor of liquor and drug. Then again he would rouse himself. He would write like a madman, and then read aloud what he had written, over and over again, until his tongue thickened in his mouth and the words turned to gibberish. He would accuse Claude of despising his poetry, and himself, and then turn to him, weeping, and plead for his love. By day he prowled endlessly from room to room. At night, when absinthe and hashish should long since have put him to sleep, he sat alone in darkness, brooding and mumbling.

"I am lost," Claude heard him say. "I am drunk. I am unclean. God have mercy—"

Then the night came when the mumbling grew louder. It rose to a cry, to a shriek, and Claude, entering his room, found him writhing on the floor, limbs convulsed and eyes staring. The seizure lasted almost an hour, ending in heavy stupor; and in the morning, when he could not rouse him, Claude called in a doctor.

"He has had delirium tremens," the doctor said. "And also he is very run down—with anemia and low blood pressure. He must have several weeks of bed rest and careful attention." He looked around him at the wild disorder of the room. "Does he have a family?"

Claude hesitated, then shook his head.

"Yes—yes," Druard murmured without opening his eyes. "Family— wife—please. . . . Wife—Isabelle—Isabelle. . . ." Then he lapsed back into unconsciousness, murmuring what seemed to be snatches of prayer.

Claude sent a message to the Rue Nicolet, and toward noon Monsieur de Bercy appeared, accompanied by two men with a stretcher. "He could rot here for all I care," he told the doctor, who had returned. "But women—" He shrugged. "Who can understand women?"

He said nothing to Claude. He appeared not even to see him. The attendants lifted Druard onto the stretcher and went out, and he and the doctor followed them.

The door closed. Claude was left alone.

And alone he remained for the days and weeks that followed. Alone with his pipe and his bottles—and his poems. There was a plentiful supply of hashish and absinthe, the rent had been paid in advance, and Druard had left enough cash behind, scattered in trouser pockets and bureau drawers, to supply him with the little food that he needed. He went out less than ever: perhaps once every second or third day on some errand or other and occasionally on long prowling walks through the city. And he had no companions at all; for, with Druard gone, he was more *non grata* than ever at the cafés, and his appearance was a signal for turned backs and emptying chairs. He didn't care. When he passed old acquaintances on the street he thumbed his nose at them. He knew that, though they wouldn't speak to him, they spoke *about* him constantly and that, at seventeen, he was already more of a legend in the *Quartier* than most men who had lived and written there all their lives. He climbed his stairs; he closed his door; he lived alone in drunkenness and dreams. And if sometimes in the aloneness there was also loneliness, he was willing to bear it. For it was the lot of all true creators. Of the Creator Himself.

Morning. . . . Or perhaps it was afternoon; time was vague. . . . He seldom undressed at night, but simply fell on the bed when consciousness flickered out, and now, as usual, he awoke fully dressed and lay motionless for a while with eyes open. The room was bright. The sun was shining. But behind the sunlight there were still moons; there were the black moons and yellow sky and white snow of his dreams; the colors fading, the forms receding. . . . And there was a sound. . . . But the sound did not fade. He listened. He raised his head a little. Someone was knocking on the door.

There had been no knock on the door since Druard left. "It's a mistake," he thought. "They'll go away." But the knocking continued. Getting up, he went to the door and opened it.

"Hello, Claude," said Germaine Lautier.

He said nothing. For a few moments she said nothing more. Stepping past him, she entered the room, and Claude looked at her without moving.

"May I sit down?" she asked. "Those were long stairs." Without waiting for an answer she took the nearest chair. "And besides," she said, "I had trouble finding you. I don't know this part of Paris very well, and when the coach let me off on the Boulevard Saint Michel I had to look around a lot. I almost got lost." She smiled. "But not quite."

Claude finally found his tongue. "How did you—"

"Know where you lived? I found out a few days ago when I went to the de Bercys. My uncle told about going for Maurice and mentioned the address. I didn't know if you'd still be here, of course, but—I thought I'd see."

There was another pause. Claude still stared. She was wearing the same school uniform in which he had last seen her—white blouse and blue skirt, to which a blue jacket had now been added—and its prim girl-ishness was sheer fantasy in the frowzy room into which nothing female had ever before penetrated. She herself, her presence, was fantastic. But differently. For the primness was only of clothing. She, Germaine, the person, seemed, as she had always seemed to him, not a schoolgirl at all, but a grown woman, poised and controlled. She sat with grace, her body straight but not rigid. Her hands lay quietly on her lap, and her violet eyes were deep and calm.

The eyes studied him. "You are all right, Claude?" she asked.

"All right? Yes. . . . Yes, of course I'm all right."

"Maurice was so sick. I didn't see him at my uncle and aunt's—they said he was still not well enough—but Isabelle told me how bad it was. How he was so weak, and delirious. She said he had suffered so. And I was afraid that maybe you—you too—"

"No, I haven't been sick."

"I'm glad, Claude. So glad."

He jerked away from her scrutiny. Going to the window, he looked down into the street, but there were only the usual random passers-by. "Who brought you here?" he demanded, turning back to her.

"No one brought me," said Germaine. "I told you—I came by coach. By myself."

"You mean your parents let you—"

"Of course they didn't. They don't know anything about it."

"What about school?"

"I told them I had a headache and left early."

"Just to come here?"

"Yes."

"Why?"

"I've told you why. Because Maurice had been so sick. Because I was worried." She paused. "And also there's another reason," she added. "Because you haven't come back to Passy."

"I didn't say—"

"No, I know you didn't. But I was hoping you would. Oh so much, Claude! Almost every day for months, after school, I'd try to fix things so I could walk home alone; thinking you might be waiting for me—across the street—around the corner—"

"I—I've been busy."

"Yes, of course you have." Her eyes went to his desk. "You've been working hard—terribly hard: I know that. It's the only way you can work." She looked back at him, and then again around the room. "But I know something else too," she said severely, "and that's that you haven't been taking care of yourself."

"I tell you I'm not—"

"No, not sick, maybe. But dirty—oh. You should be ashamed of your-self, living like this. . . . It actually smells in here." She tilted her head and sniffed. "It's a queer smell—thick and heavy; it almost makes my head spin. I suppose it's that awful tobacco of yours." She rose abruptly, went to the window and threw it open. "There, that's better. And now—where's a broom? And a mop? Or don't you even have such things?" She went to a corner cupboard and took out the few cleaning implements it contained. Then she removed her jacket and lay it over the back of a chair.

"Damn it, what are you—"

"Don't try any of your swearing on me," she snapped at him. "Just keep out of my way." Glancing at him again, she made a face. "Better yet, get inside there and clean yourself up. You're even dirtier than the room."

Ignoring him, she set about her cleaning; and for a while he watched her, undecided whether or not to interfere. Finally he shrugged and went off to the bathroom, where he slapped water on his face and pulled a comb through his hair. When he returned she was still at work, and he sat watching her again. She had swept the dirt and litter into neat piles on the floor, and now transferred them onto papers and carried them out to the bin in the hallway. Then she made the bed. She cleaned the pots on the stove and the scattered dishes on the shelves. She went into the other room and worked there a while, and when she emerged she was carrying, along with the other litter, several empty absinthe bottles. She took them out to the bin without comment; but on her next trip her hands were full of the crumpled wrappings of hashish packets, and she stopped and looked at him.

"I thought you hadn't been sick," she said.

He didn't answer.

"All this medicine. It's where the smell came from."

"It was Maurice's medicine," he said.

She threw the wrappings away and went on with her work. "There!" she said at last. "It looks almost like a place where a human being lives. . . . And now—when did you last eat?"

"I'm not hungry," he told her.

Paying no attention, she searched about until she found what little food there was: a stale half-loaf of bread, a piece of cheese, some strips of dried pork, a jar of tea. And she prepared a meal for him. At the first mouthful the dregs of liquor and hashish seemed to rise in his gorge, and he was close to vomiting; but he managed to control it and got the food down. When he had finished, Germaine cleaned the dishes and put them away. Then she sat down and said again, "There!"

Claude studied her. Her face was slightly flushed from her work, and a strand of hair had fallen over her forehead. Pushing it back, she smiled at him.

"You're very pleased with yourself, aren't you?" he said.

"Pleased?"

"At being such a good little girl."

"Some things come naturally to a girl. Haven't you found that out yet?"

"I've found out enough."

"Oh, enough. I see." She smiled slightly. "Such as that they're awful, you mean? All girls and women are awful. They should be done away with. *Le bon Dieu* should be instructed to change the specifications."

He said nothing.

"Oh Claude, Claude," she said, "how silly and foolish can you be? It's been—how long now?—almost six months since I've seen you, and I'd hoped you'd changed a little—grown up a little." Leaning forward, she laid a hand lightly on his. "Why are you like this, Claude?" she asked. "Why do you close yourself away, so lonely and afraid?"

"I'm not afraid—"

"Yes; yes you are. I know. I can tell. You may think you dislike me—that you hate me—hate all women. But it's not that, not really. I *know* it's not hating, but just being afraid—" She paused. Her hand still lay on his. "Why, Claude?" she asked softly. "Why? Can't you tell me? . . . Is it something that once happened to you with a girl? Or with someone else—someone close to you? Like your mother? Back at my uncle and aunt's, I remember, I tried to ask you about your mother, but you wouldn't say anything. Won't you tell me now? . . . Have you had trouble with her, is that it? Tell me about her. What is she like?"

For a long moment he looked at her in silence. His lips trembled, and he seemed on the point of speaking, softly and gently. . . . But then he pulled away. His hand, his eyes, the whole of him. And he leaped to his feet. "Stop it!" he shouted. "Damn it, stop prying at me and get out of here!"

Germaine didn't move.

"Did you hear me?"

"Yes, I heard you, Claude," she said. "But I'm not going. Not that way. Because—you see—it's different with me. I'm not afraid of *you*. Do you think I'd be here if I were?"

"I don't know why you're here. I don't want you here. Stop your spying and prying and preaching and let me alone!"

"Is that what you really want, Claude—are you sure? To be let alone? . . . Maybe it's what you think, but not I. I think that's just the trouble: that you've been alone too much. . . . Oh, I know you have to be alone to write —to create. No one can share that with you. But afterward, when you're not writing—when you're not a poet any more, but just a person, just a

man—don't you feel then that you want someone, need someone—?"
Her eyes went to the papers piled on his desk, which, alone in the disorder
of the room, she had not touched in her cleaning. "To create as you do, do
you have to be *always* so lonely and unhappy?"

He didn't answer. Though the sudden blaze of his anger had faded, he
was still hostile and sullen. Yet he didn't speak nor try to stop her when,
presently, she rose and crossed to the desk. He was silent as she picked up
the top two or three of his manuscript pages and read what was written
on them.

"It's strange—so strange," she said, putting them down.

"Of course it's strange. It's crazy. What do you expect from me?"

"I don't mean the poem. The poem's beautiful—like every poem
you've written." Germaine paused, looking down again. "I mean the
handwriting."

"Handwriting?"

"Yes. I noticed it from the very first: before I'd met you, even, when
I saw the verses you'd sent Maurice from Cambon. . . . How small your
writing is. How firm and neat and precise. . . . I thought then, 'How is it
possible to write such wild, free, soaring things in a hand like that?' And
I've thought about it since—wondered and puzzled about it—only now I
think I understand, because I know you. Because I know you're not really
one person, but two."

"Or a whole crowd."

"No, two. The one you want the world to see; that you want me to
see. A *voyou*. A sort of savage. A wild man. . . . And then this other one:
the one who wrote these pages: who works so hard, takes such pains, feels
and cares so deeply. The one you're alone with—who's really you." He
had turned away from her. He was trying not to listen. But he felt her
eyes full upon him, and her voice went on. "Shall I tell you something,
Claude?" she said. "Something that may make you really angry? . . . I think
that deep inside yourself, in your heart, you're a Puritan. Yes, a Puritan.
Or an ascetic; a sort of hermit monk. I think you want perfection—of
yourself, of everyone—and because you can't find it you turn on it; and
on yourself and everyone. Because you hate yourself, you want everyone
to hate you. Because you're hurt, because you're proud—oh so terribly
proud, Claude—that's the heart of it. Sometimes I think you're not satisfied to be a human being at all. You want to be more than human: a force, a
power, a sort of absolute beyond the rest of us. Like—like Lucifer, almost.
Or like God Himself."

He had turned back. He was no longer looking away, but straight at
her, staring. And now she got up and came toward him. "You can't be
God, Claude," she said softly. "Or Lucifer either. You can't, because you're
human. You may not want to be, but you are—you *are*—and you must let

yourself be. That's the whole thing, don't you see? That you let yourself. That you make yourself. For then you won't be only a great poet, but a great man. A whole and happy man."

She had stopped close before him. She looked up into his face. "Yes, you're a man, Claude," she said. "Not just a poet, but a man—"

There was a silence.

"And I am a woman," she said.

He looked down at her; at the face raised to his, so close, so glowing. That was all there was—her face, her lips, her eyes, her glowing closeness. And it was then, at that instant, that it happened: the experience he had never known before, or even dimly surmised: the experience of desire, of a man's need for a woman, that had been forever closed to him by the walls of his prison. For in that instant the walls crumbled. The gates opened. The flower and flood of his dreams streamed wildly within him, and his body trembled at its core.

"Claude, I love you," she said.

He felt his lips move. He heard them say, "Love me—?"

"Yes, yes! You must know it. You must feel it. . . . Come, hold me. Then you'll feel—then you'll know—"

Her own arms went around him. He felt her against him. He felt her arms and her cheek and her breasts and her thighs. He felt the whole of her: soft and close, tight and tender. And his trembling increased. His hands rose. His arms rose. And within him the flood rose, still higher. In a moment it would burst from him in a wild sounding cry:

Germaine! Germaine! Oh God, oh God—Germaine. . . .

But the cry never came. The flood fell. His hands fell. The walls rose again, the gates closed, the light faded, and where it had been was gray emptiness. He looked at the girl's face, so close before him; at the girl's body, the woman's body, which had, in that instant, become the face and body of a stranger. For now he was looking beyond her to the one who was not a stranger; whom he had known all his life; who stood in the shadows, watching—tall and black, tall and silent.

He pulled back. He heard his voice again. "Go away," it said. "For the love of Christ, go away!"

She still held him. Rage filled him again, and he wrenched away. "Get out, get out!" he shouted.

Germaine stood where she was.

"Are you out of your mind? Are you mad?"

"No, Claude."

"What then?"

"I love you, Claude."

"Love me?" He spat the words at her. "My God, do you know what you're saying? Do you know what I am?"

"Yes, I've just told you—I do."

"And how I live?"

"I know that too."

"*How* do you know?"

"From what I saw here when I came in. From what I've heard at the de Bercys."

"What did you hear there?"

"That you and Maurice had been living—wildly. That you didn't take care of yourselves—drank too much—"

"Drank too much—" Claude gave a rasping laugh. "Do you know what 'too much' is? We drank until we were never sober, day or night. And that's how I still drink. I was drunk last night, I was drunk when you came in, and I'll be drunk again as soon as you go." She tried to speak, but he plunged on blindly, savagely. "And I'll tell you something else," he said. "That smell you talked about—those papers you picked up—my medicine. Do you know what kind of medicine it is? It's hashish. . . . Have you heard of hashish, little girl? Do they teach you to smoke it at the school for the young ladies of Passy? They really should, you know. It would widen your education. Wouldn't you like to curl up all nice and cozy in your bed and dream of naked men and raped virgins?"

"Claude, Claude—" she pleaded.

"Oh, you wouldn't like it, eh? It wouldn't be ladylike? Not good bourgeois morality? . . . Well, it's *my* morality, little girl. My way, my life—and the hell with you. . . . And do you know what else my life is? My life with your poor dear Cousin Maurice: did his family tell you about that? They said we were living 'wildly,' but did they tell you what 'wildly' means? Did they tell you we were lovers—perverts? That we were beasts and monsters —foul, unclean—"

He broke off, panting. His eyes blazed at her, and he stood motionless, waiting, as if for her to scream and flee. . . . But she did neither. As he spoke, she had paled; but she stood straight before him, without moving, and her eyes were full on his face.

"Is that all?" she asked at last, very quietly.

"All?"

"Have you said what you want to?"

"Hasn't it been enough?"

"There is no enough. . . . Don't you understand me at all, Claude? I don't care what you say. I don't care what you've done. I care about what you are—and can be. . . . Do you want me to say it again? I love you."

There was a long silence then.

He turned away. He went to the bed and sat down and looked at the floor; and she stood where she had been, watching him.

"Claude—" she said finally.

"What?"

"You don't want my love?"

"No," he said.

"You don't want me here?"

"No."

He didn't look up. He didn't move. Long seconds, perhaps a minute, passed, and he didn't move. Then abruptly he got up. He went into the other room and closed the door. From the closet he took a half-filled bottle of absinthe and, standing in the middle of the room, drank it down in slow measured drafts. When he came out again Germaine was gone, and he sat down at his desk.

Little girl, he wrote, *you are a nigger. Tall black mother, you are a nigger. Lucifer, you are a nigger. God Almighty, you are a nigger. . . .*

That was toward the middle of April. It was early in May that Druard returned.

13

"Garçon, encore deux absinthes!"

"Oui, messieurs."

"Encore quatre!"

"Encore huit!"

"Encore huit douzaines d'ab-bab-babsumphes, tout de suite! . . . Et garçon—"

"Oui, messieurs?"

"Aussi des absumphes pour ces messieurs là-bas, avec nos compliments."

The waiter left and returned presently with a tray of drinks, going first to the nearby table where a group of four men was sitting. Then, with the tray still full, he returned to Druard and Claude. "The gentlemen will not accept them," he said.

"Not accept them?"

"No, messieurs."

"All right, put them here."

They drank all the drinks and Druard paid. Then they got up to go, and Claude went over to the other table. *"Va te faire foutre,"* he said.

The four men ignored him, and he and Druard wove off. It was raining, and Claude looked morosely up and down the street.

"And the Boul' Mich can do it too," he added.

"The whole of Paris," said Druard.

"That's right, the whole of Paris. . . . Do you know what Paris is? It's a dump. A dumphe full of absumphe. And full of bastards."

"Full of snotnoses."

"And prudes."

"And priests."

"And rain."

"It's always raining."

"And nobody talks to you."

"I hate the rain."

"And I hate Paris."

"So do I. Let's get the hell out."

"Yes—out. Fast. . . . But where to?"

"To the south."

"Right! The south!"

"Away from the rain—"

"And the priests."

"Into the sun."

"Because we're children of the sun."

"Pagans."

"And the hell with Paris."

They walked on a while. Then they were in a fiacre. Then they were in a station. Then they were in a train. At the bar in the station they had bought a bottle of absinthe, and on the train they drank from it until they fell asleep.

When the conductor roused them it was morning. The train had stopped, and beyond the window was a dock and open water. "The blue Mediterranean!" Druard exulted. Only it wasn't blue. It was gray. It was raining.

"Beyond the mists," said Claude, "lies Carthage."

"And Egypt."

"And Jerusalem."

"And Troy."

"And Babylon." Claude laughed. "The Hôtel de Babylone . . ."

They got off the train and bought another bottle of absinthe. Then they saw a boat beside the dock and got on it, and the boat pulled out. They drank for a while on the boat, and then there was another dock, and they got off and into another train, and they drank some more on the train and fell asleep again, and this time, when they awakened, the conductor was calling, "London! London!"

"My God!" said Druard. "What have we done?"

But Claude only smiled and pulled out pencil and paper.

Forever arriving, he wrote, *you will go everywhere.* . . .

"We'll go back tomorrow," Druard said.

But they didn't. They didn't go that week, or that month, or the next month, or for many months. . . . Instead, they found lodgings in Soho. Druard arranged for the income from his trust fund to be paid to him through a London bank. They bought the few clothes and other items they needed. They settled down as exiles.

It rained. It seemed always to be raining. And it seemed always to be Sunday: "that unique and monstrous British Sunday," Claude wrote in his notes, "—as gray and grim and tightly sealed as a coffin—which is enough to put the chill of death into a Frenchman's bones." Even on weekdays it was not much better. There were no boulevards, no promenading crowds, no restaurants and cafés spilling brightly out from their walls into the streets and squares. Instead of cafés, there were pubs: dark foul-smelling holes without tables or chairs, where stolid red-faced men stood three deep at bars without exchanging a word. In the pubs there was no absinthe. There were no cognac, no wine, no apéritifs, no cordials, but only warm beer and gin, and, in the more expensive places, fiery whisky. In all of them, legal closing time came at the exact moment when one was beginning to enjoy oneself, with a policeman at the door, watch in hand, to make sure it was exactly observed.

No wonder the English got out of England, Claude thought—across the seas, to far shores, into sunlight. And he wrote:

> . . . *Everywhere wasteland;*
> *facing the black skies with ruddy foreheads, go*
> *men-at-arms on ghostly chargers, riding slow,*
> *while pebbles crackle under the proud host.*

But in the wasteland there were streams; in exile, compensations. For Soho was, in most ways, more continental than British, and among the jumbled nationalities were many Frenchmen. Most of them were young; all were poor; all were Bohemian in their tastes, liberal to radical in their attitudes; and not a few were political refugees—veterans of the short-lived Commune who had had to flee France for their lives. Like Claude and Druard, they were outcasts, pariahs, rebels, and they accepted the newcomers as two more of their own kind. The turned backs and cold stares of the Boul' Mich were a thing of the past. They were greeted as fellow revolutionaries. All differences were submerged in the common hatred of fat bourgeois France, which someday they would unite to over-throw.

Lean bourgeois England did not concern them—except for its barbarous curfew and pestilential food. But there were now enough of them so that these could be at least partially by-passed in their own lodgings and small restaurants; and, for the rest, they were free to talk and argue, plot and philosophize, to their hearts' content. For most of them, the strange

Anglo-Saxon world beyond the bounds of Soho scarcely existed.

But not for Claude. For Claude, everything existed. And, unlike the true Frenchman, he was a wanderer; he was still, in his bones, "the boy who took a walk"; and soon he was embarked on long wanderings through London, from Chelsea to Whitechapel, Mayfair to Limehouse, Kew to Pimlico, into every section of the vast city. Sometimes Druard set out with him, but he would soon tire, and Claude would go on alone. When he himself tired at last, he sat on the benches in Hyde and Regent Parks, watching and listening. He drank his beers and gins in a hundred pubs, and when there was money left over (by courtesy of Druard) he went to the theater. His English, good before, was soon so fluent that he was entirely at home with it; and, discovering the British Museum, he spent long hours in its reading rooms, reacquainting himself with his favorites among the British poets. He read Shakespeare from *Lear* to sonnets. He read Coleridge, Shelley, Keats, Byron. (Ah, *there* was a Lucifer.) He discovered the works of many newer writers, and among them particularly liked Swinburne—an alchemist of the English language, as he himself was of the French.

But the core of his experiences were the walks: the watching, the listening. And for these his favorite areas were not the imperial heart of the city—Whitehall and Westminster, Piccadilly and the Strand—but the huge, sprawling, almost anonymous regions beyond. For hour after hour he would move through a gray half-world of identical streets and identical houses, blank, cheerless, featureless, a warren of millions shrouded in smoke and rain, and from there he would go on still deeper, into the true slums, into the twisting foul-smelling alleys of the docksides and the East End. Ibis was the world of which he had known the counterpart in the Paris of the bridges and the Hôtel de Babylone. But this world was more immense, more abject, more—he reached for the word and found it—more *impersonal*. And more terrible. If Paris was the City of Light, this was the City of Iron. If Paris was the capital of living, this was the capital of labor. Of rain and smoke, stone and steel. Of pounds, shillings, and pence. And of poverty. Here on the Thames, and not on the Seine, was the heart of the bourgeois capitalist world of the late nineteenth century. The new Rome. The new Byzantium. Metropolis.

He walked. He watched. He thought. And there was a change in his thinking. Two years before, as a *mioche* from the Ardennes, he had come to Paris, afire with liberal philosophy and political conviction, only to have the flame quickly smothered in the butchery of the streets and the bestiality of a barracks. And since then he had lived with and for himself: outwardly an outcast and a hooligan, inwardly a mystic, a seer, a visionary, absorbed in a private and secret cosmos of his own. But now, in the harsh gray air of London, his eyes began to see again with the old focus. Looking about, he saw not only his own visions but the world around him. He saw its wealth and its poverty, its power and its misery, the thousand inconsistencies and injustices that a new industrial society had imposed on the helpless mass of mankind. And in his reborn awareness he was resolved not only to think and feel but to act; to become again a revolutionary; to enroll again, in Heine's words, as a soldier in the war for the liberation of man.

He haunted the poorest pubs: for a change not drinking, but listening and making notes. He attended workingmen's meetings. He reread long sections of *Das Kapital* and met Marx and Engels, who were among the innumerable political exiles then in London. And with his fellow Frenchmen in Soho he talked endlessly about the problems and errors, the glories and shames, of *la patrie*. Out of all this came a resolution and an ambitious project: he would, for the first time, write politically. Out of his own experience, his own theories and passionate convictions, he would write his manifesto, his *Book of France:* a book of the Commune which had risen and fallen; of the new Commune-to-come which would rise and not fall; of the hope and vision and revolutionary dedication that would at last make of his country the great and shining thing it might be. He made his plans, his notes, his outlines. He sat down to work. He sat down on Monday. He sat down on Tuesday and Wednesday and Thursday. He sat down every day of that week, and of the next, and the next. He sat with his paper and his pencils and his notes and his plans and his project. . . .

And nothing happened.

He wrote a page and tore it up. Wrote twenty, and tore them up. He wrote a paragraph, a sentence, a line, and sat looking at them; sat looking for hours at blank pages on which he had written nothing—and tore them up. He couldn't write. The thoughts were in his head, the emotion in his heart, the will in every fiber of his brain and body. But still he could not write. "To find a tongue"—that was to write; and he could not find it. To be "a thief of fire"; but the fire was out. The spark was gone—the magic, the alchemy—and he was no longer a poet and seer, no longer the mystic "I-who-is-another," but a lump of flesh at a desk before a blank sheet of paper. And, soon, not only mind but even flesh was feckless. His hands trembled. His eyes ached. His blood seemed to scratch and claw at him as it moved through his body. At last he sprang up with a cry. He rushed in to Druard. "Come on, let's get out of here!" he shouted. "For Christ's sake out—out—out!"

And that night, in an alley in Limehouse, they found a Chinaman who sold them hashish.

During their first month or so in London, Druard, like Claude, had striven for a new pattern of life. On the very first day after their drunken arrival they had had a long and somber discussion. They had weighed themselves in the balance and found themselves wanting. And they had resolved to make changes. Not that there was any thought of separating: far from it. Druard's last defection—his return in sickness to his wife and the de Bercys and the long ordeal of his convalescence—had proven to him once and for all, he declared, that such a life was not for him. He was through forever as a family man. He was through as a bourgeois and a Catholic. His destiny was as a poet, as a free soul—his destiny was with Claude—and nothing would ever turn him from it.

Yes, Claude agreed: they belonged together. They had found in each other an understanding, a companionship, a bond of love that had become the core of their lives, and of their art. They had been made for each other, and the world could say what it liked.

But—they further agreed—they had made mistakes. There had been excess, wildness, and folly, which must be checked. And for a while in London they had accomplished this with fair success. Their drinking was more moderate (a feat in which they were helped no little by their dislike of gin and whisky); and for several weeks they did entirely without drugs (being helped in this by the circumstance that they did not know where to find them). After the ostracism of the *Quartier Latin*, their acceptance by the French of Soho gave a lift to their spirits. And London, though physically depressing, was, in its newness and vastness, a stimulant. They felt in themselves a newness, a sense of fresh beginnings. They had no fights or scenes, either between themselves or with others. They worked hard and well. They were full of plans, hopes, visions. They sustained each other. For a while, as once long before, dream joined again with dream, and flute with horn.

For a while. For a month, perhaps two. . . . But then, slowly and remorselessly, the old pattern began to re-emerge. It began with Druard's resentment of Claude's long solitary walks. ("You're always trying to get away from me." . . . "What do you think you are, my nurse?"); continued with petty arguments on what to eat, where to go, whom to see; and presently reached the old point of lost tempers and slamming doors. Claude had his first fight in a pub. Then a second. Coming home one night, they got lost, fell asleep in the street, and were arrested. They blamed each other. They wrangled. Worst of all, their work began going badly. Sallow and sunken-cheeked, Druard sat at his desk, struggling with thoughts and images that he could not bring to life; and in the next room Claude sat at his, with his notes, his plans—and his blank paper.

It was Claude who broke first. Who ran in, trembling and shouting. Who led the way to Limehouse. . . .

And after that they were back where they had been. In the Chinese quarter they found hashish and opium; in Soho itself they at last found absinthe; and soon they were living to themselves again in a hermetic world of daze and dream. More weeks went by. Summer passed into autumn. London lay as if in a cave of fog and rain, and within it the Children of the Sun moved in their own deeper cave of green pillars and blue mist. For a while they struggled against it. "We'll leave London," they said. "We'll get out of here—go south, where we meant to go. Yes, we'll go; we must go. Tomorrow." But when tomorrow came they were sick, or they were fighting—or, if they were lucky, the green-and-blue magic had done its work well, and for hours they sat at their desks writing. For that was the wonder, the marvel, the perverse core of the magic: that it was only when they were under its spell that they could truly create. Druard wove his dreams into a shining web of words. And Claude, putting aside his *Book of France*, wrote again as he had always written: out of visions and images that thronged his brain and heart. He trembled. His eyes ached. His blood clawed. But still he wrote. And when he finished there were the caves of blue haze and green fire.

They were barred from most of the pubs in Soho. They were put out of their lodgings and found others. Often they did not come home at night but slept through to the next noon in the opium dens of Limehouse, and once they spent three days in a den without emerging. When they went in Claude's age was seventeen. When they came out it was eighteen.

"We must stop."

"Yes—tomorrow."

"We must leave."

"Yes—tomorrow."

And fall passed into winter.

As before, Druard suffered the more acutely, both from the physical effects of their debauchery and from the pangs of remorse. Shortly before Christmas he had a second attack of delirium tremens and for a few weeks thereafter was too sick and weak even to go out. One night Claude awakened to find him kneeling beside his bed with tears streaming down his cheeks. "Pray with me, boy," he murmured. "For the love of God, pray with me." And though Claude repulsed him, as always, the familiar cycle continued. A crucifix made its reappearance; then a rosary; and when he was strong enough Druard tottered out to find a priest. "Don't get mixed up and confess to a Protestant," Claude shouted after him. And when he returned he greeted him with mumbled hog-Latin litanies.

A few days later he found a scrap of paper on the floor, and on it Druard had written: *My dearest wife—I am cursed; I am held by a nightmare. But I think constantly of you and our baby. Someday I shall return, and I pray God you will take me back. . . .* "Go on, get out, crawl back to her!" Claude said. But Druard's response was to lie weeping on his bed, while Claude mocked him; and then to raise his head, to stare at him, almost in terror;

to mumble wildly, "You have no heart, no pity. You are not human—not a man. You are Attila, Apollo, Lucifer, Antichrist. You are a god, a demon —*but not a man.*"

His maudlin tears and piety filled Claude with contempt. But he despised himself too (—who had once told him that?—) for his own cruelty and savagery. He tried to restrain himself from striking out, but he couldn't; Druard was a soft cloying clinging thing around his neck, an octopus strangling him, dragging him down, and he lashed and tore at him with blind instinct. Sometimes he would have the feeling of almost physical suffocation. He must have fresh air or die. And rushing from their rooms, he would again walk the streets: endlessly, tirelessly, through the rain and the fog.

But now a new and strange thing had begun to happen—for he no longer walked at random. Each of his sorties brought him to the Thames, and following it, he moved along the Embankment, past the City, past the Tower, through Whitechapel and Poplar and Limehouse, until he came at last to the docks. And here, on London's vast inland waterfront where the Thames broadens toward the sea, he found what for him was the very blood stream of Metropolis. For hours, for whole days on end, he prowled the dockside streets and alleys, through the welter of produce and goods from the ends of the earth. He rubbed shoulders with Scotsmen and Swedes, Greeks and Syrians, Arabs and lascars, Malays and Chinese. In the pubs he spoke to them in the shreds of language he had picked up from everywhere, drawing from them the stories of lives so different in background from his own, yet, in their rootless vagabondage, so strangely similar. Squatting on the pierheads in the gray northern winter, he watched the ships pull out for the ports of sunlight—for Suez, Aden, Bombay, Rangoon, Hong Kong; and his eyes and mind went with them, as they had once gone with a French barge down the Seine toward the unknown sea.

The sea was still unknown to him. His only experience of it had been on his two-hour crossing of the Channel when he had not even known where he was. But here, now, for the first time, he was at last in its presence, and the presence was not dream but reality. The tides pushing up the estuary were heavy with salt; the very air was salt; the hooting of horns, the creak of hawsers, the rattle of winches filled his ears. These were not ships of the imagination: hazy galleons, vague triremes, a child's specter ships, frail as May butterflies. They were ships of hard fact, of hard iron, of coal and machinery and cargo and tonnage. Their hulls were black, their stacks black, their smoke black in the leaden sky. They were ugly; they were dirty; they were the ships of commerce, of Metropolis, of pounds and dollars, francs and marks, pesos and piasters. But for Claude, watching them from the pierheads, they were no less ships of enchantment and wild surmise—like the Drunken Boat of his dreams—the boat of the golden birds and the far horizons.

He walked a dockside street. He entered a small drab office. He faced a bearded man across a desk and answered questions and signed a paper. "Be aboard tomorrow at six," the man said.

But at six the next morning he was lying beside Druard, while green and blue visions gleamed under his lids. "Boy, dear boy," Druard was murmuring thickly, "we must find our way back to Christ."

A week later he signed up again. And again didn't go. He *couldn't* go. His mind, his heart, his will, all of them told him "Go, go, go." And still he couldn't. The drunkenness of the ships, the seas, and the horizons was less powerful than the other drunkenness of which he had now so long been a prisoner. Like Druard, he was cursed; he was held by a nightmare. Like Druard, whom he so needed—and hated—

One of the things that he most hated about him was, perversely, his generosity. In all their time together he, Claude, had not contributed so much as a sou or farthing to their maintenance, but Druard had throughout accepted this as natural circumstance and considered his income to be as much Claude's as his own. ("Like a man and wife," Claude thought bitterly, "—but in reverse. For he is the wife and I the man. The kept man.") And now he resolved that, if he could not break away altogether, he must at least win for himself a token independence. He must find work. He must earn money. Day after day, over Druard's protests, he pored over the newspapers, wrote letters, made calls. . . . But jobs were not easily come by. London was glutted with continental expatriates, most of whom needed work to live, and his own marketable talents were almost nil. Finally, through a roundabout chain of contacts, he got a job as part-time French tutor to the children of a wealthy West End family. But it bored him to distraction. During the second session he fell asleep. For the third he arrived drunk, and was promptly discharged. Subsequently he tried a few other leads, but nothing materialized. And then he gave up the effort. "Please, *chère Maman*," he would whine to Druard when he went out alone, "give your *beau gosse* tuppence for a stick of toffee."

As always with him, the pendulum swung in its full arc. "All right," he thought, "I've made my try at being a bourgeois, and they won't have me. Now I'll go back to being myself." And in the weeks that followed he threw off restraint more wildly than ever before. As a salute to Philistia he plastered his clothes with dirt and mud. He let his yellow hair fall uncombed to his shoulders. He prowled the streets like an animal, picking refuse from the gutter, throwing it at passers-by, laughing at their anger and discomfiture. He hurled insults and picked fights in the pubs, as he had used to do in Paris. He was arrested and gloried in it. For days on end he would be drunk and drugged. He would fall in the street at night and sleep where he fell, or awake the next day in a Limehouse cellar, not knowing how he got there. Returning to their room and finding Druard asleep, he would throw himself at him in a demented frenzy. "You wanted a Hun for a lover," he would yell. "So, God damn you, now you've got one—"

"I am a drunkard, a drug addict, a pervert," he would say to anyone who would listen. And to himself: "I am Attila—I am Lucifer—I am the Antichrist."

Miraculously, he still wrote. But when or how he scarcely knew. He had reached a point where he wrote blindly, automatically—as a man breathes when sleeping—without consciousness of what he was doing, without the exercise of choice or will. And this too gave him savage satisfaction, for it was proof, he believed, that he had at last become a true *voyant:* a seer and mystic who, by derangement of the senses, was able to penetrate into the ultimate mysteries. His pockets were filled with scraps of paper. His desk, his bed, the corners of his room. He left them there. He didn't read what he had written. His eyes were too blurred, too aching to read. But it didn't matter: the words were there. The dream and the vision were there; dreams and visions such as no man had imagined; dreams of colors invisible, sounds inaudible, of forms and lights and images that never were on land or sea, between heaven and hell, but only beyond them, in a farther world—the world of eternity, of God—and of himself. He wrote the ineffable, the indescribable. He wrote revelation, the last trumpet, the apocalypse. From his green-and-blue cave he watched the earth spin past; he watched the years and the centuries. And when the centuries had passed, it was dark and he slept; but in the darkness there was still light, in the sleep there were dreams, there was thunder, there was splendor; and from the splendor sprang new centuries, and he was watching again, writing again, writing asleep, or perhaps awake—it didn't matter, nothing mattered—except the splendor, the dream, the dream blue, green, and gleaming. . . .

Then he woke and was afraid. The dream was fading. He reached for his pipe and knocked it over. He reached for his bottle and it was empty. It was not a century that was dawning, but a day; not blue and green around him, but rainy grayness. He heard the rain fall. He heard a clock tick. It ticked with terrible clarity. There was clarity in the grayness, in the room, in the litter of clothes and pipe and bottle and crumpled paper that filled the room. He picked up three of the papers at random. He read:

> . . . *I've wept too much. The dawns are sharp distress;*
> *all moons are baleful and all sunlight harsh to me.*
> *Swollen with acrid love, sagging with drunkenness—*
> *oh that my keel might rend and give me to the sea.*

He read:

> *Let them rent me at last a whitewashed tomb,*
> *with the cement lines in relief—*
> *far down under the earth.*

He read:

> *. . . It is no ship, It is*
> *a fixed canoe, its chain eternally drawn down*
> *deep in this edgeless eye of water—to what slime?*

It was Christmas time. Then January. Then February. Rain fell on Metropolis through the fog and smoke.

One day in March Druard came into Claude's room looking more than ever like a yellow fever-eyed ghost. In his hand he held a letter. "Oh God," he moaned. "Oh merciful God—"

The letter was from a firm of Paris lawyers. *We have been engaged to represent Madame Isabelle Druard,* it read, *in the suit for legal separation which she is bringing against you. The judgment will be sought in the Superior Court of Paris on five grounds, to wit: nonsupport, abandonment, habitual drunkenness, addiction to narcotics, and the maintenance of an unnatural sexual relationship with one Claude Morel.*

"They forgot swearing on Sunday," said Claude.

"It's the end. Oh God, the end. The shame—the scandal—"

"After the last year you're still worrying about scandal?"

Druard wasn't listening. He sat with head bowed and the tears flowing. "My poor Isabelle. My poor little son," he sobbed. "What have I done to you? How can I make amends?"

"You can go back and explain you've just been a little absent-minded."

"There's only one thing to do." Druard leaped up. "God, give me strength to do it—and forgive me!"

He stumbled from the room. Claude lit his pipe, returned to his writing, and forgot him. But when, a few hours later, he went into Druard, he found him unconscious on the bed with three packets of sleeping powders lying empty beside him.

He had to be taken by ambulance to a nursing home, and it was almost a week before he could return.

March. April . . .

"I must go back to Paris."

"Sure. Tomorrow."

"We must both go. We must get out."

"Yes. Tomorrow."

The tomorrows dawned in dreams and drunken mists.

Then again, briefly, the mists lifted. The light in the cave turned from blue-green to gray. And in the grayness Claude again looked at a slip of paper that he held in his hand. At first he thought it was another of his poems; but something was wrong about it. Then he saw what it was: it was not in his handwriting—and it was not a poem. It was a letter; it was addressed to him; the only letter other than Druard's—how long ago!—he had ever received. Like the one recently received by Druard, it was from Paris. But it was not from a lawyer. It read: *I have learned your address from my cousin. I think of you always. When you need and want me I am waiting.—G.*

When, an hour or more later, Druard came in, he was sitting motionless in the same place. He didn't look up. When Druard spoke, he didn't answer. Instead, after a moment, he rose and left the room and went down the stairs and into the streets. He walked the streets—for how long he didn't know. On his return to their lodgings, Druard was out, and going into his room, he sat down at his desk with pen and paper. He sat there for a long time. He wrote the date and salutation. Then he sat again. He wrote no more. Finally he got up and went out again. He walked the streets again. He came home and went to his room, and the paper was still lying on his desk. He looked down at it, and what he had written was: *April 12, 1873. Dear Mother. . . .*

That night he dreamed wildly and horribly. It began with his sister Yvette at her first Communion, and she was being married to Christ—a phallic Christ—and lay raped and broken on the altar. With a cry he flung himself upon the rapist, striking and tearing in a frenzy of rage, reaching for the eyes, the throat, the corrupted heart. But his frenzy was blind. He could find neither bone nor blood, but only flesh; and the flesh was soft, it was yielding, it changed form as he touched it; it held him, enveloped him, smothered him, as with the long twining legs of an octopus. And now the struggle was different. He was no longer striking out, but walking, stumbling; he was stumbling down dim aisles with a monstrous weight on his shoulders; and the weight was the flesh, the incubus, the *thing*, still enveloping, still smothering him, clinging ever closer, ever tighter, and now it had a voice and the voice whispered, it kept whispering, "Boy—boy— dear boy—" He was carrying it on a pilgrimage, as an offering, a sacrifice, he was carrying it through the years, through the centuries, through the dim aisles of blue and green, the aisles of cathedrals, the aisles of forests; through the forests to the river, along the river to the wide banks, past the banks, past the white cities, past the dancing files, to the high place. And the high place was the altar. He was back at the altar, but Yvette was gone, the bloody veil and the bloody Christ were gone, and in their place was the Other One: the Figure, the Queen. The Queen was black against the jungle. She was shining against the snow. She waited, motionless, and he approached and stopped before her and knelt. He knelt before his mother, and from his shoulders, at last, he took his burden, he took his offering, his sacrifice, and laid them before her—except that now there was again a change, and what he laid down was not there; only he was there; no burden of guilt, no murdered Christ or whispering flesh, but only himself, he alone. *He* was the offering, *he* the sacrifice. And he lay before his mother, before the Queen, before the tall shining figure; and he waited, the figure waited, then the figure moved. It moved closer, it bent over him, it bent to accept him, consume him, and he cried out, but no sound came, he struggled, but without movement; and the figure was upon him; its great legs, its belly, its breasts, its arms, its throat, its face and hair and eyes . . . and then only the eyes . . . it was not the body that was devouring him, but the eyes; the eyes above him, upon him, within him, the eyes watching, devouring, consuming, the eyes of omega—Ω—deep violet and gleaming. . . .

"Boy, dear boy—"

It was Druard, bending over his bed. He leaped up, threw on his clothes, rushed out.

The eyes followed him.

From then on they followed him everywhere. Through the streets, through their rooms. Through his sleeping, through his waking. Through the green halls, the blue smoke, the gray city. They looked at him from windows, from doors, from alleys, from cellars, from rooftops. Late one night, on Piccadilly, they looked at him from a small painted face under a gas lamp, and he stopped and said, "Come on."

"I've a plyce—"

"No, we'll go to my place."

He took the girl to their rooms. Druard was up waiting for him, and his eyes were feverish in his hollow cheeks.

"This is Fanny," Claude said. "We just got married."

Druard's hands trembled. He began to weep. Claude laughed, took the girl into his own room, and locked the door. After a few minutes Druard began rattling the knob and calling to him, but Claude paid no attention.

"What's the matter with 'im?" the girl asked.

"I'm a bigamist," Claude explained. "He's my other wife."

She undressed and lay on the bed, and for the first time in his life—the life of reality, not of dream—he truly saw the flesh of a naked woman. He sat on the bed beside her; he touched her flesh. But now, suddenly, it was he who was trembling. His hand was cold. His whole body was cold, frozen, but at the same time it was covered with sweat, and he jerked himself to his feet. From his pocket he drew a ten-shilling note and held it out to the girl.

She stared at him. "What in 'ell's this?" she asked.

"It's your money. You can go now."

"Go? Ye mean ye don't want nothin'?"

"No, nothing. Thank you."

She seemed about to let loose at him, but changed her mind. She looked from him to the door to the ten shillings, and then took the money and got up. "What sort of plyce is this?" she said. "A loony bin?"

"That's it," he told her. "That's exactly it."

She dressed; and he led her from the room, past Druard, to the outer door; and at the stairhead she turned and again her eyes stared at him from her painted face.

They stared at him all night.

Then May . . .

The eyes followed him.

Druard followed him.

Through the nights. Through the caves.

Then once—strangely, suddenly—it was not night, and they were not in a cave. They were on a street and it was spring and the sun was shining. But Druard did not look at the sun; nor at Claude. He walked with head bent and eyes turned away. And later, in their rooms, Claude again found a scrap of paper on the floor, and on the paper was written:

> *What have you done, O you that weep*
> *in the glad sun—*
> *Say, with your youth, you man that weep,*
> *what have you done?*

For a moment a strange feeling touched him. A tide of gentleness. Entering Druard's room he found him lying on his bed, and, going to him, he touched his hand with his own. But it was no good. The moment vanished. Druard seized his hand and pulled at it, and he jerked away, and then he was running down the stairs with Druard after him.

And so it went. No matter at what hour he got up, or how quickly he left, Druard was after him. However far he walked, Druard was at his heels. "You're going to a woman," he cried. "You're going to leave me for a woman—"

He raged. He wept. He threatened suicide. "I have new sleeping powders—and stronger ones. . . . I have my razor. . . . I'll jump from the window. . . . I'll jump in the Thames."

And he pleaded:

"All I have is you; only you. My wife is gone—my baby—everything. Even Christ is gone. There's only you. Be good to me, dear boy. Be kind —be loving—"

Then, one night, it was different. Claude stirred and rose, and Druard
pleaded, but he broke away. Druard rose to follow, but he hit out. He hit
with blind fury, and Druard groaned and sagged, and then he hit again
and Druard fell to the floor. For a wild, terrible instant he stood above
him, poised to leap, to rend, to sink his fingers like tiger's claws into the
gasping throat. In Paris he had thought of himself as an Assassin; he had
talked of "the ultimate"—of killing, of murder. But that had been *voyou*
talk, hashish dream. Now murder was in his heart and hands. He stood
still. He swayed. Eyes watched him. They were not Druard's eyes, but the
other eyes, and he swayed away from Druard, and to the door, and plunged
downstairs into the street. He ran on and on through the streets, through
the night. But still the eyes followed him; still Druard seemed to follow
him; he was close behind him now; he was touching him, grasping him,
mounting his back as he ran; he was riding his back, his shoulders, with
arms around him, clinging, strangling, and Claude stumbled and fell and
lay shuddering on the pavement.

He got up. He ran on. He had to have drink. But the pubs were
closed; there was no drink. There were only the streets, the night, the gas
lamps: the lamps stretching endlessly before him into the mist, the lamps
watching him with their thousand eyes. He ran; they watched; Druard
followed. Druard caught him, clung to him, mounted him—and still
he ran. He ran to Limehouse, through dark alleys, past blank walls. He
knocked at closed doors. But there was no answer; no one came. He ran
again, fell again. Then he rose. He stood at bay. There was one thing left—
one weapon left—the ultimate act with which he had always conquered. It
was not to kill, to murder. It was to write. And he wrote. The eyes watched
him, Druard clung to him, but still he wrote. Hunched in a dark alley of
Limehouse, he called upon the images and dreams and visions that lay
within him. He called from the depths of his soul, and they responded.
They rose, flowed, flooded up out of darkness into light. They suffused
him, transfigured him, and, transfigured, he wrote, he created, he did the
thing he had been born to do. The act of writing was his talisman. It was
his crucifix held up to the demons; to evil, to death, to dissolution. And
now he held it high. He wrote on and on. He wrote out of his dreams and
visions, and out of the torment of his spirit; and from that torment, that
agony, he produced the alchemist's magic that carried him beyond them;
that carried him to exultation, to glory; to beauty, to truth; to power, to
salvation; to godhead....

He wrote. He stopped writing. He had finished. He had finished his
masterpiece, his testament; performed again, out of his soul's own
godhead, the act of creation that would forever sustain him. A great peace
filled him, and he looked up at the night sky. Then he looked down at
what he had written; at the paper on which he had written. But there was

no paper. He looked at his pencil, but there was no pencil. His paper and pencil had been palm and finger.

He looked up again. He looked at Druard. He looked at the eyes watching him, and the eyes moved closer. He made a monstrous convulsive effort to obliterate them, to shut them out, to break, by the sheer force of will, from his prison of dreams. But even as he tried, he knew he could not. For he was not dreaming; he was awake. He was not drunk or drugged, but aware and clear-eyed. And in the clearness, the awareness, Druard was still there; the eyes were still there; they were still moving closer; they were huge, they were violet; they were deep violet caves, violet pits; and they were upon him, around him, he was within them, engulfed by them, spinning and falling. Far off, there was a terrible sound, at first faint and muffled, then louder and louder. It was the sound of his own screaming. . . .

There was a livid welt on Druard's cheekbone. His mouth worked. His eyes glittered. Behind him were the other eyes, watching.

"I am going," Claude said. "The time has come; it has to be. I am going."

He was not screaming now. His voice was very quiet. It was Druard who was screaming:

"No, no—you can't! You can't!"

Claude was packing his few belongings, and he followed him around. "You can't walk out on me like this. Throw me off. Abandon me. . . . No, no, no!"

Claude said nothing.

"Where are you going? To one of your women, is that it? To one of your dirty whores?"

"No, I'm not going to a woman," said Claude.

"Where then?"

"Just away. By myself. We can't go on with this."

"What do you mean, can't go on? . . . You just don't want me, is *that* it? You're through—*zut*—like that. After all this time—all I've done for you, given up for you—"

Claude finished his packing and closed his small grip. Druard watched him, trembling, and suddenly his rage turned to tears. "Please, please," he begged. "Dear boy, don't do this to me. No—please no. I love you—need you—Oh God, no, you can't! Not leave me alone, so terribly alone—" He seized Claude's arm and clung to it. "Please, please—you can beat me if you want—do anything you want—*anything*. But don't go. No. Don't go, don't leave me—"

Claude pulled away. With his grip he moved toward the door. "I have to," he said, still quietly. He turned and looked at Druard, and then past him at the watching eyes. "It's the only hope. The only way out."

"Way out? Way out from what? From me?" Druard's rage flooded back. "That's all it is, *hein*—that you want to get rid of me? . . . All right, God damn you, go ahead. . . . You think you're the strong one, don't you? That I'm the one that needs you, but no, you don't need me. All right, go ahead. Go and see what happens—how you'll live—who'll support you. Without me you're nothing, you fool! You think you're God, don't you? But you're not. Without me you're a tramp, a peasant lout. . . . Go, damn you, go and see! You won't eat—you won't live—you won't write. I can see it and I laugh at you. I spit at you. Claude Morel, the godalmighty poet, who will never again write a line—"

His voice screamed, quavered, broke. Claude opened the door, and there was sweat on his palm. There was sweat on his forehead. Druard watched. The eyes watched.

"Goodbye," Claude said.

"You're still going?"

"Yes, I'm going."

"No, you're not," Druard said.

His voice was different—quieter. But still trembling, still wild. His hand went to his pocket, and when he removed it it held a revolver. "I bought this for myself," he said. "My own poor miserable self, too weak to live—"

There was a pause. The only sound was his breathing.

"But now," he said, "—but now—you strong one, you godlike one—"

Claude turned. The gun wavered; it shook wildly. But it fired. Claude felt the burn of pain in his leg—his knee. He felt the splintering of bone. He saw Druard spin above him as he buckled and fell. But what he was most conscious of was neither pain nor image, but sound—a single sound—a sound that now stayed with him, strong and strangely comforting, as the rest reeled away into darkness. It was the blast of the firing gun: hard, clear, and clean.

14

Once, if I remember well, my life was a feast where all hearts opened and all wines flowed. . . .

He wrote and paused and tried to write again, but his pencil stuck. It was like a knife in his hand, jerking down. It tore the paper, and he tore the rest of the paper and threw the pencil away. He got up and walked on along the road, between the fields.

Then he came to a farmhouse. He knocked on the door and a little girl answered.

"Are you a tramp?" she asked.

"Yes, I'm a tramp," he said.

"My daddy shoots tramps. You better go away."

He walked on. The sun blazed. His knee hurt. After a while he came to a crossroads, and the sign pointing off to the right read: PARIS, 80 KM. But he kept straight on. At the next farmhouse there was a charging dog, at the next a slammed door, but at the one after that he was given a piece of bread and some cold potatoes. As he walked on still farther the sun began to set behind him, and presently it was dark. The road had left the fields and was passing through forest, and there were no more houses or barns. But it didn't matter, for the night was dry and warm. Coming to the entrance of a forest path, he turned from the road and followed it until he found a patch of soft moss. Then he lay down and closed his eyes.

And as on every night of his journey, once he closed them, he was no longer in a forest or in the countryside, but in a white room, in a bed, and he was looking up from the bed through a veil of pain and fever. Beyond the veil, figures moved, voices spoke to him. "The patella has been badly splintered," said the man in white, in English. "We have done what we can; now time must do the rest." . . . "Turn over now," said the woman in white. "Open your mouth. Raise your arm. Go to sleep now. Wake up. Turn over."

Then there were many figures, many voices, clipped and cold, and the voices beat down upon him.

"You have lived with the accused for eighteen months?"

"Yes."

"In Paris and London?"

"Yes."

"In an unnatural relationship?"

He was silent.

"As homosexuals?"

He was still silent.

"Answer me."

He turned his head.

"*Answer me!*"

"Yes," he murmured.

"You were habitual drunkards?"

"Yes."

"You were users of narcotics?"

"Yes."

"And at the time of the attempted murder the accused was—"

He faced them again. "No—no," he said.

"He was not drunk? Not drugged?"

"No."

"So. Then the assault was in cold blood? Premeditated?"

"No."

"What then?"

"It was— That is, he was—he didn't—"

"It's no use lying."

"I'm not lying."

"Tell us then. He was drunk, drugged, raving. He cursed you—raised his gun. Where did he aim the gun?"

"I—I don't know."

"Stop your lying."

"I'm not lying."

"He was in the same room with you, ten feet from you, and you don't know if—"

"I don't remember."

"Ah, you don't remember. *Why* don't you remember?"

"Because I—"

"Because you too were drunk and drugged, is that it? You'd had a fight. You were both blind, raging. You wanted to murder each other."

"No. No."

"What then?"

The pain burned in his leg; the fever welled in his brain; he turned away again.

"Answer, you!"

He was silent.

"*Answer!*"

They left. They returned. They left again. There was only the pain and the fever and the bed and the white walls, and at intervals the nurses coming and going. The nurses said only, "Turn over. Raise your arm. Open your mouth. Go to sleep." And they looked at him with cold veiled eyes.

His only testimony was from the hospital ward. He wasn't taken to court, he didn't see Druard, and it was not until several days after the trial that he learned what had happened. Druard had at first been charged with attempted murder; then this had been changed to criminal assault, and, upon the jury's verdict of guilty, he had been sentenced to two years in prison. "This man is not a felon of the usual sort," the judge had said, "but in many ways men of his ilk, and of that of his depraved companion, are even more dangerous to society than the habitual criminal. For the protection of society, and as an example to others who undermine it by corruption and vice, I therefore sentence him to the maximum penalty under the law."

So Druard had vanished: silent, invisible. And Claude lay in his bed. Because of infection and his miserable general condition, the bullet had not been removed from his knee until a week after the shooting, and even after its extraction the wound was slow in healing. Infection recurred; pain and fever recurred; his whole leg swelled monstrously, and its skin was hard and taut as a drumhead. He didn't mind the pain, however. He almost welcomed it when it came, in great nauseous waves, for it brought him up out of the pit of nothingness that lay beneath it. It was when pain ebbed that he suffered most. When he lay motionless by the hour —drained, strengthless, hopeless. When he fell asleep and dreamed and woke screaming, and the nurses came running to quiet him.

It was in a month less three days that he left the hospital. And he did not leave alone. A policeman met him at the entrance, took him to the railway station, rode with him to Dover, and put him on a Channel boat. The boat landed him in Calais. He had no bag, no possessions, and in his pocket three English pennies. So he began to walk. He walked eastward, limping. He walked all day, each day for a week, begging or filching enough food to sustain him, and at night he slept in barns, fields, or forests. Asleep, he dreamed of Druard. Awake, he thought of Druard. He thought of him in his cell in prison: his thin body stooped, his mandarin hands on iron bars, his sunken eyes looking out from depths of gray stone. And as the eyes followed him he became aware of a sensation so strange to him that at first he did not know what it was. Later he did know: it was guilt. And guilt walked with him. Guilt rose and lay down with him. Druard moved through the bars, through the stone, and walked beside him, and they were moving together, they were limping together; for Druard was limping too, he was wounded too—but not in the knee, his wounds were in his feet—two holes in the feet, two in the palms of his hands, and his arms were spread wide and limp like a scarecrow's. . . .

"You are not here," Claude cried at him. "You are there. Back there."

"No, dear boy," said Druard. "I am here—with you."

"Then go! Go back! Go away from me!"

"No, dear boy, I shall never go."

Then Claude was running. Limp and all, he was running, he was panting, stumbling, lurching down the empty road, between the fields, between the forests, blindly, wildly, on and on, until he could run no farther, until he was faint, exhausted, spent—and then at last he stopped —he stopped and turned—he faced the way he had come—and the empty road. He waited. Druard did not appear. He watched, listened, but there was no movement or sound. It was evening, the sky was gray, the sun gone beneath the horizon, and in the grayness, in the stillness, he did a thing he had not done for years. He fell on his knees—the bad with the good. He knelt in the dust of the road and bent his head. "I am alone," he thought. "Dear God—wherever you are, whatever you are—I thank you for this. I am alone."

He walked on.

The sun rose and set, the road rose and fell; it turned and twisted and forked and became another road and then another, and still he followed it, slowly, steadily, across the breadth of France. Dust rose in the summer heat, blinding and choking him, and the gravel bit deep into his flapping shoes. Then clouds came, rain came, in wild summer thunderstorms, and the rain streamed down his face and under his clothing, plastering the dust in streaks on his flesh. But he did not mind. Like the pain in the hospital, these were welcome to him. Raising his face to the torrents he felt their beat on his lips and eyelids. Beneath his feet he felt the thrust and the texture of the living earth. Once, resting, he sat for an hour by the roadside, his hands kneading the loam in a field of barley.

Later he ate the barley spikes, pulling them dry and crackling from the stalks. From a vineyard he picked grapes. At a farmhouse he was given bread and cheese. It was enough.

Some days his leg seemed all right and he scarcely limped at all. On others it swelled and throbbed and his progress was no more than a hobble. He thought of another time when he had had a bad knee—the same knee; when he had jumped from the train and fallen and then limped for the first time through the streets of Paris. "My Achilles' knee," he thought, and smiled a little.

Then one night there was something more than the knee. It had rained that evening, and he had found a barn to crawl into and fallen asleep on the straw; but in the darkness he awoke and he was sweating and trembling. At first he thought it was simply a recurrence of fever, but soon it was worse than fever, worse than anything he had ever known—a crawling of blood within him, a grinding of bones, a wild churning of every cell in his body, a rending torture, a raging hunger. And then he knew what it was. It *was* hunger. Hunger for hashish. His body yearned for it, clawed for it, screamed for it; rigid and convulsed, it screamed for balm, for easement, for soft descent into the deep blue cave. But there was no cave. There was only the crawling, the grinding, the screaming, and he writhed in the straw, flailing, burrowing, stuffing his mouth with it to keep the scream within him—until he lay still from exhaustion, still as death, his limbs thrown out grotesquely, his eyes open and glazed, his mouth open and still filled with straw.

Yet the next morning he walked on. And the next. And the next. He walked through the gravel, through the dust, through the mud, through the rain, through the sunlight. He walked past the fields and the forests, and then the fields were gone, and there was only forest, and then beyond the forest a river, slow and yellow, and beside the river, a few miles later, a town; and he came to the town and entered it and walked through its streets and squares. Faces looked at him, but he didn't see them. Once a voice spoke, but he didn't hear. He walked on from street to square, from square to street, until he came to the final street, and there he turned in and walked along it until he came to a door, and it was the final door and he opened it. There were the shelves and counters as they had always been. There was a customer fingering a tray of shoelaces, and beyond him a tall black figure watching with sharp eyes to make sure he did not slip a pair into his pocket.

Claude waited until the eyes were raised to him. Then he said, "Hello, Mother."

He was in bed again. In fever again. Walls revolved around him, but they were no longer white. A figure stood above him, but it was no longer white. It was black and tall. It moved back and forth silently, except for the squeak of its shoes.

Then his mother said, "The doctor will be here soon."

"I don't need a doctor."

"Yes, he is coming."

"I don't need—"

He was too weak to go on. The doctor came. He tried to turn away, but was too weak, and the doctor examined him. Later his mother appeared with bottle and spoon.

"I don't want any medicine."

"Open your mouth."

"I don't want—"

"Open your mouth!"

He took the medicine and slept, and when he awoke it was to a strange sensation. Something was on his forehead. He turned and saw that his mother was sitting beside him, and it was her hand on his forehead. The hand was hard and bony, but it lay quietly. He could remember no previous time when she had ever touched him, other than to strike.

Outside, at intervals, the church bells rang. It was light and then dark and then light again. His sister Yvette came in, looking much bigger than before, and said, "You will be all right, all right very soon, Claude dear. Today I lighted a candle for you after Mass." His brother Felix, looking the same as always, came in and said, "Christ, you look like someone dug you out of a hole." There were still the two old cots in the room, but for the time being, apparently, Felix was sleeping elsewhere. "For small favors, Lord," thought Claude, "we are grateful . . ."

He slept. He woke. He lay motionless, soaked in sweat, through the long midsummer days. The doctor came again and examined his knee and took pulse and temperature and prescribed more medicines. And he asked questions. It had been a burglar who shot him, Claude said: an armed burglar who had broken into his room in London and whom he had surprised at his thieving. "Ah, those English," muttered the doctor. "They are barbarians—worse than the Germans."

As a result of the long walk the knee had to heal all over again. But the knee was the least of it. Its pain, even when most swollen and throbbing, was as nothing compared to the grinding clawing torture of his hunger for hashish. Of this he gave no indication either to the doctor or his mother; when they were with him he lay quietly and silently, though it required, often, a monstrous effort of will. But when they were gone, when he was alone, there were times when will was not enough. His body became a thing divorced from will; it writhed and jerked; his jaw locked, his hands crooked stiffly into claws, and with them he tore at his bedding, his bedgown, his own flesh and bone in wild agonizing convulsion.

Nor was even this the worst. Still more terrible were the times when the seizures had passed; when he lay limp and spent on his tumbled cot and drifted feverishly into dreams. For the dreams were terrible beyond description—more terrible even than those of the last days in London—a fantasia of nameless faceless horror, choking and suffocating; and in the horror he writhed, he wallowed, he struggled with soundless screams, while he was pulled down down down into thickening darkness. He knew the darkness. Once it had been the darkness of his cave, his blue-green refuge of the pillared halls. But now bluegreen was black; refuge was gone, comfort was gone; the cave was a pit and he knew it for what it was—the pit of madness. Madness closed in upon him; it touched his eyes, his brain, it touched the beat of his heart, it held him with black arms, it possessed him; but still he struggled, still he fought, away from the arms, up from the pit, up toward the rim, grasping the rim, holding, clawing, screaming . . . and then it was done, it was over; he was lying on the rim, on his cot, in his room, and it was daylight, and all that was left were the black arms, holding him, encircling him . . . and the arms were his mother's.

"Claude, Claude! Wake up, son—can you hear me?"

"Yes, Mother."

"You are awake now. You are all right."

"Yes, Mother."

One day it was Sunday. One day it was August. There was the sun and the full moon and then a half-moon and then no moon. On one of the moonless nights the pit closed. There was earth over it; under his feet. The next night there was no dream at all, and the next day no convulsion. Two days later, when he was alone, he got out of bed and stood up. As soon as his weight was on his feet he fell down. But the next day he didn't fall. He walked across the room and back.

"I am alive," he thought. "I am going to go on living."

Why?

He stood before the washbasin on the bureau and saw himself in the bureau mirror. He saw a face of bone and chalk—as thin as his mother's, as white as his mother's—except that on each cheek, beneath the eyes, there was a patch of livid gray. The eyes themselves were those of a stranger: no longer the bright sky blue and white of his boyhood, but a pale diffused gray without feature or focus, like the eyes of a body washed up by the sea. A growth of soft light hair covered his face, and the hair of his head fell over his neck and ears. Finding a scissors, he cut it, cut it all, down to the scalp, and now his face was no longer a face at all, but a whiskered skull. Next, he found his brother's razor and shaved. His hand shook and he cut himself, and it was with surprise that he saw that his blood was red.

Later he took out the razor again and for a long time sat on the edge of his bed holding it open in his hand.

The next day he put on a sweater and carpet slippers and went down the stairs. His mother was alone in the shop, and she looked up sharply as he appeared and said, "You shouldn't be moving around yet."

"I'm all right now," he told her.

"The doctor said—"

"I'm all right," he repeated.

He spoke quietly. His mother held her peace. Finding a stool, he sat for a while in a corner while she attended to a few customers and then he went back upstairs. His heart thumped and his head spun dizzily, but there were no seizures, no dreams.

The next morning he went down again. This was Saturday—a busy day—and Yvette was helping out. But there was no sign of Felix. Indeed, it occurred to him presently, Felix was not around at all, except at night. He asked his mother about it, and her only answer was a snort. When he asked again she only said, "He has other work."

It was from Felix himself that he learned what the other work was: he was driving a cart for Guillaumet Frères, the produce merchants. "The old woman don't like it of course," he told Claude. "Thinks it's under the family dignity or something. But me, I like it fine. Here in the store it was enough to drive you crazy: on your feet all day, with the old woman yapping. Now I'm nice and cozy on my behind, with the horse on its feet —and by God, it keeps its mouth shut."

During Claude's illness Felix had slept on a cot in the rear of the store; now he moved back into their joint room. But there was scarcely any more talk between them. He scratched, he belched, he passed wind, he slept and snored, and he asked no questions at all as to where Claude had been or what he had done during his absence. They lived together as they had always lived—as two bodies, as strangers.

And now there was another stranger in the house as well: his sister Yvette. It was the season of her school holiday; she was at home or in the store almost all the time, and he saw her constantly. But she was no longer even remotely the twinkling Princess of long ago, nor even the *jeune fille* of his later memory, with flowering figure and ripening breasts. Though still only fifteen, she already seemed more woman than girl—and not even a young woman, but almost a spinster, prim and sedate, with placid manner and usually downcast eyes. As Claude had rejected the church and all its works, so had she, more and more, embraced them, until now they had become the very focus of her life. Each morning before Claude rose she was off to Mass and back again. Each evening, when the store had closed, she sat in the stiff walnut-and-horsehair parlor with her beads and prayer book. It was her intention, she had told him shyly, to become a nun ("—yes," his mother had said, "we have talked with Father Lacaze, and he agrees it is a fine idea, she has the true vocation—"); and it was a fact so strange, so incomprehensible to him that he found himself able to speak scarcely a word to her. And she too, for her part, seemed no longer able to speak to him. Sometimes when they were together in the evening, at supper or in the parlor, he would become conscious that she had looked up and was watching him; and when he too looked up she would smile. But if she was a stranger to him, so was he now to her, and in her eyes, behind the smile, were concern and uneasiness that, he knew, were close to fear.

His mother, of course, also watched him—sharply, measuringly. But she too spoke rarely, and then only about his health, his medicines, his food and sleep. There were no more gestures of affection. She was back in her shell. But neither were there gestures of impatience or anger, and whatever judgments she had formed she kept to herself. During his long journey across France he had sometimes wondered if she would accept him at all; if she would take him back into the house from which he had fled so often and with such bitterness. But the acceptance had been without question; almost without comment. Not in ten lifetimes could she have put it into words, but what she had said to him as clearly as in words was, "This is your home. You have gone away and come back, and two years have passed, and we are strangers. But I am still your mother. And this is still your home."

He, for his part, had told her little. She knew that he had been in Paris and London. He told her he had written much and earned his living at odd jobs. He told her about the armed burglar and the few other lies that seemed necessary. That he was defeated and beaten did not need telling.

One night Felix was out and he was alone in their room. Again he got out Felix's razor and stood for a while holding it open in his hand; and then he put it away and lay down on his bed. As far as he knew he had made no sound, but presently there was a knock on the door and his mother came in.

"You are all right?" she asked.

"Yes, all right," he answered.

"You have no fever?"

"No, no fever."

She seemed about to go, but stopped and turned at the door and stood looking at him for a long moment. "One must fight, son," she said at last. "One must be strong—be proud."

Then she went out, closing the door. But her image remained there before him—the tall iron-black figure, the white bony face, the pale lips, the dark eyes—and he realized that, for one of the few times in all his life, she had entered his room and spoken and left without a quarrel. And then, for the *first* time, he realized another thing: their kinship. The kinship of strength and pride that had forever divided them, but that now was subtly uniting them—if not in love (for love was beyond imagining), at least in tolerance and grudging respect. With all her might she had sought to bend him to her will—and failed. With all his might he had defied her, cursed her, rejected her, fled from her—and now he was back in her home: *his* home: the Hun, beaten and broken, who had returned to his *maman*.

In their own struggle there had been no victory for either. There never would be. They both knew it. And from their separate worlds, in their pride and loneliness, they were making a truce, a sort of peace, at last.

A visitor came. Father Lacaze.

Claude greeted him politely.

"Your little sister will someday be one of us," the priest said. "Meanwhile she comes every day to church—and your mother too, when she can. They have prayed and lighted candles for your recovery."

"Yes, I know," said Claude.

"And I have prayed too. I am happy to see you are better."

"Thank you, Father."

The priest was silent a moment, studying Claude with his sharp old eyes. "Perhaps you will be coming to church soon as well?" he went on then. "We should be happy to have you."

"Thank you. But I think not."

The priest sighed. "You are not a boy any more; you are a young man. You have been out in the world, seen and experienced much, and I was hopeful that you had changed."

"No, I haven't changed. Not about that."

"You will, in time. That I know—I am sure of. Someday you will return to us." Again Father Lacaze paused; he seemed to be waiting. Then again he sighed, rose, and smoothed his cassock down over his paunch. "Meanwhile," he said, "we shall go on praying for you."

"Thank you, Father," said Claude.

Slowly he grew stronger. There were no more seizures, no more dreams. He was still thin, but no longer skeletal, and as his hair grew and normal color returned to his cheeks his head ceased to resemble a skull. His mother bought him a new suit and the other clothing he needed, and he kept them neat. Toward the end of August he began going out for short walks.

On the street he met Georges Vuiton and Mimi Rouger. Except that she wasn't Rouger any more; she was Georges's wife. And she was pregnant. They asked him how Paris was, and he answered fine, and then they eyed him curiously for a moment and passed on.

He met old classmates from the lycée—Henri Clauson, Louis Carnot, and others—and they said, "Well, *le beau gosse!*" and "Ah, the prodigal returns!" Then again there was a question or two, a curious glance, and they passed on.

He met Michel Favre, much taller than before but still snub-nosed and freckled, and Michel said, "Well, how was it, *hein?* Did you get yourself a mistress? Were there plenty of girls?"

"Oh yes, plenty," said Claude.

"Lucky bastard!" Michel shook his head sadly. "Here they're all either married or they're children. Pfui! It's so bad I hardly bother coming up from the farm."

"You're still with your uncle, then?"

"God yes, still with my uncle. And what a life! Cows, cowmilk, cowflop; cowflop, cowmilk, cows. Great sport, I'm telling you. Come on out someday, and I'll lend you a pail and shovel."

"Maybe I will," said Claude.

He walked on. He walked aimlessly. One evening, before realizing where he was, he heard a voice shout, "Hey, *voyou!*" and he saw that he was passing the Café du Printemps.

There were the same faces, at the same tables. And now many voices:

"Hey *voyou—voyou!*"

"Where the hell've you been?"

"Come on, join the party."

"Have a beer."

"Things have been dull here. Give us a show."

"Yeah, the old *voyou* special—"

"Read us a poem—"

He quickened his pace and tried to pass by, but from a corner sidewalk-table a huge figure rose and blocked his way. "Well, the boy alchemist!" cried Fernand Archambault. And his voice, unlike the others, was warm, without mockery.

But Claude still tried to get by. "I—I'm sorry," he murmured, "I'm late. I must go—"

"Go? Go where, you young scalawag?" Archambault had a great arm around him. "Right into your old seat, that's where you're going. To tell us all about it—your life history—where you've been, what you've done." His enthusiasm mounted; his small eyes twinkled in their folds of fat. "How was Paris, boy?" he demanded. "How's the poetry, the alchemy, the magic? And how's my old friend Maurice?"

"I—I'm sorry—"

Archambault paid no attention. "Come now! We'll talk. We'll celebrate ... What would you like, *hein*—a beer? a cognac? ... No, the hell with that; this is a *real* celebration. ... *Jean, deux absinthes!*" he bellowed happily. *"Deux absinthes tout de suite!"* Raising his arm from Claude's shoulder, he gestured at the café waiter. And with the arm gone Claude turned and fled.

A few days later he met Albert Chariol.

He had assumed Chariol was in St. Quentin, where he usually spent the school holidays at his sister's, but suddenly there he was, coming toward him along the street, and they stopped and shook hands. "Well," said his old teacher. "Well, *mon vieux*. Well—"

Claude could not think of even that much to say.

"I'd heard you were back, of course. And sick. I was so sorry. I would have come to see you"—Chariol smiled ruefully—"except that I'm afraid that I'm not your mother's favorite caller."

"I'm all right now."

There was a pause. Their eyes met and moved apart. Claude knew that Chariol was studying him—not openly, staringly, as his old schoolmates had done, but studying none the less—trying to read what two years had written. And he in turn tried to bridge the years since he had seen his teacher. At first glance there seemed to be no change; the slim figure, the soft brown hair, the sensitive features, the earnest eyes were all the same as before. And yet—at second glance—not quite the same, for Chariol seemed unmistakably more than two years older. It was no specific thing about him, Claude decided, but an aura, an impression. As if the dust of Cambon summers had touched him, with a gentle filming and blurring.

"Whereas no dust has touched you," Claude thought with an inward grimace. "No dust, no years, no anything. . . ."

"Will you be staying long?" Chariol was asking.

"I don't know," he said.

"It would be nice to see you again. To talk again." The rueful smile reappeared. "There aren't too many people to talk with here in Cambon."

"I thought at this time of year—"

"I'm usually at my sister's, yes. But this summer I've been doing some special work here."

"On your stories?"

"No, no stories. They're behind me, I'm afraid. This is an assignment from the school board—a revision of the Cicero text."

"Oh."

"You were the best Cicero student I've ever had. I'd like you to come over some time and see what I'm doing. You might have some suggestions."

Claude nodded vaguely and there was another pause.

"And I'd like to see what *you've* been doing," said Chariol.

"I?"

"Yes, your poems. You must have done tremendous things these last two years."

Claude was silent.

"Don't worry, I won't make the same *gaffe* again. I won't ruffle your feathers the way I once did." For that moment his tone was light, almost bantering. Then with deep earnestness he said, "Whatever mistakes I've made—and whatever you've made—remember this: I am your friend. And if I can help you in any way, I want to with all my heart."

"Thank you, Albert," said Claude.

"So"—once more the smile—"we shall see each other?"

They shook hands. They parted. Claude went home and upstairs and into his room and sat down on the cot. He did not go out the next day. Or the next. Or the next.

Felix slept and snored there: that was all. His mother left him alone, and there was no need to block the door or to climb out the window to the privy. He sat on his cot. At long intervals he rose from the cot, went to the table, and sat with pencil and paper before him. But he did not touch them. He simply looked at them, and then out the window, and then presently he went back to the cot.

It was after he had been home almost two months that his mother knocked again and came in.

"Well, son?" she said.

He looked at her without answering.

"You are better now," she said. "It is time to think of the future."

"I'm thinking of it," he told her.

"And what have you decided?"

"I haven't."

"Well you must—and soon. You are well again. You are no longer a child, but a young man. You cannot sit here forever, like an invalid."

Again Claude didn't answer.

"I am a working woman," his mother said. "All my life, since your father left me, I have worked ten, twelve, fourteen hours a day, to support my children, but once my sons are men I expect them to support themselves. To earn their living, to have self-respect. Do you understand?"

Her voice was firm, hard, flat. Not a shout or a scream, as it had used to be. And his own voice was quiet as he answered her.

"Yes, Mother," he said, "I understand."

"I had thought once that you would have a fine career. That you would go to the university, be a gentleman, become a lawyer, banker, doctor— even, by God's grace, a priest of the church. But that is over now. You chose differently. You did not want such things."

"No," he said.

"So what will it be then? Do you want to work in the store?"

"No."

"In another store? On a farm?"

"No."

"As a laborer? As an imbecile, an animal—like your brother?"

"No."

"What then?"

"The only thing I know," he said, "is how to write."

"So—you still have that crazy notion?" His mother looked at him speculatively. "You wrote much while you were away?" she asked.

"Yes."

"And sold anything?"

"No."

"You write all these years and sell nothing, and you say that is how you will make your living?" Claude was silent, and, still watching him, she shook her head. "I do not understand you, boy," she said at last. "No, I do not understand."

She sighed. It was the first time in his life Claude had heard her sigh. . . . Then she tightened and straightened; the iron returned to her spirit. "But let God never say of me that I am not patient, not enduring. I tell you what I shall do. I shall give you one more chance. Give me the things you have written, and I shall send them to the editor of the *Journal des Ardennes*.

His wife is now a customer of mine. Since there are no decent stores in Antimes she comes to me; and her husband has been here too, several times. He is a fine man: prosperous, of good family. And most charming. I shall send your things to him, and if he likes anything, buys anything, we shall go on from there. But if he does not, it is the end—do you understand. If you cannot earn a living, this nonsense must stop!"

Claude still sat on the cot. She looked at him, waiting. "Well, let me have them," she said. "I will send them to the *Journal*—at once, today."

"I have nothing," said Claude.

"Have nothing? You just said—"

"My poems are in Paris and London."

"You can send for them then."

"No, I cannot send for them."

"You mean they are lost?"

"Yes, they are lost."

His mother drew in a deep breath, but this time it was not a sigh. Her hands were clenched, her lips tight. In the next instant, it seemed certain, the lips would open and scream at him.

But no scream came. Instead she said quietly: "Then you remember them, perhaps? You can write them again?"

"I don't know," said Claude.

"Or write something new—and better?"

"I don't know."

"Then it is time to find out. It is now near the end of August. I will give you a month: to the end of September. For a month more I will feed you, clothe you, support you, as I always have, and you can do as you like. But if you have done nothing by then, it is the end; I am through. You will work or you will get out. You will shame me no longer."

She looked down at him: face white, eyes black and burning. "If you are a writer—write," she said.

Then she turned and went out.

For a long time he sat where he was. Then he arose and crossed to the table and sat looking at the pencil and paper that lay upon it.

If you are a writer—write.

But what?

The horror was gone, but so were the dreams. The pit had closed, but so had the windows. The only window was the one beside him. It looked out on a yard, a privy, a fence, a plane tree, dust.

He looked away. The windows had never opened outward. They had opened inward. On himself. That was all he had ever written: himself. . . . But in the past he had at least known what that self was: the seer, the thief of fire, the I-who-is-another. And now there were none of these. No vision, no fire, no *other*. There was himself, and what was that?

What had happened to him? What was left of him?

Perhaps by writing he could find out.

To the Editor of the Journal des Ardennes. *Dear Sir*—he wrote. *May I submit a droll story for your Sunday edition?*

He smiled.

Permit me to begin at the beginning. . . .

And he wrote: *Once, if I remember well, my life was a feast where all hearts opened and all wines flowed . . .*

But this time he went on.

. . . One evening I sat Beauty on my knees. And I found her bitter. And I cursed her. . . . I armed myself against justice. I fled. . . . O Witches, Misery, Hate: to you has my treasure been entrusted.

I contrived to purge my mind of all human hope. On all joy, to strangle it, I pounced with the stealth of a wild beast.

I called to the executioners while dying to let me gnaw the butt-ends of their guns. I called to the plagues to smother me in blood, in sand. Misfortune was my god. I laid myself down in the mud. I dried myself in the air of crime. I played sly tricks on madness. . . .

He paused and looked from the window: at the yard, the fence, the wooden privy. Beyond the wall rose the plane tree, its leaves dry and dusty in the summer sun.

. . . And summer, he wrote, *brought the hyena's frightful laughter.*

He listened and heard the laughter. He left his room, left the house, walked the streets, and the laughter followed. The laughter of an idiot, a hyena; his own laughter. . . . And something else followed him too. Or someone else. The devil. Satan. He walked into an alley and sat on the cobbles, as he had used to sit, with paper on knees and pencil in hand. And the devil sat beside him.

"You *are the hyena," said the devil. "Go find death, with your appetites and your egotism and all the deadly sins!"*

"Ah, *I'm fed up! . . . But, dear Satan, a less fiery eye, I beg you. Look: it is for you I am writing this. For you let me tear out these few hideous pages from my logbook of the damned."*

He got up. He walked on. He walked out of the town, along the roads, along the Meuse, into the forest. He walked through the dark glades of the Ardennes and sat at the foot of a great tree.

Here, of all places, he thought, was the place of beginnings. The place he had come to as the merest child—for refuge, for escape—from his mother, from school, from church, from imprisonment. Here he had begun his revolt, declared himself a Gaul, a Hun, a savage, an outlaw. *I am of a distant race*, he had said. *My ancestors were Norsemen. They used to pierce their sides, drink their own blood. . . . I will cover myself with gashes; tattoo my body. I want to be as ugly as a Mongol; you'll see, I will howl through the streets. I want to become raving mad. Never show me jewels; I should grovel and writhe on the floor. My riches, I want them splattered all over with blood. . . .*

So—he had had his riches, his jewels, his treasure. The treasure that was his genius. And he had splattered it with blood. He had steeped it in slime, in ordure. He had found his freedom—and damnation.

He bowed his head; he covered his face with his hands. But a moment later he ripped them away. He looked up. "No, none of that!" he thought fiercely. "No self-pity—ever." "Be strong, be proud," his mother had said. And he would be, always. As he had been, always. For that, and that alone, no suffering and no defeat could take from him: that in all his life, in all he had thought and felt and written and done, he had never lost his strength or his pride.

He had his paper. He had his pencil. . . . *Was it from you, Mother,* he wrote, *that these came to me? With your bitter milk? . . . Then, thank you, Mother. And damn you, Mother . . . Was it your pride, transmitted to me, become* my *pride, that turned me against you; that made your white my black, your true my false, your good my evil?* His mother was a Catholic, fearing God and hell. Had he therefore become a pagan because God and hell have no power over pagans? His mother lived her life by the judgments of society. Had he therefore become a savage because society had no power over savages? . . . Partly, perhaps. But not wholly . . . There had been more to his life than defiance; more than revolt. In the beginning, at least, it had possessed a great affirmation. He had gone forward, unstoppably. He had broken all barriers. He had been all things that the world forbade him to be: mountebank, beggar, artist, scoundrel—priest. Yes, most of all, priest. Priest of a faith more pure and holy than any dreamed of in church or temple. Priest of the word, the image, the vision, the revelation. Of the night and the sunburst, of the storm and the rainbow.

He wrote: *I dreamed crusades, unrecorded voyages of discovery, republics without a history, religious wars hushed up, revolutions of customs, the displacements of races and continents: I believed in sorcery of every sort. . . . I invented the colors of vowels: A black, E white, I red, O blue, U green. I regulated the form and movement of every consonant, and with instinctive rhythms I prided myself on inventing a poetic language accessible some day to all the senses. . . . I was a master of phantasmagoria. I fixed frenzies in their flight. I wrote silences. I wrote the night. I wrote the Apocalypse.*

Oh yes, he had had pride. He had had genius, and the pride of genius. Consciously and deliberately he had followed his course, followed his star, transformed himself from a country *mioche,* a *beau gosse* in a blue serge suit, into a poet and a prophet, a mystic and a seer. The barriers broken, he had become the I-who-is-another, a man beyond men, a voyager beyond the walls of the mortal prison. He had embraced everything; felt himself capable of everything. In his pride he had said: *I have all the talents. There is no one here, and there is someone: I would not squander my treasures. Do you want Negro songs, the dances of houris? Do you want me to vanish, to dive after The Ring? Is that what is wanted? I will make gold. I will make remedies.*

I beg you, hold out your hand to me, he had once written. And he in turn had sought to hold out his hand to the world. *Trust in me then,* he had said. *Trust assuages, guides, restores. Come, all of you, even the little children; that I may comfort you, that my heart may be poured out for you. The marvelous heart. . . .*

But the world had not trusted. It had turned on him, spat on him, flayed him, raped him. The marvelous heart had become the ravaged heart. He had gathered it back to himself. For himself alone he would make his journey; he would unveil the mysteries—birth and death, past and future, universe and atom, totality and nothingness. Alone, in his Drunken Boat, he had sailed the wild seas of God; alone he had become one with the seas; one with God Himself.

Or so he had thought. . . .

But now?

Now he sat in the forest of the Ardennes. Now he walked the roads, stood beside the Meuse, sat in his room at night, at the old table, by the old window, while the crickets buzzed in the yard and his brother snored in his bed. Now his journey had come full circle and he was back where he had started—but now strengthless, dreamless; the golden birds still far beyond horizons, his brave boat sunk and rotted on the ocean floor.

What had gone wrong, then? On what reef had he foundered?

Had it been pride itself? The pride of Lucifer? The pride of Faust? . . ."I will make gold," he had said. Like Faust, he had been an alchemist. He had made the alchemist's descent into hell and had believed, in his pride, that from that descent he would bring back his gold; that he would bring back power, purity, vision, redemption. But he had found none of them. Or, if he had briefly found one—and that was vision—none of it was now left. "I am not more than man, not the equal of God!" Faust had cried out at the end. "I am only the worm which the foot of the traveler crushes underfoot and buries in the earth." And now he too had learned this. It was no longer *"Merde à Dieu"* that he cried, but—bitter, broken—*"Merde à moi."*

In hell he had found—only hell. The Seven Tabernacles of Hell. A symphony of hells. The hell of self, and that was the worst. The hell of jail and barracks, of vice and debauch, of lie and illusion, of drink and drug. The hell of loneliness. The hell of Druard.

And *why* Druard? Why had that happened? . . . Perhaps, in the beginning, because it had seemed the antidote to loneliness; because Druard had reached out to him the hand he had so desperately needed. But there had been more to it than that. There had been not only loneliness, but pride—again pride, always pride—for Druard, alone among all men, had seen him as he wished to be seen. *"You are not a man,"* he had said. *"You are a god, a demon. You are Attila, Apollo, Lucifer, Antichrist."* And in the spell of their companionship—in their cave of absinthe and hashish, dream and vision—he, Claude, had come to believe this himself.

He had written the testament of his childhood, of his revolt, of his escape, of his quest. Now in the night, in his old room with his brother snoring, he wrote the testament of himself and Druard. He wrote it with savageness and tenderness, venom and compassion, mockery and pity. He called it *Delirium: The Foolish Virgin, the Infernal Bridegroom*. And its last line —mocking, acrid—was *What a honeymoon!*

"Your light was burning late last night," his mother commented.

"Yes," he said.

"You are writing much?"

"Yes."

"You should soon have something ready to send to the *Journal*."

"Yes, soon."

Then the door closed again. Felix was out, and he lay on his cot.

"You are not a man," Druard had said.

Not a man, not a man, not a man . . .

And now no longer a demon; no longer Lucifer.

What then?

"You *are* a man," another had said.

A man to whom? To his mother, his sister? To Mimi Rouger—the farm woman—the London whore? . . . To the one who herself had said it?

Love must be reinvented, he had written.

To suit himself?

He had shut women away. He had shut love away. He had followed his own path—proudly, relentlessly—trying to be not as other men were but as different as possible from other men. He had tried to achieve his "derangement of the senses," and he had succeeded, and in his youth and pride he had regarded as sacred the disorder of his mind. "I must make my soul monstrous," he had said; and by monstrous he had meant prodigious, encompassing, Faustian, godlike. But in doing so he had attained another sort of monstrosity as well: a monstrosity of debauch, of vice, of self-mutilation and self-destruction that had brought him to the rim of the pit.

He rose and went to his table. At the top of a page he set down— *Delirium Compounded: The Alchemist of the Word*. And he wrote: *My justification was my poetry. "I am a poet," I said. "That is the root of the tree, the foundation of the building, the heart of it all: that I am a poet." But soon—how soon!—I discovered that there is no place for a poet in the modern world. So I created my own world. I created it out of strength and pride, out of genius and vision, out of dream and desire, and as I fashioned it I looked upon it and I saw that it was good.*

But it was not good.

For the world that he had thought to make was not a world. It was a refuge, a cocoon, a cave, and in that cave he had walked through darkness: a somnambulist. In his outward life he had not been the great free soul he had fancied himself, but only another adolescent rebel, a *voyou*, a cheap Bohemian. And as a poet he had been—just that: a poet. In his arrogance he had become convinced of his power to find a new tongue, to "steal fire from heaven," to open windows that had forever been closed to men. And it had been self-delusion. He had merely wallowed in the onanism of words, of image, of uncontrolled fantasy, and what he had conceived to be his liberation had been, instead, even deeper imprisonment. . . . *I called my poems* Illuminations. *I should have called them* Hallucinations. *For that is what they were: the distillations of a false alchemy, of pride and blindness, leading me on toward a pit of darkness. The windows of the soul are still closed. The Tree of Good and Evil still stands. In my frenzy of living and of creation I achieved no mystical union with God—but only chaos. It was a debacle. It has left me bankrupt. I seized beauty, I seized truth, I seized freedom; and my hands are empty. Howling underneath the leaves, the wolf spits out the lovely plumes of his feast of fowls. And like him I am consumed.*

He returned to his bed. He slept. He dreamed. . . . But the dreams were quieter now. The black terror had faded. The pit had closed. . . . Sometimes, in the nights that followed, he rose again and went to his table.

Dreams, he wrote. *Dreams have been the enemy. They have crowded round too thick.*

And—*I have done all I could. I can do no more.*

And—*I sought self-realization. And what was achieved? Self-crucifixion.*

And—*De profundis, Domine—what a fool I have been!*

Fragments.

He could write nothing more. Without the frenzy of living, the frenzy of creation, he was no longer a madman. But he was also no longer a poet. If the madness was gone, so too was the foundation, the root, the heart of his being.

What was left was . . . fragments.

He had descended from his own cross, but he could not kneel at the other. "No, mother; no, sister; no, Father Lacaze. No hymns, please. No rosaries. No holy water."

He had returned to his beginnings—to Cambon—but in Cambon he would forever be an alien. "No thank you, Albert—no Cicero. No thank you, Michel—no cowflop."

What then?

He had re-entered the world of men. He must walk among men. But could he? Could he himself be a man, or was he maimed and ravaged beyond repair—a thing of shreds and fragments, like the dreams that had been his life? Had he reached final disintegration and dissolution, or was there something, somewhere in the world, that could restore him, make him whole? . . . Faust, in the end, had been saved. Could *he* be? . . . Where could he turn? To what? Or to whom? *To become a man a man a man a man a man.* . . .

He sat deep in the forest, and the forest was dark. Overhead, leaves and branches mingled and intertwined and made a roof—like the roof of a cave; but in the roof, high above him, were two holes, two breaks in the shadow, and beyond them he could see the sky. It was violet blue and gleaming, and through the holes it seemed to watch him, like two eyes.

It was early fall when he said to his mother, "I am going away again."

"Away? Where?" Then she thought she understood. "Oh, you mean you have finished your writing? You are taking it to Antimes—to the editor of the *Journal?*

"No, I am not going to Antimes."

"Not Antimes? Where then? What for?

"I am going on a pilgrimage."

"A pilgrimage?" She looked at him blankly.

"Not to Jerusalem, Mother," he said. "To Paris."

15

. . . I think of you always. When you need and want me I am waiting . . .

The paper was crumpled, the words smudged with dirt. But they were still there. There before his eyes, as he stopped and read; there in his pocket, as he moved on. The leaves of the chestnut trees were brown and red, and they were falling. They swirled about his head and crackled under his feet, while he walked on through the streets of the city.

His mother—for his mother—had not been difficult. "Paris?" she had demanded. "Again Paris? Why?" And he had answered, "To see an editor." "Who might buy something?" "Yes." "He has showed interest?" "Yes." And at last she had conceded that a Parisian magazine might promise more to a poet than the *Journal des Ardennes.*

She had given him enough money for his train fare (third class) and a week of frugal living. He had folded the dozen-odd pages he had recently written into an envelope and taken the early morning train. His new suit was neat, his face clean, his hair combed; and there had been no hiding from ticket takers, no leap onto ties and cinders. It had been noon when he reached the Gare de l'Est, and now it was half past two and he was on the Champs Elysées, approaching the Etoile. The timing was right.

And it was still right when, a while later, he walked through the prim and sunlit avenues of Passy and stopped at the curb in front of the now familiar school. For it was only a few minutes after his arrival that the doors opened and the girls came out. In their blue jackets and white blouses they streamed down the steps, toward him, past him, chattering their way along the pavements and fanning off down the tree-lined streets. His palms were cold. He felt his heart thump. He watched and waited. And the stream flowed past and thinned, and still he stood there. He stood until there were only a few stragglers, and then the teachers came out, singly and in pairs; and then they were gone and there was no one. A concierge appeared, locked the door, and disappeared behind it, and he was alone on the street among the falling leaves.

It was not until several minutes later that the obvious occurred to him: that she was no longer at the school. That she was the same age as he—eighteen, almost nineteen—and that, in the natural order of things, she would have graduated the previous spring. His mind groped and fumbled. . . . Graduated. No longer a schoolgirl. In the deep cave of his dreams, of his self-absorption, it had been only he who lived, who experienced, who grew and changed. He had forgotten that others lived lives, others grew and changed, as well.

Oh yes, he had done a thorough job on his derangement of the senses. . . .

He moved away from the school. He walked slowly, and for a while aimlessly. Then resolution came. Looking around, he took his bearings; he turned a corner, walked several blocks, turned another corner, and followed still another tree-lined street; he passed a house, and a second house, and before the third house he stopped and waited a few moments, and then he walked up the path and pulled the bell cord.

He heard a ringing inside. He felt the beat of his heart. Then a maid, in a cap and apron, opened the door, and he said, "Is Mademoiselle Lautier at home?"

"Mademoiselle—?"

"Yes."

The maid eyed him distrustfully. "I—I am not sure," she said.

"Would you find out, please."

"Who should I say is calling?"

"A friend. An old friend."

The maid hesitated. Then she said, "You will wait, please." Another moment of hesitation followed, as she made a half-movement to close the door; but she decided against it and left it open. From the stoop Claude could see her cross a wide foyer and ascend a staircase, not unlike those of the de Bercys' house in Montmartre.

Again he waited. He could see nothing but foyer and stairs. Then the maid reappeared, coming down the stairs, and there was someone following her. But it was not Germaine. It was a young man in his early twenties, tall, well-built, and handsome, and he crossed the foyer to Claude and said, "Yes?"

"I would like to see Mademoiselle Lautier," Claude said.

"About what, may I ask?"

"I'm a friend. An old friend."

"Oh?"

The young man's eyes were blue—violet blue—but they were not gleaming. They were narrowed and sharp and they looked at Claude steadily. "I am Mademoiselle Lautier's brother," he said, "and I'm afraid I must ask you to tell me a little more."

"More?"

"Your name, for instance."

Claude didn't answer.

"You do not choose to tell me your name?" Young Lautier waited. "Very well," he said, "I will tell it to *you*. You are Morel—aren't you?"

"Yes, I am Claude Morel."

There was a moment's silence. Claude saw the face tighten, a hand move. Then face and hand were gone, and there was only the door. The door was heavy and it swung fast and hard. Standing close, he was hit on the face and shoulder and the bad knee, and he reeled back onto the stoop and almost fell, but not quite. The door slammed and he stood facing it. Clenching his fist, he rushed forward and struck at it, and a sharp pain flashed through his knuckles. The door did not even quiver. There was no sound from inside the house.

For a while he stood where he was, and the only sound was his breathing. Then he turned away. From the other side of the street he looked across at the house, but all the windows were curtained. His hand throbbed. His knee ached. After a few minutes he walked slowly down the leafy street.

He walked. . . .

Again he walked. Always he walked.

He passed a clock and it said four thirty. He passed another and it said six. He was in the Bois de Boulogne, in the Etoile, on the Champs, in the Place de la Concorde. He was on the Rue de Rivoli, and it was night, and the shop fronts glittered, and the gas lamps flared. Off to the left now, where the streets were narrow and the lamps dimmer, were Les Halles and the slum warrens and the Hôtel de Babylone. But he didn't turn left. He kept straight ahead and then turned right. He crossed a bridge and the

Ile de la Cité and then another bridge and was on the Boulevard St. Michel. He walked up the Boul' Mich between the lights and sounds of the cafés.

He passed the entrance of the Rue de Lacque. He came to a café—one of the old cafés—and found a table and sat down. A waiter came and asked what he wanted, and he said, "A lemonade."

"We have no lemonade."

"Then some other juice."

"We have no juices."

"What *do* you have?"

"Spirits, wine, beer."

"Very well then, *un vin rouge.*"

The waiter brought it, with its saucer, and it was so long since he had had a drink that even wine seemed strong to him. He sipped it slowly. Then, setting it down, he brought out paper and pencil. *Dear Germaine* —he wrote.

And that was all he wrote.

Dear Germaine—what?

Before, it had seemed so clear, so well-defined. He would go to Paris, on his pilgrimage. He would go to her: the one who waited, who had said, "I love you"; the one of whom he had been afraid but now must fear no longer. He would say to her, "I am soiled, ravaged, fragmented. I have deranged my life, as I have deranged my senses. I have come to the blank end of nothingness, to the rim of the pit. And now only you can help me. Only you can cleanse me, heal me, make me whole, make me a man. That above all—a man." . . . And she would take him, accept him. And in her acceptance he would find strength again: the strength to live, to feel, to think, to work, to write. . . . Oh yes, to write—still to write. For that was part of it, the heart of it, the root and foundation. And all he knew. . . . He had not lied to his mother when he had said he was going to Paris to see an editor. That was part of the plan too. He would go to Herz of the *Nouvelle Revue*; he would show him his new work, tell him of his new life; he would offer everything he had to Herz, everything he would do in the future, and Herz, in return, would give him the work he had once offered, make him a reader, a subeditor, tide him over the period of trial and adjustment. For the first time in his life he would not only write, but make a living from it. He would support himself—support Germaine—as she, with her love, would support him. His loneliness and apartness behind him, he would become at last a man among his fellows. A man with a woman, a man living, a man working. A man. . . .

His original plan had been to go first to Herz, and then on to Germaine with job and livelihood in his hand. But it had not worked that way; first things had come first, and his feet had taken him from the Gare de l'Est to Passy, beyond the power of his will to change their course. As it turned out, it had been a horrid debacle. Humiliation and anger still burned in him. Even as he thought of it, his hand tightened around his wineglass, and he wished the young snot of a Lautier would pass by so that he could throw it in his face.

But at least nothing had happened that was irremediable. . . . His hand relaxed. He sipped his wine. . . . He could still reach Germaine: by letter, another visit, somehow. And she would come to him—that he knew. Whatever the obstacles, whatever the penalties, in her strength and love she would come to him. . . . All that was needed was rearrangement. Now Herz first, she second—the original sequence. That was why he had come here, to this particular café: because it was Herz's regular place; because in all the months he, Claude, had lived in the *Quartier Latin* he had scarcely known Herz to miss a night.

He finished his wine. He looked around. Herz was not to be seen. But at a large nearby table were other familiar faces and figures: a group of writers, two other editors, a critic, a journalist. They were hunched around their glasses, talking, arguing, as they had always done; indeed, Claude thought, as if they had not ever left the table since he had last been there. But as he turned and saw them, they too saw him. And their talk stopped. In the yellow light of the café's lamps their eyes watched him, fixed and glittering.

For a few moments none of them spoke; the usual café hum continued around him. Then, through the hum, came a voice, loud and clear:

"*Crapule*," it said.

"*Cochon*."

"*Enculé*."

"*Tapette*."

The general hum faded. Other heads turned. One of the writers at the big table half rose from his seat.

"Go back to your sty, pig," he said.

"Don't bring your filth here."

"Who let you out of your sewer?"

"And why?"

"Yes, why?" The one who had half risen was leaning forward, glaring. "Why you and not Druard? They put poor Druard in jail, but let you loose."

"The little lamb," said another.

"The little viper."

"There's the famous old British justice for you! They put a great French poet in jail. Degrade him, shame him, kick him when he's down. And the one who pulled him down? Oh no, he goes free as air."

"To take a walkout."

"To come back here again."

"With his boasts—"

"And his filth."

A figure loomed before Claude. "If you know what is good for you, *salaud*," its voice said, "this will be the last time you show your face around here."

Claude said nothing.

"Do you hear me, *salaud?*"

He still said nothing. The man stared at him, and he stared back—as if unseeing, unhearing. Then the man moved away. He went back to the big table, and the talk continued. The café still hummed and the eyes still watched.

Claude beckoned to the waiter.

"Another *rouge*, please."

And this one, too, he drank slowly. He sat straight in his chair. He held his head high. At intervals he turned and looked around, past the big table, down the length of the café, and at last he saw what he was looking for. One of the tables that had been empty was now occupied by two men who had just come in. The first whom his eye fell on was a stranger to him, but the other was Herz.

He finished his wine. Then he got up. Passing the big table, he made his way down the aisle of watching eyes. When he came to Herz's table he stopped and said, "Good evening."

The two men looked up. The stranger's eyes were blank; Herz's, as always, were soft and sad behind his glasses.

Neither spoke.

"Good evening," Claude repeated.

Herz looked at him for another moment. Then he said, "Go away." His voice was gentle—as soft and sad as his eyes.

"I—I only want—"

"Go away, boy. Please—go away."

Herz turned his head. He drew a folded manuscript from his pocket, spread it open on the table, and, with his companion, bent over it.

"Monsieur Herz—"

A waiter came. *"Pardon—"* Moving in front of Claude, he set down two drinks, and the saucers rattled. *"Pardon—"* and he was gone. There was no sound at all now, not even the humming, as Claude walked away under the watching eyes.

He passed the big table. He went to his own. He sat down. Presently his own waiter came and said, *"Encore un rouge?"*

He nodded, and the waiter turned. Then he said, "No. No—*une absinthe.*"

He still sat straight. His face was expressionless. The waiter brought bottle and glass and poured the drink, and he drank it slowly. The effect of the wine had been quick and heady, but the absinthe was different—slow, deep and coiling—and he could feel it spreading through every cell and adit of his body.

When the drink was gone he ordered another.

"Better get two," said a voice from the big table. "One in memory of your boy friend."

The eyes still watched him, except those of Herz and his companion, who were deep in conversation. The lights above them seemed no longer yellow but a yellowish green.

"*Garçon!*" He reached for his money. . . . Then he put it back. No, the hell with that! . . . "*Garçon*, another absinthe. Two." He indicated the empty chair beside him. "One for my friend who will be joining me."

Raising his newly filled glass, he turned to the big table. "To French literature, messieurs," he said. "To beauty and truth and the great art with which you serve them."

He drained the glass. Then he drained the other. He looked out past the rim of the café awning at the crowd that moved by on the Boul' Mich. It was the same crowd as always—the same that was in the café: writers, artists, students, loafers: the parade of Bohemia. And among them, usually apart from them, the women. The charwomen in their broken shoes; the whores in their shiny shoes—shiny dresses—bags swinging, rumps swinging, eyes tired and watchful. The eyes of one of them met his, and he almost beckoned. But he didn't. "No, no more Fannys," he thought. And she went by. The parade went by. . . . Then along with the parade came a new figure; new but familiar; not a woman but a man. Claude first saw the red cloak, then the black beard, the chalk face. Dar Misheram went by, and this time he did beckon. But Misheram did not see him. He moved on, his lips moving, his head raised to some unimaginable vision beyond the gas lamps, and Claude rose to intercept him. "Dar! Dar!" Suddenly it was of great importance to intercept him, to speak to him: the one man in all the *Quartier*—all Paris—who would share his table and his aloneness.

Then a voice spoke:

"Claude—"

But it was not Dar Misheram's. It was not from the café. As he turned, a figure detached itself from the passing crowd and in an instant was beside him, close against him. A hand held his; a face looked into his. "Thank God, oh thank God!" said Germaine.

Then he was sitting again, and she was sitting beside him. Her hand still held his. She was talking on—softly, tensely:

"I've looked everywhere, Claude. The last hour. Maybe two. Up and down the boulevard, in the side streets, the Rue de Lacque, the cafés. I was sure you'd be here, like you used to be. Here somewhere—"

He stared at her. "But how—how did—"

"I was home when you came there. Upstairs. I didn't know it was you, of course, but I heard the bell and my brother going down, and then the door slam. When he came back I asked who it was, and he wouldn't say, and then I knew it had been someone for me; and I kept asking, I kept pestering, and at last he told me it was you; and then I waited, I waited until I had my chance and ran out, and I ran a few blocks and took a coach and came here, and since then I've been looking and looking—" The words had come tumbling out, but now suddenly she stopped. She caught her breath and smiled and her hand pressed his tightly. "And now I've found you!" she said in triumph.

Claude sat motionless. He still stared. At the figure that magically, incredibly, had appeared beside him. At the hand on his, the sleeve of her coat, at its shoulders, its collar; at the face above the collar, so well remembered, turned to him, watching him, glowing with excitement and fulfillment. It was still the same face, half a girl's, half a woman's—perhaps more a woman's now—but still the same—with its rich brown hair, wide brow, full mouth, soft cheekline. With its eyes—yes, most of all the eyes —the same as ever; not green or greenish yellow, as was everything else wavering about him, but blue and clear and deep and steady, the blue of O, omega, violet-deep, violet-blue. . . .

"Oh Claude—dearest—"

He closed his own eyes. Blue turned to green; green slowly coiling. . . . Lips touched his cheek.

Blue returned.

"—I was so miserable before. So lost and afraid, afraid I'd never find you. . . . And now so happy. . . . Claude, do you know something? Every day—yes, every day since you went away—I've thought of you, prayed for you; prayed that you were all right, that you'd come back. The note I wrote you to London: you got it? Yes, I know you got it. That's why you're here. . . . Oh darling. . . . It wasn't easy to write it, you know; nice *jeunes filles* aren't supposed to do such things. But it was even harder not to do it again; not to write every week, every day. . . . And then when you didn't answer it was the worst of all. I imagined all sorts of things; terrible things; that you really meant it when you turned away from me. . . . And then I wanted to die. Yes, truly. My family could tell you: how I was at home. They thought I was sick—wanted to call doctors. And they were right, really: I was sick. Sick at heart. . . . Until today. Until now. . . ."

The rush of words stopped. There was a pause. When she went on it was slowly and very quietly: "Because now you've come back," she said. "You came to me once before—that day at school—remember? And now again. After two years, again. And now I know you want me."

Another pause. This time she smiled. "So I've come twice, too," she added. "Once before, once now. That makes us even."

He looked at her. That was all he could do: look at her. At her eyes; at their violet blue. Away from the other eyes, the other tables, the blur of voices, the haze of green. Through blur and haze one voice came clearly: "The sod's got himself a chicken. Poor Sister Maurice must be rattling his bars."

Germaine did not seem to hear. Or if she heard, it meant nothing to her. The waiter appeared and asked, "Something for the lady?" and Claude shook his head.

"Oh yes—yes, please!" she said. "I've never had a drink at a café, and I've wanted to for so long. And now's the perfect time—with you—to celebrate—"

"What will it be?" asked the waiter.

"A—a—" She looked at Claude, then at the empty glasses. "Whatever monsieur has been having."

"A vermouth," said Claude.

"A vermouth—good! Two of them. Yours are gone, and this is one drink we must have together."

She was still holding his hand, and she continued holding it while the waiter left and returned, and then with her other hand she raised her glass. "To us, darling," she murmured. "Not to you, not to me. But to us."

Her eyes glowed. They remained fixed on him as she bent her head to drink. And then she was talking again—happily, gaily, excitedly—half woman-talk, half girl-talk—her eyes still on his face, her hand still in his hand. Claude heard her voice, not the words. Behind him he heard other voices—*and* the words.

He heard, "Faggot."

He heard, "Queer-looking whore."

He heard, "Bet she's a he. . . . You know, one of those. . . . Let's find out."

The words hung in green haze. Germaine talked through the haze. Then she had stopped talking. Her eyes were different.

"Is something wrong, Claude?" she asked.

"No. . . . No."

"You're sure?"

"Yes, I'm sure."

She smiled. "When we're together, nothing can be wrong."

But now she was conscious of something in him—and around them. She began talking again, but stopped. She raised her glass and put it down. Her eyes were no longer on him, and her hand, in his, was suddenly tight and tense.

"Claude," she murmured, "they're all staring."

"Yes."

"At us. Why, Claude? Why?"

"How the hell should I know?"

His voice was savage. Suddenly he jerked to his feet. He fumbled in his pocket, threw money on the table, pulled her roughly up.... "Come on." ... In another moment they were part of the crowd on the Boul' Mich.

"Claude—Claude, what is it—?"

He didn't answer. He elbowed on through the crowd, and the gas lamps glared green.

"Where are we going, Claude?"

"I'll take you home."

"Home?"

"Where else is there to go?"

"To your place."

"I don't have a place."

"Then we'll find one. Anywhere—it doesn't matter. I have some money.... Oh, Claude, what is it? What's happened? ... I *came* to you, don't you understand? To stay with you. To be yours."

"Mine.... Christ!"

She was still talking. She was questioning, arguing, pleading, her eyes searching his face with incomprehension and fear. And though the words were soft and gentle they cut into him like knives. All his brain and body were filled with knives, piercing, tearing, rending; as sharp and terrible as the knives of his old hunger for hashish.... "Yes, *mine*," he thought. "Mine to do what with? ... To take to a room, to lie down with, to hold; to hold and hold and then release and turn away and lie in darkness and say at last, 'I am sorry. I cannot love you. I am not a man.' To rise in the morning, to walk the streets, among those who hate me, past the frozen stares, the turned heads, knowing nothing the world wants, having nothing the world needs, and to return to you each evening and say, 'I am sorry. I cannot support you. I am not a man.'"

"Claude—Claude, listen—"

But all he heard were the knives. The click and whir and grind of the knives. The long green knives of the Assassins.

He plunged on. She clung to his arm. Her face was raised to him.

"Claude—dearest—"

But now everything was green. U—green. The green of absinthe, coiling, spinning; the green of lights and lamps and stone and flowing faces; the green of night and Paris and the flowing boulevard, as they fled swiftly, dimly down its pillared halls. Blocks vanished behind them, opened ahead, and now they were running; he was lunging, dodging, battering his way through the crowds, and she was clinging to him, calling his name; and how far they had come, or where they were going, he didn't know, but then they had come to a final block and there were no more beyond it; there was a square, a bridge, the river, and they were running across the square, past the crowds, into the open, through a green gleaming—and then others were running, others were shouting, breaking out of the crowd, drawing closer, and he saw the uniforms and the tricornes and heard the voice yelling, "There! There they are—" and he saw young Lautier, Germaine's brother, pointing, running, and the police running, all running together, their faces green, their clubs green, green and long and raised, like knives. . . .

Then no knives, no green, nothing.

. . . And later, grayness. Gray stone. A stone floor. He was lying on the floor and raising his head, and from a corner of the cell a face was watching him. At first it was a gross face, bleared and bearded. Then it changed and was thinner—thin and fragile—with high cheekbones, high forehead, slanted eyes. The eyes watched him for a while, and they were full of sadness. Then they faded, the face faded; and he was alone.

As he had been always alone. . . .

In his room. At his table. By the window. Beyond the window the yard was gray with frost, and the branches of the plane tree above the privy stood brown and bare against the winter sky.

Pencil and paper lay before him. Taking the pencil, he wrote: *To the Editor of the* Journal des Ardennes. *Dear Sir: May I continue my little story?*

Two months had passed since he had last written. Two months in three acts and a prologue. Or, perhaps, one act and three epilogues. Listing them backward, he had now been home for ten days; he had been on the road (with stopovers) for fifteen; he had been in jail for thirty. Add to them one day—the first—the Day of the Knives. Total: fifty-six. Two months. Or close enough.

His mother had received him quietly, as before. She had let him go to his room and close the door, and it was not until he had been back almost a week that she knocked and entered and stood tall and black before him.

"It did not go well?" she asked.

"No."

"The publishers did not buy your things?"

"No."

"So then you have wasted two months, *hein?* You should have done in the first place what I told you to and let me send them to the *Journal* at Antimes."

"Perhaps."

"Well anyhow, we will do it now. Here, give me your papers." She put out her hand. "I will send them off today."

"No," said Claude. "Not today. They're not ready yet."

"Not ready? After all this time?"

"I still have more to do."

His mother's tight lips grew still tighter. Her eyes kindled. The outburst was close, but she controlled it. "I see," she said. "And how long now will this 'more' take you?"

"I don't know," he said.

"You don't know?" Her lips were white. Her clenched hands were white. "Well, if you don't I *do*, and I will tell you. It will take you exactly one week and no longer. Not by a day, not by an hour. A week from this minute you will give me what you have written to send to the *Journal;* or it is the end, do you understand? The end of this nonsense. Forever—"

She turned and went out, and he sat alone at his table. He sat and looked from the window: at the yard, the tree, the privy—at nothing—and then he folded his arms on the table and laid his head upon them. How long he remained there he didn't know; but presently a strange thing happened, for he became aware that he was no longer alone, and, raising his head, he saw that his mother had re-entered the room. She was standing at the door and watching him, and as their eyes met she said quietly: "Be strong, son. Be proud. Be a man."

Then she turned and went out again.

Yes, be a man. But I am not a man. I am fragments.

I was a captain, a master mariner, sailing my Drunken Boat. But now the boat is piled up on the reef: a wreck, a derelict. I was a mountaineer, a climber of the peaks. But I climbed too far, too high; and I fell. I committed the sin of pride —I knew the hubris *of the ancient Greeks—and God has long known what to do with pride; the gods with* hubris.

I am fragments. Put the fragments together and there is still no man. The blood is bad, the mind warped, the body ravaged. I can give neither friendship to man nor love to woman.

I am a beast, a brute, a nigger.

He left his room and the house. He walked. He walked through the back streets and out of the town and along the roads and the river to the forest. Again he plunged deep into the forest: the dark forest of his beginnings.

Very well then, I am a nigger.

An outcast. A criminal. . . . Yes, a criminal too, for he had been judged. Priests, professors, masters—they had all judged him. Life had judged him. Love had judged him. And all had found him wanting. "You are not a man," they had said. And he said, "No, I am something better. I am a force, a spirit. I am poet, prophet, alchemist, mystic, seer. I am more than man." But they said, "No, you are less." . . . And they were right.

He had tried to heighten, to intensify, his life to the ultimate pitch, to embrace all experience, to transcend his individuality and become the I-who-is-another. But all he had accomplished was to lose the I-who-was-himself. Like Faust, he had sold himself to the devil—to the Demon of the Absolute. And the Demon had claimed its own. He was not a man, but what was left of a man: a death's head, the *caput mortuum* of his own alchemy, the ash and dross that was left when the flame went out.

Very well then. I am ash and dross. But I still AM. *I still exist....* And he would continue to exist. To go on. To be that which he was—steadfastly, remorselessly—and the judges could take it or leave it. If there was no seed within him, there was iron. If no fire, there was stone. Man or nigger, he could still be strong, still be proud, with the strength and pride of his dark heritage; of his aloneness, his apartness; of the black bitch, the Nigger Queen, who was his mother.

He had been damned. He had been in hell. But he could be saved.... How?... How was a nigger saved? A pagan? A savage?

I shall enter the Kingdom of Savages, the Kingdom of Ham. My day here is done; I'm quitting Europe. Sea air will burn my lungs; strange climates will burn my skin. To swim, to trample the grass, to hunt, to smoke the kill; to drink liquors strong as boiling metal—like my dear ancestors around their fires.

A smile. The old smile. Slow, sardonic....

I shall return with limbs of iron, dark skin and furious eye; people will think to look at me that I am of a strong race. I shall have gold; I shall be idle and brutal. Women nurse these fierce invalids, home from hot countries. I shall be mixed up in politics. Saved.... Ah yes. SAVED.

Ah yes. But with the smile.

Then, smile fading; *ah no.*

Salvation was not in that. Not in return. Not anywhere in the world he had lived in; not in anything he had known or done.... Above all, not in what he was doing now. In writing. In words.... For what were words to a nigger?

Dear God, no more words! I turn from them, leave them. I bury the dead in my belly. My pilgrimage is not to Paris, not to centers, capitals, portals, towers, but to the far places, the wild hidden places; the seas, the deserts, the forests, the forest rivers. On the riverbank, see—the black dancing files. The savages, my brothers. The niggers, my brothers. Shouts, drums: dance, dance, dance, dance! ... And beyond the dance the tall one, the black shining one. The Nigger Queen. The one who waits. The one from whom I came and to whom I shall return.

No more words. But what were these?

No more dreams. But what were these?

The papers were high on his table, and his mother looked at them.

"You have written a lot," she said.

"Yes."

"It is almost a book."

"Yes. My Savage Book. My Nigger Book."

"*What?*"

"Those are my names for it."

"*Un tas d'idioties!* Well, you will change them, let me tell you, before I send them to the *Journal.*"

Words and dreams. Dreams and words. He had been damned by them. He had been in hell.

"I am not a prisoner of reason," he had said in his pride. But he had been a prisoner of unreason, and now reason must be born again. He arose in the night, and the only sound was Felix' snoring. He went to his table and he needed no lamp, for the window was bright with the winter moon. Taking a pencil and paper, he wrote, and what he wrote was a prayer: ... *The world is good. I shall bless life. I shall love my brothers. These are not childish promises; nor the hope of escaping old age and death. God is my strength; yes, I praise God. And let my soul, oh God, redeem its promise, in spite of the night alone and the day on fire.*

The prayer of a nigger, he thought. Of a pagan, a savage. The prayer to the God of the godless.

But still a prayer ...

And if he could pray he could live. Not as he had lived before—no. *No.* Not as the sleepwalker, the illusionist, who imagined himself to be God. Perhaps not as others lived: the sheep-men, the ant-men, who imagined nothing. But yet live—as himself. As the new self he would put together from the fragments of the old.

Much would be lost. Much would be left behind in hell. But still he would rise out of hell. ... *God of Judgment: I repent my sins, but not my dreams. I have been damned by the rainbow, but still I shall follow the rainbow —beyond the seas, beyond the deserts, beyond encompassing night. In the night always—always—my eyes will awake to the silver star, and I will walk in the night, I will walk with the Magi, toward the morning, toward the rainbow, toward the Christmas on earth that is to come.*

The night had paled. Morning came. But not Christmas morning. In his bed, Felix turned heavily and swore in his sleep. The room was cold and gray. And outside it was gray too: a grayness of yard and wall, of boarded privy and naked tree. The light did not illumine. It hid more than it revealed. It hid the moon, the stars, the gleam of night, the shining firmament.

... As he must now hide his own, he thought; his own inner firmament of word and image, dream and vision. ... Close the soul away. Clothe it. Cover its nakedness. A soul is a fearful thing, displeasing to God and man. ... No more vision, no more dream. Faust is dead; and Apollo; and

Lucifer. There is a yard and the privy, the house and the street; the court-room, the factory chimney, the cash drawer. One must live in the world that is. One must be absolutely modern.

Welcome then, new day! Hail, new world and new life!

But first, a final look backward. A long farewell look into the paling sky. . . . *In that sky, once, I saw endless beaches covered with white nations full of joy. Above me a great golden ship waved its flaming pennants in the breezes of morning. I created all festivities, all triumphs, all dramas. I invented new flowers, new stars, new flesh, new tongues. I thought I was acquiring the powers of God. . . . Well, bury the dead. Bury imagination and memory: an artist's and poet's priceless gift flung away. For if I cannot dream I cannot write; if I cannot see I cannot sing.*

Goodbye to that.

And goodbye to you who sang with me. My foolish virgin. My companion of the magic caves: weak, gentle and corrupt. Together we tried to dream our dream of glory, and, holding hands we went down into the pit.

Goodbye to you.

And to you other, too: the one who, in my extremity, my damnation, I thought might raise me from the pit. In you, in your deep violet glow, I dreamed another dream, a dream of woman; but that too was illusion, hallucination, a flickering of chimeras in the pit.

Goodbye to you all.

I shall climb from the pit, but I shall climb alone. I shall go on alone. I have been in hell, but now my Season in Hell is over. And I shall be free to possess truth in one soul and one body.

"Goodbye, Mother," he said.

"Goodbye?"

"The work is finished—on my table—and I'm sure the editor of the *Journal* will send you a great deal of money. I have given it a new title; just right, I think, for the *Journal*. I have called it *A Season in Hell*."

His mother did not seem to hear him. She was looking at his face, at his clothing, at the small canvas bag that he carried slung over shoulder.

"But *you*—" she said. "You say goodbye. Where are you going?"

"On another pilgrimage," he said. "And this one may take longer."

16

The trees were tall and black, like the trees of the Ardennes. But it was not the Ardennes in which he now walked. It was the *Schwarzwald*, the Black Forest, of southern Germany. At the forest's edge, as in the Ardennes, there was a river, but it was not yellow and slow-coiling like the Meuse. It was the upper Rhine, clear, swift, and urgent, and following its bank he came to a bridge and crossed it, and then he was no longer in Germany but in Switzerland. He was in the city of Basel that was now his home.

From Cambon, this time, he had headed not southwest but southeast; not toward Paris but through the Argonne, Lorraine, and Alsace. At first he had not known where he was going, except that it was away again. And then one day he *had* known: it was to Switzerland, the historic land of exiles. The first city he had come to was Basel, and he had stopped there. He had gone to an inn, and presently, when it was discovered that he had no money, he had talked the proprietor out of calling the police and into giving him work. For a month he washed dishes and beer glasses. Then a merchant who drank his beers at the inn gave him a job in his warehouse. Then the merchant's fifteen-year-old son began having trouble with his French at the *Realschule*, and Claude became his tutor; and presently sons of other well-to-do Baselers were also having trouble and he was tutoring them too. When he had enough pupils he quit the warehouse and gave his whole time to teaching, and he did not, as he had in London, either fall asleep or arrive drunk at his appointments. "Now I am an *echter Herr Professor*," he thought. And for the first time in many months he smiled.

He wore the clothes his mother had bought him for the last trip to Paris. And he took care of them. He washed his face, cut and combed his hair, ate at regular hours, slept at night from ten to six. On the streets he bowed politely and said, *"Grüss Gott—guten Tag—wie geht's—jawohl."* All he still needed, he thought, were apple cheeks and cow eyes and he would out-bourgeois the Swissest burgher who ever folded hands over paunch.

One thing only remained of his old self: the need to walk—and walk. Between tutoring appointments he wandered the streets of the city, and on Sundays and other appointmentless days he went farther afield: either southward through the meadows of the canton of Basel, or north across the bridge and the Rhine into Germany and the Black Forest. He walked through the days of autumn: beside the murmuring river, under the sunset of leaves, across the banks of moss and crackling cones and acorns. He walked through the hours and miles and did not tire, and he thought, "I have my strength again, I am well again; even the knee is well, the Achilles' knee, and the infection gone, and the bad blood now pure." In the purity of a forest stream he knelt and washed his face; he plunged his wrists deep and felt the coolness against his blood; he sat beside the stream in the fading light, in the thickening darkness, until it was night —but the night of God, not of the pit—and then he rose and walked on, through the black aisles to the river, along the bank to the bridge, and on into the city and Frau Borchers'.

Frau Borchers was a widow who had neither family nor other lodgers nor curiosity. She had simply one room on the top floor of her house, well removed from her own, and almost the only time Claude saw her—for he ate his meals out—was each Saturday morning when he knocked at her door and handed her the money for his week's rent. He lived in privacy, even in anonymity, for she had never so much as asked his name. On the few occasions she spoke to him she simply called him *monsieur*, with a German accent. So did his pupils. No one else called him anything.

"I, Claude Morel," he thought. "I, Attila. I, Lucifer."

Then, to his pupils: *"Je suis, j'ai été, j'étais, j'avais été, je serais, j'aurais été. . . .* The past conditional, yes. . . . *J'aurais été, tu aurais été, il aurait été.* . . . Do you understand? *Verstehen Sie?* Now repeat please. . . ."

"Gut."

He taught French, but he taught it in German. He had begun thinking in German—almost thought of himself as a German (*jawohl, Herr Feldwebel Gunst*, my friend, my brother); and his new tongue, his identification with the solid stolid burghers of Germanic Basel met the deepest need of his mind and soul. If there was loneliness within him, it was the calm loneliness of self-containment. If there was a void, it was the void of peace. . . . Or so he believed. So he willed it to be. . . . The last root had been torn up, the last cord cut—with Cambon, Paris, France, with everything and everyone in the past. *Ils avaient été.* They had been. And now were no more. He was himself no more, but someone else; again the I-who-is-another, a changeling, a mutant. In time, if all went well, even memory would be gone.

But that time was not yet. For one day in early winter, as he was walking down the main shopping street of the city, he found suddenly that he had stopped, that he was standing before a window, and that he was experiencing the strongest sense of *déjà vu*—of "this-has-happened-before"—that he had ever known. The window was of a toy store, and he had passed it many times; but now it was no longer on the Freiestrasse in Basel but on a small side street in Paris, and he was not a young man of nineteen but a boy of fifteen, a yokel in the great strange city, and he was again staring into the window, that selfsame window, at the bright ranks of toys. He would remain where he was for another moment. He would look around for *flics*. Then he would enter the store. On the counter near the door would be a box of balls, rubber balls of many colors, and he would seize one, a red one, and turn and run; he would run down the street and turn a corner, and then he would stop and look around again, and there would be no one behind him, and he would bounce the ball, once, twice, three times, and smile and put it carefully in his pocket.

Now it would happen. He waited. . . . He entered the store.

"What can I do for the gentleman?" asked a woman behind the counter.

"I am looking for a present."

"A present—surely. For a boy or a girl?"

"A girl."

"Of what age?"

"Of—" He stopped. Four years passed. Yvette was almost sixteen. "I have made a mistake," he mumbled, and left the shop.

Then he was in another shop down the street—a jeweler's—and a man was bringing trays of brooches and bangles.

"How much is this?" asked Claude, holding one up.

"Forty francs, sir."

"Forty—" Claude swallowed. "I—I was—"

The man removed the trays and replaced them with others. "These are our cheaper items," he said. "Not gold, you understand. Merely plated."

"Yes, of course. Plated." Claude looked through them and fixed on a small heart-shaped locket with a blue stone at its center.

"Seven francs," said the jeweler.

He took it. He gave the jeweler the Cambon address and a franc extra for postage. He made out a card, writing *From an admirer*.

Leaving the shop, he had a franc left in his pocket, but he would get three francs from a tutoring session that afternoon and six more from two sessions the next day.

Christmas came. Then the new year. Outdoors there was snow, and indoors there were irregular verbs. Then one day he was again walking down the main shopping street, past the toy store and the jewelry store, and as he came to the latter the jeweler looked out through the window and saw him and beckoned.

When Claude went in he said, "You are the one who bought a little locket a few weeks ago, to be sent to France?"

"Yes," said Claude.

"And your name is Morel?"

"Yes."

"I have a letter for you then." The jeweler took an envelope from a drawer and handed it to him, and Claude saw that it was addressed to him in care of the shop and that the handwriting was his mother's. "I was about to return it to the post office," the jeweler said. "You should let people know where you are living."

"Yes," said Claude.

"And not make such a nuisance for others."

"Yes," he said. And as an afterthought, "Thank you."

He went out. He went home. And it was not until he was in his room that he opened the letter. . . . *You do not bother about me*, he read, *and I see no reason why I should bother about you. Yet once again, as always, I shall try to do my duty as God directs me.* There followed a recrimination about his failure to write and mention of the return address on the gift package for Yvette. *Whether this will reach you I do not know, but at least* (again) *I shall have done my duty.*

Then:

As for the gewgaw for your sister, it was a silly and vulgar extravagance, and I have assuredly not given it to her, nor indeed even told her about it. The one mitigating aspect is the indication that you are somehow earning money, and I only hope it is in a manner that would not bring disgrace to your family.

And then:

At least your having money must mean that you are no longer wasting your time scribbling. As I promised, I sent your last effort to the Journal des Ardennes, *and a few weeks later it came back without comment—I imagine because the editor is a friend and wished to spare my feelings. What further can be done with it I have no idea, but I do not imagine you are concerned about it, now that you have apparently put such foolishness behind you. Nevertheless, I shall put it in the drawer of your table until either I hear from you or you return home.*

For remember this: this is still your home. And however ill you treat me, I shall still be your mother and perform my duties. God be with you and lead you from the path of sin and error.

He tore the letter up. He reached for a sheet of paper. *Dear Sister*, he wrote. . . . Then he stopped. What was the use? His mother would intercept that too. . . . He took another sheet. *Dear Mother*. . . . And stopped again. *Dear Mother*—what?

For a long time he sat looking down at the four words on the two pages; at the fine, precise script that now seemed that of a stranger. Along with the card to Yvette from the jeweler's, this was the sum total of his writing in the six months since he had left Cambon.

February passed. . . . *J'ai, tu as, il a, nous avons, vous avez, ils ont.* . . . And now, in addition to his schoolboys, he had two fashionable ladies who were taking conversation. . . . *Voilà la plume de ma tante. S'il vous plaît, où se trouve la salle a manger de l'hôtel?* . . . All with a Baseler accent.

He took longer walks: through the forest, through the snow. He tried not to return to his room until late at night, so that he would be exhausted and ready for bed immediately. But bed was one thing, sleep another. And increasingly he could not sleep, but only toss and turn, and then rise and pace the floor, and at last stare down from the window into the empty street, until gray daylight came and it was time again for irregular verbs.

Then the night came when it happened differently; when he turned suddenly from the window and went to his table, almost ran to it, panting, trembling, and sat down with paper and pencil. But this time he did not write *Dear Sister* or *Dear Mother*. He wrote in capitals: A SEASON ON EARTH. And then: *My Season in Hell is over. I am free. The new season begins. Season of earth, snow, flower, mountain, castle....*

> *O seasons, O castles,*
> *what soul is without sin?*
> *without desire, that holds life in bondage?*
> *O new season, proud castle,*
> *is the hour of freedom the hour of life?*
>
> *or*
>
> *of*
>
> *nothing. Le néant.* Torn paper. Blank paper. Void.... And the void was not peace; it was emptiness. Emptiness of paper, of word, of mind, of heart, of soul. The Magi who had walked the night were gone, and there was only night; only void; void that ached and trembled to be filled. He had climbed from his pit —into another pit. From the blue-green cave into a cave of blankness. The dreams were gone. All that had been was gone. There would be no more dreams, no more Magi, no more visions, no more drunkenness.... But what instead? What besides void? ... "Dear God," he prayed, "when will morning come? When will a vent pale in the dark corner of my vault?"

If he could not create, he could still absorb. If he could not give, he could still receive. He went to the library of Basel; he rejoined *les assis;* through every hour of every day, when he was not earning his living, he sat in the dim rustling quietude, reading and studying. Life was not dream but fact, he told himself; the end of life not vision but knowledge. And in his new knowledge-hunger he ravened and battened. You are a teacher of language, he thought; very well, then *know* language; and he plunged into philology and etymology, into root and variant, into Sanskrit, Urdu, Arabic, Spanish, Russian. From there he went on to history, from history to politics, from this to economics, sociology, anthropology, law. Only one field he left almost untouched: literature. He read no novels, no essays, no plays, no poetry. Above all, no poetry—with one exception. And that was Goethe's. For now it seemed to him that Goethe alone, among the poets of the modern world, had been able to maintain balance and value, to see with equal clarity the outward and the inward, to encompass all knowledge, all experience, and yet maintain himself intact and whole.

Perhaps he himself, if he studied enough, if he labored enough, could make himself such a man and such a writer: a Goethe of a yet later day. Knowledge was the key. And objectivity. And outwardness. Above all, outwardness; the seeking of truth beyond the self; the turning from the inner dream, the private vision that in the end led only to self-devouring and self-destruction. Time was when he had thought himself a being apart: a seer, an alchemist, an "other." But Goethe had understood Faust better than he. He had known that his dreams led only to damnation, and that to be saved he must become again a man among men. And now he, Claude, knew it too.

In his deepest heart, perhaps, he had known it always. Twice before in his life he had striven to become such a man: once when he had gone to Paris to fight for the Commune, again during the early days in London when he had tried to write his *Book of France*. But the first time he had been too young, too vulnerable, and the second too deeply sunk in the blue-green cave. Now he was older, wiser. Now the cave was behind him. That cave, at least—that deepest one—and he would find his way from the other. By knowledge. By labor. By the strength of his will that would only fail with death.

Je serai, tu seras, il sera, nous serons. . . . Oui, voilà la plume de ma tante. Et où se trouve, s'il vous plaît, le royaume de Dieu?

He taught. He read. He walked. He climbed the stairs to his room. In his room he sat at his table, he looked at his sheets of paper, he looked at the one sheet on which he had written A SEASON ON EARTH . . . and at the other sheets on which he had written nothing; and he thought, no, not yet, not so soon, so easy. But someday—someday—

In the void there was study. In the void there was labor. And then, one evening, as he read in his room, something else as well: a thing not inward but outward, a sound and movement, and for the first time since he had been in Basel there were steps on his stairway and a knock on his door.

"Come in," he said in German, and the door opened.

"Boy, dear boy," said Druard, smiling, "you sound like *un vrai Prussco!*"

He seemed the same, and yet not the same, as before. He was still thin, gaunt-cheeked, and sallow, with the same full-domed high forehead and small trimmed beard; but he was dressed in conservative bourgeois fashion, and his tense febrile mannerisms were gone. Sitting across from Claude, he was quiet and self-possessed. His long, delicate hands lay relaxed on his lap, and his voice, when he spoke, was gentle and soft.

"So you are surprised?" he said. "Yes, of course. Instead of two years I was detained only eight months."

Claude said nothing.

"After the sixth month I was allowed to apply for a reprieve. There was a little delay, but it was granted, for my conduct, you see, had been very good. The one stipulation was that I leave England, and that I wished to do anyhow."

Claude still said nothing. He simply stared.

"You haven't spoken, boy—not a word of welcome. What's the matter: still too surprised?" Druard smiled. "Yes, of course you're surprised," he said. "Why wouldn't you be? That was part of the pleasure of coming. . . . But now that it has happened, you might at least say you're glad."

He waited; received no answer. Then, the smile fading, he leaned forward earnestly. "Boy, dear boy," he said, "you aren't angry? You haven't hardened against me? . . . No, no, you couldn't. You mustn't. What's past is past, don't you see? We did bad things—foolish, wrong things, both of us—but they're over now, and we must forget and forgive. . . . Yes, forgive. The blame was not all mine, you know that. Yet I've forgiven you, with a full heart; and you must do the same. . . . Is it your leg, boy: is that what you're thinking of? It's all right now, isn't it? Stand up, walk, let me see. Yes, of course, it must be all right. I've prayed for it. Night and day, all the time in prison, I prayed for it. That you would be well again; that we would both be; that God would heal us in our bodies and souls."

There was another silence. Then Claude said:

"How did you find me?"

"Through your mother," said Druard.

"My mother?"

"Yes. It's an interesting story. A rather touching one, really. . . . When I left England, of course, I returned straightway to Paris. And it was terrible —terrible. I'd written my wife from prison—every week, sometimes two and three times a week—and now I tried to go to her, to see her and my little son; but she wouldn't let me. Her lawyers said she insisted on going through with the legal action. I went to the house, but her father blocked the door and threatened to call the police. So I turned away. I stood in the street. From an open upper window I heard a baby crying, and then I was crying too. Standing there alone in the street, I wept bitter tears."

Druard passed a hand over his eyes. Then he went on:

"Well—I left. What else could I do? I went to the *Quartier*, to our old place, but it was occupied by strangers. Then I walked the streets. I went to the cafés. I saw many of our old friends and spoke to them, and some made it clear that they were friends no longer, but others were kind and warm; they welcomed me back, tried to buy me drinks, and though I refused the drinks and told them that was all over, I sat and talked with them. I asked about you. That was what I wanted to know most: about you. But they knew nothing. They said you hadn't been back; they had no idea where you were. Some even acted as if they had never heard of you. So I went on my way. I found a little room and moved in and kept to myself. Oh how alone I was! With my wife and baby gone; with my old friends, even the kind ones, now like strangers. All that was left was you, dear boy—if I could find you. I knew I *must* find you. Somehow, somewhere, I must find a way.

"Then one day, suddenly, the way seemed clear to me. I took the train to Cambon. I went to your mother. I found her in the store, behind the counter, just as you had used to describe her to me, and at first she acted as you'd described her, too—cold and suspicious and wanting me to be off on my way. But I was patient, I persevered—and I also, I confess, was not above using a stratagem. I didn't give her my true name, of course. Whether you'd mentioned it and she'd have known it, I had no idea, but it seemed wiser in the circumstances to assume an alias. So I became a Monsieur Durand. And since it seemed wiser, too, after what you had told me, not to be a poet, I became by profession an editor. A forgivable lie, I think, and as it turned out, an effective one, for her attitude quickly changed. 'Ah, and you are interested in my son's writings?' she said. And I said yes. And she said, 'You will pay money for them?' And I said yes. Which was in a way a mistake, because she tried for the next hour to get me to pay there and then; but also not a mistake, because, after I explained twenty times that I must first see you in person, she at last told me you were in Basel. So on I came. I didn't, of course, have your address, but I imagined there would not be many young Frenchmen in Basel and that a few inquiries would be enough to locate you. As it turned out, I was right. I arrived only this morning, and the first person I asked—my innkeeper —knew of you. And so, thanks to the good Lord and your good mother, here I am!"

In the telling of the story he had grown animated. Several times he had smiled. But now, reaching its end, he became serious again; his eyes were earnest, almost pleading. "So you see," he said, "I wanted very much, tried very hard, to find you. Won't you at least give me some greeting, some welcome, in return?"

Claude rose. He went to the window and stood looking out at the night, and then suddenly turned back to Druard. "What do you want?" he demanded, the words jerking out of him. "What do you want of me?"

"Want? What should I want? . . . To see you, that's all. To be with you again."

"No! Damn it, no! It's no good."

Druard was silent a moment, watching him. Then he shook his head and said gently: "You don't understand, dear boy. No, not at all. I don't mean what you think, but something very different. Truly. . . . You've changed: I can see that. But I've changed too. Deeply: in my heart—in my soul. What do you think I did during those months in prison? I looked inward at myself. I meditated. I prayed. I prayed to God to cleanse, to purify me, to grant me the strength to find His grace. And God answered me. Yes, He did! In the depths of my cell, of my misery and degradation, He saw me and He answered. He reached out His hand to me and gave me strength. . . . No, boy, it is not the old Druard you see. Not the weakling and the fool. Shall I tell you something? I have not had a single drink in all the months since we separated. Nor will I ever again for the rest of my life. Hashish? Opium? It seems incredible to me now that I could ever have known such madness. . . . Oh no, it's not for such things that I've come to you. We've learned our lesson: both of us. And from that lesson we'll go on to a new life—a wonderful life—all we once hoped and dreamed it might be. No more folly; no more vice and sin; but living as God wills it—simply, decently. Working together, writing, creating. Yes, that above all: creating. As we were born to do."

His eyes kindled. His voice was again edged with excitement. And now he too rose and crossed to where Claude was standing. "To write, boy—that must be our lives, our dedication. At first when I was in prison, after those terrible things that happened, I was sunk in despair. All was blankness, blackness, hopelessness, and I was sure I would never write again. But then the change came: slowly, but wonderfully. As I found my way back to God, everything changed, and I began to write again. At first just fragments, lines, snatches; but then whole poems—finally I had a full notebook of poems—and I think they're good, as good as anything I've ever done. I must show them to you, of course. That's been the one trouble: that until now I couldn't show them to you. After our two years together, nothing I write seems really written, really *done*, until you've seen it, felt it, distilled it, and then given it back to me. . . . And it must be the other way too. Oh yes. I must see all *you* have written. Everything. We will talk it out, feel it out, feel it through to its essence. We will be poets again, together. Create again, together. . . ."

He paused and looked at Claude questioningly. "You look at me so strangely," he said. "You're shaking your head. Why? What have I said that is wrong?"

"I have nothing to show you, Maurice," Claude said.

"Nothing to—"

"No, I have written nothing."

"Oh?" Druard looked puzzled. Then he half smiled. "Nothing, you say?" Putting a hand in his pocket, he produced a folded manuscript.

"Is this nothing then?" he asked. "The finest thing you have ever done—"

Claude stared. "What is that?" he demanded.

"It is called A *Season in Hell.*"

Claude took the manuscript and opened it. He saw his own hand-writing. He read: *Once, if I remember well . . .*

". . . and it is magnificent," said Druard. "Wild and terrible, perhaps; a nightmare rather than a piece of writing. A flagellation of yourself—and, I might add, of me. But that's of no matter. It is magnificent. A work of genius."

"Where did you get it?" said Claude.

"From your mother, of course."

"My mother?"

"Yes, I asked her all about you, naturally. What you'd been doing—and writing. And then she told me about this. She let me have it."

"Let you have it? She thought you were an editor and let you have it for nothing? No, you're talking about someone else; not my mother."

"I confess it wasn't easy," said Druard. "For a long time she kept demanding money. But at last I talked her out of it, and she simply gave it to me."

"I don't believe you."

"You can ask her when next you see her."

"But why? Why?"

"Because she knew I was coming to see you. Because she believed and trusted me."

"Why should she trust you?"

"Because . . . well, it's rather interesting, really. I spent three days in Cambon, you see, and I saw a great deal of your mother. We talked of you constantly—of your life and work and problems, and of her unhappiness and concern for you—and in the end she realized that I too was concerned, that I too loved you. At the end of those three days we were, in a strange way, very close. We talked of God and faith; of the tragedy of your lack of faith, and of what might be done about it. Together we prayed for you. We went to church and—"

"You *what?*"

"We went to church and prayed. As I had so often before, alone. And she, alone. Now we prayed together, we two who love you, and—"

That was as far as he got. His voice was lost in the sound of Claude's, and the sound was half laugh and half roar.

"To church! Holy Christ! You and she—in church!" . . . More laughter. More roars. . . . "Oh my God, you damned fraud—"

Druard stiffened. He stepped back as if struck. "What do you mean —fraud?"

"What do you think I mean? What do you think you *are?* . . . You liar, you hypocrite. You drunkard, you dope addict, you pervert, you wallower-in-*merde*—"

Druard's stiffness became a trembling. Of his hands, his lips, his whole body. With immense effort he controlled it; and he controlled his voice as he spoke again:

"No. No, dear boy. That was true once, perhaps. In the past—the dead past. But no more. You must believe me. . . . That's what I've been trying to tell you. And why I've come here. Because it's different now, all different. The blackness is gone now. The sin, the evil. I've found the way out at last—the way back to Christ—and that's why I'm here, boy—for that reason and that only. To show *you* the way. To help you, guide you; to save your soul as I am saving my own."

"Fine! Bravo! Hallelujah! . . . Now it's time to pull them out."

"Pull them out?"

"Your rosary. Your crucifix. To paw them, wave them, drool on them. . . . Only excuse me for not staying." Claude moved quickly across the room. "There's all the vaudeville I want right here in the beer halls."

"No, no boy. Stop. Wait." Druard moved after him. "Where are you going?"

"Out. Away from this. Anywhere—nowhere. But out!"

Claude reached the door. He went out and down the stairs. Druard followed quickly.

"Boy—dear boy—"

At the downstairs door he caught up with him. Claude did not break away again, and they walked down the street through the spring evening. For a while neither spoke. Then Druard said:

"I didn't mean to upset you. Truly. I haven't come all this way for that. To fight with you, as we used to; to have trouble and misery. Only to see you, be with you, talk with you again."

"Then talk sense," said Claude.

"Yes—yes, we will talk sense. Both of us. Quietly, reasonably."

They turned into the main street. Around them were lights, sounds, people, and again for a while they walked without speaking. Then they reached the river. They did not cross the bridge, into Germany, but turned and walked along the nearer bank, through the city's suburbs. Here it was darker and quieter again. The only light was from occasional gas lamps along the riverside path; the only sound the murmur of the Rhine.

"It's lovely," said Druard. "Do you walk here often?"

Claude nodded.

"Still the boy who takes a walk, eh? Around a block—around a continent—" Druard smiled, then he added: "You know, I've come to like walking too. Since—well, since it's all changed. I find I think clearly when I walk; feel clearly. I've even composed whole poems." Druard paused. His eyes fixed on Claude gently. "And now tell me about yourself, boy," he said. "What have you composed? What have you been writing?"

"What you have in your pocket."

"Yes, I know—and it is marvelous. But since then, I mean. Here in Basel."

"I told you before. Nothing."

"Nothing? Good God! What *have* you been doing then?"

"Teaching. Giving French lessons."

"To earn your living, yes. But beyond that? For yourself? *Out* of your own self?"

"I've been reading."

"That's all?"

"Yes, all."

"You've written nothing at all?"

"Not a word."

"I can't believe it. It's incredible—monstrous. For you of all men on earth: a seer, an alchemist, a great poet."

"I *was* a poet," said Claude.

"Was?"

Claude indicated Druard's pocket. "You've read what I wrote there. Do you think it's some kind of joke? . . . No. No, Maurice, it's no joke. It means what it says. It means finis, quits, goodbye."

"What in God's name are you talking about?"

"It seems quite clear to me."

"You plan never to write again?"

"Exactly." Claude was silent a moment. "Or at least never again as I wrote before. No more poems, no more visions, no more dreams."

"But those things are *you*, boy. Your heart, your soul, your essence, all of you. You can't waste genius like that—simply throw it away."

"Yes, I can. I have."

"You're mad. Mad!"

"No, I think not. I think rather it's the other way around."

"The other way—?"

"If I went on as I *was* I would go mad. I would go mad and die."

The path led on before them beside the glinting river. But now suddenly Claude stopped. He turned quickly and began walking back toward town, and it took Druard several moments to catch up with him.

"Go on by yourself, why don't you?" said Claude. "You can compose one of your poems."

"No, no." Druard's breathing was hard. "I'll stay with you. That's why I came, boy—to be with you. And now I thank God for it, more than ever, because I see how upset you are, how distraught, how miserable."

"I am fine, thank you," Claude said savagely.

"No, you are not fine. You're in agony. Do you think I'm blind? You're unhappy, confused, lost; and I say again, thank God I've found you; that I can be with you again, share with you, help you."

Claude did not answer. He seemed not even to be listening.

"Don't reject me, boy," Druard pleaded. "It isn't just for myself I ask it, but for your own sake—truly. We need each other: you no less than I. I told you this once in anger, when you decided to leave me; now I say it again in friendship and love. Without me, you've been lost, haven't you? Unable to write, to create, to be your own true self. What I said is true, and you know it. From each other we draw companionship, stimulation, the strength and will to create. . . . It's begun already, can't you feel it? Simply from being together again. Wait and see: there'll be no more emptiness for you—no more darkness and loneliness—but creation again. You'll be yourself again. Feeling, dreaming, writing; writing more beautifully than ever before. . . . Yes, yes, boy, I'm right, and you know I'm right. The fire isn't dead in you; it's only sleeping. And now it will wake again, flame again. Yes! Wait and see. . . ."

They had retraced their steps along the river. They swung away from it. They were once more in the town, on the main street, among the lights and the crowds, and then they were at the corner of a side street, and there Claude stopped and turned to Druard.

"Well, goodnight," he said.

"Goodnight?"

"This is my street. I'm going home."

"I'll come with you."

"No."

"Then you come with me, to my place."

Claude shook his head. "Goodnight," he repeated. *"Frater, ave atque vale.* When my fires are well stoked, *mon vieux,* I'll join you on Parnassus."

He made as if to move away, but Druard seized his arm. "No, no," he protested. "You can't—not like that—not just walk away, as if I were nothing to you. Please, dear boy, please! I've come so far; this means so much to me; to us both. And we've just begun to talk, to get together again. . . . Please. . . . All right, we won't go to your place, if you don't want to. Or mine. We'll go somewhere else—anywhere—where we can sit and talk." He looked around almost desperately. "Yes, there's a place just down the street. A café. A—what is it they call it here?—a *Bierstube.* We'll go there. Yes—come. Please come."

"I thought you'd stopped drinking," Claude said.

"Who's talking of drinking? We'll just talk, boy, talk. With maybe one glass—one only—for old time's sake."

He all but dragged Claude along the street and into the tavern. It was low-ceilinged, smoky and crowded, but in a corner they found an empty table and sat down, and after a moment a waiter appeared.

"So, what will it be, boy?" Druard smiled. "Our ceremonial cup for the occasion."

"Swiss goat's milk is very good."

"Goat's milk? Hah! Come off it. I mean a real drink. Only one, but a real one. A drink to us, boy. To reunion; to the future."

"*Wünschen Sie Bier oder Schnapps, meine Herren?*" asked the waiter.

"Schnapps, that's it. *Mais oui. Jawohl. . . .* Two schnapps, if you please," Druard said delightedly. And then to Claude: "Yes, that's just right— perfect. No giddiness, as with brandy. No poison, as in absinthe. A simple harmless drink of good cheer for two old friends reunited."

It was ten o'clock.

"*Wünschen Sie—*"

"*Noch zwei, bitte.*" Druard laughed. "My German is getting good, *hein?* In a few days I'll be an *echter Schweizen.*"

And when the drinks came: "*Prosit! Skoal! Salud! Santé!*" He leaned forward across the table. "Come on boy, drink up. What's the matter?"

"Nothing," said Claude.

"So then—glasses up! Bottoms up! . . . There. That's better, *hein?* No absinthe, no poison; just a little friendly bourgeois schnapps. A most salutary and beneficial beverage, guaranteed to cure rickets, sweeten mother's milk, and bring red roses to the cheeks of cadavers."

Druard laughed again. "No cadavers, we. No, no longer. Not ever again." Setting down his glass, he laid a hand on Claude's arm. "Oh my boy, dear boy," he said, "it's good to see you again!"

It was ten thirty.

Claude felt the drinks. He felt them in his throat, his chest, his stomach, his arms and legs. The only place he did not feel them was in his head. His head was clear: crystal-diamond clear. Or did that perhaps mean that he felt them there most of all?

Druard was talking. Still talking. And now he was back to poetry. "Wait and see, boy," he was saying. "Wait and see. In a few days—just a few, together—and it will all be different. You'll be yourself again: yes. Writing, dreaming, creating—"

Claude nodded. "I am already."

"Already?"

"Yes, I'm composing a poem now. It's called *La Plume de ma Tante.*"

"What?"

"It goes: *J'aurais eu, tu aurais eu, il aurait eu.* That's the first stanza. Then the second goes: *Nous aurions eu, vous auriez—*"

"Very funny."

"Who's being funny? I once wrote a poem of vowels; now I'll write one of verbs. Both V's, don't you see? Symbolic. Esoteric."

"Stop mocking. I'm serious. Utterly. I'm talking about your life, boy. About your work, your genius, the pure flame within you—"

"Oh, you mean about schnapps? ... *Psst, Kellner—noch zwei*.... All right, then we'll talk about schnapps."

Eleven.

"*Psst, Kellner!*"

Druard patted the red-checked tablecloth. "I miss the towers," he said. "The lovely leaning saucer-towers. The damn Swiss have no towers. No absinthe. Only mountains. Brrr—"

He looked around through the haze of pipe smoke. "Only mountains and fog. Look at the damn fog—all gray. On the Boul' Mich the fog's green and blue. Deep gleaming blue...." He pushed back his chair. "That's what we need, boy—a smoke. A real smoke, I mean; the blue magic smoke.... Come on, we'll find it. We'll find Dar Misheram."

He started to rise.

"Look out you don't slip," said Claude.

"Slip? I'm not drunk. Why should I slip?"

"In the blood."

"Blood? What do you mean, blood? Where?"

"On the floor: all around you—up to your ankles. The blood of the Lamb. You've got His ninety-six wounds all bleeding again."

Druard stared around him. He stared at Claude. He sank back in his chair, and his forehead shone with a film of sweat. "Oh God," he murmured.... And then: "I was joking. You know that, boy. Just joking —as you were before."

"Yes, of course," said Claude.

"Two old friends, they must joke sometimes, no? About their follies. About the old times." Druard's face was twisted; his hands trembled. He reached for his glass, knocked it over, brushed it aside. "But those times are gone, boy," he said. "I have changed—you must believe me. In tears and agony I have changed. I have seen my sins and renounced them forever. I have found my way back to God."

"Yes, of course," said Claude.

Eleven thirty.

"... and that's why I've come to you. The only reason. To help you too to find your way.... Don't close your heart, boy. Accept Him. Love Him. Love Him and He will give that love back a thousandfold. He will reach out His hand, sustain you, transfigure you ..."

Druard's eyes gleamed. His voice was soft and impassioned.

"But there is no halfway with Him," he said. "As He gives wholly of Himself, so too must he who seeks Him.... And that's why I've really come, boy—what I want to tell you about: how we can seek and find Him together.... Look. Listen. You've heard of the Trappists, haven't you? Of course you have: the most strict and austere of all the orders of monks. Well, I've been in touch with the Trappists. First by writing from prison; since then by many personal calls. Specifically I've gone to their monastery at Chimay; I've spoken to the superior about the conditions for a novitiate, and he thinks it would be possible for us to qualify. Yes, you and me. Think of it, boy! We could put the follies of the world behind us; give ourselves wholly to Christ. We could pray together, serve God together, work together. Yes, work too. Write. Create. The order has no rule against that. Living purely, we could create purely—create as we never have before—humbly, devotedly, gloriously; not for ourselves alone but for the Holy Spirit; not for the glory of man but the glory of God—"

His hand fumbled for Claude's. His eyes filled with tears. "Say you will, dear boy," he pleaded. "Say you'll come with me, tomorrow, to Chimay. The superior there is a dear old man—blessed, sainted. He will welcome us to refuge, to peace, to the arms of our Father. Our sins will be cleansed away, and we will be renewed, reborn. . . . Say you will, boy. For your soul's sake, and mine. Say you will. Swear to it. Here—swear—"

He reached into his pocket and there was a clicking of beads.

"Leave that damn thing where it is!" said Claude.

"No. No. You must accept it, swear to it. Together we will pray to it. *O bone Jesu, miserere nobis. Sancta Maria, ora pro nobis*—"

Claude rose. He threw money on the table. He turned and made for the door.

"No. No, dear boy. No!"

Druard lurched to his feet. He ran after him. At the door he stumbled and almost fell, but righted himself and ran on. Then they were outside, in the night: first on the main street, then on a side street, in darkness, Claude striding, Druard running and calling; and at last Druard caught him.

"Go away," Claude said. "For the love of that Christ of yours, go away."

"No, no, I won't. Please, boy—please, dear dear boy—" Druard was weeping. "Don't turn on me; don't leave me. No, no—please—I couldn't stand it. . . . You're all I have, don't you see? My family's gone; my wife and baby. All gone—everyone, everything—with nothing left but you and God."

He grasped Claude's arm. He grasped his hand. "Please—please, dear dearest boy. I love you, don't you see that? I still love you—need you. As you love and need me—yes—as you did before, as you always will—"

He had pulled Claude to a halt. Trembling and sobbing, he embraced him. "Tell me you love me, boy. Tell me—tell me—"

Claude moved back from him. "Let me go, Maurice," he said.

"No, I won't. You can't go! Not now nor ever—"

"Did you hear me? Let go."

"No. No, dear boy—"

Claude hit him. At the last instant he closed his eyes so that he did not see the blow but only felt it; felt with his fist Druard's beard and his lips and his teeth, and the teeth crumbling; and then there was a sound, a low strangled moaning sound, and then his hand was at his side again, his eyes were open, and there was Druard on the pavement. He was not unconscious, but half lying and half sitting, his face raised; and the face was a skull's, and the skull's eyes were weeping; and the mouth was a hole, and in the hole was blood and broken teeth.

The hole was mumbling. It said, "Forgive me. Please—I didn't mean. . . . No. Forgive me, boy. I forgive you . . ."

A hand was raised. It tried to grasp Claude's knees. The hole said, "Forgive. Forgive and love each other—in Christ . . ."

Then face and hole were gone. There was only the dark street stretching away before him and the sound of his own footsteps on the pavements of the sleeping city.

In Olten he bought food and a rucksack; in Lucerne more food. Then his money was gone. He odd-jobbed his way through the central cantons of Switzerland, and when there were no jobs he begged or stole.

He was going south. Spring was well on toward May. Yet each day it grew not warmer but colder, for he was approaching the mountains. For two days he moved through dark slanting forests of fir and spruce and heard the wind wail in the treetops above him. The next morning there was frost on the earth. And that evening, above tree line, he came to the opening of a high Alpine pass and a hospice perched on the boulders near the snout of a glacier.

The monks at the hospice were not Trappists. They were Franciscans. They spoke. And they told him that though it was full spring in the lowlands and early spring here at the hospice, up above, at the top of the pass, it was still deep frozen winter. "Nothing can get through yet," they said, "—and probably not for another month. If you want to cross over to Italy now, you had better go around to the west, into France, where the mountains are lower."

He thanked them. He put the cheese and bread they gave him in his rucksack. He slept on a pallet on the floor beside the embers of a fire. And the next morning at three, while the monks still slept, he left the hospice and began the ascent of the pass. It was black and cold, then gray and cold, and he had no heavy clothing; but through the morning the work of climbing kept him warm, and there was only a thin film of snow on the hard ruts of the road. His knee did not bother him. His body was fit from the months of walking in the Black Forest. And he moved quickly and steadily. Soon the hospice, behind him, was no more than a speck on the boulder slope far below.

But above him was a world of whiteness. And now he entered the whiteness. The film of snow became a blanket, then a billow; the road vanished beneath the billows; and he climbed on, slowly, gropingly, through a trackless sea of snow. At intervals he stopped to rest: not sitting, for there was nowhere to sit, but leaning his weight against the white drifts. Toward midday—or what seemed to be midday—he ate his cheese and bread. A while later it began to grow darker. It was not the darkness of evening, however, but of thickening clouds, and presently new snow was falling. From behind the snow came wind, quickly rising. It hissed spuming along the white drifts beside him and howled on the peaks high above.

It grew colder. Much colder. He himself should have been growing cold—in his flesh, bones, and blood. But he did not feel it. Perhaps he was getting numb, he thought. But he did not feel that either. Nor even tired. He rested less often than before. On he pushed, up and on, on and up, and within him it was neither coldness nor numbness nor tiredness that he felt, but a great lifting surge of strength and will. He raised his head. Waves of snow beat against it, stinging his flesh and his eyes. But beyond the snow, beyond the gray scud above him, he could see faintly the white line that marked the top of the pass.

He climbed on. The wind sang. His heart sang.

Their song was wild and savage and free.

17

He followed the road of the centuries. The road of the barbarians and the conquerors. The road of kings, cardinals, bankers, pilgrims, poets, painters, lovers, tramps. He followed the road of dreams, and it rose to its crest, and it fell away, and now the white of snow and the gray of rock were gone, and the earth was green, the sky was blue. Beyond the Alps lay Italy. Beyond the clouds was the sun.

He came down into the valleys. He walked beside the Lombard lakes. Near Como, for a week, he worked on a farm, and in Milan, for two weeks, in a spaghetti factory. With his savings he bought a gallery seat at La Scala and saw Verdi's *Aida*. He walked out to the Convent of Santa Maria delle Grazie and stood looking at the bleak and faded majesty of da Vinci's *Last Supper*. He sat on a bench in the Piazza del Duomo, feeding the pigeons, and then rose and went into the cathedral—the first time he had entered a church since the year of his first boyhood flight from Cambon to Paris. He moved slowly through the great dim vault; he passed the recessed shrines, the burning tapers, the crypts, the fonts, the confessionals, the vast fluted pillars soaring up into shadowed stillness; he came to the altar and stood before it; he looked beyond it at the white waxen effigy impaled on the towering cross. He was not alone. At the altar rail were many figures, mostly women, black-shawled and kneeling, and for a while he stood behind them listening to the whisper of their prayers. Then the figure directly before him rose and moved off. The place was empty. The place seemed to be waiting. The other figures, the altar, the white effigy: all were waiting. . . .

But he did not move forward. He turned away. He went out of the cathedral into the square—into the sunlight and the crowds. The life of Milan was in its streets. Crowds were everywhere. And he was part of the crowd. He made no decision as to where he would go—what street he would follow or what corner he would turn—but let the crowds lead him, guide him, carry him where they would. All his life he had gone counter to others; his course *à rebours*—against the grain of the world. But now at last he went *with* the grain, gladly, joyfully, letting the world impose its will on him, losing, submerging, dissolving himself in the crowd. He was a man among men, a drop in an ocean. Of all the thousands among whom he moved, not one had a name. And he had no name. Nameless, he would move among his fellow men—without anger, without fear.

He left the spaghetti factory. He found a job as busboy in a restaurant. His name became *Pssst*. And though he did not care greatly for dirty dishes or being pushed by waiters, he liked the crowd and bustle, the light and sound. Indeed, he more than liked them. He needed them—in his deepest self. In the rooming house where he lived he kept his door open, so that as much light and sound as possible would come in. A closed room was like a cave to him. Like a pit. One night as he slept his door accidentally closed, and he awoke to a feeling of suffocation that almost overcame him before he rushed to the door and threw it open.

In mid-June he left Milan.

He let the roads lead him, and the roads led south. He came to the plain of the Po, crossed the river, and came to Reggio Emilia. Here his savings ran out and he tried to find work. But there was no work. Milan, a growing industrial city, had been busy and prosperous, with jobs for the asking; but now he was in farming country, the spring crops had been blighted by drought, and Reggio Emilia, the country's market center, lay in poverty and stagnation. He scavenged barely enough to keep going and went on to Bologna. But it was the same there. In the city fabled for its feasts and gourmets he was able to find barely enough edible garbage to keep himself alive.

Leaving Bologna, he continued south. The road climbed, the plain of the Po fell away behind him, and he was now again in mountain country. This was not the Alps, however, but the Apennines. There were no soaring peaks, no snowy passes, no wind or storm, but only rank upon rank of worn sculptured hills spreading away under the sky of Tuscany. The sky was blue and flawless, its horizons notched by the silhouettes of hilltop towns and castles, and the earth beneath was brown, green, and silver, checkered by vineyards and olive groves and striped by long dark files of cypress and poplar.

The land gleamed in antique beauty under the sun. But like the plain of the Po it offered little food. The grapes were sour, the olives as hard in their flesh as in their pits, and hunger walked like a shadow beside him. Begging at farmhouses, he was turned away. Raiding barns and yards, he found bare bins and coops. Always in his wanderings he had found the poor more ready to give than the rich, but here they had nothing to be given, or even stolen. His eyes went up from the valleys to the hills, from the farms and villages to the high castles and villas. And late one afternoon he climbed a winding road up a hillside, came to a pink-and-gray stucco villa, and boldly entered its gate. Beyond the gate was a formal garden. He saw graveled paths, clipped hedges, banks of flowers, marble statues. He saw a fountain and a pool, and beside the pool, on a marble bench, a woman sitting alone. She was a woman of perhaps forty, richly dressed, full-figured, with almost startlingly white skin, dark lustrous hair, and even darker deep-shadowed eyes. And as he approached she looked up, but otherwise did not move, nor did she speak, until he was close beside her and was about to speak himself—but didn't, because she was looking at him so strangely—and then she smiled, with her dark eyes and her red lips, and rose with slow grace and put out her hand to him.

"*Benvenuto, caro amico*," she said gently. "I have been waiting for you."

There was no poverty in her villa. He was served a dinner fit for a ducal palace and slept the night in a canopied bed. In the morning a maidservant brought breakfast to his bedside, and as he ate there was a knock on the door and his hostess entered. As on the previous evening, she studied him a while before speaking. Then again she smiled, and this time said:

"No, I was not wrong. It is even righter now, this morning."

"Signora?"

"Your hair, your eyes, your bones, your coloring. You are the true Northman, the true barbarian. Teuton, Visigoth, Viking, Vandal."

"I must correct you, Signora. I am a Hun."

"A Hun? No, I think not. The Huns were shorter and darker, and besides they did not invade Tuscany. . . . Anyhow, we will not argue the point. For me you are *il Vandalo*—the Vandal. . . . And so come now. We will get to work."

Then he found out what she had been "waiting for." She was an artist, a painter, and she wanted him as a model. "I have been painting here for

six months," she said. "The landscape, the garden, my servants, the peasants. Lord, how many peasants—I think every one in all of Tuscany—and
I am sick of them! Sick of their brownness, like the earth. '*Dio mio*,' I have
prayed, 'send me a man who is not brown, not old, not an Italian. A man
from the north—white, golden, and young; not brown and old and full of
dust, like Italy, but young as the wind is young, savage and free.' ... Yes, I
have prayed. And now I am answered. Come! To work! My painting will
live again. It will have the life of wind, and of fire."

She posed him in the garden, standing spread-legged atop a low wall,
and as costume she supplied a strip of muslin loincloth.

"But the Vandals wore—"

"Who cares what they wore? Do you think I am doing a drawing for a
child's picture book?" She changed his stance slightly, stood back to study
it, and then directed a manservant as he set up easel and canvas. "Don't
you see what this will be?" she said. "Not a reproduction, a stupid copying,
but a thing of the spirit, of the imagination.... Look. Turn and look
behind you. You see the background, the old hills—as old and prim and
dead as in a painting of Giotto's. Here in the foreground, the garden. Old,
too, and prim and dead; full of marble and memories. And in the center of
it, you. You as I shall paint you: not as a mere man, a person, but as a force,
an element—the wind from the north; the young, the fresh, the pagan; the
barbarian, *il Vandalo*, come to breathe life into death."

She painted through the morning and the afternoon. Through the
next day, and the next. She did not show him her work, but covered the
canvas at the end of each session and had it carried inside; nor, after the
first morning, did she speak to him, except to give occasional instructions
about his posing. She painted with an intensity, almost a frenzy, of concentration. Each time when she lay down her brush she would seem suddenly
drained and exhausted, and then she would go into the villa and he would
not see her at all until she was again ready to paint. He had his meals alone,
waited on by the maid and manservant. He walked alone through the
halls and loggias, across the terraces and gardens, soaked in sunlight and
stillness. Apparently there was no family, no one at all in the villa, except
his hostess and the servants.

He was still nameless. She had asked him not a single question about
himself and called him simply *il Vandalo*. And he knew her only as Signora.
The Signora painted, she vanished, she sent for him when she was ready
to paint again, and the rest was food and sleep, sunlight and stillness....
"The roads have led me to the house of Circe," he thought. "I am caught
in a dream, a hallucination." ... But he did not mind; he made no effort to
break out. For years he had lived in his own dreams, and they had turned
into nightmares. Now the dream was someone else's, and perhaps it
would turn out better.... "Or perhaps," he thought, "I shall wake one

morning and look in the mirror and see, not myself, but one of Circe's
pigs." . . . Well, that would be all right too. And no great change. With will
dead, imagination dead, what was man, after all, but a pig?

Resolution, however, came not in the morning, but in the evening;
not in a mirror but in the garden where he posed for her painting. Dinner
over, he walked out alone into the garden, in the fading light, and came
to the low wall, followed it—and then suddenly stopped. For the easel,
which had always been taken in at night, now stood in its usual daytime
place. It held the painting. The painting was uncovered. And it was
finished. Approaching, he stood before it, motionless, staring; he saw the
background of Giottoesque hills, the foreground of garden, all prim and
ancient as the Signora had described them; and in their center, emergent,
dominant, he saw himself—or, rather, the image that had been born of
himself. There were eyes, sky blue, blue-flaming. There was golden hair
and a body white and gleaming. It was a body in its wholeness, for the
loincloth was gone and it was nude. . . . No, nude was not the word; the
word was naked. . . . For this was no classic form, no figure from antique
frieze or museum wall, but a thing of flesh, of sensuality, barbarous and
obscene. "It will be a force, an element," its creator had said, "come to
bring life into death." And the life it had brought was the life of the phallus.

He stood rooted, frozen—like one of the garden's marble statues.
Then there was a faint sound in the stillness, and he turned, and there was
another figure behind him. The woman was there, the Signora, her face
white, her eyes dark, in the twilight. The eyes seemed to be smiling; the
red lips were smiling. "As you have come to me," she said softly, "now I
have come to you."

She came forward slowly. She was wearing a dark silken robe, but now,
as she advanced, it opened and fell away, and it was no longer only her
face that was white but the whole of her—her shoulders and breasts and
belly and flanks and thighs—and she was naked now, naked as the figure
in the painting, as she stopped and stood before him, her body arched, her
breasts high and swelling. "Take me," she said. "Take me, Vandalo—with
your strength, with your lust. With the lust of the life you have brought
me."

She moved still closer. She pressed against him. Her arms drew him
down toward the soft grass, and against the grass her flesh was white and
gleaming. The flesh trembled, waited—the flesh of Circe—and now it *was*
dream, it *was* hallucination that held him, for as it waited it changed. It was
no longer gleaming white but coarsely reddish; the face was coarse and
broad, the face of a French peasant woman; then thin and painted, like a
London whore's. And he had pulled away; he was trying to rise. But the
arms held him. And now, again, they changed, the body changed—not
back into whiteness, but growing darker, turning to blackness—the shoul-

ders, breasts, and belly, the whole nakedness now black and glinting; and the face too, and the hair—all, all of her black, except only the eyes—for the eyes, which had been black, were now a deep violet-blue. . . .

It was time for waking. But he didn't wake. It was still in dream that he had freed himself and risen and moved away. He moved on out of the garden, through the twilight; and the twilight was violet-blue. It enveloped him, cradled him, watched him, as he moved on swiftly into the gathering night.

He came to Florence. He stood in the hall of the Accademia and looked at the miracle of Michelangelo's *David*. "He too was possessed and cursed," he thought. "He too knew the loneliness and emptiness of man without woman. But in that emptiness he created truth and beauty that will live as long as the turning earth."

Hungry again, he looked for work. He found it as a delivery boy for a leather-goods store, and, like the busboy job in Milan, it kept him in motion and among crowds. But there was one difference from Milan. Here, at night in his squalid room, he did not keep his door open but closed it tight. With his first wages, he bought a pad of paper and pencil and for long times sat in flickering candlelight on his cot (for there was no table) with the pad on his lap. He wrote: *My Season in Hell is over, my Season on Earth begun. And I am free. . . .*

The pencil hung motionless.

Free? Free to do what? To run? Still to run, forever to run: from home, church, school, employment; from Cambon, Paris, London, Basel; from mother, family, friends. From women. . . . *I shall be free*, he had written, *to possess truth in one soul and one body*. But what was truth? And *how* possess it? Could he be said even to have a body—he who could not perform the prime function of the body? Did he still have a soul—or had he left it behind him in the deep blue-green caves?

Question: Why had he left Basel? *Answer:* Druard. . . . But it had only partly been Druard, and he knew it. It had been also irregular verbs. It had been *la plume de ma tante*. It had been climbing upstairs and climbing downstairs. It had been the library. . . . Yes, most of all the library. The reading, the studying. Goethe. For even as he studied, even as, with half his mind, he planned his future as man and writer, he knew with the other half that he could never become such a man, such a writer, as Goethe. . . . It had been writing alone in his room at Frau Borchers. Writing—and writing nothing.

As he was writing now.

Question: Well then? Why was he here? Where was he going? *Answer:* He was going south. To the sun; to the sea. To the blue sea of his dreams and the lands beyond the sea. To the lands where his father had gone, the lands of waste and desert; and beyond the desert the storms; beyond the storms the forests, the jungles, the jungle rivers, the black nations. To the Kingdom of Ham, land of niggers, of savages, where black was life, black was flesh, and not illusion and hallucination. . . .

The candle guttered. He slept. He dreamed. The old dreams; the wild shining dreams. And the next morning he left Florence and walked south.

The roads led up. The roads led down. He was still in the Tuscan hills, and they rose and fell before him like the waves of a brown ocean. It was full summer now. The sun flamed down from an iron-blue sky that lay clamped on the earth like the lid of an oven. From under his feet dust rose and hung motionless in the air. Dust covered the hills, the valleys, the groves, the vineyards, and lay in yellow-brown drifts in the yards of farmhouses. In Florence he had earned enough money to buy only a very little food, and by the fourth day it was gone, with nothing anywhere to replace it. Even the stream beds he passed held dust instead of water, and to his hunger was now added thirst.

At the Signora's villa, with its sumptuous meals, he had put on weight, but now quickly he lost all he had gained, and more. His clothes hung from him, his hands and wrists were skeletal, and when he put hand to face he felt deep hollows between cheekbone and jaw. Also, for the first time in months, his knee began bothering him. And his progress was slow. It was his plan to cut over to the Mediterranean and follow it southward, and he knew that the coast was no great distance from Florence; but now day followed day and still it did not appear. He trudged on through scorched hills, through the dust, through the oven of sunlight; trudged and stumbled, stumbled and rested, rested and rose, and trudged on again. He had come down into Italy from the Alps, along the route of conquerors. Now he was on a different route, a route of flight to the sea. "It is my Anabasis," he thought, "my March of the Ten Thousand." Except that on this march there were not ten thousand souls and bodies, but only one.

There were more hills, more valleys. Up, down—down, up. There was still another up, and the end of the up, the crest of a hill, and on the crest he stopped, he stared ahead, he put out a hand as if to touch what lay before him, and his cracked lips smiled. For the down-slope before him did not end in a valley, and beyond it was no hill. At its base, instead, there was a plain, spreading to the west, and at its far side a city, and beyond the city, beyond the dust-brown miles of the parched land, a sweep of deep and dazzling blue.

"Thalassa! Thalassa!"

The old cry of the Ten Thousand croaked up from his throat. . . . "the sea! the sea!" . . . and an old woman, prodding a donkey through the dust of the road, looked up at him fearfully. Then he was moving on, down the slope, toward the plain and the city, toward the shining apparition that lay beyond.

The plain was even hotter than the hills, the dust thicker and more choking, and through the dust the sun beat down on him like a hammer of brass. Along the road he looked for something with which to cover his head, but there was nothing; nothing but dust and bare fields and the silver glinting of leaves on the fruitless olive trees. He found himself thinking of the leaves of Cambon in their summer dryness, but they had hung stiff and motionless, while these seemed to dance and shimmer in the blaze of sunlight. He turned his eyes away. From the lowland plain the sea was no longer visible, but at each slight rise of the ground he strained them ahead for a possible glimpse of its blueness. He strained for the smell, the taste, the faintest breath of the sea.

It was midafternoon now; the sun's heat should have been waning. But it did not wane. It grew more intense. In such heat, ordinarily, he would have been soaked in sweat; but there was no ounce of moisture in him to come out in sweat, and the sun bathed him as if in a dry burning stream. He raised his head to it, defiantly. He bent his head and plodded, doggedly. And then it seemed to him that he was no longer plodding but swimming; he was swimming, floating through the burning stream; and the stream was carrying him, rolling him, rolling him gently on—and then not gently —for there was a lurch, a bump; he had gone down on the road with one knee. And then he had righted himself and was plodding again.

The sun. The sun.... It was what he had dreamed of, yearned for, through all the years. The barbarian of the north, the heathen, the Vandal —he had come seeking the sun; to be a child of the sun—

And now he had come to it, found it. It was no longer outside him but within him; not a distant fire in the sky but a fire in his bones and blood. "*Thalassa!*" he had cried, but it had been the cry of illusion. For there was no sea. There was no city, no goal, no end to the journey, but only the sun and the dust and the endless road.... And now, presently, not one road, but many roads.... For he had come to an intersection; there were roads in all directions; and he was turning, revolving, to select the road he would take. He was wheeling, spinning—and then standing still. Or perhaps not still, for the spinning continued: a spinning of roads, like the spokes of a wheel: of the fields and the dust, of the sky and the sun. He fixed his eyes on the sun, to stop it, and the sun obeyed. It stopped spinning, hung poised —and then it struck. This time it was not with a hammer. It was with a thousand brass lances, and the lances pierced him, long and flaming, splintering with blinding light in his eyes and his brain.

Then the light went out. There was only blindness, only darkness....

... And, later, whiteness.

Whiteness of ceiling, of walls, of sheets and pillow, and of a woman's figure beside his bed. "It is another dream," he thought. "I am back in London, in the hospital, and my knee is in a cast."

But his knee was not in a cast. And when the nurse spoke it was in Italian. "You have had sunstroke," she said, "but you are all right now."

Then the white uniform was gone, and there was a green one. (In London it had been blue.)

"Your papers?" said the *agente di polizia*.

"Papers?"

"Your identification."

"I have none."

"No, we know you haven't. And you are not Italian."

"No."

"What are you?"

"A Hun."

"What?"

"Or maybe a Vandal."

"We happen to know you are French."

"All right, I'm French."

They prepared papers for him. *Name: Attila Bonhomme* (taking his word for it). *Status: alien-vagrant*. And a few days later, when he was discharged from the hospital, he had, for the third time in his life, a train ride with a policeman. At the French frontier station at Mentone the immigration officer asked, "Are there any criminal charges against him?" The policeman said, "No." And he was back in France.

Back in France. Again walking, still walking. . . .

But it was different now, very different. For now at last he was by the Mediterranean. Though it was still summer the heat was gentle, and the sun shone smiling on the bright cities of the Riviera; on hill and valley, headland, bay, and beach. Once, long ago, in *The Drunken Boat*, he had written of "Europe, land of ancient parapets." He had not seen them then, but he saw them now: the walls and cliffs and bastions of the homeland rising high and proud out of the southern sea. He followed the parapets. He stared out from them at the sea. He clambered down from them and bathed in the sea. He had never been in salt water before; his only swimming had been in the muddy coils of the Meuse, above Cambon. But all his life he had known it in his imaginings—felt it, smelled it, wrapped himself in it, in the canvas sail of his boyhood bed—and now he came to it as to a thing long remembered and well loved. Like the Drunken Boat itself, he plunged, raced, wallowed, dived—gave himself to the sea, became drunk with the sea.

He moved on. The Riviera was behind him. He came to Marseilles. Finding his way to the Vieux Port, he went up and down the docks, into

offices and hiring halls, along gangways and decks seeking a berth on one
of the dozens of ships that thronged the harbor. But he found nothing.
In London, two years before, he had signed onto ships twice within
a week, only to turn back from them into the blue-green caves. On the
Riviera there had been jobs for the asking, but he had wanted them only
as stopgaps. Here there was nothing. When he truly cared, truly tried,
there was nothing. "Where are your papers?" he was asked. "Papers?"
"Your seaman's papers." "I have none." And there was a shake of the head.
Marseilles crawled with paperless men—with wanderers, outcasts, vagabonds, jailbirds—all of them seeking escape by ship from the assorted
fates and furies that pursued them.

Longshoreman's work, however, was available—and he took it. For
ten hours a day he heaved boxes and crates and sacks and bales, from
wharves into ships and ships onto wharves, and at night he slept in one of
Marseilles' replicas of the Hôtel de Babylone. Twice, while helping load
an outgoing freighter, he tried to stow away—once hiding in a coal bunker
and once (salute to the past) in a W.C.—but both times he was found and
thrown ashore. In the evenings he frequented the waterfront bars, for it
was there, more than on the wharves, that occasional shipboard jobs were
offered the paperless; but from there too he was often ejected, because he
bought no drinks.

Still, one night, a chance appeared to be developing. In one of the bars
he met a mate off a Greek tramp; Claude was the only one present who
could manage even a few words of his language; and the man seemed to
like him. Finishing a drink, he said, "Come on, let's go," and Claude went
with him, assuming they were off to another bar. But in the street the
mate turned, looking at him meaningfully, and said, "All right, where is it?"

"Where's what?" said Claude.

"Your room."

"What do you mean, my room?"

"You know what I mean."

Claude tried to walk off, but the mate caught his arm. He tried to pull
away, but the mate held it tightly. "Don't worry, chéri," he said, "I have
plenty of money." Then Claude hit him and left him lying in the street.

For several hours, then, he himself walked the streets. Then going at
last to his lodging house he lay sleepless on his pallet. "Why—why?" he
asked over and over. "Is there still a mark? Do I wear a bell like a leper?"

In the morning, as he washed, he looked into the cracked, fly-specked
mirror. He saw a face that was no longer a boy's but a man's; the softness
gone, the roundness gone; now lean, brown, and leathered, with cropped
sun-bleached hair and hard metal-blue eyes. And his body, too, was hard;
for though he had gained back the weight he had lost in Italy, it had been
not in flesh but only muscle and bone. He held an arm out before him:

the arm of a stevedore. He closed the hand into a fist: the fist that had felled the mate—that had felled Druard. "I have given up being a poet," he thought, "and become a stevedore. Now perhaps I shall give that up and become a prize fighter."

"Truth in one soul and one body," he thought. . . . "Perhaps the one truth of life is a blow in the face."

He swung his baling hook. He hoisted his crates. He walked the wharves, boarded ships, entered offices, talked to captains and mates and agents. And the answer remained "No." He walked the streets and into the bars and out again, and one evening, as he came out of one, a hand touched his arm and a voice asked a familiar question: "Your papers?" And turning, he faced two sergeants of the French Army.

"My papers?" he said.

"Your army service papers. Let's see them."

"I have none."

"Have none?"

"I—I mean not with me. I left them at home."

"You have done your service already?"

"Oh yes."

"In which unit?"

"In—in—I mean I served only a few weeks. I have a bad knee; I was discharged."

"And you have the discharge papers at home?"

"Yes."

"All right, we'll go home."

The sergeants fell in beside him, and they walked a few blocks in silence.

Then one asked, "How much farther?"

"Not far," said Claude.

"It isn't far to headquarters either. And we have good facilities there, including quick assignment to penal battalions."

They turned a corner, walked a block, came to a second corner. And this one Claude knew. Just around it, off the intersecting street, was an alley ending in a low wall, and as they made the turn he jerked suddenly away. In an instant he was in the alley, in darkness; then over a wall, in another alley, another street. It was a crowded street, and he moved with the crowd, away from the waterfront, away from the Vieux Port, until he was on the other side of town. Here he came to railroad tracks, and following them, reached the city's main freight yards. On a siding he found a string of cars that seemed ready to move, and, after a search, a car with an unlocked door. It was loaded with crates of produce, but there was room on top of the crates, and he climbed in and lay down. An hour passed; perhaps two. Then the train started.

"All right," he thought. "I'm a sailor on wheels."

The wheels turned. He was on this train. He was on that. Or when there was no train, or he was tired of trains, he walked. He was in Nîmes, Toulouse, Bordeaux, Limoges, Lyon, Bourges, Tours, Nantes. Or he was in the country between, where the fields were turning brown with autumn. He went where the roads led, or where the freight cars rolled, and it didn't matter. In some of the cities he found odd jobs. In two, as his train pulled in, he was picked up by railway police and spent a few days in jail. After that, except when he had a job or was looking for one, he kept away from the centers of towns and frequented the makeshift communities of tramps and vagrants that were always to be found in the outskirts. He sat at their fires, heard their tales of woe, watched them drink themselves into stupor on liquor they had got from God knows where. "These men are my brothers," he thought. "The misfits, the rejects, the outcasts—my companions of the road." But they were companions only in physical presence, and he had nothing to say to them, nor they to him. Even among the outcasts, he was an outcast.

One morning he awoke to find a face bending over him. It was a whiskered face, with bleared eyes and stumps of teeth, and he stared for a moment and then leaped up, trembling. *"Putain de merde,"* said the tramp, "I'm just lookin' for my bottle." But Claude backed away silently, and the image followed him for days.

Then, another morning, he awoke in a freight car, and the train was pulling into a city. Through the slit-opened door he watched the suburbs go by; and the suburbs were huge, they were endless, and suddenly he realized where he was. Pushing the door wide, he leaped to the tracks, climbed an embankment, and walked in the opposite direction from the train's: away from Paris.

It was November now, and growing colder. There was frost on the ground—then snow—and he headed back south. But the going was hard; the railway police had increased their forces, and he was arrested twice in one week. Taking to the roads, he walked; but this was hard too, for he had no warm clothing, and in winter there was no work on the farms. One night, in a snowstorm, he slept in a leaky barn and awoke wet and freezing, and a few hours later chills and fever began. "Where are you now, sun?" he asked. But when he moved on it was not toward the sun. It was back the other way—to the north and east. He found the nearest railway tracks and a northbound freight train, and this time he was not caught, but rode for eight hours, and got off at a junction and walked again; through the snow, along the roads, between the dark walls of forest. His legs shook, his breath rasped, his laboring body burned and froze; but he walked on all night, and by morning reached the yellow river and, an hour later, Cambon. He passed the Place de la Gare and the Place du Sépulcre and came to the store and went in, and the tall black-clad figure behind the counter asked, "What can I do for you?"

"I'm sick, Mother," he said.

Then she recognized him. But no flicker of emotion touched her face. When she spoke again it was as if he had been gone eighteen minutes instead of eighteen months.

"You look it," she told him. "Well, you know where your bed is. Get into it."

For two weeks he lay in bed with pneumonia, and for the next two he convalesced. "I suppose I should be appreciative," his mother said, "that this is at least your favorite hospital."

She nursed and waited on him, as she had before, but, apart from talk of food and medicines, that was almost the sum total of their conversation until the day he rose and went downstairs. Then, as he entered the store, his mother was serving a customer, and when the customer had gone she turned on him in anger. "So that is still your great pleasure," she flung at him. "To taunt me. To shame me."

"Shame you?" he said.

"Showing yourself in front of people like that. The son of a decent respectable woman in those torn filthy rags."

"I have no other clothes."

"Well then get yourself some. At once."

"I'll be glad to. If you give me the money."

"Use your own money."

"I have none."

"What do you mean, you have none? You had enough to send that extravagant nonsense to your sister."

"That was more than a year ago. I was earning money then."

"And you've earned nothing since?"

"Not enough to save."

"What about your writing? You've been paid for that, haven't you?"

"I've done no writing."

"Your old things, I mean. The ones Monsieur Durand wished to buy."

"Monsieur Durand?"

"The gentleman from Paris. The editor who came to see me and then went on to Basel."

"Oh."

"He found you, didn't he?"

"Yes, he found me."

"And he bought your poems?"

"No."

"I don't believe you. That was the reason he went to Basel."

"All right, don't believe me. But he didn't."

"Why? Why not?"

"Because he—" Claude paused. "Because we didn't get along," he said.

"Didn't get along? . . . For the first time in your useless life someone offers you money; for the first time you meet someone who is not trash but a fine decent Christian gentleman; and you stand there and tell me 'we did not get along.' . . . *Pour l'amour de Dieu*, what must I listen to? What perversities—what insanities—"

She was interrupted by the entrance of another customer. It was an elderly woman who wanted a variety of small kitchen items, and as Madame Morel assembled them for her she looked curiously at Claude. Several times she seemed on the point of speaking, but changed her mind, contenting herself with a final over-the-shoulder stare as she took the parcel and left.

"Anyhow," snapped the Widow Morel, wheeling back at him, "I will not have this humiliation of a tramp in my family. Here—" Opening her cash drawer, she slapped a fifty-franc note on the counter. "Go and make yourself at least *look* respectable."

Claude took the note.

"But there is one thing I want clearly understood," she added. "I am not giving you this money; I am lending it. And when you find work—if such a miracle ever happens—you will pay me back. Fifty francs, if you please, at five per cent interest."

"Forty-one francs," he corrected her.

"What do you mean, forty-one?"

"There is the little matter of the extravagant nonsense you were just talking about."

"What do you mean?"

"The locket I sent Yvette from Basel. You didn't give it to her."

"Of course I didn't."

"What did you do with it?"

"What do you think I did?"

"I think you sold it—right here at the store. Meaning you owe *me* nine francs."

"Nine? That's ridiculous. I sold it for only six."

"I don't care what you sold it for. I know what I paid. Seven Swiss francs for the locket and one franc for postage. And eight francs Swiss equals nine francs French."

His mother stared at him. Her lips were tight, her black eyes hard, but behind the tightness and hardness was a certain grudging admiration. "Well," she said at last, "—well. You've become quite the businessman, haven't you?"

"I wonder where I learned," said Claude, and went out.

Over the past year he had occasionally thought of sending his sister another gift. But he hadn't, for he had known his mother would intercept it as she had the locket. And now Yvette was not home. The previous fall, having finished with school in Cambon, she had gone to Cambrai to enter a convent for advanced studies, and in another year, if all went well, would begin her postulancy as a Carmelite nun.

"So that will even things up for you," said Claude. "One child to God and one to the devil."

"No, two to the devil," his mother corrected him. And she glared across the room at his brother Felix.

For Felix was still there. And still driving a cart. "If you need an assistant," Claude told him, "I can offer you a Grade A coolie from the Marseilles docks."

But nothing came of it. He didn't work. He scarcely went out. He sat in his old room and looked from the window at the back yard and the wall and the privy. He sat at his table and opened the drawer and looked at the stubs of pencils and yellowing sheets of paper. And then he closed the drawer and left the table and lay face downward on his cot.

He had come home to die. But he had not died.

One evening, after he had been back some six weeks, he was sitting in the upstairs parlor with his mother and Felix, when there was a knocking on the door of the shop. Felix went down to answer it. Claude heard the sound of male voices, and when his brother came back upstairs he was grinning.

"Well, *au revoir*," Felix said.

"Where are you going?"

"I'm not. You are."

"I?"

"You've two callers downstairs. They're wearing nice blue uniforms with sergeants' stripes, and they'd like to have a little talk with you."

His mother looked up sharply. "Well," she said. "Well. So you have employment at last. . . . And you will please not forget, when you are paid," she added, "that you owe me forty-one francs."

"Plus the interest," said Claude. "I'll have to figure that out."

In the hall he called down the stairs: "One moment, messieurs." Then he went into his room. When, a few minutes later, Felix followed him, it was to feel a cold draft from the open window.

18

Tumult of cities: in the evening, and in the sun, and always. . . .

He returned to the cities. He lost himself in the tumult. Crossing into Germany, he came to Frankfurt, to Cologne, to Bremen and Hamburg; then, doubling back westward, to Brussels, Antwerp, Amsterdam, Rotterdam. He moved through the streets, boulevards, squares, and alleys; past factories, freight yards, warehouses, wharves. Always, after a time, he returned to the wharves—the seaports. He stood on the parapets of Europe and looked out to the sea.

He walked through the polders of Holland and along the parapets of the dikes. Coming to Rotterdam, he made the familiar round of ships, offices, and bars—with the familiar result. He worked with a crew paving the streets and slept on a pallet in one of Rotterdam's Hôtels de Babylone, and when he had raised a few florins he stopped paving the streets and simply walked them. With his knowledge of German, he was soon able to read Dutch, and he practiced on the street signs. Among the signs were many posters for recruitment in the Dutch Colonial Army, and one day, coming to a recruitment office, he went in. This time there was only one sergeant instead of two. His uniform was blue, but of a darker shade. And now it was not the sergeant who came for him, but he who came to the sergeant.

The man looked him over. He looked him over, as another sergeant once had, six years before, in the barracks at Antimes. But he did not laugh. He did not say, "In this army we have no nursery school." Instead he said, "You will be sent to Java."

"That's all right," said Claude.

"The term is six years."

"That's all right."

There was an examination, a document, a signature. And a few days later a uniform. He sold his civilian clothes for ten florins—the largest commercial transaction of his career—and for two weeks drilled with other recruits at a camp in the outskirts of Rotterdam. Then they were marched to the railway station, rode by train to the port of Den Helder, and boarded the troopship *Prins van Oranje*.

"So I am a soldier," he thought.

But by request—not conscription.

The parapets sank into the sea. There was only the sea. And the ship was its hub and its fulcrum.

He had been on a ship twice before—once going to England and once returning—but the first time he had been drunk with absinthe and the second time drunk with shock and misery. Now he was not drunk. But still there was drunkenness; for now at last he was on his Drunken Boat, his boat of dreams. It was still winter. The sea was gray. The sky was heavy with cloud and storm. But it was not the *Prins van Oranje* that bore Claude onward; it was the Argo, bound for Colchis and the Fleece. Beyond the windlashed northern ocean were the calms of motionless and blue eternity. Beyond the clouds were the starry archipelagoes, the golden birds, the thousand mornings of the day as yet unborn.

He stood at the rail, and mind and spirit rushed outward. Then he went to his hammock, on the bunk deck below, and there they veered and turned inward. This was the third stage of his journey, he thought; of his flight from the pit, from his Season in Hell. The first had been to Basel, to the haven of learning and knowledge—and a new hell of loneliness. The second had been to Italy, to the sun—and to sunstroke; to a hell of rootless feckless wandering. And now he was on the third: still moving, still seeking. But this was different, he thought. Different because now, for the first time, he was not alone; for the first time he was not only in a crowd—a stranger, an outsider—but part of the crowd, of a group, of a unit, a unit with a function, a purpose, a goal. Say what you would of colonialism, it was a force in the world, a current, a great tide. Very well, he was part of the world and now part of its tide: Soldaat Claude Morel of his Dutch Majesty's Colonial Army, soldier in the march of Europe's century of dominion.

Elsewhere, perhaps, the tide was raging like the Atlantic storms; but in the bowels of the *Prins van Oranje* it was thick and sluggish. It washed through the bunk deck in a rumble of snores, as if from five hundred close-packed Felixes. It seeped through cabin and companionway to the shuffle of boots, the clank of mess tins, the groans of the seasick, the scrape of latrine brushes. It pressed down on Claude, trying to sleep, in the shape of the lump of the soldier above him, who was too heavy for his hammock.

This particular soldier's name was Dirk Uden, and he was a farm boy from Friesland with a red face, as broad as his buttocks, that was made for smiling. But the smile never appeared. When the face was not contorted with nausea it was blank with apathy, and his eyes were blank too, whether turned to shipmates, ship, or sea.

"Things will be better next week," Claude consoled him.

"Better how?"

"We'll be in the Mediterranean. Out of the storms. In the sun."

"I don't like the sun."

"Well, in six weeks then. We'll be in Java."

"What's good about Java?"

"Everything will be new—fresh. We'll see the other side of the world; strange things, strange people."

"I don't like strange people."

"Why did you enlist then? You're a volunteer, aren't you? Why didn't you stay on the farm?"

"Because I don't like cows."

There was no Fleece, no day unborn, for Dirk Uden. Nor for any of the others in Claude's company of infantry. Their eyes were not on the horizon but on their cards and dice; their dreams not of sun and strangeness but of women and beer.

"They make the beer from rice out there."

"Rice, for Crissake."

"Yeah. And it tastes like piss. Only weaker."

"Me for gin then."

"Gin, hah. Gin's for officers."

"What about women? I suppose they're just for officers too."

"No, they're plenty of women."

"They're supposed to be good too."

"And cheap."

"But they all got clap."

"If you get clap you get sick leave. That's the life for me."

Claude turned to the rail. He lived at the rail. The routine of shipboard was simple and rigid: inspections, drills, lectures, meals, sleep. But between times there were long hours of leisure, and he spent almost all of them on deck and alone. Finding a seaward niche between a lifeboat and a davit, he made it his own domain, closed off from the grunt of voices, the roll of dice, the slap of cards. He watched the sea. He heard the breathing of the sea. He felt the salt of the sea on his lips and eyelids and the deep throb of the ship's engines in his bones and blood. He watched the sky. He watched the grayness thinning, the clouds dissolving, the sun emerging. At night he watched the masts sway tall and naked against the brightening stars.

. . . From the same desert, the same ocean, in the same night, always my tired eyes awake—always. . . . Always the Kings of Life, the three Magi, awake, to rise in the darkness, to continue their journey. . . .

The first land was Spain, low and dim off the port bow. Then, nearer and clearer, the coast rose. It became cliffs; it became Gibraltar; and the ship turned east. But it was not on Europe's last parapet that Claude's eyes were fixed. It was to the other side, to the south, to Africa. There was no parapet there. No rock. No fortress. There was only yellow beach, purple hills, and above them sky and sun.

Then Europe and Africa alike were gone, and again there was only the sea. But this sea was different; it was not ocean-gray but deep gleaming blue, and the horizons bounding it were the skylines of earth's heart and center. Ships passed them daily: steamships and sail-ships, freighters and liners and men-of-war, plowing the ancient furrows of the triremes and galleons. And occasionally land passed too: the tip of Sardinia, the cliffs of Malta, the old hills of Crete lying brown in the sun. Claude's fellow Argonauts neither knew where they were nor cared. "That was England, *hein?*" said Dirk Uden, as Malta sank away behind them. "*Vervloekt*, where's Java?" complained the cardplayers, as they moved on past Crete toward Suez. The engines rumbled, sergeants shouted. Land appeared ahead. "*Vervloekt*, aren't they going to let us off?" . . . "I need a woman." . . . "I need a beer."

They passed through the Suez Canal. Dark faces looked up at them from the banks, and pink faces looked down, incurious and sullen.

"The bastards! They don't let us off."

Then they were in the Red Sea. Sweat poured from them. The bunk-rooms reeked. All metalwork was too hot to be touched, and the decks shimmered as with the fumes of a furnace. The sun of Italy that had struck Claude down had been weak and pallid compared to this white flame of the tropics, but still he endured the flame, still he welcomed it, sought it, all but alone on the deck through the burning glare of the days. Now, for the first time in their journey, land was constantly in sight: the coasts of Egypt, the Sudan, Eritrea, and the Somalilands, sweeping endlessly through the miles. And through the miles and days he watched them—an image unrolling as if in a dream.

The image unrolled but it did not move. Only the ship moved, panting, burning; the land lay transfixed in heat and sunlight and at night spread like iron under the glitter of the stars. Nothing stirred on it. It was waste-land, desert. It was sand and gravel and rock, broken at intervals by low hills and hummocks, rising bare and forlorn against the parched bare sky. There was not only no life to be seen, but none to be imagined. A man, a horse, a camel—even a snake or a toad or a spider or an ant—would have seemed as out of place as in a landscape of the moon. It was a world of cinders and ashes; of stillness, of death.

And yet it was not death that Claude saw under the sun and the starlight. His eyes moved on past death, past desert and wasteland, and what he saw was vision and magic. He was the *voyant* again—the seer, the alchemist—and in the alembic of alchemy death changed into life. He was no longer staring at a coastline, but moving toward it, moving through it; he was moving through the desert, the wasteland, and it was no longer hostile but welcoming, not strange but familiar; it was the land-scape of his old journeys, of his dreams. Beyond the desert were the hills, and the hills grew higher. They became a great wall, a range, an escarp-ment, and he was climbing the escarpment, he was breaching it, he was past it; he had reached the world beyond, the lost world—of Cimmeria, of Abyssinia; he had come to the deep hidden places, to the green forests, the yellow rivers, the black nations, the dancing files. And this world, too, though it was lost, was not strange. He had seen it often. He had seen it always. But this time the seeing was even clearer than before; it was with a purity of vision and projection of which he had not been capable even in the days of his boyhood dreaming; and he thought, "Yes, it is still there. It is not gone, not dead. And I am not dead either—self-murdered—but still alive, still journeying, still following the rainbow toward the sun and the star. . . ."

An old instinct moved his hand. It groped through his pockets. But the pockets were empty.

They docked at Aden to coal. But there was no shore leave. Motionless at its wharf, the oven of the ship grew even hotter, and coal grimed the sweat on arms and faces.

Then they crossed the Arabian Sea. They docked at Bombay. There was no shore leave either—except for officers—and for two days the men leaned on the rails, bored and restless. Here was the long-imagined East, and Claude gazed out at it: at the shacks and temples, the slums and palaces, the cranes and warehouses, the cows and vultures. In his ears was an unending dim babel of voices and in his nose the smell of spice and urine. On the wharf an Englishman in khaki and topee shouted orders to a crew of coolies. Beyond, on the street, a man in rags lay sleeping, his head pillowed on a heap of dung. The cows moved by him; the crowds moved by him; crowds by the hundred and thousand streaming from every street and alley and doorway of the teeming city. As the Red Sea coast had been emptiness, so was this fullness—fullness and glut—of sound, movement, and life. Behind the façade of the city Claude could feel the depths of the vast labyrinth that was India. Beyond the visible thousands on this strip of waterfront he could feel the breath of unseen millions.

Again an old impulse stirred him. He would desert, jump ship, wait his chance, and get away in the night. He would enter the city, the labyrinth; sink and lose himself in those millions. But when night came he went no farther than the rail. He stopped and thought: "But why? To sink, to lose— what is that? And what will it profit? To lose oneself, one's identity, is not to find life, but to renounce it; to sink toward death. I have tried it before—in Europe, in my own country—and found only loneliness, only void. And how much deeper the void would be here; how much more certain the journey toward death. . . .

"No. That I know now: I do not want to die. Not now. Not yet. This journey is to Java, and other journeys will come in their time."

He turned away from the night, from the city, from India. Descending to the bunkroom, he joined a crowd at a card game, threw down a florin, and said, "Deal me a hand."

They came to Java. To the port of Tanjong Priok, near Batavia. Off to one side they could catch a glimpse of the capital city; to the other was a sweep of bright palm-fringed beaches. But they got to neither. Debarking from the ship, they entered a bleak cantonment of barracks, warehouses, tin-roofed shacks, and dusty compounds. They were issued rifles. They oiled the rifles. They dismantled and reassembled them. They shouldered them and marched for hours in the compounds, while the dust rose and the sergeants shouted.

That seemed to be the entire population of Java: sergeants.

Packs were issued, inspections held. A general reviewed them in a march-past and told them that they were now the Third Battalion of the Fifth Regiment of His Dutch Majesty's East Indian Army, and that the honor and glory of the Motherland was in their hands. As the general spoke, he stood on a raised platform under a canvas canopy; but the troops had no canopy, and three members of Claude's company toppled over in the heat. He considered toppling too, but thought better of it, for he had been told that the food in the hospital was even worse than in the barracks.

After two weeks they moved. A newly built railway line had its terminus at Tanjong Priok, and they were loaded into slat-sided freight cars and headed off to the interior. Now for the first time they saw non-Dutch, nonmilitary Java: roads and villages, fields and paddies, mango trees, banana trees, bamboo trees, and, above them, rank upon rank of soft green-brown hills, terraced and planted to their very crests. Hump-backed zebu cattle were everywhere. And people were everywhere. There was as strong an impression of myriad humanity as on the waterfront of Bombay, but instead of the squalid compression of a great city there was the ease and flow of countryside. Everything seemed on a miniature scale: hills and fields and carts and houses and people—most of all, the people —like figures from the pages of a child's picture book. Brown oval faces with gentle eyes were raised to them as they passed. Brown bodies moved, slender and lithe, in the fields and paddies. All the men and children and most of the women, were unclothed from the waist up, and their flesh gleamed soft and warm in the golden sunlight.

The train moved on. Its steel clanked. Its engine belched black smoke. From the cars the troops eyed the women hungrily and shouted obscenities in Dutch.

Then the hills grew higher, the country wilder. And the railway line ended. They camped for a night in the outskirts of a town, and the next day went on through terrain that was partly cultivated and partly virgin forest. They gained altitude, and it grew cooler. And ahead were the tall cones of great volcanoes.

They did not, however, march all the way to the volcanoes, but, after three days marching, reached the end of their journey in a broad upland valley. Here was another cantonment, a sort of outpost fort, still in the process of being built, and one of their first jobs was to help complete it. Another was to keep an eye on the neighboring hill tribes, some of which had been making trouble; and a third was to begin clearing a right of way down to the railhead for the tracks that would soon be laid all the way to the valley.

"Then when it's all done they give us a glass of beer each," said the company wit, "and a look at a woman through a spyglass."

They drilled. They shouldered their rifles and packs. They stacked their rifles and shouldered picks and shovels. Later they drilled again.

"*Eén, twee, drie, vier,*" barked the sergeant. "*Eén, twee, drie, vier. . . .*"

On the ship and in Tanjong Priok there had been many sergeants. Now—at least for Claude's platoon—there was only one, and his name was Houttekamp. He did not look as a Dutch sergeant should. He was not red-faced, not beef-necked; he could not have weighed more than a sun-shriveled hundred-and-thirty pounds. But in all other respects he was built according to the traditional specifications, and his men accorded him the traditional hatred.

Eén, twee, drie, vier. Eén, twee, drie, vier. . . . Sunday was usually drill-less; but the Sunday came when inspection was unsatisfactory, and for two hours they tramped the parade ground under the flaming sun.

"*Eén, twee, drie, vier. . . .*"

And then, "*Halt!*" The sergeant moved along the ranks and stopped in front of Claude. "You do not enjoy drilling?" he asked.

"No," said Claude.

"No, what?"

"No, Herr Gunst."

"My name is Houttekamp."

"I beg your pardon. I thought it was Gunst."

"What are you talking about?"

"I had an old friend called Sergeant Gunst. He yelled just like you do, and I got mixed up."

"Oh, I see." The sergeant's dark face grew even darker. "Well, you will remain here after the others are dismissed. Perhaps a little individual attention will assist you in enjoying drill—and remembering my name."

"Yes, Herr Gunst."

The drill continued. Rifles swung. Boots thumped. "All together now!" Houttekamp shouted. "*Eén, twee, drie, vier. . . .*"

The men responded. Their voices barked. One barked rather louder than the others:

"*Eén, twee, drie, vier,*
Sergeant Houttekamp, kiss my rear. . . ."

Again, "*Halt!*"

Again Houttekamp approached. "French swine—"

He spent two weeks in confinement and two more on latrine duty, and in the process he decided to desert. But by the time he was released he had changed his mind. . . . No, he thought, it was no good. It would be the same pattern all over again—revolt and flight, aloneness and outsideness —the very pattern he had joined the army to break. It was not freedom that he needed now; for five years he had had nothing but freedom, and it had all but destroyed him. What he needed was exactly the opposite: conformity, a sense of belonging, submission to the will of the world— and to discipline. He would submit to discipline, if it killed him. Or until he killed Houttekamp.

More weeks passed. He kept out of trouble. He drilled and marched and cleared forest for the railway tracks and helped throw up earthworks against the "troublesome," though invisible, hill tribes. The heat gradu- ally grew less, and that was good. But simultaneously the rains came, and that was not good, for rain in Java was not like rain in Europe; it flooded down relentlessly, day after day, in the deluge of the monsoon, and their world was a sunless airless slough of steaming mud.

Many of the men came down with fevers. Several died. The encamp- ment became a place of sodden ghosts, but, perversely, Claude grew even stronger and flourished. The last of his boyish softness was gone now, from both face and body, and he was lean, leathery, and hard; so hard, indeed, he thought with satisfaction, that a mosquito would starve or break its beak before it could coax a drop of blood from his flesh.

Inwardly, too, he felt a new hardness, a new containment and control. In Italy, during his lonely wanderings, he had set himself a stern goal: to face the world without anger and without fear. And now at last he seemed on the way to its attainment. The incident with Houttekamp had been an outbreak of the old *voyou* he once had been. After that, he kept his mouth shut. He drilled, he marched, he shoveled, he did his work. As the shell of his skin had become too tough for the mosquitoes, so would he make the shell of his spirit impermeable to everything. Make the armor sound, he thought, and the shield mighty. Then in time, perhaps, he would reclaim his sword and his spear.

The "platoon of Felixes" lived their lives around him. If lives they could be called. They drilled, marched, and shoveled; they ate and slept; they snored, belched, farted, and scratched; they wiped the mud from their clothes and rifles. Dirk Uden, the farm boy from Friesland, wiped by the hour, his mouth slack, his eyes fixed blankly on the barracks wall. One morning he awoke with fever and was sent to the hospital, and three days later he died. First he had got away from cows. Now he had got away from mud.

Some two miles from the camp was a town. It offered rice beer and whores, and was the troops' Saturday night refuge. But Claude never went there. Indeed, he did nothing with the other men except what routine required of him, and lived wholly within himself. They, for their part, accepted him as a "queer one"—the Frenchy—and left him alone. Sergeant Houttekamp, after a few unsuccessful attempts to goad him into further insubordination, also left him alone. There were a half-dozen-odd known and active homosexuals in the platoon, but none ever approached him. Apparently the suns and storms of two years had obliterated all marks that they might once have recognized.

The only one to make friendly overtures was a young lieutenant, whom Claude had early on recognized as an educated and sensitive man. And the recognition, it seemed, had been mutual, for one day, when Claude had been to his quarters on some errand, the lieutenant tried to detain him.

"I have a few books," he said. "Perhaps you might like to borrow some."

"No thank you, sir," Claude replied.

"You don't care for reading?"

"No sir."

The lieutenant tried another tack. "What did you do before?" he inquired.

"Before, sir?"

"Before you joined up. Back in Europe, what did you do?"

"I paved streets, sir."

"Oh?" The lieutenant showed his surprise. "And before that, may I ask?"

"Before that?" Claude considered. "A longshoreman, sir. Also a busboy, a delivery boy, an artist's model, and a cleaner in a spaghetti factory. . . . Then, too, I have been a ratcatcher and a pimp," he added.

And the lieutenant gave up.

He was, however, not wholly without human companionship. Sometimes he left the camp and tramped through the rain—not to the town where the other soldiers went, but to the smaller villages of the district —and there he slowly made acquaintances among the people. It was not easy. For one thing, there was the problem of languages, for, though he was still a master of tongues, he had no books on Javanese, and the villagers were poor preceptors. And for another, more important, there was the barrier of fear. The natives did not seem to hate the Dutch—they were too gentle for hatred—but they were afraid of them; mortally afraid of their faces, their uniforms, their strangeness, their brutality. Claude was the first outlander ever to come among them who had not wanted either a drink, a woman, or to requisition them for labor; and for a while they were uneasy and guarded in his presence. In the end, however, he won them over. When he came they welcomed him with garlands and food, and when he left they begged him soon to return.

Ndoro-sabrangan, they called him. Lord-from-over-the-sea. And they asked why all the others were so different.

"Because the others don't like niggers," he told them.

"Niggers? What is that? We do not know such a word."

"You are niggers," he said. "And so am I."

Then he walked out beyond the villages, into the forest. He followed deep jungle paths, like green tunnels, and the sky was gone, the rain a faint pattering high overhead. He was a familiar of the forest, a child of the forest. Memories of the Ardennes and the *Schwarzwald* thronged his mind as he moved on through stillness and aloneness. And yet this was not at all like the forests of the north. There were no outcroppings of rock, no cones and acorns underfoot, no Gothic aisles of light and shadow, but only greenness, only an endlessly repeated pattern of leaf and frond and vine and liana, like flowing images upon a screen.

Behind the screen was silence. Silence absolute and transfixed. In the green gleam ahead great bluish blossoms hung from a vine, gleaming as with an inner light of their own. Beyond them the screens ranged off into dimness: tall, looming, still. . . . Then, in the next instant, no longer still, for there was a screech, a rending of branches, faint shapes in the branches, plunging, struggling, screaming. . . . And then gone. There was only silence again. Only the emerald screens. As Claude moved on, the screens opened ahead and closed behind. The blossoms seemed to be watching him, as if with deep violet eyes.

He returned to camp. To wiping mud. To his rifle and shovel. To *eén, twee, drie, vier*.

Now the principal job was clearing the way for the railroad. Large gangs, it was said, were working at the other end, from the present railhead up toward the valley, and they, on their end, worked down toward the eventual meeting place. As the clearing progressed, they of course moved farther from their barracks, until the distance was too great for daily back-and-forth marching and they bivouacked out in the bush.

The bivouacs were large ones, for so was the enterprise. At the top were a few civilian engineers and senior officers, under them the junior officers, then the noncoms—the Houttekamps, then the troops to the strength of six platoons. But the troops were now no longer at the bottom of the ladder, for under them, in turn, were several hundred native laborers who had been requisitioned for the job. As a result—in spite of rain and mud and other camping-out discomforts—the members of the Third Battalion of the Fifth Regiment of His Dutch Majesty's Colonial Army had it rather better than usual. For their hated shovels were now in Javanese hands, while they themselves carried only their rifles. After months of menial labor and indignity, the White Man's Burden had at last been properly distributed: with the European as *ndoro*—master—and the brownskin as *budak*—slave.

The rifles did not go unused. Occasionally shots sounded. More often butts rose and fell. For the Javanese were not willing workers; most had been dragged forcibly into service from their fields and paddies and bamboo huts; and while there was no concerted revolt among them, there were constant escapes and escape attempts. "Absolute discipline must be maintained. We must show always who are the masters," the word came down from the higher levels. And for the first time since their arrival the new troops responded with a will.

The slave labor for Claude's platoon had been secured from one of the villages near the encampment which he had visited on his wanderings. They had talked with him, fed him, garlanded him, and he knew almost all by appearance and many by name. But he did not call them by name now. He did not look at their faces. He gave his orders quietly, impersonally, and looked past their naked sweating bodies toward the jungle screens.

"Without anger," he thought. "Without anger or fear . . ."

The loss of fear was easy; as easy and sure as the loss of hope.

But anger died harder.

Among those he stood guard on was a man named Pandap. He was small and brown and gentle, as they all were, but not quite so gentle as the others, nor so submissive, with a certain youthful fire, a ready smile, a quick mind. This Claude had seen back in his village. Neither fire nor smile, to be sure, were in evidence now, as he chopped and shoveled through the days at the brown jungle loam; but Claude knew that the mind was still working, that it was not wholly sunk in animal apathy and docility. One day, while hacking at the forest's edge, Pandap had moved almost imperceptibly away from the others, and Claude had been sure he was on the point of making a break for it. On another, a soldier had cursed and shoved him, and there had been a quick dangerous gleam in Pandap's eyes and teeth. Neither time did anything happen. But then a third day came, and something did.

This time Houttekamp was involved. Approaching Claude's particular area while the men were carrying out cut brushwood, he watched Pandap for a moment, was displeased by his slowness, and kicked him hard in the rump. The little Javanese went down, and his load scattered around him.

The sergeant kicked him in the side. "Get up!" he roared.

Pandap got to his feet and began picking up the brush; but again he was not fast enough for Houttekamp, and this time the sergeant hit him with his fist. Once more he went down. There was another kick; a rain of kicks.

Then Claude came up.

"That's enough," he said.

Houttekamp whirled on him. "What?"

"I said that's enough. Stop it."

"Stop it? I come and do what you should be doing, and you tell me to stop, *hein?* You give orders to your sergeant, *hein?*—you insubordinate bastard." Houttekamp's face was twisted with rage. "I'll show you how I'll stop, all right," he shouted. "First this nigger and then you—"

He swung back to Pandap. He swung his booted foot. The Javanese was still prostrate, and the kick was aimed at his face; but it never reached it. For Claude's rifle swung faster. It seemed to leap of its own will from his shoulder, to leap butt first at the sergeant's head; and then it struck, the sergeant swayed and went down, and Claude stood over him, and only then, in the sudden stillness, did anger die. . . .

He jerked Pandap to his feet.

"Come on!" he said.

Then the jungle enveloped them.

19

They moved between the emerald screens, through the sodden web of the forest. Now and then they came to a clearing or vestigial path, but the paths either petered out or veered off in the wrong directions, and for the most part they had to shove and claw their way through the undergrowth. Sometimes there were snapping or whining sounds behind the screens. An animal screeched. A bird cawed. Then there was stillness, broken only by the sucking sound of their feet in the muck. When they stopped to listen there was total stillness. Apparently they were not being followed.

They moved on without speaking. There had been no discussion of what to do or where to go, but Pandap obviously had a plan, and Claude was certain that it was to make an arc around the railway route and the army post which would head back to his own village. It was all right with Claude. Pandap led and he followed. They crept on through the hours, and when it grew dark they sat down in the driest place they could find, at the foot of a giant teak tree.

Claude sat motionless, his body hunched over and his head in his hands; and Pandap watched him solicitously.

"You are tired, *ndoro?*" he asked at last.

"My name is Claude."

"You are tired—Clowde? You are sick?"

"No, I'm all right."

But he wasn't all right. He was sick. And the sickness was deep: deeper than flesh and blood and bone. His rifle was leaning against the tree beside him, and he looked at it; at the butt of it that had hit Houttekamp. He did not regret hitting Houttekamp. Not the specific blow at the specific man, for the man was a swine, a *crapule*. And yet sickness was within him. It was not the sergeant's face that he saw, but others: a face stunned and reeling, the mouth dark with blood, as Druard slumped to the pavement. The face of the Greek mate in Marseilles. His own face in the mirror the next morning, his own fist held up, himself looking at the fist and thinking: "Perhaps the one truth of life is a blow in the face."

Those earlier blows had been with the fist. This one had been with a rifle butt. Perhaps next time he would reverse the rifle and use it as it was designed to be used; strike as modern man was equipped to strike. "Why not the whole way? Why not murder?" he had asked when he was Attila, when he was Lucifer. Now, as a mere man, would he do what Lucifer could not?

Pandap as well was looking at the rifle. "It is too dark to hunt," he said. "And also they might hear us."

Getting up, he foraged about in the undergrowth, and returned with a booty of fruits and berries. They ate. They dozed. They waited through the night. And at dawn they were off again.

The second day was like the first, and the third like both of them—except that toward the end of the third they came to the edge of the forest. Pandap's instincts had been true; his village was only a few miles away across the plain. And when darkness came they crossed the open land and reached it. Their welcome was tremendous. There were shouts, laughter, garlands, embraces, and then a feast with bowls of *sego* and rice beer, and Claude drank for the first time since the night he had left Basel. And finally he went to sleep in Pandap's hut, with Pandap, his wife, and their three children lying on their woven mats beside him.

In the morning, however, the celebration was over, and Pandap's face was grave as he brought Claude a breakfast of mangoes and tea.

"There have been Dutch patrols around," he said. "They do not know anything yet, but soon they will, and there will be trouble."

"I must leave then," said Claude.

"Yes, you must leave. And for that I have a plan. It is to go to another village—not near here but about four days away—across the jungle and the slopes of the volcanoes. It is a village I know well; I have there a brother and many cousins. There are no Dutch, no army, and you will be safe."

"If I can find it."

"You do not need to find it. I will take you."

"No, this is your home. You'll be all right here. Even if the patrols come back you'll be all right; they can't tell one of you from another."

Pandap did not argue. His reply was quiet and final. "I am only a peasant," he said. "A simple coolie. But I am also a man, with a man's feelings, who will remember all his life what you have done for him. Do you think I will just sit here and let you go alone through strange country? No, we will go together to my brother's village. I will make you known to them, and then when you are all right there—when you know what you will do next—I will come back here."

Claude tried to speak, but he wouldn't listen. "So, it is settled. We will go." He got to his feet, then paused, his eyes on Claude. "But first," he added, "there is a change to be made."

The change was of clothing. Claude removed his uniform, and it was taken out and burned, and Pandap brought a length of batik cloth, and wrapped it around him as a sarong.

"Now the boots," he said.

But Claude shook his head. "I couldn't walk half a mile without the boots."

Pandap furrowed his brow. He called his wife. His wife called other women, and they called their men, and soon half the village was crowded into the hut, staring at the *ndoro sabrangan* in sarong and army boots. At first they were solemn and shy. Then a woman giggled. A man laughed. In a moment everyone was laughing, and Claude loudest of all.

"If someone comes too close," he said, "I'll sit on my feet."

Then something else was pointed out. Something stranger than his feet. His hair. His sun-bronzed skin was dark enough to pass for Javanese, and at a distance his features, like his boots, might go unnoticed; but his light hair shone like a sunburst among the blacktopped natives. There was more laughter—and a conference. A straw hat was brought, but it was not enough, and there was another conference. Then Pandap's wife had an idea, and she and several of the other women went out, returning presently with baskets of nuts. Seating Claude in their midst, they cracked open the nuts, ground the kernels until they were pulpy, and dyed his hair with the blackish juice.

Finally they moved back to look at their handiwork. They nodded. Then they laughed again. Someone pointed at Claude's eyes, and they roared with laughter, for though his hair was now purple-black, the eyes were still a light northern blue.

"No, you're not going to spit in them," Claude said. "I'll just keep them closed, and Pandap can lead me."

The limit had been reached in tailoring and cosmetology, and nothing could be done about Claude's excess height. Food was brought and packed into two straw baskets which they slung on their backs. Claude fastened his bandolier under his sarong and wrapped his rifle in bamboo matting. Then they left the hut. They walked down the village street, and the whole population followed them, jabbering and laughing, and Claude thought, "It's not like an escape at all, a thing of life and death, but like going off to a picnic or a masquerade ball." But then they reached the end of the street, and suddenly the jabbering stopped, the laughter stopped, and there was only silence, only dark eyes gravely watching him, as he turned to say his thanks and his goodbye.

"Goodbye, *ndoro*," said Pandap's wife.

"Claude," he corrected her.

"Goodbye, Clowde."

"Goodbye, Clowde," echoed the others.

And then he and Pandap walked on.

For this journey they had first to travel several miles through open country, between the fields and paddies, but they saw no sign of the Dutch, and though Claude's tallness brought stares from some passers-by, this in itself was nothing to worry about. In a few hours they had gained the forest, and this time there was a forest trail. They moved on until it was dark, ate from their baskets, and slept.

In the morning they were on their way again. They reached the slopes of the nearest of the volcanoes, and the land began to rise, the vegetation to thin, as they climbed up out of the tropics into the temperate zone above. The forest was now like the forests of Europe. The emerald screens were gone, and in their place were bare tree trunks and long mossy aisles. Then, still higher, the trees grew smaller, they too fell away, and the trail led over open mountainsides and bare plateaus. Behind them the flatland spread away like a dim green sea. Ahead and above, the volcanoes raised their crests skyward, some gleaming in sunlight, others barely discernible in cloud and rain. Claude had learned their names from the village people—Papandayan, Merapi, Kalut, Semeru, Lamongan—and now they sounded in his mind as in a litany. Their high silent world drew him on, enveloped him. The world of railways and barracks and rifles and red-faced Dutchmen was lost and gone.

—Except that he still had his rifle. On entering the forest he had discarded its bamboo sheath, and now he carried it at the ready, hoping to add to their supply of food. On the high slopes game was plentiful. Twice they sighted wild pig and once a herd of the small deer called muntjac, and each time he took aim and fired—and missed—as the beasts scuttled quickly away. "Now you see what sort of soldier I was," he told Pandap, laughing.

When the next game appeared Pandap tried his luck. And missed too.

The recoil of the rifle all but knocked him down, and they laughed again and moved on.

By evening they were wholly above the trees. Rain fell. It grew cold. But they found a cleft in the mountainside, almost a cave, whose walls and floor were heated by the volcano's inner fire, and there they spent a dry, warm night. In the morning, when they first stirred, there was a sudden scurrying, and two rabbits, who had apparently slept with them, dashed out of their sanctuary.

"Seems that word's got around about our shooting," said Claude.

All that next day they moved through high valleys beneath the towering cones. Occasionally there were clumps of trees and patches of moss and grass, but for the most part their way led over great beds of lava and cindery ashes. The shell of the earth was cold, bleak, lifeless, yet beneath the shell burned the fires of life, and sometimes that life burned irresistibly through it, and they came to beds of sulphur, to jets of steam and water, to boiling wells and mud caldrons, with the earth around them gleaming green and yellow and red. High above, too, steam poured from the volcano's crater and mingled with the clouds and sunlight and quick passing storms.

On Papandayan's farther side, late in the third day, they began their descent, again spending the night in a warmed refuge and reaching the end of the lava slopes early the next morning. And here, on a great burned cliff projecting from the mountainside, they came again to the world of men—or what had once been men: an ancient, ruined, lonely temple facing out toward the plains beyond. They moved through silent aisles and terraces, past crumbling walls and columns and sculptured pyramids, and, from the ground, toppled stone faces looked up at them with sightless eyes. Here there were rats and spiders, and in the air above, crows wheeling and cawing; and Claude shot at them, and missed, and continued shooting until his bullets were gone. Then, unfastening his bandolier, he threw it away. And he laid the rifle on the ground beside a stone face. "Now another culture," he thought, "has left its memorial."

For the rest of the day they continued their descent: first across alpine grass and scrub, then through the slanting forest and on down again into jungle. But Pandap knew his way; in the jungle, as before, they followed well-worn trails; and toward evening the last of dense growth fell away, and they came out on the plains on the other side of the volcanoes. In the dusk and then in darkness they followed a road between fields and paddies. They came to a village and passed through it, and then to a second and stopped. Pandap called out and voices answered. People poured from the huts. Torches gleamed in their faces. And their journey was over.

The village was called Sambol. With its bamboo huts, its mud street, its zebu-drawn carts, its brown gentle people, it was indistinguishable from

Pandap's village—or any other in Java—except that it was even quieter, even happier, than any Claude had seen before. For here there was no nearby army post, no uniforms, no patrols, no loud red-faced invaders in quest of beer or women or slave labor for a railway. Many of them had not so much as seen an outlander before, and Claude's brownness and sarong and sleek black hair did not lessen his strangeness. They stared at his tallness, and at his eyes. *"Mikla-takan,"* they called him. In their back-country dialect it meant "Sky-eyes."

But if they stared they also smiled. They welcomed him. When Pandap had told his story they embraced him and brought him food and garlands and made him one of their own. That night he slept in the place of honor in the hut of Pandap's brother, Kitong. And the next morning when he arose, the men of the village were already at work building a new hut close by.

"Will it be big enough for you?" asked Pandap.

"For *me?*"

"Yes, of course. You must have a place of your own."

"But I will be going soon."

"Going—where? . . . No. No, *ndoro*. No, Clowde. You must stay here. It is safe, truly. There are no soldiers, no Dutch at all. And the people are proud and happy to have you."

So, as it turned out a few days later, it was not Claude who left, but Pandap, setting out back across the volcanoes toward his own village. Claude remained in Sambol. He slept in his new hut. He became part of the household of Kitong, and of Kitong's wife, Mati, and of their four naked laughing children, and of Mati's younger sister, Kuru, who cleaned his hut and served his meals and watched him silently with shy grave eyes. He became part of the village, and the village accepted him—as had Pandap's before it; except that here it was an even deeper acceptance, for it was not as a mere friend, a visitor, but almost as one of their own selves.

The rains fell. The sun shone. The days passed. He sat in front of his hut, in the shade of a pandanus-leaf awning, and watched the life of the village. He walked down the street, among the women and children and cattle and pigs and chickens. Joining the men, he walked on out of the village in the early morning, until they came to the rice paddies, and there he took off his boots and entered the paddies and worked in them all day, his back bent, his legs submerged to the knee in brown water, and his arms to the elbow; and in the evening he returned to the village, he ate with Kitong and his family, he went to his own hut and lay on his mat, and his back ached and his hands and feet felt bloodless and shriveled; but at last he slept, and in the morning went back to the paddies. From the brown water, now and then, he lifted his eyes. He looked at the pale yellow-green of the rice leaves and at the dark gleaming green of the fields beyond. Once green had meant other things to him: the green of a vowel, of pillared caves, of tearing knives. Now it meant rice, a field, a meadow, growth, life. What God had meant it to mean. . . .

God? What God? The God of the bamboo villages? Of the stone faces on the volcano? Of the gun-swinging Dutchmen? Of serge suits and umbrellas?

Of a drunkard vomiting in a baptismal font?

The days passed. And he stayed in Sambol. There had been no conscious decision, no act of will, but still he stayed, and now his back no longer ached and he went barefoot all the time, and he was no longer *ndoro*, nor even Clowde, but simply Mikla-takan: Sky-eyes. He lived in poverty. He lived in labor. He lived in warmth—the warmth of earth and growth and flesh and smile and laughter—and it enveloped him, filled him, as with the warmth of the sun. "At last I am a child of the son," he thought, "a child of God the Father." And so he would remain. So the days would pass. Days without end. . . .

Until a day came—and, with it, ending. Or, rather, a night, for it was dark and he was lying on the mat in his hut, waiting for sleep, when he heard whispering voices outside, and after a moment Kitong appeared carrying a lamp.

"Mikla-takan," he said softly.

"Yes?" said Claude.

"Ah, you are awake. Good. We did not wish to awake you from sleep and dream."

"What is it?" Claude asked.

"We have a present for you."

"A present?"

"Yes." Kitong turned to the doorway and beckoned, and two other figures appeared. They were his wife, Mati, and her young sister, Kuru. "You have now been among us for more than a moon," said Kitong. "When my brother brought you he said you were a good man, a friend to us—like one of us. And he was right. You too have been a brother."

Claude had risen. Kitong paused and then he said, "You have stayed, and we hope you will stay always. But a man cannot live alone; it is not the way of nature. So we have brought you a companion, a wife, so you will be alone no longer."

He stepped back a little, and the two women moved forward. For a moment they stood together before Claude, and Mati's arm was around her sister; and then she too stepped back and the girl Kuru stood there alone. She was wearing a bright sarong that fell from waist to knees, but the rest of her was bare, except for flowers. In her black hair was a frangipani blossom, around her neck was a garland of blossoms, and beneath the garland her shoulders and breasts gleamed golden in the lamplight.

She raised her dark eyes to Claude, smiled shyly, and lowered them, and Claude looked at her, and then at Mati and then at Kitong, and tried to speak.

But Kitong forestalled him. "No, Mikla-takan," he said, "it is not what you perhaps think: that we have brought Kuru against her will. You see, she has smiled at you. Now she stands alone. She has come not because we made her, but of her own self, so you will be no more alone. To be your woman, your wife—"

"And may you be happy together," murmured Mati.

Then it was they who smiled, at Claude and at Kuru, and in the next instant they had faded back, they were gone, the lamp was gone, and in the hut there was darkness and beyond the door the pallid moonlight. Claude could not see the girl. She made no sound. He could only feel her. He felt her moving softly to his mat and sitting down on it, and then lying down. He felt her waiting. And he too waited. He waited a long time: first standing where he was, then sitting in a corner of the hut, finally rising and moving and sitting on the mat beside her. There too he sat a long time, and, as time passed, the moon climbed and grew brighter, until he was able to see her; and he saw that now the sarong was gone and she was wearing only the blossoms and beneath the white of the blossoms was her flesh—naked, waiting. Her eyes were closed, and then open, watching him. He could hear the sound of her breathing.

The moon shadows moved. She had closed her eyes again. Then he spoke her name.

"Yes, Mikla-takan?"

"You are lovely," he said, "and you are good. You must not be hurt. You must not be angry."

"I shall not be angry," she murmured.

He touched her hand and it closed on his, drawing him toward her. But he pulled gently away. He pulled back and up, raising her to her feet, and across the hut and through the doorway into the moonlight. He led her to Kitong's hut and stopped and released her; he returned to his own and lay down on his mat; and for hours, in the darkness, through the honk of pigs and the hum of cicadas, he could hear the faint sound of a woman's sobbing.

He pulled on his boots, and they were tight and stiff on his feet. Then he went to Kitong's hut. Kitong, Mati, and the four children were at breakfast, and his place at the mat was waiting for him. But Kuru's place was empty. And he did not sit down at his own.

He stopped in the doorway and said, "I have come to say goodbye."

Kitong rose and stood awkwardly. "You are going, *ndoro*?"

"Yes, I am going."

"First eat with us," said Mati.

"No—thank you. I must go now, early. I shall have a long journey."

The children stared at him. Mati took several yams and mangoes from a bowl on the mat and, rising, put them in a basket and gave it to him. "At least with these you will not go hungry," she said.

"Thank you," he said again.

She did not answer; Kitong did not speak. Only their eyes spoke. Their eyes said, "We were wrong. You are not one of us. You are a white man, a *ndoro sabrangan*. And we are not good enough for you. Kuru is not good enough—"

For another moment Claude stood there. He half raised his hand and dropped it. "Well, goodbye then," he said.

"Goodbye, *ndoro*."

"When you see him, say my goodbye to Pandap."

"Yes, *ndoro*."

"And to Kuru."

"Yes, *ndoro*."

He turned and left. He walked down the village street. He walked out of Sambol and down the road and past the paddies and on to the west. All that day, and the next, and the next, and the next. . . .

He skirted the volcanoes. He kept to the plains. Circling back in the direction from which he and Pandap had come, he approached the army post, and the line of the railway, but stopped before he reached them and followed a parallel line across country toward the coast. Where else was there to go but to the coast—to Batavia? To the world he had left and to which he must now return.

The sun shone. The rain fell. Sometimes he followed roads, sometimes he crossed fields and paddies, sometimes he beat his way through jungle. When the food Mati had given him was gone he lived off the country, and he avoided towns and villages as much as possible. For a few days his boots bothered him badly, and he limped as he had used to in Europe with his "Achilles' knee." But as he moved on the boots softened, the blisters healed, and he consumed the miles with a long steady stride.

As he neared the coast, however, the land was more thickly settled, the roads were crowded, and it became impossible to avoid the villages. Several times he saw Dutchmen, both military and civilian, and on at least one occasion barely missed a confrontation. And even where there were no Dutch, the Javanese eyed him curiously as he passed, staring at his tallness, his face, and the crown of his head. Above all, at his head—and he soon found out why. For one day, stooping to drink from a sunlit pool, he saw that his hair had grown out until it was now in two layers: the outer still black with dye, but the inner his own flaxen blond.

Something obviously had to be done, and that same night he did it.

The part of the country to which he had come consisted less and less of small native farms and more and more of large Dutch-owned plantations; and moving from one plantation house to another, he at last found the chance he was looking for. Though it was already dark, this house had no lights in its windows, and yet it was too early for its occupants to be asleep. They must all be out, he decided, and when a watchful wait confirmed his opinion, he took quick action. Running to the rear of the house, he forced a window, climbed in, and groped his way upstairs to what seemed to be the main bedroom. He threw open a wardrobe and found women's clothes. Another—and there were men's. From a rack he took a linen suit, from a drawer a shirt, and shedding his sarong, he pulled them on. The suit was too short and too broad for him—the owner was obviously another square-rigged Dutchman—but it would have to do. Now only one more thing remained, and that too he accomplished quickly. Off the bedroom was a bathroom, in the bathroom a tin tub, and beside the tub a cake of soap. Thrusting the soap into a pocket, he retraced his steps—through the bedroom, down the stairs, out the window, into darkness.

Fait accompli, he thought: the most ambitious theft of his career. But as he moved on he decided, no, it was not a theft at all but merely an exchange, for had he not left his sarong neatly folded on the Dutchman's bed? After a bit of washing it would be just the thing for the next reception at Government House.

He moved through peanut and tobacco fields. Finding a storage shed, he broke in, spent the night, and in the morning had a breakfast of peanuts. Then he found a secluded pool, took out his soap, and set about the business of his hair. It took a long time; the dye had soaked deep, and even after an hour his reflection did not look quite right. But at least the fantastic layer cake was gone, and the hair, if streaked and dirty, was no longer that of a freak. Like his clothing, it would do. When he rose and walked on he was again a European.

But being a European presented its problems, too, for white men did not travel on foot and alone through the fields of Java. He had thought about this during the night; he had taken his bearings as best he could; and now he cut sharply to the north, where, a few miles distant, he should come to the railway line. His calculation proved correct. By midmorning he reached it, and by noon, following the track, he came to a station. A while later, a coastbound train pulled in. And late that same afternoon he opened a compartment door, clung for an instant to an iron bar, and jumped from the platform into the freight yards of Batavia.

This time he did not fall. He did not even soil his white linen. "Shall I go toward Montmartre or the *Quartier?*" he thought. "Or simply walk for a while along the boulevards?"

Where he walked was, first, through alleys and past warehouses. Then he came to the Chinese district of Batavia and had his first glimpse of an Oriental city as he had long imagined one to be: a labyrinth of streets and lanes and warrens, of shops and teahouses and pagodas, of pointed concave roofs and red doors and carved black dragons and lacquered balconies. Then these, too, were behind him and he came to the new city, the Dutch city, and around him now were square buildings and trim compounds, pink faces and broad buttocks, the cleanness, flatness, and dullness of a provincial town in the Netherlands.

But within the dullness, he well knew, there was danger. For here, if anywhere, was where he would be caught.

He was dressed like a prosperous planter, but he had not a florin in his pockets. Many times in his life his pockets had been empty, and he had filled them by finding work; but to seek work here would be the surest way to disaster. Though to a Javanese he could pass as Dutch, he could not to a Dutchman, and there were so few other Europeans in Java that the mere opening of his mouth would beget suspicion and inquiry. He had a three-way choice: to be caught; to remain a fugitive (and either starve or be caught); or to get out. Walking on through Batavia, he followed the waterfront to Tanjong Priok.

Here, of course, there was the greatest danger of all: the camps and depots and sentries of the army from which he had deserted. But here too were the harbor, the ships, the only way out. Remembering the location of the guard posts, he carefully detoured them; but once he made a mistake, a challenging voice rang out, and he ran, with his loose clothes flapping about him. He found a corner in an empty warehouse and hid there until dark. Then he tried again: moving furtively along the base of the wharves, a shadow among shadows. There were many ships in the harbor, but more than half were out at anchor and unreachable, and, of those at dock, all seemed to be Dutch, and therefore as much to be avoided as the streets of Batavia. He moved on. He searched desperately. He began to despair. And then at last, toward the very end of the wharves, he had such luck as he could not have dreamed of, for there before him, moored to a dock, was the black hull of a foreign freighter. On its stern was the name *Nottingham Castle;* above it the Union Jack. And a tide of smoke from its stack and a rattling of winches on deck indicated that it would soon be casting off.

Bound where, Claude of course did not know. Nor did it matter. The East was full of British ports of call: Calcutta, Rangoon, Singapore, Hong Kong, Sydney. The coasts of Borneo and wildest Papua. . . .

It was too late and too chancy to try to sign on, and the gangway was full of lights and moving figures. But at the ship's stern it was dark and quiet, and a mooring rope slanted up to the deck, no more than twelve feet above. He grasped the rope. He pulled. He climbed. He reached the rail, and the deck, and moved along the deck to the nearest lifeboat, and there he loosened the canvas cover, climbed in, and replaced the canvas. A while later there was a throbbing of engines, and he smiled. Twice, back in Marseilles, he had tried to stow away on a ship and failed, but this time he was doing better.

> *"Calcutta, Rangoon, Singapore, Hong Kong, Sydney,*
> *The coasts of Borneo and wildest Papua. . . ."*

"What? What's that? demanded the captain. "What bloody nonsense are you talking?"

"I am composing a poem, sir."

"A poem? It sounds like a geography."

"It's a geographical poem, sir. A work of the imagination."

"Oh, I see." The captain nodded grimly. "Well, you'll have plenty of time to let your imagination work in the stokehole," he said. "And you'd best fix your geography on Liverpool, because that's the first place you're going ashore."

Finished with Claude, he spoke to his mate. "Turn him over to Mr. Mackenzie. At all coaling stations he's to be locked up, and if he makes any trouble he'll be locked up the whole time." He shook his head and snorted. "I've had stowaways with cholera. I've had 'em with plague. I've had 'em with leprosy. Now I've got one with poems—"

"Maybe it's because he's French," he added later. "I've yet to meet the Frenchman that wasn't balmy."

But this last Claude was not there to hear. All he heard was the thump of engines, the hiss of steam, the rattle of coal. All he saw was black coal, black iron, and the red mouth of a furnace. Batavia and Liverpool were half a world apart, but already, in a matter of hours, of minutes, he had made an even longer journey. The green forests and fields of Java were as remote as the images of a long-gone dream.

He was the only white man in the stokehole crew. The rest were Indian, Burmese, Malayans, small gnomelike men from the coasts of British Asia, of the sort he had often seen on the Thames dockside during his days in London. But then they had been strangers, no more than passing shadows from an unknown world; whereas now they were his companions, his peers, his fellow workers. Together they swung their shovels, feeding the yellow fires of the *Nottingham Castle*. Together they moved its cargo of sugar toward the tables and teacups of Imperial England. For one day he had been a European, a bourgeois—though a bankrupt and hunted one —in a white linen suit. Now the suit was gone, and in its place were dungarees. The dungarees were black, his body was black, his face was black. He was a nigger again: a nigger among niggers. . . . Stooping, scooping, heaving. Stooping, scooping. . . . To the rhythm of pistons, the hiss of steam.

He had seen it before. Known it before. . . . *On the riverbank, look—the black dancing files. The savages, my brothers. The niggers, my brothers. Shouts, drums: dance, dance, dance, dance!* . . . The riverbank was now a pit. The dance was of coal, sweat, and fire. But beyond the dance was still the tall one, the black shining one. Iron-flanked. Flame-mouthed. Consuming.

Stoop, scoop, heave. Stoop, scoop, heave. . . .

Then bells clanked and they leaned on their shovels. Other hands took the shovels, and they climbed long ladders up out of the pit. They ate: for the lascars, rice and curry; for Claude, bully beef and porridge (the one concession to his whiteness). Then they slept; and, as on the *Prins van Oranje*, it was in hammocks and in layers, but here the layer above did not sag into Claude's face, for there were no rumps of the dimensions of Dirk Uden's. And there were neither farts nor belches from the lascars' carcasses of skin and bone. The only sound in the darkness was the occasional sound of a voice murmuring a high sad singsong above the throbbing of the ship.

He went up onto the deck. And the sun struck at him. It was not with heat, however—its heat was nothing after that of the stokehole—but with a blaze of light that reeled in his head and slitted his eyes. It didn't matter; there was nothing to see; nothing but miles of water, endlessly the same, for the ship was cutting straight across the Indian Ocean toward Aden, and with no land ever in sight. And even with land there would still have been nothing; merely coasts unrolling in one direction when they had formerly unrolled in the other; the façades of cities, islands, continents to which he might come, at which he might stare forever, but forever from outside, apart, alone. As he had come to Java. As he had moved from ship to shore to barracks to bamboo hut, across fields and forests and mountains, and then back to ship again; and what had it all meant except the feel of movement, the compulsion of movement, the unending changing changeless journey of the boy—the man—who took a walk?

"I shall become part of the world," he had thought. "Part of the crowd, a group, a unit, with function, purpose, and goal." So he had joined the Dutch Colonial Army. He had entered the world of Dirk Uden and Sergeant Houttekamp.

And he had fled it.

"I shall enter another world," he had thought. "The world of field and forest and greenness and growth and life." So he had gone with Pandap. He had lived the life of Pandap and Kitong and Mati and Kuru, a sky-eyed Javanese peasant in a peasant village.

And he had fled it.

He had fled, going he knew not where. Farther, he had thought—

always farther. To the coasts of Borneo and wildest Papua. And instead he had boarded a ship for—Liverpool. For England, Europe; borne back again to the ancient parapets. He felt the hulk of the *Nottingham Castle* beneath his soles. He felt its slow deep rumble in his bones. It was no Drunken Boat, this—no Argo, no cruiser of the star-archipelagoes—but a squat black wallower of the trade lanes, with sugar for London's grocers in her holds and the almighty pound sterling emblazoned on her logbook. It was a ship of iron, of coal, of smoke, of naked fact. The ship of flight, return, retreat.

Bells clanked. He went below. Turning his back on the mockery of sea and sun, he climbed down the long ladders into the stokehole; he swung his shovel; he fed the mouth of flame. And he thought: "Yes, I am back in the pit again. I have merely exchanged a green pit for a black pit and am writing the next chapter of my Season in Hell."

As always, since the long-gone days in Paris, he lived almost wholly within himself. "The niggers, my brothers," he had said. But the lascars were not his brothers. They were so many sooty gnomes with whom he worked, ate, slept, lived in the closest possible physical contact, and whom, as *men*, as living souls, he did not know at all. It was not a matter of language; he had quickly picked up enough of their tongues for communication. Nor were they unfriendly or withdrawn. It was, rather, that when he talked with them, tried to know them and draw them out, there seemed to be nothing to know, nothing to draw, nothing beneath flesh and voice but a dark morass of animal appetite and lethargy.

"I know good woman Liverpool."

"But beer too damn expensive Liverpool."

It might have been the Dutch. It might have been Germans or Italians or Swedes or Frenchmen. It might have been his own brother, his blood brother, Felix, who, of all brothers anywhere, was most totally a stranger.

The British crew and their officers he knew scarcely at all. Since the first day he had glimpsed the captain only once or twice, at a distance, and the others were merely figures and faces, on the deck, in the companionways, in the engine room adjoining the stokehole. They rarely spoke to him; most often they seemed not even to see him. With one exception —and as the days passed Claude became more conscious of the exception, which was Mr. Mackenzie, the chief engineer. He was a Scotsman from the Clydeside, with a broad dungaree-clad beam, a broad square-planed face, and eyes that gleamed gray and clear through the engine-room grime. And though, for a long time, he no more than nodded or gave an occasional order, Claude knew that the eyes were watching him curiously.

Then, finally, the day came when he was going off duty, and the lascars had gone up the ladder before him, and there suddenly was Mackenzie looking him up and down.

"Things goin' all right with ye, lad?" he asked.

"Yes, all right, sir," said Claude.

"A bit more of a lark than ye bargained fer, maybe?"

"A lark, sir?"

"Stowin' away, I mean. Endin' up in a stokehole. I'll make my bet ye have nae been in no stokehole afore, have ye?"

"No sir."

"Well, I hope yer enjoyin' yerself."

That was the end of the first conversation. But a few days later the chief spoke to him again.

"Well, I'm still waitin'," he said.

"Waiting, sir?"

"For ye to do somethin' daft. The cap'n said to keep a close eye on ye; that ye looked like a bad one, a real daft one. He said, the day they found ye, ye spouted poems at him, no less."

Mackenzie eyed him quizzically, but Claude didn't answer.

"Whose poems, eh? Some Frenchy's?" The chief laughed. "By God, that I'd 'a like to 'a heard! Only I'd 'a liked it even better if ye'd given him Robbie Burns."

Claude smiled.

"Ye've heard of Robbie, have ye? The great Scotsman. Ye've read him, yes? And d'ye like him? ... No, don't tell me. If ye say yes, I'll ask ye what does a Frenchy know. And if ye say no, I'll clap ye in irons ... Well, anyhow—" The chief's eyes narrowed. "Where d'ye get all this, eh? Poems and Burns and all. Not pitchin' coal, I'll wager. Not hoppin' ships around the islands."

Again Claude said nothing.

"What were ye doin' afore this? There in Java?"

"I—I worked in the rice fields."

"And afore that?"

"I was in the army."

"And deserted, eh?"

"Yes."

"And afore the army, what were ye? Back in the old country—in France —what did ye do there?"

"I was a street-paver," said Claude. "I was a longshoreman and a busboy and a pimp and a ratcatcher and—"

"And a goddamned liar," said Mackenzie.

But he did not give up as easily as the Dutch lieutenant.

". . . Or if not a liar," he went on, the next day, "a goddamned fool, and that's worse. . . . Oh, I know yer kind, my lad. The world's yer enemy, eh? Ye can't find yerself, and that's the world's fault. Ye go from this to that, from here to there, not knowin' what ye want or where yer goin', and sure enough, the world kicks ye in the pants and, bong, yer down a stokehole."

Again the gray eyes looked Claude up and down. "How old are ye?" he demanded.

"Twenty-one," said Claude.

"Twenty-one—hah. Old enough to know better and too young to know anything. But yer educated—I can tell that. You and yer poems, and knowin' Burns, and English, and the way ye can jabber with them brown monkeys. Ye didn't learn all that in a stokehole, I'm tellin' ye, or doin' any of that other stuff ye were talkin' about. Ye had school, didn't ye? Sure, ye had plenty of school. And then ye got tired of it, eh? Ye told school where to head in, and yer old man to shove it, and off ye went. See the wide world—lure of the East—all that stuff. Aye, lad, I know plenty about it; I did it myself."

They were standing on the chief's platform before the engine's control panels, and his big hand slapped hard against the metal plates. "Only I had more sense than you," he went on. "Not so much education, maybe—not so much out of books—but more sense. I had a trade. A profession. I could make a ship go. If I wanted somethin' out of the world, I could give it back somethin' it needed.

"And there's another thing I had besides, and that's somethin' to come back to. And I've got it now. I mean a wife; a wife and bairns. D'ye know how many bairns I've got? I've got five. Five of 'em and the old woman, all waitin' for me there in a little cottage by the Clydeside. Oh, I grant ye a man's got to get away; he can't live his life tied to aprons and nappies. But he's got to come back too. He's got to have roots. A home. A home and a trade, lad, them's the two great things, and without 'em a man can have the whole world and still he's lost, lost, lost."

A bell clanked. A voice came down from the bridge through the speaking tube, and Mackenzie reached for a lever. Then he stopped. "No, you do it," he said, pointing. "There—that one. Pull it toward ye three notches."

Claude pulled, and the lever moved. There was no noticeable effect, but the chief nodded. "Better than heavin' with that shovel, ain't it, lad?" he said.

In the days that followed he sometimes called Claude again onto the platform and talked of the ship's engine. And as he talked the engine changed. It became for Claude, as it was for him, no longer a mere image, a giant of iron and coal and fire, but a machine, an organism, a sum of parts, each with its place and function and relationship to the whole. It was plate and bolt, rod and shaft. It was pipe and joint and valve and gear and wheel and piston and cylinder. It was oil and grease. It was dial and lever. And, above all, it was something beyond itself, outside itself: the eye that watched the dial, the hand that moved the lever. It was the men who had conceived and built it; the men who fed and tended it. It was Chief Engineer Mackenzie: peering, listening, adjusting, controlling. It was Mackenzie searching patiently for a deep hidden scraping, disappearing with wrench and hammer into a maze of pipes, emerging finally with a grinning face as black as the lascars', and announcing, "Well, the fookin' old fooker should behave herself now."

Mackenzie had watched Claude. Now it was Claude who watched Mackenzie. He watched the square frame, the square face, the keen and cool gray eyes, and for almost the first time in his life he found himself trying to see through another's eyes. What the Scotsman saw was, assuredly, not vision and dream, but neither was it blackness, nor were his mind and perception sunk in apathy. Claude looked at the engine and saw a symbol: a Moloch, a Belial, a god of iron and fire and smoke to whom man was a servant. Mackenzie looked at it and saw a machine: a thing made by man, controlled by man, to be *his* servant. And as their eyes saw, so it was—for each of them differently. For the engineer—master; for the stoker—slave.

The master pulled his levers. The slave wielded his shovel. They came to Aden and coaled, and Claude labored in his pit while the black tide roared down around him. Then they moved up the Red Sea, through the furnace of the sun, and to the west was the country of dreams, the vast deserts of Africa. But this time Claude scarcely glanced at Africa. He scarcely went on deck, but stayed in his pit, in his furnace of iron, with the coal, with his shovel, with the flaming maw. He looked up from the maw to the railed platform where Mackenzie stood before his dials and his levers.

And one day he washed the grime from his hands and knocked at the door of Mackenzie's cabin.

"Could I borrow some of your books, sir," he asked.

"Books, lad?" said the chief. "I don't have—"

"I mean your manuals. About engines, boilers, compressors—all of that."

"Oh."

The chief led him in. From a shelf above his bunk he took a pamphlet and handed it to him. "Here," he said, "this is fer the kiddies' class. See how ye do with it." Then, as Claude turned to go, he smiled and added, "So ye been thinkin' a bit about what I said to ye, eh? . . . Well, go on thinkin'. Think and read. Think and ask yerself some questions. And maybe it won't be just at Liverpool that ye climb up out of a stokehole."

He put a big hand on Claude's shoulder. "Remember what I told ye, lad. A trade—a trade. Somethin' the world needs. . . . And the other thing too: don't go it alone. No. Get yerself a lass, a wife, that'll give ye bairns and a home. A trade and home—those two, lad, and the seven seas are yours."

Their eyes met for an instant; then Claude turned away. He could think of nothing to say.

"All right," said Mackenzie, "yer down now. Yer in the hole. The world's kicked ye in the pants, and yer ass over ears in a pile of coal and mad at everybody. . . . All right, so there ye are. And what will ye do about it? Go on lyin' there or pick yerself up?"

He stood at the door as Claude went out.

"Well, good readin' to ye. And here—here's somethin' to go with the readin'." He reached into a pocket and brought out a cigar. "Nothin' like a good smoke to clear the brain cells and give ye confidence." His hand thumped once—hard—on Claude's shoulder. "Aye, confidence, lad, that's the magical word. Good luck to ye. And when yer down and yer beat and the world's all agley, don't ye ever forget what Robbie Burns said . . . no sir. He said, *'A man's a man for a' that.'*"

Claude read in his hammock. He climbed down to the stokehole. The iron maw flamed and the ship wallowed on.

20

"So for once," said the Widow Morel, "you come home without being sick."

"For your delicious food, Mother," he explained.

"Food, bah! All day I work myself to the bone here in the store—for ten, twelve, fourteen hours—and then I am supposed to become a cook and work all night. . . . I suppose you ate better in this crazy Lava place you have been off to."

"Not Lava, Mother. Java."

"Lava, Java—what does it matter? First it is one crazy place and then another. And for what, *hein?* Tell me that—for what?"

"I'm a professional tourist," Claude said. "I try out all the international hotels."

"Oh, you are the smart one, aren't you? So successful; so pleased with yourself." His mother's black eyes snapped at him. "If you were so pleased and successful in Lava, why did you not stay there? Why have you come back again?"

Claude didn't answer.

"To go to work like a man, at last?" She snorted. "No, that is too much to expect. For more writing, I suppose. More scribble scribble scribble on old pieces of paper. . . . Well, this time at least, maybe you will have something to write about. A travel book, *hein?* I have heard such books sell well, and maybe at last you will make some money."

"Like Victor Hugo? Your old idol, Monsieur Hugo."

"Like any self-respecting man who can earn a living. Who has something to sell that others wish to buy." Madame Morel bit her lip. Then she thought of something. "There was this editor who came here two years ago to buy your things. The nice one who went to church: Monsieur Durand. He would still be interested, I am sure. Why do you not go to see him?"

"Because—"

"Yes, I know. Because this; because that. Always some excuse. Always any excuse: to do nothing, sell nothing, earn nothing. Only to sit in your room, lie on your bed, and then at last, when you get up, to climb out the window, run away, disappear—"

Her voice was growing shrill, but she cut it off. "Oh I am sick, I am disgusted," she said, and she went downstairs to her shop and her counter.

The two of them were alone in the house. Six months before, Felix had fallen into a drunken sleep while driving his cart, smashed it in a ditch, and forthwith lost his job with Guillaumet Frères. And after several weeks, during which he had neither found nor tried to find another, Madame Morel had put him out. Now he was in Antimes, working as a laborer for the Department of Roads. Or so she had heard, for it was no concern of hers. Nor was he. A common *manouvrier*, a drunkard and an imbecile, he had had his last chance to disgrace her, or to so much as enter her door. He was no longer her son.

And Yvette was gone too: still at the convent in Cambrai, where she was now a postulant in the Carmelite order and would soon go on into her nun's novitiate. "So she is also lost to me," said his mother. Then, scorning her self-pity: "But at least I can be proud of her. Two men-children and one girl I have, and the men are an imbecile and a godless lunatic, and she is the only one of whom I can be proud." Suddenly she lashed at Claude. "You are the one I had thought to be proud of," she said. "You, the rare one, the brilliant one. You could have been a doctor, a lawyer, a magistrate —anything. And look at you: a wastrel, a tramp, a no-good. And, God help me, an atheist. Why I do not put you out like your brother I do not know. Why I stand this mockery of all I hoped for, worked for, slaved for—"

Again she cut herself short. She went down to her counter. In the days that followed she kept her peace, and they lived together almost in silence. Occasionally he helped her in the store, but only at the busy hours when there were many customers to take care of, and the rest of the time he went out for walks or closed himself in his room. She did not burst in on him or even knock. Almost the only times they were alone with each other were at meals, and there, from beginning to end, the only sound was the clicking of pewter on china. Seated within three feet of each other, they were as far apart as when he had been on the slope of a volcano on an island in the antipodes.

"Why have you come back again?" she had asked. And he hadn't answered. He didn't know. His father before him had walked out and vanished forever, but when he took his walks—made his endless escapes and flights and journeys and voyages—it was always in a great circle that brought him back to this street, this house, this room, this table. . . . Why? . . . "This is your home," his mother had once said. And once, when he had come back from London and lay fevered and writhing in the pit of hell, he had opened his eyes to find her hand on his forehead. He looked at her hand now, white and bony, cutting tough veal with a knife. He looked at her black sleeve and her black dress and the silver crucifix at her throat, and then at her face, also chalk-white and bony; and then she looked up and their eyes met, and they both looked quickly away. He no longer hated his mother. He did not love her, could never love her—probably could never love anyone, no more than could she—and perhaps that was the heart of it all. But out of that very lovelessness, and their loneliness, he would have liked to speak a word, to make a gesture. To touch *her* hand for an instant. To say, "Yes, this is home."

He could not. They sat in silence: the two of them. And then he thought, "No, not two, but three;" for another sat beside them, and between them. "Like the demon of the old Greeks—Alastor," he thought. "The evil genius of a house; the curse that haunts and torments a family from generation to generation."

Downstairs the bell clinked. Customers came, and he stood with his mother behind the counter. He said, *"Bonjour madame; bonjour monsieur."* He said, "Yes, I have been away. Yes, now I am back." And when the customers had gone, he went out too.

He did not seek out his old friends. He went straight to the library, to the dustbin of *les assis.* Now, however, he did not go to the right wing, as he had used to, but to the left, where over the door a sign read, SCIENCE —MATHEMATIQUE—TECHNOLOGIE. He piled books before him and, hour upon hour, day after day, he read them through. Beginning at the beginning, he read of Thales and Archimedes. He read Copernicus and Galileo and Newton and Faraday and Volta and Helmholtz and Watt. He took endless notes, filling pages with equations and formulas, until he reached the point when the shelves of the small library had nothing further to offer him.

Then he went to the house where Albert Chariol had lived, which he had visited so often in years gone by. But his old teacher was no longer there; the landlady looked at him curiously and told him he had been gone

for over a year. Gone where? he asked. To Paris, she believed. Where in
Paris? She did not know.

He went to the Lycée de Cambon. He entered the office of Monsieur
Izard, and the headmaster, too, eyed him curiously, and then recognized
him and said "Oh." He was scarcely cordial. He did not ask Claude to sit
down, and kept looking around nervously, as if afraid his very presence
was spreading a disease through the school. But he told him what he
wanted to know. Chariol had left in the fall of the previous year and was
now an instructor in literature at the Sorbonne, in the University of Paris.

Claude found a job. Applying to Guillaumet Frères, he was accepted,
and for two weeks drove a cart, as had Felix before him. On the first
morning of the third week, however, he stayed at home. He packed a few
belongings. He waited upstairs until he heard his mother engaged with
a customer in the store, and then he walked down and through the store
and into the street and to the station. For he had saved enough money
from his job so that no longer walk was necessary.

Chariol's eyes were bright and warm. "So tell me everything, *mon
vieux*," he demanded. "From the last moment I saw you. The whole story
—*everything*." He poured a vermouth for Claude and one for himself, and
sat facing him, smiling and eager. "Ah, it's fine to see you, you crazy good-
for-nothing, after all these years. . . ."

He had not been hard to find, but quite the opposite. Scarcely had
Claude entered the Sorbonne to make inquiries than he had encountered
him in a hallway; and Chariol, unlike many of the Cambonards, had recognized him immediately and forthwith seized him in a happy embrace. At
that time they had talked for only a moment, for he was on his way to a
class and had other classes following. But they had met again by arrangement at the end of the day, and now they were together in Chariol's cozy
book-lined flat off the Boul' Mich—a few blocks from the university, and
no more than that, in the other direction, from a small side street called
the Rue de Lacque.

"Well, it is like the old days," Chariol had said as they entered. And so
it was, with one exception. In the old days they had been a man and a boy.
Now they were two men.

If Claude had changed, so had the teacher, but with him it had not
been a matter of aging. Indeed, quite the contrary; for, whereas the last
time Claude had seen him he had seemed almost middle-aged, dulled and
smothered by Cambon's dusty ennui, he was now youthful, animated,
full of sparkle and enthusiasm. And it was obvious that though this was
heightened by his pleasure at the reunion, it was also a fixed and inward
change in himself.

"So you see," he said, smiling, "I have got away too. I have also made my escape." And he told Claude how at last, after years of hoping and despairing, of applications and interviews and rejections and reapplications, he had at last been accepted by the Sorbonne and received an instructorship. "And it has been all I hoped for," he added. "Yes, more than that. A chance to teach minds that really want to learn; to get away from the old fuddy-dud routine."

"No more rhetoric? No more Cicero?"

"No, no more of them. At last I'm teaching stuff that's alive, that's breathing. I've a course in modern poetry that comes right up to Baudelaire; a course in the novel—Flaubert, Stendhal, Balzac, Hugo. And my students, ah!" Chariol blew a kiss with his hand. "No more Henri Clausons and Louis Carnots and Jacques Bruns, no indeed. Now I even have students who are writing themselves—essays, poems, stories, all sorts of things—and I'm doing my best to help them."

"And your own writing?" Claude asked. "How is that coming, Albert?"

Chariol shook his head, but smiled again as he did so. "No," he said, "that's over. For me myself, no more writing. It took me a long time to find out what you'd known all along: that I was third-rate—hopeless. But once I did know, that was that. I will be what I am, I said: not a third-rate scribbler, but a teacher. Perhaps someday a first-rate teacher. A true helper, a critic, an editor to those who truly can write." He paused and looked at Claude and somehow his smile changed. "As a matter of fact," he added, "I've already been doing some editing of a sort. In a while I'll tell you about it—"

He jumped up and refilled the glasses. "But first I want to hear about yourself. More—still more. *Mon Dieu*, what a time you've had! What places you've seen! England, Switzerland, Italy, the Riviera, Germany, Holland. And Java. Of all places, Java. Tell me more, boy; all about it. I don't mean geography—what was outside—what you've seen. I mean what you've *done*, really done. What a wonderful harvest you must have from it all!"

"Harvest?"

"What you've felt. What you've written. Your poems. . . . You've brought some of them with you, I hope."

Now it was Claude's turn to shake his head.

"What? Why not? You must have known how anxious I'd be—" Chariol stopped. A thought came to him and he frowned unhappily. "Good Lord, it can't still be that trouble, that foolishness of years ago?"

"No," Claude said, "it isn't that."

"What then?"

"I have no poems."

"You *have* none?"

"I haven't written since I last saw you. In over three years."

Chariol stared at him incredulously. "No," he said. "It's not possible. It isn't true."

"Yes, it's true, Albert."

"But why, boy? For God's sake, why? Writing was food and breath to you. Your whole self—your whole life."

"Yes, I know."

"And yet you—"

"Yet I stopped." A thin smile touched Claude's lips. "The same as you," he added.

"But there's no comparison. It's utterly different."

"All right, there are differences. You stopped your writing for one reason, I for another. But mine is finished as well as yours."

"But why? Again why? For what possible reason?"

"Because it was evil. Because it was sick."

Chariol still stared. He sat in silence. Then abruptly he jumped up and paced across the room. "I don't understand," he said. "No, I can't begin to understand. A boy of your gifts, your genius. And now no longer a boy, but a man—and throwing it all away." He swung back on Claude and his voice was angry. "You talk of evil, of sickness. What are you saying now —that's what's evil and sick. To throw away all you have, all you can give to the world, as if it were rubbish—nothing." He slammed a hand down on a table. "No, you're lying; I still don't believe it. It's fantastic. Insane."

Claude said nothing. Chariol waited. Then he burst out: "You've not been writing. For three years, you say, you've written nothing. What *have* you been doing then? Besides chasing around the world—running away from yourself. What are you doing now, *hein?* What are you going to do for the rest of your life?"

There was another pause. Then Claude said quietly: "That's what I've come to talk to you about."

"Oh, to talk to me about?" The voice was still harsh, but the eyes were curious. Chariol sat down again. "Well, let's have it. Go on—tell me."

"I want to enter the university."

"The university? Here?"

"Yes, here."

"Mmm—I see." Chariol's anger was now wholly gone. He looked at Claude with new hope and eagerness. "You mean you see now, at last, how wrong you were to leave school as you did. That you want to go on with your studies. Prepare for the Sorbonne."

"No, not for the Sorbonne."

"For what, then?"

"For the *Ecole Centrale.*"

"The *Centrale?*"

"Yes. I want to be a scientist. An engineer."

"An engineer—" Chariol let the word hang. He looked at Claude as if he had taken leave of his senses. "Good God, boy, what are you talking about?"

"That's why I've come to you, Albert. To ask your advice—your help. How do I go about applying? What courses will I need to matriculate?"

"Have you gone wholly crazy?"

"It's not crazy," said Claude. "I know something about engines now. I've worked with them. And I've read a lot—thought a lot. The world we live in has no place for poets. It belongs to the scientists, to the engineers."

"But—but—" Chariol groped for words. "It's fantastic! Impossible! To get an engineering degree?—it would take you years; an eternity. Good Lord, boy, at school you could scarcely handle algebra or elementary physics. And you talk of *engineering*. It's impossible, utterly impossible. Even if you were serious, which I don't believe for a minute."

"I'm serious, Albert."

"Then stop being. Now. This minute. Back at Cambon they all said you were cracked, and I'm starting to think they were right."

Chariol had sat down. Now he got up again. He made a jerky movement with his arm, as if pushing the whole subject away.

"You mean you won't help me," said Claude.

"Of course I won't help. I won't even discuss it." Chariol came close and all but shook a finger in his face. "All right, you lunatic, I've listened to your nonsense; now you're going to listen to me. And if I have to treat you like a child it's because you asked for it. . . . You're a writer, boy— remember? A poet. You have it inside yourself to be one of the great poets of France—of the whole world—and you know it; you've known it all your life."

"I don't—"

"Shut up. I'm talking now. And I'm talking to a poet—not to some crackpot who thinks he's an engineer." Chariol pulled up a chair. "Look —listen. I'm going to tell you something you don't know and that may just possibly be of some slight interest to you. What would you say if I told you right here and now that your poems are going to be published?"

Claude looked at him blankly.

"Yes, published! And I don't mean in some obscure little magazine, but in a book—a book all your own—by one of the best firms in Paris."

He paused for effect, and the glint returned to his eyes. "Perhaps you remember I mentioned before that I've been doing some editing? Well, what I've been editing, my boy, just so happens to be *your* work. . . . Yes, just that. Exactly. . . . In the past year I've made quite a collection, you see. I've collected and edited and annotated and been around a bit, and the distinguished house of Messieurs Boniface et Fils stands ready at this moment to print the selected writings of one Claude Morel."

Claude's face was still blank. "What writings?" he said, and his voice was toneless.

"As I've just said—a selection. *My* selection. From all the things you wrote in Cambon and here in Paris and in London."

"How can you? They're lost."

"No, they *were* lost, perhaps. But now they're found. Oh, it took a while all right—it's incredible you'd strew them around like that—but I think most have turned up. *The Drunken Boat*, the vowel sonnet, the *Illuminations*—I've all of them. And your long one: *A Season in Hell*—"

"*A Season in Hell?* That's impossible."

"No, not impossible. It's right there in a drawer—in your own handwriting." Chariol started to rise. "Do you want to see it?"

"No. Leave it there. Leave it!" Claude's voice was suddenly hard and strident. With an effort he controlled it, and now it was he who stared incredulously at Chariol.

"How did you find it?" he demanded. "How? Where?"

Chariol smiled. "It took a bit of detective work," he said, "and it's really a rather fascinating story. . . . It began with your mother, of course. Back before I left Cambon I went to see her; I told her how much I'd always admired your poems—that I thought them incredibly good for a boy of your age; and I asked her to let me take them to Paris, on the chance that I could find a publisher. Well, as you know, your mother was never very partial to me. At first she wouldn't talk to me at all. Then she said she didn't have them; that they'd already been sold—to a Monsieur Durand, a Paris editor, who had come to Cambon especially to buy them. It sounded most peculiar to me; in fact I didn't believe her. But what could I do? When I got here, though, I still kept on the trail. I inquired here and there and everywhere about an editor named Durand, and, as I'd expected, there wasn't any such person. But as I got around I began hearing a name that was strangely like it. Not of an editor but another poet. A man I gathered had been a friend of yours."

"Druard."

"Yes, Maurice Druard."

"You got them from him?"

"Well, yes and no. It wasn't simple. . . . I was sure now that Druard was Durand, or vice versa, and soon I learned that you hadn't only known him, but that you'd lived and traveled together. He was the man I wanted —I knew that. But finding him was another matter. I inquired all over the *Quartier*, and everyone knew him, but no one knew where he was. He's a real queer one, I gather—trust you to find queer ones—and I had a dozen different stories. That he was dead, in prison, in an asylum, in a monastery. But anyhow, I kept asking and looking, and finally I got a lead that took me to his family—well, sort of his family: his ex-wife and her people, over in

Montmartre. When I mentioned his name, they gave me the same fishy eye as your mother; they said they had no idea where he was. And when I mentioned yours—you must have made quite a hit there—they showed me the door. I thought that was the end of it then; that I'd reached a blank wall. But a week later the most astonishing thing happened. I received a note in the mail that said, 'Dear Sir: My cousin has told me of your visit, and I think I have what you are looking for. Would you come to see me?' And the next day, after classes, I took a bus out to Passy."

"Passy—"

"Yes, Passy." Chariol smiled. "Well, I've made a bit of a mystery of it so far, but now we've reached the ending. I met a very charming old friend of yours, Claude. A young lady you may have half forgotten, but who, I assure you, has not forgotten you."

"*She* had my poems?"

"Yes—she. Mademoiselle Lautier."

"How had she got them?"

"That's the most fascinating part of the story. She'd got them from Druard—but without his knowledge. A year or so ago, apparently, he had some sort of a breakdown and was sent to a sanitarium; but before they emptied out his place she went there to look for your poems and found them and took them home with her. She is not only a charming, but a very remarkable young lady, this Mademoiselle Lautier, and I might add, a great admirer of your work."

There was a pause. Claude sat motionless. His feet were flat on the floor and his hands flat on the arms of his chair.

"And she gave you these—things?" he said.

"She more than gave them to me," said Chariol. "As I say, she's a remarkable girl; a brilliant girl. She herself had been working on them: copying them out, arranging them. When I met her, she was about to try, on her own, to interest a publisher. And since then we've been partners."

"Partners?"

Chariol smiled again. "In the Claude Morel Private Promotion Society. We've worked together on the selection, the editing, the search for a publisher. And it was she, I might add, who really won the day with Boniface."

Claude still did not move. Leaning forward, Chariol thumped him on the shoulder. "So, how do you like that for a story, *hein?* A detective, a mysterious lady, a happy ending, everything! Let's see you match that, *monsieur l'ingenieur*, with your slide rule and blueprints."

He leaped to his feet. "Another drink to top it off. Yes. To our soon-to-be-published Bard of Cambon." But then, suddenly he looked at his watch. "No, we'd be late; we'll have it at the restaurant. Come on, boy—" Once more the smile. "I've still another little surprise for you. After I saw you this morning I took the liberty of writing a note to my co-editor, and I'm pleased to announce that we'll be three for dinner."

He swung into his coat and held out Claude's. "Come on, come on!" he commanded. "No poetic trances, please. Or do you now have engineering trances?" He laughed and all but pulled Claude to his feet. "All right, forward and onward. Can't keep a lady waiting, you know—especially when she's your editor."

He continued talking, keen and animated, as they descended the stairs and walked the half block to the Boul' Mich. And there he hailed a fiacre. Getting in, he slid across the seat and turned to continue talking, and then abruptly leaned forward and peered from the door. "Claude—" he called.

The coachman swiveled around.

"Claude—" Chariol repeated. And then louder: "Claude! Claude!"

"So?" said his mother.

He didn't answer.

"So you are back again. Back with nothing. Back *for* nothing. Only to lounge about, to mope, to shut yourself in your room." When still he didn't speak her voice grew shrill. "Well, I am telling you, this time it will not go on for long. You will go to work—at once, before the month is out —or else I will do with you what I have with your brother."

"Yes, Mother."

"You will find employment; earn money."

"Yes, Mother."

"And when you have earned it you will first of all pay your debt to me."

"Yes, Mother. Forty-one francs."

"No, it is more. It is now over a year at five per cent interest. But I will be generous; I will call it only a year. That means forty-three francs and five centimes."

Claude reached into his pocket. "Here are the five centimes," he said. "I'll pay by installment."

He went out. He went to the library. He entered the wing marked SCIENCE—MATHEMATIQUE—TECHNOLOGIE and took books from the shelves, but sitting with them at a table, he left them unopened. His mind went back to Paris, to the morning after he had left Chariol, to the entrance of the great technological school called the Centrale—and himself standing before it. He had stood there a long while, and several times he had started to go in; but each time he had stopped at the threshold, and at last he had turned away. He had done so because he had known Chariol was right. To be accepted at the school of science, even to enter its lowest classes, he would have had to retrace his steps to the lower forms of the lycée; to do the work not of weeks or months but of years. If he could do it at all. Certainly, one who had not been able to master even elementary physics or algebra could not do it on his own.

The books remained unopened. He put them back on the shelves. Leaving the library, he looked into the other wing, where he had spent so much of his boyhood; but he did not go in. He went out into the street and through the town and along the Meuse and into the Ardennes. He took a walk. And when he was tired of walking he sat under a tree, and after a while, from old habit, he took from his pocket a piece of paper and pencil. He wrote: *Once, if I remember well* . . . and crossed it out. He wrote: *From the bituminous desert flee in confusion, with sheets of fog spaced in hideous bands across the sky that curves, recedes, descends, formed by the most sinister black smoke that Ocean in mourning can produce: helmets, wheels, ships, rumps. The battle.* . . . Then he threw pencil and paper away. A bird flew down from a branch, snatched the pencil and flew off. "Hey, write me a poem," Claude called after it. "A sonnet on ships, a rondel on rumps."

But the bird had its own poem. Perched in a treetop, it dropped the pencil. It sang. It sang high and clear and free in the silent forest in the fading light, and he listened until the light was gone and the song was done, and then rose and moved on in the darkness.

Etre de beauté, he thought. Being and essence and inmost core of beauty. . . . Why could he not sing like that? Without agony. Without madness. *Without the red and black wounds and the whistlings of death.* . . .

One day, again, two sergeants came, and this time he went with them. At the induction center they filled out forms in triplicate, and from them he was passed on to a doctor. The examination was routine until the doctor saw his right knee, and then he pursed his lips and looked closer.

"An old bullet wound, *hein?*" he said. "Where did you get it?"

"In the British campaign," said Claude.

"The British—?" The doctor eyed him. "Oh, I see—a wise one. And what other service have you had, may I inquire?"

"The Cambon campaign, under Feldwebel Gunst. The Java campaign, under Sergeant Houttekamp."

The doctor felt the knee. He tapped it. He moved it about. "It's always the wise ones, the no-good ones, who get off," he said sadly. And on the triplicate forms he wrote: *Imperfectly healed fracture of patella, with deterioration of adjacent tissue. Leg would stiffen with extended marching or under severe field conditions. Candidate unfit for army service.*

Glancing around, he saw Claude's face at his shoulder. "Stop that!" he barked. "Stop that laughing and get out. At once. *Fous le camp!*"

Then two letters came—in the same mail.

The one from Chariol was long, and he didn't read it. The other was short, and it said: *Dearest Claude—You are still the same, I see. But that is not so strange, I suppose, for I am still the same too. Perhaps you remember my letter to London. After three years I have nothing to add or subtract.*

As before, it was signed only with an initial—G.

"So?" said his mother.

But still he didn't answer.

He closed his door. He lay on his cot. There was no canvas now, no sail; it was no boat but only a cot, and he lay on it motionless for hours. When he rose he went to the table and took another pencil and piece of paper. And he wrote:

Candidate unfit for:

A   *army service*
B   *engineering*
Γ   *dinner with lady editor*
        . . .
        . . .
Ω   *anything*

Candidate will submit in triplicate: one for Father, one for Son, one for Holy Ghost. File reference: CM—ooooo—omega.

This paper, too, he threw away. He lay down again and looked at the ceiling, and all he saw was the ceiling. He looked at it steadily, for hours, for days, and then suddenly he rose and went out and walked the ten kilometers to Antimes and found his brother Felix. In Antimes, Felix had been unable to get a job as a carter and was working for the township as a laborer on a road-grading gang. "One of my old professions," said Claude. And for a week he joined him: swinging a pick and shovel, listening to Felix's complaints about their mother, and in the evenings drinking cheap wine with him in a workingman's bar.

"And what next?" he inquired.

"Next?"

"Are you going to pave roads forever?"

Felix shrugged. Then he belched. "Why not?" he asked.

"You and hard work? It sounds peculiar."

"It's not so bad. If you keep away from the foreman you can just go through the motions. The hours are all right, and there's no smell of horseflop. You get enough for a *rouge* and a *fille* on Saturday night."

"And that's enough?"

"What the hell else is there?"

"I wouldn't know," said Claude. "I'm just asking."

He went back to Cambon. From his week's pay he gave his mother three francs and said, "That makes the debt an even forty."

"Still at five per cent," she reminded him.

He walked off again—to Cambrai. He sat on a stone bench in a hallway in the convent of the Carmelite Sisters and looked at the pale and robed young novice nun who was his sister Yvette. This time he had no ball, no scarf, no locket, and the hair he had used to pull was hidden under her tight coif. The only thing unchanged was her eyes, and he looked at them curiously: the light blue eyes, so much like his own, that saw such different things.

She asked for *"chère Maman."* She asked for *"cher* Felix." She said how tall and strong he looked, how much he must have seen and done, and that she had prayed for him every day of his absence. And he in turn told her something of his travels: of Switzerland and Italy and Holland, and especially of Java and its brown gentle people.

"Are they Christians?" she asked. And when he shook his head she was sad. "But it will happen in time," she said. "All blessed things happen in the Lord's good time." And she went on to tell him of the missionary work of the Carmelites and how eventually she herself might be sent abroad and have the wonderful chance to work among the heathen. "But that, of course, is still many years away," she said. And her smile was as gentle as the Javanese' own.

After an hour an older nun appeared and coughed quietly, and he left. "Mother, brother, sister," he thought. "Flesh of flesh. Blood of blood."

Back in Cambon, he stopped in the square in front of the church and stood looking at the spot on the pavement where he had once chalked the words MERDE AUX PRETRES—MERDE A DIEU. Turning, he entered the church and stood for a while in the stone shadows, facing the altar. The church was empty, but before the altar, nevertheless, he saw three kneeling figures—three figures in blue serge—Yvette, Felix, himself. Then there was a change and there were only two figures. They were larger, older. They were his mother and Druard. (No, excuse it: not Druard—Monsieur Durand.) And as he saw them there was a sound in the stillness, and the sound came from himself.

Then there was another sound—of soft footsteps; a stout black-clad figure approached; and Father Lacaze said quietly, "This is no place for laughter."

"Yes, I know. I am sorry," said Claude.

The priest was close now and peering at him. "So it is you," he said. "You have come back to Cambon."

"Yes."

"And now here—to the church."

"Yes."

"To blaspheme again? To laugh at God?"

"No, Father, not for that," said Claude.

There was a pause. Then the priest said: "How has it gone with you, my son? All these years, all over the world—how has it gone?"

"Not well, Father."

"What has been the trouble?"

"I've been alone. Too much alone. Everywhere I've gone, I've been among men, lived among men; and yet everywhere I've been alone."

"If you put out your hand to men, they will put out theirs to you."

"I've tried," said Claude.

"But at the same time you must put out your hand to God."

"I've tried that too. In my own way."

"In your own way is no good. There is only one way—the Church's." Father Lacaze stood silently for a moment; then he took Claude's arm. "Come, my son," he said. "We will begin your return to the Church of God."

They walked in the dimness between the pillars and stopped before the confessional. "Come," the priest repeated. "This is the beginning of grace. Then we shall see what follows." He opened the door of the booth and waited for Claude to enter. But Claude stood motionless before it, as he had once before, years ago.

"You will not, my son?"

"No, Father."

"Why not?"

"I cannot."

"Then you still do not believe?"

"Not this way—no."

Father Lacaze sighed and closed the booth. Then he walked with Claude to the door. "When you *do* believe," he said, "—when you are truly ready—come back to us. We shall be waiting."

"Thank you, Father," said Claude, and left.

"This is your home," his mother had said.

Cambon was his home.

And he was a stranger.

He passed young men in the street, and it was not until they had gone by that he recognized them as Pierre Berthoud or Henri Clauson or Louis Carnot or Jacques Brun. He rounded a corner and made way for a family group of a man, woman, and two small children, and then, turning, he saw that the parents were Georges and Mimi Vuiton. Georges shambled. Mimi waddled. Under the black dress which had once hidden such strange and evil secrets was now merely the unmistakable evidence that she was carrying still another child.

Then, in the center of town, he was face to face with a trim citified young man, and a long moment passed before he realized it was Michel Favre.

"My God," he said, "—mustache, jacket, necktie, shoeshine. What sort of a farmer are you?"

"No farmer at all," said Michel. "I'm a banker."

"A banker?"

His old friend pointed across the street. "There, at the Banque du Nord. I don't quite own it yet," he conceded, smiling, "but give me time."

He had, he told Claude, now been off his uncle's farm for almost three years. For two of these he had gone to accounting school in Reims and then had returned to Cambon and got a teller's job at the bank.

"And you like it?" Claude asked.

"Well, right now, as I say, I'm hardly running things. Lots of it's dull and routine. But in a few years it will be different, I can promise you that. I'm going to make my escape from Cambon, the same as you did."

"Escape—how?"

"The bank has branches all over France; all over the world. And it's growing every day. Let me tell you one thing, *mon vieux;* in case you don't know it: this is the age of banks. Of industry, commerce, investments, loans, money. The world's going to change and expand like none of us ever imagined, and banks are going to be right at the center of it, running the whole thing."

He talked on enthusiastically. His eyes shone as they had used to in the old days when he talked about girls. But there was no mention of girls now. Only of capital, income, debentures, exchange rates; of the future of the world, of banking, and of Michel Favre.

"It doesn't sound much like Cambon," said Claude.

"Cambon—what a place! The last outpost of the Middle Ages. The only thing is to get out: as you did—as I'm going to. To stay here's like dying; dying and still walking around. Have you seen how everyone is: full of dust and rot? Have you seen any of the old crowd from school, and what's happened to them?"

"I've seen a few. . . . I saw Georges and Mimi."

"That's just what I mean. Poor Georges—a blacksmith's helper. And Mimi: an imbecile, a drudge, a birthing machine."

"Have you married?" Claude asked.

"Me? Good God, no. . . . Oh, I will some day. But first things first, my boy. I promise you it won't be in this town, or to something like Mimi."

Michel shook off the depressing thought. He asked Claude about himself and his travels. Not about the romance of travel—about blue seas and tropic coasts and tall masts and golden birds—but about production and trade and exchange and currencies. . . . Was there hope of the lira being stabilized in Italy? Were irrigation projects really under way in the Middle East? Did Java depend wholly on a one-crop export economy of sugar, or were the Dutch in favor of diversification? . . . And how about Claude: Claude himself? Had he done well? Had he been working for others or himself? Had he made good connections? Above all, good connections. "Believe me, *mon vieux*, that's the main thing, the big thing. In this world of ours it's not *what* you know but *whom* you know."

"Well, I met a man called Houttekamp," said Claude. "And another called Pandap—"

He found himself looking at the ground. He was looking for a stone: a stone to kick. He would kick it to Michel, and Michel would kick it back, and they would kick it back and forth, faster and faster, until they were racing down the street in a fine cloud of Cambon dust.

But in this part of town there were no stones. There was solid pavement, and on the pavement Michel's shined city shoes. There was Michel consulting his watch and saying, "Well, *mon vieux*, it was pleasant. We'll meet again, talk some more." And then they had shaken hands, and Michel had crossed the street and was holding the door for an elderly customer at the entrance of the Banque du Nord.

He lay on his cot. He looked at the ceiling. Then suddenly he leaped up and went downstairs and out. Again, as with Felix at Antimes, he took a job as a road laborer—but this time worked for only a day; and that evening he went with his wages to the Café du Printemps. He sat at a table and looked around him and saw both strange and familiar faces. But the familiar ones either were turned away or glanced at him blankly. And the face he was looking for he did not see.

The waiter came, and he ordered a beer. "Where's Monsieur Archambault?" he asked.

"Arch—?"

"The fat gentleman who was always here."

"Ah. Ah, yes—Monsieur Archambault, who made magician's tricks." The waiter shook his head. "He is dead, monsieur. About a year now. As his old friends say, he ran out of magic at last."

Claude drank his beer, and the waiter returned. *"Encore une?"* he asked.

"No, a cognac."

When the cognac was gone he ordered an absinthe. Then a second and a third and a fourth. Other than to the waiter he spoke to no one; and no one spoke to him. It grew late, and the café cleared out, and with the last of his money he had a final absinthe, while the waiter carried off glasses and mopped table tops. Then he got up and went home, walking carefully and steadily along the darkened streets.

He climbed the stairs to his room. He lay again on his cot. "Now I will sleep," he thought. "Now I will really sleep." But there was no sleep. The late moon rose over the yard and the privy, and the moon was green. The room was green. The absinthe within him coiled slowly, green and gleaming; it moved through his bones, through his blood, through his tissues; it ran into his head, his eyes, his brain, and there it burst like a fountain into vision and dreams. But they were not sleeping dreams. They were waking dreams. They possessed not only his mind but his body. And again he leaped from the cot—wildly, tremblingly. He lunged to his table, his chair. He clawed for paper and pencil. He found them, held them, and wrote. He did not light his lamp; the green moonlight was enough. The inward light of his vision was enough, and he wrote strongly, fiercely, as he had used to write—in the Rue Fontard, in the Rue de Lacque, in the flat in Soho, in London—deep in the magic of the blue-green caves.

The pencil flew in his hand. The pages littered the floor. For an hour his pace continued, his frenzy held . . . and when at last they slackened it was only slightly, only as it had used to be, and of no matter, for now, as then, he knew the alchemy of replenishment. Archambault's magic had run out; but not his. His was at hand, and he reached for it. He reached for his bottle, for the green magic of absinthe . . . and his hand groped, it fumbled, it knocked the lamp on its side; it groped farther, it searched, his eyes searched; but there was only the lamp, only paper and pencil, only the table and the chair and the cot and the moonlit room. He thrust the chair back and it toppled over. He searched the room. He searched under the cot, between its sheets, in the cupboard, the closet, the corners, over every inch of the floor. He dug into the papers on the floor, flinging them aside. Returning to the table, he rifled the drawers and flung their contents about the room.

There was no bottle. There was no magic.

He looked around wildly, and he could scarcely see. For soon, now, there would be no moonlight either; no light of any kind; only darkness. He tried to cry out. To strike, to act, to move, to do something to stop it. But there was nothing to do. The light faded; the green gleaming faded. They were out, they were gone; the magic, the frenzy were gone. He was back on his cot in the darkness. . . .

And then the darkness was grayness, and it was morning, and he rose. He picked up the mass of papers and pushed them into the wastebasket, and he put the other things he had scattered back in the drawers. For a long while, then, he sat at the table, pressing his hands against its bare surface until their trembling stopped. At seven he went in and had breakfast with his mother.

"So again you are writing," she said.

He shook his head.

"You were up late in the night. When you are up late it is always for writing."

"Once it was. But not now. I was sorting things—putting them away."

"You do not intend to write?" she said.

"No."

"Why not?"

"Because I have nothing to say."

"Nothing to say?" The Widow Morel's white face grew whiter. Her lips tightened. "*Mon Dieu*, you used to have plenty to say. When you were a child, a mere schoolboy, that was all you could do: say, say, say. And now that you're a man—that you've traveled, experienced, know things that maybe someone would pay to read about—you say no, you have nothing. . . . What kind of talk is that? What sense does that make, *hein*?"

"It's the truth, that's all."

"The truth—"

"Yes, the truth. *Your* truth. You've won, don't you see? You were right and you've won. It was all foolishness, emptiness; the games of a child—"

He got up. He returned to his room and lay again on the cot. But he no longer jammed the door, as he had used to, and later his mother opened it and came in. She, too, did not come as in the old days—in a burst of words and anger—but slowly, quietly, at first with no words at all. She went to his chair and sat in it, stiff and upright, her bony hands clasped in her lap and her eyes on the window. And then she turned to him and said:

"I am getting older. For years I have worked in my store—ten, twelve, fourteen hours a day—and I cannot do it much longer. Your brother is gone, your sister is gone, and I cannot do it alone." There was no self-pity in her voice. It was as hard and flat as if she were taking inventory of merchandise. "I have been thinking much about it," she went on. "I have also been thinking much about you and what you have done with your life, and I am prepared to make you an offer. It is that you work with me in the store. I do not mean as you have sometimes done, simply helping at the counter. I mean running it with me, as a partner."

Claude turned and looked at her. He sat up, and still he looked at her. He would have thought it as likely for her to cut off her hands as to offer to share her money or authority.

"Well," she said, "what do you think of it?"

"I think that first I will say thank you, Mother. Thank you—for the first time in my life."

"You will do it, then?"

He shook his head. "No, Mother. I can't."

"Can't?"

"It is not for me. I am not a storekeeper."

He lay down again. She talked on. Then she left.

But a while later she returned.

"Then I have another suggestion," she said. "I am tired of the store anyhow. I am tired of pins and pots and spools and yard goods and customers who pick my bones for a bargain. Most of all I am tired of the shame of it; of fetching and carrying and wrapping and waiting on the riffraff of Cambon, as if I were some sort of servant. I who come from one of the best families in the Ardennes; who was raised as a lady, a gentlewoman, and lived as one, until I made the mistake of marrying your father, and then everything changed. . . . Anyhow, I have had enough of it. There is no more need to work and humiliate myself to death. If you do not want the store I shall get rid of it. I shall be done, through, finished."

"Where would you go? What would you do?"

"I would buy a farm. Land is wealth. Land is dignity. I would at last have dignity again and live out my life as a gentlewoman."

"Do you have the money?" asked Claude.

"I have some. I have not thrown my money away. And for the store I could get more. In the past months I have made some inquiries, and there are places available. A deal could be made with the bank. . . . But I could not run a farm alone: that is obvious. A farm needs a man, and I could not afford to hire one. That is why I am speaking to you now."

"You mean I should be the man?"

"Yes."

"To run it with you? As with the store? As partners?"

"Yes."

"But I know nothing about farming."

"You could learn. We could both learn," she said.

Again Claude looked at her. At the stranger who was his mother and his mother who was a stranger; at the mother he had hated, he had cursed, he had fled, yet always had returned to; the witch-mother, bitch-mother, bigot and tyrant; at the Christ-woman, stone-woman, iron-woman (who thought herself a gentlewoman); at the black ghost of his childhood—of his dreams—the Nigger Queen. But this time he looked deeper, more steadily—no longer with a child's eyes, but a man's—and he saw beyond the iron and the blackness; he saw an aging and tired and proud and lonely woman. And again, as on the evening at suppertime several weeks before, he had the sudden impulse to put out his hand, to touch hers, to join their pride and loneliness together. . . .

But again he didn't. Again he couldn't.

No more than he could do anything but again shake his head.

"You will not do that either?" she said.

"No, I am not a farmer."

"So—you are not a farmer. You are not a storekeeper. God knows, you are none of the things I hoped you would be. And now you say you are not even what you hoped to be—a writer."

"No," said Claude.

"For the love of God, what *are* you then?"

"I don't know," he said. "I don't know." And then, after a pause: "I think perhaps I am not anything."

The next morning, before daylight, he left. Walking to the empty Place du Sépulcre, where six streets converged, he stood at its center and spun about with eyes closed. When he opened his eyes he followed the street he was facing. It led north.

2 I

The roads spun. The earth spun like a wheel. And he followed the spokes.

He was in Belgium again. He was in Holland, Germany, Denmark. He was a carter, a millhand, a digger, a dishwasher. He was a walker of the countrysides, through the dust, through the snow. He was a sleeper in lofts, in alleys, in barns, in hayricks.

Sometimes he looked back.

To Cambon . . . to a woman, tall, black, holding out money . . . and he fled from her. "What *are* you?" the woman asked. "I am not anything," he said.

To Paris . . . to a girl in school uniform, holding a book . . . and he fled from her. "You are still the same, I see," she called after him. But he did not answer.

Then there were books by the hundred, the thousand. Or at least the pages of books. He was in a printing plant in Stockholm, and his hands had been black for three months.

The proprietor had been watching him (as once Mackenzie had watched him), and one day he called him to his office. 'You are French," he said, "but your Swedish is now excellent. I have bought the rights to a French work, but my translator had left me. Perhaps you would like to try your hand." And he handed Claude a book called *Vers Parnassiens*, by Yves Balmer.

Claude took the book and the next day brought back the first page of his translation. The printer looked at it, reading slowly; and then he looked up at Claude, and his face was not the same as the day before.

"Do you think this is funny perhaps?" he inquired coldly.

"No, I think it is sad," said Claude. "Very sad."

He was in Glasgow, by the River Clyde, and he asked for Mackenzie. There were hundreds of Mackenzies. There were hundreds of ships, wharves, warehouses, smokestacks, engines, factories. There was work in a whisky distillery, and a few blank days, and no more Scotland.

He was back in France: in Lyon—in a suburb. He was carrying a black cardboard case, and in the case were bottles, but they were not of whisky. They were bottles of *La Duchesse* perfume (trial size, fifty centimes), and he carried them from door to door and knocked. Half the women in France seemed to look like his mother, the other half like Mimi Rouger; and with the Mimis he occasionally made a sale.

The roads spun.

"I am going south," he thought.

But they spun him east.

He was in Munich, Vienna, Budapest.

He was in a tent—a huge tent—in a bright light. And his hand was raised. . . . *"Holgyeim és uraim,"* he said. "And now, ladies and gentlemen: For the first time in Debrecen, indeed in all this section of Hungary, Waltzuger's Consolidated International Circus and Carnival takes pride in presenting the toast of twelve capitals, the phenomenon of our generation, the queen of aerialists, Mademoiselle Cosima!"

He backed into the shadows and the girl appeared: a girl of eighteen, pert-faced, clean-limbed, trim and lithe and glittering in cloth of gold. She pirouetted. She curtsied. The band brayed as she climbed agilely up the rope ladder to the high platform beneath the canvas roof; and then she swung from the trapezes and soared between them like a golden bird. On her bodice she wore a spray of flowers; and at the climax of her act, as she reached the platform from her last spinning flight, she unfastened it and threw it downward. It was her gesture to the audience, or so the audience thought. But the flower did not fall among them. It fell, as always, onto the tan-bark, into the shadows beyond the gas lamps, where Claude stood waiting to make his next announcement. And Claude knew it was no accident.

Nor was it an accident that, later, when the show was over and the carnival grounds were dark, Cosima was sitting on the steps of her dwelling-wagon, as he walked by toward his own. She spoke his name softly, and he stopped, and she said, "It's still early. Won't you come in a while?"

"I—I—"

"I have some coffee brewing."

"Thanks, I don't like coffee."

"Well, just to talk then." The girl smiled and moved over on the steps. "Here. Sit here," she said. "No need to go in. It's a lovely night."

Claude stood close beside her, but he didn't move.

"Please," she said.

"I—I can't."

"Can't?"

"I have to—" He gestured vaguely out toward the darkness. He started to go. But the girl reached out and took his hand. Her young face, raised to his, was no longer smiling, but earnest, almost pleading.

"What's the matter, Claude?" she asked.

"The matter?"

"What are you afraid of? Why are you always running away?"

He didn't answer. Her dark child's eyes were fixed on his face. She was wearing a loose dressing gown, open in front, that showed the young flesh of her chest and shoulders and the gold cloth of her bodice.

"You've been with us five months," she said. "All through Germany and Austria, and now here. Every day, every night, you've been with us. And still not with us. Still off by yourself—a stranger."

Again Claude said nothing. Her hand tightened a little. "Sit down," she said. "Talk to me.... You're different from the rest of us, I can tell that. You're not really circus. You're—oh, I don't know. You speak so many languages. I've a feeling you know so much, have done so much.... Tell me, Claude. Talk. It will be good for you. You're so alone always. With no friends, no family, no girls—"

"No golden birds."

For that one moment his eyes met hers. Then he looked away again.

"Birds?" said Cosima. "What do you mean, Claude? What are you talking about? Tell me. Talk to me—please."

But he had gently released his hand, and now he walked away into the darkness. He walked slowly until he came to another, larger wagon, with bright light in the windows; and he went in. Under a hanging lamp was a table; on the table were cards, coins, bills, cigar stubs, bottles, glasses; and around it sat five men and a woman. One of the men was a giant. One was a midget. The third was tattooed, the fourth was an albino, the fifth had three arms. And the woman had a thick henna-red beard that fell to her waist over vast bulging breasts.

Between her and the giant was an empty chair, and Claude took it. "Well, goddammit, about time," squealed the midget. "How long do you expect us to wait for you?"

"You be polite to my Schnickelfritz!" roared the bearded lady.

Claude poured out a glass of slivovitz and put his money before him. The three-armed man dealt the cards. The bearded lady caressed his leg under the table, and he smiled. *I alone*, he thought, *have the key to this savage sideshow.*

"I am going south," he thought.

And he went a little south, but mostly west.

He came to Spain. He walked the roads, and learned the language, and it was easier than Swedish or Hungarian. But when he came to Cadiz and stopped, and found work, he had no need, professionally, for the gift of tongues.

The tools of his trade were shovel, rake, and barrow, and he stood with them behind the wooden *barrera* until each bullfight was ended and then moved out into the arena. Every one of the other thousands in the Plaza de Toros was talking, shouting, screaming, but, at the very center of the arena, his part was silence. He swung his shovel. He pulled his rake. He put the flesh and feces of bulls and the entrails of horses into his barrow and covered the blood that remained with dirt and sand.

"What have you done before?" the bull-ring manager had asked when he hired him. And Claude had assured him: "I have much experience with latrines."

So now he was gaining more experience. "And it is good," he thought, "for it is my true profession. I was a failure as a salesman; no good as a circus barker. I am a latrine man by true vocation, and I shall cultivate my garden."

That was Voltaire and his Candide (who had come to Cadiz too). And also there was another who had once written: *I called to the plagues to smother me in blood, in sand.*

Now he had his sand and his blood. He trundled them in his barrow. They clung to his feet, his clothing, his hands and face. He shoveled and raked, and when he was done the ring was fresh and immaculate for the next slaughter, and as he left he bowed ceremoniously to the unseeing thousands. Then he was again behind the *barrera.* He stood among the swaggering picadors, the restless banderilleros, the aloof and brooding matadors, awaiting their turns; and the trumpets blew, the bull's feet thundered, the Dance of Death resumed. First, cape and charge. Then lance and horse guts. Then dart and bull blood. Then cape again, sword, sword thrust: the Moment of Truth. *"Olé!"* cried the thousands. And above the roar of men's voices rose the shriek of the women's *"olé! olé!"*—higher, wilder, more savage; lusting shrilly for the kill.

The bull bled red. The bull bled black. It was black and still and dead; the air was filled with *olés!* and flying hats and cushions; and from a box a fragile girl in a lace mantilla leaned forward smiling, radiant, and threw a rose to the matador. Claude hawked and spat. He shouldered rake and shovel and, pushing his barrow, moved out into the arena for his own Moment of Truth.

"I am going south," he thought.

And he went south.

He came to Gibraltar and crossed the straits—and was in Africa at last. Not dreaming it. Not watching it pass, still a dream, a mirage, from the deck of a ship. . . . He was there. Truly there. . . . He was in Tangier, then Oran, then Algiers. The sights and smells and voices of Africa were all around him. And the voices said, *"Garçon! Psst, garçon!"*

For he was a waiter in the Café du Lys on the Rue Michelet.

"Garçon, deux bières."

"Oui, monsieur."

"Tout de suite."

"Oui, monsieur."

By now he knew Arabic too. But in downtown Algiers one needed no Arabic, for almost everyone was French. More than half were army French. . . . Which was why he was there.

Africa. At last, Africa!

And—

"Psst garçon, deux absinthes."

"Oui, monsieur," he said *"Deux absumphes."*

"What?"

"I said two absumphes. That is the way it is pronounced in *le beau monde* of Paris."

"Enough of your insolence."

"It is not insolence. Merely a correction."

"What's the matter with you? Are you drunk?"

"No, monsieur, it is you who are drunk."

Then he was no more at the Café du Lys. He was at the Café du Boulevard. But it didn't matter; in fact the Boulevard was better. For it was near Army Headquarters, its patrons were mostly officers, and officers were the ones who might help him in his search. Moving among them with tray and glasses, he searched their faces. He searched his deepest memories. And once, seeing a colonel of infantry, a tall spare man with blue eyes and blond-gray hair, he approached with a queer thumping of the heart.

"I beg your pardon, sir," he heard his voice say, "but are you Colonel Morel?"

The officer glanced at him coldly. "What?" he demanded.

"Is your name—perhaps—Morel?"

"No, it is not Morel."

"Do you—do you by any chance then—know a Colonel Morel? Or a General Morel?"

"No, I do not know any Morels: colonels, generals, or privates. And now if the inquisition is over, will you be so kind as to serve my drink."

"But of course, *mon colonel.* Where would you like it: down the neck or in the face?"

Then he was no more at the Café Boulevard. He was at another café, but not as a waiter—as a customer, spending his tip money—and for the first time since Glasgow he got drunk. In his drunken sleep, later, eyes looked at him, eyes he knew, and a voice said, "What is wrong, Claude? Why do you do this? Do you want others to hate you because you hate yourself?"

But again he did not answer.

And the next day, after again drinking at a café, he went to Army Headquarters. He progressed from private to corporal to sergeant—the eternal sergeant—and the sergeant said, "Yes, of course, *mon brave*, that is just why we are here. To supply names and addresses of ranking officers for the benefit of drunken bums."

Then he said, *"Fous le camp!"*

It was like the old days.

And as in the old days, too, Claude now roamed the city streets. He found no new work. He sought none. He lived, as he had so often lived before, on refuse and random windfalls: now in the French quarter along the harbor, now in the Arab district, the Casbah, sprawling and labyrinthine on the hills above. At night, he slept in doorways and alleys. And by day he walked. He no longer searched for his father; that was foolishness, childishness. He searched for nothing. He simply walked.

But at night, on his stone beds, he now dreamed of his father. His father, the colonel; his father, the general; the general on horseback at the head of his troops—his sword pointing to distant battlements, his sleeve bright with golden stripes. He, Claude, was a soldier in his army. He followed him. He marched behind him. He was always behind him; he never saw his face, but only sword and sleeve; until they reached the battlements and the defenders fired and the bullets struck him and he fell to earth. Not his father. He himself. He lay wounded, he lay dying; but his father was unhit, unhurt; and now at last his father turned, he was bending over him, Claude saw his face... but it was the wrong face. It was not his father's, not a Morel's at all, but broad and flat-planed, with gray eyes and sandy hair. It was a stranger's—and yet not a stranger's. The wrong face —and yet the right one. The right man. It was his father, Mackenzie, and Mackenzie lifted him up. He slapped his back. He handed him his gun. He said, "All right, lad, no more o' this nonsense now. Up and at 'em. Ye may be a little hurt, lad, but ye ain't dead, and what's a wound or two, a scar or two? Remember, a man's a man for a' that—"

Mackenzie moved on.

"For a' *what?*" thought Claude.

Then it was morning—and his turn to move on.

He moved back west. He came to Fez and Meknes and Rabat, and from Rabat he looked out at the Atlantic Ocean. Then he moved east. He retraced his steps across Morocco and Algeria, and came to Tunis, and went on to Tripoli, and in Tripoli he was arrested for vagrancy and put in jail. By this time he was tired and hungry, and jail was welcome.

The city was Turkish—or at least held by the Turks—and, while imprisoned, he was able to get a few books and learn the language. The warden was impressed by this. When Claude had served his term, he called him to his office and offered him a job.

"No thank you," said Claude. "I don't care to be a jailer."

"It is not exactly as a jailer," the warden explained, "but as the prison clerk. You see, we have much difficulty finding someone who can read and write, and the records are in bad shape."

So Claude became the prison clerk—a *fonctionnaire*, an *assí*. In his fine, careful script he wrote up the records, including his own. He translated for the Turkish jailers and Arab prisoners. He had a desk and wore a fez and was called *effendi*. This went on for five months, until, one day, after a protest by the prisoners about the food, the warden had them all brought into the courtyard and flogged with knouts. That evening Claude stayed at his desk later than usual. He stacked the records neatly in a corner, set a match to them, and, when the night guard appeared and set about fighting the flames, walked down the cell block opening all the doors.

Then, leaving the prison, he walked on, to the east, out of Tripoli.

Communications were poor in Turkish North Africa. He was not jailed again until he reached Bengasi—and then, again, only for vagrancy. In Derna he begged. In Tobruk he stole. Beyond Tobruk, in a mud village, a woman and child stared at him as he passed.

"Who is the strange man?" the child asked. "Where is he going?"

And the woman answered, "He is a holy man on a pilgrimage."

Then there was only the sky, the sun, the earth, and the earth was brown and bare. From horizon to horizon, across the desert wastes, there was no movement of any kind, save only of a single figure slowly walking and of the dust that rose in puffs from beneath his feet.

The feet were shod in tattered sandals, and the legs above them were bare to the knee. Across the right kneecap was a band of dead white, a swath of scar tissue, but the legs elsewhere were a dark earthen brown, as were the man's hands and arms and neck and hatless face. His frame, beneath faded shirt and chopped-off drill trousers, was almost skeletal thin; and the face was thin too, high-boned and hollow, the face of an ascetic hermit of the desert. Indeed, in line and coloring, it could have been that of an Arab, had it not been for the hair, cropped and bleached pale by the sun, and the eyes, even paler, seeming almost white, as white as the scar, in the burned brownness of flesh.

How old this man was it would have been hard to say. There was no drag in his step, but no spring; no film in his eyes, but no light. He was a figure—that was all—without age or identity. A figure walking. A figure alone.

The horizons opened ahead and closed behind. The sun rose and set and rose again. He was walking east. In the morning his shadow followed him; at midday it was beside him; in the afternoon it led him, and he followed it until it lengthened to the horizon, and then faded and was gone, and it was night. In the night he sat on the earth and opened his small pack. He took from it the food he had found at the last village or oasis, and the strip of canvas that was his bed and blanket. In the dark, the sun's warmth seeped from the sands. It grew cold. The stars blazed cold as diamonds. Under the canvas he lay wrapped in his own arms.

He was alone. Alone by choice. *I shall be free to possess truth*, he said, *in one soul and one body*. And he had said it not in humility, as he had thought, but with the same pride, the same *hubris*, that had filled and driven him in his boyhood. . . . And with the same result. For what truth did he possess —here, now, in his aloneness? . . . He was not even one, but a thing of fragments. Self-crucified, he had nailed himself to a cross of rejection. Self-mutilated, he had cut from himself and cast away all that had given him identity and function. He had been drunkard, dope addict, pervert. He had been damned. But at least, in his damnation, he had sung, he had dreamed. Now, no songs—no dreams—nothing. Now the desert. And the night.

He had forsworn all old goals, hopes, ambitions. He had set his course by a new star. The meaning of life, he had decided, was in its living; in experience for its own sake; in the alchemy, not of word, but of deed—of forever doing, acting, moving. So he had moved, on and on. . . . To what? To where? . . . He had moved through cities and nations. He had "found a tongue," learned languages, he could learn all languages, and yet knew *no* language, for he could speak to no one. A mute, a stranger, he had passed without communication through the cities, through the world of men, and now he had come beyond them, to the desert. He had come down the rivers to the ocean of the desert, and there, alone, he had foundered, like the Drunken Boat of his dreams.

He too was a derelict. Fragments, flotsam. It was easy to take a faulty machine apart—be it ship of dreams or the life of man—but to rebuild it again was another matter. To rebuild one needed knowledge and skill; the skill of an engineer. The world belonged to the engineers. The ones with sure hands, cool eyes. The Mackenzies. . . . And to those others too: the Michel Favres. The machine men and the money men. The men who dealt in realities.

"Realities," he thought, "One: machines. Two: money. Three: politics." That was all. . . . No, not all. There was a fourth.

"Four: women."

The rest was chimera and illusion. The word, the image, the dream, the journey, the search: all he had lived his life by was illusion: first during his Season in Hell—now, no less, in his Season on Earth. . . . For what had he found in his years of wandering, save again the caves and the sea bottom, the desert and the night? What had it been but a running, a flight? A flight to what? To find what? . . . God? His eternal soul?

"What shall it profit a man," Christ had asked, "if he gain the whole world and lose his own soul?" . . . "And I ask in return: 'What if he gain his own soul (—ah yes, that one soul in one body—) and lose the whole world?' "

He lay on the sand, alone, beneath his strip of canvas.

He watched the stars. He slept.

And in the morning he moved on.

He crossed the wastes of Tripoli, came to the wastes of Egypt. Ahead, out of the emptiness, rose a column, the ruin of an antique temple, and reaching it, he stood at its base looking upward. "There is home," he thought. A home for a holy man on his pilgrimage. "I will climb it and live on its top: a new-day stylite, a pillar saint." Then his cracked lips smiled. For it was unclimbable. He would have needed friends, followers to lift him up. Or, better yet, a derrick. A machine.

He lay at its base through the night. He looked up at the stars. "Once this was a place of prayer," he thought. And he tried to pray. . . . He heard a voice, a priest's. "*You* could have been a priest," it said. . . . Then another, a girl's. "You are a sort of hermit monk," it said.

He had risen. He was kneeling.

And his mother said, "You will wear your blue serge suit."

Druard touched his hand and said, "We will be Trappists, for the glory of God."

And then he stood. He moved away; first through dark, then through daylight. His shadow followed him, passed him, led him. The dust rose from his feet and hung glinting in the sunlight.

To the north, invisible across the miles lay the Mediterranean, and beyond it Europe. To the south were only miles, only desert. He had seen this desert before. He had come to it, entered it, crossed it. He had moved south through the miles until the miles were behind him, until the wastes were behind him; he had passed the end of the wastes, through the darkness and whirlwinds; he had come to the true Africa, black Africa—to the green forests, the yellow rivers, the white cities, the dancing files. To those who waited. . . . Who, perhaps, still waited. . . . If he sought them. If he turned south. If he followed the dream.

He turned.

He followed it.

Through the rest of the day he moved on to the south, and when night came he still moved on. In this direction there were no villages, no oases, and in the darkness he did not even stop and sit and spread his canvas on the earth. Indeed, he no longer had the canvas. He had dropped it. He had dropped his pack. He moved on without rest, without food, without water; and the stars gleamed, the stars faded, the dawn came, and then the sun; and still he kept on, under the flaming sun, through the whole of the next day, into the night.

"It is far," he thought. "The dream is longer, the end more distant." And again his cracked lips smiled. "I have come—what?" he thought. "Twenty miles? Twenty-five? . . . It can be no more than two thousand to the borders of Cimmeria."

Once he had walked south into the eye of the sun. Now he walked into the maw of night. But the sun would come again, the sun of Africa —brighter, more terrible by far than the sun of Italy—and when it came, he knew, his journey would be over. When it came he would stop at last. He would rest. He would not spin and fall, but sit quietly down. He would rest; he would sleep. And this time there would be no hands to raise him from sleep; there would be no awakening, no whiteness, no hospital walls, no *agente di polizia*. There would be only sleep; sleep without dream; all dreams dissolved, all journeys ended.

As his was ending now. . . .

For again the dawn was coming. He was still moving, still walking on; but he could no longer feel the tread of his feet on the desert earth. He could no longer see the earth slipping by, nor when he raised his eyes could he see the horizon ahead. The horizon was gone. The dawn had come and gone. And in its place was the sun. And he thought, "Now the time has come. Now I will stop and rest."

He *had* stopped.

But he did not rest; he did not sink to the ground. He still stood and looked ahead—into the rising sun; and he thought, "It is the dream, it is illusion," for ahead was south, the sun could not be ahead; but still it was, the sun huge before him. . . . Nor could the sun's light be green. But still it was. The earth beneath was green. . . . And he was walking again, he was moving toward it ("—again into the green cave," he thought; "into the green-pillared hall—"). But it was not a cave, not a hall, but a field, a vast sweep of fields; and he moved on to the east, not the south—as he had moved all night—into the fields of cotton, into the delta of the Nile, and around him was no longer the bareness of desert, but greenness and growth and life. Around him were brown figures, moving, stooping, tending the earth; before him was brown earth, brown water, long ditches of water, brown aisles in the greenness; and now at last he fell forward; he was lying on the earth, in mud, with his face in the water, with the brown figures bent over him and hands lifting him up.

He came to Cairo.

He came to Port Said.

The ships moved in slow procession past Port Said: some northward into the Mediterranean, some southward into the Suez Canal. Twice before he had seen them: from the decks of the *Prins van Oranje* and the *Nottingham Castle*. But now he saw them from the land. From the wharves and jetties of the city that stood at the gate to the far horizons.

A southbound Danish tramp needed a deckhand, and he signed on. On its day of departure he came to the dock, reached the foot of the gangway —and stopped. Then he turned away. A few docks farther on was a Greek tramp, bound north, and it needed an oiler. Again he signed on. And, that evening, sailed out on it.

It took him to Limassol, and he walked across Cyprus. Another ship took him to Piraeus, and he walked through Greece. He came to Athens and Corinth and Delphi, and here too there were ruined temples to ancient and long-dead gods, their columns rising to the sunlit sky. He saw them and moved on; past the temples to the fields; through the fields, past moving figures; and the figures' eyes were not raised to the sky but bent to the earth beneath them.

He took a ship again. He came to Italy. Again he walked through Italy; this time not south but north—and then west; this time not watching the castled hilltops but the fields around him.

Then he entered France. Again, as so often before, he walked through France, bearing still to the north and west; through the fields, the pastures, the orchards, the vineyards. In a village on the Rhone he rested on a bench in the square, and across the square was a columned church, and on the steps a priest stood, watching him.

"When you are ready," Father Lacaze had said, "come back to us. We shall be waiting."

And he thought, "No—no, Father, that is not why I have returned." And rising, he moved on.

"When you need and want me, I am waiting," another had said. And to this he did not answer . . . not yet. . . but still moved on.

Then he was again on the long roads of the countryside. It was early autumn, the time of harvest, and the crops were high. And here again, as in Egypt, Greece, Italy—as everywhere—the fields were full of moving, stooping figures; but here the figures were Frenchmen, the people his own. Toward evening, reaching a farmhouse, he turned off and knocked at its door, but he did not, as he had used to, ask for food or a night's lodging.

"Can you use another hand in the fields?" he said instead.

The farmer looked him over. "Where are you from?" he asked.

"From the south, monsieur."

"Hmm—"

"I am strong, monsieur. I am young. I will work hard."

"I cannot pay much. Only a franc a day and keep."

"That is enough," Claude said.

22

Months passed. Seasons passed.

He stayed on.

He harvested. He planted. He hoed and spaded and furrowed and manured and drove carts and milked cows and cleaned barns. He had never before worked on a farm and had had no previous experience in these things. But he watched others, he learned, and while learning worked so hard that he could not be faulted for an occasional mistake. In time he made no more mistakes. And still he worked hard. He worked from dawn to night: through the months, through the seasons. . . .

The farmer who employed him was named Leduc. And Leduc was puzzled. "He's a queer one," he told his wife. "I've never seen a man work like that, even on his *own* place." But it was a queerness that he found not bothersome, for the labors of farm hand Morel were saving him the wages of two other men.

On Saturday nights the single men from the roundabout farms went in to the nearest town for drinking and whoring. But Claude did not go with them. Nor, on other nights, did he join in their talk or card games. They called him *le muet*—the Mute—and *le moine*—the Monk. But they treated him with instinctive, if uncomprehending, respect.

He moved alone through the fields. He followed the furrows. Sometimes he stooped and felt the earth with his hands, and sometimes he picked it up and let it run in brown streams through his fingers. Once, long ago, he had done this same thing. It had been on his walk home after London, his journey upward from the blue-green caves. But then he had been a passer-by, a wanderer, a transient of the roadside. The earth he touched now was earth he had plowed and sown.

His journey was over. True, there was yet one stage remaining—a final stage to the north. But still it was over. The anabasis had ended. The beginning of its end had been at its farthest extremity: in the desert of Africa. The end of the end had been on the road that now ran beside him: in his stopping, his turning, his knocking at a farmhouse door. Beyond the horizons he had found—nothing. Beyond the door he had found peace.

In peace now, alone, he knelt in the field. And now, at last, he could pray. "Do you see me, Mother?" he asked. "I am praying, giving thanks. Do you see me, priests, professors, masters? Do you see me, Druard the Holy? I am kneeling to God."

He arose. He worked. He worked every hour, every day.... *To give one's whole life, every day:* that was it. That was all of it.... Not to seek, not to roam, not to dream; but to work. To work the soil that was the life of earth, the life of man—and heaven and hell could take care of themselves.

In peace he returned from the field. He entered the house of Leduc and sat at supper with the farmer and his wife and five children. Madame Leduc's face was broad and red—like that of another farm woman he had known long ago; but it was also soft, her eyes were soft, her voice was gentle; for her man was with her. The children sometimes argued and fought, sometimes shouted and cried, but they too were gentle within, for they were happy and loved.

And in the darkness of the night, alone, Claude heard a voice, a man's voice—but not Leduc's; the voice of another man he had known who had had a wife and five children; the voice of Mackenzie, saying, "Remember what I told ye, lad: a trade—and a wife and bairns. A trade and a home —those two, lad—and the seven seas are yours. . . ."

There had been a time for coming. Then there came a time for leaving. When it came he knew it, and he went to Leduc and told him.

"Leaving?" The farmer was distressed. He had never had such a worker as Claude, and would never find another. "Why?" he asked. "What is wrong? Where are you going?"

"Nothing is wrong," Claude said. "I am going home."

Home.

The store the same. Upstairs the same. The piano keys carved on the table top and the tough veal on the plates at supper.

"I owed you forty francs," he said. "Three years and four months at five per cent makes six francs, sixty-six and two-third centimes interest. Seeing as it's a family transaction, I'll call it seventy centimes, which makes a total of forty-six francs, seventy centimes."

He counted out the money, and his mother recounted it and put it away in the cash drawer. She was the same too, unchanged by the years: her face white and gaunt, her eyes glinting black, and her hair also still black, with no softening of gray.

"And here is something else," he said, handing her a folded paper.

"What is this?"

"A reference."

She opened the paper and read what the farmer Leduc had written. "So if you are still interested in a farm," said Claude, "we can talk business there too."

His mother looked at him sharply. "Before, it was you who were not interested."

"Before, I knew nothing about farming. Now I do."

"That is what you have been doing all this time?"

"Not all of it, but some. I know now how to run a farm."

"Do you have money?"

"No. At least only a hundred francs or so. Nothing toward buying a farm."

"You are away for over three years. You are a strong grown man of —what is it now?—almost twenty-five. And yet you come home with next to nothing."

"You should be used to that by now, Mother," he said.

"Hmm—yes." Her lips tightened. "So it is *I*," she said, "who am supposed to finance this farm?"

"That was your idea before. To sell the store. To talk to the bank."

The Widow Morel rubbed her bony chin. "Well, I shall have to think about it," she said. "I understand that interest rates on mortgages are criminally high."

"As high as five per cent?" asked Claude.

They were alone in the house. Yvette had gone on from Cambrai to another Carmelite convent in Lille, whence she came home on a brief visit only once a year. Felix, still banned from the house, had now not been heard of in some eighteen months. On his last appearance, according to Madame Morel, he had come at night, drunk, shouting up from the street that he wanted money; and she had slammed the shutters tight. He might or might not still be in Antimes. She didn't know. She didn't care. "All I can do," she said, "is to pray to God for his soul."

Her eyes fixed on Claude. "As I have prayed for yours through all these years," she added.

His room was the same. The cot, the chair, the table. It was late fall, and beyond the window the yard and plane tree were bare and brown. The privy needed a coat of paint.

"It will have to be done before we sell the place," he thought.

A lot of things would have to be done.

There was nothing in his room except the furniture, and the few items of clothing he had brought home with him. The cupboard was empty. The drawers were empty. Or so he thought until, one day, opening a drawer at random, he found a small flat paper-wrapped package. It was addressed to him and was postmarked Paris. One corner of the covering had been torn away, and he saw that inside there were two books.

He took the package in to his mother.

"It came a long while ago; I had forgotten it," she said. Then she noticed the torn wrapping. "I thought it might be something valuable, so I looked. But it was only two books."

"Yes, only books."

"There is a letter there too. In the same drawer. Did you see it?"

"No, I didn't."

His mother shrugged. "I am sure it is nothing important either."

Back in his room he reopened the drawer. Reaching far in, he found the letter and brought it out. It was in a blue envelope, also postmarked Paris, and was dated several months later than the package. He knew the writing on the envelope. He had seen it twice before. He took the package and letter to the table and sat down.

First he opened the package, all the way, and took out the two books. The first was bound in blue with white lettering, and the lettering read: SONGS OF DARKNESS *by Maurice Druard*. He turned the pages, reading a line here, a line there. Then he came to a page and on it a poem called "London Night."

He read:

> *What have you done, O you that weep*
> *in the glad sun—*
> *Say, with your youth, you man that weep,*
> *what have you done?*

He pushed the book away. He looked at the second. This one was bound in red with black lettering, and the lettering read: SELECTED POEMS AND PROSE, *by Claude Morel.*

Again he turned pages.

He read:

> *I shall not speak, I shall not show my heart,*
> *but still, within that heart, a fire will burn—*

He read:

> *I shall travel. I shall hunt in the deserts. I shall sleep on the pavements of unknown cities—*

He read:

I have seen star-archipelagoes and islands
in skies that call the wanderer, fierce, forlorn—

He read:

Once, if I remember well, my life was a feast where all hearts opened and all wines flowed. One evening I seated Beauty on my knees. And I found her bitter. And I cursed her—

He read:

God of Judgment: I repent my sins, but not my dreams. I have been damned by the rainbow, but still I shall follow the rainbow—

He pushed this book away.

He looked at the blue envelope.

He looked at it for a long time, but did not open it, and then he rose, leaving it on the table, and took the two books and left the room. He went downstairs and through the door and into the street, and then he followed the streets through the town and its outskirts, until he came to the road along the bank of the Meuse. There, standing on the bank, he dropped the books into the river. He did not fling them, but merely opened his hands and let them drop, and the yellow Meuse took them, turned them slowly over, and sucked them down.

At supper his mother said, "I have an appointment at the bank tomorrow. They have a piece of property off the Antimes road in which they think I may be interested."

"And I?"

"I, what?"

"Do they think *I* may be interested?"

"That," said his mother, "has not yet been discussed."

Later, he went to his room. He sat again at his table and looked at the blue envelope he had left there. And this time he opened it.

Dearest Claude, he read—*Now for the third time I write to you. Perhaps it is foolish, perhaps it is wrong, but still I must do it—this once more. A while ago we sent you a copy of your book, and one of Maurice's, and we had so much hoped to have word from you. Perhaps you are off again on your journeys and have not received them. Perhaps you will not receive this letter. But still (again)—I must write it.*

Claude, what is the matter? What are you afraid of? Why do you run away? Before, you were a boy; it was perhaps natural then. But now you are a man and it is different. . . . Why, Claude—why? . . . If it were to someone, something

*—anything—that you ran, I would understand, but it isn't; I know that. It's to
emptiness, to nothing. You are so terribly wonderfully alive—the most alive and
thinking and feeling of anyone I have ever known—yet you run from life, hide
from it. What do you find in your hiding, Claude? I feel it can only be a sort of
death.*

*This is not an easy letter to write. Women are not supposed to write such
letters. But if you are a strange man, perhaps I am a strange woman. And not to
write it would be, for me, a sort of death.*

*So then.... Twice before I have written you. Twice you have come to me. Will
you come again? It does not have to be to Paris; I know there is something about
Paris that upsets and torments you. Nor do I mean that you should come as a
writer, to talk of your work; for I know that is torment for you too. I ask you to
come simply as a man to a woman. I will not hurt you, Claude. I will not judge or
question or make demands. I will only help—if I can. If love can.*

*Foolish letter? Wrong letter? ... Yes, of course. And also no.... I could not
have written it if I did not know that in your deepest heart you love me too.*

The signature, as before, was simply—G.

The Widow Morel came back from the bank.

"They are all thieves, of course," she said. "Thieves and connivers. But
they say they have a buyer for the store who will pay a good price, and the
property on the Antimes road seems worth a look." A young man from
the bank, she added, was picking them up the next morning to take them
out there.

The young man was Michel Favre. Spruce and businesslike, he drove
up in a two-horse carriage, helped Madame Morel in, and off they went.
It occurred to Claude that this was the first time in all his life that he and
his mother had left the house together bound for anywhere but church.
He and Michel had already met in the street and had talked briefly and
awkwardly, with even less to say to each other than on their previous
meeting, three years before. But now Michel was full of talk and enthusiasm: about acreage, freeholds, deeds, mortgages, quitclaims. Madame
Morel listened stonily and interrupted with occasional pointed questions.
Claude silently watched the bobbing rumps of the horses.

Reaching the property, they first inspected the farmhouse. It was old
and needed refurbishing, both outside and in, but generous allowance,
Michel pointed out, had been made in the really fabulously low terms
the bank was privileged to offer. Barn and outbuildings were also in poor
repair. "But allowance has been made for that too, and with an efficient
farm manager—"

"My son will manage the farm," said Madame Morel.

"Your son? Then Felix is returning?" Michel looked from Madame

Morel to Claude and said "Oh." Then he smiled. "Well, times have changed," he said.

"Yes, times change," agreed Madame Morel. "Often it takes long, but they change."

She returned to reinspect the interior of the house, and Michel and Claude walked out across the fields. "It's good land," said Michel. "The best in the area. My uncle wanted to buy it once, but couldn't, and he was always sorry."

"Your uncle with the cows."

"Yes, with the cows."

As he so often had done on Leduc's farm, in the south, Claude bent and picked up a handful of earth. He felt it, smelled it, let it run out between his fingers.

"Yes, by God," he said, "—they change."

They walked on again: Claude walking slowly, easily; Michel with short hops and side steps to avoid getting mud on his shoes.

"What happened to your plan?" Claude asked.

"Plan?"

"Of leaving. Clearing out of here. What you talked about three years ago."

"It's not all that easy, I'm afraid."

"But you still want to?"

"Want to? God, yes. And it isn't just wanting. I'm still planning, working on it, pulling all sorts of wires. And one of these days, not too far away, it's going to happen." Michel's eyes kindled. His voice took on the edge it had used to have when he was a schoolboy, planning great adventures in the Bois d'Amour. "As a matter of fact, I'm on my way already, really. When you were here last I was an apprentice teller. Now I'm assistant manager of the real-estate division, and in another year or two I should be manager. From there on it's just another step to junior officer, and the Banque du Nord moves its junior officers around to give them experience."

"Such as to Paris?"

"Paris, Algiers, Saigon, everywhere. The whole world."

Claude looked at his old friend and smiled. "A man with dreams, eh?" he said. Then he added: "You know, maybe we could have saved each other a lot of trouble that Christmas morning nine years ago. You should have been the one to walk out of your uncle's barn, and I should have stayed and milked the cows."

As they walked on the going got muddier. Michel looked down at his shoes and then back at the house. "I think maybe your mother will be wanting me," he said.

"Go ahead," Claude told him. "I'll be along soon."

Then he walked on alone. Ahead of him now were trees, the edge of the Ardennes Forest, and there was no wall nor fence, for the farm property, Michel had told them, extended on into the forest for almost half a kilometer. He moved on between the trees, through the brown and gray of November. He sat on the great roots of an oak, as he had used to sit, and looked down the dim aisles of the forest. But now he saw no red-fanged werewolves, no prowling Huns. He saw a stand of timber, and he thought, "They'll pay two francs a cord for that at Vervet's sawmill." Then he thought: "And when the land is cleared it will be good for grazing or an orchard."

That night his mother said, "Well, it is robbery, of course, but in these days, I suppose, one must expect to be robbed. . . . One thing I shall insist on, though: that we inspect the place more thoroughly, inch by inch, before I put down so much as a sou. I will take care of the house and you of the grounds and we will go out every day until we are satisfied, starting tomorrow."

"No, I can't start until next week, Mother," he said.

"Next week? Why? Why not until next week?"

"Because first," he said, "I am going to Paris to bring back a wife."

The chestnut trees of Passy, like the plane trees of Cambon, were brown and bare. He walked past the school and down a street and along another, and then he came to the house and went up the pathway and pulled the doorbell. A maid answered—not the same maid as before—and he said, "I should like to see Mademoiselle Lautier."

The woman looked at him blankly.

"Will you tell her please that Monsieur Morel is here?"

The maid shook her head. "I cannot tell her, monsieur, because there is no such person."

"This is the Lautier home, is it not?"

"No, monsieur."

Claude stepped back. He looked at the door, the number, the façade of the house. "Then whose home is it?" he asked.

"This is the home of Monsieur and Madame Gregoire."

"How long have they lived here?"

"About three years."

"And the people who were here before—the Lautiers: do you know where they have moved?"

"No, monsieur. I do not know them at all."

He turned away. He walked through Passy to the Seine, and along the Seine in the winter dusk. . . . "I shall go to Montmartre," he thought. "To the Rue Nicolet, in Montmartre, and ask the de Bercys." . . .

But even as he thought it he decided against it. If he was a stranger to them the de Bercys would tell him nothing. If they recognized him they would slam the door.

He had a better idea: he would find Chariol. Chariol would know where she was—she probably no longer lived with her family anyhow. Crossing the river, he walked through the *Quartier Latin*. At this hour of the evening the Sorbonne offices would be closed, but Chariol might well be still at his old lodgings off the Boul' Mich; and there he went. No such name, however, appeared on the list of tenants. The concierge knew no Monsieur Chariol. "But wait—" A search of a cabinet in his dim cubicle produced a list of former tenants, and there was the name of Chariol, all right, with a forwarding address—18 Rue Martine.

This walk was a short one. Around a corner, down the boulevard, around a second corner and past the Odeon. Then Claude was at another, and rather more prosperous-looking, building of flats, and among the names on a board in the lobby was that of Albert Chariol. Claude went up a flight of stairs, found the right door, and knocked. And the door was opened by his old teacher.

"Good evening, Albert," said Claude.

For a moment Chariol's face was as blank as the maid's in Passy. Then blankness tightened into a stare. The light in the hall was dim, and he stepped forward a little; his eyes narrowed into a squint, then rewidened into a stare, and he said, "No, no, it's impossible. It can't be."

"Yes, Albert, it can. It is."

Chariol threw an arm about him. He pulled him close. Then, still holding him, he turned and led Claude into the flat, and there, in the brighter light, studied him all over again.

"How different you are, boy," he said. "My God, yes—how you've changed!"

"It's been a long time, Albert."

"Yes—long. Too long."

Chariol had changed too, of course. He was heavier than before, both in face and body. He wore a short brown beard and pince-nez. But the eyes behind the lenses had lost none of their old warmth; nor had his smile nor his handclasp, as he bade his old friend welcome.

"Here, give me your things," he demanded. "Come in—sit down. And start talking. Lord, boy, after all this time we're going to be talking the whole night!"

"I—I can't, Albert. I've just come to ask you—"

"You can ask all you want. All night long. First we're going to have a drink; then dinner. Just the three of us for dinner—perfect." Chariol turned and called: "Darling, come out here—right away, this minute! I've a tremendous surprise for you."

There was no immediate answer; and looking in the same direction as Chariol, Claude became aware of the room he had entered. It was a cheerful, warmly lighted room, lined with books. And the books were familiar; they were the same as they had always been, on the walls of Chariol's lodging. But the rest was not the same. It was very different. The cheerfulness, for one thing, for Chariol's other rooms had been austere. And the furnishings: they were bright, neat, almost rich-looking. On a table was a vase with flowers. At the windows were flowered curtains. On the far side of the room was another door; and now the door opened and a woman appeared.

"Darling, look," said Chariol happily. "Look who's here. You won't believe it."

The woman approached. She was young; she was tall and beautiful; she moved with grace. Her face was oval and soft of line, but the forehead was broad and high under light swept-back chestnut hair. She came toward them quickly, half-smiling; then, all at once, no longer quickly, not smiling, her face gone suddenly white and bloodless, her eyes dark in its whiteness, a deep violet-blue.

"Claude—" Germaine said. That was all. Just once: "Claude—"

Claude said nothing.

Chariol beamed. "My dear, may I present an old friend of yours?" he said. "Old friend, may I present my wife?"

There was a silence.

Then Chariol laughed. "Yes, of course you're surprised—the two of you. Speechless. Who wouldn't be? *Mon Dieu*, I should be speechless myself. Only I'm too happy. It's incredible—poof! just like that—and the three of us together at last."

He squeezed Claude's shoulder. He kissed Germaine's cheek. "Yes," he said, "this is really he. Really she. You are really each other. Claude—Germaine. . . . Madame Germaine Chariol," he added fondly.

"How are you, Claude?"

Her voice seemed small and distant. It was the eyes that were close; close and enormous. He tried to look away, but still he saw them. He wanted to turn and flee, but could not move an inch.

"You're so tall, Claude," the voice said. "So thin and brown. You've changed."

"Of course he's changed," said Chariol. "Who hasn't?" Again he laughed. "And I most of all, eh boy? Old bachelor Chariol now the married man; you'd never have thought it of me, would you? . . . And the wonderful thing, of course, is that it's you who's responsible. Yes you, you rascal. You and your poems. Morel the matchmaker: that's you. . . . Well, now at last we've the chance to say thank you."

He had taken Claude by the arm and all but forced him into a chair. Germaine had not moved. "Sit down. Sit down, my dear," he told her.

"*Mon Dieu*, there's so much to talk about it's hard to know where to begin."

He himself sat down. He leaned forward. "Your poems, yes: that's the most important thing. We sent you a copy of our little book to Cambon. A long time ago, that was. . . . You've seen it, of course? We'd hoped to hear from you about it, but I suppose you were off again, chasing around the world."

There was a pause.

"It had no great sale, to be sure. Books by new poets never do. But it got into the right hands, I can tell you that. You're being talked about where it matters. France will catch up with you—the world will catch up: wait and see."

Again a pause.

"We sent you another book too. Druard's. He asked us to. . . . You haven't seen him at all, have you? Or corresponded. . . ." Chariol shook his head. "Poor Maurice, what a mess he's made of his life. He is a great poet, yes. His last things are his best ever: exquisite, works of genius. But for the rest, it's awful—awful. He tried to enter a monastery, you know; but it was hopeless. He begged his wife to take him back. Hopeless too. Besides his poems he has nothing; only drink, drugs, loneliness. . . . I met him through Germaine, of course. We see him now and then and do what we can for him. He lives only a few blocks away, in the Rue de Lacque. Germaine tells me you two once lived there together, and I suppose that's where he was happiest, so he went back. But he's not happy now. Mother of God, no! As I say, we try to help a little, but—"

Chariol shook his head again, this time briskly. He shook the somber thoughts away and, leaning forward, put a hand on Claude's knee. "But we've better things to talk about than Druard. I mean you, boy. *You*." He chuckled. "I still call you 'boy,' you see. It's ridiculous, isn't it? My God, you must be—what now? Twenty-four. Twenty-five. Fantastic! But anyhow, you're still a boy to me. A crazy *mioche* from the Ardennes."

Another chuckle.

"So go on, boy—it's your turn now. Talk. Talk all night. Tell us everything. . . . Where have you been? What have you done? What have you written? . . . The last time I saw you there was all that nonsense about no more writing, remember? Insanity. Childishness. Shall I tell you something, boy? In the whole history of the world there has never been a true writer who gave up writing. And you are a true one if one ever lived.

"So go on, tell us. How has it gone? What have you done? Have you some of your things right there in your pocket?"

Claude did not answer. He had not heard. Chariol sat not two feet away, but he did not see him. He saw only the figure behind him; the figure still standing silent and motionless. He saw the face, white as the face of the drowned. He saw the eyes, violet-blue as the sea.

Then the figure moved; Chariol turned. "Where are you going, dear?" he asked.

"It's time I saw to dinner," Germaine said.

"Dinner—good Lord, of course. And the drinks. I'm still so excited I've forgotten everything." He jumped up. "So—first things first. The drinks. Stay with Claude, dear, while I get them, and we'll toast reunion. After that, there'll be plenty of time for dinner."

He went quickly to the door and out.

Claude sat where he was. Germaine stood where she was. A horse and wagon rattled by on the street below.

"Don't, Claude—" she said softly.

"Don't what?"

"Don't look at me like that."

His eyes did not move.

"*Why* do you look like that?"

He did not answer.

"Why, Claude? Why? . . . What's the matter? What did you come here for?"

"I came to see Albert," he said.

"Yes, of course, to see Albert. I understand that. But—"

"I came to ask where I could find you."

Now it was she who was silent.

"I received your letter," he said.

"My letter?"

He took from his pocket a blue envelope. "I came to answer it," he said.

She moved closer. She looked down at the envelope. For an instant her eyes met his, and then turned away.

"Oh Claude—no—"

"Your note," he said, "—and I was answering."

"But—" Her voice was the merest whisper. "But that was *three years ago*."

"Three years—"

"Yes. Yes, Claude—"

She turned back to him. She stood before him. Her lips moved, but soundlessly. Her hand went out a little and returned to her side.

"How long have you been married?" he asked tonelessly.

"About two years," she said.

"Have you children?"

"No."

There was a long pause. Then—

"I have no children either," he said.

There was a voice from the next room. "Darling, where are the vermouth glasses?" Chariol called.

Germaine turned. "In the left-hand cupboard, where they always are."

"No, they're not."

"All right then—wait a second."

She left the room.

Claude rose.

He crossed to the foyer, got his coat and hat and went out the door, closing it quietly behind him.

He walked down the Rue Martine. He came to the boulevard. He walked down the Boul' Mich. The winter night was cold, and there were few strollers. The cafés were glassed in and the glass rimed with frost.

At the entrance of a café he turned suddenly in. There was an empty table and he sat at it, and a waiter came. His face was familiar to Claude, but the waiter did not recognize him.

"*Oui, monsieur?*"

"*Une absinthe.*"

The absinthe came, and he sat with it. Once he raised it, and then set it down. He revolved the glass slowly in the saucer and watched the play of greenish light. After a while he put change on the table and left, leaving the drink untouched.

He walked another block on the boulevard. He turned right. He walked half a block on the Rue de Lacque, entered a doorway, climbed two flights of stairs. The second landing was dark, as it had always been, but a thread of light showed under the door before him. He raised his hand to knock.

But he held his hand.

For he was conscious of something other than light that came from behind the door. It was not something he saw, but that he smelled, tasted —knew. It was very faint, but it was there: subtle, sweetish, pervading. . . . And then he was conscious of something else as well. And this was sound. . . . From behind the door, too, came the sound of a voice. Very low. A mere mumbling. Like the sound of a voice in prayer . . . or in delirium.

He turned and went down the stairs. He walked east on the Rue de Lacque and south on the Boul' Mich. He followed the Boul' Mich until it ended, then other streets and avenues, but bearing always to the south, keeping his course by a star that burned bright before him above the rooftops. Three times before he had gone south, toward the horizons, and turned back from them. But this time—the last time—there would be no turning.

Slowly the city fell away behind him. He moved through suburbs, and then on into the countryside. It was still night, still cold, but he walked evenly, steadily, as a man walks who has plenty of time.

The country roads were empty, and he walked alone.

He was one soul, one body.

One.

PART II
THE DISPOSSESSED

"No more words. I bury the dead in my belly."

23

To the north was desert, to the south the sea. Between them, black and bare, stood the walls of a long-dead volcano, and around the volcano—on its slopes, in its crater—was the city of Aden.

Aden burned. Aden fried. In that midsummer of 1880, no breath of air moved down from the Arabian highlands, no wisp of rain moved inward from the Indian Ocean. Above the land there was only the tan dust raised by the camel caravans; above the sea, only the black smoke of the ships. Dust and smoke met and mingled and sifted down into the city. Above them—above the crater of the dead volcano—flamed the live volcano of the sun.

Aden was British: the Empire's fortress and coaling station on the route from Suez to India. And since the opening of the Canal, eleven years before, it had grown from torpid village to small metropolis. Few of its sweltering thousands, though, were Englishmen. Most were Arabs, from the surrounding areas of Yemen, Muscat, and Oman, drawn in from their desert villages by the lure of work and wages. There were many Indians, too—for Aden was administratively part of India—and many Somalis, from the nearby African coasts. There were Greeks, Syrians, Armenians, Jews. And, in lesser numbers, and with better status, there were Western Europeans of assorted nationalities and occupations. Merchants and traders, clerks and officials. Germans and Swedes, Italians and Frenchmen. Among the French were Monsieur Paul Colbert, Consul of the Republic, and Monsieur Emil Gorbeau, proprietor of the import-export firm of Gorbeau and Company (Aden), Limited.

The two were very different, both in appearance and temperament. Colbert, a Marseillais, was slim and sharp-faced, tense and mercurial. Gorbeau, from the Breton coast, was broad, solid, stolid, phlegmatic. But they were about of an age—in their early fifties; both had been long in Aden; and they were close friends. Scarcely a week passed in which Gorbeau did not visit the consul on some matter of business, and the consul in turn would brief him on matters political and international. Usually—and perhaps with an assist from Colbert's temperament—such matters were in a state close to crisis. And seldom had they been more so than on an ovenlike July afternoon in 1880 when the two, in their dusty, sweat-stained linens, sat in the consul's office over cool, but not cooling, drinks.

"*Eh bien,*" said Colbert, "we are used to the British, with their conniving and grabbing. First here, with Aden itself. Then all up and down the Red Sea, all over Africa. . . . But the Italians: *nom de Dieu!* Who are the Italians to get into such things?"

"I could have told you—"

"Of course you could have told me. I could have told you. I *did* tell them—the Quai d'Orsay—over and over. The Italians are moving in on Eritrea, I tell them. No, no, they answer, it is only a little private trading company there at Assab. Wait and see what happens, I say. So they wait —and now they see. Now the little private trading company is the Italian government. With warships, troops, forts."

"They are not going to stop there either," said Gorbeau. "They have their eye on Abyssinia."

"Of course they have their eye on Abyssinia. Everyone knows it. Even the Quai d'Orsay knows it—now; and they're all in an uproar. And they expect me to stop it. *Me*, mind you. What do they think I am? An army? A navy? I should stop the Italians all by myself, and for the consulate here they give me hardly enough money for spittoons and rubber stamps."

Colbert bit his lip. He shook his head. He clapped his hands, and an Arab boy appeared, and he ordered the drinks to be replenished.

"It is the money of course," he went on, "that is the heart of the trouble. They expect me to outwit the British Empire, to throw the Italians out, to make France supreme on the Red Sea. And what do they give me? Five thousand francs a month. Out of that I am supposed to live, run this office, pay a staff, entertain. Out of five thousand miserable francs I am even supposed to handle repatriations; to pay the way back to Marseilles for every no-good drunken tramp of a Frenchman that jumps ship or gets stranded here. The police hand me a dozen a month, and I am supposed to house them, feed them, and send them home. It's murderous, I tell you. And on top of that they expect me to wage a private war against Italy."

The boy brought the fresh drinks, and the consul eyed his glumly. Then a sudden thought raised his head.

"By the way," he said, "I hear you lost one of your clerks last week."

Gorbeau nodded. "Yes, old Colignac, poor fellow. The malaria burned him out at last and he had to go home."

"Well, you need a replacement, don't you?"

"Not one of your tramps, thank you."

"This isn't a tramp, the one I'm thinking of. He's not— Well, he's different."

"Different, how?"

"For one thing, I'm sure he's not a drunkard. I can tell by his eyes. They're queer eyes—very queer—but not a drunkard's."

"But he's a derelict?"

"Well—yes, I suppose you'd have to say that. He has no money, no clothes, nothing. Yet, as I say, he's different. There's something about him. . . . Anyhow, I think you could use him; at least as a stopgap."

"And, quite incidentally of course, get him off your hands."

"I didn't—"

"No, naturally you didn't." Gorbeau smiled; then he sighed. "All right," he said, "send him around to see me."

The consul brightened. "No need to. He's here right now, downstairs—doing some odd jobs for me." Again he clapped his hands, the boy appeared, and he spoke to him briefly. When the boy had gone, he opened a drawer, took out a paper and handed it to Gorbeau. "Here's his police form. Not much on it, you'll see; he's not very communicative. But it gives you something at least."

Gorbeau glanced at the document; then up at the door as the boy reappeared. Behind the boy came a man: a tallish, very thin man dressed in soiled and ragged cotton. His face seemed to be made of bones and leather; very dark leather, the face darker than the young Arab's. But the hair was no Arab's. It was light: a dusty yellow streaked with gray. Nor were the eyes an Arab's. They were light too. In the dark face they seemed almost white. . . . Yes, Gorbeau thought, the consul had been right. They were strange eyes. Very strange.

The boy left. The man came forward and stood silently before the consul's desk. "This is Monsieur Gorbeau, one of our leading Aden merchants," the consul said to him. "He thinks he might have work for you."

The man remained silent. Gorbeau again glanced at the police card.

"Your name is Morel?" he said.

"Yes."

"From Cambon, in the Ardennes."

"Yes."

Gorbeau's eyes went up sharply. "You do not look like an Ardennais."

"I have lived many places." The man spoke softly and slowly. "Perhaps that has changed me," he said.

"Hmm. . . . It says here you are twenty-five."

"That is correct."

Gorbeau studied him. "You are sure? You are *only* twenty-five?"

"Yes, that is my age."

"There is nothing written here after 'Occupation.'"

"I have no regular occupation."

"What sort of work have you done?"

"I've farmed. I've been to sea. I've been a waiter, a factory hand."

"Ever handled merchandise?"

"Yes."

"Where?"

"In a store."

"Where?"

"In Cambon."

"Can you read and write?"

"Yes."

"Can you do figures?"

"Simple ones."

"Hmm. . . ." Gorbeau rubbed his chin. He looked the man up and down. He looked at his eyes.

"Why did you come to Aden?" he asked.

"To find work."

"And you have not been able to?"

"No."

"You are prepared to do hard work—dirty work?"

"Yes."

"For small pay?"

"Yes."

Gorbeau re-examined the police card. He turned it over. Then he looked at the consul. "He was in police custody for five days?" he said.

The consul nodded. "Before they notified me."

"But there were no criminal charges?"

"No."

"Only vagrancy?"

"Yes."

Gorbeau pursed his lips. He rubbed his chin again. Then he looked up. "Come to my office tomorrow at eight," he said. "Gorbeau and Company, on Queen's Way. I cannot promise anything, but we shall see."

He turned away. The consul nodded. The man went out. When he was gone the two friends again sipped their drinks.

"Yes, he is different all right," said Gorbeau. "A strange one. . . . his face, his voice, the way he stood there. . . . And then his eyes," he added. *"Mon Dieu,* those eyes!"

The eyes were open, looking up at the sky. And it was full of stars. He knew the names of the stars now, for early in his journey he had bought a chart of the heavens to help him find his way in the trackless nights. The star he had followed south was Fomalhaut. It was in the constellation of Pisces, and its magnitude was 1.3.

Almost every night he looked up at the stars, for almost every night he slept outdoors. On much of his journey it had been of necessity: in doorways, alleys, fields, forests, deserts. Now it was from choice. He had been given a small room with a cot in the rear of the Gorbeau warehouse, but beyond the room was an open storage yard and soon he had moved his cot out into it. There was no danger of rain. What there was danger of, for most Europeans, was mosquitoes; but not for him, and he did not even use a net. Sometimes the mosquitoes came and whined and lighted on him, but he did not even bother to brush them away, for he knew they would find no blood but merely blunt their needles on his leathery skin. After a while they would give up and whine angrily away, and he would laugh at them. He did not laugh often, but he laughed at the mosquitoes.

Under the stars, he slept. And when he awoke he often, at first, did not know where he was, for he had slept outdoors in so many places. First in France, even in the winter nights. Then in Italy (again); then in Greece (again); then down through Levantine Turkey to Egypt and Cairo. From Cairo he had planned to go up the Nile, but there too, as here in Aden, he had been arrested, and the police had taken him to Port Said (again) to put him on a ship bound for France. He had got away from them, but it was too risky to go back to Cairo; so he had gone to the docks and hidden in warehouses. He had slept there, found his food there, and at last found a ship as well; this time a ship going not north but south (—no, there would be no more north, but only south, always south—); and had gone on through the Canal to Suez and the Red Sea. He had signed on for Bombay, but at Suez he jumped ship. He had found a job here, a job there; finally a berth on a small coastal trading boat that took him south to Jidda, in Arabia; and from there he had continued on down the Red Sea—south, always south—to Port Sudan, to Massawa, to Hodeida, to Assab. And at last to Aden. He had been to Aden twice before—on the *Prins van Oranje* and the *Nottingham Castle*—but no farther, each time, than the coaling wharves. This third time he came ashore. He walked the streets. He looked for work. He fell asleep under a palm tree on the lawn of a public building, and when he awoke two policemen stood over him. Five days later, Monsieur Paul Colbert, the French Consul, had come to the jail and reluctantly signed a paper.

Now he slept again and woke.

He was still in Aden.

Why?

Because of the consul, for one thing. Because of Gorbeau and a departed invalid named Colignac. They were why he was *still* there. But why had he come there in the first place? "To find work," he had said. But why in Aden? Why not in Bombay? Or Calcutta? Or Colombo or Singapore or Shanghai or San Francisco or Rio or Quebec or St. Petersburg?

Why? . . . No, not why. No matter why. His Season on Earth continued; he was here; that was enough. He was out of the deep caves, in the world of men, beneath the sky and stars. . . . *From the same desert, in the same night, always my eyes awake to the silver star. Always* . . . And through the desert, through the night, the Three Magi moved on in their own journey, toward their own star. Always. . . .

He watched them for a while. Then they faded and it was morning.

Gorbeau and Company was a going and growing enterprise. Emil Gorbeau, former merchant of Nantes, had, like so many Frenchmen, been fired by the dreams of de Lesseps, and soon after the opening of the Suez Canal had migrated to Aden with a capital of a few thousand francs. He had worked hard, made good deals, prospered; and by 1880 his company ranked only slightly behind the two largest British mercantile houses in the city. Its trade was complex and multidirectional. From Europe came cheap manufactured goods that went out by caravan into interior Arabia and by dhow and small steamer to the Somali coast of Africa; and from Arabia and Africa came raw produce that moved on to the factories and shops of Europe. Little merchandise was either bought or sold in Aden itself. But Aden was the trading post and transshipment point—the heart and center of the enterprise. The office on Queen's Way was jammed with ledgers, invoices, waybills, documents; the adjoining warehouse and wharf with the wares and staples of three continents.

Gorbeau habitually employed a staff of three Europeans—a chief clerk, a warehouse superintendent, and a general assistant—and with the departure of one Colignac and the advent of Claude, the number remained constant. Claude became the assistant. In the office, behind the ledgers, was another Frenchman, Marcel Rappe, and in the warehouse, among the crates and bales, was an Irishman named Neil Fitzsimmons.

Rappe was small, bald and ageless. He talked little. He worked prodigiously. Order and neatness were his passions, and this manifested itself not only in his office and records but in his person as well. Aden was an oven, yet his linen was always crisp. It was a dustbin, yet his shoes always shone. His fringe of hair and mustache were carefully trimmed, his spectacles carefully wiped and glittering; and behind them his eyes were sharp, black, and usually fixed on his ledgers. He seemed the French *fonctionnaire par excellence*, a man with his niche, his desk, his forms, his rubber stamps. He should, Claude thought, have been an accountant in Dijon or a postmaster in Reims, and what had brought him to this far and frowzy outpost was a mystery.

What had brought Fitzsimmons was, on the other hand, obvious. It was that old bringer and dispatcher, Adventure. A tall, red-haired, ramshackle man of perhaps thirty, he was as talkative, at least in spurts, as Rappe was taciturn, and Claude had been with him no more than a few hours before he knew that he had (1) run away from his County Sligo home at fourteen, (2) worked on ships and at odd jobs in many parts of the world, (3) come to Aden because it was the jumping-off place for Africa, and (4) gone to work for Gorbeau because he hated the British. What he did not say, but Claude noted, was that he was lonely, restless, and a drinker. But he did his drinking only at night. In the warehouse he worked hard; as hard as Rappe in his office—but in his own way, the same way he talked, in sudden spurts of energy and spirit. When a job was done, he would often sink into lassitude, lying stretched on a bale in a doorway or on the wharf and staring broodingly out to sea.

Claude's work was where he was needed, and he was needed more in the warehouse (—or godown, as he learned to call it, for in Aden everyone used the East Indian name). And this he preferred, though the labor was harder, for here was the very taste and smell and essence of the blood-stream of world trade. Perhaps a third of the space was given over to the goods of Europe: bolts of cotton and calico, pots and pans, knives and pins and beads and glassware—the inventory of his mother's store, replenished once each week and multiplied tenfold—on their way to desert tents and jungle compounds. And filling the other two-thirds was the bulkier crude produce of desert and jungle, bound outward to north and west. In one section, tall stacks of hides: of leopard, cheetah, zebra, monkey, antelope. In another, a ton of shells (for the buttons of Europe). In still others, great bins of coffee and durra, the African grain. At the bins stood rows of Arab boys and Somali women (only Somalis, the women, for all female Arabs were in purdah), measuring, sorting, wrapping with mat and bark. When each bale was ready stevedores hoisted it off with their hooks and ropes. More coffee and grain poured in. Nothing stood still. Everything moved. In and out. Out and in.

There were other bins too. Of spices. Of gums. Of resins. Of myrrh and musk and aloes and opopanax. In Europe these would become soap, flavorings, medicines, perfumes. They would become the incense burning at the altars of cathedrals and churches. "We must be especially careful with our sorting of the incense gums," Gorbeau had cautioned. "The Catholic Church is the biggest buyer and is very particular." And Claude had nodded and was especially careful. "For you, Mother—For you, Father Lacaze—For you, Druard the Holy," he thought, as he worked at the bins with his helpers. "From all good Moslems and your son and servant, with best wishes for an aromatic Communion."

He worked in the godown. He worked on the wharf. The produce for Europe was loaded onto lighters that were then moved out to the freighters at anchor; the wares for Africa into native dhows that pulled alongside. There were no forests in Arabia, and the dhows were built of teakwood brought from Malaya. They were heavy and high-pooped, and, with their slanted masts and heavy lateen sails, looked as if they would capsize at the first swell. Yet they were among the most seaworthy of ships; for uncounted centuries the Arabs had sailed them along the coasts and across the seas, as far as India and Ceylon, Java and Zanzibar. To the nearest shores of the Somalis was only some hundred and thirty miles, and the dhows often made it in a day and a night. Then a few days later they would reappear, their pots and pans and cottons replaced by hides and coffee and shells and gum. There would be an unloading—a reloading. Endlessly.

Claude worked hard. As hard as on Leduc's farm by the Rhone. In Aden, as in most tropical cities, work began early and ended late, with a break for rest at midday. But Claude rested only at night. At noon he left the godown and the wharf and moved on through the city. In the oven heat no one else walked so much as a block if he could help it, but he walked as he had always walked: steadily, tirelessly, in and out, up and down. The sun burned down on his bare head, but he did not feel it. Nor did he sweat. He had no juices for sweating, any more than he had blood for mosquitoes.

In earlier days Aden had been wholly contained within the crater of its volcano. Now, in its new incarnation, however, it had burst out from its black rim and sprawled out at the base into the modern dockside area called Steamer Point. Here, on Queen's Way, were the headquarters of Gorbeau and Company. And here too were most of the other trading houses, the banks, the shops, the hotels and bars, the piers and coaling wharves that made the city an international entrepôt. Ships hooted, winches creaked, gangways rose and fell. Through the streets passed the produce and wares of three continents, creaking slowly along in camel and mule carts. And in the streets, too, were the ships' human cargo: British army and civil service officers from the P. & O. liners on the India run; their ladies in white linen with parasols; merchants, tourists, officials from all the countries of Europe; bound for—or from—Bombay, Rangoon, Penang, Batavia, Hong Kong, Sydney, Zanzibar, Capetown. There were the crews as well, and their officers; from the liners, the packets, the tramps, the coalers; sooty lascars from the stokeholes, red-faced jack-tars from the crow's-nests; men from Norway and Sweden, France and Germany, Holland and Belgium, England and Scotland. Most of the engineers were Scotsmen, and most looked like Mackenzie. Once, on Queen's Way, Claude thought he saw Mackenzie, but on approaching closer he found the man was a stranger.

Everyone was a stranger.

All right—he was used to that. And he no longer wanted any fathers —Mackenzie or otherwise.

He walked on the waterfront. Among the crates and bales; past the sweating stevedores; past the dhows and lighters and barges and coal bunkers, and the coal soot sifted down like a mist, filming his face and hands. Behind the film was the red sail of a dhow moving seaward. Across the harbor the desert glared in the sun.

He left Steamer Point. He climbed the slopes to Crater Town. Here, beyond the break in the black rock, was the old city, a different city. Here the world was shut out, and the ships and horizons. The white and pink faces were gone, and there were only dark faces: the faces of Arabs, Somalis, Indians, Negroes. Almost all were men. It was a city of men. The few women to be seen were no more than muffled, veiled figures glimpsed fleetingly in a courtyard or on a balcony. It was a city of camels and goats; of goats by the thousand. A city of dust and filth and stench and offal. Some of the offal was animal and some was human, but it was the human that made the stench.

On one side of him, now, was the ruin of an old Turkish fort; on the other, a mosque. From the minaret of the mosque came the singsong of a muezzin calling Islam to prayer. "He should have incense," Claude thought. "A kilo of certified Gorbeau incense to burn in his tower, to take the stink out of Allah's nostrils."

Ahead was the main market, the souk, and he moved slowly through its labyrinthine aisles. The most crowded and active section was that given over to the selling of khat. Those old staples of the East, opium and hashish, had been (more or less effectively) outlawed by the master British; but khat was legal, it was brought into Aden by the dhowfull, the fleet-full, from the coasts of Africa, and its sleek green leaves filled the booths and bins of Crater Town. As narcotics went, it was a mild one; a bundle of leaves had to be chewed for hours before it took effect. But the Arabs of Aden had plenty of hours. Through the days and the nights they sat in the streets, in the alleys, along the walls of the market, chewing patiently, like cows, like camels, until at last they entered the trance of their seeking. Passing among them, Claude was as if invisible. Their eyes were glazed. Green foam was on their lips. And he thought, "No, no incense needed here. They have their own short cut to Allah; their own green caves of dream and refuge."

He moved on. Through stink, through fester; through sun and dust and dung and flies. The khat-chewers were gone now, and instead there were children. The children's eyes were not glazed. They were dark and liquid, ringed with pus and flies. Beyond them, in the street, lay a dead donkey, wrapped in a crawling corset that shone black in the sun.

"A, black, the glittering of flies," he thought. And then—"Why A? A, black?" An old image rose, flickered briefly, and was gone.

Then there was a different black: the black of rock. He was moving up out of the streets, out of the town, onto the slopes above them; onto the inner walls of the crater. There were still men here, but no houses. Instead of houses there were caves—not green but black, black holes in the rock —and the men sat in the holes and watched him as he passed. They sat without anger, without fear. Without even khat. They sat through the days and nights—and the years.

Above the caves were goats. Above the goats, nothing. Here the flesh of earth, even its dust, had been ripped away and its hideous bones laid bare. There was only rock and lava, black crags, the burning sun. "You are no longer on the earth at all," Claude thought, "but in hell." He had been in hell before, to be sure; he had had his full season there; but that had been a hell of his own making, whereas this was the hell of reality. Aden was an inverted hell, with its pit at its summit, and he had come up through its seven circles to its ultimate level, to the central fire pit of the sun.

He felt an inward smile. . . . Well, why not? . . . He had once been Child of the Sun. He had once been Lucifer, and here was Lucifer's home.

He climbed on. He reached the rim of the pit. The world reappeared. Standing on the flange of Aden's crater, he looked out over city and harbor, desert and sea. Above the desert hung the dust trails of the caravans; above the sea, the smoke trails of the ships. The smoke streamed in three directions: southeast, toward the Indian Ocean and Asia; northwest, toward the Red Sea and Europe; southwest, across the Gulf of Aden, toward Africa. And between the smoke trails, tiny between the black hulls of the steamships, were the colored sails of the dhows. Far to the southwest was a single sail, a red sail—perhaps the one he had seen earlier from the wharves in the harbor—and he watched it until it was out of sight.

In the morning I shall draw my boat up on strange beaches. I shall enter the Kingdom of Savages, the Kingdom of Ham. . . .

Turning, he moved down through the circles of hell to the wharf and the warehouse.

Neil Fitzsimmons did his roaming at night. To the bars and to the brothels. "Come along. Come on, goddammit," he would say to Claude. "What sort o' man are ye anyhow?" Sometimes he would say it with a growl, sometimes with a grin that showed a gleaming gold tooth.

To the brothels Claude would not go. ("I prefer my own bed," he said. "It's better for astronomy.") And though occasionally he went along to a bar, he drank nothing stronger than lime juice or ginger beer.

"What's wrong with ye, feller?" the Irishman persisted.

"Nothing," said Claude. "I'm just not a drinker."

"The hell yer not. Yer an old boozer; I can tell one when I see 'im."

"I used to drink, yes."

"And—?"

"And stopped."

"Took the pledge, eh? But took it fer rale." Fitzsimmons shook his head. "Well, it takes all kinds, they say." He swallowed his whisky and called down the bar: "Hey, Jocko, one more o' the same!" Then again to Claude: "Pledges, Jesus. The pledges I've took—and busted—"

He told of a heroic spree in Liverpool, and another in Capetown. After the third drink he told of his women: one in London, one in Naples, one in Sydney. "But the one in Sydney, the little Aussie, she warn't like the others," he said. "She was the rale thing, that one. The rale goods, and I loved 'er. The one woman in the whole damn world I ever loved, outside me mother."

After the fourth drink he told of his mother. He told of his boyhood, his running away, his adventures on ships and in cities. The whisky went down, and the loneliness welled up, and for an hour he talked steadily, roaming back and forth through his life.... Then finally he stopped. He stared broodingly into his glass. He looked at Claude and said, "Well?"

"Well, what?"

"Yer turn now, lad. Let's have it."

Claude shook his head. "There is nothing to tell."

"Nothin' to tell? Ye was born here this evenin', ye mean?" Fitzsimmons' eyes had been misty with whisky and memories. Now they were hard. His voice grew belligerent. "Goddammit, I sit here spillin' me guts out, and ye never open yer face. Three months we've been together—every day, side by side—and ye've never opened it. Dammit, man, talk. Talk! Where've ye been in yer life? What have ye done? Who the hell are ye, anyhow?"

"I am Claude Morel."

"Claude Morel. Well now, ain't that interestin'. Fancy that. And I was mistakin' ye the whole time fer the Maharajah of Maragoochi." The Irishman thumped the bar. He took another drink. "All right," he said, "yer name's Morel. Yer a frog. Yer an old boozer that's given it up.... And what else? ... Answer me, man, goddammit. Where ye been? What've ye done? What are ye? Who are ye?"

"I am nobody."

"Nobody?—Crap!—Everybody's somebody. So come on, let's have it. Who *are* ye, ye bloody sphinx?"

It was a moment before Claude answered. He shook his head slowly. Then he said, "No—no, Fitz—there's nothing to tell you. There's just what you see. Just arms, legs, face, body. No I—no I at all. There is no I." He smiled slightly, remembering. "I—is *another*."

"Is anoth—"

Fitzsimmons' glass was halfway to his lips. He drained it, slammed it down, and stood up. "Lemme out o' here," he said.... "Hey, Jocko, how much? ... By Jesus, now I see why ye took the pledge. Yer loony enough without the booze."

There was a week when the warehouse was quiet. But the papers had piled high in the office, and he was given one of the ledgers to bring up to date.

"Hmm, hmm—" said Monsieur Rappe noncommittally when Claude

finished his work. And at the time there was no further comment. But a few days later he beckoned him to his desk and cleared his throat.

"I see you have done bookkeeping before," he said.

"No," said Claude.

"No? You told Monsieur Gorbeau you have worked in a store."

"Yes, I have. But not as a bookkeeper."

"Hmm." Rappe's eyes, from behind their glasses, appraised him sharply. "That is interesting; quite interesting." Again he cleared his throat. "At least you have done much writing, I gather."

"Writing, monsieur?"

"These entries of yours. Your script. It is not the work of a man unfamiliar with pen and ink."

"I studied penmanship at school, of course. It was one of my good subjects."

"Hmm. I see." Rappe let it pass. "In any case," he said, "it seems to me you are wasting your time in the warehouse. Or, more important, the company's time."

"I do not follow you, monsieur."

"As you have probably observed, we are a successful concern. A growing one. Soon my time will be wholly occupied as office manager and we will need a full-time clerk."

"Oh."

"I intend to recommend you for the position to Monsieur Gorbeau."

"That is kind of you," said Claude, "but I would not be interested."

"Not interested?" Rappe stared at him. "*Mon Dieu*, my good fellow, why not?"

"Because I am not *un assis*."

"A what?"

"I do not like to sit down. I do not like desks or papers or pen and ink."

"You prefer crates and bales?"

"Yes."

"And manual labor?"

"Yes."

"And working side by side with stinking Arabs and Somalis?"

"Yes."

Rappe opened his mouth. He closed it again. Then he shrugged and returned to his work.

"Thank you, nevertheless," Claude said to him. "I am glad you are pleased with my bookkeeping."

The chief clerk ran the office, but Gorbeau ran the business. Broad, rumpled, and slow-moving, he seemed much of the time to be doing nothing in particular. But somehow he was always on hand when a decision had to be made. Both in the office and godown he watched every-thing, missed nothing, surveying his domain with the small sharp eyes of a Breton trader.

He talked little. To Claude, once he had hired him, he spoke scarcely at all, except to give an occasional order or explain how something should be done. It was his wife who was the talker. Although she took no part in the business, Claude, after a few months with Gorbeau and Company, knew her better than he did her husband.

Madame Gorbeau was a Parisienne. She was friendly and animated. Though well into her forties, and no beauty, she took meticulous care of her face, figure, and clothing, and ran a household of which she was justly proud. "In such a place as this," she would say, "the nice things, the civilized things, are all the more important."

Claude went to her home on errands and for an occasional odd job. She smiled at him, talked to him, and one day had him stay for tea. "It is one of the British customs I have grown fond of," she said. "Others, I confess, I can do without. But tea is pleasant. It is *sympathique*."

As she poured she looked at Claude with interest. "I gather you know the British well, Monsieur Morel," she said. "You speak their language so fluently." Claude looked at her with surprise, and she laughed. "Oh, I know more about you than you may think. For instance, that you speak English with Mr. Fitzsimmons. Not to mention Arabic with the godown workers. In short, that you are quite a linguist. . . . Sugar? Milk?"

"Thank you," said Claude.

"You must have traveled much."

"Yes, some."

"And studied, too. One does not learn much by the simple act of travel. Just look around you at the Europeans here in Aden, and you will see what I mean." Again Madame Gorbeau smiled. "But I am sure you have already —to your distress. It cannot be a very congenial place, I am certain, for a person like yourself."

"Like myself, madame? I am not—"

"Oh come now, do you think I am blind—or deaf? That because you are dressed as a workman I cannot tell you are an educated, cultured man?" She raised a hand quickly. "Don't be worried now. I am not going to ask questions. I am not going to pry. But I am not a fool, you know. I have not lived all my life in such a place as this."

A houseboy brought in cakes and bonbons and set them on the table between them. "Here," she said, pointing, "try one of these; I think you'll like them. They are a favorite of my son."

She looked up. "Perhaps you didn't know we had a son?"

"No," said Claude.

"He is nineteen now, and in Paris, at the university. We miss him

greatly, of course. But—as I say—what is there here for him? He must
have an education, absorb the culture of his homeland; then he will come
back and enter the business. Meanwhile we must get along without him.
Without many things."

She shrugged. "One does the best one can. For my husband it is
not difficult. His wants are simple; he is the businessman through and
through. But for myself—no, for such as myself there are problems. For
such as you, I should think. To live, a plant must have roots; and a human
being too. And what roots can one strike in such a desert as this? What
food is there for the mind, the spirit?"

She sighed. "As I say, one does one's best. Or at least a few of us. We
arrange an occasional concert, a showing of paintings. And thank the
Lord there are books. I have quite a few, as you may have noticed. Many of
the classics—the best. Do feel free to borrow any, if you care to."

"That is kind of you, madame, but—"

"And some new books too," Madame Gorbeau brightened. "My son
sends them to me from Paris, and he has excellent taste. Lately he has
become interested in poetry; particularly the modern poets—I believe
they call themselves Parnassians. . . . Here, let me show you." She rose and
crossed to a table on which was a small pile of new volumes. "I myself
did not know any of the names before." She picked up the books one by
one. "Leconte de Lisle—Stephane Mallarmé—Yves Balmer—Maurice
Druard—"

Claude had risen too.

"Most men do not care for poetry, of course. But if you are interested—"

"I—I am sorry, madame—"

"Sorry?"

"That I must go," said Claude. "I didn't realize how late it was, and
there is work I must still finish at the godown."

"Oh." Madame Gorbeau showed disappointment, then covered it with
a smile. "Yes, of course, I understand," she said. "I know that husband of
mine is a taskmaster."

She accompanied Claude to the door. "Well, another time perhaps—"

"Yes, madame, and thank you. Perhaps another time."

That night—as on every night—he lay on his cot in the warehouse
yard, looking up at the stars. They blazed and wheeled; then faded. . . .
Then were gone. . . . There was no longer sky but a ceiling; he was in a
room, in a room with a woman; and the woman said, "I have a son. I miss
him greatly;" and he said, "I must go," and he went away. He came to
another room, far off; he was lying on his cot in this room; and there was
another woman, a black figure, standing above him, and her hand, cold

and bony, was on his forehead. She had no face, but she had eyes, and the eyes, too, were black, and filled with midnight loneliness.

Then he awoke, and she was gone. A mosquito whined away into darkness, and the stars returned, burning huge and bright above the warehouse yard.

He lay still for a while. Then he rose. He went through his own cubicle into the warehouse and through the warehouse into the office. Lighting an oil lamp, he sat down at Rappe's desk, took a sheet of paper, and dipped Rappe's pen in the inkwell.

Dear Mother, he wrote—

Twice before he had written that—only twice in his whole life: once from the deep cave of London, once from the gray void of Basel. And neither time had he written more.

Now, however, he went on:

Dear Mother,

As you have perhaps gathered, I have changed my plans, and will probably again be away for some while. This time, however, I am not wandering. I have employment with a commercial firm, and I think you would be pleased at how hard I am working.

I of course regret any inconvenience my actions may have caused you and hope that, nevertheless, you have gone ahead with your project of buying the farm. I cannot, to be sure, contribute anything substantial toward the purchase price; but, mindful of the fact that you were counting on me to run the farm, I feel I should help in the hiring of a man to take my place. I am therefore enclosing herewith one hundred (100) francs, representing about one half of my savings to date.

Since my personal needs are few, I hope to be able to continue to do this in the future.

With best wishes for your health and welfare, I am, most respectfully, your son,

                                        Claude

P.S. The intended marriage of which I spoke to you did not materialize.

24

September—
. . . and after your disgraceful behavior I should have nothing more to do with you. However, I am still your mother and know my duty. Each time I go to church I pray you will see the error of your ways, give up your pointless wasteful life, and come home.

November—

. . . No, Mother, I will not come home. Nor should you want me to, for now, for the first time, I am making what the world calls a "success." My salary has been raised, and I am therefore sending you, this time, two hundred (200) francs. Are you not proud of me? . . . Do you have the farm? . . . Do you note any improvement in the smell of incense at the church?

January—

. . . Yes, I have bought the farm. I was robbed and swindled, of course, as well as in the price I was paid for the store. The land is second-rate. Last summer's wheat was a failure. The man I have hired to run it is a hopeless incompetent, yet I must pay him twenty francs a week. It is a scandal.

March—

. . . I think you will perhaps find the land better suited to garden vegetables than to wheat. And I am sure you can hire a better man if you pay more than twenty francs . . . My expenses have been low and I am therefore enclosing two hundred and fifty (250) francs. Do you think Michel Favre is making this much at the bank?

April—

. . . I will thank you to keep your advice to yourself and allow me to run my farm as I see fit. . . . How is your health? And your weight? Are you eating well? . . . I gather you are at last working hard and have some regard for the value of money. Should not your salary soon be raised again?

June—

Enclosed please find four hundred (400) francs. . . . I am eating very well, thank you. Rump of goat and camel's liver are the favorites here, but I miss your veal. . . . Have I mentioned that we have as much dust here as in Cambon? But of course we have a volcano to compensate.

He signed the letters, sealed them, stamped them.

"I am a writer again," he thought. "Author of *Prose Poems from the Fabled East*. Of *Illuminations: Revised Version*."

Aden burned. Aden fried. For perhaps two months, at midwinter, the temperature dropped a few degrees and wisps of breeze drifted up from the Indian Ocean. Then the wisps faded and died. The oven rekindled. Along the stagnant sea front the sheds and godowns lay flat and crushed in the sun, and above them the great lava crags gleamed with black incandescence. Over all curved the parched sky, clamped to earth and sea like a lid of brass.

It was a mineral world. Without trees, without grass, without soil; with no single drop of sweet water. For the few who could afford it, water was brought in from east and west in the holds of ships. For the rest, it was distilled from the sea on the broad sand flats beyond the city. High on the crater walls were the ruins of vast cisterns, built by an ancient race to catch the rains that must once have fallen. But no rain fell now. The black jaws of the cisterns gaped empty at the empty sky.

At long intervals—once a month, once in two—the sky changed. It turned from brass to lead. Clouds moved in. A wind rose. With the wind, however, came neither moisture nor freshness, but only sand; and for a day, or a day and a night, the sand would blow, beating in on the city in brown waves from the desert beyond. When the wind died, that was all that was left. More sand. More dust. It lay mixed with the soot on the wharves and jetties. It filled the streets and alleys of Crater Town. On the black scarps above, it coated the flags and cannons of empire. The sun returned to its sky of brass, and burned on the dust. It glinted on the pus-ringed eyes of children, on the green foam on the lips of the khat-chewers, on the flies and the dead goats and the offal.

In the bar of the Three Kings Tavern, Neil Fitzsimmons slammed down his glass. "Christ Jesus," he said, "I've got to get out of here!"

"There are plenty of ships," said Claude.

"Yes, plenty. And I'm takin' me one. This week, tomorrow—anywhere —so long it's out of this goddamn hole." Fitz raised his glass again, drained it; then he eyed Claude with sudden excitement. "Tell ye what, lad—we'll go together. The two of us. You and me, right out of here, whoosh, like that—what d'ye say?"

Claude shook his head.

"No? Why? Christ Jesus, why not? This isn't a city; not even part of the earth. It's hell, that's what it is. The goddamn center of damn bloody hell."

"That is a distinct possibility," Claude conceded.

"But ye won't leave? Ye want to stay here, ye balmy frog. Hell's fer you, eh? Ye like it, ye love it."

Claude shrugged and smiled a little. "Perhaps I'm used to it," he said. "As we say in the frog pond, *ici je suis chez moi.*"

But it was not the Irishman who was to be the first to leave Aden. Early in July, Gorbeau called Claude into his private office. Though he had of course been there often before, it had been only for brief visits, to receive instructions or answer a question; but this time Gorbeau offered him a chair and a cigar.

"You have been here now about a year," he said.

Claude nodded.

"And how does it go with you?"

"All right."

"You are satisfied? You are happy?"

"Happiness, monsieur, is a—"

"In your work, I mean. Do you think we have treated you fairly?"

"Yes."

"No complaints about salary?"

"No."

"By now you must have saved a fair amount. I notice you live very simply."

"My wants are simple."

"And so you send money home."

"Yes."

"To Cambon, I assume. You have a family there?"

"I have a mother."

"And—a young lady, perhaps?"

"No, no young lady."

"You are deeply attached to your mother, then? You take good care of her."

"I do what I can."

"But you yourself do not want to go home?"

"No."

Gorbeau puffed on his cigar. Through the smoke he studied Claude with his small shrewd eyes.

"I have been thinking of your work for the firm," he said. "I of course know that Monsieur Rappe has spoken to you about coming into the office."

Claude said nothing.

"That he has suggested it several times."

"Yes."

"And each time you refused."

"Yes."

"Why?"

"Because it is not my sort of work."

"What *is* your sort of work, may I ask?"

Claude hesitated. "What I am—"

"What you are doing? Sorting coffee beans? Moving crates? ... Monsieur Rappe, as you know, does not agree with you. Nor, may I add, does my wife."

"Your wife, monsieur?"

"I know too, of course, that she has spoken with you. That she is, in fact, quite interested in you—and, I may add, quite baffled. She cannot understand why a man of your background and education—"

"I have not so much education," said Claude.

"No? My wife thinks you are a university graduate."

"She is wrong, monsieur."

"Wrong? Hmm. . . . Well, it's none of her business. Or mine either. The past is past; I am interested in the present—the future. That is why I called you in."

Gorbeau paused and exhaled a cloud of smoke. "As you are aware, our business, on the whole, has been good. Whatever one may think of Aden as a place to live, it's the center of a whole new developing trade area. It has grown enormously. We have grown with it. And I intend to grow further.

"To be specific. . . . Roughly half our trade is with Africa, both in imports and exports. The gross figures last year were highly satisfactory, but the net was not. It should have been more, much more, and there is only one reason why it was not. As you know, we do our African buying and selling at Zeila, on the Somali coast. Hamid Nomoury is in charge there, and he is a good man—for an Arab. But the setup is wrong. Zeila itself buys little and supplies none of our merchandise; almost everything goes in or comes out by caravan. The caravans are uncertain. Their rates are exorbitant. What they carry in is finally sold for three times what we are paid in Zeila, and for what comes out we pay three times the value. You see what I am getting at. All these middlemen must be eliminated. The traders in Zeila; the caravan owners; the traders inland. We must buy, sell, and transport our own goods, all the way from here to the farthest consumers and sources of supply; in other words, establish our own African enterprise. It cannot all be done at once, of course, but a start can be made. Right now. And that is what I propose to do."

He paused, as if waiting for Claude to speak. But Claude said nothing.

"Have you heard of the city of Harar?" asked Gorbeau.

"In Abyssinia."

"Yes, in Abyssinia. More or less, at least. It's on the edge of the highlands where Abyssinia begins; but not part of its kingdoms—not Amharic or Christian." Gorbeau took a map from a drawer and unrolled it. "See," he said, "—there. About two hundred miles inland. To the east, on this side, are the Somalis; north and west is Abyssinia; south and west is unknown country. But Harar has been Moslem for centuries. Until about seven years ago it was ruled by native Arab emirs and shut tight as Mecca. But then the Egyptians moved in. The British were behind it, of course —they always are—but they've been so busy planting flags along the coast they haven't had time to move in after them. So there it is—Harar—wide open at last, with no one in it; not a single trading firm. The one who gets there first is going to control the trade of half of northeast Africa."

Gorbeau puffed at his cigar. He looked at Claude. "Well, what do you think of it?" he asked.

"I'm not an authority on such matters," Claude said.

"I don't mean the general plan; that's my concern. I mean for yourself. I have been thinking about this carefully and I feel you are the man for the job."

"What about Fitzsimmons? He's been here longer than I. He knows the business and would like a change."

Gorbeau shook his head. "No, Fitzsimmons is no good for it; you know that as well as I. It's you who are the right one. . . . You've been with us only a year, that's true. You came to me out of a jail, and from God knows where before that. But you're still the best man I've been able to find in Aden. You're self-reliant. You're steady. Wherever you got it, you have an education; you know languages. That is of extreme importance in this assignment—to know languages. Arabic, to begin with. And the ability to pick up dialects as you go along."

"What would be expected of me—besides talking?"

"I would want you to leave for Zeila as soon as possible. With you you would take a full cargo of trade goods and at Zeila transfer them to a caravan. Our *own* caravan: that is of the essence. Nomoury will help you organize it. Then you will go up to Harar. Arriving there, you will sell our trade goods; you will buy raw produce; you will confer with local merchants and officials, open a trading post, and continue buying and selling. We will send up further goods by our own caravans, and you will continue to send down African produce."

"And for how long would this be?"

"For yourself, I would say about a year. My hope, of course, is that this will become a permanent part of the business, but once the trade is established there should be no need for you to stay there. Perhaps you will find a competent Arab to take over—like Nomoury in Zeila. Or someone can be sent up to take your place. In any case, that's for the future. The thing now is to get the enterprise started."

Again Gorbeau paused. He waited.

"If you are thinking of money," he said, "I believe you will find me reasonable. For a start, I am prepared to pay you half again your present salary, plus a two per cent commission on profits. Then we will see how things develop."

There was another pause.

"The life may be hard, of course; sometimes even dangerous. I think it only fair to point that out. But you strike me as a man who doesn't care greatly about such things. . . . Anyhow—" Gorbeau pushed back his chair, "—there's my offer. As I say, I want to put the plan into effect at once. Think it over and give me your answer tomorrow."

Claude rose and shook his head. "No. No, monsieur," he said. "There is no need to wait until tomorrow."

"Goddamn," said Neil Fitzsimmons, "so this is what ye've had up yer sleeve. Aden's too good fer ye; hell itself's too good fer ye. Off ye go to bloody Africa to roll in the mud with the heathen."

"They won't be heathen long," Claude said. "I'm taking a kilo of certified incense along to convert them."

"Never mind the goddamn blasphemies. . . . Ye crazy frog. What d'ye expect to get out of it, eh? Harar, fer Christ's sweet sake! Buryin' yerself out there, three million miles from nowhere—"

Fitzsimmons didn't wait for an answer. They were in the godown; bales of coffee were moving in; and he plunged vehemently back to work, shouting orders, hauling and heaving with the stevedores.

At intervals, however, he came back to Claude.

"Dammit," he said, "I asked ye, I begged ye, to take off with me. But no, ye wouldn't. Ye liked it here. Ye was stayin' here."

And the next time: "Christ, man, I c'd understand if it was on yer own. If there was a chance fer big money, a rale killin'. Hell, fer that I'd go with ye meself."

And the next: "Why's it you he sends, tell me that? Why not me? I been here longer, ha'nt I? Worked like a dog here fer all these years, and this is the thanks I get. . . . Well, you'll see. He'll see. I'm gettin' out too, like I told ye: only not to some mudhole in Africa, no sir. I'm takin' a ship, lad—a big ship. To big places. To London, Rio, Frisco, New York—"

He went back to work: heaving, straining, pushing, and shouting at the Arabs. And after all the coffee was in, he went out onto the wharf and sat with his back against the godown wall looking out across the harbor. When, later, Claude emerged, he was asleep. His face was slack, his mouth open, and his gold tooth glinted in the sun.

"Here, I have something for you," said Marcel Rappe. "I have had it specially made." He handed Claude a flat rubber pouch with drawstrings. "If you keep your ledgers in this at all times except when you are actually using them, you will have no trouble from dust, moisture, mold, or insects.

"You will remember, please," he went on, "to send a summary of transactions down with each caravan. As for sending actual money, use your own judgment; but bear in mind that all Arabs and Africans are dishonest. Any losses, either in Harar or on the caravans, will of course be your responsibility."

He consulted a page of notes to see if there was anything else. "And yes," he said, "—one other thing. Remember at all times that you are not merely an individual, but a representative of the House of Gorbeau —and also of France itself. Whatever the difficulties, prestige must be maintained. In the running of the business, of course; in individual relations; and"—his bright-lensed glance flicked up and down—"in personal manner and appearance."

"Yes, of course," said Claude.

"I suggest you make out a list so that nothing will be forgotten. Of clothing, accessories, household items, et cetera. For instance—" Rappe wrote on a pad, "—soap, cleaning fluids, brushes, toiletries—"

"And shoe polish," Claude added.

"Yes, shoe polish, of course." Rappe jotted it down. "Black, brown, white. For the white, incidentally, I suggest Hornsby's 'Evergleam.' Even though it is British, I have found it quite satisfactory."

Monsieur Colbert, the consul, nodded as Gorbeau spoke. "Yes, yes," he agreed, "it is good. It is smart. Fine things can come of this, Emil.

"Not only for you," he went on, "but us all. For France. The British and Italians are everywhere on the coast, and we are nowhere; but this will steal a march on them sure enough. Put us behind them—right on the inside."

"We are only a company, not an army," said Gorbeau. "Don't expect miracles."

"Miracles, no. But results, yes. The first Western trading company up there in the interior, right on the border of Abyssinia—*mon Dieu*, what influence it should have! I'm writing the Quai d'Orsay all about it in my next dispatch, and maybe it will help stir them at last off their fat behinds."

The consul nodded again, with satisfaction. Then he looked at his friend and his expression changed. "My only concern is for you," he said. "It's a risky affair, after all."

"Yes, there is risk, of course. From bandits, desert tribes, even the Egyptians in Harar. There's no telling how they will take to it."

"And what about your own man?"

"Morel?"

"Yes, Morel. Are you sure he's reliable? That you can count on him? After all, you know where you found him. And where *I* found him."

"I think he will be all right," Gorbeau said.

"Meaning you trust him?"

"Yes, I trust him."

"Why?" Colbert's eyes were sharp and questioning. "What do you know of him? What have you found out."

"I have found out nothing," said Gorbeau. "Yet—"

"Yet what?"

"Yet I think he will do." The merchant paused a moment, considering, and then he added, "I think he is a man who is afraid of nothing. And who wants nothing for himself."

On the last night in Aden Claude lay out on his cot in the yard. He watched the stars. He watched bright Fomalhaut. "So you are still following it," he mused. "You are going to Africa."

Question: What do you think of that?

Answer: I do not think anything.

With apologies to Monsieur Descartes: I do not think, therefore I am. The *I* who thought—who felt—is *another.* And he is dead.

In the morning, for the perhaps the hundredth time, he supervised the loading of a dhow. But this time, when it was done, he did not climb back onto the wharf. He merely turned and looked up, and there was Gorbeau, and Gorbeau leaned down and shook hands.

"So good luck, *mon vieux,*" he said.

"Thank you," said Claude.

"We'll expect word from Zeila within a week, and from Harar as soon as you can manage. Send the first caravan down when you've enough produce to make it pay. We'll send the second one up when we get the next shipment from Europe."

Claude nodded. Gorbeau straightened and waved. The Arab captain shouted, ropes thudded on the deck, and the great green lateen sail creaked slowly up the mast. Broad, squat, and heavy-bellied—like its owner watching from the wharf—the dhow edged out into the crowded harbor.

For an hour it seemed scarcely to move. The tan water clung to it. The heat pressed down on it. A freighter to starboard weighed anchor, hooted, spewed smoke, and in ten minutes had disappeared through the harbor's mouth. The dhow inched on. The docks and godowns inched past. Above them the black fangs of Aden's crater wall were clamped rigid and still into the burning sky.

"*Ayeee, ayaaa—*"

The helmsman chanted. The captain dozed. Claude watched the shore. And slowly, very slowly, it slipped past; it receded; the docks and godowns receded; the volcano receded, wheeling black and glittering in the midday sun. The harbor mouth drew nearer: on one side a jetty, on the other a long sandspit, each with a lighthouse. They were close to the lighthouses, abreast of them, beyond them—and at that instant everything changed. The water was now no longer tan but blue. The limp sail stirred and bellied. The teakwood timbers creaked. "*Ayeee, ayaaa—*" came the cry of the helmsman, louder and shriller. And they moved out from the prison of Aden into the sweep of the sea.

For a while they followed the coast westward. Here they were on the great traffic lane leading from Aden to the Red Sea and Suez, and ships steamed past in stately procession. Then in the late afternoon, they veered south; the ships vanished, the coast vanished; far astern, the black smudge that was Aden's volcano sank below the horizon, and there was only the

THE DAY ON FIRE 347

sea. As the sun sloped away the wind freshened still further, blowing up from the northeast and driving them on. The mast swayed. The sail hummed. Spray rose from the prow and streamed sternward, touching Claude's face with fresh coolness, and he stripped off shirt and trousers, the better to feel it on the whole of his body. The heat and dust of Aden were no more than a memory, lost behind them; the desert of Africa unimaginable ahead.

To the north now, toward sunset, was the strait of Bab el Mandeb, and here the wind shifted and struck them broadside, and the dhow rolled in the troughs of the sea. From below, presently, came a rattling and thumping, as the cargo shifted, and for an hour Claude worked in the hold with the Arab crew, moving bales and boxes and retying ropes. When he came back on deck it was night. The crew made a charcoal fire in the iron stove amidships and cooked the evening meal of rice and goatmeat. Sparks from the fire blew out over the black water, under the stars.

Then there were only the stars. The fire was out. The crew slept, sprawled or huddled about the deck, except for a helmsman, now the captain, at the wheel, and a lookout in the bow; and even these two seemed almost to be sleeping, soundless and motionless in the dark. Claude too, stretched on the afterdeck, lay as quiet as if asleep. But he was not. Listening, he heard the hum of the sail and the swish of water against the hull. Watching, he saw the mast sway in long arcs against the stars.

He had seen it before: on other boats, under other skies. From the deck of the *Prins van Oranje*, of the *Nottingham Castle*, of the boats in which, over the years, he had crossed the Mediterranean, the Adriatic, the Red Sea, the North Sea, the Baltic. And before that he had seen it too: not from a deck at all, not from a ship, but from a cot, a cot covered with canvas, the cot in the room of his boyhood, the room that was prison, the room of dreams. Oh yes, he had seen them, always seen them. The mast . . . the night . . .

> *the star-archipelagoes and islands*
> *in skies that call the wanderer, fierce, forlorn . . .*

He had seen them, known them, followed them, searching, asking. Asking:

> *is it within these depthless nights you sleep in exile,*
> *O hosts of golden birds, O day as yet unborn?*

As still he searched, still traveled, still moved on into horizons. Except that now it was in no Drunken Boat, no boat of dream or words. . . . *No, no more words.* . . . This was a boat of teak, of iron, of pitch, of rope, of canvas.

It was bound from the port of Aden to the port of Zeila. It was owned by Monsieur Emil Gorbeau, merchant, trader, and commission agent. It carried a cargo of cotton, calico, pots, pans, knives, pins, beads, glassware. Under his head, as a pillow, were three ledgers in a rubber pouch, with drawstring, presented to him by Monsieur Marcel Rappe.

The stars wheeled. The boat moved on. He slept. And in the morning, when he woke, the sun was shining on the coast of Africa.

In the nights that followed there were no stars. There was a ceiling. And he looked at the ceiling. *"Me voici,"* he thought. "Here I am. In the house of one Hamid Nomoury, in a village called Zeila."

Question: What has brought you here?

Answer: Your life has brought you here.

AUTOBIOGRAPHY. *In a room barred by a chair, when I was a boy, I got to know the world. I illustrated the human comedy. In a wine cellar with Faust I learned history. At midnight revels I met all the mistresses of the old masters. In the pavillions of the City of Light I learned the classical arts and vices. Now, in a palace encircled by the entire Orient, I complete my prodigious work and spend my illustrious retreat. I have brewed my blood. My duty is done. I am from beyond the tomb, and no messages.*

Except, of course, to one. As a good French son, to *the one*. . . . And he wrote:

September 8—

Dear Mother:

You will be pleased to know that I am advancing in the world. I am no longer a warehouse employee but a traveling representative of my company —un vrai homme d'affaires; *and no longer in Aden but in the town of Zeila on the Somali coast. I shall not be here long, however, for in a day or two I leave for the interior. My destination is a city called Harar, near the border of Abyssinia, where I am to open an office and trading post for our firm.*

A few days in Zeila will be more than enough. It is a dismal place: flat, baked by the sun, full of sand and dust and flies and dung. In Aden the dung was mostly from goats. Here it is from camels, and the piles are bigger.

Right now that is what I am mostly involved in. Not dung, but camels. About twenty are needed for the caravan to Harar, plus five or six drivers, and I am now buying and hiring. In this I am being helped by our firm's representative here, who is pleasant enough, and eager to please me, but, like most Arabs, slow in thought and action; and though I had planned to be here only two or three days, it is now the fourth, and I shall probably not be off until the end of the week.

In any case, it may be some time before I can write again—and that will be from Harar. My salary, as you know, has again been increased, and I have instructed the Aden office to send you, each month, one half of my pay. I also, of course, hope to make considerably more from my percentage of profits, but that is a matter for the future. In reference to the comment in your last letter, there is no reason for you to worry about my losing my funds. I have bought a money belt, which I wear at all times around my waist, beneath my clothing, and it is even safer than your cash drawer at the store.

Sometimes I have to remind myself that there is no longer the store, but now the farm. As your—shall we say—junior partner I should appreciate your sending me periodic reports of income and expenses.

Respectfully, your son,

Claude.

October 14—

Dear Mother:

I am still in Zeila. They are not used to ferangi—that means Europeans, foreigners—here, and since last I wrote you I have been subjected to much delay and annoyance.

This has all been concerned with the organization of the caravan. Until now our firm has itself operated only as far as this, trading with the interior through Arab caravans that come and go, but the first step in our new expansion was to organize our own. And in this I have been balked and harassed at every turn.

The camels have been no problem. Indeed, I bought them during my first few days here and have had the expense of feeding them ever since. But the drivers are another matter, and I have had a hard time finding them. The reason is not lack of men; there are plenty of them, half-starving and desperate for work. It is that, up till now, all caravans have been owned or controlled by a rich Arab trader called Abou Dakir, who is not pleased by competition from newcomers. Everyone is afraid of him. Even our agent, Nomoury, is afraid. "You had better take one of his caravans," he keeps telling me. But that is not what I am here for.

Well, anyhow—at last I have the men—five of them. We shall leave tomorrow and expect to reach Harar in two weeks, where I shall write you again. But of course the mails from there are apt to be uncertain.

I am glad to see from your recent letters (the latest of which has been forwarded to me from Aden) that you no longer question my motives for being in this part of the world, or feel that I am wasting my time. . . . No, the time-wasting is in the past, I reassure you. I am now your own true son: working hard, making my way in the world, letting myself be put upon by no one, including Monsieur Abou Dakir. Really, dear Mother, you should by now be quite proud of

Your respectful son,

Claude.

P.S. I trust you are saving the stamps from my letters. In case you are unaware of it, Monsieur Duplessis, clerk of the Cambon District Court, is an avid collector, and would, I am sure, be glad to pay twice their face value.

October 14—

Dear Father . . . Father Mackenzie . . .

You see, I have a trade. I have a home. I write home. Are you proud of me too?

25

"Ayeee, ayaaa—"

There was again the sky. Again the sea. But the sky no longer dipped and wheeled above it, for the sea was a sea of land.

"Ayeee, ayaaa—"

No helmsman here. It was a camel driver, prodding a rump with a long stick. There were five of them, and twenty camels, and one mule, and Claude, and they were all that lived or moved in the vast waste of space and stillness.

The first day out from Zeila had, to be sure, been different. First in the town itself: threading the narrow streets, crossing the market place, passing the white mosque, the trading sheds, the rows of mud- and-wattle huts, among the crowds and goats and flies and dunghills. Beyond the streets were mud flats, and then sand, and then salt. Salt was the one product of Zeila, and the main cargo of outbound caravans; and for several miles around it the earth was pocked with white gleaming pits in which dark naked figures toiled like ants. Then, as they moved on, the ants were gone, and the whiteness, and all of Zeila, all life and movement except their own. Their course was southwest. To the south and east, falling slowly away behind, a burned black headland notched the glaring sky; and far ahead, barely visible in the haze of heat, sprawled a low range of tawny hills. The rest was sea: a sea of flatness and of dust. Out of the dust, here and there, rose the bare bleak branches of a camel's-thorn, and into the flatness ahead, centuries old, ran the faint trail into Africa.

They followed it. Through stillness. Through emptiness. And the dust rose from the slow tread of the camels. The only sounds were the occasional clinking of tin in the swaying loads. And, now and then, the voice of a driver, calling:

"Ayeee, ayaaa—"

Claude rode on the mule. He had not wanted it, but Hamid Nomoury had insisted, claiming that a caravan leader must be mounted—if not for comfort, then at least for prestige—and a mule was easier for a European than a camel. Slung on his back was a gun, the best that Gorbeau had been able to find in Aden. And he had not wanted this either; he had wanted to leave it in Zeila. But here Nomoury had been even more insistent, saying, "It is impossible—I will not hear of it—that you go into such country without arms."

"I thought it was the northeast route that was dangerous," Claude had said. "Through the Danakil country."

"Yes, the Danakils are the worst. But the Somalis can be bad too. The inland tribes through whose country you will be going are not like the people here on the coast."

"Several caravans have come in while I've been in Zeila. None have had any trouble."

"No, that is true," Nomoury conceded. "But let me point out, monsieur, that these caravans are all Arab. They belong to Abou Dakir."

"And he controls the Somali tribes?"

"I would not say he controls them. I would say he has—well—influence with them. His caravans are safe. But a stranger's, a competitor's—" Nomoury shrugged. "No, if we are transporting our own goods we must be prepared to protect them."

Claude in turn, had shrugged. He had taken the gun.

". . . So now you are a soldier again," he thought, as they moved out into the desert. "Old soldier Morel, late of his Royal Dutch Majesty's Colonial Forces. Only now no longer a private, but an officer, a commander of troops. . . . Sergeant Houttekamp, take note please. Dear Father, take note. Are you proud?"

From his mule, at the end of the procession, he surveyed his troops, his army of five, spaced out among the camels ahead. One was an Arab, the others Somalis. All were ragged and barefoot. Each carried a stick for the prodding of rumps. "Shouldn't they have guns too?" Claude had asked Nomoury, "—if the trip is such a risky business?"

But the agent had shaken his head.

"You mean they'd be more risk than the tribesmen?"

"No, I would not say that. But—well, they are new men. We do not know them. It is always best if men one does not know are unarmed."

"Even if we are attacked?"

"Yes, even if you are attacked."

So the men had their staffs. They had the rags on their backs. The four Somalis, like most of their people, were themselves scarcely stouter than the staffs: tall, gaunt, angular, almost skeletal. The Arab, on the other hand, was short, almost dwarfish. His body was frail and crooked, and his

face a hobgoblin's, with a black pointed beard. His name was Egal, and he
ranked as head driver, for he had made the trip to Harar many times. The
Somalis took his orders without argument, and he in turn took Claude's.
He knew the way. He knew camels. For a week they moved on without
trouble or incident.

The sun flamed. The dust hung in the air. From his stores Claude took
a length of cotton cloth and, with Egal's help, made it into a kaffiyah, the
Arab headdress. It mitigated the heat, but not the dryness, and he was
perpetually thirsty; but their water, carried in goatskin bags, was soon so
stale and foul that thirst was almost preferable to its quenching. Unaccus-
tomed to riding, he developed sores on his buttocks, and for the first time
in years felt a stiffness in his right knee. So presently he turned the mule
into an auxilliary pack animal and went afoot, as did the others, beside the
camels. Immediately he felt better, more natural, more himself.

"Yes, of course, myself," he thought. "Whatever that is." Himself—the
boy, the man, who took a walk.

He walked. Through the dust. Through the miles. Distance was im-
measurable, meaningless, in that empty world, but he estimated that
they averaged some twelve miles a day. They started off each morning
at first light, traveled until midday, rested two hours, and then moved on
again until dusk; and he himself, on such a schedule, could have made
almost double the mileage. But the camels could not be forced beyond
their normal plodding pace—any more than the sun could be forced more
swiftly ahead through the heavens.

It was all right with Claude. He had plenty of time. He had a lifetime.

At their noonday halts they slung a strip of canvas on the drivers' staffs
and rested in its shade. At nightfall they camped wherever they happened
to be, for there was no spot better than another—no trees or grass or trace
of water. The camels were unloaded, hobbled, and turned out to graze on
the thornbushes, and the men built a fire of camel dung, which they kept
and dried, and cooked their unvarying meal of rice and jerked mutton.
While they ate, and afterward, Claude would often try to get the Somalis
to talk. He wanted to learn their language, and also as much as he could
about their land and people. But they were shy and taciturn. They ate and
then they slept. Each night a goatskin tent was set up for him, but he used
it only to store his ledgers and few personal belongings, sleeping out, as
did the others, with his gun beside him.

There was never enough dung for an all-night fire, but they took turns
keeping watch. And often during his turn, Claude saw moving shapes in
the darkness and the glint of yellow eyes, watching. How animals could
live in such a waste—where they found food and water—Claude could
not imagine. But they were there, nevertheless: by day invisible, but by
night emergent, prowling, always watching. Now a band of jackals, now

hyenas; once (he thought) a leopard, but the shadow was so slim, so swift, he could not be sure. They did not come close. They did not attack. At the first stirring in outer darkness the camels would move in toward the camp-site; the man on watch would shout; the shapes would vanish. One night Claude seized his gun, sighted, and fired at two yellow eyes, and there was a screech, a wild clawing, and, in the morning, a thin trail of dried blood in the dust. "So, you have improved since Java," he thought. "One day—who knows?—you may be Morel the Great Hunter."

The next night the eyes were there again: still watching, still waiting. But at least they preferred the shadows of beasts to the shadows of men.

And the only men they saw, during this part of their journey, were those of other caravans, in the blaze of daylight, moving past them from the interior toward the sea. In the first week there were only two of these; both small, like their own; both carrying the usual outbound cargoes of coffee and grain and hides and gums. But on the eighth or ninth day, in the late afternoon, a third appeared, approaching slowly over the wastes ahead, and this was a procession of a different sort. It was far longer than the others, but its length did not consist of loaded camels. The only camels were spaced at intervals, with armed Arabs atop their humps, and between them was a long dark straggling chain of men afoot.... Or at least they seemed men until they came closer. And then they became women and children. Perhaps two hundred of them.... A few brown-skinned: Somalis or Issas or Shoans from Abyssinia. But most were black: night-black and naked in the desert dust. They carried loads. Their backs were bent. They moved in utter silence, their eyes fixed on the earth.

There were no slaves in Aden; the British had wiped the trade out. But Claude had seen them in Zeila, herded in pens near the market place: the sound ones being assorted, fattened, awaiting shipment by dhow to the ports and markets of Arabia; the weak and sick being left to die untended where they lay. Once, seeing them, he would have felt outrage and anger. But here he had turned away, feeling nothing. And he turned away now. Once the world had been his—or so he thought: to shape, to change, to bend to his will.... But no longer.... *Priests, professors, masters, generals, emperors: you have won. The world is yours. Yours to rule. Yours to change. Not mine.*

"By Allah, that's a good lot," said Egal, watching the procession. "Another ton of piasters for old Abou Dakir."

By the time the two caravans had passed it was almost dusk. Presently Claude called a halt, the slaves halted soon after, and the camps were no more than a mile apart on the empty waste. For a while fires winked in the night. Then they went out, and all was black, all was still. In the stillness Claude lay out beside his tent, watching the stars. Then he slept ... and woke ... and waking, knew that something was happening. The camels were stirring, edging in closer to the camp, and as he roused himself one of the Somalis appeared beside him and pointed out into the darkness. He peered. He saw a shadow. But it was shadow different from those of the previous night; the shape not of a beast but of a human being. It came toward them slowly, swaying and stumbling, and then it was no longer on its feet at all, but on all fours, crawling; and now Egal and the other Somalis had wakened too and stood beside Claude; and they watched as the figure crept on, past the camels, past the ashes of their fire, and crouched motionless at their feet.

It was a Negro girl: black, naked, her hair and body streaked with dust.

Egal spat and swore in disgust. "For this," he growled, "we have our sleep disturbed."

He gestured to one of the Somalis, and the man jerked her to her feet. Her head lolled to one side. Her eyes rolled, showing the whites. The black flesh of her body was no more than a hide covering the bones and when the Somali let go of her she sagged and crumpled again at their feet.

"And it is not even one of the good ones; it is a walking corpse," said Egal. Then, looking over her shoulder: "Well, at least they're coming to get her."

Out in the darkness there was the sound of shouts, the glint of lanterns. Claude went to the goatskin bag, poured a cupful of water, and, kneeling, put the cup to the woman's lips. Her eyes rolled again, her mouth opened; she tried to seize the cup, but spilled it, and the water rolled down her chin and through the dust on her shrunken breasts. Claude rose to refill the cup, and she crept after him. Then Egal said, "Don't waste our water, sidi. Here they are." And three Arabs appeared beside them with guns and lanterns.

Now it was they who jerked the girl to her feet. One of them uncoiled a rope from under his burnous.

"No, she will stay here," Claude said.

The Arabs looked at him curiously.

"Here, with us. Do you understand?"

The one with the rope went on uncoiling it. The other two half raised their guns. Egal shifted nervously and said, "Sidi, she belongs to them. What do you—"

"She's for sale, isn't she?" said Claude.

"For sale? Yes, of course. They are all for sale, when they get to Zeila or Arabia. But this one will never get there. Look at her. She is sick—dying. In two days she will be hyena food."

"So I will buy her."

"Buy her?"

"Yes." Claude turned to the slavers. "How much do you want?" he asked.

"Sidi, you are mad—"

"How much?" Claude repeated.

The Arabs eyed him warily. They consulted. "Eight hundred piasters," one of them said.

"I will give you two."

They consulted again.

"Five," they said.

"All right—five."

Claude went into his tent, took the money from his belt, and paid them. "Now go," he said. "Leave the girl and go."

Again the slavers eyed him. Then they shrugged and left. "You are mad, mad, mad," Egal repeated, his gnome's face full of anger and disgust. "If you want a woman so badly, why did you not at least go over to their caravan where there are plenty to choose from. This one is sick, I tell you —half alive—hopeless. If you want her, you had better get at it quickly, before she's a corpse."

Again he spat. "Five hundred piasters! Ai! Ai!"

He turned away, lay down, went back to sleep. The Somalis slept. Claude spread a strip of canvas and laid the girl on it and sat beside her in the darkness. From his kit he took some medicines, mixed them with water, and tried to get her to drink. But she could not swallow, and her head rolled limply to one side. Once she turned it back to him. Her eyes opened, the whites gleamed, and from her lips came low groaning sounds. Then her body stiffened and convulsed. Her ribs and pelvis heaved up as if the bones would burst through the flesh. Then she subsided. She lay still. And she died.

"So what did I tell you?" said Egal when he rose in the morning. "Ai, ai—that's the easiest five hundred piasters Abou Dakir ever made."

He turned away and, with the Somalis, readied the camels for the day's march. But Claude, interrupting them, took picks and shovels from the stores and said, "First we will dig a grave."

"But it is not necessary," Egal protested. "She is only a nigger—a heathen—and by nightfall the hyenas—"

"We will dig a grave," Claude repeated, "—deep enough so that the hyenas cannot find her."

The miles unrolled. The waste spread parched and scabrous, gleaming in sulphurous light. Each day, often for hours on end, mirages lay before them: vast sky-blue lakes and seas that receded remorselessly into the sea of dust. For the most part the dust lay flat as a table, broken only by the thornbushes, but sometimes it buckled into humps and hollows, and they moved on as if over the waves of a petrified sea. Then, one day, something took form far ahead that was not a mirage: the first range of hills they had seen since the first day out of Zeila. And two days after that they entered the hills.

The hills were not high. They were bare, tawny, crouched about them like lions, the manes of their ridges stiff against the burning sky. They entered the range by way of an old wadi, or watercourse, but no trace of moisture remained among its gravel and stones. And the slopes above the hills were seamed by other, smaller stream beds: the veins and arteries of what had once been living earth lying, now dry and withered, in the wasteland. At one point the slopes steepened and closed in, and they passed through a deep defile, peering warily ahead, behind, above them. But nothing moved. Nothing was there. Beyond the defile they climbed steeply for an hour, reaching a wide plateau, and here, finally, there *was* movement, there was change; the sun faded, a wind rose, the dust blew, and for an hour they stopped, huddling muffled beside the camels, while air and earth raged around them. Then the storm ended, as abruptly as it had begun. The wind vanished, the sun returned; the hills lay bare and still and lifeless as before. The violence that had briefly risen and subsided seemed no more than the sudden twitching of a corpse.

Farther on along the plateau, the dust gave way to gravel, and on the way down from it, to stones and tumbled rocks. Here the camels had hard going, swaying and stumbling awkwardly as they descended, and presently one went down and lay sprawled and floundering on the incline. Its front right leg was broken. Egal spat and swore and took Claude's gun and shot it, and then the Somalis, with their knives, cut out pieces of flesh and entrails, and its load was distributed among the other beasts.

They moved on. They came out of the hills, and the hills receded behind them, and on the next day, across the flatland, there arose what seemed to be still another mirage; but Egal pointed and said "Biyo Kaboba," and in the evening they came to the one oasis between Zeila and Harar. No other caravan was there. They had the haven to themselves —the trees, the shade, the soft earth, the water. And for a full day they stayed there: resting, bathing, and drinking, drinking, drinking, from the miraculous trickle of water that welled up from the earth. It was a haven, however, that was not without hazards. In the sand beside the spring were the tracks of many animals, and when dark came, the waste beyond their clump of trees was filled with moving shadows and watching eyes. They tied their own animals in close beside them. They kept careful watch. But it was not enough. Late in the second night there was a quick commotion, a snarl, a braying scream, and, as the men rushed forward, a lean shape bounding off into blackness. It was not a camel that had been attacked, but the mule. And it was dead.

"So now we have a third kind of meat," said Egal philosophically.

Then the oasis, like the hills, was behind them. There was only the waste again: waste of earth, waste of sky. They moved under the sky, through the stillness, through a caul of silence; the men spaced out among the camels, moving together, yet each alone, each sheathed in solitude, as in the cotton veil of his headdress. Once or twice a day—no more now —there rose the thin cry, *"Ayeee, ayaaa—"* And five times each day the drivers spread small faded rugs and knelt and murmured prayers toward Mecca. Mecca was to the northeast, behind them. They turned to pray, and then turned again and moved on. Only Claude did not turn. He did not look back at all, but only ahead, to the west and south, to the empty land, the empty sky; and the land remained empty—barren, still—but into the sky, each afternoon, there came the sun, moving up from behind and passing them, moving down ahead to the horizon, and at the end of day the sun streamed red and huge into his squinting eyes. He watched it set. He watched the dusk, the night, the stars. Lying out beside his tent, he watched Fomalhaut burning in the sky; and as the night passed it grew brighter, with his eyes closed it was still there, bright, burning, and in the morning still there, brightest of all—only now no longer the star but again the sun. In the rising sun the drivers knelt and prayed and he stood and was silent. Then they loaded the camels and moved on. . . .

> *forward.*
> *The march, the burden and the desert;*
> *from the night alone,*
> *through the day on fire.*

The fire cracked the earth. The dust was fissured with dry wadis, and between them the flatness buckled up again, this time not into hills but into knobs and hummocks and bare knuckles of rock. The rock was darker than the dust. It was black, bituminous. At midday it glistened darkly in the sun, and in the morning and evening threw long shadows across the waste. The shadows undulated: rising, falling. They thickened and closed in about the caravan, moving with it, slowly, in stillness, across the tortured earth. They seemed to move not only as the sun moved, but with an inner endowment of their own.

The drivers watched them. They turned. They listened.

"Your gun is loaded, sidi?" Egal asked.

Claude nodded. "But there are only rocks," he said.

"Yes, now only rocks. But this is the bad country. We must watch."

And later he said, "I think it better, sidi, we rest by day and travel by night."

Claude did not object. Reversing their schedule, they slept under the sun and moved under the stars, breaking camp each evening after sunset and halting again at the first graying of dawn. In the daylight, they stopped in as open a place as they could find and kept two men on watch at a time, lest one alone should fall asleep in the heat. In the night, they were themselves no more than moving shadows on the waste.

Thus two nights passed, and two days, and toward dark of the second day they rose again and prepared to go on. As before, they had camped in as open a place as possible; but it was not wholly open—there was no such place; and a few hundred yards away a line of black rocks rose in a low ridge against the sky. The ridge was to the west, and for the past hour, as the sun declined, Claude had watched its shadow deepen and move slowly toward them across the flat. Now it had reached them. The sun was down. The time for leaving had come, and they set about loading the camels.

It was the camels that first gave warning of something wrong. They shifted restlessly. They heaved suddenly to their feet before their loads were secure. They raised their heads and sniffed the air with flared nostrils. At first the men swore. They whacked and prodded. Then they too raised their heads, and looked and listened. There was nothing to hear; nothing to see. Nothing but dust and shadow, the same as always. . . . And then, a moment later, *not* as always, not the same but wholly different, wholly changed; for now they saw the shadows within the shadow, the moving forms, the running men. . . . The men were running toward them. They were black and half-naked and carried shields and spears. Rising up from the rocks on the ridge to the west, they raced down the slope and across the flat, and their spears glinted in the somber twilight.

The camels jerked and thrashed. The drivers seized their knives, and Claude his gun; and the gun, he knew, was all that mattered, all that stood between them and quick thrusting death. As they moved, the attackers knew they had been seen and broke the stillness with a savage howl, coming on, it seemed, even faster than before. At first they had seemed a dark wave, a tide, but now Claude saw there were not many of them. Perhaps a dozen—fifteen—that was all. And they were not circling in on the camp, but coming together, closely spaced, from the ridge. *"Les sots!"* he thought. "The fools! Thank God for fools—" Kneeling behind a still-unloaded bale, he raised the gun. He aimed. He waited.

Then he fired. The gun's magazine held six cartridges, and, working the bolt, he fired them at intervals of a few seconds, sighting at the center of the oncoming line. With the first shot, the howl changed; it became a sound of surprise and dismay. With the second and third, the advance faltered; a figure swayed, stumbled, and fell. With the fourth, the others stopped. "Now they will drop," Claude thought. "They will come on crawling." But they didn't drop. Only the one who had fallen was down. "The fools! The damned savage nigger fools—" He fired again, and they withdrew slowly. Again, and they turned and fled. By the time he had reloaded his gun, there was only stillness and silence between themselves and the ridge.

Then it was the drivers who shouted. They stamped, they leaped, they all but danced—the tall Somalis throwing long arms skyward, the shrunken Egal beside them like a prancing doll. "They didn't know we had a gun," Egal yelled. "But we showed them! We taught them!"

The Somalis grinned and showed their teeth. "*Ai, ai*," they chorused. "*Allah, Allah, ai—*"

When their jubilation had subsided, they turned again to the desert. They watched and waited. Claude waited. But the tribesmen were gone. All except the one who had fallen and whom they could now barely see, in the thickening darkness, a sprawled motionless form in the dust of the waste.

"Come on," said Egal. "We will go look at the dead one."

Claude remained where he was while the others moved out into the dusk. When they returned they were carrying the dead man's possessions —his spear, his shield, a few beads—and they showed them to Claude.

"Did you bury him?" he asked.

"Yes, sidi," said Egal. "To please you."

Claude nodded and was about to turn away, but one of the Somalis stepped forward. "And these, sidi," he said, "we have brought for you."

He extended his hands, palms cupped together, and in the palms, faintly visible in the darkness, were two oval objects about the color and size of small plums. "They must be smoked over a slow fire," he said. "And this we will do for you when we reach the country of wood."

Claude looked at the plums. The plums that were testicles.

"They are yours, sidi. Take them."

Claude did not move or speak.

"You are a man who wants women: we have seen that with the slave who died. When we reach Harar you will have many women, and if you keep these by you when you are with them it will make you like a bull among men."

He raised his palms. Claude shook his head slowly.

"You do not want them, sidi?"

"No. No, thank you."

There was a pause. The Somali shrugged and put the testes in a fold of his robe.

"It is not a *ferangi* custom," Egal told him. Then his goblin's face grinned. "And besides," he added, "I think the sidi is enough of a man already."

They moved on through the night. Their attackers were gone, and there was only the waste. In the waste, when dawn came, they made their next camp and rested.

When they rested by day, Claude lay in his tent, and he lay there now, half awake, half sleeping. Beyond the shield of the tent, he knew, the sun had risen. It was rising, brightening, gleaming with a strange yellow glow; and then it was no longer the sun at all, but a gas lamp—a lamp hanging above him, above a café table—and he was leaning across the table toward Druard. ". . . So I let her have it," he said, "with a big rip, clear to the chin. Oh, it was quite a sight, I tell you: all the guts and things—like an open book. I never saw so much blood; so red and thick. . . ."

Then the café was gone. There was another lamp, another table, and he said to Druard: "It could be done, you know. Not just in talk, but really done."

"For God's sake, boy—"

"No, not for God's sake. For Satan's. And our own. If we've given ourselves to him, we should give to the ultimate. If we're Assassins, we must be true ones. . . ."

Then Druard was gone. He was alone.

And it was *done. Really done.*

There was neither lamp nor sun now, but shadow, the shadow of trees, and he was in a forest, in the Ardennes, a blue-eyed Gaul in fur and leather, and the blood of his slain enemies was glittering on his hands. He came to the edge of the forest, and there was a field and a house and a door, and he opened the door and saw a woman. She stood in a low bare farmhouse kitchen, and her face was broad, her hands red, and she held out her arms and said, "You have killed. You are a man." She sat on a bench on a terrace by a marble statue, and her face, too, was of marble, her eyes of jet, and she held out her arms and said, "You are a man." She lay on a woven mat in bamboo-striped moonlight, and her face and hair and breasts were soft and brown, and she held out her arms and said, "You are a man." Then he was out of the house, under the trees again, but they were no longer the trees of a forest; they were the trees of an avenue; and the avenue led on, on through a city, and at its end, far, far at its end, was the violet blue of the sky, of the eyes of a woman. And he came to her and knelt and said, "I am a man. I have come." And she smiled. The grave eyes smiled. And she, too, held out her arms to him, but she held them differently—not wide, but close together; not to receive but to give—and her gift was in her hands, in her cupped palms; the gift of life, the victor's trophy. . . .

Then there was a voice. Not her's. Another's. "Sidi, sidi," it said. "What is it? What is wrong?"

He sat up, trembling.

"You cried out," said Egal.

"It was a dream."

"Yes, I thought a dream. Do not worry, sidi. Sleep. They will not come back."

Egal crept from the tent.

He was alone again.

And he thought: "No, they will not come back. They *must* not come back." They were dead. Dead as the camel, the mule, the slave girl, the tribesman. "I bury the dead in the earth. In my belly." Dead words, dreams, images, hopes, regrets. Dead heaven and hell. Dead God and dead Satan.

He had killed a man.

So—he had killed a man.

He had killed him, not for Satan, no more than for God, but simply because, if he had not, he would have been killed himself. It had been quick, easy, almost casual. He had shot in self-defense; in defense of others; in defense of Gorbeau and Company; in defense of pots, pans, calicos, buckets, jackknives. In defense of civilization. The savage from the forest had met the savage from the desert, and civilization had been saved.

Here lies a nameless nigger.

"Here lies my gun."

He reached out and touched it, and it was real. It was there. His money belt was there. His ledgers were there. And he reached out and touched them too. He touched nothing else, because there was nothing else to touch. The rest was dream, phantasm, hallucination—like the mirages of the desert.

In the evening—up. In the night—forward. Ledgers packed, belt fastened, gun ready.

> *I have buried the dead in my belly*, he thought.
> *And the time of the Assassins is here.*

They moved on.

Through the waste. Through the nights.

Then one morning, as the night faded and they searched for a campsite for the day, another caravan appeared out of the southwest. The trains halted close together, and the drivers talked. They were only five days out of Harar, the others said—and the intervening country was "good." From there on, Claude and his men again rested by night and traveled by day.

The sun flamed. The earth shimmered. Mirages rose and gleamed and dissolved, and they plodded on through the horizons, as it seemed now to Claude they would plod forever. . . . But it was not forever. On the morning of the third day he became aware of a slow change. . . . The earth had been flat. Or it had risen and fallen in waves. But now it was different —rising but not falling, rising gradually, steadily through the miles—as they moved up a great tilt of the land. The earth's color and texture changed too. It was darker, heavier; no longer merely dust. And wisps of air stirred across the sweep of the wasteland. That night Claude woke to find the sweat had dried on his body, and the next morning the sun beat less fiercely than before.

All that day, too, the slope continued—steepened. Far ahead, it surged up into what was not a mirage but a range of hills, and the hills were not tan but purple, and through the purple ran streaks of green. Then for the first time there was green around them—a pale and withered green, to be sure, but still green, not tan, the green of life—among the thornbushes the green of leaves and stalks and strips of grass. A miracle rose up: a tree. Beyond it more trees. And, among them, animals. Throughout the journey animals had been no more than eyes, than moving shadows, but these were plain in the sunlight; a hare, an oryx, a herd of zebra, a pair of tiny dik-dik antelope bouncing away on matchstick legs. Claude shot the oryx ("—Morel the Hunter," he thought. "The killer. The killer of a man—now an oryx—"); and the Somalis skinned it, and that night they ate fresh meat. They drank fresh water too, camping beside a spring in a stand of sycamores.

Then the last day but one . . . and they climbed still more steeply. The waste was wholly gone now: a vast gleaming plain spread below and behind them. Ahead, the hills were closer, higher, greener; trees and plants were greener; sycamore, locust, begonia, euphorbia. They were no longer on a smooth slope but among the hills, the trail twisting on through valleys, up ridges. With every step they were higher. With every foot gained the earth burgeoned more brightly. And toward evening there was another miracle. Clouds gathered. Rain fell. When the rain stopped, mist descended and swirled softly about them in the hills.

Then the last day . . . and the sun again. The sun soft and mellow, almost cool in the rain-washed sky. And still they climbed toward the sky, up the valley, up the ridges, and on the crest of a ridge Egal pointed and said, "Kondudo," and there ahead, to the south and west, above the hills, was the squat flat-topped mountain that was the watchtower of Harar. They moved on toward it, past it, still ascending, and now their pace was even slower than in the desert, for the camels were now higher than they liked, out of their natural milieu, and their feet dragged, their breathing rasped in the thin air. But they kept on; on this final day they did not stop at all; and now at last they were in country not only of greenness, of life, but of human life, passing herdsmen and huts and then villages of huts, huddled, spike-topped, made of mud and thatch, from which dark faces watched them silently as they went by.

"I am the first European they have ever seen," Claude thought. "The first white man in their country. But they do not know it." They could not know it. For there was no whiteness in his face. He wore the kaffiyah and burnous of the desert. "And that is as it should be," he thought. To come as an African to the Africans, a nigger to the niggers.

They moved on. Up another valley; past a wooded slope; to another ridge. They topped the ridge, and there it was.... *Harar*.... Spread on a hillside facing eastward, it lay all before them: a maze of mud, of thatch, of brown stone, no brighter than the villages, but larger, a hundredfold larger, a huge sprawl of city slanting up to the evening sky. A thick dark wall surrounded it, fronting the slope before them, curving away to each side, out of sight: a wall of towers, bastions, parapets, scarred by the centuries. Beyond it were more walls, walls of houses, tiering upward; above them terraces, rooftops, minarets, domes; between them streets, squares, alleys, steep stairways; a honeycomb of city, of mud and thatch and stone and breathing life, crouched on its hillside beneath the setting sun.

For it was evening now. The sun sank. The walls stood somber. By the time they reached them the gates had swung shut, and, with other late-comers, they had to camp for the night on the slope outside. Here there was wood for a fire, and they built one and sat around it in the darkness, their camels hunched in close around them shivering gently in the cold. Through the slits in the walls they could see other fires and flickering lamps and hear voices, as Harar stirred in the night. A man laughed, a child cried; from far away the sound of a flute rose and fell. Then the sounds faded. The lamps dimmed. Their fire dimmed. There was only the night and the stars.

Lying beneath them, Claude waited for sleep. For the morning.

In the morning we shall enter fabulous cities. ...

And he would be the first. The first to see, to know, to tread those ancient stones of Africa. The first Barbarian of the North. With his pots and pans and pins and yard goods. With his belt and ledgers and gun. With the dead in his belly.

Then the morning came. The gates opened. They moved in. There were soldiers, officials, noise, questions, confusion. There was a crowd around them, pressing close, staring, talking; brown faces, and black faces ... and then another face, a different face ... a figure coming toward them across the square; a large figure, tall, broad, in a brown robe, with a brown beard; and he came quickly and greeted them and said, "*Salaam. Marhaba. Salaam aleikum.*" ... Then he stopped. He looked at Claude. At his face, his eyes. Now his own eyes were staring. And he said, "*Mon Dieu! Mon Dieu —un européen!*"

A big hand enveloped Claude's. "You speak French, perhaps? ... Yes? ... Ah—good. Excellent!" The face beamed. The voice boomed. "I am Father Hippolyte Lutz of the Capuchin Order. Welcome, my son. Welcome."

26

NOTES, he wrote in the back of a ledger.

Then:

The green flag of Egypt flies on the governor's palace. There are Egyptian soldiers in the barracks and on the walls. But Harar is not Egyptian. Except that they are Moslems, they are as much strangers—ferangi—here as a European. As I. More than I; for they are here only to rule, and I am here to buy and sell. When you buy you are still a ferangi, but when you sell you are something else.

The people are called Hararis. But that is a matter of geography, not blood. By blood they are Arab, Somali, Issa, Amhara, Shoan, Galla, Shankalla, both pure (whatever that means) and in every conceivable mixture. Those who are mostly Arab, Somali, and Issa are Moslem. They are in the majority, and the city is full of mosques, minarets, and chanting muezzins. The Amharas and Shoans, from Abyssinia, are Coptic Christians, and their churches are small. The Gallas and Shankallas are pagan: they come from the south and west, and the G's are partly negro, the S's all. Most are slaves: some living here, some on their way through with the caravans to the coast. The girl who died in the desert was a Shankalla, and there are many like her. Niggers, pagans, slaves. The flesh of Africa.

No, I am not altogether a ferangi.

I walk through the city, the streets. Or, rather, I climb the streets, for they are steep, twisting, full of rocks and mud. The only level place in the city is the great market square, the souk, from which the streets radiate out, and up or down, to the seven gates in the walls. The market itself sprawls over the center of the square. Bounding it are: (1) the chief mosque, (2) the palace, (3) the barracks, (4) the headquarters of Gorbeau and Company. "You must find a good place," Gorbeau told me. "A place of importance—prestige." And I did. No one knows that Sidi Morel is a pagan and a nigger. They think him a very important fellow.

Well, why not? What is a man except what others think he is?

I walk through the market. Ours is the only place that is housed in a building; the rest is stalls, sheds, awnings, or simply heaps and piles under the open sky. There is coffee, coffee everywhere. There are bananas, and hides and gums and khat (which is grown here), and the local grain that is called durra. And there are animals. Not many camels; here it is too high, cool, and damp for them. But donkeys, mules, goats, small horses, fat-tailed sheep, and humpbacked zebu cattle. And, of course, dung. And flies. In one section is the salt that has come up from the desert: great grayish bars, like boulders, speckled with flies and urine. And to one side is a pen for slaves on their way down. This is the only part of the market that does not vanish with darkness. Guards with guns patrol its walls of thorn and wattles, and from inside comes a low steady whispering moan, as if of the sea at night.

From the square I enter the streets. Besides being steep, they are narrow and twisting, and if you meet a mule there is an impasse. Walls of mud and brick scrape the elbows; but in the walls there are doors, and behind the doors a labyrinth. There are houses, huts, sheds, rooms, courtyards, alleys, terraces, roofs, cellars, one next to another, above and below one another, even within one another, like nests of Chinese boxes. There are coffeehouses filled with turbaned men; men smoking their hookahs in wreaths of blue smoke; men chewing khat leaves with green foam on their lips. And women can be seen too, everywhere, for purdah here is not strict. The women in Aden wear black, but the Hararis wear color: blue, green, pink, lavender, with swinging skirts and beneath the skirts tight trousers, and on their arms and throats silver bracelets and bangles. Some sit at looms in doorways. Some merely sit—and wait. For Harar is full of brothels. Egal, however (who would like to be my procurer plenipotentiary), is anti-brothel and pro-slave girl. A slave, he claims, is: (1) less likely to be diseased, (2) always there when wanted, (3) in the long run, cheaper.

Academic.

What is nonacademic is the rain. When I first arrived it fell only rarely, but now it rains two and three times a week. It falls on the square and streets and turns them to mud, but mud is welcome, blessed, after a year of sand and dust. Beyond the city it falls on the hills, and the hills shout with green. The streams shout, carrying the rains south, always southward. Eventually, it is said, they all reach the same river: the Web Shebeli, River of Leopards. But no one in Harar seems ever to have been there.

The rains, however, do not not long at a time. They come usually in the late afternoon, and then they stop, and the sun reappears, setting, and when it is gone it is dry and cool. In the cool darkness the city changes, draws into itself. Except for the slave pen, the square is empty; the streets are empty, the doors closed. And the seven gates are closed too, with guards and baying dogs on the walls to watch for shifta—*bandits—and wild beasts. From my roof, as from our camps in the desert, I can see the beasts, their eyes, their shadows, prowling, circling. The land is theirs now: all but the huddled darkness within the walls. The darkness, locked and silent, waiting for morning. By day Harar stands up bright and proud on its hillside: market, fortress, metropolis, city of men. At night it is itself an animal, crouched and wary in the African night.*

NOTES. . . .

Notes for what? For the *Journal des Ardennes?*

He tore the pages from the ledger and crumpled them. On another sheet he wrote:

Dear Mother:

A caravan for the coast leaves tomorrow, so I hasten to write you. In the caravan there will be many slaves, and it is too bad I cannot send you some for the farm, where they would be very useful. Ha, ha!

Our business continues to develop, and now I am a real storekeeper: my mother's son. But there are many problems, many obstacles. First and worst, there are exorbitant duties leveled on all that enters or leaves the town. Bribes are not only expected but demanded. To ask for credit is hopeless, and to give it is to cut one's throat. Also the exchange situation is most complicated. The official currency is the Egyptian piaster, but the Maria Theresa thaler is the most commonly used, and there are also francs, pounds sterling, Turkish piasters, Greek drachmas, and Indian rupees—plus much straight barter—with of course no bank to handle anything. Tell Michel Favre when next you see him that, on my return, I shall be prepared to take over as president of the Banque du Nord.

I am glad the remittances have been reaching you from the Aden office. There is a Monsieur Rappe there who is most reliable and whom you would greatly admire. In a letter accompanying this one I am asking him to send you an additional one thousand (1,000) francs, representing a share of my percentage profits to date.

You inquire about my health. I am glad to report that it is excellent. And you need have no concern, either, for my spiritual welfare, for there is a Capuchin priest here who is an old hand with heathens. His name is Lutz, and he is from Alsace, which makes him now, technically, German. But he himself is as French as a cuirassier of the Garde Républicaine—and almost as hairy. Perhaps I can sell him some incense for his church.

Respectfully, your son,

Claude

The house on the square, like all the houses of the city, was square, flat-roofed, made of stone and mud, but it was one of the few that had two stories. Built by the Egyptians for the use of government officials who had never materialized, it had been vacant at the time of Claude's arrival, and after much palaver he had managed to rent it. It was a good place, the right place, not only for prestige but in size and location. The square was both market and caravan terminus. It was the heart of Harar, crowded from dawn to dusk. And the building was large enough both for present purposes and for such expansion of activity as might follow. On the ground floor front were store and office, behind it storage rooms, and behind them, in turn, a spacious courtyard; and from one corner an outside stairway led up to a long second-floor balcony, off which there were more rooms for storage, offices, and living quarters. Claude occupied the largest of these, but used it for little more than holding his few personal belongings. By day he was in the office, the store, the market, around the town; and by night he slept out on the balcony on a folded rug. Close beside him were the blossoms of the jacaranda tree that rose from the courtyard. And beyond the blossoms were the glittering stars.

"*Ayeee, ayaaa—*"

The caravans came and went. The market hummed. From the market great crowds spilled over into Maison Gorbeau—merchants, traders, agents, shopkeepers—and he spent the hours buying and selling. Egal, aging and weary of caravans, had asked to stay on with him and served as foreman and general assistant; a Somali called Ahmed handled the moving of merchandise; and upstairs there was an ancient Harari, Mohammed, who cooked and cleaned. But otherwise, Claude did everything himself: from earliest morning, when the city first stirred, until late at night, when it slept, and he sat alone with his ledgers in the dim light of an oil lamp.

"On the whole it goes well," he wrote to Aden. And it was so. In the beginning, to be sure, there had been difficulties, for as a white man, however unwhite, he was automatically suspect, and the Egyptians, though theoretically avid for foreign trade, had greeted him with upturned palms that were not strictly symbols of welcome. A 100 per cent tax had been levied on his imports. The rental for the store was set fantastically high. And even when he succeeded in opening it, no one at first came, except, one night while he slept, a band of thieves. But he was patient, he persevered; and things improved. A few well-placed bribes reduced tax and rental. An honorarium to the Egyptian garrison commander removed the threat of theft. And soon the simple equation of supply and demand was taking care of the rest; for he had goods that Harar wanted and money to pay for what Harar had. Up from the coast came the pots, pans, pins, knives, and yard goods. Down went the coffee, hides, fruits, gums, and grains. As the traffic grew, the store grew, and in six months it was established, accepted, as the principal trading post in the city.

There were other factors, too, in its success. For one thing, the company took no part in the slave trade, and thus did not compete with the Arab entrepreneurs in the most lucrative of their activities. And for another, Claude, after his own trip up, was content to use the established caravans rather than organizing his own. "Our own will come in time," he wrote to Gorbeau. "But for the moment, I think it wiser not to push too hard." And Gorbeau wrote back commending his caution and diplomacy.

Most important of all, perhaps, in the company's development was, as his employer had foreseen, Claude's gift of tongues. Arabic, to be sure, he had already known, and this was the principal language of commerce and politics; but to it he had soon added fluent Somali and enough Amharic, Galla, and Issa so that he could talk, in his own speech, to everyone with whom he dealt. And for this he was soon famous in the city: the *ferangi* who was not a *ferangi;* the outsider who, alone among its inhabitants, could speak in all the languages of many-tongued Harar.

He walked through the market, the square, the streets. And voices followed him:

"*Salaam*, Sidi Morel—"

"If you please, Sidi Morel—"

"A word with you, sidi—"

"*Mashkur*. We thank you, honored sidi—"

He returned to the store. He moved through the warehouse among the crates and bales; stood in the courtyard directing the loading of a caravan; sat in his office while merchants filed in to see him. His gun stood unloaded in a cupboard. His belt lay in a locked drawer, his ledgers on a table, and each night he placed money in the one and careful figures in the other. When it was done he closed up and climbed the stairs. He lay on his rug on the balcony and looked up at the stars.

"Well done, Monsieur Rappe?" he asked.

"Well done, Mother?"

Beside him, the jacaranda blossoms stirred in the faint breeze of the African night. Within him, a ghost stirred and smiled.

There were two other *ferangi* merchants in the city: Spiranthos, a Greek, and Mardik, a Syrian. Both had been there for many years, ran small shops off the market square, and at first strongly resented Claude's coming. They had, he knew, intrigued against him with the Egyptian officials; they had done all they could to harm his business; they had even, he suspected, been the instigators of the early burglary of his store. But with them, too, he had been patient and forbearing. He had called on them. He had pointed out that his business was primarily import and export, whereas theirs was retail local trade. He had given them first choice, at dealer's prices, of merchandise received from Aden. When Mardik's Somali wife fell ill with fever, he called again, bringing medicines, and when Spiranthos lost much of his stock in a fire from a tipped brazier, he loaned him a thousand piasters to tide him over.

The two were still suspicious, still waiting for the mailed fist of big business to strike them. But thereafter they stopped their outward active hostility and left Claude alone.

With the Egyptians, too, he succeeded in getting along—though on a different basis and at higher cost. There were the bribes, the "honorariums," the contributions to the fund-for-this and fund-for-that, and when a high official visited the store and expressed admiration for this or that new importation, Claude was not so dull or boorish as to withhold a gift. In the Accounts Payable Ledger there was a section called bakshish, and it comprised some 20 per cent of the firm's total expenditures.

Early on, he had met the governor, Hajj Pasha. And the pasha was not unfriendly. A fat, mustached, bulge-eyed man, who had once been Egyptian minister to Belgium, he spoke both French and English, favored European clothes, especially uniforms, and considered himself a spearhead of civilization in Darkest Africa. "Since the opening of the Canal it has all changed," he told Claude. "Egypt is now at the crossroads of the world, a power no less than England and France. It is our duty, our destiny, to expand southward; to open the continent, bring light into darkness."

"If you can keep the Europeans from bringing it first," said Claude.

"Europeans, Egyptians—it is all the same. We are Moslems and you are Christians: that is the only difference. We are both civilized, both men of the modern world. We can work together. We must. That is why, in spite of much opposition, I have been glad to welcome you here. To co-operate. To smooth the path for you."

"It would be still smoother, Your Excellency," Claude pointed out, "if the duties were not so high."

"Yes, yes, I know: duties—taxes. Alas, governments must live, no less than people." The governor sighed and rubbed his several chins. "We have of course already greatly reduced your duties," he said. "But I am a fair man, a reasonable man. Perhaps—I am not promising, mind you, but just perhaps—we can do something further for you."

"It would be much appreciated, Your Excellency."

"Hmm, hmm— Well, we shall see. It is a tricky matter, of course; it must be handled judiciously. But I am sympathetic, Morel. As I say, you are welcome here. You are important. Like our government itself, you are a civilizing force: opening the gates to Africa, fostering trade, bringing the world, the goods, the techniques of the nineteenth century to these poor backward people. . . . Hmm—yes—your work must be helped. I shall think about it; talk to my staff. And perhaps something further can be done."

"Thank you," Claude said and made ready to go.

"And by the way, Morel—" said Hajj Pasha.

"Yes, Your Excellency?"

"Let me compliment you on the variety and quality of the merchandise in your recent shipments. The Irish linens you sent over were much appreciated. And the Turkish cigars were excellent."

"Think nothing of it, Your—"

"It was most generous. Indeed, the cigars were so good that I was wondering if in your next order to Aden—"

"Of course," said Claude.

"And also, perhaps, some of those tinned foods from France. The pâté, particularly, and the asparagus: they are delicious. . . . Then, too, I have been hearing of this new type of filament pressure lamp. They are made in Germany, I believe, and if you could—"

"Of course, Your Excellency."

The governor slapped his desk with his ringed fingers. "This is the sort of thing I have been talking about," he declared. "Trade, import, exchange, the flow of goods. It is our hope for this city—for all Africa. To trade, raise its standards of living, enter the modern world, instead of living as it has through the Dark Ages on this abominable slave traffic—"

Claude nodded—"Yes, Your Excellency"—and took his leave. A Galla slave held the door for him and another escorted him to the palace entrance. Outside, in the square, a new caravan had arrived from the south, and slaves were being herded into the pen, while officials counted them. The municipality of Harar received a payment of one hundred piasters each for every man, woman, and child who passed through the city.

"Sidi Morel?"

"Yes," said Claude.

His visitor was a small, elderly man—as small as Egal—and pale, for an Arab, with a round bland face and watery eyes. But his embroidered robe and kaffiyah proclaimed him a man of importance, as did the men behind him, in the doorway, who were apparently his retinue.

"Ah, I am glad," he said, "for I have heard much of you. Perhaps you in turn have heard of me. I am Abou Dakir."

"I bid you welcome, sidi."

"Thank you. . . . And thank you, no," he added, to Claude's invitation to sit down. "I am merely passing through Harar and can stay but a moment. This is my home, of course—or one of them—but unfortunately I have been able to spend little time here of late. The life of a trader, you know. One must be here, there, everywhere. Visiting one's markets, supervising transport, seeing to one's business." He smiled. "And Africa—even our small part of it—is very large."

He paused and dabbed with a silk cloth at his watery eyes. The men behind him stood motionless, and their eyes were not damp, but hard and black, and they stared fixedly at Claude from under desert hoods.

"But as I say," Abou Dakir continued, "I have heard of you much —indeed, since you first came to Zeila—and have promised myself the pleasure of meeting you. Now that pleasure is realized."

"Thank you," said Claude. "And what may I do for you?"

"Do? . . . Oh no, you misunderstand. It is I, rather, who have come to see if there is anything I can do for you."

There was a pause. The little Arab looked around him. "This is a fine place you have here," he said. "And I gather your business is good."

"It's all right," said Claude.

"You have no complaints?"

"Complaints?"

"With the caravan service. You have found it satisfactory?"

"Yes, quite."

"Good. Good." Abou Dakir nodded. Then, his voice changing a little: "I may tell you in all honesty, Sidi Morel, that I was most impressed when I learned of your forming your own caravan in Zeila. Impressed, for I thought, 'There is a strong, a courageous young man; a man I would like to know, to do business with.' But at the same time, I confess, unhappy. For I thought too, 'He is also a rash young man. Self-willed. Foolhardy.' I was concerned. But I see my concern was groundless. Apparently you had no difficulties, no misadventures, on the journey?"

"No," said Claude.

"Good. Good. You did well. . . . But it is well too, I think, that you have since decided to use our service. We have the experience, you see. We know the desert, the local tribes. And I have always believed in the maxim, 'Each man to his proper function.'"

"Yes, that is reasonable."

"You agree—good. I had hoped you would. I have said to my colleagues, 'This young man is strong-willed, yes. But he is also a Frenchman, and the French are practical, they are realists. They are not like the British, who are forever interfering, meddling, trying to impose their will on others.'" Abou Dakir paused. "As they are trying, for example," he said, "to interfere with *my* principal business."

He did not elaborate. It was not he, but Claude, who glanced out the door and across the square to the pen of thorns and wattles.

"I gather," he said, "that your company has no plans to interfere."

"No," said Claude.

"You will continue to deal only in your present types of merchandise?"

"Yes."

"And to use our caravans for your transport?"

"Yes."

"Good. Good." Again the old man nodded. "As I say, each man to his function; and there will be no difficulties. . . . Meanwhile, you are sure there is nothing I can do for you?"

"Quite sure, thank you."

"You have an ample supply of goods, I see."

"Yes."

"And enough help?"

"Yes."

"If at any time you need further help—good dependable help, laborers or servants—I should be glad to supply them. . . . Or women too, of course. There are, in fact, several rather nice specimens in my present consignment."

"I have an old Somali who cooks and cleans for me."

"I was referring to a rather different type. One in particular that might interest you. She is an Arussi Galla; a chief's daughter, I believe; very young, very pretty. Actually she is consigned to the Sultan of Hodeida, but I could send on a substitute; and since she has not yet been fattened you could have her at a bargain price."

"Thank you," said Claude. "But—"

"But you are not interested." Abou Dakir shrugged. "Well, it was merely a friendly gesture. Another time, perhaps." Again he dabbed at his eyes and then bowed slightly. "So I must be going," he said. "*Salaam*, sidi. We shall meet again, I trust."

"*Salaam*" Claude replied.

The Arab turned and went out, and his retinue followed him silently. Across the square, presently, there was much shouting and cracking of whips, as the slaves were herded out from the pen into caravan file.

There was another visitor to the store: a frequent one: Father Hippolyte Lutz. Almost every day the Capuchin stopped by during his rounds of the city, examined Claude's merchandise with lively interest, and tried to make casual friendly conversation. But Claude avoided him as much as he could, busying himself with chores in the warehouse or plunging deep into his bills and ledgers.

"You are a Catholic, my son?" the priest had asked him early on.

"No," he had said.

"A Protestant?"

"No."

"What then, might I ask?"

"A Zoroastrian."

Father Lutz had not pursued the point, but neither had he taken offense, as Claude had hoped, and stayed away. On the contrary, he had returned the next day, as friendly as before, and continued to come through the weeks and the months: sometimes merely for a "*bon jour*" and a wave of the hand; sometimes, when Claude gave him the opportunity, to sit and talk. He was a man of perhaps forty or forty-five: big, indeed huge, vast in frame and in girth, with a broad weathered face, a great bush of beard, and a robe that cascaded in brown billows to his sandaled feet. The only part of him not built to scale were his eyes, which were small, indeed tiny, and brown and bright. When he smiled or laughed, which was often, they all but disappeared in the folds of his flesh. At other times they watched Claude keenly, steadily, seeming to probe him with shrewd surmise.

After his rebuffed attempt he did not, for some time, speak again of religion. He spoke of Harar, its people, its sights and sounds, its smells, and offered to show Claude such parts of the city as he did not yet know.

He spoke of Abou Dakir and the slave trade—sadly; and of the African land and its people—fervently. He talked a great deal about food. Several times he bought imported items from the supply in the store, and once, in return, and as a gift, he brought Claude a basketful of freshly picked pomegranates.

He had, it developed, come to Harar some six months before Claude. And it had been by way of neither Aden nor Zeila, but across the breadth of Abyssinia from the Nile and Khartoum. Indeed, his original assignment had been to the Abyssinian kingdom of Shoa. "But they are mostly Christians there," he said. "Coptic Christians. And my welcome was less than cordial. In fact I was thrown out." His eyes crinkled in a smile. "The Shoans are in some ways quite civilized, you know; almost as advanced in intolerance as we Europeans. . . . Anyhow, they wanted no de-Copting, no part of our Roman Church. 'Goodbye, please,' they said, and I moved on. I came here. The Moslems, to be sure, love me no more than the Copts. But they are not fanatic here; they let me stay. And I in turn have tried to show that *I* am not fanatic."

He had only the smallest of churches: a mere cross-topped hut of mud and wattle that he had built with his own hands. His converts had been few —and these wholly from among the lowest, the poorest, the pagan fringe of the Moslem city. "But I am patient," he said. "I doubt if I am a wise man, but I am a patient one, and I know that the human soul cannot be driven, even to Christ. I am grateful to be allowed to stay here; to help, to counsel, to lead a few, perhaps slowly, on the true path. And then, in time, more of my order will come. We will build real churches, open schools and hospitals, establish missions. Above all, we will fight the curse of slavery."

"Not forgetting," said Claude, "to replace the African kind with your own."

Again, Father Lutz did not join the issue. For a moment he looked at Claude with sorrowful eyes; but then the moment passed, and when he left he was again his usual self, moving brown and broad-beamed and cheerful through the market place. For an instant, as Claude looked after him, he seemed to change, to become someone else. Not another priest. Not Father Lacaze. He was the engineer, Mackenzie. Halfway across the market he stopped to talk to a group of Hararis at one of the stalls, and presently Claude could hear his deep voice booming with laughter.

The next time Father Lutz came it was with an invitation. "It would be nice if you paid me a visit," he said.

"No, thank you," Claude told him. "I don't convert that easily."

The priest smiled. "I do not mean to church. I mean to my home for dinner. Even Zoroastrians eat, do they not? And as two bachelors we could pass a companionable evening."

Claude made excuses, but the priest persisted, and the next night, reluctantly, Claude went to his house. It was in the poorest part of town, and from the outside scarcely distinguishable from the hovels around it; but within, though plain, it was neat and comfortable, and oil lamps on the walls threw a cheerful glow. "Welcome. Welcome, my son," beamed Father Lutz, as he had when Claude first entered the city. And then, seeing Claude's stare, he laughed. "You will please excuse my costume for an informal occasion?" he asked; for he was wearing only cotton trousers and an undershirt. "I would not wish it told in Gath or published in Askelon, but in this climate, confidentially, my robe itches like the devil's own."

He had neither cook nor servant, but the meal he produced was delicious. And with it appeared a jug of red wine. "From the private *cuvée* of Hippolyte Lutz," he announced. "The Harari grapes are really not bad, you know. Scarcely Burgundian, but still not bad. I pick them myself, wild, up in the hills, and then I work like an alchemist—and *voilà!*"

He started to pour, but Claude shook his head.

"You do not care for wine?"

"No thank you; I don't drink."

"Hmm—a pity. You miss much." The priest poured for himself. "Well, some more food then. Come, come, my son—eat up. You are all skin and bones."

He himself ate hugely. He drank with relish. When the meal was over he opened the top button of his trousers, leaned back in his seat, and gazed happily at the ceiling.

"You should have the governor for dinner," Claude said.

"The governor?"

"He's a *bon vivant* too. He likes food, wine, cigars."

"Cigars—*mon Dieu!* I have not had a cigar since I left France. Where does he get them, the lucky devil?"

"From me. I import them from Aden. Would you like some too?"

"Would I?" Father Lutz's eyes sparkled. "Would I! That is the one thing I dream of at night—other than sacred matters, of course. A fine mild fragrant cigar." He rounded his lips and puffed at an imaginary cheroot. He refilled his wineglass. Then he looked at Claude and chuckled.

"You find me a queer one, don't you?" he said.

"Queer?"

"A priest who likes food, wine, cigars. And admits it." He sipped from his glass. "Well, I am luckier than many, to be sure. A Trappist, for instance. Or a Carthusian. Lord, the life *they* have to lead! Fortunately my order does not require mortification of the flesh. I would have a dreadful time of it, I am afraid—having so much to mortify."

His chuckle swelled to a laugh. He patted his stomach. He belched and said, "*Pardon*." Then for a few minutes there was a silence, and he watched Claude musingly in the yellow lamplight.

"*You* are the mortifier, aren't you?" he said.

"I?"

"Yes. The apostate Trappist. The Zoroastrian ascetic. . . . You do not, as I have seen, drink wine. Or, I gather, smoke. You do not consort with women. You scarcely eat. You scarcely speak."

"There is still another item you have forgotten," said Claude. "And what is that?"

"I do not pray."

"No, I imagine not." The priest paused. "Tell me then: what *do* you do, my son?"

"I do my work."

"Yes, of course—your work. And when your work is done?"

"I sleep."

"That is all?"

"Yes."

"It is enough?"

"Yes."

"It is not only the flesh you mortify, then, but the mind as well?"

"My mind is my own," said Claude. "And I do with it as I see fit."

"Which is to shut it away? Starve it? Destroy it?" Father Lutz studied him with his keen brown eyes. "Do you think I cannot see that you have a mind?" he said. "That you are a man of education, intellect, spirit?"

"I am a man of trade. I buy and sell. I run my store."

"And supply cigars to governors and priests?"

"Exactly."

There was a silence. The bright eyes watched him. Claude stood up.

"If this is all you want of life," the priest said, "why are you then so bitter and so lost?"

"I am not."

"No?"

"I live as I choose to, that is all. As you do. To myself. Alone."

The priest shook his head. "No, about me you are wrong; my son," he said, "I am not alone. There is a difference between us—a great difference —for, you see, I am never alone."

His eyes moved and changed. They were no longer looking at Claude, but past him, toward the wall behind. And, turning, Claude looked too and saw the crucifix.

He turned again, quickly. He moved toward the door. "Do not go, my son," said Father Lutz gently. "Stay a while; it is still early."

"No, I must go."

"I had hoped we could talk a bit. Not of Trappists or Zoroaster, but of what you choose. Or we could play cards. Do you know bezique? It is a pleasant way to pass an evening."

"I am sorry—"

Claude stood at the door, and the priest shrugged and rose. "Well then, at least you must come again," he said. "And next time please bring an appetite."

"Yes, perhaps I shall. Goodnight—and thank you."

"Goodnight. Thank *you*, too." The priest went to the door and shook hands, and a smile showed through the great bush of his beard. "*Mon Dieu*," he said happily, "I can hardly wait to get my teeth into one of those luscious cigars."

The rains fell. There were mud and mosquitoes.

The rains stopped. There were dust and flies.

The flies were thickest around the privy in the courtyard, and, with Egal, he built a new one and dug a deep hole. There was no need for a lock, for there was no mother to disturb him, but instead, he nailed a tin can to the wall and in it burned gums and resins which he took from the warehouse. "Now I have my own church," he told Father Lutz, "—the Temple of Dysentery. Incense is supplied free to communicants, but they must bring their own holy waters."

He made little use, any longer, of his office. When he was not in the warehouse or the privy, or around the city, he would sit on his balcony or under the jacaranda tree, talking to buyers and sellers, or with his ledgers spread on his knees. He could sit now as the Africans sat, without chair or stool, squatting by the hour on his haunches, rump resting on heels. Usually he was barefoot; he wore only cotton trousers and shirts; and when he developed an infection of the scalp he shaved his head and wound a turban around it to keep off the sun. Only his eyes kept him from seeming wholly an African: the eyes pale blue, cold, glacial, in the dark bronze of his face.

The seasons passed. The earth turned. In her letters, occasionally, his mother wrote of events in Cambon, France, Paris, the world. But they had no meaning for him. "All such things are now incomprehensible to me," he wrote back. "Like the Moslems, I know that what is, is—what happens, happens—and that is all." As the earth turned, the sun rose and set, the muezzins called from the minarets, the eyes of the wilderness ringed the city at night. The world beyond was the caravan, coming, going. It was the cry of the drivers, the bale in the warehouse, the cigar in the face of Hajj Pasha or Father Lutz. It was the figures he wrote in his ledgers, endlessly, patiently, squatting in the courtyard under the jacaranda tree.

What happened, happened. One day the old cook, Mohammed, climbed the stairs with a load of firewood, laid it neatly beside the oven, and then himself lay down beside it and died. The next week Claude discovered an error in his accounts that took him four days to rectify.

Sometimes he left the courtyard and the store. He walked through the town. He walked beyond it into the countryside. With Egal and a train of donkeys he visited the villages in the hills, taking with him merchandise he had received from Aden and bringing back such local produce as was available. The earth was red and rich and living. High on the hillsides stood the sycamores and locust trees, the acacia, mimosa, and flowering begonia, the green-spiked euphorbia rising like candelabra against the sky. There were fields of green khat, of yellow durra, and long slanting meadows filled with zebu cattle. In the valleys were lakes: not mirages, not dried beds of salt and soda, but blue-green lakes of gleaming water, as fresh and living as the earth. The land shone. The land burgeoned under the sun. Only the villages were poor—and the people. But they did not know it. They were ignorant, benighted, dirty, diseased; but they did not know it. They sat in the mud in front of their huts, pushed their single-stick plows through the red earth, ate and slept and copulated and waited for death, and said their prayers to Allah, and, to be safe, to the old gods of Africa as well.

They did not, however, Claude knew, greatly believe in the efficacy of their prayers. Allah and the Thunder King both had their own plans. What was, was. What happened, happened.

So he moved among them: the *ferangi* who was not a *ferangi*, who spoke their languages, dressed as they dressed, came not as a sidi or pasha on a camel or caparisoned horse, but afoot, like a Somali or Issa, behind his plodding train of mules. He came and sat beside them, and traded knives and pans and cloth for hides and grain, and then left and moved on to the next village; and when he had been to the last village of a circuit he would send Egal back to Harar with the mules and produce and move on for a few days through the hills, alone. For these two things within remained unchanged from the old days: the need to walk and the need for solitude.

He walked down through the valleys, and up to the hilltops. Once he walked farther and higher than before, leaving the trails, climbing through brush and forest, to the flat summit of Mount Kondudo, and there he sat, almost the full day through, his eyes fixed on the horizons. To the east and north was the desert of Somaliland, flat and glaring in the sunlight, the waste he had crossed on his journey of pilgrimage. Beyond it were Zeila and the sea, beyond them Aden and the world, but these were as invisible to the mind as to the eye, and soon his eyes moved on. They moved to the north and west, and there were hills: first the hills of Harar, then others behind him, range upon range of hills spreading away, farther, higher, into the purple uplands of Abyssinia. At these he looked for a while, measuring, musing, and then his eyes moved again, to the southwest, the

south. Here the hills fell away again. There was flatland, plain, wilderness
—the vast wilderness called the Ogaden. But it was not like the wilderness
to the northeast; not dust but earth, red earth; not bare but flecked with
grass and thorn; not veined with empty wadis but with flowing streams,
the streams from the hills, living, moving, the green veins and arteries of
the living land, flowing on to the horizon, to the south. All, always, to the
south. Out of the hills of Harar, out of Moslem Africa, known Africa, into
the lands beyond. The lands of leopards, lions, elephants, ivory, gold. Of
green forests and yellow rivers. Of beating drums; black dancing files. The
lands once known, then lost, that lay hidden, waiting. . . .

For whom?

The sun gleamed. The earth gleamed. Then the sun set and it grew
dark, and he slept on the mountaintop under the stars; and in the morning
he descended and crossed the fields and returned to Harar. He checked the
produce that had come in with Egal and the mules and sorted it out into
the warehouse to await shipment with the next caravan. He bargained
with an Arab who wanted knives and a Somali selling khat. Then for the
rest of the day he squatted under the jacaranda tree, bringing his ledgers
up to date, and when it was evening he took them upstairs, slipped them
into their dust- and damp-proof pouch and locked them away with his
money belt and gun. Since the old man, Mohammed, had died he had
not hired another servant, and he prepared his own frugal supper. As he
ate, Father Hippolyte Lutz paid a call, talked cheerfully of this and that,
and suggested he come to his place for a game of cards; but he declined
and, when the priest had left, sat out as usual on the balcony, in the starlit
darkness. Egal and the Somali helper, Ahmed, were gone for the evening.
He was alone. Content alone. "No, Reverend Father," he thought, "I do
not need your company. I do not need your cards or your food or your
wine or your prayers or your God. As you said, I am the mortifier. I am
the renouncer, the anchorite." . . . He smiled. . . . "Can you see me now,
Druard, old ghost—you pious fraud, you holy devil, with your gabble of
Chimay? Where are you now? Drunk, drugged, and reeling in a gutter of
Paris? It is I who have found the retreat, the sanctuary: the monk in his
monastery, the silent Trappist in his cell."

Fomalhaut blazed in the southern sky, over the Ogaden. But he no
longer watched it. He turned and faced the wall and waited for sleep. For
sleep without star, without dream. Each night was the same as the last,
each day as the last; and they would be the same forever. . . .

Until one night, suddenly, not the same; for he had awakened, and
there was a sound—not the usual sound of night, of baying dogs or stirring branches, but from the store downstairs—and he knew that, again,
someone had broken in. He got his gun from the cupboard, loaded it,
went down the steps. Opening a door, he entered the store and stopped.

He looked and listened. At first there was only darkness and stillness; but then, as he advanced, there was again a faint sound, a stirring. A shadow moved, slowly, warily; then as Claude called "Stop!" a figure darted with sudden swiftness across the room toward the warehouse door. Claude raised his gun, but did not fire. Something about the figure—its size or movement—stopped him and, instead, he dropped the gun and ran in pursuit. The figure entered the warehouse, vanished briefly, reappeared at a far door and struggled to open it. And there Claude caught it. The figure became flesh, the shadow a body, and he seized it and jerked backward and the body fell; and then Egal appeared with a lantern, and he and Claude looked down into the face of a boy.

Besides the lantern Egal carried a club, and he raised it. But Claude held his arm.

"Get up," he said. And the boy stood.

He was brown, thin, almost naked, and the face was barely level with Claude's shoulder. In the light of the lantern it seemed all bone and eyes —the face, simultaneously, of a child and an old man—and the eyes were wide and wild, filled half with defiance, half with fear.

Egal snatched at his hand and pulled something away. It was a half-eaten plum. He searched his rags and found another plum, a few dates, a strip of dried meat.

"What else have you taken, *hein?*"

The boy was silent.

"And where is the rest of your gang?"

Still the boy said nothing, and Egal swung around with the lantern to peer into the darkness. For an instant Claude turned as well, and as he did so the boy ducked quickly past him, making another break for the door. But again Claude caught him, and this time held him fast.

"He is alone," said Egal, turning back to them. "So we will fix him, yes? Will I call the police, sidi? Or will we do it ourselves?" Claude did not answer at once, and he again raised his club. "I think we do it ourselves, sidi. We do it better ourselves."

Claude held the boy by the neck. Under his fingers he felt the bones of his spine and the cords of his throat. That was all there was: bone, cord, skin—without flesh. "No, wait," he said. He jerked the head up. He looked at the dark frightened eyes.

"What is your name?" he demanded.

No answer.

"Where do you live?"

No answer.

"Who are your parents?"

No answer.

"I will make him talk, sidi," said Egal.

Claude shook his head. "No, this kind you cannot *make* do anything. I know them." He released his grip on the boy. "Wipe your nose, snotface," he told him.

The boy stared at him.

"Wipe it—do you hear me?"

The boy raised a hand slowly and dabbed at his nose.

"I will get the police," said Egal.

"No, no police," Claude said. "No *flics.*"

"But he is a thief."

"No, not a thief. He is a *voyou.*"

Egal looked at him uncomprehendingly. The boy still stared.

"And you are hungry, *hein, voyou?*" said Claude. He pointed at the floor. "All right, pick them up."

The boy looked where he pointed. Slowly he stooped and picked up the plums, the dates, the strip of meat that had been dropped there.

"Now stand there. Wait."

The boy stood, waiting. Claude took the lantern from Egal and crossed the room. He opened a cupboard and took out a loaf of bread and, returning, gave the loaf to the boy. "Next time you should try Les Halles," he told him. "They have a better assortment."

He laughed. Then, going to the outer door, he swung it open. "All right, on your way," he said. "Out with you, *voyou. Fous le camp!*"

For another moment the boy stood motionless. Then he turned, ran, vanished, and Claude laughed again and closed the door.

Now it was Egal alone who stared at him. "What do you do, sidi?" he protested. "He is a thief. He will come back."

"No, not a thief," Claude repeated. "We won't see him again."

But in this last he was wrong. . . .

For the next day, sitting under the jacaranda tree, he looked up from his ledgers to see the boy in the courtyard. He had with him a sack and a sort of improvised shovel and was poking among the debris and dung left recently by an unloading caravan. When Claude called to him and beckoned he did not run away, but approached and stood before him quietly.

"You are looking for something else to steal?" Claude asked.

"No, sidi," said the boy.

"What then?"

"I am making clean."

"Clean?"

"Your place here. It is dirty. I thought you would like it clean."

"Oh, I see." Claude eyed him. "Thank you."

"No, it is you I thank, sidi. For last night. You did not beat me, or let the other one beat me, or call the police."

His voice was soft. His eyes were soft, with the wildness gone from them.

"You did not speak last night," said Claude.

"No, sidi."

"Why not?"

"Because I was afraid."

"And now you are not?"

"No, sidi."

Claude studied him again. He half smiled.

"I may go on cleaning?" the boy asked.

Claude nodded and returned to his ledgers. When next he looked up, the debris in the yard was gone, and the boy had found a rag and water and was washing the walls of the privy. And when still later it was dusk and Claude rose to go inside, he was still there, standing quietly against a wall and watching him.

Claude took a coin from his pocket and held it out to him. But the boy shook his head.

"When you do work," Claude said, "you should be paid for it."

"No," said the boy. "I do not want to be paid."

"Here, crazy one, take it. And now off with you."

He put the coin in the boy's hand, but still the boy did not move.

"Did you hear me?" said Claude. "Go."

"Go where, sidi?"

"To your home."

"I have no home."

"To wherever you want, then."

"I want to stay here."

"Here?"

"Yes, sidi. Please, sidi. Let me stay. I will work hard—do anything. Please, sidi. Please—"

Claude looked at him. He bit his lip. Then, very slowly, he smiled. "No *fous le camp* for you, *hein*, *voyou?*" he said.

The boy's face was raised. His eyes were huge, dark, and pleading. "Please, sidi," he murmured. "Please, please let me stay—"

Claude still watched him, still smiled. Then he shrugged and turned toward the warehouse.

"All right," he said. "Stay."

NOTES, he wrote. . . .

A caravan came in today. Many come, of course: from the east, the north, the west: from Zeila, the Somalilands, the Galla country, the Abyssinian kingdoms of Tigre and Shoa. But this one was from the south, the Ogaden, where the rivers flow. It was Abou Dakir's. Another ton of piasters for Abou Dakir. It brought ivory, musk, gold dust, the plumes of birds, the skins of giraffes, zebras, leopards, lions. And slaves.

The slaves carry the loads. They are the only merchandise that can carry merchandise, and therefore the best investment. For Arabs, that is. We Christians do not make such investments. We serve the Lord and keep our guns well oiled. The skins piled high on that black lashed back will look more becoming on the back of Madame la Comtesse as she leaves Maxim's for the opera.

Father Hippolyte Lutz puts down his cigar and raises his eyes to Christ crucified. I do not raise mine. I look level across the square at the slaves, the merchandise, the pagan niggers, as they come up out of the south, out of Africa. I see a hundred. Behind them, a thousand, a hundred thousand. Each with his load, his cross, his march to Golgotha.

I see a million murdered Christs, their eyes somber and true. . . .

He tore the page from the ledger.
NOTES—for what?

27

"So what is your name?" he had asked.

"Ali," said the boy.

Claude shook his head. "That is no good. There are too many Alis. Every time I call you half the boys in Harar will answer."

He thought it over. Then he smiled.

"You will have a new name," he said.

"Yes, sidi?"

"From now on you are Voyou."

"Va-yu—"

"All right—Vayu." Claude laughed. "Hey, Vayu"—he clapped his hands —"bring me my ledger and pen."

"Yes, sidi."

"And the warehouse needs sweeping, Vayu."

"I shall do, sidi."

And the new Vayu ran off, laughing too.

As it developed, the name was ill-chosen, for once fear and hunger were gone, there was nothing of the *voyou* about him. He was polite, softspoken, gentle. He did instantly what he was told to do, and when not told, found ways on his own to make himself useful. Soon he was not only choreboy and errand-runner, but had taken old Mohammed's place as cook and housekeeper and was an integral part of the ménage. Egal, at first gruff and suspicious (—"Wait and see: he will clean us out good and plenty"—), came reluctantly to accept him. Ahmed, the Somali, accepted him. After a month it was hard for Claude to recall what it had been like before the boy came among them.

In different ways, he appeared now both older and younger than on his first midnight appearance. Older in that, with proper food, he grew quickly in flesh and bone; younger because simultaneously he lost the wizened furtive look of hunger and hardship. His body was smooth, lithe, and brown; his face brown, oval, fine-boned, with a thatch of wild black curly hair. But the hair was now all that was wild. The rest was softness, grace, gentleness. His eyes were large, dark, and liquid, like the eyes of an antelope.

He did not know his age. ("All right," said Claude, "we will give you an age: fourteen.") Nor did he know where he came from, or who his parents were, or where, if ever, he had had a home. As long as he could remember he had lived in the streets of Harar, sometimes alone, sometimes with gangs of other homeless boys: sleeping where he could, eating scraps, foraging, scavenging, stealing, being caught, being beaten . . . until at last the night had come when he had been caught but not beaten, when a man had held him by the scruff and looked into his face and did not strike the face, but suddenly, strangely, laughed.

"And now at last, sidi, I have a home," he said.

"Yes, Vayu."

"And now, too, I have a father."

Dear Mother. . . . So Felix is married. Bravo! And to a barmaid in Antimes. Halleluiah! Your cup indeed must runneth over, and now you have a real professional to refill it. . . . And Yvette a full-fledged nun, so that at least you have a son-in-law you approve of. What does one send a Bride of the Lamb as a wedding gift? Not a rubber ball; not a locket; not a Somali leopard cloak for Maxim's and the opera. So I content myself with the fond wishes of a damned but loving infidel. . . . No thank you, there is nothing I need. And yes, I take care of myself and my appearance. Indeed, next to the governor (who wears medals) and Father Lutz (who wears his beard), I rank as the third most fashionable foreigner in Harar. . . . Yes, I can appreciate the problems at the farm and hope the new handy man is better than the preceding six. Here, as in more enlightened lands, seven is considered a lucky number. I am instructing the Aden office to send you another thousand francs toward the reduction of the mortgage. . . .

Dear M. Gorbeau. . . . The consignment shipped from Aden as of August 4 has been received, in good condition except for certain items of tinware dented in transit. I am writing Nomoury in Zeila directing him to take greater care in the packing of caravan loads. . . . In my own current shipment, which this

letter will accompany, you will find a new, and I think better, grade of raw
opopanax gum, perhaps suitable for incense in the more solvent dioceses. . . .
I am glad M. Rappe was satisfied with the last accounts receivable statement.
Please assure him that the ledgers remain dry and dustless and thank him for
the new tin of Hornsby's Shoe Polish that he was kind enough to send me. . . .
Yes, I am aware that I have now been a year in Harar, but, with your permis-
sion, I should like to stay on. I am content here. And not lonely. . . .

He was content.

"*Je suis chez moi,*" he thought. "I have found my home—my niche."
He had roamed the world; he had crossed seas, deserts, mountains,
continents, until he had come to the very edge of the world; and here on
its edge, on its farthest margin, he belonged. The world of his birth, of
his youth, was gone. He had come beyond it at last. He was outside. Yet,
outside, he was now, for the first time in his life, not an outsider, not a rebel
or fugitive. He did his work. He lived his life. What happened, happened.
He had passed at last beyond rages and boredom, beyond anger and fear.

From under the jacaranda tree he watched the activity of yard and
warehouse. From his balcony he looked across the square, across the rooftops, to the walls of Harar. But now no farther than the walls. Not to the
south, to the green valleys, the streams flowing down into the Ogaden.
Not to the west and the purple mountains or the north and east and the
flaming wastes. He had crossed those wastes, he made his journey; now
they were behind him; and behind them, in turn, immeasurably remote,
dim and lost, was what was now, to him, the *outside*. Europe and France,
Paris and Cambon, even Aden and Zeila, could as well have been specks on
a planet of Fomalhaut. From the planet signals came: motes borne on the
light-years. . . . *Felix is married. . . . Since the hide market is now depressed. . . .*
The new hired man is a loafer, a sot. . . . In ref. yrs. of July 12. . . . And he, in turn,
sent signals back: across the light-years, into the void.

But he did not look into the void. He looked at his ledgers. He looked
up and gave instructions to Egal, Ahmed, Vayu. He counted pots and
hides. He talked to buyers, listened to sellers. . . . "Good morning, sidi. . . .
Salaam aleikum, sidi. . . . For eight thalers, sidi. See—the finest quality. Rare.
A bargain. . . ." And when the deal was made he thumped a paper with one
of the six new rubber stamps that Rappe had sent him from Aden.

Above the entrance of the store was a sign in Arabic script that he had
painted himself. It read MAISON GORBEAU, and below, in smaller letters, C.
Morel, gérant. Sometimes he looked at it and smiled; and smiling, thought,
"So there you are at last. *Monsieur le gérant, le directeur, le commerçant, le*
fonctionnaire." . . . Yes, he had his niche. He "belonged." He belonged
more thoroughly, more truly, than any of the other *ferangi* in Harar—than
Hajj Pasha the Egyptian or Spiranthos the Greek or Mardik the Syrian or

Father Lutz the Alsatian—for he alone lived wholly the life of a Harari. Each of the others, in varying ways, had brought with him something of his past, of the world he had come from: in his clothing, his habits, his language, his race, his religion. He, Claude, had brought only himself. One soul—one body. No, not even these two. Only one: a body. Soul had been left behind with all the rest: in the wastes, on the sea bottoms, in hell. On the planet of Fomalhaut.

He lay out on the balcony. Around him were the city, the walls, the desert, the night. . . . *From the same desert, in the same night, always the tired eyes awake. Always.* . . . But not now. Now it was only on an occasional night, the rare and troubled night, that, waking, they watched the darkness, watched the star, the Three Magi on their journey; and he thought, "They are still there—the dreams, the specters. They are not gone but only hidden." And it was he who hid them, who turned his eyes away, who had found his new cave in which he dwelt as a mole, a troglodyte, self-walled, self-blinded, self-drugged, with the counting of crates and bales for absinthe and the balancing of ledgers for hashish. Then the cave opened. The tomb opened. The night trembled and the star burned. . . . But only briefly. For he closed his eyes. He turned away. . . . He turned to the wall and slept, or went down to the office and worked by lamplight on the ledgers; and soon night and star were gone, the cave closed in again; and then the cave grew brighter and it was morning, and there were voices and movements in the courtyard and warehouse, and Vayu brought him his coffee, and the first merchant said *"Salaam aleikum,"* and thus again began the day of *un gérant, un directeur, un commerçant, un vrai fonctionnaire.*

Dear Mother, he wrote, *I am very busy here, very industrious. I work ten, twelve, fourteen hours a day. And on Sundays, sixteen, for the greater glory of the Lord.*

When work was done, when day was done, he would sit at ease on the veranda or under the jacaranda tree, and there Vayu brought him his supper. Several times Father Lutz had again asked him to his tiny home —for a meal, a game of cards, an evening of talk—but he had declined; as he declined, too, the occasional invitations of others. He did not go to the coffeehouses, nor did he ask anyone to come to him as a guest. When night fell, Egal and Ahmed vanished into the labyrinth of the city and returned only to sleep. His only companions of the darkness were his ledgers—and Vayu.

The boy, he had soon discovered, was remarkably bright. Though he had not, of course, had an hour of schooling in his life, he was curious and quick to learn, and soon knew as much about the store, its methods and merchandise, as Egal or Ahmed, or even Claude himself. And in the evenings he was full of questions about the unknown world beyond

Harar and pounced like a hungry cub on every scrap of information he received.

After one of his visits to the store, and a talk with Vayu, Father Lutz approached Claude. "He is as intelligent a boy as I have known," he said. "Let him come to me for an hour a day and I will teach him."

But Claude shook his head. "No thank you, Father. No psalms. No rosaries."

"I do not mean religious teaching. I mean simply reading, writing, a few figures. It is a shame for such a fine young mind to stay in darkness."

"Darkness? What darkness, Father? Of the sun? Of youth? Of being healthy and happy?"

"He will be happier with some education. With answers to his questions. With tools for his mind to make use of."

"Perhaps," said Claude. "But, with your permission, I shall supply the answers and tools myself."

The priest sighed and left. Claude smiled. He watched Vayu—and smiled. And one day in the courtyard, as the boy stood before him, he said, quite suddenly, "All right, school is convened. The class will now come to order."

Vayu looked at him, uncomprehending.

"The Lycée Morel will now hold its examination of candidates for baccalaureate degrees in the liberal arts and humane sciences. You will stand at attention, Candidate, and answer such questions as I, the headmaster, put to you."

Uncomprehension became misery. "Sidi, forgive me. I do not—"

"Silence! ... So now. The first question: literature.... How many words, placed one after another, does it require to: (a) save the world, (b) save a soul, (c) save your skin?"

Vayu stared at him.

"Well?"

No answer.

"You do not know?"

"No, sidi."

"Not one of the three parts?"

"No, sidi."

"Hmm ... Well, next question: science ... If it requires ten grams of nitroglycerin to blow the leg off one soldier, how many grams does it take to exterminate the inmates of a hundred-bed hospital?"

He waited.... "Well?"

"Sidi, I—"

"If you know, answer. If you do not know, say 'I do not know.'"

"I do not know."

"Very well. Third question: politics.... There is a new mayor of a city.

There are many criminals in the city. What percentage of their earnings do the criminals pay the mayor so that the police will keep the children off the grass in the park?"

"I do not know, sidi."

"Fourth question: economics.... You are a child of ten. You work in a fine new woolen mill, eighty hours a week, for which you are paid five francs. The rest of your family together earns forty francs a week, and the cost of housing and food is fifty-two francs. Where will the family go for its summer vacation?"

"I do not know."

"Fifth and last question: theology.... God is everywhere. He sees everything. What does he say?"

"I do not know."

Claude rose. He cleared his throat. "The examinations of the Lycée Morel," he said, "are now at an end, and it is the finding of the Board of Regents that Candidate Vayu has achieved a perfect score. Next on the program is the ceremonial prize-giving, for which you will please comb your hair and put on your blue serge suit."

The boy was motionless; numb with confusion.

Then Claude laughed. "You will put on a clean loincloth," he said, "and march up the aisle, and the headmaster of the lycée will award you your prize."

"A prize?" Vayu came alive. His eyes sparkled. "You mean a present, sidi? You will give me a present?"

Claude nodded.

"Oh, sidi—"

"But first you will have to answer one more question.... No, don't worry, it's not a hard one.... You must just tell me what the prize should be; what you would most like to have."

Vayu did not have to think. "I would like a *krar*," he said instantly. "Oh, sidi, that would be so wonderful—the best of all—if I could have a *krar* —please—"

So Claude bought him a *krar*—an Abyssinian banjo made of sticks and stretched skin—and Vayu took it and held it lovingly and plucked the strings and sang a song. And now Claude learned that, along with his brightness, he was musical too; for the strings twanged true, the voice sang true, and in the evenings thereafter, with the day's work done, they sat often together in the yard or on the balcony, while Vayu spun thin sweet music in the quiet darkness.

Once—only once—in the dark, the boy paused and his eyes fixed on Claude. "You too, sidi," he said. "I sing you the songs of Harar; so now you sing me the songs of the place where you come from."

But Claude shook his head. "No, I know no songs, Vayu," he answered.

"You are the *chansonnier*. It is for you to sing and me to listen."

The months passed. Rains came again. The days were not afire but gray and misty. The nights were cold but he was not alone.

In the hill country to the northwest—the long spur of the Abyssinian highlands known as the Chercher—there were stirrings of trouble. This was the borderland country between the Moslem Somalis and Danakils and the Christian Shoans and Amharas, and ever more frequent reports kept reaching Harar of raids and counterraids, alarums and excursions. These, to be sure, had gone on past all memory. They still held to the old African pattern: the surprise attack, the burned village, the dead (and castrated), the raped, the enslaved—to which, in times past, no one not immediately involved would have paid the slightest attention. But now their number and scale were increasing, and their significance too; for more was involved than mere tribal warfare. On the one hand, in the east, the growing pressure of European colonization along the Red Sea coast was driving the desert dwellers farther inland; and on the other, in high Abyssinia, the rivalry of the two kingdoms of Tigre and Shoa was raising both to a warlike ferment that spilled over in all directions. No longer was it merely tribe against tribe, but, increasingly, race against race, almost nation against nation. Up toward the hills swarmed the Moslem nomads, crying *"Allah! Allah akbar!"*—"Allah is great!" And down from them, black and savage, swept the Coptic warriors on their highland ponies, shouting the name of the Virgin—*"Mirian! Mirian!"* Ringed around them beyond the wastelands were the eyes of imperial Europe: of France, Italy, Germany, England—and Egypt, the pawn of England: watching, waiting, taking this side and the other: moving slowly closer, maneuvering warily into position, for their bid for the vast shining prize that was Africa.

Thus far, there had been no decisive battles, no invasion or conquest; and in Harar things went on as before. The Egyptian garrison kept order; the caravans came and went; the Moslem Hararis, accustomed to life in a city of mixed breeds, made trouble neither for the Abyssinian Coptic minority nor for the tiny Catholic flock of Father Lutz. But, roundabout, the violence spread, the rumblings grew louder. . . .

And in his palace on the square, the governor, Hajj Pasha, slapped his desk in anger, so that the rings clinked on his pudgy fingers. "So it has come to this now," he said to Claude. "Have you heard the latest report? Last week, in the village of Bulba in the Chercher, twenty Somalis were shot by Abyssinian raiders. Shot, mind you. Not speared or knifed, but shot. They have guns."

Claude nodded. "The march of progress. They are getting civilized."

"Civilized!" Hajj Pasha snorted. "A fine sort of civilization. The savages in the bush have guns, like a regiment, and we here in Harar, the representatives of the Imperial Egyptian Government, have barely enough to keep the hyenas from the walls. I write to Cairo. I explain, urge, plead. And what do they send me? Words, excuses, nothing. With nothing I am supposed to defend the city against all the savages of Africa."

"No, not with nothing, Excellency," Claude assured him. "I have just received a new shipment from the coast: some more linens, pâté, asparagus, cigars. Egal will deliver them this afternoon. And perhaps the pâté and asparagus tins can be melted down into bullets."

From the palace he went on, with a gift of cigars, to Hippolyte Lutz.

"With my congratulations, Father," he told him.

"Congratulations, my son?"

"To the church militant. On the Seventh Crusade. I hear our brothers from Abyssinia are killing the Saracens like roaches."

The priest shook his head sadly. "Yes, there has been new violence," he said. "It is a pity, a tragic shame."

"A shame? But we are winning, Father. The Shoans now have guns and bullets. Guns for Mirian. Bullets for the Lamb. They say the slaughter has been marvelous—"

"My son, why do you—"

"—and that there are now so many smoked Moslem testicles that they are a drug on the market."

The priest turned away. "When you are like this," he said gently, "there is no use in our talking. Please go now, my son. You had better go."

"All right, I will go, Father," said Claude. "And I hope you enjoy the cigars."

The fighting was only to the north and west. The caravans—Abou Dakir's caravans—moved back and forth unmolested between Harar and the coast, and the goods of Maison Gorbeau *(C. Morel, gérant)* moved with them. One day, however, a caravan that was not Abou Dakir's arrived in the market square; or, rather, the tattered remnant of a caravan, for all that was left of it were five loadless camels and two half-starved and terrified drivers. It had been attacked, the drivers reported, near the oasis of Biyo Kaboba; its proprietors, an Italian and an Armenian, both new to the desert, had been killed, along with the rest of the drivers; and these two had barely escaped with their lives and struggled on to Harar. . . . No, they said, there had been no cries of *"Mirian!"* Nor of *"Allah akbar!"* It had been a raid in the old style—for plunder. And the plunder had vanished into the desert.

It did not vanish for long, however. The next regular caravan from the coast was one of the largest in memory, and along with the shipments for Maison Gorbeau and the other usual local importers, was a great mass of crates and bales stamped *Manicotti & Gulbanian*. They had been bought, it was said, from one of the desert tribes. That tribe had got them, apparently, from a second tribe. And the second tribe—there were shrugs, outspread hands—who could tell? Some tribes were no better than *shifta* —bandits—and it had obviously been bandits who attacked the first caravan. The second caravan had kept a sharp lookout; they had feared bandits themselves. But they had met only the one tribe, a most respect-able peace-loving tribe, from whom they bought the merchandise—and that was all they knew. The rest was inscrutable, a mystery. A misfortune of the desert.

". . . Ah yes, a true misfortune," echoed Abou Dakir, dabbing at his pale eyes, when, a few weeks later, he came to Harar with his retinue and again paid a visit to Maison Gorbeau. "But alas, these two gentlemen, these *ferangi*, did not understand the hazards of the country. Africa is in ferment; the desert seethes with unrest; yet they were either unarmed, or, having arms, did not know how to use them. And so—" He shrugged like the others. Then he added: "But there is no need for me to tell you such things, Sidi Morel, for you are no longer a *ferangi*. You know the desert —Africa—the problems of trade and transportation."

"Say, rather, I am still learning them, Sidi Abou," said Claude.

"Very well, learning. But learning well." The old Arab looked around the store. "I see your shelves and bins are full," he said. "Your business prospers, I gather."

"It is all right."

"Good. Good. . . . And the caravan service: that is still satisfactory?"

"Yes, that is all right too."

"Good." Abou Dakir nodded. "We strive to please our customers, of course, but it is not always easy. As we were just saying, there are problems and hazards; such hazards as recently befell these unfortunate *ferangi*." He paused and stroked his bland beardless face; then took a silk cloth from his burnous and again dabbed at his eyes. "I have found myself wondering," he went on—and now the eyes fixed Claude steadily—"if you might not be interested in again trying your hand with the caravan trade."

"I?" Claude returned his gaze, curiously. "No," he said. "No, Sidi Abou, I think not."

"Your one venture was successful. You could be successful again."

"Like Manicotti and Gulbanian."

"No, not like them. You misunderstand me. I am not suggesting that you again become my competitor; that might be awkward indeed. I was thinking, rather, that something might be worked out on the basis of asso-ciation—of mutual advantage."

"Will you explain, please," said Claude.

"Yes, I shall explain. But first I shall go back a little. You will perhaps recall that when we first met, some eighteen months ago, I said I was favorably impressed by you. From the first reports I had had from Zeila;

from your management of your caravan. And your conduct since you have been here has impressed me too."

"Meaning that I have managed no more caravans?"

"Yes and no. If you had, it might, as I have said, have been awkward. And you know that. But I do not think—and here is the interesting thing, the important thing—I do not think it has been fear that has deterred you. No, from what I know of you, you are not a fearful man. You have courage, confidence, resolution. But you are also reasonable, and I think that is why you have acted as you have. You have come to a world that is strange to you, but you have not tried to change it to suit yourself; to change a continent and a civilization from what they are into what you might wish them to be."

"That," said Claude, "might present certain difficulties."

"Quite. Quite. Yet it is astonishing how many Europeans attempt it. The British are the worst, of course; they seem convinced that they have been divinely appointed to rule the world. And then there are the missionaries—of all countries. They are great ones, too, for prying into other people's affairs."

"I would not know, Sidi Abou, about either British or missionaries."

"No. That is my point about you: you are different. Your philosophy, I would say, is that of the East rather than of the West. One accepts life as it is and things as they are. What is, is—"

"What happens, happens—"

"Precisely." Abou Dakir paused. Then his pale eyes again fixed on Claude. "And now I shall get to the point of why I have come to see you. . . . You are a young man," he went on, "and I am an old one. Recently, for the first time, I have been feeling my age, finding my long business trips most fatiguing, and I have recognized the need of finding a younger man to travel in my stead and assume the supervision of my caravans. My thoughts turned first, of course, to my own sons. I have eighteen of them, of various ages and by various wives, engaged in family enterprises from Jidda to Zanzibar. But—it is not pleasant for a father to say this, yet I must—but none of them, not one, is capable of the assignment. I am a rich man, as you know; and they are a rich man's sons—soft, lazy, and incompetent. They could not conceivably direct such enterprises; nor, for different reasons, could any of the subordinates now working for me. And that is why I am here, why I have come to you: to ask if you would be interested in such an assignment."

"To run your caravans between here and Zeila?"

"No, not to Zeila. That is routine, easy; my assistants have been doing it for years. I am thinking of far greater enterprises: of my caravans to the south. You have seen them, of course, here in the market square, as they pass through Harar."

Claude nodded.

"And you have seen what they carry. Not grain or hides or coffee or such rubbish, but the true wealth of Africa. Ivory, gold, gems—"

"—and slaves."

"Yes, slaves. Of course, slaves. The greatest wealth of all: in their thousands, their millions—"

Again he paused. Claude said nothing.

"—the best, the most profitable of all merchandise," said Abou Dakir. "The only merchandise in the world that provides its own transportation. But hard to come by; for it must be hunted, you see—hunted skillfully, patiently, relentlessly—and there are not many men who are capable of this. I am one—which, if I may say so, is why I have been so successful. And you, I believe, might be another."

"In short, your are suggesting I become a slaver."

"Words, Sidi Morel, have different meanings on different tongues. If it will please you more, let us say you will still be a merchant, with an expanded inventory."

Claude shook his head. "I am afraid it is an expansion," he said, "that my employers would not approve."

"I was not thinking of your employers, but of yourself alone."

"Meaning that I should leave Gorbeau and Company?"

"Leave it—or devote only part of your time to it. From what I know of your work here, that would not be difficult. It is mostly routine, is it not? Bookkeeping and such, that an assistant, a clerk, could take care of."

Claude did not answer, and the old Arab continued: "This would still be your headquarters, your place of business, but you would make, say, one trip a year. To the south, the Ogaden, the Web Shebeli, and beyond: into the heart of black Africa. For your firm you would bring back gold, ivory, gems, whatever wealth you can find, and for me you would bring my particular form of wealth. At a generous commission. If you are concerned as to what your firm might say to this, there is no reason for them to learn of it; you will be a thousand miles removed from the prying eyes of Aden. Monsieur Gorbeau will get his gold, ivory, and the rest, in far greater quantities and more cheaply than he can get them here. I shall get what I want. And you will profit from both. Whatever you earn now in a year I promise you you will make tenfold in one trip to the south. And after a few years, a few trips, you will be one of the rich men of Africa."

Abou Dakir was silent. He waited. But still Claude did not speak.

"Well?" said the old man at last.

Once more Claude shook his head.

"You will not do it?"

"No."

"You are not interested?"

"No. Thank you, but—no."

"I was wrong about you, then. You are a true European after all. One of the reformers, the missionaries, the hypocrites."

"No," said Claude, "I am not one of them."

"What then?"

"Simply a merchant, Sidi Abou. A trader. A dealer in pots and pans."

"And that is all you want in your life? To deal in pots and pans? To be a clerk, a shopkeeper?"

"Yes, that is all I want."

"You are sure?"

"I am sure."

Abou Dakir rose. His retinue ranged itself for his departure. Then, for a long moment, he looked at Claude with his pale watering eyes. "Well, so be it," he said. "You are a strange one, all right—even stranger than I had thought. In my experience of men, and it has been a long one, there are two things that they crave above all others, and these are women and wealth. But with you, I see, it is different. Once, eighteen months ago, I offered you a woman, and you did not want her. Now I have offered you wealth, and you do not want it. . . . Well, I repeat: so be it. One must go on learning." He shrugged and smiled faintly. "Perhaps at last I have met a true dweller in the Garden of Allah—the man who wants nothing."

He preceded his retinue to the door, and there he turned. "Until we meet again, Sidi Morel," he said, bowing.

"Until we meet, Sidi Abou."

"My compliments."

"And mine."

"*Salaam.*"

"*Salaam aleikum.*"

The rains grew heavier, the nights colder. In the darkness, now, he no longer sat on the balcony or under the jacaranda tree, but in his little room above the store. The room was snug. Vayu brought firewood and cooked his supper, and, supper over, they sat together while the fire burned on, and he worked on his ledgers, and Vayu sang. When he raised his eyes the boy smiled, and he smiled back. And he thought: "No, thank you, I shall not become the nineteenth son of one Abou Dakir. I am no longer a son to anyone, first or thousandth: to a father-slaver or a father-engineer or a father-colonel or a father-who-is-God.

"I have moved up a peg, you see. I am a father myself."

Outside, the mist shrouded the rooftops, weaving like a gray sea between the minarets of the mosques. It hid the stars. It hid hillside and meadow. It hid plain and valley, desert and mountain, wrapping the city in a caul of stillness and peace. Up from the valley, across plain and desert, crept the long caravans of the damned: backs bloody under the lash, eyes rolling, knees buckling, the smallest and weakest falling at last, while the hyenas moved closer. In the mountains, and behind them, were the raids, the gunfire, the burning villages, the cries of *"Allah!"* and *"Mirian!"*—the cries of the wounded, the raped, the maimed, the destroyed. And beyond these, still farther, watching, waiting, were the newcomers, the *ferangi*, the barbarians of the north, with their boots and beads and Bibles and bigger guns, moving warily in toward bloody conquest. Africa trembled. Soon it would be convulsed. It would be no longer the black but the red continent —red with the blood of multitudes.

But in the city on the hillside it was neither black nor red, but quietly gray with weaving mist; and in the snug room above the store the embers glowed, a boy sang softly.

"Qu'importe?" asked Claude Morel. Of the eyes of the boy. Of the page of his ledger . . .

> . . . *what do they mean to us, my heart: the sheets of fire*
> *and blood, a thousand murders, the long caterwauls*
> *of rage and fear, sobs from all hell that echo through*
> *a world in torment?*
>   . . . *Nothing.*
>   *Le néant.*

Then he looked up and Vayu was watching him.

"You are writing, Sidi Claude," the boy said.

"Yes, I am doing the week's accounts."

"You said you had finished them."

"I made a mistake. I must do them over."

Claude tore the page from the ledger and crumpled it. The boy still watched him. Then he said:

"Please teach me to write, Sidi Claude."

"To write? Why?"

"I should love to know. Please show me how."

"And if you knew, what would you write, *hein?* Tell me that."

Vayu considered. "I would write words," he said.

"Yes, words. Exactly—words. And what good is that? Words are for speaking. *Good morning. How are you? I am hungry. I am thirsty.* It is when words are written that the trouble begins."

"Trouble? I do not understand, sidi. Father Lutz has said that—"

"I do not care what Father Lutz says. Are you living with him or with me?" Claude blazed with sudden anger. "Words, words, words. They are lies—poison. Do you hear me? Poison!"

He rose, and Vayu shrank from him. Then, as suddenly as it came, his anger faded; he put a hand on the boy's shoulder and smiled; and he said, "I am sorry. Forgive me. I am upset tonight—perhaps the mistake in the accounts. Go on now, it is late. It is time we slept."

But long after Vayu had gone he sat alone in the room watching the dying fire. Its glow faded, it went out. He sat in darkness. But still in his mind he saw it, and the mind's fire did not die; it swelled, it brightened, it blazed; it was no longer the fire in a hearth but the fire beyond—the great fire, the world fire, the fire of war, of rage and fear, of sobs, of slaves, of murder, of burning villages and the mouths of guns. The fire of blood. . . . *Cry blood! Blood and the golden flame!* . . . He heard the voices, howling: "Princes, lords, tyrants, perish! Evil dies, God prevails! *Allah—Mirian —liberté—vive la Commune!*" He saw the charging hordes, the armies, the warriors; the warriors with guns, with spears, with knives, with clubs, with fire; the bearers of fire, the *pétroleurs*, the freedom fighters. He saw the boy with his torch and his can of benzine; the barricades, the burning buildings, the fires of freedom. Liberty and equality, equality and fraternity, fraternity and blood, blood and the golden flame—to save the earth, to save mankind, for God, for righteousness—and on the pavement, in the flame's bright gleaming, the blood dripping dark from the mouth of a child.

He had seen them then, and he saw them now. Murdered and murderer. The hero-assassins. The flame of glory and the flame of hell . . .

And the other flame, too. The pure. The inward. The flame of Prometheus, of the thieves of fire. That too he had known, nurtured, cherished, borne in glory and pride: the flame of word, song, image, dream, creation. . . . Or so he had thought. . . . But that too had been lie and illusion: a lie that led not to the heights but the depths. To the cave and the tomb. To death. To hell.

Both flames were out. The fire was dead. He sat in darkness. In the darkness, later, he lay on the cot in the quiet room, and he thought: "So I have left hell. I have made my pact with Satan and with God, and they have let me out. Or what is left of me. The I-who-was, who was another, is perhaps still there, a corpse, a shell, in the niche of his tomb; but the I-who-am, remains, has found a niche at last in the world of men. In my niche I am content. I exist. I am. I am alive—a man. A man of stone, perhaps, of fragments broken and reassembled. But still alive, a man—*for a' that*.

Life and death were not absolutes. There were degrees of each. Once he had been too much alive; he had wanted too much, dared too much, aspired too greatly; aspired to the highest and lowest, to the star and the slime, to alpha and omega, to godhead itself. And that, of its own essence, in its overextension of life and life's powers, had become not life supernal but a sort of death. Now he had forsworn all that. He had turned away; withdrawn into his niche, his shell, his sheath of stone. And in so doing, in coming halfway to the blank, the void, of death, had found at last a sort of twilight life. Most men, to be sure, lived their lives exactly so. Neither in the blaze of noon, fired by a golden flame, nor in a night of stars between the gulfs of space, but in the twilight, the gray marches, the pale dim world between, without glory, without blackness, without tumult or vision. And now he was one of them.

> Seen enough . . . known enough . . . dreamed enough.
> Now to see no more, know no more, dream no more.
> Now to be one with the crippled and blind.

With the boy, Vayu, who could not read nor write. With the Hararis, mumbling, "As Allah wills. What happens, happens." With Egal and Ahmed, heaving their bales; with Hajj Pasha eating his pâté; with Marcel Rappe wiping his pen points. With all ant-men, sheep-men, pig-men, ox-men, fox-men everywhere: the laborer with his load, the clerk with his figures, the merchant with his cash drawer, the soldier with his gun. "I am your brother, Dirk Uden, of His Dutch Majesty's Colonial Forces, who crossed the earth, unseeing, unknowing, to find in the mud of Java a dreamless death. I am yours, all pawns, all slaves. And yours, too, all masters of slaves: Abou Dakir, Sergeant Houttekamp, Feldwebel Gunst and your tribe—sergeants and captains, generals and emperors—who suck your strength and your lifeblood from the weakness of others. I am your brother, messieurs les fonctionnaires, les assis, on your calloused rumps, with your files and stamps. And yours, old friend Michel, in your shrewd thousands, with your francs and your centimes. Even yours, priests and hierarchs—Father Lutz, Father Lacaze, and the rest of you, with your bishops and popes, your beads and your bromides—for I too have now sold my soul to the godlets of conformity and closed my eyes to the visage of God. I am brother to you all, in your twilight, your blindness. And most of all, I am brother at last to you, my blood brother, Felix. Felix the Happy, the Wise: the Zero, the Cipher. I salute you and I join you. With you, each day, I rise, I eat, I sit, I grunt, I itch, I scratch, I swear, I drink, I belch, I yawn, I sleep, I snore. Yes, come to me, Felix; take my hand; we are brothers, men together. For if this is what makes a man, I am a man."

> . . . a man a man a man a man. Behold the man:
> Ecce homo!
> No, Father forgive me:
> Ecce homunculus . . .

He closed his eyes. He slept. (Perhaps he snored.) There was no fire now, no blood or golden flame, but only the quiet darkness of the room, the niche, the snug cave in the night and the mist. Then from the night outside there was a sound. There was the thump of feet on the steps leading up from the store; then a thumping on the balcony, and the door opened, and Felix came in. There was light now, and he looked around and said, "Good, the old bitch isn't here."

"And you are not either," said Claude.

"Oh yes I am." Felix belched. "You called me, didn't you? So I came. Damn nice of me, if you ask, but I'm glad of the chance." He sat down on the edge of the bed. "About that list of yours, I mean," he went on. "It was very interesting—yes, *mon brave*—very homey, down to earth, all of that. But, I must point out, with an omission. There is one other little thing, you see, that makes a man."

"Go," said Claude. "This is my room. Go and leave me alone."

"No," Felix answered, "you are wrong. My brother the genius is mixed up. This is no longer your room, but ours, and we share it together. Just as, according to you, we share our activities."

His thick lips grinned, his small eyes glinted. And now they were no longer both on the bed, but only Felix, and Claude was watching him from across the room.

"So we shall share," said Felix amiably. "It will be a privilege to assist in the education of my little brother, the genius."

"No," said Claude. "No."

But Felix laughed and said, "Yes, *mon brave*, yes." And then he clapped his hands and called, "Hey, my girl, we are waiting." And the door opened, and a woman came in. She was a barmaid, dressed in black, with a full voluptuous figure, and she carried a tray on which were two glasses filled with a green glowing liquid. "Ah, that's my girl, my little peach, my own true sweetie," said Felix happily. Then to Claude: "You see how nice it is; how friendly and cozy. There are those, alas, such as our sainted mother, who do not approve of barmaids; who would prefer us to have a duchess or at least the daughter of a fashionable plumber. But from them would you get such service, such amenities?" He took a glass and raised it. "Come, my boy, my dear brother the genius—a drink together. A toast to the one little thing you forgot that makes a man."

He drained his glass. Claude did not move. Or at least he did not seem to move; but the other glass was in his hand, it was raised, it was empty. He felt the absinthe deep within him, glowing, coiling, and Felix grinned and said, "Fine, that's my boy. Now the preliminaries are done and we can pursue the main business of the evening. I hope my instructions and demonstrations will be clear to you, and you may feel free to ask questions at any time."

He turned to the woman. He gestured. He sat on the edge of the cot, with his knees spread, and the woman approached and stood between his knees, and he closed them and held her. He raised his hands and held her for a moment at the waist, and then his hands moved slowly over her black dress: first upward, along her back, then over the shoulders, stroking, kneading, and down across the breasts to her belly and thighs. The woman's dress was tight. Breast and thighs bulged beneath it. She did not move, but stood straight and stiff as the hands moved over her, and Felix said to Claude, "Observe, please, the mechanics of the first phase. She is unaroused, passive, in fact rather dull. In this phase considerable patience and muscular energy are required of the gentleman, but results, as you shall see, are gradually obtained."

His hands moved on. They stroked, lingered, probed, moved on again: from belly to thighs, from thighs to buttocks. And now gradually, as Claude watched, the woman changed. Her head went back, her eyes closed, her breathing became deeper. The body that had been stiff and still began itself to move; at first gently, almost imperceptibly, with a slight rhythmic undulation of arms and legs; then more and more actively, and in all parts, in shoulders, breasts, belly, thighs, buttocks, until the whole of her flesh under the clinging dress quivered and writhed to the touch of the hands.

"Now further observe, please," said Felix, "that we are entering a second phase. She is now interested, aroused, feeling a certain pleasure; but of course far from satisfied—and here again one must give certain assistance."

The woman's movements became more violent, her writhings a barbaric dance. Her back was arched, her pelvis thrust forward, and her breasts swelled as if about to burst from their restraining sheath. . . . Then they did burst. . . . With what seemed a single sudden motion Felix ripped the sheath away, and they were bare. Another motion, and thighs and belly were bare. The woman stood naked before him, dancing, writhing, as if in the act of coitus itself. Then Felix pulled her down, and she was on the cot beside him, and they held each other; and now her eyes were open, dark and smoldering, her mouth was open, tongue crimson, teeth bright and sharp, and with her mouth she sought him, with her hands, her arms, her thighs, her secret flesh. And Felix turned and said to Claude, "Now, you see, things have progressed a bit. Now we are in the grip of what is known as lust."

Claude stood motionless, rigid. The sweat poured from his body. With all the strength that was in him he tried to move, to turn, to wrench himself away and run from the room into the mist and the night. But he was held transfixed. And Felix went on: "It is a simple word—*lust*—little brother: of only four letters and one syllable, comprehensible even to geniuses. It should not, let me point out, be confused with that other word of four letters and one syllable, also beginning with *l*, which is properly

used in reference to mothers, dogs, children, and God. Lust is applicable
only to the relationship between the sexes, and leads only to one act. The
act which you absent-mindedly omitted from your list of what makes a
man.

"Any questions? . . . No? . . . Well then, to proceed—" Felix turned back
to the woman. "You will note, please, that various changes have taken
place in our companion. I do not mean only the obvious ones of costume
and behavior, but more subtle changes as well. When she appeared, for
instance, she was a specific woman—my wife. She had a name—which,
I regret to say, happens to be Bertha. Her hair was brown, her eyes hazel,
her skin a bit sallow, and, as perhaps you noticed, she had a small mole
on her right cheek. But now, please observe, all these features are gone.
At least to you. To me, perhaps, she is still my wife, called Bertha. But to
you she has no name, no identity—or any such as you may wish. She is
Aphrodite, perhaps, or Madame Pompadour. A French farm woman or
an Italian signora. Her name is Mimi or Kuru or Cosima. Or Germaine.
That is a nice name, don't you think? Germaine. Most *distingué*. But it is up
to you. . . . As is the rest. . . . Her hair, for instance: what is it now: brown,
black, or blonde, or light chestnut? Her skin: sallow or pink or milky
white or black as Africa? Her eyes: hazel, brown, black, gray? Or perhaps a
magical deep violet-blue?"

Felix rose from the cot. The woman lay there. "Now I have played my
little part," he said, "and she is yours. Yours as you wish her. The Virgin
Bride, the Fairy Princess, the Whore of Babylon, the Nigger Queen. She
is all of them. She is Maya. She is woman, sex, flesh. And you lust for her."

"No," said Claude. "No—" His voice was a whisper in the stillness.

"Yes," said Felix. "Yes. . . . You are a man, are you not? At last a man,
like the rest of us. And if you are a man you lust: that is the First and Great
Commandment."

"No, I do not. . . . I cannot. . . ."

"Rubbish! *Merde!* Come on with you. None of your damn prudery; this
is all *en famille.*" Felix pulled him toward the cot. The woman waited. Her
arms were out, her legs spread. Her flesh waited. "She is not mine any
more," said Felix. "She is yours. I brought her for you. For my little brother
the genius, who is now a man. For *le beau gosse*, for mama's darling, who is
now a man a man a man a man a man. . . ."

Claude trembled. Again he tried to turn, to break away; but Felix held
him, pulled him on. "Come!" he ordered. "Forward, *gosse*—there's man's
work to be done!" . . . Then he stopped. "*Mon Dieu*," he said, and his voice
had changed. "How stupid. Now It is I who am doing the forgetting. . . . I
have a gift for you, brother. A little gift that is quite important."

He let Claude go. His arm went to his side, then up again, and Claude
saw the glint of steel, the blade, the long curve of a Somali knife. . . . Then

the knife was gone. Felix stood motionless. His arms were outstretched, his hands cupped, and in the cup he held his offering.

"A little gift," he said, "for the mama's darling who is now a man." Claude did not speak. He did not move.

"Take them," said Felix.

"No . . . No . . ."

"They are yours."

"No . . ."

"Yes, yours. Look. Look down at yourself, brother, *and you will see.*"

Claude did not look down, but at his brother's hands. The hands were close. The face was close. The face had changed. It was contorted. It was laughing. Felix was laughing, and his laughter rose and swelled until it filled the room, the stillness, the darkness, the night around them. . . . And then it faded, receded, it was gone, he was gone. . . . And in the night, presently, there was another sound, another voice, and the voice said, "Sidi, Sidi Claude, what is it? What is wrong?"

In the tent in the desert it had been Egal. Now it was Vayu. He held a lamp in his hand, and Claude rose from the cot.

"What is it, sidi?" the boy repeated. "You are sick? There is something the matter?"

"No," said Claude. "No. I am all right."

"You called. You cried. . . . You were dreaming, perhaps?"

"Yes, dreaming."

"And perhaps heard the hyenas?"

"Hyenas?"

"They are loud tonight outside the walls. They are howling and laughing."

"Yes," said Claude, "perhaps I heard them."

There was a pause. He stood motionless. Vayu watched him.

"But you are all right now, sidi?" the boy said.

"Yes, all right."

"It was only the dream?"

"Yes."

"You are sure? You are not sick? It was nothing else?"

"No, it was nothing. Nothing."

28

But it was not nothing.

The dream recurred. Felix returned. And the woman. The terrible dream-woman of his boyhood.

He struggled against her, strove to exorcise her. But still she came. She mocked him with her flesh, with her desire—and with her violet eyes. She held out her arms, and he approached, and she vanished, and again, as in his boyhood, he awoke spent and trembling in the night.

He heard Felix's laughter, receding.

He heard the laughter of the hyenas.

It was a thing beyond his control—and his understanding. For most men, he well knew, sex was an imperious master: a need, a hunger, as strong as that for food. But for himself it had been different. Since those dreams of his adolescence, since the shame and misery of his early failures, he had been free of its dominance, in his life and his dreams alike. In the wild years, the mad years in Paris and London, it had not been sex that drove him—not the perverted desire of a Druard—but his very lack of desire; his pride in his difference, his contempt of man's bondage to woman. And when, later, after his fall, his black season in hell, he had sought out Germaine of the violet eyes, it had been because she, among all women he had known, seemed to offer not flesh but spirit, not the bondage of lust but freedom and peace.

So he had thought. So he had believed. . . . But why then, now in his exile, did desire rise like a monstrous specter? Why did the violet eyes watch him, mocking, from the face and flesh of a rutting whore?

He could not answer. It was Felix who answered. "Because you are at last a man," he said. "And if you are a man you lust."

But what of a man who knew lust without fulfillment? Who knew it only in dream—alone?

His real world, his daytime world, was womanless. In all the years since he had walked for the last time away from Paris he could recall only two occasions when he had actually been with a woman—the day in Aden when he had had tea with Madame Gorbeau; the night in the desert when he had bought the dying slave girl—and both were now far in the past. In Harar he knew only men. The few women who came into the store were veiled featureless figures who appeared silently, bought pins or a pot or a strip of yard goods from Egal or Vayu, and vanished as anonymously as they had come. And the women elsewhere were anonymous too: nameless, faceless, without feature or identity. They were shapes passing in the street, seen fleetingly in a courtyard or on a balcony, sealed off in a world of their own; a world so remote from his that, like the world of Europe, it could as well have been on a planet of Fomalhaut.

Or so, too, he had thought. . . .

Until the change began. Until the dreams began. For with the dreams there now came a change that was not only inward but outward, and for the first time he was conscious of the women of Harar. Of their movements, their voices; of the bodies beneath bright skirts and bodices; of silver bangles on dark arms and throats; of dark eyes watching him through colored veils. It was a new awareness, strange and disturbing. And as uncontrollable as his dreams. Part of the reason—true, if unacknowledged—why he had come to the Moslem world was that it was a world of men, with women hidden and sequestered, and thus, for long, he had found it and lived his life as he wished. But now that he had changed, it too had changed—or seemed to have. For there were women everywhere. Half of Harar, as of mankind, were women. And he alone, among the men of the city, moved among them as an alien, a stranger.

Other men lived with women, lay with women. Thought of women, talked of women.

Abou Dakir had come to offer him a slave girl, shrugged when he refused her, and gone his way—presumably to various of the mothers of his eighteen sons. Egal had discoursed for his benefit on the comparative merits of slave girls and prostitutes, and, finding him uninterested, now went off on his own in the evenings in quest of one or the other. As did Ahmed the Somali. The merchants, Mardik and Spiranthos, each had a Harari wife and a brood of mongrel children. And Hajj Pasha, the governor (whose three wives had remained in Egypt), was known to have six concubines, who followed each other in palace residence in business-like weekly rotation. Where there was a man there was a woman—or women; perhaps hidden, unseen, but still there; waiting in the palace, the house, the hut, the brothel, for the man to come to her; and the man came. The coffeehouses closed. Footsteps faded in the streets. The doors of the city closed, and the lights went out, and in the darkness man and woman lay together as one. Only he was womanless, with his pen and his ledgers. With Vayu and his *krar*. With himself and his dreams.

Even Vayu was turning from boy into young man. In the store, Claude would notice him talking and joking with the younger women who came in, and in the evenings, sometimes, he would sit with a girl in the courtyard under the jacaranda tree. Then the time came for another trading trip into the countryside, and Claude took Vayu with him instead of Egal. With their mules and merchandise they moved from district to district, and one day toward evening, as they approached an outlying village, they passed a stream at which a woman was drawing water. There was no one else there. She was alone: a young Somali woman, bare to the waist, with soft brown skin and mane of ebony hair; and as they went by she raised from the stream a leopard-skin bucket, swung it onto her head, and walked away. She walked slowly, with grace, her body tall, straight, and slim. And the setting sun shone on the bucket and the raised arm that held it, on her hair and shoulders and bare body, on the firm breasts and pointed nipples, turning her flesh to rich gleaming gold.

The mules clopped on. But Vayu had stopped; he was staring. And Claude stopped beside him, questioningly.

"The woman—" the boy murmured.

"Yes," said Claude, "I see the woman."

"She is beautiful."

"Yes—in the sunset."

"She is the most beautiful I have ever seen. A queen, a sultana. . . . Oh sidi, you must have her!"

"Have her?"

"Yes, for yourself. You have been too long without a woman. It is not good for a man—not right."

Claude smiled. "You are an expert on such things, *hein*, little one?"

"I am not so little. I am a man myself—almost. I know that every man needs a woman. . . . Yes, you too, sidi. You are lonely, I have seen it. That is why you cry out at night: because you are lonely and need a woman." Vayu looked again at the slim golden figure. "Such a one as this," he said, eyes shining. "So fine, so beautiful—"

"We have let the mules get ahead," said Claude. "Come on. They are almost to the village."

"Yes, we go to the village." The boy grew excited. "There we will find the woman's family and buy her. Did you see, sidi?—from the way she wears her hair she is not married. Her family will sell her for only a few knives, or some cloth and beads, and you will have a woman more beautiful than any in Harar."

Claude did not answer, and they walked on.

"You will do it, sidi? Yes? You will buy her and take her home?"

Claude shook his head.

"No?" The boy's face fell. "Why? Why not, sidi? Why do you not want so beautiful a woman?"

"Because I have no use for her."

"No use? Oh sidi! When I am bigger—a whole man—"

"—then I shall buy her for *you*," Claude told him, smiling. "If she is not, by then, a grandmother."

Vayu chattered on. They reached the village. They sold cloth and cutlery, bought coffee and hides, and when their trading was done they pitched their tent beyond the village, ate their evening meal, and slept. In the night Felix came and brought the woman. Her skin was still golden, but her hair was now chestnut, her eyes violet-blue. And Felix laughed and said, "For a few knives, *mon brave;* for some cloth, some beads." . . . His laughter grew louder. . . . Then Vayu stirred and said, "The hyenas are close tonight, sidi. I will go out and see to the mules."

They moved on. To other villages. To the west and southwest. Skirting the spurs of the Chercher, they came to the borders of the Galla country, a land of plains of blue distance. The rainy season had ended, and the sky was cloudless above them, but the earth was still green and watered, fecund, thrusting with life. It was the season of beginnings, of growth, of nature's myriad procreation. The cattle mated in the fields, the wild game in the brushland, the birds in the trees, the very flies in the dung on the trail. And it was the same in the world of men, in the Galla villages: tiny clusters of human life, mating, breeding, repeating the endless pattern of generations, unchanged and untouched by the centuries. In one to which they came there was a mass wedding in progress; in another, a ceremonial of circumcision; in a third, a nightlong orgiastic dance with frenzied drumming to the tribal gods of seed and fertility. Sex and worship were one; sex and sustenance; sex and life. Even sex and death. In the Galla burial grounds, beyond the villages, tall carved stone phalluses rose in ranks from the earth, symbols in death's own purlieus of the dream of life everlasting.

They moved on: through the world of beasts, through the world of men. And everywhere there was the thrust of life—and of the phallus. It was neither brain nor heart that the African warrior cut from his enemy and hung as trophy and talisman from the walls of his hut; neither brain nor heart in which resided man's ultimate function. The god of life was Priapus, and the purpose of life was his service. . . . "Yes, it is thus," thought Claude. *"Ecce homo.* Behold the man: the creator; the seed sower. Man, who can never die because he carries within him the gift of life beyond life." . . . And, with Vayu, he moved on. Back to Harar, the store, the room, the days and nights. In the nights Felix came. He brought women. He brought the gift of life. He laughed.

"Ecce homunculus. . . ."

Dear Mother:

As an experienced businesswoman, you can perhaps advise me on certain problems of inventory which I find bothersome. I have been keeping one record (A) of items of merchandise as they enter the store and another (B) of over-all sales. But in my monthly checkups I often find discrepancies and am wondering if by keeping a third record (C) of stock on hand at certain regular intervals I could substantially reduce the margin of error.

Dear M. Gorbeau:

You will note from the accompanying statement for M. Rappe's attention that gross income in the past quarter has increased by some 6 per cent, and I trust this will please. Also that expenditures have been somewhat reduced, owing to the fact that my Somali warehouseman has left and I have not found it necessary to replace him.

He himself did the work of the departed Ahmed, heaving crates and bales, unloading caravans, helping with all the hard and menial work in warehouse and courtyard. It had been his hope, at first, that this would tire him to the point of sleeping soundly and dreamlessly. But it did not work; the dreams still came. And presently he found it having the contrary effect of his sleeping scarcely at all. His dealings with buyers and sellers, plus the added physical labor, now took up the whole of his days, so that all of his bookkeeping was done at night, beginning when Vayu put down his *krar* and went to bed, and continuing often until the sky grayed in the east. At most, he slept two or three hours of the twenty-four; and now at last he no longer dreamed. For the dreams, he had discovered, did not begin until he had been asleep for some time, and he had managed the trick of forcing himself awake before they seized and held him. Felix still came—or tried to come. His steps sounded on the stairs, the balcony. He opened the door of the room. But in that moment Claude defeated him. He woke. He rose. He went on to the next day's work in store and warehouse, and the next night's with his ledgers.

"It is not good, sidi," said Vayu. "You work too hard. You are tired and will be sick." But he did not feel tiredness. Only a gray wakefulness. Only the gratefulness of a man from whom a fever has ebbed at last, leaving coolness and peace.

"Peace," he thought. "*Salaam. Salaam aleikum.* I have found the peace of the dweller in the Garden of Allah."

My garden has high walls. They shut out dreams. They shut out visions. They shut out earth and sky, ocean and continent, life and life's burden, man and man's fate. They shut out slaves, masters, raids, wars, tumult, glory, the golden flame. They shut out woman, and the need of woman; all that I do not need or want— and my wants are few. I shall make a new list for you, my brother Felix: my NOT- LIST. *To wit . . . I do not dream. I do not think. I do not read. I do not write. I do not hunger. I do not thirst. I do not lust. I do not covet. I do not hope. I do not fear. I do not laugh. I do not weep. . . . This time, is my list complete? If not, perhaps it will be soon. Soon, perhaps, behind my walls, I shall do nothing; not even work. I shall need and want nothing* (with a salaam to Abou Dakir). *I shall* BE *nothing. And then I shall have reached the shrine in the heart of the garden.*

When the time came for the next trip into the countryside, he sent Egal and Vayu. He remained in Harar, in the store. Indeed, he now scarcely so much as left the boundaries of Maison Gorbeau; his world was the shop, the office, the warehouse, the courtyard, his room. In the evening, with the day's business done, he would sit for a while under the jacaranda tree, and then, when darkness came, go up to his room with his ledgers and close the door. Only occasionally did he sit out on the balcony, as he had used to: looking across the roofs of the city, watching its lights wink out, listening to its night sounds—a distant song, a whisper, the slap of sandaled feet in a hidden alley, the baying of dogs on the ancient walls. And the city's walls were not so high as the garden's. He could see beyond them: to the plains, the wastes, the valleys, the tiering mountains. Above, he could see the stars. And under the stars, just beyond the city, the other lights—dim, yellow, moving; moving like glowing disks, circling, watching, as the hyenas kept their vigil in the night.

Nor were the city's walls so stout as the garden's, for often the hyenas breached them. Singly, or in pairs or small groups, they would find an opening and enter, and Claude would see them in the streets and the square: silent slope-backed shadows prowling about the slave pen on the square's farther side or nosing at the gates of his own closed courtyard. He did not shoot at them, for they could not get in; and besides, they were performing their age-old accepted function of consuming the filth and refuse of the city. Nor did he shout, to frighten them away. He merely watched them, silent and unmoving, until they felt his presence and raised their heads and watched him too—ears cocked, teeth bare, eyes burning yellow—and then at last they moved again, they turned, they slipped away and were gone; and only then, when they were gone, when there was nothing left but stars and stillness and the sleeping city, did he hear the shriek of their laughter flowing back to him through the night.

They came under the stars. They came through the mists. Then a time arrived, in the season of rain and mist, when they came differently, and for another purpose. An epidemic swept the city, a wave of fever and convulsion; and it was both nameless and uncontrollable, for there was no hospital in Harar, no doctor or nurse or modern medicine—nor even a knowledge, among most of its people, that such things existed. Prayers rose to Allah, and incantations to older darker gods. Charms and amulets were turned in febrile hands. But the hands grew weaker; the sickness spread; death was everywhere. Those who were not stricken were too busy, or weak, or fearful, to bury the dead, and, following ancient custom, simply laid them out in street and alley, while the governor decreed a sunset curfew and the opening of the seven gates in the night. So again the shadows came, with the glinting teeth, the yellow eyes; but this time not furtively, not in small bands but by the swarming hundreds, filling the darkness of the city; and in the morning the streets were bare, the dead were gone.

What happened, happened. If there was no hospital, neither was there a morgue. . . .

But toward evening of the next day Father Hippolyte Lutz appeared at Maison Gorbeau, his broad face pale above his beard, his robed bulk heaving with agitation. "Now they are not only putting out the dead," he said, "but the sick as well. There are hundreds of sick lying in the streets."

Claude shrugged. "It is their way here. They are afraid of the sick."

"But it is barbarous, murderous. We cannot simply stand by and do nothing."

"No? What then?"

"We must work through the night. Get at least as many as possible off the streets."

"So that tomorrow they will be dead one way instead of another?"

"So that we shall at least have done what we can. As civilized men. As Christians."

"I am neither civilized," said Claude, "nor a member of the cult you refer to . . ."

But in the end, with another shrug, he accompanied the priest. And through the night that followed, with Egal, Vayu, and some of Lutz's small flock to help them, they moved through the dark city; among the shadows, among the yellow eyes; wielding clubs, hurling stones, searching out the still living from among the corpses and carrying them to the safety of the Maison Gorbeau courtyard. . . . Or to safety, at least, from the hyenas. . . . But not from death. For once they were there nothing further could be done for them, and by morning, as Claude had foretold, they too were corpses, stretched in stiff rows beneath the jacaranda tree. No one, of course, came for them. There was neither place nor means for burial. So when night returned they were back in the street. . . . And, the next morning, gone. . . . Not only their flesh gone, but bones and nails and hair and clothing as well; with only the skulls left, and a few buckles and bracelets and silver amulets; and then, in their turn, human scavengers came, and all that remained were the skulls.

Claude turned away. He went back to the courtyard, the warehouse, the store. But with the epidemic still raging no one came to the store, and toward midday he closed it and went up to the balcony with his ledgers. Sitting cross-legged on his folded rug, he entered a column of figures; turned a page, entered another; turned again . . . and then the change began. First it was the page itself that changed. The day was dull and sunless, but the paper seemed to glare as if in brilliant light. The ruled lines wavered, the figures blurred and merged, and the pencil moving over them felt thick and heavy in his hand. The hand, too, felt thick, and he could not control it. It was sweating and trembling, all his body was trembling, he was filled with fever; and this time it was not the fever of dream but of the flesh, of blood. The pencil fell from his hand, the ledger slipped from his lap. He tried to rise, but could not, and instead fell back on the rug; and then the rug was spinning, his head was spinning; a wave of nausea swept through him, and he retched and vomited. But still he could not get up. When the convulsion had passed he lay limp and strengthless. Where nausea had been there was now numbness and torpor, and the glare of the paper had dissolved into dimness and shadow. It was no longer only his hand that felt heavy and thick, but the whole of him—body and limbs and lips and tongue and eyes—and his tongue could not speak, his eyes could not see; the very blood was thickening in his veins, filling, flooding, drowning him, and he seemed to be sinking in a warm dark sea.

He did not wholly lose consciousness, but neither could he wake nor move. Only the sea moved, around him, within him, and he wallowed in its flow like a derelict—a Drunken Boat. Time stopped. Time raced. And it was the same, for there was no time. There was only the sea. Through its vast tide, later—an hour, a day, a week?—he heard sounds; he heard voices. He was being moved. Hands touched him. Then the hands were gone. Or if not gone, they were different; they were the hands, not of men, but of the sea; and the hands moved him, rolled him, lulled him, drew him down and down into blackness.

He lay in the slime of the sea's bottom. In the sea's deep hidden night, alone. Then he was moving again; the sea bore him upward; where blackness had been was weaving shadow and twilight, and then the twilight brightened, it glowed and shone, and the sea cast him up into the eye of the sun. He was on a beach, a beach of sand, on the sand of a desert, and the sea was gone now and there was only the desert, and he moved on across its wastes, under the flaming sun. It was as if the earth itself, the day itself, were on fire: a caldron of heat and light, an intolerable blaze of illumination. It was around and within him: a golden flame. And the flame consumed him; consumed his flesh and bone and blood until there was nothing left—no body or mind or heart or soul—nothing; and yet not nothing, for he himself was left; a thing of fragments, of ashes, of burned blackened stone—yet *still* himself—moving on through the wastes to his destination.

And now at last the desert, too, was behind him. He came to fields, meadows, forests, and followed long roads through the countryside. He came to cities and entered them, following their thousand streets through the days and nights; and then the cities were behind him and he was on a road again; on a road by a yellow river, and he entered a town. Here, too, he walked the streets, he sought the end of his journey—the familiar street, the house, the store, the room above the store, his house

and home. But it was not there. The house had become a farm and was
somewhere else, and he could not find it. He found instead a park, called
the *Bois d'Amour*, and it was full of people, of men and women, of boys
and girls, and they called to him, but he did not answer; he still went on;
and beyond the park was a forest, and beyond the forest a garden, and now
he entered the garden and closed the gate. He examined the walls and
found them wanting, and slowly, patiently, he made them stronger, filling
their chinks with bales of merchandise, raising them higher with stacks
of ledgers. Then the wall was firm, solid, impregnable. It shut out the sea
and the desert, the fire and the fever. No man could now breach it—and
no woman. He moved toward the heart of the garden, and at its heart was
a shrine.

At the shrine he rested. He waited.

He watched the day fade and the night close in, and with the night
came the stars. And now he knew that he had been wrong, that his wall
was not impregnable, but could still be breached from beyond. For it was
not high enough to shut out the stars; nor thick enough to hide the other
lights, closer than stars—close, yellow, and gleaming—that now moved
slowly, silently in from the darkness around him. The wall had changed. It
was torn, crumbling, broken. It was no longer a wall at all, but a ruin, and
through the ruin the lights approached in a great circle; the long shadows
drew nearer. Still he waited. He thought, "No, there is no wall, no refuge
or sanctuary. Now, as they come for all men, they have come for you."

. . . And they came. They were close now. They shouldered in through
the darkness over the broken wall; their circle narrowed and tightened;
and now, finally, they were no longer shadows but the beasts themselves
—the night-comers, the destroyers. He saw the pointed ears, the muzzles,
the fangs, the glowing eyes. Of the wolves of the Ardennes. The hyenas
of Harar.

He heard the sound of laughter.

But it was not the beasts' laughter; they made no sound. Nor was it
Felix's, for he was far away. It was the devil who laughed. And now Satan
sat beside him on the shrine's crumbled stones, as he had once before,
long ago, on the stone streets of Cambon, and he said, "So we meet again,
my friend. My friend, the brother to wolves and hyenas."

Claude did not speak, and Satan's laughter rose. "For you are yourself
wolf and hyena," he shrieked. "Remember? Do you remember? You are
not a man but a hyena, and now at last you have returned to your beginnings, and your own kind has come to claim you."

Then the laughter faded. The devil was gone. Claude waited—alone.

And he thought: "Yes, of course—alone. As you have always been. In
the sea, the desert, the forest, the towns and cities. On the roads you have
traveled so long and so far, and now at last at roads' end in the shrine in

the garden. Alone, you have made your journey; alone, you have reached its end; and in the end you *know* the end—know what it is you have been seeking."

He looked up. He saw the eyes of death. He saw the eyes move closer. ... But he did not flinch. He was not afraid.... Fever had long since drained from him: the fever of blood and flesh, and of dream, and of life. Hope and despair, anger and fear were gone from him, and he was calm, he was at peace; he put out his hand to death and welcomed it; he spoke to death, saying, "I am ready. Take me. Accept me."

He touched death; seized it, clung to it—as if to a hand. And the hand seemed to be drawing him onward. It drew him through darkness, through the forest, through the sea, through fire—into the yellow eyes of fire—and the eyes were upon him, above him . . . a face was above him: the face of death . . . and then not of death: another face . . . the face of Hippolyte Lutz, broad and bearded, bent above him, and beside it the face of Egal, the face of Vayu.

"His eyes are open," a voice said. "He is waking. He is better."

"Yes, he is better," said another voice. "The fever is broken."

Claude watched the faces. He watched them for a long time in silence. Then a third voice spoke—faint, remote—and it was his own.

"Vayu is crying," he said. "What is the matter? Why is he crying?"

"He is crying because he loves you," said Father Lutz, "and now he knows that you will live."

Vayu was there through the nights and the days. Egal came and went. The priest came in the evenings and sat by the cot.

"I suppose it's all owing to your prayers," Claude said to him.

"No." Lutz smiled. "Oh, I prayed a bit, I admit; you couldn't very well stop me. But no, it was not prayer that saved you."

"What then? One of your saints, perhaps? It wasn't the devil, I know that."

"It was God's will." The priest paused for a moment. "And your own," he added. "I have never seen a man with so strong a will to live."

On his next visit he brought fruit and soup. He had prepared the soup himself, and, while Vayu heated it, described in detail its compounding from sundry admirable ingredients. "Like the potion of a witch doctor," he said cheerfully, "—which is what you think I am anyhow."

While he fed Claude (and, at intervals, himself) he talked of happenings in Harar, of the epidemic that was now over, of the war in the hills that was not over, of the comings and goings of caravans—and finally, again, of soup, specifically oxtail soup, and how much better a place northeast Africa would be if it contained some good sound Alsatian oxtails. "But you have seen these sad zebu cattle," he said disconsolately, as he emptied the soup bowl. "In a whole herd, *mon Dieu*, there is not tail enough to nourish a weaning infant."

Claude rose from the cot. He sat on its edge, stood up, crossed the room, and went out on the balcony. A buzz of voices rose from the store below. A caravan was unloading in the courtyard, and from wall to wall the enclosure was filled with crates and bales, with camels and mules and horses and moving men. Beyond the walls, the square, too, was filled. The crowds flowed through the market, around the stalls, past the governor's palace, in a tide of color and noise and stench and teeming life. The epidemic was over. The dead were dead, the living living. The sound of the living beat with a din on Claude's ears. The sun, hot and glaring, beat on the stones, the dust, the stalls, the swirling tide of the crowds and struck back into his eyes with blinding brightness.

He returned to his room. To its stillness and shadow. He sat again, motionless, on the edge of the cot, and there he still was when, in the evening, as usual, Father Lutz made his appearance.

"Well," said the priest, "the patient is up. He makes progress."

Claude did not answer.

"He is well again. Whole, sound, alive."

Still Claude said nothing, and the priest sat down. Usually he met Claude's silence with a flow of casual volubility, but this time he too sat silently for several minutes, watching him fixedly with bright brown eyes.

When at last he spoke again, it was to say one word, and he spoke it quietly. The word was "Why?"

Claude looked at him.

"Why are you alive?" said Father Lutz. "Why did you struggle with all your will and might to live?"

Claude looked away.

"*Why?*"

The priest waited. Then he said, "You had thought you wanted to die, hadn't you? But you were wrong. You wanted to live."

"No catechism please, Father," said Claude.

"Yes, the time has come for a little catechism. And if you won't answer me, my son, I shall answer myself."

Again he paused. And Claude said nothing.

"Very well," said Father Lutz, "I shall tell you. You lived because you are filled with life. And I am not speaking of your body. I am speaking of your mind, your heart, your soul—and they are on fire with life."

Claude looked at him again. In the brown gauntness of his face his eyes were cold and opaque. "I will thank you, Father," he said, "to leave my soul to myself. You know nothing about it—or me."

"That is not true," said the priest.

"What do you know of me?"

"I know what I have seen and felt since you came to Harar. And now I know what I have heard while you lay sick in this room."

"Heard? What did you hear?"

"You had high fever, my son. You were delirious. In your delirium, it so happens, you talked much more than is your habit."

"What does that mean? It was the talk of fever—of dreams."

"It was in fever, yes. It was in dream. But it was *you*. The you you once were—and still are, beneath your shell."

"I see. And what, may I ask, is that?"

"It is many things, my son; but one thing above all others." The priest paused, and his eyes bored into Claude's. "I know now that you are a man of letters," he said. "A writer—a poet."

"Now it is you who are delirious."

"You deny it?'

"Yes."

"What are you then?"

"A merchant, a trader."

"A merchant of Illuminations, you mean? A trader who sails the seas in his Drunken Boat?"

There was a silence. Then Claude rose.

"That is enough, Father," he said. "You had better go now."

"No," said the priest, "it is not enough. And this time I shall not go."

"Then I shall."

Claude moved toward the door, but Lutz, rising too, held his arm. "No, you will not go either; you will hear me out. For once in your life you will listen to someone." He pushed Claude back onto the cot and stood before him. "Even if that someone is a priest—and you hate priests."

Claude made as if to rise again. But he did not rise. For a long moment he looked up at Lutz, then bowed his head and sat motionless and silent.

"I do not mean to pry, my son," said the priest gently. "Nor to cause you pain. But such pain as I can cause is, I am sure, as nothing to what you cause yourself. . . . You are a man of mind and spirit: I have seen that from the beginning. And now I know more as well. That you are a man of great learning, great vision; a writer and poet—"

"I was a writer once. Back in France. Long ago."

"But no more?"

"No, no more."

"The boy, Vayu, tells me that he has seen you writing. That you write often, here in this room late in the night."

"I write my ledgers. I keep my accounts."

"And that is all?"

"Yes."

"Vayu says it is not all. He is not educated, but he is very bright; he can tell figures from words. And he says it is not always figures that you write. That you write words—often many pages of words—and then stare at them a while and tear them up."

Claude did not answer.

"Why?" demanded Lutz. "Why do you tear them up? Why are you afraid of writing?"

"I am not afraid."

"Yes, I think you are. And not only of writing but of many things. Of life itself. It is plain in all you have done since you have been here in Harar. In all you have *not* done. In the way you have sealed yourself up as if in a tomb."

"You call this store a tomb? It is crowded from dawn to night."

"I am not speaking of crowds. I am speaking of *you*. However many people you see, you still have no true contact with them, and you know it. You have shut yourself away from them too. As you have from your writing, from your true self—from everything. Like a hermit in his cave—"

"Or perhaps a Trappist in his cell?"

"Yes, I remember our little joke about Trappists. And Zoroastrians. But there is something, my son, that *you* have not remembered. The Trappist mortifies only the flesh, to cleanse the spirit. You have not cleansed your spirit. You have only strangled, starved it, tried to kill it. . . . And even in that you have not succeeded, have you? For what you thought you had killed is still there: your own self—what you truly are—under the shell, the mask, in which you try to hide."

Claude had turned his head away. He did not seem to be listening. But the priest persisted:

"Has what you have just been through taught you nothing?" he asked gently. "You had reached the point where you held life to be worthless and meaningless; yet when the epidemic came—when the sick lay in the streets and I came asking for your help—you gave me your help. You risked your life to help others. . . . And then later, when you yourself were sick. . . . You had thought you wanted to die; that there was nothing left for you but death. Yet when death came close you fought for life. You did not sink down into your tomb, but rose up from it. You became again a poet, again your true self. . . . No, do not deny it. I was here beside you; I heard you. It was not I who saw the light of your Illuminations or followed golden birds in a Drunken Boat. . . . You were a poet again. Alive. On fire with life. It was not death you sought, but the very sources of life—your youth, your home, your family, your identity. All that you really are, and have renounced and fled."

Lutz paused. Claude said nothing. Then the priest said:

"Speak to me, my son. It will help you. Tell me what it is that you have fled from; that you fear. Tell me about your life before you came here. About your work, your home. Your mother and sister."

Claude's eyes met his.

"Yes," said the priest, "you dreamed of them. You were trying to find them. . . . Your sister is a nun, is she not?"

"Yes."

"And your mother—"

Claude was silent.

"She too is a deeply religious woman, I gather. Pious, stern, righteous. Because of that, you turned from her—but still you need and seek her. As, later, you turned from others—first from women, then men, from all your fellow beings—believing you were sufficient to yourself, but still needing, still seeking them. As you have turned from life, from love, from the source of love that is God Himself."

"So we have come at last to God," said Claude.

"Yes, of course, my son—we have come to God. Where else should we come but to the end and the beginning?"

"The end and beginning for you, perhaps. For me, the beginning is birth and the end is death."

"And there is nothing more? There is no God?"

"There are many gods. Have you heard of Allah? Have you heard of Yahveh? Have you heard of Zeus, Jupiter, Odin, Mithra, Brahma, Ra, Ahura-Mazda, Baal, Osiris? Within a hundred miles of Harar there are enough gods to supply one for every day of your life, without repeating."

"And these, to you," said Father Lutz, "are all the same?"

"Yes."

"The same as the God of whom I speak? The one true God—our God the Father?"

"There is no—"

"Stop!"

Lutz's voice had changed. It was harsh and strong. "Stop, my son," he said. "I will not let you say it. Not because of myself, but because of you; because you do not believe it. *You believe in God.*" He paused, his eyes fixed unwaveringly on Claude's, and when he resumed his voice was again low and gentle. "That, too, I have seen in you. In your life here. In your sickness and fever. Within yourself you are a man of faith, a seeker of God. I would guess that few men have ever sought him with more will and more longing. . . . But then something went wrong, did it not? Somewhere along the way you strayed; you erred, you sinned. Was it the sin of pride? I rather think so. And pride brought you not to strength, as you had hoped, but to weakness. To misery. And in your misery you turned on God—as you have turned on men, and on yourself." He paused again and put a hand on Claude's shoulder. "I am not preaching to you, my son," he said. "I shall not speak of confession or absolution or the sacraments of the church. In a way I am speaking not even as a priest, but as a man, and all I ask is that you allow *yourself* to become a man again; to open your mind and heart to yourself and your fellows. And then again you will find your way back to God's love and mercy."

"I have never seen His mercy. I have never known His love."

"No? What was it then that sustained you in sickness and fever? That filled you with the strength to fight back from death to life?"

Claude did not answer.

"What was it, if not His mercy, that held out a hand in lonely darkness? What, if not His love, that you saw when you opened your eyes? . . . Do you remember what you saw? You saw a face; the face of a boy; of Vayu. And Vayu was crying. He was crying because you had lived, and he loved you. And in that love, my son—of man for man, of soul for human soul —is the core and essence of the love of God."

Still Claude was silent. Lutz was silent. Then, presently, he rose.

"I shall go now," he said. "I should like to stay and pray with you, but I know you would refuse; so I shall go and pray alone. I shall pray that you may open your heart to God's mercy and love. That you may open it to your fellow men. To yourself." He went to the door, and there he turned, made the sign of the cross, and added quietly: "May the blessing of God Almighty, the Father, and the Son, and the Holy Ghost, descend upon thee and remain with thee always. Amen."

Then he was gone. From far away—beyond the house, the square, the walls, the city; beyond the miles and years—there was a faint sound, as if of laughter. A voice called, *"Merde. Merde aux pretres. Merde à Dieu"* . . . receding, fading. But in the room there was only stillness and a man alone, head bent, in the gathering dusk.

A week later he left the room. He went to work. He moved among men: in the store, the warehouse, the courtyard, the square. He rejoined the living. And the sun did not blind him.

At the end of the first day's work he was tired and went early to bed. And he slept, but did not dream. In the nights that followed, too, he slept early—and did not dream. Sometimes in the darkness he awoke and went out onto the balcony. He saw the roofs of the city, the minarets, the stars, and under the stars, beyond the city wall, the dim sweep of the land. On the land, as always, there were moving shadows, yellow eyes; and often they moved inward, circled the walls, breached them, and shadows and eyes then prowled through the city streets. They came into the square, approached the gates of the courtyard, stopped and listened, looked up at him. . . . But now they were hyenas, animals: that was all: the filthy, familiar scavengers of Harar.... *"Fous le camp!"* he shouted down at them. And the shadows ran, the eyes vanished.

There was no dream, no fever, no visitation in the night. It was as if a final fever had burned the dreams away. As if death, in touching him and then receding, had lost its power and given him back to life.

"The sickness was good for you, sidi," said Vayu, smiling. "You are better now than before. You are stronger and happier."

And it was true. Or almost true. For if happiness—or what men meant by it—was a chimera that would forever elude him, he was at least slowly groping his way up from the pit of nothingness. He worked as hard as before. But work was no longer a drug: it was work, and no more. Before, the people with whom he dealt, the visitors to Maison Gorbeau, had been merely figures, faces, voices, with no identity as human beings; but now, for the first time, he began truly to know them; to talk with them, to listen, to share in the casual give-and-take of daily living. From the beginning, in Harar, he had thought of himself as not a *ferangi*, since he spoke and dressed and lived as did the people of the city. But it had been an outward, superficial thing; inwardly he had been wholly the *ferangi*—the stranger, the outsider—as he had been through all his life to all men everywhere. Only now, at last, did he begin to feel a strange and subtle difference: a kinship, a community of interest with others, a consciousness that he was not wholly an exile behind the walls of his apartness, but a human being among his fellows, a man among men.

Death had touched him. He had thought that he was waiting for it, that he would embrace it when it came. But he had not embraced it. He had fought and defeated it.... Father Lutz had been right: he had willed to live.... "Why? *Why?*" the priest had asked him, and then moved on, inevitably, to talk of God. But if it had been God's hand that had drawn him up from the pit of darkness, it had been a human hand as well—a hand warm and strong and living. It had been human faces to which his eyes had opened. A boy's face; and the boy had been crying.... "Do you remember that?" Father Lutz had asked. And the answer was, yes, he remembered. And would remember forever.... In all his dreams, all his visions, that was one thing he could never before have imagined: that a fellow being would cry for him. That a fellow being could love him.

Was it possible that he at last could love in return? Or, if not love, at least give something of himself; put out *his* hand to others?

He tried.

... During the hours of work, with those who came to the store. In the evenings, with Egal and Vayu. Then the evening came when, instead of going to his room at the usual hour, he left the store and crossed the square, and following one of the streets, came to the entrance of a coffee-house, and there he turned and went in. The place was crowded, full of smoke and voices and clinking cups and brown faces, and the faces turned to him, staring in surprise. But then they smiled; the Hararis welcomed him, and for an hour he sat among them, drinking coffee and talking. A few nights later he went again, and stayed longer. He ate his dinner, dipping his fingers with the others into a great bowl of stewed mutton and onions. Later, the water pipes were passed around, and he took his turn —and burst out coughing. The Hararis laughed and thumped his back. "You are not used to it, Sidi Claude," they told him. (For now they called him Claude.) And he said, "No, it is a long time since I have smoked—and never from a hookah."

He took to walking again: around the city, through its alleys and byways, watching the life that swarmed in them, stopping to talk at shops and stalls. Then, one day, he found himself passing the store of the Greek, Spiranthos, and there too he stopped and went in. He had no business to transact. He simply visited for a while, chatting about this and that, and then went on his way. A week or two later he was invited, and went, to a party celebrating the marriage of one of Spiranthos' numerous daughters. He called on Mardik, the Syrian merchant, was invited to dinner —and stayed.

Every month or so, Hajj Pasha, the governor, held a reception of sorts in his palace, and now for the first time Claude attended one. The pasha's concubine of the week, a half-westernized Somali who was not in purdah, made an appearance, and he talked with her for several minutes. And he talked, too, with the occasional women who came shopping to Maison Gorbeau.

Then there was a night on which he stood in a narrow street beneath a balcony, while dark eyes looked down at him and a voice called softly. He did not answer. For several moments he did not move. Then he entered a door, climbed a stairway, and came to a dim, thickly carpeted room in which there were perhaps a dozen women, unveiled and wearing only flimsy shifts, sitting on piles of cushions along the walls. All looked at him. All smiled. Then an older woman, in the usual Harari dress, appeared and said, "Welcome, Sidi Morel. *Salaam aleikum.* We are pleased that after all this time you pay us the honor of a visit."

Some of the women were fat, and some thin. Some were black, some brown, some almost white, and in their features were all the racial strains of Moslem Africa. Yet what distinguished them as a group was not variety but likeness: each with oiled hair, scarlet lips, and kohl-painted eyelids; each cast in the stylized mold of their ancient trade. Claude had never before actually been in a brothel. But he had seen prostitutes by the countless thousand; he had once, even, long ago, been a pimp on the streets of Paris; and for a moment it almost seemed to him that he was back there . . . or on a street in London, under the gas lamps, seeing the painted and empty face of a whore called Fanny. But then he was again where he *was*. In Harar. In the room of carpets and cushions. And the madam was leading him respectfully around the circle of the women; and she was saying, "Would you like this one, honored sidi? . . . Or perhaps this one? . . . Or this?"

They completed the circle. And she said, "So, which one will it be?"

He did not answer at once, but looked back around the circle. Then he answered, "None. No, I think none—thank you; not now."

"None, sidi?"

"Not tonight—no. Another time—"

"My girls are good ones. They are young, skillful, clean."

"Yes, I am sure. I shall be back. Tonight I merely stopped in to—" He hesitated. "To see for myself," he said. "To get acquainted."

The woman was baffled and disappointed. But she remained polite. "Ah, I understand," she said. "To get acquainted—yes, of course."

"So goodnight." He went to the door. "And thank you."

"You are welcome, honored sidi. And I hope you will come again."

"Yes. Yes, indeed," he said. "I shall come again."

He went out. He walked the streets. But not in flight; not in fear or fever. "All things in their good time," he thought, smiling inwardly. And he walked on, slowly, until he reached the house of Father Hippolyte Lutz; and there the priest looked up at him in pleased surprise and rose quickly to welcome him in. "I thought I would finally accept that invitation to play cards," said Claude. "But, first, I'm afraid, you will have to teach me."

So Lutz taught him to play bezique, and in the weeks that followed they played on many evenings, sometimes at the priest's, sometimes at Maison Gorbeau. As on the night when they had first dined together, Lutz usually took off his robe, and he laid his rosary with its wooden cross on the table beside him. On the wall above them, when they played at his house, hung the larger cross, with the white waxen figure. But he looked neither down at the one nor up at the other. Nor did he speak of crosses or Christ or the church or any part of religion, but only of deals and points and aces and kings, and how, if Claude's luck was as good in business as in gaming, he would shortly be the wealthiest man in Africa. With one big brown hand he slapped the cards down. With the other he tugged at his beard. He laughed at his triumphs, moaned at his defeats and demanded vengeance. The priest was lost in the cardplayer. Only once, when a game had ended and they were saying goodnight, did he speak, for a moment, personally, putting a hand on Claude's shoulder and saying gently, "Well, it is good to play, is it not, my son? Relaxing for the body, the mind, and the soul." Only at long intervals in their games did Claude look up to find Lutz studying him with his bright brown eyes.

Again they dined together. Once—twice—then often. Claude ate well and drank Lutz's homemade wine. One night he again brought the priest a box of cigars, from a new caravan shipment, and this time smoked one himself—and coughed, as he had with the hookah. Lutz smiled, puffing contentedly on his own. "Vice comes hard to you, eh, my son?" he said. "But do not despair; with practice one becomes a master."

Usually, Claude met him only in the evenings. But one day, passing Lutz's house, he glanced in through the open door and saw him seated at his table, surrounded by a group of Harari boys. Lutz waved and called him in, and for an hour he sat by while the priest conducted a class in the Arabic alphabet and simple arithmetic. And then, when the boys had gone, he stayed on for a while, and Lutz talked of his teaching problems: of the lack of books and materials, of the pupils' lethargy, of the suspicion and hostility of their parents and, even more, of the city's few Moslem teachers, who believed that all knowledge worth possessing was to be found in the Koran.

"Whereas we enlightened ones know," said Claude, "that it is in a book called the Bible."

"Alas, I cannot use the Bible," Lutz said. "The one condition on which I am allowed to teach to Moslem boys is that I use no Bible at all."

Claude left. But a few nights later, when next they met, it was he who broached the subject again.

"In these classes of yours," he asked, "you give no religious instruction?"

"No, none," said the priest.

"No Bible, no lives of saints? No hymns or prayers or catechism?"

"No."

"But only lay subjects?"

"Yes."

"Then perhaps you can use an assistant," said Claude. "I am not, as you know, too bad at languages, and I could come for, say, an hour each afternoon."

Lutz beamed. He took Claude's hand. "I cannot tell you how glad I would be," he said. "For my pupils, for myself—and for *you*."

So Claude went to the priest's each day and became a part-time schoolmaster. And inevitably, before the first week was up, Vayu begged to be taken along.

"You mean you are not satisfied," Claude demanded, "with the fine education I have already given you?"

"Education, sidi—?"

"At the Lycée Morel. Where you were the prize pupil and won your *krar*."

Vayu did not answer. His face was sad, his eyes puzzled.

And Claude smiled and said, "All right, come along then." And Vayu went with him, delighted, to the priest's.

He did not, however, go for long. For he was so much brighter than the other boys, so far ahead in interest and capacity, that after a few weeks he was no longer learning anything in the classes, but merely sitting by and waiting for the others to catch up. "So we shall have to withdraw you," Claude told him, after talking with Lutz. Then added, as the boy's face fell: "But other arrangements have been made through the courtesy of the Board of Education. The Lycée Morel will again go into business—with a revised curriculum."

He himself still went to the priest's for his hour a day. But now Vayu stayed home. And in the evenings, when the store was closed and they had had their supper, teacher and pupil sat together on the balcony in the light of an oil lamp, and Claude opened the gates of the world to the boy's seeking mind. Already, in the classes, Vayu had learned the fundamentals of letters and numbers, and now quickly they moved on to reading and writing, to more advanced arithmetic, to the elements of geography and history, language and science—indeed to anything and everything that Claude was able to teach him. The boy's curiosity was boundless. He asked questions by the hour. He practiced his writing and his sums. But above all, as his capacity grew, he loved to read. The only book generally available in Harar was the Koran, and this he and Claude read through together, chapter by chapter, verse by verse. Then Claude wrote to Aden asking for other books; but they would be long in coming, and meanwhile Vayu was avid for more. "There are no more," Claude told him. "Not in all of Harar." But Vayu knew better. The next day he left the store on his own, returning in due time with a thick blackbound volume, and that night they began reading from one of Father Lutz's Bibles.

"It is rather neat, rather nice, don't you think?" said Claude, when he next saw the priest. "—That what is forbidden to you is permitted to *me*."

He prepared himself, warily, for the questions Vayu might ask—about the meanings of Christianity and the functions of the church—and resolved to answer as straightforwardly as he could; without piety, to be sure, but also without iconoclasm. He could have saved himself his concern, however, for the boy's thoughts were far from either faith or theology, and his pagan mind accepted the Scriptures, as it had the Koran, without probing their religious content. His questions, his interest, his excitement were for the text itself: for its stories, its images, its phrases, its words. He was as enamored of words, as drunk with words—with their meaning and form and color and texture—as Claude himself had been, years before, as a boy of his age.

"I had thought words were just sounds, sidi," he said. "Sounds that you spoke—sounds that you heard. But these are different. They are like—" he paused and groped, "—like something alive," he said. "So strange and so strong—"

And Claude nodded and said, "Yes, Vayu, that is true. Words are strange. Words are strong."

For he too, as they read, felt again the power of words; the magic, the alchemy that had once ruled his life. As a boy, to be sure, he had found no magic in the Bible. That alone, among all books, he had despised and rejected, as the book of cant, of priests, of hierarchs; the book of the mind's enslavement; the book of his mother and her cold and sterile piety. He had hated the Bible, feared the Bible.... But, now, no longer. Now hatred and fear were gone. For he was no longer that boy, but at last a man.... With Vayu, in the quiet nights in the Moslem city, he read the Scriptures as he had once, long ago, read the poets, and he saw now that these too were poetry, filled with vision and dream. Alone, after Vayu had gone, he sometimes sat and read on, and the spell of reading filled the emptiness of the long years of fear and flight.

Once, late in the night, the boy awoke and came to him and found him sitting in the yellow lamplight, his hands clasped on his table, his head bent to the open pages.

"You are praying, sidi?" the boy asked, as he looked up.

"No, not praying," he answered. "Only reading."

"You do not ever pray—like the saints?"

"No, I do not pray."

But when Vayu had gone he smiled. He let his fancy roam. Getting pencil and paper, he sat for a while, musing....

AUTOBIOGRAPHY (*Revised Version*), he wrote.

And then:

I am the saint at prayer ... on the terrace ... like beasts grazing down to the sea of Palestine. I am the scholar of the dark armchair. Branches and rain beat against the casements of the library.

He went back to his journeys.... *I am the walker of the highroad through the dark woods. The roar of rivers covers my steps. I see for a long time the melancholy golden wash of the setting sun.*

And still farther.... *I am the child abandoned on the jetty, gone out to the high sea; the* mioche *following the lane whose forehead touches the sky.*

The path is rough, he wrote. *The hills are covered with scrub. The air is motionless. How far the birds and the springs are! This can only be the end of the world—Ω—going forward.*

Forward...

From alpha to omega,
From omega to alpha.

He did not destroy what he had written. He wrote again the next night. And the next. And now, truly, it was as if a tomb had opened—the tomb of his belly, where the dead were buried; the tomb of his mind, his heart, his spirit—and the words flowed up. The images, the visions, flowed up.

He was no longer a shell of stone filled with ashes, but a living being: in his outward life at last a man among men, in his inner self again a writer, a creator. Almost every night now, after his reading with Vayu or his games with Father Lutz, he would sit down with pencil and paper and write without fear or inhibition: impressions of the day, imagined conversations, snatches of verse, whatever came to his mind. Rewriting the notes on Harar which he had once torn up, he decided that, when finished, he would send them to the *Société de Géographie* in Paris. He might even send off a poem or two: to—what was the name?—Messieurs Boniface et Fils ... (*you will recall me perhaps, gentlemen, from your great success with my earlier works*). ... Or to Herz and his *Nouvelle Revue*. Or to Chariol. And his wife. ... For the first time in years he allowed himself consciously to think of such things—and such persons. Of their faces, their names. Of the name of Germaine.

Fear was gone. The deathly emptiness was gone. Now he could think of the past, and it was only that—the past, that was gone—with no power to hurt him. He could live under the sun, through the day on fire, without fever; in the dark, through the night alone, without the whisper of death. He could look with clear eyes past the walls of his exile to the deep violet-blue of the evening sky.

He had found life again. He had found the beauty of living. It was not the beauty he had sought before—the *être de beauté* of his Paris days: the core, the essence of beauty, beyond human grasp, rending and shattering, that had led him to the edge of madness and the pit of hell. This was a beauty of the natural world; free of fever and darkness; calm, serene. The beauty of sunrise, of dusk, of the stars at night. Of the wide African land, its green valleys, its purple mountains. Of the tawny lion in his pride, the bright leaping gazelle, the great flights of birds through the sky above the city. And of the city itself on its hillside; its ancient stones, its streets, its towers, its homes, its people. Above all, of its people. Of the tall Somalis with their spears, the Gallas with black skin and silver bangles, the veiled Harari women with their dark liquid eyes, the brown Harari children with their shouts and laughter. Human beings, he now saw, were beautiful: man, woman, child, all of them: in their flesh and their spirit.

To live.

To love.

They were the same. He knew that now. And he knew now, too, that the source of all his failures, all his sorrows, had been his inability truly to love another human being. He had been alone, always and forever alone, in his rebellion, his struggle, his flight, beneath the shell of his apartness. He had lived his life alone, gone down toward death alone, and only at the very moment of death had a fellow man reached out his hand to him, and he had reawakened to life, a new vision of life—to eyes that wept tears for him because he was loved.

That was why—now, at last—he in turn could reach out his hand to others.

He worked until sundown; then he left the store. He went to the coffee-house, and there he drank, smoked, and talked with the men of Harar. Later, in the street, he came to the house of the balcony and the watching eyes, and as he passed he waved and smiled, thinking, "Soon. Yes, this too —soon. One night, not far away, I shall go in again, and this time stay, like other men." . . . But on this night he went on. He went to Father Lutz's. For two hours he stayed there: playing bezique, sipping wine, talking, laughing, slapping cards on the table, and in the end winning two piasters which he put in Lutz's poor box. Walking home through the silent streets, he felt within him the glow of the wine, the glow of companionship—and then beneath them, deeper, stronger, the glow of word, of image, of the writer's magic, the poet's vision; the glow of mind and heart that was the source and wellspring of all life.

The store was dark. Egal was out. But upstairs, as always, Vayu waited for him, and since the night was cold he had made a fire in the room. Often, at this hour, they read together, but tonight they did not read. Instead, they simply sat together before the fire, and Claude felt its warmth softly mingling with the warmth within him; and then Vayu took his *krar* and strummed it, while he sang the sad sweet songs of old Harar. Claude closed his eyes, and the fire-gleam touched his lids. Then he opened them, and in the gleam was Vayu, singing. The light touched his moving hand. It touched his arm, his shoulder, his throat, the smooth brown-gold of his young body—the body slim and strong and lithe—and the touseled hair, the singing lips, the cheeks, the eyes. The eyes as deep and gentle as the eyes of a fawn. The eyes that had wept for him. That now met his own and smiled.

He reached for pencil and paper. The boy sang on. And he wrote:

> *It is repose in the light,*
> *neither fever nor languor,*
> *on a bed or a meadow.*
> *It is the friend, neither violent nor weak:*
> *the friend.*
> *It is the beloved, neither tormenting nor tormented:*
> *the beloved.*
> *Light, and the world not sought. . . .*
> *To live.*
> *To love.*

He put the writing aside. The singing had stopped. Vayu was watching him. The firelight seemed no longer to come from beyond but from within him. He was part of the fire, child of the fire; child of the sun and moon and stars, of all light everywhere; and Claude felt the light, he leaned toward it, he reached out to it, he touched it; he touched the glowing flesh, the warm bright living flesh. He caressed it gently. . . . And then he spoke.

"Dear boy," he said. "Dear boy—"

The words hung in stillness.

In firelight.

Vayu did not move, for a moment Claude did not move. Then he withdrew his hand. He stood up.

"What is it, sidi?" the boy asked. "What is wrong?"

He did not answer. He stood motionless, looking at Vayu; and Vayu, too, rose—and backed slowly away.

"Sidi—sidi—" he said. "What is it—what has happened, sidi? . . . Your face—your eyes—sidi. . . . Your eyes. You are sick again. . . ."

Claude wheeled and went to the door. The boy called after him. But he did not turn. He went out onto the balcony and down the stairs and through the courtyard into the market square. Crossing the square, he entered a street beyond, and for the rest of the night he walked the streets. No one was abroad. The city slept wrapped in darkness. Only the hyenas were not asleep: prowling the darkness, following him, circling him: watching him steadily with their yellow eyes.

Through the stillness, from beyond the walls of the city, came the shriek of distant laughter.

29

The walls were down again, the shrine crumbled, and the eyes watched through the broken stones. In the night there were again the steps on the stairs, on the balcony; then the opening door; but now it was no longer Felix who came—nor a woman. It was Druard. He put out his hand, and the hand was white in the darkness, and he said, "Dear boy, I have come. You have called me at last, and I have come."

The walls were down. But now not only in sleep and dream. Through the days, too, the eyes watched him, the voice spoke to him, the hand reached out white and dead from the past; and he knew that, however far he had fled, through the miles and the years, it had yet not been far enough. For miles and years were not the only measures of man's journey. He had not gone back, in his flesh, to the world of his youth. And no man could go back through time. But he had returned none the less, within himself—in permitting himself again to think, to feel, to write, to come alive—and the mouth of hell had reopened to receive him.

He groped again through hell. The hell of self. The hell of solitude. And now his outward life underwent still another change. He let Egal and Vayu run the store. He did not go to the coffeehouse or to Father Lutz's, or indeed into the streets at all, and when the priest came to Maison Gorbeau he would not see him. He did not even turn to his ledgers—to the old familiar drug of bookkeeping. He did nothing. He sat alone.

Vayu brought him his evening meals, but he scarcely touched them.

And the boy said, "Sidi, what is wrong? You are sick again. I can see."

"No, I am not sick," he said.

"Then why do you not eat?"

"I am not hungry."

Then Vayu left, but later he came back. And this time he asked, "We will read tonight, sidi?"

"No, we will not read."

"Then I shall play the *krar*."

"No. No *krar*."

"But sidi—why—what is it? It is weeks now since we have read or—"

"So it is weeks," said Claude. And he lashed out with sudden anger. "Stop bothering me. Go—do you hear me? For God's sake go and leave me alone!"

The boy recoiled. He left again, hurt and uncomprehending. And Claude sat alone. All through the night he sat alone on the balcony, watching the sky, the stars—the bright star Fomalhaut blazing in the south —and when it faded, when dawn came, he rose at last and went downstairs through the store and out into the square. From the square he took the street to the southern gate of the city, and when he reached it the gate was opening for the day; and he went through it and down the hill and across the countryside, bearing south and then east toward the mountain Kondudo. For the first time in more than two years he climbed Kondudo, and for a long while, again, he sat on its flat summit, on the top of the watchtower of Harar, looking off to the south; looking at the streams, the green valleys, to the land beyond, toward the great plains, the great sky; from the edge of the civilized world to the world beyond.

The next day he spoke to Egal.

"You now run the store well," he said. "As well as I do."

"Thank you, sidi," said the little Arab.

"So for a while I am going to let you run it alone."

"You mean you are going away?"

"Yes."

"As you have before—to the villages?"

"No, not to the villages. This will be a longer trip—much longer. To the south."

"The south?" Egal looked at him in surprise. "But how can you, sidi? How is it possible? Everything to the south, and from it, is by way of the caravans of Abou Dakir."

Claude nodded. "Yes, I know."

"He is more jealous of that than of any other route. And you remember what happened when we came here from Zeila."

"I remember."

"But you will risk it and go anyhow?"

"Yes, I shall go anyhow," said Claude. "But the risk will not be so great as you think."

Again he closed himself away. He sat alone. He waited. And when, a few weeks later, Abou Dakir again appeared in Harar, he went to see him.

"*Salaam. Salaam aleikum,*" he said to the old merchant. "I have come to ask if you are still in need of a nineteenth son."

He wrote to Gorbeau:

> *The time has come, I am convinced, for us to extend our range still farther: into the area, south and west of here, the true heart of Africa. It is there that the real wealth of the continent lies: gold, silver, gems, ivory, the hides of strange beasts, the plumes of strange birds—all of untold potential value in the markets of Europe. Thus far, as you know, I have been able to buy such items only in small quantities and at the high prices charged by Arab traders. But now the opportunity has been presented for me to go south myself, and by the time you receive this I shall already be on my way. During my absence the store will be in charge of my assistant, Egal, a competent and trustworthy man, and routine business will proceed as usual. I shall write again immediately upon my return, with what I am confident will be an extraordinary report. But just when that will be it is of course hard to say.*

And to his mother:

> *I am about to leave on an extended business trip, and it may be some time before you next hear from me. When you do, however, it will, I think, be with a remittance many times the amount that I have thus far been able to send you.*

He assembled his trade goods.

He conferred with Abou Dakir.

For such a trip the caravan would be a large one: many times the size of that in which he had come up from the coast. There would be eighty camels and mules. There would be sixty men—Arab, Somali, Galla, and various combinations thereof. There would be sixty guns, twenty cases of ammunition, and enough staple foods—flour, salt, coffee, sugar, and the like—to supplement for several months what they would shoot and forage on the way. Still, the animals, on the outward journey, would be lightly loaded, for the only other considerable item would be Claude's trade goods. In the old tradition of African commerce, the bulk of the caravan would carry merchandise in only one direction.

In charge of the transport—and of certain specialized operations —would be one of Abou Dakir's old hands: a tall, somber, and scar-faced Arab named Houreh Nasruddin. But Claude was to be in over-all command, with the power of decision in all major matters and the respon-sibility to Abou Dakir for the success of the venture. He would, in fact, exert every effort to insure that success, not only in his own interests but in Abou Dakir's as well. And in return, he (and/or Gorbeau & Company) would be granted free transportation, all necessary protection, and a one hundred per cent commission-free title to all goods acquired through his own trading and enterprise. A contract was drawn between them. It was signed and sealed. And the old Arab nodded and dabbed with his silk cloth at his watering eyes. "So good fortune to us both, Sidi Morel," he said. "You are the only *ferangi* I have known whom I would dream of trusting with such a project; and I hope you will find it more profitable than your recent sojourn in the Garden of Allah."

Soon all was ready.

For the last time he reviewed with Egal the details of the store's opera-tion. He gave instructions to Vayu that he should at all times do as Egal ordered.

"Please—please—will you not take me along, Sidi Claude?" the boy begged.

But he shook his head.

"I would be no bother. I would work hard—truly. I would be of much help to you."

"No," Claude said. "You must stay here."

"Oh sidi, please—"

"*No!*"

Then Father Lutz appeared. And his eyes were disturbed and ques-tioning.

"So what is it that I have heard, my son?" he said gently. "That you are going off on a trip?"

"That is correct," said Claude curtly.

"May I ask what sort of trip?"

"For business."

"For business only—that is all?"

"For what else should it be?"

"I had thought perhaps there might be other reasons." The priest paused. Then he said, "You have been so different lately, my son. You have not come to me: to teach the boys, to dine, to play cards. You have not come at all; and when I have come to you, you would not see me. You have kept to yourself, shut yourself off, even more than in the old days. And I have been concerned as to what is wrong."

"Nothing is wrong," said Claude. "I have been busy, that is all. And now I am going on a trip."

"For Abou Dakir."

"For Maison Gorbeau. For myself."

"But with Abou Dakir's caravan."

"So?"

"With slavers."

"I am going on my own sort of business. It has nothing to do with slaves."

"How can you travel with slavers and have nothing to do with slaves?"

"Because I—" Claude broke off. "Because it will be the way it is," he said flatly. "What affair is it of yours?"

"It is my affair when I see you about to do something that is not in your true nature. A thing you will regret; that will give you pain and remorse."

"I'll decide for myself what I'll regret. And what I'll do, as well."

Claude turned away, but Lutz did not let him go. "No, do not turn from me, my son," he pleaded. "Stay—please—and speak to me. Tell me what it is, what has happened, that you are again so lost, so bitter."

"There is nothing to tell. I am leaving tomorrow. I am busy. Will you go now and leave me alone!"

"To go off in shame with slavers?"

"Yes, to go off with slavers. To go where I choose—do what I choose." Claude wheeled back on him, and his eyes glinted with cold anger. "Who are you to talk of slavery? You—a priest. . . . What is a priest if he is not a slaver? Of the poor, the ignorant, the superstitious, the gullible. What is your whole religion but slavery: to myth and ritual and cant and lies? You're slavers as much as the Arabs—more than the Arabs; they only take men's bodies but you take their souls. . . . All right, take them. Go back to your flock, rattling your beads, and do what you want to their souls. But leave mine alone, you holy fraud. Leave mine alone!"

Again he turned. This time he broke away. Father Lutz called after him: "My son—Claude—please, my son—" But he did not stop. He went to his room. He locked the door and sat alone. Later, Vayu came and knocked and spoke his name, but he did not answer.

During the night he took out his neglected ledgers and brought them up to date; then slipped them into their rubber pouch and locked them away. He oiled and loaded his gun. He filled his money belt with assorted gold and silver coins and strapped it around him beneath his clothing. He put a few personal items in a haversack. Then, toward morning, he lay on his cot in the darkness . . . and Druard came and stood beside him. His face was white, like a skull's, with black holes for eyes, but in the depths of the holes was a yellow glow: the glow of the eyes of a hyena. At his waist he wore Father Lutz's rosary, and in his hand he held its crucifix, which he raised before him. "I have come, dear boy," he murmured. "You called, and I have come, to show you the way to Christ. . . ."

Then it was dawn, and Claude rose. Leaving the room, he went downstairs, through the store and courtyard into the market square, and there, already, the caravan was assembling. For a few hours he was busy with final preparations: supervising the loading, checking his trade goods, conferring with Nasruddin, setting the order of march. And by midmorning all was ready. As caravan leader, he would ride at its head, preceded only by two foreguards with ready guns; so it was he who first mounted his kneeling camel, swayed upward, and moved slowly off toward the southern gate. Egal and Vayu watched from the steps of the store, and, as he went, they waved and called after him. He raised a hand in return, but did not call back. Nor did he look back as he crossed the square.

> *Forward:*
> *the march, the burden and the desert. . . .*
> *To whom have I sold myself?*
> *What lies shall I uphold?*
> *In what blood tread?*

But there was no answer. In the fields beyond Harar there was no lie, no blood, no desert, but only the sun beaming gently from a gentle sky. The season of rains had just ended, the land was green and living, and the streams poured down the valleys toward the south. For some time, in the first valley, Harar was visible behind them, gray and sprawling on its hillside. Then, topping a low rise, they entered a second valley; and it vanished. At intervals, they passed through villages, and, between them, through pastures and planted fields. Toward midafternoon, they neared Mount Kondudo, skirting its wooded slopes, and then it too receded behind them, finally sinking from sight beyond the lower intervening hills.

The first night they spent in a grove of sycamores beside one of the streams; the second—after a day's journey in similar country—on the outskirts of a large village called Bubassa. A caravan staging post of long standing, it boasted a coffeehouse, brothel, and other amenities, to which most of the men repaired for the evening. But Claude remained in camp with the few assigned to guard duty. He had been to Bubassa before, on his

short trading trips with Egal and Vayu, and its produce was not of the sort
for which he was searching now.

Indeed, many days—even weeks—would pass before the caravan
would have any function save simply to move on. The sources of gold,
ivory, and such were still far to the south, and so too were the sources
of the merchandise which the others were seeking. For this was still
Moslem country. Almost the whole of the Ogaden, that lay before them,
was Moslem. And Abou Dakir, however ruthless otherwise, however
easy the prey that presented itself, would under no circumstances permit
his men to touch peoples of their own faith. They camped. They spent
the night. They moved on. On the march, now and then, could be heard a
clanking of chains, as a load shifted on the back of a mule or a camel. But
five times each day the caravan halted, as the men dismounted, spread
their rugs on the earth, and facing back toward Mecca, prayed to the God
of Islam.

Bubassa was the farthest south that Claude had previously gone.
And beyond it the country changed. It was still hilly, but the hills were
different; no longer soft and green, with pastures and forests, but bare,
harsh, rugged; and the trail wound through steep defiles between high
tumbled rocks. Hitherto, only the fore and rear guards had ridden with
guns unslung, but now almost all the men held theirs at the ready, on the
watch for game. And at intervals they were rewarded. There would be a
sudden movement in the brush and rock; a flash of brown or gray, as a
gazelle appeared—or an eland or oryx; and then shots would ring out, and
when an animal fell a few of the men would dismount and drop behind to
flay and dismember it. Once, too, there was an encounter of another sort,
as, rounding a bend in the trail, they found themselves in the midst of a
band of baboons. There were hundreds of them, chattering and scamp-
ering in the brush, and now whole volleys of shots were fired—not for
food but for the simple pleasure of slaughter. The baboons ran, leaped,
screeched, as they tried frenziedly to scramble to shelter; but they were
crowded so thickly that they piled up onto one another in their flight, and
the men, shouting and laughing, went on shooting into the piles. This
time, no one stopped or dismounted. The dead lay where they fell, and the
wounded dragged themselves among them, shrieking. The shrieks were
still audible when, a while later, the caravan stopped by a stream for water
and the midday prayer.

Claude had not joined in the shooting. But neither had he tried to stop
it. Or, indeed, spoken at all.

He spoke little at any time.

Nasruddin, his second-in-command, rode habitually at the rear of
the long train, to handle stragglers and mishaps. Even when they were
together, in camp or at the wayside halts, he remained somber and taci-

turn, and their conversations were limited to a few words each day about their course, their bivouacs, and the routine of the march. With the others he had so little communication that there were only a handful whom he knew by face or name. One was a cook's assistant, called Abdul, who brought him his meals, which he ate alone. Another was a driver, Sharaf, who was assigned to the care of his trade goods and the pitching of his tent at night. The rest were scarcely men to him at all, but mere white ghostly figures, with their veils and their guns, swaying behind him on their camels through the hours and the days.

What Abou Dakir had said about him to Nasruddin, or Nasruddin to the men, he did not know. But they seemed to accept him, without curiosity or hostility. They did their endlessly repeated work of loading and unloading. They cared for their animals. They made their appointed marches. One day on the march they had turned their guns on baboons; and on another day, farther on, they would turn them on a different, more valuable species, whose shrieks might well be even louder. What was, was. What happened, happened. They were following their ancient trade, as had their fathers before them; and one *ferangi* among them was one *ferangi*—no more.

During the third and fourth days out of Bubassa the country changed again. The hills fell away behind, the land sloped steadily downward, and ahead, under a high wide sky, appeared the plain of the Ogaden. Here at last was the landscape, not of northern, but of central Africa: neither green broken highland, like the region of Harar, nor yet bare stony desert, like the wastes of Somalia, but a sea of land, sparsely covered with grass, rolling on into distance so vast that one could see in its sweep the very curve of the earth. The land itself was of reddish laterite, the grass pale yellow, dotted everywhere with thorny acacia, and the streams that crossed it, still flowing southward, were now miles apart, no more than thin flowing threads in the surrounding stillness. For the land was utterly still. It was hot and dry. The moisture of the season of rains—less here at any time than in the hills to the north—had now sunk into the soil, drawing all greenness with it, leaving only the red of earth, the yellow of grass, across cloudless, sun-blazing miles.

Descending onto the plain, they came to the villages of the upper Ogaden. These were nothing like Bubassa, or even the lesser villages of the hill country, but merely tiny huddles of mud-and-grass huts, thrown up for shelter by the nomadic tribes while their cattle grazed a certain area, and then to be abandoned when the herds moved on. Yet their inhabitants were not savages. They were not Negro but Somali—and Moslem. And they knew and welcomed the men of Abou Dakir. Food was offered, women brought for their pleasure, advice given on the whereabouts of game and water. And if it was thought strange that the caravan leader had eyes of a color never before seen except in the sky overhead, no indication was given by either word or action.

"*Salaam*," they were greeted. "*Salaam aleikum*," they were bidden goodbye.

Peace to the slavers. . . .

Then the last village was behind them. The last men, last huts, last grazing herds of scrawny cattle. They moved on into the empty plain.

Or, rather, the plain that had seemed empty from the distance, for now that they were on it Claude found that it teemed with life. Gazelle and antelope were everywhere, moving in great waves across the scrubland. There were hartebeest, wildebeest, wild pig, zebra. There were giraffe and ostrich, their long necks swiveling as they peered warily from above the thorn trees, their long legs carrying them swiftly off across the grassland; and birds by the myriad thousand, nesting in the trees or winging in convoy across the sky. They were not yet in the country of elephant or buffalo, but, as they moved on, they came to an occasional rhinoceros bulling through the bush, and in the shallows of the now-sluggish streams were hippopotamus and crocodile. Each early morning, as they set out, the ferment of life was at its height, and the movement of the caravan was only a minute part of the great stirring in the wilderness. Then, as the sun climbed and blazed, there was a withdrawal, a quiescence; they alone seemed to live and move on the plain, riding on through empty stillness . . . until the sun declined and evening came, and then again, with sudden magic, the world about them came alive. Finally, with darkness, it underwent its final change, as under the moon and stars, shadowed but sleepless, it became the domain of the carnivores. Of lion and leopard, of jackal, bush dog, and hyena. Of the fang, the claw, the shadow, the yellow eyes.

For if life was everywhere, so too was death, in its immemorial pattern. Scarcely a morning passed on which the harbingers of death did not appear in the sky ahead: the black shapes of vultures wheeling, hovering, over a kill. And the ritual of which they were a part was as fixed as that of the turning earth. At its center, beneath them, was the sacrificial victim —zebra, wildebeest, or antelope—and upon it, tearing, rending, the killer king, the tawny lion. The attack had been made during the night, by a lioness; almost always it was the female who was the actual executioner. But once the prey lay dead, the male had moved in, driving his mate away, and it was he who first feasted, rumbling and gnawing in the morning sunlight. Then came the turn of lioness and cubs, and while they ate, the lesser actors in the play assembled: the hyenas, jackals, and bush dogs, watching, waiting, waiting, moving slowly closer, until their turn came (in that order—always the identical order) to snatch such prize as they could. And after them, at last, came the vultures, flopping heavily down onto the carcass, hiding it from sight with their black wings—until nothing was left but bones and hoofs and teeth and shreds of hide. But even then, with the last vulture gone and stillness everywhere, the cycle continued, as the ants moved in, by the thousand and million, to complete the ritual under the noonday sun.

In the world of beasts—of beast devouring beast—the lion was alpha and the ant omega. But now man had come to that world, and man was both: a surer, more deadly killer than ant and lion and all between them. The caravan shot for food, and sometimes sport; not a single animal at a time, but by the dozen, by the score. And now Claude, too, began to shoot —for hides. With a squad of men to help him as trackers and beaters, he ranged back and forth across the line of march, finding game everywhere, and soon a whole string of the camels and mules were laden with his prizes. At first his bag consisted mostly of easy victims—the same zebra and antelope and such that were the prey of the carnivores; but then he turned to the killers themselves, the far more valuable lions and leopards, and their proportion swiftly increased as he learned the tricks of the hunter's trade. Indeed, as a hunter he now won the respect of the slavers: partly for his marksmanship, which, with practice, had become excellent; even more for his apparent lack of fear at even the most dangerous of encounters. He alone would go out at night to a blind in the brush to confront the cunning and unpredictable leopard. And faced by a charging lion, he would wait far longer than the others before at last firing the shot, quick and true, that would bring it down.

"For Madame la Comtesse," he thought, "—your chic cloak for the opera. For Monsieur le Directeur—a fine rug for your office." At the end of two weeks in the Ogaden he estimated the worth of his bag at no less than ten thousand francs.

They moved on. It grew hotter and drier. The streams, now, were no more than brown sluggish trickles, and the dust rose in red plumes from beneath the tread of their plodding file. Several of the mules sickened and had to be slaughtered. One of the drivers died. Others, at intervals, became feverish and weak and had to be roped, during the day's march, to the backs of their camels. But still each day's march was completed; still they made their ten to twelve miles between dawn and dusk; and by the end of the third week were at a point roughly halfway to the Ogaden's southern boundary—the fabled Web Shebeli, River of Leopards. According to Nasruddin, the Shebeli, even at this season would be a true river, full and flowing, and beyond it would be rains and forests. This was the country of their destination, of their quest: the margins of black Africa; the land of elephants and ivory and gold and slaves. "There we will find as many blacks," said the somber Arab, "as here there are zebra and gazelle. And it will be easier hunting too, for they are not so good at running or hiding."

The part of the Ogaden they had now come to was itself not wholly devoid of human life. Every second or third day a cluster of huts rose up out of the brush ahead, and they rode through a dusty and forlorn village. Occasionally they passed a small nomad caravan or encampment. But the people were still Moslem. They were abysmally poor—with scarcely enough for their own subsistence, let alone produce for trade or plunder. And, ignoring them, the slavers moved on. The wealth of animal life, however, did not diminish, but throve and teemed on the arid plains; and each day the guns fired along the line of march and the store of meat and hides grew larger. Indeed, Claude's own bag of pelts was now so big that its transportation had become a problem, and, rather than carry it farther on the outward journey, he decided to make a cache. In the flat country, almost bare of landmarks, this too posed a problem; but at last a rocky hillock rose up beside the trail, and, finding clefts and small caves in its sides, he unloaded his pack animals and stored his goods in their depths. The hillock was unmistakable in its stony solitude, and he would stop and retrieve them on the return trip.

The return . . .

It was a thing he had scarcely thought of before; nor did he wish to think of it now. . . . His return with what? With his hides. Perhaps with ivory and gold. And with slaves. . . . His return *to* what? To the store, the ledgers, the fine profits in the ledger's columns. To Father Lutz and his crucifix. To Vayu and his *krar*. To the days behind the walls that he must forever keep high around him; and the nights of crumbled walls, of phantoms, of yellow eyes in the darkness. . . . Here, now, on his journey, there were no phantoms. When eyes circled the camp at night, they were the eyes of beasts—no more—and when he fired his gun they were gone. On the journey there were no walls, but only the plain; and he moved on through the plain. He rode, he hunted, he shot, he killed. He ate and slept and rose and moved on again. And that was all of life, all he asked of it: to move on. Since the days of his boyhood when he had trudged out from Cambon onto the dusty roads—when he had set sail for the horizon in the Drunken Boat of his dreams—he had been truly alive, truly his own self, only in movement; in bursting out from the walls that held him; in moving on always, toward the ends of the earth, toward the sun and the stars.

As he was moving now. As each night he sat out before his tent, alone, and watched Fomalhaut blaze in the southern sky. As each day he rode on beneath the flame of the sun, on his swaying camel . . . his Drunken Camel . . . farther, deeper, into the void of the miles.

Priests, professors, masters, he asked—*do you see me now? Do you judge me now? No, you cannot; because now at last I have passed beyond your ken and your power. I have passed beyond the utmost boundary of your world, into the world beyond. I have escaped, left you behind. . . . You have heard this before, you say? Yes, you have. But then I wrote it. Now I do it. Now at last I am what I was born to be: the outcast. I am Hun, pagan, nigger, savage; and I enter the kingdom of savages, the kingdom of Ham. As a savage I go, and as a savage I shall return. Untouched by you; untouchable; a creature from this other world, this other planet. It is my eyes, now, that will glow at night like the hyena's. My hair will be streaked with the fat of lion and leopard, and my hands with gold dust and the blood of slaves.*

The hillock and its cache receded behind them. He would return to them . . . when he returned. Now his eyes were fixed only ahead, and ahead was the plain and the sweep of the miles. There were no more hillocks, scarcely so much as an undulation of the earth, but only flatness, grass, dust, distance. Even the acacias were now low and truncated, their tops flattened out as if by the beat of the sun. And here, as they advanced, the game dwindled. On one day they sighted only a few antelope and zebra; on the next, a single distant eland; on the next, nothing. The only life that stirred was in the dust: the domain of lizard and toad, scorpion and ant. Around them now, from the flat earth, rose the shapes of great ant hills: twisted towers of red earth as high as a man on a camel's back.

Still the plain unrolled. They crossed dry stream beds, seas of yellow grass. The grass, knife-sharp, cut the feet of the plodding animals, and the trees, when they brushed beside them, cut their flanks. The trees gave no shade. They bore no leaf or blossom or berry, but only thorns, spikes, daggers, swords. They seemed to be made not of living wood but of black rigid iron.

Three camels and a mule went lame and had to be shot. A second man sickened and died. The meat of the game they carried went putrid and was jettisoned, and their water was brown and stinking in its goatskin bags. . . . But such things were routine to the men of the caravan. And now to Claude as well. . . . They moved on, mile beyond mile, into distance beyond distance, until at last, once again, the world around them began to change, and they approached the southern limits of the Ogaden.

The change began, not in the earth itself, but in the air. In wind. For weeks they had moved through a sunlit blaze of utter stillness, but now the wind rose and swept the plain, rippling like waves across the seas of grass. The dust raised by their passing no longer hung motionless above them, but blew swiftly away to the north, and on the horizon appeared other dust, great columns of dust, whirling in spouts as red as flame. One night Claude awoke to an unfamiliar sound, the distant rumble of thunder, and the next morning the sky to the south was purple with storm clouds. Then the earth too began to change. It rolled. It rose. It buckled. They passed through a region of low scrub-covered mounds; beyond the mounds were hills; and when they had crossed the hills, winding through steep passes and rocky chasms, they came out into the valley of the Web Shebeli.

Here they were again in inhabited country: a land of nomadic tribes and scattered villages. But the villages were larger than those of the upper Ogaden, and the people more prosperous. They too were Moslem. They were tall, gaunt, brown-skinned, with thin lips and noses; and they were proud and warlike, carrying spears and knives and thick shields of rhinoceros hide. Like the tribesmen to the north, they knew and welcomed the men of Abou Dakir, but, unlike them, they had goods to trade, and for the first time Claude came into possession of hides which he had not himself hunted—as well as, at last, of ivory. There were no elephants in the region. The ivory had been obtained by the tribesmen on their own incursions across the Web Shebeli: sometimes by hunting, sometimes by raids on other villages. And from these villages, too, they had brought back slaves; for beyond the river the Moslem world ended and black pagan Africa began.

In the tribal huts, at night, chiefs and warriors described to them the country that lay ahead. It was country, to be sure, that Nasruddin and most of his men already knew; but still there were aspects that were forever changing—with the cycle of seasons, the movements of tribes—and the slavers were not ones to conduct their business in haphazard fashion. Here Claude was supposed to play a role of importance, for neither Nasruddin nor any of the others could read, and he was in charge of the rough maps by which they would keep their bearings. But Nasruddin seemed to know very well what he was about, without benefit of cartography, and Claude's route-tracing and notations were of use only to himself.

"In another three days," he said one evening to the Arab, "we should reach the Shebeli."

"No, in five," said Nasruddin.

"I figure it as only thirty miles."

"In a straight line, perhaps. But if we go straight we come to a place that is no good for crossing. It is better to cross farther to the south, and that is also nearer to the country we should go to."

"Where there are elephants? And gold?"

"About gold I do not know. But there are elephants—yes," said Nasruddin. "And also there are the Worombu."

"Worombu?"

"They are a tribe: black, rich, with much ivory. . . . You have seen the slaves in the villages here? Most of them are Worombu. I have not myself had experience with them, but they are said to be strong and hard workers. And at the same time poor fighters."

Claude said nothing more. And in the morning they rode on.

For five days they rode—still across the plains, across the red earth and seas of grass—and toward evening of the fifth, as Nasruddin had predicted, they came at last to the river called the Web Shebeli. It was no Nile or Congo: perhaps two hundred yards in width and, at the place where they had reached it (for Nasruddin had been right about that too), no more than a few feet in depth. But after the weeks in the arid Ogaden it seemed a vast reservoir of coolness and refreshment, and they spent three days on its nearer bank, resting and renewing their strength. During the second night Claude again awoke to the sound of thunder, but this time it was not distant. Presently it was rolling and crashing overhead; the sky was streaked with lightning; and then the sky opened and poured down the miracle of rain.

Here there were more animals than they had seen anywhere on their journey. Each morning and evening plains game by the thousand came down to the water to drink, and following them, stalking them, came the carnivores—lions in great roaring prides, behind them hyenas and jackals, on the flanks the swift lonely leopards that gave the river its name. A short way upstream was a papyrus swamp, filled with bellowing hippopotamus, and downstream lay broad sandbanks, the home of crocodiles and storks. When Claude shot at the crocodiles the storks rose into the air in mass panic: the beat of their wings as loud as thunder, the spread of them all but hiding the sky.

The river itself was of course the chief reason for the profusion of animals. But another was the absence—until their own arrival—of men. During the three days of their halt small groups of Moslem tribesmen appeared along the northern bank, on quick hunting forays or to fetch water for their villages. But there were no permanent habitations; no other caravans appeared; and on the far side there was no sign at all of human life. According to Nasruddin, the nearest of the black tribes lived several days' journey from the south bank, as did the Moslems from the north, leaving the river and its marginal country as empty frontier between two Africas. It was crossed only at long intervals by scouts or raiding parties from either side, and by such travelers as the men of Abou Dakir.

On the fourth morning they forded the Shebeli. At its middle the water was too deep for the mules to hold their footing, and they had to be swum across unloaded; but there was no problem for men or camels, and the passage was made without mishap. Toward midday they were on their way again, by sundown some five or six miles into the land beyond, and here they pitched their camp, cooked the evening meal, and posted their guards for the night. They were in the heart of a wilderness. Around them everywhere were wild beasts, and, ahead, the domain of black savages. In such country, not long before, a caravan would have set half its men as guards against possible attack, but they used no more than on any night during the journey. For they were guards with guns. It was no longer tooth or claw or tusk that was king in Africa; no longer bow or knife or spear or poisoned dart. There was a new king now—king undisputed—the gun. And the guns were theirs.

There was no attack. There were only the familiar yellow eyes, watching. Late in the night there was again thunder and rain. And then stillness. When they arose the sky was clear; dawn stood in the east like a vast cliff of golden light.

They moved south and west. For another day it was across a broad featureless plain, indistinguishable from the Ogaden. But then again the land sloped upward; leaving the Shebeli valley, they topped a range of hills; and beyond the hills a new world spread before them. For here, at last, there was not only flatness and distance. There were other hills, squat and massive, tiering away into the silent miles; and between the hills, valleys; and in the valleys streams and greenness. For the first time since leaving the highlands of Harar they came to grass that was not yellow, to trees that were not mere skeletons of spike and thorn. There were trees with leaf, with blossom, that gave shade and shelter. There were giant baobabs, their trunks as thick as the pillars of old temples, their branches twisted grotesquely against the sky.

The sky itself had changed as well; indeed was now constantly changing through the cycle of the hours. On their third day beyond the river they arose and moved through the morning beneath a dome of stainless clarity. Then, toward noon, clouds moved up from the south, at first white and gentle, then gray and darker, hiding the sun, as a wind rose, and suddenly the world around them was blotted out in rain and storm. The rain did not last long. By late afternoon the sun reappeared; but now no longer clear in the sky, now dim beyond cloud and weaving mist. The land had turned from brown and green to gleaming silver. The hills were purple. And as evening came, their shadows, purple too, moved out into the valleys, engulfing them; but, above, the sky, now filled with clouds and beams of sunset, shone with a wild and fiery turbulence.

Night came—and a lurid moon. In the moonlight the land spread about them vast and primeval, transfixed in the stillness of space. Or, rather, in what seemed like stillness until their own minute sounds had subsided—until the cook fires were out and the tents sealed in darkness— and then clear through the darkness came the mighty hum of the wilderness. The hum filled Claude's ears as he sank toward sleep. It followed him into sleep, rising, falling, becoming part of sleep, part of body and brain; and deep in his sleep it seemed to change, to deepen, to be no longer a hum but a beat, a throbbing; neither the sound of insects in their billions, nor yet of murmuring thunder—or not these alone—but the throbbing beat as of a pulse in fever, as of the dark deep rhythm of distant drums. He was asleep—then awake—and the sound continued. But he had no fever.

Lying in the darkness, he listened; through the whole night he listened; and in the morning Nasruddin nodded and said, "Yes, we are coming close now. They were drums."

The next day, for the first time, they moved warily and circuitously. The caravan was too large, of course, for any long-range concealment, and the wooded areas, which now increased, were impassable to the camels. But they kept their course as close to cover as they could, following the curve of the hills and the forest's edges and avoiding the middle of open brush-land. And ahead, now, went a small patrol, searching each new vista with sharp eye and ready gun. Insofar as the eye could see, however, it was still a land of beasts; of lion and rhino, zebra and antelope, the familiar game of the Ogaden; and now too of elephant—the first they had seen—moving in gray lumbering herds across the broad savannas. This, above all, was what he—Claude Morel, hunter, trader—had come to find: elephant, tusk, ivory, for himself, for the House of Gorbeau: and his hand itched on his gun. But he did not shoot. No one shot. They moved on warily, silently . . . watching . . . and listening.

Then two hills rose close together, ahead, and they passed between them, topping a long draw and looking out from its crest across a sweep of valley. Again Nasruddin nodded. "Yes," he said, "we are there: in Worombu country." But there was no sound to be heard, no throb of drumming; no wisp of smoke rising from forest or brushland. As they descended the slope toward the valley floor it was through stillness immense and absolute.

Or through stillness, at least, of earth. For, in this world they had come to, the air was never still. Now, in the windless silence of noon, it gleamed and glittered with sunlight; touching the hills and trees, it made their very immobility seem a sort of vibrant preternatural movement. The sky was blue and bare. The earth was green. And then no longer green, but silver —a vast silver plain between purple mountains—and the sky, too, was silver and streaked with long trailing clouds. As the afternoon passed, the silver darkened. The purple of the hills seeped into plain and sky. The sun receded. A wind rose. Where silence had been was now the hum of the wind, and from behind it, presently, came a deeper wilder sound—the sound of thunder. It came from before them, from the south. It grew louder. It roared above them in the sky, and the sky was no longer purple and silver but purple and black and streaked with lightning, then sky and earth alike grew dim and vanished in a tide of rain.

Through the rain Claude rode hooded on the swaying back of his camel. Before him the camel's head loomed in the storm like the prow of a ship, and beyond it was only the storm. The advance patrol, out ahead, was lost in deluge and murk, and so too was the long file of the caravan plodding behind. He was alone in the rain, in his hood, in his slow swaying movement—as he was alone within himself. As he had been alone throughout the whole of the journey. In the weeks since leaving Harar his sole communication with others had been a few words each day with Nasruddin, with Abdul the cook, with Sharaf the driver; his sole activity, other than endless riding, the intense recurring ritual of the hunt and kill. Except for these brief interludes, he had, with each passing day, sunk more deeply into the hood, the caul, of his own apartness, his own identity.

And what was that: his identity? Who was he now, this Claude Morel, once the scourge of Paris, *le petit mioche* from the Ardennes?

Hunter? Trader? . . . No, no more. Not now. He had found his elephants, his ivory, and he had passed them by. . . . He was something else now. A slaver. A leader of slavers. Across his knees, under his burnous, his gun lay ready—but not for elephants. For men. For slaves. The gun was king, and he was king, the king of slavers, come to claim his kingdom in the land of darkness.

In the dark world beyond the world. Untouched. Unknown. . . . And yet, *to him*, not unknown; to him long familiar, through all the years of his life. . . . For it was no new journey on which he had come; it was an old journey, the eternal journey; and he needed no map to guide him— no more than did Nasruddin or the others—for he too carried with him the map of memory. *From the same desert, in the same night, always his eyes had waked, always:* to the silver star, the star in the south: to the Magi's journey. And with the Magi he too had journeyed. Across the horizon in his Drunken Boat; across the seas to the coasts of the sun; across the wastes beyond, the burning desert—farther, deeper—until he came to the end of the desert, and the sun was gone . . . as it was gone now: in storm, in tumult . . . as now still he moved on, hooded, silent, alone, *through the land of Cimmeria, land of whirlwinds and darkness.*

He was a slaver.

He was also a pilgrim.

And it was the pilgrim, now, who rode on into darkness; who watched the darkness slowly brighten, the whirlwind slacken, the rain cease; and behind the storm was the sky, the sky of evening, immense and shining in deep violet-blue. Across its breadth arched a rainbow, and beneath the rainbow the earth, too, shone and gleamed in the light of the setting sun. And this, also, he had seen before. He had seen it always—the land beyond Cimmeria; the lost land, the promised land—and it lay before him now, as it always had lain, in the world of vision, the world of dream. Again he saw green jungles, yellow rivers. He saw within the jungles the glint of gold, of orchids, of tawny lions, of scarlet birds; along the rivers, the tribes, the savages, the files of dancers; dancers by the thousand, black, naked, glistening, their eyes rolling whitely, their hair laced with threads of gold. He heard wild music and the beat of drums, and the beat was like thunder, but deeper than thunder; as deep and secret as the beat of his heart. And he thought, "Yes, it is the land of the heart that I have come to at last. Of the secret heart—of the inward eye." It was the land of dream that he had known as a boy, and left, and lost, and forever sought through the years of his journey. The land of illusion: *fabulous . . .*

. . . and false . . .

For now illusion faded. The sun had gone, and the rainbow, and the great vistas, and around him were rock and trees and hills, gray in evening light. "It will soon be time to stop for the night," he thought. And then he rounded the spur of a hill and, beyond it, found the advance patrol waiting. "We have found them, sidi," its leader reported. "They are in the next valley."

"They?"

"The Worombu."

Behind Claude the whole caravan had halted. One of the men was sent back to summon Nasruddin, and the leader continued with his report; but Claude scarcely heard him. What he heard was another sound, beyond the voice, deep and rhythmic. A sound that now, he knew, was not illusion. The sound of drums.

Then Nasruddin rode up. There were questions and answers. The patrol had gone perhaps a mile beyond their present point and, topping the next rise in the land, had looked down upon a Worombu village. It was in a valley similar to the one they were now in, but more thickly forested and with a river at its center. The village was in a clearing on the river's bank and surrounded by forest. It could easily be approached without detection, unless, of course, there were guards at outlying positions. But they had seen none such. And were sure that they themselves had not been seen. Having heard the drums in advance, they had dismounted from their camels and kept in good cover while at their lookout point on the hill.

Was the village a big one? asked Nasruddin.

Yes, it was big.

And crowded?

Yes, there were many people. Many women and children.

And the men? What did they seem to be doing? Why were the drums being beaten?

"They are just back from a hunt, I think," said the patrol leader, "and are preparing a feast."

"So?" said Nasruddin. He nodded slowly. "That is good."

"Yes, it is good. It could not be better. All night they will eat and drink and dance, and in the morning they will still be drunk or asleep."

"And it will be easy."

"Yes—easy."

Nasruddin turned, and his eyes went up to the ridge of the hill beyond them. In the silence there could be heard again the thump of the drums. "By the time we went up," he said, this time to Claude, "it would be too dark to see more. I suggest we make our camp here. Then late in the night we move, so that at dawn we are on the top, and ready."

Claude said nothing.

"If Selim here is right—and he is usually right," Nasruddin said, "the blacks will see nothing, know nothing. It will not be necessary even to surround them, but only to go down quietly into the forest and then move toward the river."

He paused.

"Most of the men are experienced and know what to do. We will enter the village in two ranks: the first, fully armed, to take care of the men; the second with whips and chains to round up the women and children. It should take little fighting. In a few minutes all should be finished."

The others nodded. They looked at Claude. But still he said nothing.

"The plan is agreeable?" said Nasruddin.

A long moment passed. Then Claude, too, nodded.

"You have any further instructions?"

"No."

The word went back along the line of the caravan. The pack animals were deployed and unloaded, but now the sky was clear and no tents were pitched. As the sun went down the men turned to the north and knelt in prayer; then prepared their supper, keeping the cook fires low. When they had eaten they sat about in the darkness, readying their guns and cartridges, and the clink of iron could be heard faintly in the stillness. Then the moon rose: a half-moon, gold and gleaming. And in its dim light they lay on the ground and slept, wrapped in their burnouses.

Claude did not sleep. He lay on the ground, as did the others, but his eyes were open. He watched the moon and stars. The camp was silent now, and utterly still, save for the occasional shifting movements of tethered animals. But from beyond the stillness came the other sound: the drums. And again their beat, in the vaulted darkness, was like the beat of a secret heart.

An hour passed.

Another.

The drumming continued.

The time set for moving on was four o'clock. It was eleven. And then midnight. And then one. The moon climbed the black miles of the sky, and still Claude watched it; watched the stars. Still the drums sounded, filling the night, filling his blood and his brain.

It was two.

In the dead of night, years before, in a town in the Ardennes, a boy had used to rise from his bed of sailcloth and set out alone upon his journeys. Now, in a camp in Africa, a man rose from his bed of earth. Claude's gun lay beside him, but he did not touch it. He left it. Moving quietly between the sleeping figures, he passed the last of them, passed the tethered grazing animals, and came to open ground. Off to his right now was one of the caravan guards, a white-hooded figure squatting motionless on a rock. Claude picked up a stone and threw it beyond him, and while the guard turned his head toward the sound of its fall, moved quickly into the nearby brush. In a few more moments he was in a stand of trees, and when presently he looked back there were only the trees, and the camp was gone. For a time the ground was level. Then it began to rise, and he moved up out of the floor of the valley onto the hillside beyond. Here there were alternating patches of forest and open land, and, in places, rocks underfoot; but the moon gave enough light to see by, and he climbed steadily on. There was no movement anywhere, other than his own; no hint of wild beasts' shadows, no gleam of watching eyes. There was only the sound of his own steps on the hillside—and beyond it, through it, the sound of the drums.

The hill was neither high nor long. As he ascended, the beat grew quickly louder, more pervading, until he could no longer hear the slight sounds of his own making, and he moved through a tide of drumming, as if through a storming sea. Then the ground leveled off; the hill was beneath him, and from its crest he looked down into the valley of the Worombu. Even in the darkness he could see that, as the patrol had reported, it was well forested. He could see the dim flow of a river. But these were mere fleeting images as his eyes fixed on the valley's center, beyond the forest, beside the river; on the bank of the river that, there, shone in firelight; on the village etched in firelight, on the huts, the open clearing, and in the clearing the moving figures, swaying, dancing, the figures black and leaping against red flame.

The brightness of flame seared the night. The tide of the drums now engulfed it. For a few moments Claude stood motionless, transfixed, on the crest of the hill. And then he was moving again. It was not back that he went, toward the camp and the caravan, but on and down; into the valley before him, toward the village, the flames. As he descended, the trees swung up from below and the flames became only a glow in the night sky above them; but the drums beat still louder, ever louder, and now, within the beat, he could hear the shouts and cries of human voices. Soon he was down the slope. He was beneath the trees, in a forest. And still he went on, through the forest, through darkness—until again the darkness brightened and, ahead, the black boles of the trees stood up like columns against walls of fire.

Then the fire was closer, and he saw that it was many fires. It was a great ring of bonfires on the bank of the river, and around it were huts of wattle and thatch, and within it the clearing—and the Worombu. A few yards from the clearing he stopped. "I have come to the end of my journey," he thought. And in that same instant—of stopping, of ending —he knew at last why he had come on the journey; that he had come not as a slaver but as a pilgrim, and no more; that the journey was part of the pilgrimage of all his years.

. . . For my pilgrimage is not to Paris, not to centers, capitals, portals, towers, thrones, but to the far places, the wild hidden places, the seas, the deserts, the forests, the forest rivers. On the riverbank, see—the black dancing files. The savages, my brothers. The niggers, my brothers. Shouts, drums, dance. Dance, dance, dance. . . .

He moved to the very edge of the forest. He saw the dancers. He saw the long files, the thumping feet, the swaying bodies; the bodies black, naked, glistening; teeth glistening bright, and eyes, and plumes and beads. On the fires lay the smoking carcasses of great beasts, and as they passed, the dancers ripped off the flesh and devoured it, dancing on. In their hands they held gourds, and they held them high, pouring drink down into their mouths, upon their faces—dancing on. The drums were wilder now, the dancers frenzied: on one side the men, on the other the women, the two lines approaching each other, withdrawing, approaching again, and each time nearer, the men shouting, the women shrilling, their bodies alike convulsed and leaping in savage rhythm. At the center of the men was one taller than the rest: tall with feathers, bright with beads, his feet pounding, his arms flailing, leaping high against the flames: the men's leader—the chief—the Nigger King. And opposite him a woman: tall, too, and black and naked, her blackness gleaming, her head shaved and gleaming: leaping, whirling, dancing: the chief's woman—the Nigger Queen.

The fires blazed. The drums thundered.

Fires, drums, shouts, dance, dance.

Hunger, thirst, shouts, dance dance dance dance. . . .

Claude stepped out from the forest.

He moved past the huts and the fires and into the clearing and stopped.

The drums stopped. The dancing stopped. The only sound left was the crackling of the fires.

For a long staring moment the Worombu stood motionless. If they were going to attack, it would be now. But they did not attack. Instead, the tall one, the chief, raised a hand and made a single guttural sound, and instantly the women turned, scattered, and vanished into the huts. There was another pause. Then he spoke again. And the men moved forward. Approaching Claude, they made a circle around him and again stood motionless. . . . Or almost motionless, for many swayed, as if still dancing.... They were drunk: with dance, with palm wine, with the frenzy of their revels. Their eyes rolled whitely. Their beads and feathers glittered in the firelight.

None of them spoke. At first Claude, too, did not speak, but merely held out his hands, open and empty, to show that he had no weapon.

Then he said, "I am your friend. Your brother."

He spoke in one of the Shankalla dialects that he had learned from south-country Negroes in Harar. But there was no response. He tried another—with the same result. All that was left to him now was a smattering of one of the Bantu tongues, and he did not know if the Worombu were Bantu. But he made his try. He said again, slowly, clearly, "I am your friend. Your brother."

And this time there was a change. There was recognition. A murmur passed through the great circle around him, and the chief—the tall one —moved slowly forward.

"But there are others near," Claude said, "who are not brothers." He pointed toward the forest and the hill beyond. "There is a caravan of Arabs. Of slavers."

The chief was close to him now. He had stopped. He was not swaying, like most of the others, but he too was drunk. His eyes were clouded and wild and rolling, and his lips jerked back from his white filed teeth.

He repeated the single word—"Slavers—"

"Yes," said Claude. "In the next valley. They will come soon. So you must go—go fast. To the south, to the forests. And hide."

Still the chief stood motionless. Only his eyes and lips moved, and only the same word came from his lips.... Then suddenly he turned. He shouted. He shouted the one word, over and over, to the circle of tribesmen, and the night rang to the sound of his voice.... For a few moments it was the only sound, and then the others, too, broke their silence. At first it was with a renewed murmur—no more. But then, swiftly, the murmur rose; it was broken by grunts and cries; and the cries rose and multiplied until they became one cry, a concerted howling and roaring that filled the clearing and the firelit darkness. Drunkenness rose again, filling voice and body, and the black bodies were no longer merely swaying, but again twitching, stamping, leaping, as if in a new dance of savage fury. The drums reawakened: rolling, booming. The chief leaped to the beat—higher, wilder than the rest—arms flailing, face raised to the moon. And beside him now appeared a new figure, a witch doctor, masked and horned and with painted body, and his high thin shriek rose even above the din of the howling and the drums.

As the shriek continued there was another change. The circle had broken. The men were milling about the clearing, running in all directions—to the clearing's edge, between the fires, into the huts. When they emerged from the huts they were still running, still leaping and howling, but now in their hands they carried spears and clubs and shields. Massing in the center of the clearing, they stamped and shouted themselves into an ever-wilder frenzy around the now demonic figures of the chief and witchman, and then, with a mighty roar, broke toward the forest and the hill beyond.

Since he had last spoken, Claude had been ignored, forgotten. But now he tried to interpose himself. He stepped again in front of the chief. "No! No!" he said—and now he too was shouting, yelling, straining to raise his voice above the tumult. "Go the other way—escape—take your women and children. . . . You cannot fight them, attack them. They are too strong. They have—"

There was no word for what they had; no word for *fusil, Flinte, fucile, bondikia*—GUN. The Worombu had never seen a gun; could not imagine a gun. And yet he shouted it—in French, Arabic, English, Italian, German; in every language he could think of—wildly, hopelessly, without meaning or effect. No one heard, much less understood. No one seemed even to see him, and he was shoved aside, all but swept from his feet. Trying to move with the tide, he seized the arm of the chief, still shouting, still pleading; "No! Stop! Stop! No! They have guns—guns—guns—"

Then the tide overwhelmed him. Something struck him on the back, throwing him forward, and he fell to his knees. Trying to rise, he was struck again, fell again, and rose a second time—only to see a club hanging poised close above him. He saw the club descend; he felt it strike, felt the impact, the shock. And then saw nothing, felt nothing . . .

. . . Until, presently, he was again conscious of movement. And of pain. The movement was his own, and he was still trying to rise; and the pain was within his head, like the throb and beat of the drums. . . . But the real drums, now, were silent. The clearing was silent, except for the crackling of the fires. Looking about him, struggling to focus his eyes, he saw that he was still at its center. That all the men had vanished. But he was not alone, for now others surrounded him: the women and children of the village, watching him curiously, fearfully, with black firelit faces and white staring eyes. They were not close around him, as the men had been, but far back at the clearing's edge, between the fires and the huts; and as he gained his feet they withdrew still farther; but still they watched him—staring, silent.

"Go! Go!" he shouted at them. "Go run, go hide—"

They made no sound, no movement.

"Go hide in the forest!" His voice was a croak in the stillness. "Go, go now—hide—or you will all be slaves—"

Still no one moved. Finally it was he who moved. A faint sound came to him—not from the fires, not from the village, but from farther away —and, raising his eyes, he looked beyond the village, beyond the treetops of the forest, to the hill in the north, and on the crest of the hill he saw torches and running figures against the sky. . . . Then he too was running. Across the clearing, toward the forest, toward the hill and what lay behind it. . . . Reaching the forest's edge, he found a path and followed it, still running, stumbling, swaying, as he moved on between the trees. The fires were gone now, and there was only darkness. There was no sound save the thump of his feet on the packed earth of the trail. . . . And then that sound, too, was gone. The earth, the trail were gone. The earth had fallen away; it had opened into a pit; he was falling, pitching forward, hurtling down into the pit. In the darkness he saw a spike rise to meet him, and he twisted away; but another spike struck his leg; and still he fell, twisting, writhing—until there was a second blow, again a blow on the head, and he had stopped falling, he had stopped moving, he lay still. And again there was pain, there was blackness.

And then nothing.

30

Out of nothing, later—much later—came the flickering of light. The blackness was gone. But not the pain. Pain flooded back: into his head, his shoulder, his side, his leg. For a while he lay with pain, wrapped round by pain as by his burnous; then slipped again into unconsciousness.

Then again he awoke, and the light was steady. Above, beyond the rim of the pit, were trees and sky and dappled sunshine, and even at the bottom, where he lay, it was bright enough to see clearly. He had fallen onto red earth—soft, but strewn with half-buried rocks. Around him the walls rose vertically, perhaps ten feet, to ground level, and spaced between them, erect and spearlike, were the dozen-odd wooden spikes of the animal trap. Two of the spikes were twisted askew, and a third had been broken off near the top. For a while Claude looked at it, and then, raising his burnous, saw the point projecting from the flesh behind his knee. With a sharp, sudden movement he pulled it out. Then, tearing a strip from his burnous, he made a binding to stem the blood.

It was the right knee, the Achilles' knee. . . . "So you are back in London," he thought: "No, not London; there someone else did the bandaging. You are back at the Gare de l'Est and still a dud at jumping from trains." He got slowly to his feet, and the knee ached, but the pain was bearable. Nor was the pain too bad in his shoulder or side; at least nothing had been broken. It was his head that hurt most: the head twice struck, by a club and then a rock. He put his hand to it, but the wounds were indistinguishable in the tangle of hair and earth and clotted blood.

Standing now, he looked up—and the pit revolved. Then it stopped. For several moments he listened, but heard no sound, and suddenly he felt the impulse to call out. . . . To whom? . . . He did not call. He began trying to climb the walls. But the earth was loose and crumbled in on him, and he could gain no more than a foot or two before he slipped back exhausted. He waited. He rested. He looked at the spikes. Then, breaking them off, he made a crude ladder of hand- and footholds, and with these worked himself up the side of the pit. His head throbbed; his knee ached and trembled; there seemed no ounce of strength left in bone or muscle. But at last he got a hand over the rim, and then his good leg, and clawing and writhing, he pulled himself up onto the forest trail.

The trail was empty and still. But in the trees above him there was a faint sound, and, looking up, he saw a great red bird perched high on a branch. For a moment the bird watched him curiously; then cawed and flew away, its wings scarlet in the sunlight. Beyond the treetops Claude could now see the sun, and he judged it to be about midafternoon.

He moved slowly along the trail toward the village, and around a bend came upon the first dead: a Worombu lying face down, arms flung out, with a bullet hole high in his spine. A bit farther on was a second body; then two close together, and still another alone. This last one was close to the edge of the clearing, and now Claude came to the clearing and saw the village. Or what had been the village, for it was that no longer. It was an ash heap, a charnel. Every hut was gone, burned to the earth, and what debris remained was indistinguishable from that of the previous night's bonfires. No trace of flame remained. Here and there a wisp of smoke rose curling into the windless air, but for the most part all was cold, gray, dead—as dead as the corpses that were strewn everywhere across the wreckage.

For here the dead lay, not singly or in pairs, but by the dozen and the score. Most were Worombu—male Worombu—black, naked, crumpled, their feathers and beads forming a bright nimbus around them against the gray of ash and cinder. But there were a few women too, and children, and, scattered widely about, an occasional figure in Arab burnous and kaffiyah. There were no wounded, no hint of movement or of flickering life. The slavers had done their work thoroughly and professionally, leaving only dead Worombu; and their own injured—probably few—had been carried off.

What had happened was as clear in Claude's mind as if he himself had been witness. The Worombu, wild, drunk, and howling had poured into the next valley to attack the caravan camp; but long before they reached it the sentries had heard them, the camp was ready; ready with a force unknown and omnipotent—the new king of Africa—the gun. And at the first volley the savages had turned and fled. They had fled back across the hill into their valley, to their village, and the slavers had followed, and this was what was left. Claude raised his eyes past the treetops to the hill, and its crest stood utterly still in the sunlight. The caravan and its human booty were by now probably a full half-day's march away to the north or east. He looked at the river, the banks, the forest walls, and they too were still. If there had been any survivors, they too were gone.

"*I* am the survivor," he thought. "I have come to the far place. To the savages, my brothers; to the niggers, my brothers. And now my brothers are gone, and I survive."

He moved through the clearing, among the dead. Some of the dead had been charred and lay faceless in ashes. Some lay prone, with faces hidden. But most had their faces turned up to the sun—to him—and as he passed they watched him with white dead eyes. He limped over to the riverbank, and then along the bank a short distance, away from the dead. Crouching beside the water, he drank. He washed his wounded knee and, again tearing a strip from his burnous, tied on a fresh and better bandage. He washed the earth and dried blood from his hair and with probing fingers felt the double wound in his scalp. Luckily it was only the scalp that had been broken, with no apparent damage to the skull.

"Luckily—" he thought. "Why luckily?"

For a while he sat by the river—the flowing water—the water of life. Then he returned to the place of the dead. At the clearing's edge he stopped, and the eyes still watched him; and then suddenly he was conscious of a change, of something different, of eyes that were watching —but differently—and at the far side of the clearing he saw a movement. For an instant he was truly a savage himself, frozen with awe and terror.... The dead had risen.... Then he saw more clearly. He saw a standing figure, a woman's figure, black and with staring eyes—but the eyes were living—and as he advanced a step, the figure turned and ran and vanished into the forest.

He called out, and the call was high and wild in the stillness. Hobbling as fast as he could, he crossed the clearing and called again, but there was no sound in response, no hint of movement among the trees.... Rather it was the trees themselves that seemed presently to be moving; to be slowly revolving around him, swaying in and out of focus.... He took a few more steps, and his knee buckled, and he fell. Trying to rise, he fell again, and this time he lay where he had fallen, too weak and spent to move. He lay at the forest's edge, the clearing's edge, and looked with dull eyes at the ashes, at the dead. And with dull brain he thought, "Yes, you have finished your journey at last. You have come at last to the place you have been seeking and have found the shrine in the heart of the garden."

But it was not the shrine. He slept ... and woke. And waking, he was conscious of change. It was raining. The sky had darkened, there was lightning and thunder, and the rain beat down into his face and eyes and plastered his torn and filthy burnous into a tight sheath about his body. Across the breadth of the clearing it beat upon the ashes and the dead.

There had been another change too. An inward change. But at first he did not know what it was. Then, suddenly, he did know: he was hungry. In the place of death he was alive—and hungry. And after a few minutes he rose to his feet. His knee shook but held him; his head ached but was clear; and leaning against the tree trunks for support, he moved slowly into the forest. Here the rain was only a sodden dripping, and for perhaps an hour he foraged through the twilit gloom, hunting for berries and roots. But such berries as he found were hard as bullets; the roots were tough and bitter; and for every morsel he could swallow there were a dozen mouthfuls spat out. Then an idea struck him and he returned to the clearing. Searching out the sites of the Worombu fires of the previous night, he grubbed about in mud and ashes, looking for remnants of their interrupted feast. But there was only mud, only ashes—and bones. Only the dead men, away from the fires, still had flesh on their bones.

The dead watched him, and he watched the dead. "So here is your chance," he thought. "Nigger, savage, Vandal, Hun, Lucifer: here is your chance of a lifetime. Think how fine it would be—how *formidable* —to return to Cambon, to stop by at the Café du Printemps, to say, 'Your pardon, messieurs; you remember me perhaps? Your old friend, *le voyou*. Your old friend, *le beau gosse*. But with a slight change, messieurs, I must explain—for *le beau gosse*, you see, is now a cannibal.'"

Among the dead were the few slavers who had fallen—three, four, he counted—their burnouses white, like shrouds, among the dark bodies of the Worombu. And counting them, he had another thought: the thought of a gun. Here in this world a gun was of such importance that the survivors would have retrieved all they could; but there was at least a chance that they had missed one in the wild confusion, and now, picking his way through the mud, between the corpses, he made his search. At the first corpse he found nothing. At the second, nothing. At the third and fourth, nothing—until, turning to leave the fourth, he saw a wedge of wood projecting from beneath the edge of the burnous, and in a moment the wedge had become a gun butt and he held the gun in his hands. In a pouch at the man's waist he found a dozen bullets; on the other men more bullets, to a total of almost fifty.

Sitting at the edge of the clearing, he cleaned the gun with his own tattered clothing. There was now no game to be seen; it had obviously been frightened off, first by the Worombu fires and then by the din of conflict. But it would come with darkness. And darkness was approaching quickly. The rain had stopped. The clouds had passed on, the sky was clear, and in the still, clear twilight he sat ready, waiting.

Then it was dark, it was night. And he must have slept again, for when he next looked up the night was filtered with silver and the moon stood already high above the treetops. It was not, however, the moon that had wakened him—but a sound; a sound low and close, a sound in the clearing. And now, peering across the clearing, he saw what had made it. He saw the shadows moving. He heard the tearing of flesh and the crunch of bone, as the hyenas held their feast in silver darkness. He reached for the gun; and slight as the movement was, the hyenas felt it. Their heads went up, their ears cocked, and yellow eyes shone in the dimness. He picked a pair of eyes, raised the gun, fired; and the eyes sank, the shadow sank, and the other shadows turned, ran, and vanished. There was neither sound nor movement in the clearing as he went out toward its center. The beast he had shot twitched and trembled slightly as he stood above it, and he put a second bullet into its head and dragged the carcass back to the edge of the forest.

"So—" he thought, "I shall only be a cannibal once removed."

Then he sat again. He waited. The moonlight glinted on the corpses, on the river, in his eyes—on closed eyelids—and when he awoke again it was morning.

The carcass still lay beside him. But it was not at the carcass that he looked. It was beyond it, along the edge of the forest, at the woman who stood watching him.

This time she did not run. As he sat up and then rose she remained utterly still; nor did she move as he approached, except to crouch and bow her shaven head. Looking down at her, he had an image of another place, another time: of the dying slave girl crouched beside him, years before, in the Somali Desert. But this was no slave, he thought. It was the one Worombu woman who was now not a slave—or dead; nor was she a thing of skeletal bones, but tall and firm and full-fleshed in her nakedness. . . . Then another image rose—from the night of his coming, the night of fire and drums—and he saw again the dancing files, the dancing women, the tall chief's woman, the Nigger Queen. . . . Was this one she? He could not tell. It was not night now. There were no drums, no fire, no frenzy. If she was queen, it was queen of mud and ashes. Of tattered loincloth and broken beads and flesh torn and bloodied by forest brambles. A queen who crouched, who cowered; who looked up at him now, silent and fearful, her eyes staring white in her black mud-streaked face.

He stood before her and said in Bantu, gently: "I shall not hurt you. Do not be afraid."

But if she understood, she gave no sign. She remained crouched and mute, her eyes staring. And then the eyes moved past him to the carcass of the hyena.

"I shall not hurt you," he repeated. "See, I have food. We shall eat."

The hollowness of hunger filled him, and, leaving her, he returned to the carcass. He bent over it—and stopped—for in that instant it occurred to him that he had no knife. And no fire. The great fires that had burned in the clearing were dead and cold, no more than sodden ashes; and such implements as he had had—matches, flints, knives, hatchets—were lost and gone with the vanished caravan. His possessions were a torn burnous, a gun, bullets. And, beneath the burnous, his money belt. For the first time he was conscious of the belt, hot and heavy and chafing about his waist, and, unfastening it, he threw it down upon a rock. "Ah yes, exactly what I need," he thought sardonically, "for the carving and cooking of *hyène sautée.*"

Turning, he saw that the woman had moved. She had approached silently until she was standing close by, and in her hand, held out to him, was a spearhead of sharpened stone. He took it from her and smiled and again bent to the carcass, and for a while he lost track of her as he hacked and sawed at the sinewy flesh. "So we are savages—we shall eat it raw," he thought. But they did not have to eat it raw. When he rose and looked about him it was to see the woman squatting over a pile of brushwood, rubbing two other spearheads together. And in a moment there were sparks. And in another, fire.

"*Bravo!*" he said. "*Ça va bien, ma jolie.*"

And for the next hour they waited silently while their meal cooked on the crackling flames.

The meat was tough. Its smell was strong and nauseous. But they ate ravenously, tearing and rending, and the sound was not unlike that made by the hyenas themselves at their ghoulish feast. . . . The thought drew his eyes up and across the clearing. Since wakening he had been aware of nothing but hunger—and the woman—but now, suddenly, he was again conscious of where he was; of the mud and ash and flesh of the charnel that once had been a living village. . . . The other hyenas had not returned. No lions or leopards or jackals had appeared, and the clearing lay still in the morning sunlight. But the air above was not still. It was full of movement, of circlings, of black wings and claws and beaks and croaking voices, wheeling lower, closer—and now the first of the vultures landed, plopping heavily to earth, and soon mud, ash, and flesh had all but vanished under a black tide of flapping wings.

Claude's hand touched his gun. Then left it; for what was the sense in wasting bullets? He rose and shouted, and a few of the nearer vultures flew up, with strips of black and red flesh dangling from their beaks. Then they descended again. The others had not moved. The mass of them would not move and fly away until their work was done—or until night came, and with it the earthly carnivores—and the next morning's sun would rise on a sweep of mud and ash, and nothing more. Claude slung his gun. He could eat no more. The woman, too, had finished eating, and now she rose and wrapped what was left of the meat in large leaves which she plucked from the edge of the forest. Then Claude set off around the edge, and she followed, carrying the meat; but then she made a sound —the first he had heard from her—and, turning, he saw her pointing, and, beyond her, his money belt on the rock.

"For the vultures, too," he thought. But then, changing his mind, he went back and got it. "No, for us," he said. "Perhaps on our promenade we shall find a little bistro, and there we shall stop off and buy an ice and pastries."

They continued around the clearing. He did not look again at the tide of vultures. Nor did the woman. This was her village, her home that they were leaving; that lay in ruins, destroyed. Beneath the devouring birds lay —who? Her husband? The tall one, perhaps: the chief, the Nigger King? Or perhaps another: one of his men: hunter, warrior, dancer—and now corpse, Whoever it was, he was gone. Father, brothers were gone. And the women too: mother, sisters. And children. Perhaps her own? . . . He did not know. The rest were gone, and she was there, and that was all he knew. Somehow she had escaped; run into the forest, hidden, vanished, been overlooked. And now here she was. She—and he. Perhaps earlier—on the day before, while he had lain unconscious in the pit—she had come back to the village and wailed and howled among the dead. But she did not now; and he was grateful. The dead were dead. The gone were gone. And they remained. Moving on around the clearing, they reached the river's edge and knelt and drank.

When he rose his knee buckled and he almost fell. The woman watched and waited. Then he limped along the bank, and she followed him. Passing the place where he had been the day before, he kept on for another few minutes, until the bank disappeared in swamp and under-growth and he could go on no farther. Retracing his steps, he went back past the clearing, past the place of vultures, following the bank in the other direction, until, here too, it became swamp and brush, again forcing a halt. Turning, he looked at the woman and pointed upstream and down. "A village?" he asked. "More Worombu? Another tribe?" But she did not answer. He repeated the questions, in the same words, in others, using every Bantu word he could think of. But still she was silent: staring, shaking her head.

Then they entered the forest. It was his intention to cut straight through to the open land, where he could see the contours of the valley, and then follow the valley south to the next tribal village; but the forest was dense, it was almost jungle, and hours passed while they groped and zigzagged through its mazes. Thorns and branches tore at him, ripping to shreds what was left of his burnous, leaving his flesh as torn and welted as the woman's. His knee trembled and ached, then stiffened and ached, and pain returned, drumming, throbbing, to his head. At one point they stumbled onto a trail, and he took it for the one on which he had fallen into the pit; but they came to no pit, to neither clearing nor brushland, and presently the trail petered out and they were back again in trackless forest. Another hour passed—or so he judged—before, at last, the forest thinned, light showed between the trees ahead, and they came out from between the last of them into open country.

But even here the light was not bright. The sky was now gray, shrouded, sunless, growing darker by the moment as prelude to the afternoon rains; and without the sun, after their zigzag journey, he could not tell one direction from another. Ahead were hills, to each side other hills, but which were south, and which were north or east or west, he did not know. They seemed larger than the one he had crossed, entering the valley; broader and taller, with pointed cones, like volcanoes . . . the volcanoes of Java . . . except that the volcanoes of Java had been tall and still, and these were tall and moving; they were circling about him, slowly—then faster and faster; they were revolving, spinning—like the spinning roads of Europe, of the Place du Sépulcre—and then gone; and he was lying on humpy earth with a black face bent above him. It was raining, and he was lying in the shelter of the forest's margin, with the rain drumming above him, and the pain in his knee was a great turning saw-edged knife.

The woman was crouched beside him, and he spoke to her. "I cannot go on," he said. "You must go alone. To people—the next tribe—the next village."

As before, she was silent and motionless.

And he grew angry. "Go," he ordered. "Do you understand? Go!"

He pushed her. He pointed: in what direction he did not know. "Go—go!" he repeated. "If you stay here you will die."

At last she rose and moved slowly away, and he lay alone under the trees in the rain. He felt the belt around his waist and the gun under his hand, and the thought occurred to him that he might have given them to her. . . . Then he thought: "For what? What use would they be to her?" . . . And the gun, at least, might be of use to him when it was his turn with the hyenas; or before that, in different fashion, if the pain in his leg did not relent. He closed his eyes. He listened to the rain on the leaves above him. Then the rain stopped and there was only a slow dripping, fading to stillness . . . and the stillness deepened . . . until at last, within it, he heard a slight sound, a soft movement; and he opened his eyes to see the hyenas, but saw, instead, the woman returning.

"Go—go!" he said again.

But she came close and knelt beside him. In her hand she held a gourd filled with water, and she put it to his lips and made him drink. Then she gave him food: first a strip of the meat which she had carried from the village, and afterward fresh-picked fruit of a kind he did not know. While he ate, she busied herself with still another thing she had brought: a handful of shrubs, which she now ground fine between two stones and mixed with earth and water into a greenish paste. And when that was done she pointed to his knee and, removing the binding, spread the paste thickly on the swollen, broken flesh. Within a few moments, to his astonishment, the pain began to ebb. By the time the binding was back on, the knee felt cool and numb. And thus it remained through the hours that followed, as daylight faded to dusk, and then dusk into night, and still they sat at the forest's edge, in blackness and silence.

Again he closed his eyes. He lay back. He slept. And when he awoke again it was daylight.

The woman was already up. And she had obviously already been out on another foraging trip, for beside her was the gourd newly filled with water, and more fruits and shrubs; and she was again grinding the shrubs into a muddy paste. Her shaven head was bent to her work, and her face was composed and expressionless. It was a strong face—not a girl's but a woman's: the bones heavy and strong, the lips heavy and thick, the nose broad, with flaring nostrils, between long slanting scars on either cheek. A wholly Negro face; a savage's face. And the body, too, was a savage's: black and lithe and all but naked, squatting, knees high and rump on heels, while two stones ground and thumped against the forest earth. As Claude watched her, she turned and saw him, and he said, *"Bonjour, madame.* Since we cannot talk in Bantu, let us try in French." But again there was no answer; and presently he rose and stood upright, and his leg was stiff, but held him, and did not hurt. While he moved back and forth to ease the stiffness, she went on with her work, and when she was finished came to him, unbound his knee, and again applied her green paste. "Thank you," he said. "You are kind. And it is wonderful." But she was already silently bringing the fruit and water; and when they had eaten and drunk they moved out from the forest onto the open savanna.

With pain gone his mind was clearer. He saw now that the axis of the valley lay at right angles before them, running to right and left along the edge of the forest. But he did not go in either direction. Instead, with the woman following, he cut straight across the valley to the nearest hill and, climbing to a level above the treetops, turned and looked out over the land below. Directly ahead, beyond savanna and forest, he saw the river, and on the near bank the empty clearing that had been the Worombu village. To the left of it—to the north—the river curved away, and there rose the hill over which he had come into the valley. His eyes quickly passed over these, however, moving on to the right—to the south. For the first time, in daylight, he looked down the farther sweep of the valley, along the river, the rim of hills, the miles of forest and brushland. And across the miles he saw what he had hoped to see: the beacon of the next village: a thread of smoke rising from the earth into the still morning air.

He took a bearing on it. Descending to the valley, with the woman following, he turned toward the south—but in that same instant a change came over her. She ran quickly up beside him. She stood before him, blocking his way. With her eyes, her hands, her arms, her whole body, she pleaded with him not to go on.

He looked at her in surprise. "There is a village," he said. "Another tribe. They will take you in—care for you."

She shook her head. Her hands were clasped in supplication. For the first time she spoke to him—spoke actual words—in her own language. "*Nya—nya!*" she begged. "No—no!"

"They would not help? They are not friendly?"

"No."

"They would harm you?"

"Yes. Harm—kill. Kill . . ."

Claude had stopped. She fell to her knees before him. "*Nya, nya,*" she pleaded, and her voice was a low sobbing moan.

He hesitated. A few moments passed. Then he raised her up. "All right," he said gently. "Stop crying. We will not go there."

The woman understood him. Her face changed, her eyes shone, and grasping his hand, she held it to her cheek.

"But where then?" said Claude.

It was not the woman he asked, but himself. . . . "*Where then? Where now?*" . . . For weeks past he had asked no questions; he had simply moved on; through the weeks, through the miles, on a journey fixed and pre-ordained. He had been a pilgrim—and now the pilgrimage had ended. He had lived a dream—and now the dream was done. He looked on ahead, to the south, and from where he stood he could not see far, for the trees and hills blocked off the view; but still, in his mind's eye, he could see beyond them; he could see the valley, the river, the miles, the thread of smoke; and beyond these more threads, more miles, more rivers and valleys and ranges, spreading on into distance, spreading on without end, into the wilderness. . . . Then he turned. He looked north. He saw the northern hill—the hill over which he had come; and beyond it was the route of his pilgrimage; beyond it the known world, the Ogaden, the highlands, Harar.

The dream was done, the pilgrimage ended. "Come. We will not die. We will live," he said to the woman.

And they headed north.

It had taken the caravan four days to travel from the Web Shebeli to the valley of the Worombu. It took them nine to make the journey in reverse.

On that first day they came up out of the valley, crossed the hill, and reached the campsite where he had left the caravan. Here he had hoped to find some remnants of food, or perhaps an implement or two that would be of use to them, but all that remained were footprints and dung. There was water nearby, however—a small stream by which they spent the night—and in the morning a second hope was realized when game approached to drink. From the concealment of the brush he fired at an antelope, and it went down. But at the sound of the shot the woman fell too and lay screaming in terror, and he was a long time in persuading her that no harm would come to her from his stick of death. Then the rest of the morning passed while they cooked and ate, and it was afternoon before they were ready to set out. The woman filled her gourd with water, and Claude slung what was left of the antelope over his shoulder. But at this the woman protested. Taking the carcass from him, she balanced it artfully atop her shaven head, and then in turn balanced the gourd upon the carcass, so that, as they marched off, she resembled a sort of ambulating tower. Claude laughed. It was the first time in a long while that he had laughed. And he said, *"Eh bien, ma jolie,* each sex to its appointed duties."

He carried his gun. His bullets were tucked into his money belt.

During the rest of the day, and through the second and third, they followed the route of the caravan. He did not like following it, for he knew that the caravan, too, would be moving slowly, with its column of slaves; but he was also reluctant to leave the trail, for it was well marked and offered water at known places. Early in the fourth day, however, he made his decision. In the first light of dawn, while the woman hauled water and prepared the last of the antelope meat, he trudged ahead toward a rise in the land to search for warning signs of dust or smoke in the northern sky. And again, as before, he saw none—but this time saw something else. On the trail, just beyond the crest of the rise, was a form, a *thing,* black and motionless—yet at the same time not motionless, for the blackness churned and glittered—and approaching closer, he saw the ants, the heap of ants, in their crawling thousands, and beneath them the half-devoured body of a Worombu child. Turning back, he rejoined the woman. He said nothing to her. But when, soon after, they moved on together, he bore off to the northeast, and they left the trail.

The land was enormous: vast in plain and brush and seas of grass. The hills had fallen away, and the forests too, and the trees were scattered thorny acacias, with, at intervals, a great baobab raising its gnarled and shrunken branches against the sky. Claude plotted their course by the baobabs. And by the sun. At night he watched the stars—watched Fomalhaut blazing bright in the southern heavens—and in the morning turned his back to where it had been and began the march.

His knee, amazingly, was all right. Even when the last of the magical paste was gone, it remained all right: a little stiff, perhaps, so that he moved with a slight limp, but free of pain and able to carry him through the miles. His head had long since ceased to bother him. It was his feet that bothered him now, for the soles of his boots were wearing through; and on the fourth night the woman wove new soles of coarse grasses and he put them as linings inside the old. The woman's own feet, of course, were bare. Her body was bare, except for the strip of loincloth and the few broken beads that hung over her breasts. And his body, too, was now almost naked, for he had kept ripping away at his burnous for fresh bindings for his leg, until all that was left was a strip around his middle, scarcely wider than his money belt, and another that he had wound around his head to ward off the sun.

On the woman's head, during the fourth and fifth days, there was only her gourd, for the antelope meat was gone and they encountered no game. In this country, too, there were neither fruits nor edible plants; and they were hungry. But at least there was water. And on the sixth morning, suddenly and inexplicably, they were surrounded by game. Indeed, when Claude awoke at first light it was to find a herd of eland grazing only a few yards away, and in a matter of moments he had his kill. Again the woman was frightened. Waking with a scream, she lay huddled and trembling, her hands covering her face; but this time, thanks to hunger, recovered more quickly and was soon preparing their meal. As, later, they moved on, the game increased and multiplied. There were gazelle and antelope by the hundred. There were herds of zebra and wildebeest. And at intervals, too, they sighted larger beasts on the grasslands: giraffe, buffalo, rhinoceros, elephant, lion. At one point they passed close to a bull elephant whose tusks must have weighed a full two hundred pounds: a small fortune in ivory.... "Yes, of course—a fortune," he thought. "To slip in my money belt. To balance on milady's head."... He did not shoot. They had food; all day he did not shoot again. And the animals, in turn, did not attack. Once a rhino eyed them, lowered its horn, grunting, and began a lumbering charge, while Claude waited with ready gun, but then abruptly changed its mind and thumped off into the bush. And once, in high grass, they came within a mere yard or two of a pride of lions; but the lions were busy over a feast of zebra and only rumbled, twitching their tails, as they passed.

The woman stayed close beside him, but showed no fear. Her fear was of sound—of the crash of the gun. And also, he later discovered, of thunder; for toward evening of that day, for the first time since they had left the valley, a storm gathered and broke upon them, and as long as it lasted she refused to move on, but lay prone on the earth, stiff with terror.

That night, with wild beasts still around them, they built a larger fire than usual and did not stray far from it. Now and then they could see the glint of eyes in the darkness, but nothing came close; they sat in flickering stillness. . . . And they themselves did not break the stillness. They did not talk. . . . Throughout the journey the woman had spoken scarcely a word, and Claude little more. Their life had no kinship to words. To live was to move, to find food, to find water, to eat, drink, rest—and move on. Yet now, watching her in the firelight, he found himself trying to pierce behind her silence, to imagine what lay hidden in her mind and heart. She was a savage—yes; but also a woman, a human being; and a human being had thoughts and emotions. Her village and her world had been destroyed, her people killed, enslaved, and she alone was left: alone in the wilderness with a man with a stick of death: a man such as she had never seen before, himself a killer, an enslaver. Yet only once had she declared herself in word or action. She had refused to go south. To the north, now, she went silently, unquestioningly, afraid only of the sound of thunder and gun, showing neither grief for what was gone nor apprehension of what lay ahead. What did she expect? What could she conceive to lie ahead? . . . He could not even surmise. No more than he could surmise, now that he tried to, what lay ahead for himself. . . . All that lay ahead, plain and sure, were the miles, the march, the wilderness, and beyond them the Web Shebeli. Sufficient unto the day was the march toward the Shebeli; to the night, their food, their water, and their fire.

The fire was sinking, and he piled it higher with brush and thorn. The woman was asleep now, lying on her back with head turned toward the flames, and their light gleamed on her shaven skull, her scarred cheeks, and the black bareness of her body. After a while she stirred slightly; her lips moved; faint sounds came from them. And he knew she was dreaming.

But of what?

The next day was the seventh, and now the country changed again. During the morning the land sloped slowly up before them, climbing at last to a low ridge which they crossed about midday, and beyond it was a downward slope, another plain—but a plain that was virtually desert. They were, Claude was sure, at last in the valley of the Shebeli, but the river was still hidden beyond the miles, and all that could be seen was red earth, yellow patches of grass, stunted thorn trees. There were no animals, no streams or water holes. And the earth grew drier as they advanced. A wind rose, lifting the dust from the earth, and blew it about them in red whirling spouts.

The dust grated under his eyelids. It was in his nose and mouth and throat. And thirst began: racking, tormenting. During the whole day's march, however, he denied himself a drink from the meager supply in the woman's gourd—only to find, when they stopped for the night (and it was his own fault, for he had neglected to warn her) that she had consumed almost all of it as she followed after him. They still had food: the remains of the eland. But it was now dry, bloodless, gritty with dust, and left them thirstier than before. Before lying down to sleep he allowed the woman and himself a swallow apiece of the remaining water; in the morning a second swallow. And that was the end of it.

As they trudged on, he kept a sharp lookout for a possible source of replenishment; but it was without real hope, for the land was utterly barren. Nor was there any hope of rain. Two days before, when they had had no need of water, the skies had opened and poured down a deluge; but now that they longed for it, were desperate for it, the skies were as bare and barren as the earth. What Claude *had* hoped was that on this eighth day they would reach the Web Shebeli; but that did not happen either. Sundown found them still trudging through a waste of dust and thornbush, and there they spent the night, while a hot wind blew and the dust sifted over them in a smothering blanket.

For the first time they did not build a fire. They scarcely ate or slept. And in the morning, long before first light, they were again on their way. . . . The hours crept past. And the miles. And while it remained dark it was not too bad; at least movement was better than lying still in the dust. But then dawn came, and sunrise, and from then on it was not earth at all over which they seemed to be moving, but rather through a flaming oven of heat and light. Claude's eyes ached, and he kept them slitted against the glare. His lips were swollen and cracked, his throat all but closed, and he could not force so much as a drop of saliva from the parched membranes of his mouth. Looking at the woman, he knew that she too was suffering, consumed by heat and thirst. But she made no complaint; said nothing at all. Hour by hour, mile after mile, she moved on behind him—silent, patient—a haunch of eland and her empty gourd still poised as before upon her shaven head.

Toward midday they rested. He had to rest. And when he rose he swayed and almost fell. His leg did not hurt. After the days of walking it was no longer even stiff. But it had no strength. Nor did his other leg. Nor his body. His body lurched and floundered, uncontrollable by his will; his head spun; and into the spinning, through slitted eyelids, poured the blazing tide of the sun. They went on—again rested—went on. Through the blaze now, when he turned, the woman was only a wavering shadow. And ahead were other shadows, in the blaze, in the dust: wavering, weaving . . . the shadows of hummock and hollow and thorn and sifting dust . . . and then, beyond them, another shadow—longer, darker—a long green shadow, a mirage. They approached the mirage. It was close now.

He stumbled and fell and stood up, and it was very close. It was a mirage he knew, that he had seen before; and he was coming down the hills of Italy in the sun-flame; he was moving through the desert of Egypt into the eye of the sun, into the delta of the Nile; and there before him again was the green of growth, the glint of water—and a voice croaked *"Thalassa! Thalassa!"* They were moving into the mirage, between trees—themselves in shadow, in coolness. They were on the bank of a river. They were lying prone on the bank, in cool grass, cool mud, their faces bent to the river, and the river flowed over their faces and into their eyes and mouths and throats and bodies.

They remained by the river.

Throughout that night and the next day they did not move from the spot at which they had reached it: lying on the bank, resting, sleeping, bestirring themselves only to perform the few essential acts of self-sustenance. Since they were again in animal country they made a fire against the darkness. And in the morning game came by the hundred to drink from the river, and Claude made another kill—a young spotted gazelle. Its flesh was tender and full of blood and brought the strength back into their bodies; and while he still ate—for, with thirst gone, his hunger was enormous—the woman went off into the trees and returned with fruits and berries. Later, they slept again, and when he awoke he bathed in the river. The woman, however, would not go in, in spite of his urging. Though she came from a riverside village, water was apparently another of her fears, and she would go only close enough to drink or to scoop it up in her hands. Yet in this way she too cleansed herself; and then they ate again; and then it was dark and again they slept.

In the morning they moved on. But they did not cross the river. It was neither broad nor swift, and Claude himself could have easily swum it, even carrying his gun. But for the woman it was another matter, and so he moved upstream along their own bank, on the watch for a ford. The ford he had crossed with the caravan was, he estimated, some fifteen to twenty miles in that direction—the northeast—and if he found nothing sooner it would again provide passage. It was still all-important, of course, not to run afoul of the slavers, but at the same time he could not risk wandering too far afield into trackless wilderness. They had had enough of that already; and besides, his bullets would not last forever.

They moved slowly. They rested often. Unlike the river of the Worombu, the Shebeli had open banks between trees and water that could be easily followed, and for the most part, too, they were straight and unindented. Toward late afternoon, however, they came to an inlet and, following its shore, reached its innermost point—a hidden place of still waters and green shade trees. Here a small stream flowed out into the river; the earth was carpeted with moss; and beneath the trees, at one point, was an interweaving of branch and leaf that made a small natural bower. And here they stopped again. They ate their evening meal. They spent the night. In the morning they rose to go on again. Claude put on his boots and picked up his gun—and then stopped and looked around him. He looked at the still water and the tall trees; at the green of leaf and moss and bower, the blue of sky above them, the gold of sunlight streaming in bars through the foliage; at the light, the stillness, the peace. . . . And then he turned and leaned his gun against a tree trunk.

"No, let us stay a while," he said.

And they stayed.

That day passed, and that night, and then the next and the next, and many more; and his knee was now wholly healed, he was well and strong; the woman was well and strong, and they could have gone on; but still they stayed in the bower beside the quiet inlet. They had such shelter as they needed. They had ample food. Small game abounded everywhere along the riverbank, and though there were larger beasts as well, the occasional sound of his gun and their nightly fires kept them safely away. Finding fish in the river, he made a trap to catch them. The woman gathered fruits and berries. She cooked. She fashioned implements from sticks and stones. And from long grasses and tree fronds she wove a mat on which they slept in the bower when the moss grew damp during the night.

Fish swam up into the inlet, but there were neither hippo nor crocodile, and Claude was in and out of the water many times each day. He swam along its shores, plunged deep into its cooling depths, lay floating with eyes closed on its surface web of sun and shadow; then, emerging, lay on the soft moss of the bank, beneath the trees. He lay. He dozed. He waked. He watched the weaverbirds. The weavers were small and bright and yellow and lived by the hundreds in their woven nests which hung like strings of pouches from the branches overhead. Great workers, they were forever patching their nests, storing food, hurrying off on aerial errands; flashing about like tiny balls of sunlight, while their chatter filled the stillness of the bank. Of other sounds there were few. Now and then the roar of a lion—but always distant. The crackle of their fire; the caw of a larger bird; the splash of a fish. And finally the softer, slower splash of Claude's own body, as he moved out again into the gleaming water.

At certain hours of the day the inlet's surface was a perfect mirror, and seeing his own image, he laughed, for he was tressed and bearded like a prophet. And the woman's hair, too, had grown considerably in the weeks they had now been together. It was not to any great length, to be sure, but enough so that she could no longer be called shaven, and the change had brought a certain new softness to her face. As with him, the outward marks of her ordeal had disappeared. Her thorn and bramble cuts were healed; her skin—except for the tribal cheek scars—was smooth and unblemished; and from certain shrubs in the forest she extracted an oil with which she coated it daily, so that it glistened silken black in the sunlight. When he had first seen her she had been wearing as ornament only the shreds of beads; and these were long since gone. But now, in their place, she wore a necklace and bracelets of twisted vine, and in her pierced ears two plugs of antelope bone that she had scraped and polished to the color of ivory. She still would not go into the water; when now and then he tried to persuade her she grew frightened and ran away. But he often found her at its edge, leaning over to peer at her reflection, and then again he would laugh, as when he had seen his own.

"One day we shall go to a *grand magasin* and buy Madame a cheval glass," he told her. "And then on down the boulevards in the fashion parade."

She smiled. Sometimes she smiled now. But, still, rarely spoke. And he knew nothing more about her than he had at the beginning—except her name.

Her name was Nagunda.

—Or something like Nagunda. When he had asked her it had been no more than a murmur on her lips, and he had heard it as that, and it was good enough. And he had asked her no other questions; for to what purpose would they have been? She had brought her name with her. She had brought herself. And all the rest was gone: her home, her tribe, her family, her past—gone in ashes and mud and death and the chains of slavery. Of what matter what she had been as a Worombu?—for she was a Worombu no longer. No more then he, here and now, was a Frenchman, an Ardennais, a Cambonard. They were two beings, that was all; man and woman; and past and future alike were remote and lost beyond the emerald screens of the riverbank.

Time flowed like the river: slowly, gently. The days came and went, the sun rose and set, and the moon waned from full to half to nothing—and the nights were dark—until it reappeared and swelled and grew, and then at last, again, was round and full. He hunted. He fished. He bathed. He lay on the moss of the bank and watched the weaverbirds; he watched the still inlet, the tall trees, the shining sky above the treetops; and he thought, "So you have come to your garden. You have found what you were seeking. And it is not the Garden of Death but the Garden of Life." Then he rose. He bathed again. The sun slanted away into dusk, and he sat on the bank, and the fire glowed, and Nagunda brought him his evening meal; and when he had finished it was dark, and the fire glowed brighter, and for a while they sat beside it in the stillness, and then lay down on their mat in the bower.

Once during the night, every night, he awoke and, arising, replenished the fire. Usually when he returned to the bower he fell asleep again immediately, but with the full of the moon he was wakeful and lay with eyes open, watching the inlet. In its farther reaches it was silver and black. Closer in, where the firelight touched it, it was silver and red, and the shore, where the fire stood before the bower, gleamed in a blend of flame and moonbeam. The light filtered into the bower. It lay on his eyes, his face, his body. It lay on the body of the woman, Nagunda, who lay beside him, glinting on the oiled black flesh of her breasts and stomach, on her vine-braceleted arm outflung across the mat. Her face was in shadow, but within the shadow, too, there was a flicker of light, of reflection, and he knew that her eyes were open. Her body moved slightly, and it was not in sleep. Her hand moved and touched him, and his hand touched her. It touched her hand, her arm, her body; the smooth oiled flesh, the flesh of woman. A few moments passed—and more—and he was close to her now, touching, holding her. He was lying against her, against her flesh, her body; and then no longer against her but upon her, a man upon a woman . . . and the thing that never could be, was; the thing that had never happened, happened . . . and he was upon her, within her, and she rose to meet him, and he was deep within her, his flesh within hers, and for an instant it was one flesh, *they* were one, and his seed flowed, the seed of life, of manhood. . . . And it had happened. It was done. And they were two. They were lying again side by side in the bower, in the fire- and moonlight, and the light did not grow brighter, it did not blaze; and there was no thunder in the sky, no shaking of the earth, but only the light and shadow, only the two of them in stillness; and then presently, in the stillness, the first sound that either of them had made, as the woman, eyes closed now, snored softly in her sleep.

The days came and went. And the nights. And the moon waned again into darkness. In the darkness, once, Druard came, but he did not speak; he passed by silently; and his eyes were sad in his skull-like face. Once Felix came. But he brought no woman. He did not laugh. And he too moved on and vanished—leaving the woman who was already there.

She was there in the darkness. There in the sunlight. Her skin was not white, nor her hair chestnut brown; and her eyes were not violet-blue. All were black. She was black. She was an African savage. Her name was Nagunda. And she was there.

The days passed. He hunted, fished, bathed. He lay on the moss of the bank in the fading sunlight, and then in the bower at night, with Nagunda beside him—a man with a woman—and when the sun reappeared he arose and again hunted their food. For a month the sun alone had been his calendar, but now the hunt too was a teller of time, for his supply of bullets was running low. He had fifteen left, and then a dozen, and then ten. And on the day he used the next he returned to Nagunda and said, "The time has come for us to go."

Again she asked no question. She spoke no word. Balancing meat and gourd on her head, she followed him silently around the inlet and along the shore of the Web Shebeli. They walked for the rest of that day, and then the next, and half the next; and then they came to a ford and crossed it, and on the far side cut diagonally northeastward toward the caravan trail. He was no longer concerned about meeting the caravan; by now it would be far across the Ogaden, perhaps almost to Harar. And when they reached the trail there was no sign of other, more recent traffic. They plodded on. They had water and food. Enough food so that he had to shoot for meat only once, using a single bullet: leaving eight. And on the fifth day from the Web Shebeli they came to the first of the Ogaden villages.

Nagunda was afraid. She trembled. But he took her arm, and she walked on, and they reached the center of the village and the assembled tribesmen. He could not tell if he was recognized. He did not know what they might have been told by the slavers. But he knew that *they* knew what a gun was—and he held his gun ready.

"*Allah maak,*" he said. "*Salaam aleikum.*"

"*Salaam,*" said their chief. "And who are you?"

"I am a traveler from the south. I am on a journey to the north."

"What do you want here?"

"I want two camels. And food. And some cloth for a burnous."

"We have no such things."

"Yes you have. I have seen them."

The men looked at him. They looked at his gun. At Nagunda. "What can you give in exchange?" said the chief. "This gun? This woman?"

"One camel," said another, "is worth twenty women."

"No, not the gun or the woman," Claude said. "I shall give you money. Gold and silver."

He took coins from his money belt and held them out. They glittered in the sunlight. And the eyes of the tribesmen glittered too.

"That is not enough," said the chief.

"I have more."

"Let me have it."

"When you bring the things that I need."

There was a consultation. Then the chief gave orders, and three men went off in various directions. After a while they returned: one leading two camels, one with a length of cloth, one with two sacks containing flour and dried dates.

"Now give me the money," said the chief.

Claude took about half his coins from his belt.

"No, all of it."

"This is more than enough."

"No—all."

Claude hesitated. The tribesmen waited. There were about fifty of them in the surrounding circle, and the circle was closer than before.

"All of it," the chief repeated.

There was the money belt. There was the gun. . . . One gun. . . . Claude unfastened the belt and held it out, and the chief took it and emptied it and then he nodded; and the man with the camels approached. The camels knelt, and the sacks and cloth were tied onto their backs, and then it was the turn of Claude and Nagunda. Nagunda was again afraid. He was sure she had never seen a camel before, let alone ridden one. But she was less afraid of them than of the tribesmen, and with Claude's aid she mounted. The camel swayed up. Claude mounted the other, swayed up, and took the lead rope of hers in his hand. The circle of tribesmen opened, they rode out through the village, and still he held the rope in one hand and his gun ready in the other. But there was no movement behind them. No one followed. The village receded, and they rode on through the hours, across the grasslands, and still there was no movement, no stirring of dust, on the flat horizon to the south.

He avoided the other villages. They encountered no one. Following the caravan trail, they found only faint footprints and dry crumbled dung, as they moved on through the miles of the Ogaden. They threaded the belt of hills and gorges, descended to the plains, and continued across them, day after day: across the red earth, the seas of grass, the flat and thorny wilderness sweeping endlessly to the north. Here the season of rains had not long since ended, and they found streams and water holes. The flour and dates they had got from the tribesmen reduced their need for meat, so that he had to expend a bullet on game no more than once a week. For himself, from the new cloth, he had fashioned a crude burnous that kept off the sun, and for Nagunda a sort of robe of the kind worn by Somali women. At first she would not wear it; but as time went on she grew curious, tried it, liked it—became proud of it—draping it each day in new ways about her body, adorning it with stripes of mud and pins of thorn. She had gradually lost her fear of her camel, and he no longer had to lead it. She rode behind him—as once she had walked behind him —silent, unquestioning, through the miles and the days.

At last, out of the flatness ahead, rose a hillock. The remembered hillock. He had little hope that his cache of hides would still be there. And he was right. Nearby were the remains of a caravan camp; the caves and clefts in the rock had been ransacked; his bag of lion and leopard belonged no longer to himself or Maison Gorbeau, but to the commercial kingdom of Abou Dakir.

They too made their camp beside the hillock. They ate, they slept, they moved on. They moved on toward the north—toward the end of the journey—and roped to their camels were one half-filled sack of dates and one of flour, and the partly eaten haunch of a newly killed antelope. There were no hides. There were no ivory, no gold, no money, no slaves. There was the food and the camels and a gun and four bullets. There was a woman, a black woman: riding behind him through the day, lying beside him in the night.

The sun rose and set and rose again, and they were alone under the sun.

A man and a woman.

Two souls and two bodies.

31

It was Egal who saw them first. He was standing on the stoop of Maison Gorbeau, talking with a Somali trader, and suddenly he raised his head and stared—and continued staring—and then ran out across the market square as fast as his short crooked legs could carry him. "Sidi!" he cried, and his gnome's face was beaming. "Sidi, it is you! You have come back. It is you!"

Claude and Nagunda were on foot. One of the camels had sickened and died in the northern Ogaden; the other he had sold in Bubassa in exchange for food and a few piasters. From Bubassa they had walked. And now at last they walked through the great square of Harar—and stopped —as Egal reached them and seized both of Claude's hands in his own.

"Oh sidi, sidi!" said the little Arab. "We had thought you were dead."

"No, I am not dead, Egal," Claude said.

"We heard from the men of Abou Dakir—"

"What did you hear?"

"That you were lost—had disappeared. That the savages had killed you."

"No, they did not kill me. I got away."

"Thanks to Allah."

Egal released him at last. . . . "But now come," he said. "You have walked, yes? You are tired, thirsty. Come in and rest, and I will bring you coffee." He seized Claude's arm and led him toward the entrance of Maison Gorbeau, taking no notice of Nagunda, standing off to one side. "Ah, it is so fine, sidi—such a surprise. And the new sidi—*he* will be so surprised—"

"The new sidi?"

"Yes. You do not know, of course. He has been here now for some months, and—"

But by now they were up the steps and in the store. To the right was the office, and the door was open, and Claude saw the man at the desk inside. He saw the bright white linen, the polished shoes. He saw the balding head and glinting glasses bent to an open ledger; and then he entered the office, and the head was raised, and he met the quick sharp glance of Monsieur Marcel Rappe.

"I am busy now. You will please wait," said Rappe brusquely. He bent back toward the ledger—and stopped. He looked up again; his face changed; what had been a glance was now a stare. *"Nom de Dieu!"* he said. And again: *"Nom de Dieu!"*

"Salaam aleikum," said Claude.

"We—we thought you were dead."

"Yes, Egal has told me."

"But—"

"But I am not—no." Claude smiled a little. "I hope it is not too inconvenient."

Rappe arose slowly and came around the desk. He did not offer his hand, but stopped a few paces away and surveyed Claude from head to foot.

"It is the ensemble," said Claude, "of the well-dressed Ogaden tribesman."

"You were among them all this time?"

"No, not for long."

"Where then?"

"I have been in Cimmeria."

"Cimmeria?"

"The land of whirlwinds and darkness.... It is a mythical country. But most interesting." Claude unslung his gun and sat down. "If you will permit me—" he said. "My feet are tired."

"You have walked far?" asked Rappe.

"Yes, far."

"You have no caravan?"

"No."

"You have brought nothing back?"

"I have brought one companion."

"I mean goods—produce. No hides or plumes? No ivory or gold?"

"No, nothing."

"And the money you took with you?"

"That is gone."

Rappe started to speak again, but changed his mind and cleared his throat instead. Then he moved back behind the desk, and Egal came in with coffee.

"It is like the old times, sidi," he said, pouring. "I am so happy—so glad."

Egal went out, and Claude sipped the coffee. Rappe sat silently, watching him.

"But you, I gather, are not," said Claude.

"Eh?"

"Not so glad I am back."

Rappe again cleared his throat. "I am of course glad you were not killed," he said.

"But—"

"But there is more to it than that, I am afraid. These are serious things that have happened."

"Precisely what things, monsieur?"

"Your abandonment of the store. Your disappearance for all these months."

"I could scarcely control the length of my absence."

"Perhaps not. But you could have controlled your going in the first place."

"I wrote to Aden that I was going."

"Yes, you wrote. But you did not wait for an answer, did you? You did not give us any details, any information at all. Most particularly"—Rappe's voice was hard and edged—"you did not say that you were going with slavers."

"It was the only way to get to the south."

"Hmm—the only way. So you go to the south. With slavers. You disgrace the good name of Maison Gorbeau, which has never had any part in such things, and to top it off, you return with *nothing*."

Claude finished the coffee and set down his cup. "The expedition was not a success," he said. "And I made mistakes; I grant you that. In the next few days I shall send my report to Monsieur Gorbeau."

Rappe shook his head. "No, that will not be necessary. You will give it to me. Why, may I ask, do you think I was sent here?"

"I have been wondering," said Claude. "I would have thought it would have been Fitzsimmons."

"Fitzsimmons is no longer with us. He proved unsatisfactory—wholly unreliable." Rappe's sharp eyes glinted behind his glasses. "Unfortunately the firm has been having considerable trouble with that sort of thing."

"And you are in charge of putting it to rights."

"Yes, I am."

There was a pause. Then a figure appeared in the door. It was not Egal, but a man unfamiliar to Claude—a young Harari—and he put a slip of paper before Rappe, waited silently for his signature, and then left.

"I see there are changes here too," Claude said.

"You mean Hussein? Yes, there was too much for Egal alone. I hired him about a month ago."

"And Vayu?"

"Who?"

"Vayu. The boy. Was he not here when you came?"

"Oh, that one—yes. He was here, but not for long."

"You mean you discharged him?"

"Yes."

"Why?"

"He was no use at all. Hopeless. A mere child—a ragamuffin."

"I see. And where is he now?"

"Now?" Rappe shrugged. "How on earth should I know?"

"You have not seen him since?"

"No, of course not."

Claude rose and walked to the office door. The store itself looked the same as ever: the long counter, the shelves, and on the shelves the assorted cloth, hardware, and cheap jewelry that were Maison Gorbeau's chief stock in retail trade. It smelled the same: of hides, gums, and coffee—though these were out of sight behind the storeroom door. There was, at the moment, a single customer in evidence, and Egal was waiting on him. The new Harari, Hussein, was not there. But now, suddenly, through the front door, Claude saw him gesturing angrily on the stoop outside.

Then he heard Nagunda's voice. And he himself went outside. Nagunda had apparently tried to enter the store, and the man had seen her, and now he was pushing her down the stoop, while she struggled against him.

"Let her alone," Claude told him. "What has she done wrong?"

"She is a Shankalla, a bushwoman," the man said. "They come only to beg, and we do not want them around."

"This one is not a beggar. She is with me."

"With you?"

"Yes, let her by."

The Harari looked confused, but he stepped aside, and after a moment went back into the store.

"Come," Claude said. And Nagunda mounted the stoop. "Come, you're tired. I'll take you upstairs where you can rest."

He started toward the outside stairway that led up to the veranda and his old dwelling room. But before they reached it Rappe emerged from the store.

"I had not known our interview was over," he said coolly.

"I'll be back shortly," said Claude.

"So? And where are you going, may I ask?"

"To my room."

"And this—woman?"

"I am taking her there."

Rappe came closer. Stopping, he inspected Nagunda, as before, in the office, he had inspected Claude: slowly, deliberately, from head to foot. Then he turned to Claude.

"This is the 'companion' you spoke of?" he said.

"Yes."

"But you meant 'slave.' Not only do you associate with these filthy Arabs, these slave hunters, but you come back with one of your own."

"She is not a slave," said Claude.

"No? What then? Your concubine?"

"Say, rather, my wife."

"Your wife?" For the first time since Claude had surprised him Rappe's face lost its rigid composure. "What sort of joke is that?" he said. *"Quelle espèce de bêtise?"*

"It is no *bêtise*. She is my wife, my woman. And I am taking her upstairs."

Claude made as if to move past, but Rappe interposed himself. "Oh no you are not," he said.

"Not?"

"Most certainly not."

"And what do you suggest I do with her?"

"I don't care. Tell her to go. Sell her to your Arab friends. Whatever you like. But I am not having any black whore or slave—or whatever she is—in my establishment."

"*Your* establishment?"

"Precisely."

"After four years, monsieur—"

"After four years," said Rappe, "it is a wonder to me that there is any store left at all. Four years of mismanagement, neglect, consorting with all sorts of riffraff—with slavers. Finally disappearing altogether, so that I have to be sent from Aden to take charge."

"Oh, I see. It is you who are now in charge here?"

"Yes."

"And I am to take your orders?"

"Yes."

There was a moment's pause; and now it was Claude who, with slow deliberation, looked Marcel Rappe up and down. His eyes were like chips of ice in his dark leathery face, and his voice, when he spoke, was quiet.

"*Va te faire foutre*," he said.

Suddenly Rappe's face, too, was dark—with rushing blood. "What?" he demanded. "What did you say? Whom do you think you are talking to?"

"To *un assis*, monsieur. *Un grand fonctionnaire*. A fine gentleman who may take his Hornsby's shoe polish and shine his behind."

"*Crapule! Salaud!* And what are you, may I ask?" Rappe's countenance was apoplectic. "You are a slaver. A renegade. A disgrace to this firm—and to all Frenchmen."

His voice had risen. Eyes turned to them from the market square, and a crowd began to gather. Egal and the Harari clerk emerged and stood watching: the first unhappily, the second with wide eyes.

With an effort Rappe got hold of himself. "In any case," he said, and his voice was again cold and precise—"I do not intend to provide an exhibition for this *canaille.* . . . When you regain your senses, I shall be in my office, and we can discuss matters. But first this woman must go, do you understand? I will have no slaves or whores here, and that is final."

He turned and walked quickly back into the store, his heels clicking on the wooden planking. The crowd went its way. The Harari followed him in. But Egal came to Claude, and his goblin face was full of worry. "There is something wrong, sidi?" he asked. "There is trouble between you and Sidi Rappe."

Claude, too, was calm now; his voice still quiet. "Yes, there is trouble," he said.

"So what will you do?"

"First I shall go and find some food for my wife and myself."

"And then?"

"Then we shall see."

Gesturing to Nagunda, he moved away; and turning, he noticed for the first time the sign above the store entrance that he had placed there long before. It now read:

MAISON GORBEAU
M. Rappe—Gérant

He did not go back. He found a room in a house on one of the steep streets off the market square, and he and Nagunda moved in. The moving, initially, consisted of their bodies, the clothes on their backs, and his bulletless gun; but with the money remaining from the sale of the camel he bought food and a few basic implements and furnishings. Their ménage was squalid and primitive—but less primitive than anything they had had before in their months together. They had a straw pallet, a blanket, a brazier for cooking. And Claude showed Nagunda how to use a knife and a match.

On the third day Egal found them and looked about with dismay. "I have searched all over for you, sidi," he said. "And Sidi Rappe, he wants also to see you."

"So?"

"Yes, he has asked me to bring you to the store."

"And my wife?"

"Your wife?" Egal stared at Nagunda. "No, sidi, he said nothing about that."

"Tell Sidi Rappe," said Claude, "that I am accepting no invitations that do not include my wife."

No amended invitation came. But Egal returned. "If you will no longer be at the store," he said, "then I, Egal, will leave too."

"And do what?" asked Claude.

"Come with you, sidi."

"But I have no business, no work. Not even for myself, so I have nothing for you."

Egal frowned. He was unhappy. He argued. But in the end it was decided that, for the time being, he would stay with Rappe. Every few days, however, he paid a visit to Claude's new domicile, usually bringing with him foodstuffs or other articles from the store, and though Claude protested it was with no great vehemence. "All right, let us call it my bonus," he said finally, smiling. "A farewell token of appreciation from Maison Gorbeau."

One day he sat down to write a letter. . . . *Cher Monsieur Gorbeau.* . . . But he got no farther. And instead, the next day, he sat down to another.

Dear Mother, he wrote. *It is many months since you have heard from me, and I hope you have not been concerned. The long trip of which I wrote you is now over, and I have come through it in good health. But unfortunately it was not a financial success; indeed, it has resulted in the termination of my employment with Gorbeau and Company; and for the time being, therefore, I shall be unable to send you further funds. This is a situation that, of course, I hope will soon be rectified. And meanwhile, if you are pinched, I suggest you speak to Michel Favre, at the bank, about a second mortgage on the farm.*

As for myself, I am living rather more simply than before—but well enough —and I have a native woman to keep house for me. How about yourself? I hope you are comfortable and not lonely. Does Yvette get home occasionally from the nunnery? And do you hear anything of Felix? It is now quite some time since I have had occasion to think of him . . .

During the first week or two he went out rarely. He made the room livable. He spent much time with Nagunda, who had to be patiently taught every act and aspect of city living. She cooked for him. She cleaned and fetched and carried, and learned the use of soap and pots and buckets and a broom. She never went out, asked no questions, showed no curiosity in the life of Harar that swarmed about them. By day she worked, and when she was through working sat silently in a corner, her knees high, her rump on her heels, as she had once sat on the forest floor in the Worombu valley. At night she lay beside him on the straw pallet, and they slept together as man and wife.

Soon his money was all but gone. And though Egal still brought food, this could not go on forever. Tossing his last piaster, he designated heads as Spiranthos the Greek, tails as Mardik the Syrian; and Mardik came up; and he went to him. The Syrian was short and fat and buttery, with eyes like two raisins in his yellow face. And his initial greeting to Claude was reserved and wary, for he had obviously heard what had happened and believed that a man in trouble brings trouble. But when he learned why Claude had come he unbent. Why yes, he thought, there might well be a place for Monsieur Morel in his mercantile establishment. It was only a small one, of course; nothing like the great Maison Gorbeau. But at least it was growing—yes. He had high hopes. Already, he was pleased to say, he had well outdistanced the wily Greek, Spiranthos. "And in time, my friend, who can tell?" he said; and now the raisin eyes were shrewd and smiling. "With your experience added to mine, perhaps we shall soon be showing a trick or two to our good friend Monsieur Rappe."

So Claude went to work for Taklu Mardik—at a wage less than Egal's at Maison Gorbeau. He who had been the city's leading merchant was now not a merchant at all, but a merchant's assistant, a clerk. Behind the counter of Mardik's shop he sold pins and pots and yard goods, as he had once, as a child, in another shop far away. He was no longer *monsieur le gérant* or *honored sidi*—a man to be reckoned with, to be deferred to—but merely one among nameless thousands in the swarming city. Threading the market square, he sometimes, through the doorway of Maison Gorbeau, saw Marcel Rappe seated at his desk, immaculate in white linen and glinting spectacles, while a line of tradesmen waited to see him. And sometimes, too, he saw the governor, Hajj Pasha, proceeding here or there with his uniformed escort. But Hajj Pasha, now, did not in turn see him; for his eyesight was poor when it came to citizens who neither paid taxes nor were a source of Strasbourg pâté or Turkish cigars.

Claude did not care. . . . *Qu'importe?* What did it matter? . . . He did not consider leaving Harar, for Harar was home: as much of a home as he had ever had. *"Ici je suis chez moi,"* he had once said. "I am at home here. I have found my niche." And now he was back in his niche, and if it was smaller and more obscure than before, it was still a place that was his, in which he belonged and functioned; and in it, now, he was not alone. Through the days he worked busily in Mardik's store. Leaving it, he moved through the crowded streets, the crowded square. He went to a coffeehouse. For an hour he sat there, drinking, smoking, talking—talking with the other men of the city, the merchants, traders, and clerks, about the things of the

day—and then he went home through the streets, through the street of
the balcony and the watching eyes; but he did not stop there; he did not
look up, but went on; he went on home, to the tiny room, to Nagunda;
and she was waiting, she gave him his supper, and when supper was over
and the lights were out, they lay together in the darkness as man and wife.
He was a man with work, with a home, with a woman. A man among
thousands. A man. . . .

The days passed. And the nights.

Then one night there was a knock on the door, and Claude opened it,
expecting Egal. But it was not Egal. It was a taller figure that stood there
—a younger figure—lithe, slender, with a wild shock of hair and shining
eyes. And as Claude stared, in the dim light, the figure moved closer and
seized his hands, crying, "Yes—yes, it is I, Sidi Claude. It is Vayu—"

They came together into the room, and still Claude stared, for the boy
had grown half a head in the months since he had seen him. "Oh sidi," he
went on, the words tumbling upon each other, "it is so fine—so wonderful.
We thought you were dead—yes—gone, lost—and I felt so sad. But today
I came back to Harar—I too have been gone—and I see Egal and he tells
me and so I come—I come running—" Vayu paused for breath. His eyes
searched Claude's face. "You are well, sidi. You are all right, I can see. I am
so happy." Then his own face changed; his eyes grew worried. "But you,
sidi—you are happy too, yes?" he said. "I mean to see me—that I am here.
You are no longer angry?"

"No Vayu," said Claude, "I am not angry."

"You were before. Before you went away, and I did not know why; but
you were angry and would not speak to me, and I was sad, I cried; it was
so awful. What I did wrong I did not know, but I will not do it again, not
ever, I promise. If you will tell me what it was, sidi—truly I will never do
it again."

"It was nothing," said Claude. "That is past, done with."

"And we are friends again. Oh, that is so fine, so good—"

The boy's eyes shone again. He squeezed Claude's hands. He all but
danced. And now Claude pressed his hands in return, and smiled, and said,
"Yes, it is good. And I am happy too. I am just surprised; I didn't know
where you were. . . . You said you have come back. You were away too,
then? Where?"

"I have been out to the villages. I and Father Lutz."

"Father Lutz?"

"Yes, I am with him now."

"*With* him?"

"Yes, sidi. When you left I was of course still at the store. For many
months I was there, with Egal, the same as always. But then the new sidi

came, the *ferangi*, and he did not like me. He told me to go, and I went, and for a while I was like I used to be—around the streets, with no work, no house, nothing. Then I saw Father Lutz. In the street—he saw me—he took me home. He said I should stay. And I stayed. I have worked for him. I have cooked, kept clean, made errands, everything. And he has let me teach—" The boy's voice grew proud. "Yes, sidi, in the school, he lets me teach—the small boys—the alphabet and sums and how to read—and he says I have done well, that he needs me, and when last month he goes out on a trip to the villages, he says I should come too, and I go."

Claude's smile was now full and warm. "So—I am glad, boy. It has been all right with you."

"Yes, all right, sidi—"

The smile changed a little. "And now, to go with all this, I suppose you are a Christian."

Vayu's face changed too. His eyes were again worried. "With—with the Father you know how it is, sidi," he said stumblingly. "He is a priest. He thinks all the time of such things—"

"And he baptized you?"

Vayu hung his head. "Yes, sidi," he murmured. Then he looked up earnestly. "But it means nothing, sidi. Truly. Do not be angry. I am not a good Christian—no. You understand. It was only for the Father—to make him happy. Truly I am not a good one at all—"

Claude's smile became a laugh. "I am not angry, Vayu," he said. "I understand."

"Oh sidi, thank you. I am so glad." The boy's face was bright again. "And anyhow," he said, "it does not matter. For now I will not be with the Father any longer but again with you, and we—"

He broke off for Claude was shaking his head. "No? You will not take me? Oh sidi—you *are* still angry then?"

"No, not angry, Vayu—believe me. But I have no work for you now. Didn't Egal tell you that I am no longer with Maison Gorbeau?"

"Yes, he told me. But he said you were with Mardik."

"With Mardik, yes. But only working for him. I am no longer the big sidi. I cannot hire anyone."

"Then I will work here. I will cook, clean."

"There is not room. There is only what you see. And besides—" Claude indicated Nagunda, who was squatting silently by the brazier, preparing supper. "Besides, you see, I have someone—"

Vayu could not but have seen her when he came in the door, but for the first time he showed awareness. "She is a Shankalla?" he asked.

"She is like a Shankalla. From far to the south."

"You brought her back with you?"

"Yes."

"And she takes care of you?"

"Yes."

"And is your woman?"

Claude nodded. "Yes, Vayu, she is my woman."

There was a pause. The boy's face was sad. Then he looked up at Claude, and it changed and was not sad. "I am glad, sidi," he said. "For myself I am sorry, that I cannot come here and stay. But for you I am glad—that you have a woman. . . . You have needed a woman, sidi. Remember—how I told you?" He looked again at Nagunda, and he smiled. "Remember when we went to the villages, you and I—like I now go with the Father—and we see the girl at the stream with the leopard-skin bucket, and I say you should buy her, but you say to me no? Well, so now you have a girl—a woman. And that is good. This one is not so pretty, sidi. No, the other she was a princess, a sultana, and this one is not. But still she is a woman; she is yours. Yes, I am glad, sidi."

Claude was smiling too. "Thank you, Vayu," he said.

"And maybe in a while," said the boy, "you will have a bigger place and I can come. Maybe you will be partner of Mardik, head of Mardik, like you were of Gorbeau, and then I will come there, and work, and be with you again."

"Yes, maybe that will happen."

"For that is what I want, sidi. What I want most of everything: to be with you. The Father is good, he is kind to me, but it is not the same. Nothing can ever be the same as it was with you. . . ."

The brazier steamed and bubbled. Supper was ready. And Vayu stayed.

"I will come again, Sidi Claude," he said later, when it was time for leaving. "I will come every day to see you, here and at Mardik's—please; do not say no; please—and then soon, one day, I will come and things will be different and I will not go. I will stay with you, like before. I will be with you, always—"

Claude did not say no, as he went with him to the door and said good-night. And Vayu left as he had come: face bright, eyes shining.

The next night there was another knock. And it was Father Hippolyte Lutz. His long beard came into the room with the broad face and brown robe behind it, and he stood shaking Claude's hand while his small eyes appraised him shrewdly.

"Welcome, my son. Welcome back," he said. "Vayu has told me he is no longer in your bad books, and I hope the same holds true for me."

"I am glad to see you, Father," said Claude quietly.

"Good. Splendid. A general amnesty." The priest smiled. "And so here you are at last. And I am glad too. Although to me, I confess, it is no great surprise. Everyone else seemed to have given you up—to think you gone, lost, dead—but not I, my son. Oh no. Our Sidi Morel will be back, I told them. He will survive, win through. His strength is as the strength of ten —though not, perhaps, for the traditional reason."

He chuckled. "So I was right and you are back," he said. "But with some changes, I see." His eyes moved around the squalid room and fixed on Nagunda, who was squatting as usual beside the brazier. "Vayu told me you had brought home a—" he hesitated, "—a companion," he said. "And that I was sorry to hear."

"Were you?"

"Deeply, my son." Lutz was no longer smiling. "I was saddened, as you know, when you went off with the men of Abou Dakir. But at least I did not think that you yourself would return with a slave."

"She is not a slave," said Claude.

"No? What then, my son?"

"She is my wife."

"Your wife?"

"Yes, exactly that. My wife. My woman."

"But—"

"But we are not what you called married? No. We have not had the sacrament of your church. . . . But still we are married. We have performed our own sacrament." Claude's eyes met the priest's and held them, and he said: "What I am saying to you is the truth. She is not a slave. We are man and wife."

There was a pause. Lutz returned his gaze. Then he turned and went to Nagunda and stood beside her. "Welcome to you too, my daughter," he said gently, in Somali. "Will you tell me your name?"

It was the first time since Claude and she had been together that anyone other than he had spoken a word to her. She raised her eyes, but only for an instant, casting them quickly down again; and she did not speak.

"Her name is Nagunda," said Claude.

"Does she know any of the languages of Harar?"

"I have taught her a few words of Arabic. But she is shy and afraid."

"Yes, of course she is—in such a strange new world." Stooping, Lutz laid his hand on her head. "Welcome again, Nagunda," he said in Arabic, slowly. "I hope you will be happy here. And we shall do all we can to help you."

Again Nagunda looked up, and this time it was for longer. Her lips moved, and for a moment it seemed she would speak—or smile. But then she bent her head; she remained silent; and it was Lutz who smiled down at her as he turned away.

"There is a Shankalla woman who comes to my church," he said to Claude, "and who knows the ways and languages of the south. With your permission I shall ask her to come here—during the day, while you are gone—and I think it may be good and pleasing for Nagunda."

"Yes, that would be kind of you," said Claude. "She is by herself too much, and she is lonely."

The priest nodded. Again he looked around the room. Then again at Claude. "And you, my son?" he asked after a pause. "Is there, perhaps, anything I can do for you?"

"For me? How for me?"

"Since I returned yesterday from my trip I have been around the town a bit. I have been to Maison Gorbeau and know the trouble there, and I am sorry."

"By now, I daresay, you are an old friend of Monsieur Rappe."

"I know Monsieur Rappe—yes, of course. I still go to the store occasionally, and every Sunday he comes to my church."

"He is most devout, I am sure."

"Yes, he is devout; and at heart a good man, I am sure. But—well—rigid, unimaginative. A very different sort of man from you, my son." Lutz smiled a little. "But then, most men are different from you, are they not?"

No answer was expected or given. He went to the door, and then he turned and again shook hands. "In any case," he said, "welcome back. And if I can be of any help, I shall be pleased."

"Thank you," said Claude, "but *I* have no need for a Shankalla woman. . . . Or of prayers," he added, and now it was he who smiled.

"I was thinking rather of something more—practical."

"No, thank you, Father. I have all I require."

"You are sure?"

"I am sure."

Once again the priest looked around the room. At its bareness and squalor. At the stone floor, the straw pallet, the brazier. At the woman beside the brazier, black, crouched, and silent, with the scars of a savage tribe etched long and deep into her cheeks. He looked at Claude—into his face, into his eyes—but the eyes were opaque, and he turned his own away.

"So—I will come again," he said, "—if I may."

"Yes, of course," said Claude.

"And you too must come to me—as you used to. I am still a good cook, you know. And a bad cardplayer."

"I am afraid I can no longer bring cigars. You will have to get them from Monsieur Rappe."

"I shall manage without them, my son. Bring your wife instead. She will be welcome too."

The weeks passed. And the months.

He worked at Mardik's. At first he earned barely enough for food, for rent, and for his and Nagunda's few other basic needs. But old customers followed him to the Syrian's shop; soon sales had increased by some fifty per cent; and in a month he had gained a raise, and in two months another. Mardik, to be sure, was a merchant not noted for openhandedness. But he knew a good thing when he saw it—or at least when it clanked on his counter—and he knew, too, that Spiranthos the Greek was watching his new clerk with covetous eyes.

Claude had not asked for the raises. Nor when he received them did he change his way of living. He worked a full ten hours a day. Leaving the store in the evening, he went to a coffeehouse for a cup and a pipe. From there he went on home to supper, to Nagunda; to sleep the night with Nagunda; and in the morning at seven he returned to the store.

He had work. He had a home. He was not alone.

Vayu he saw almost every day, either at the store or his dwelling, and each time the boy stayed as long as Claude permitted and ended up by pleading that he could stay for good.

"But there is no space in my one room," Claude told him.

"So I will sleep in the courtyard."

"And no job in the store."

"But yes—it is growing now. You are so busy. You need a helper."

"Mardik will not pay for a helper."

"He will if you ask him. If you say you must have me. Please, sidi—"

"No, Vayu, I cannot do that. Not yet."

"But soon, sidi? Yes? Please, sidi. Maybe soon."

"Yes—maybe soon."

Egal, too, appeared often. And he too wanted to work again for Claude, but was less importunate. He brought gossip of Maison Gorbeau. ("The retail sales are much down. . . . The caravan rates have been raised. . . . The Harari clerk is an imbecile.") And once he said: "Sidi Rappe, he is worried, I will tell you that; for he does not understand the people here, or how to deal with them. One day, for sure, he will come and ask you to go back with him—even with the woman." And the gnome's face crinkled into a complacent grin.

Father Lutz came, dropping by now and then for a few words and trying gently and patiently to speak with Nagunda. And sometimes, returning home, Claude found his Shankalla there—a fat black woman named Onuz, who, as soon as he appeared, invariably rose and in quick silence took her leave. Despite Lutz's repeated invitations, however, he did not take Nagunda to the priest's. Nor did he go himself for cards or supper, for he did not want to leave her alone in the night.

Sometimes, of course, he saw Marcel Rappe, passing in the streets or the market square; but Rappe did not approach or speak to him, and at most nodded coolly as they went by. The Greek merchant, Spiranthos, was, however, another matter; for he had taken to greeting Claude at every opportunity, inviting him to his shop and home, in a strenuous effort to lure him from his rival, Mardik. And the result was that presently, for the third time—and without asking—Claude received an increase in pay from his employer.

Dear Mother, he wrote one evening: *Your return letter has been received and there is no point in your railing at my loss of my position with Gorbeau and Company. I have, I am glad to say, now found other employment, and while it is not yet so remunerative, I have advanced rapidly, and I am happy to be able to send you at least the token amount of one hundred francs. I would like to make it more, but. . . .* He paused in his writing. He looked up and across the room at Nagunda; at her black face, her broad nose, her scarred cheeks; and he smiled. . . . *but I have undertaken certain obligations,* he wrote, *which make it impossible for me to do so at this moment. . . .*

That night, for the first time in months, he dreamed. It was not of Felix, nor of Druard—they were gone and lost—but of his mother; and he was entering her house; he was holding Nagunda's hand and leading her toward his mother, and he said, "Mother, may I present to you my Certain Obligation. Mother and wife, may I present you to each other— my Nigger Queens." . . . Then his mother put out her hand, but whether to strike or caress him he could not tell; and he saw the hand, he felt it, and it was hard, white, and cold; he had seized it, was clinging to it, drawing it to him; he was drawing her body to him—his mother's—yet not his mother's—for it changed now, it was different, and what had been hard was soft, what had been cold was warm, and it was not his mother he held, but the other—Nagunda; and she was beside him, close against him, not in dream now, not in sleep, but warm, soft, stirring, living, and he sank deep into the living warmth of Nagunda's flesh.

She was flesh. A body.
She was a woman. His wife.
But she was also a savage, a creature of the Stone Age torn from her tribe, her village, from all she had ever known or experienced, and transplanted to a world of whose existence, a few months before, she had been wholly ignorant.
And her adaptation was slow and painful.
The simplest acts of everyday living had to be taught to her—and taught again and again. To light a lamp and to cook with charcoal. To draw water from a well. To handle a broom, a knife, a spoon, and pots and pans. Even to sit occasionally on a stool or bench, instead of on the floor on her haunches. Most difficult of all was the problem of language; for her tribal

Bantu had no words for most of the objects and acts in which her new life involved her, and she showed little facility for learning Arabic or Somali.

Still Claude persisted: patiently, doggedly. Each evening, during supper and after, he struggled to teach her a few words and how to put them together; and slowly she reached the point where she could understand simple statements and questions. But there was little resemblance to the earlier sessions of the Lycée Morel; none of the response, the spark, the excitement that had marked the teaching of his pupil, Vayu. Nagunda was docile, complaisant; she tried to please. She repeated words and phrases after him, parrotlike, and with enough repetition they stuck in her memory. But there was no contributing force from within, no curiosity or reach for meaning; and even when her vocabulary had become sufficient to her simple needs, she spoke scarcely more than she had before. It was not only lack of words, Claude knew, that held her silent, but, far more, that she had nothing to say. Her body was his. And her attentions and labor. But her mind and spirit were as remote as ever, hidden deep and unfathomable in the primitive past.

Even after a few months in Harar she scarcely ever went out; for the crowds in the streets terrified her. She made no friends among the women of the neighborhood, and when Egal or Vayu came sat silent in a corner—or, still silent, brought them coffee or food when Claude so directed. Only with Father Lutz did she seem gradually to become at ease, answering him when he spoke to her in his deep gentle voice and sometimes raising her eyes in a shy smile. And Claude gathered, too—though he seldom saw them together—that she responded to the Shankalla woman, Onuz, for the latter came often and stayed long, and once even induced Nagunda to go with her to Father Lutz's.

"So—you were not murdered in the streets," Claude said to her, smiling, after this event. Then he asked, "And how was it for you? Did you enjoy yourself?"

"Yes," she replied, "it was nice."

But when he tried to get her to tell more he was unsuccessful. Even with him, alone, she could not give voice to what was within her and could say only, over and over, "Yes, it was nice. It was very nice."

One—almost the only—aspect of city life which she had taken to easily was the wearing of clothes. Early on, he had bought her a Harari costume, to replace the makeshift robe acquired in the Ogaden, and she reveled in its bright colors, in its shawl, bodice, tight trousers, and flaring skirt. Also he had brought home from the store a small mirror—scarcely the cheval glass he had talked of on the inlet of the Web Shebeli, but still a mirror, the first she had ever seen—and before it she preened herself happily by the hour. If she did not consort with the neighborhood women, it was obvious that she at least watched them, for she was trying assiduously to shape her hair, now some three or four inches long, into an approximation of their coiffure. And she had taken to hiding her cheek scars with oils and salves and adopted the Harari style of kohled eyes and reddened lips.

Claude watched her and smiled. And mused. "So, she is a woman," he thought. "A savage—but still a woman." . . . Or, rather, three. . . . One was this woman, the outward, the visible, now scarcely distinguishable from other dark-skinned women of Harar. The second was the woman of silence, of withdrawal, the croucher in corners, the bush creature captive and afraid. And the third was the woman of the nighttime, of clothing laid aside and flesh laid bare; of fear gone, of loneliness gone, of everything gone, stripped away, except the flesh of her womanhood; of *his* woman, his wife, his Nigger Queen. . . .

The other women did not matter. What mattered was the woman who had made him a man.

One evening after work he sat alone at a table in a coffeehouse. Presently there was a movement at the street doorway, and several men came in, most of them young and tall, but with one at their center who was small and old, and this one approached and sat down beside him.

"*Salaam*, Sidi Morel," said Abou Dakir. "I felt it would be most unfriendly to pass through Harar without paying my respects to my old associate."

"That is kind of you, Sidi Abou," said Claude. "Will you not join me in a cup of coffee?"

"With pleasure," said Abou Dakir. And the coffee was brought and he sipped it slowly.

"So, it is long time since we have met," he said. "More than a year, I think, since you set out for the Web Shebeli."

"Yes, more than a year," said Claude.

"And much has happened."

"Much."

"As it chanced, I was not hereabouts when the caravan returned. My affairs took me to Zanzibar. Then to Lamu and Mukalla and Zeila. For an old man, alas, I must do much journeying. . . . But in Zeila, at last, I received reports of the venture."

"From Nasruddin."

"No, not from Nasruddin. Had you not heard? Nasruddin caught fever and died on the trip between here and Zeila. It was from others I had the reports—and among them, of course, that you had been lost."

Claude said nothing. Abou Dakir sipped his coffee, and the steam rose into his pale old eyes. Producing his silken cloth, he patted at them gently.

"They not unreasonably assumed you were dead," he went on. "That you had been killed by the blacks—probably somewhere in the forest—for they said they had searched but could find no trace. I was most grieved, I assure you. To lose first you, my deputy, and then later Nasruddin, seemed too high a price to pay for a few paltry piasters' profit.... As I say, I was traveling much at the time. From Zeila I had to return to Zanzibar, and it was not until quite recently that I heard you were not lost, not dead, but had returned at last to Harar. Need I add that I was most happy about it?"

The old man paused. "In a business such as mine," he said, "I employ many men." He glanced up briefly at his retinue, who were standing by, ranged silent and waiting near the coffeehouse door. "Most of them are like these—the same sort that were with you in the caravan. Strong, hard, fearless; in their own way remarkably loyal. But not, I must say, with great judgment or ability. To be frank—well—expendable. When such as they fail to return from an expedition it is perhaps regrettable, but not important; it is the will of Allah. When one such as yourself, however, is lost —ah, that is a different matter. A trusted lieutenant. A man of integrity, dependability. It is like losing one's own right hand. And that is why I am so pleased at the good fortune of your return."

At his raised glance the waiting men had moved—a little closer. But now he had lowered it, again dabbing at his eyes; and they remained where they were.

"Indeed, it is an interesting thing about the expedition," said Abou Dakir, "that in spite of various troubles and mischances, it too, in the end, had good fortune. I may say, in fact, that it was one of the most successful I have ever sent out. The Worombu, by and large, are excellent specimens, and most of them arrived at the Red Sea markets in good condition and were sold at very gratifying prices. Also, the hides brought back were magnificent—far more and far better than usual. The hunting was expert, I gather, and the establishment of a cache a truly brilliant idea. The profit from the hides, you may be interested to know, was almost as great as that from the slaves."

There was another pause. Abou Dakir put his finger tips together, and his pale eyes seemed almost to be smiling. "In short," he said, "the venture was as successful as I had hoped. The merchandise is sold. The lost trader has returned. As you Frenchmen—or perhaps it is the British—say: 'all's well that ends well'; eh, my friend?"

Claude raised his cup and drank and set it down again. The old Arab watched him over the arch of his fingers.

"With you it *does* go well, I trust?" he asked.

"Well enough," said Claude.

"Good. Good. I understand you have made a new connection."

"Yes, with Mardik the Syrian."

"And you have broken with Maison Gorbeau."

"Yes. The new management and I did not agree on various matters."

"Sidi Rappe, you mean?. . . Hmm, yes—I can well understand. You are most different types. Frankly, I much preferred dealing with you; this Rappe is the sort of *ferangi* I do not much care for." Abou Dakir paused and shrugged. "But it does not greatly matter," he added mildly, "for the situation, I rather think, will soon be changing."

Claude looked up sharply. "Changing?" he repeated. "Changing how? What do you mean?"

"I mean there is a distinct possibility that Sidi Rappe will not be here much longer. Or Maison Gorbeau either."

"Why? What has happened?"

"Nothing has happened—just yet. But it will soon. Quite soon, perhaps. And then things may be quite different." The old Arab brought out his cloth and dabbed again at his watering eyes. "You were away for some time, my friend," he said. "Even when here, I gather, you lead a rather sequestered life and are perhaps not aware of certain forces at work—shall we say—behind the scenes. . . . What I am referring to is that, within a few months, the Egyptians will, in all likelihood, leave Harar."

"The Egyptians?"

"Yes. The esteemed Hajj Pasha, his functionaries, his garrison; all of them."

"Why?"

"The reasons are complex—all part of the struggle for power here in Africa—and I shall not bore you with the details. You may take my word for it, however, that our friends from down the Nile will not be hereabouts much longer."

"And who will take their place?"

"That is a matter of conjecture. It is the British, of course, who have been behind the Egyptians, and there is talk in Aden and elsewhere that they themselves will move in." Again Abou Dakir paused. "On the other hand," he said, "the British are well-known devotees of the unexpected, and there is talk in other quarters that they may not."

"In which case, who would?"

"In which case, I rather think, *my people* would."

"Your people?"

"The Arab people. The Moslems. Not false, westernized, bastardized Moslems like the Egyptians, but the true forces of Islam: the ones who first settled this country, who live in it, and to whom it rightfully belongs."

Abou Dakir once more made an arch of his fingers.

"You have perhaps heard of the Emir Ismail Abdullah?" he inquired.

"In the Somali desert—"

"Yes, in the Somali desert. And you know why he is in the desert. His family were for generations the rulers of Harar—until the Egyptians came, with British arms and connivance, and forced him out. But now the Egyptians are going. The British might come, and then again might not, for I understand they have many things on their minds elsewhere. If they do not, you will hear much more about the Emir Ismail; and things in Harar may be quite different from what they are just now."

"And quite pleasing to you, Sidi Abou," said Claude. "Or so I gather from your expression."

"But of course pleasing to me. I am a Arab, am I not? I am a patriot. I wish my people to be free.... And besides, it so happens that I am an old friend of the Emir Ismail. Quite a dear friend, indeed. He would not strangle me with taxes and tribute, as do the Egyptians, nor try to put me out of business, as would the British. Quite on the contrary, I should be a free man in free trade in my own country. It would be the others who would be out of business, who would have to go. Maison Gorbeau, for instance, and your countryman, Sidi Rappe. Perhaps even others—the smaller fry. Perhaps all outsiders, all *ferangi* and infidels, and Harar would again be a Moslem city for Moslems only...."

He let his voice trail away. He raised his cup, drank the last of his coffee, and seemed about to rise. "Well, so much for coffeehouse gossip," he said blandly. "It has been a pleasant meeting, Sidi Morel, and I trust we shall meet again—here or elsewhere."

Claude's eyes were fixed on his. "Why have you said all this?" he asked.

"And why not?" Abou Dakir affected surprise. "What is it that men talk of in a coffeehouse, if not politics, trade, the events of the times? It seemed to me to make a few minutes of perhaps interesting conversation."

"And also—"

It was a moment before the old man answered. "And also," he then said, "because I thought my speculations might be of certain use to you."

"As a warning?"

"I prefer my own word. As speculation."

"Very well, then. And why do you tell me such speculations?"

Abou Dakir considered. He smiled a little. Then he said: "As a point of fact I rather wonder about that myself.... Perhaps it is for the same reason I have not asked many questions about the caravan trip and your disappearance. Or about the black woman, not wholly unlike a Worombu, whom I am told you brought back with you from the south.... For the same reason, let us say, that I have not summoned to the table the three men of mine at the doorway, who, as you see, are alertly waiting for a possible signal."

Now he did rise. His men drew closer—but only slightly—and then they stopped and waited. "Suppose we leave it at what I told you once before," he said. "That you are, somehow, different from other Europeans; that you are a *ferangi* who is not wholly a *ferangi*. Not quite, yet almost, an African—"

"And your nineteenth son?"

"My nineteenth—?" Abou Dakir looked puzzled; then suddenly smiled again, almost broadly. "Ha, yes, I remember. My nineteenth. . . . But we shall have to make a change in that. My youngest wife, the one in Zanzibar—do you know what she did, by Allah? On my last visit she presented me with a new son—a fine boy, a fine surprise—and now *he* is the nineteenth. So that you must move on to twentieth. . . ."

He laughed. It was the first time Claude had seen him laugh. "Well, I must go," he said. "These are busy days for me, with busy times ahead. *Salaam*, my twentieth son. *Salaam aleikum!*"

The season of rains came and passed; then the season of dryness and hot dust-laden winds. Abou Dakir did not reappear. The Egyptians gave no hint of planned departure. Bits of news and rumor came to Harar with the caravans: of heightening political tensions along the Red Sea coast; of British, French, and Italian maneuverings; of trouble in Cairo and the Egyptian Sudan; of continued raids by the Abyssinians into the Somali lowlands and counterraids by the desert tribes of the Emir Ismail. But in the city itself all remained as before. The caravans came and went. The market place hummed. The Egyptian sentries in dirty khaki and torn fezzes languidly patrolled the perimeter of Hajj Pasha's palace, and Hajj Pasha smoked the Turkish cigars he received—now by courtesy of Marcel Rappe—from Maison Gorbeau.

Claude's life remained as before. He went from home to store to coffeehouse to home, through the streets and squares of the unchanged city. He conferred with Mardik. He dealt with his customers. He saw Vayu and Egal and Father Lutz, and avoided Spiranthos (who still courted him) and Rappe (whose nods when they passed in the street were becoming noticeably less frigid). "He will speak to you soon," Egal continued to prophesy. "He is having much trouble and needs you back." But thus far Rappe had made no actual approach; and Claude, for his part, went about his business and spoke to no one of the "speculations" he had heard from Abou Dakir.

He and Nagunda had finally moved. Their new quarters were larger, cleaner, and better furnished, with carpeting on the floor and a low Arab-style divan to sleep on in place of their former straw pallet. He had bought her more clothes, which she found endlessly fascinating, and she spent much time putting them on and taking them off and posing, in various combinations, before the mirror. She still, however, rarely went out, and then only for brief intervals with the Shankalla woman, Onuz, remaining as shy and frightened of the Moslem Hararis as she had been at the beginning. And even with Claude himself she was as silent and withdrawn as ever. For a time he had tried his hardest to penetrate into her mind, to teach and guide her, going even beyond the fundamentals of languages to other knowledges and skills, the acquisition of which would make her at least a semicivilized person. But it had been fruitless. He had met only blankness and apathy. And in the end he had given up. She knew the few words of Arabic and Somali that were essential to her getting along. She knew how to cook, clean, take care of their dwelling. And that was the sum of it. In the evenings now when he came home—as in the evenings long before when they had been alone in the wilderness—scarcely a word passed between them. Their only intercourse was that of the night, of the bed, of their lying together in darkness. The intercourse of man and woman; of their bodies, their flesh.

Looking back on the years of his life, he was not unaware of a certain irony.

One evening he stayed later than usual at the coffeehouse. On another, a week later, he returned to it after supper at home and sat for a few hours smoking and talking with the men of Harar. Then the night came when he took a different route, following the steep crooked streets until he came to Father Lutz's, and there he played bezique, as he had used to, while the priest thumped cards and boomed defiance, and Vayu sat in a corner smiling happily and playing his *krar*.

"*Eh bien*, it was pleasant, was it not?" Lutz said when he left. "You must come soon again, my son—and this time bring your lady."

But Claude did not bring Nagunda.

"She is shy. She is afraid," he said, when, on his next visit, Lutz asked for her. "It is better I do not force her to things that are hard for her."

"She did not seem afraid when she was here," said the priest.

"Here?"

"When she has come with Onuz, once or twice. She was shy, yes—and quiet—which is natural in strange surroundings. But I do not think she was afraid."

Claude did not argue the point with him; but later, on his way home, he argued it with himself. . . . "She is unhappy," he thought, "and I should do something for her. But what? She would be more unhappy out than she is at home. And she is lonely too—but what can I do there? She is as lonely, as withdrawn, when I am with her as she could be by herself alone. Only in bed, in copulation, are we truly together. Perhaps it is different for her with the woman Onuz—even with Lutz—but between *us* there is nothing else."

For several nights he stayed home with her. He tried to talk, to interest, to amuse her. But though she tried to please, and served and caressed him, she responded only to his body; not to words, not to thought. . . . "And how could she? How could I expect it?" he asked himself. Even among her own people it would not be expected. Savages did not expect companionship from a woman. Nor did Moslems, for that matter. Or Hindus. Or Chinese. Only Europeans, white men, expected their women to be companions, and it was too much to ask of a woman of another race.

Still, he *was* a European, a white man. However far he had come, whatever things he had done, he was still that; and from a woman, now that at last he could have a woman, he needed more than a body. . . . He stayed at home, and he was bored and restless. He paced the room and then the courtyard, and then went out and paced the streets. But this time he did not go to Father Lutz's or to a coffeehouse, but simply walked; he walked for hours, up and down, in and out, through the streets and squares and alleys of the city; he walked to the high places and saw the city's walls and the land beyond and the squat bulk of Kondudo rising in distant darkness; he walked until there was only darkness, with the city's lights all out and only the glow of stars in the night, and the eyes of hyenas; and still he walked, restless, prowling, until the night was almost over, and then he returned home and to his bed and took his woman in his arms; but when the next night came, he was still restless, still prowling, walking on and on through the city, alone. . . .

And a few days later, in the store, he spoke to Mardik.

"The store has done well lately," he said. "Business has been good."

"Well, not too bad," said Mardik cautiously.

"It has been good, but still not good enough. We have a large stock on hand. We should expand."

"The store is big enough. And there is an extra room in back."

"I do not mean the store. I mean to expand our market. To sell not only here but out in the villages—and also to buy there—as I used to when I was with Gorbeau."

Mardik thought it over. Then he shook his head. "No," he said, "I do not like traveling, or those dirty villages. And besides, with my family—"

"I am not suggesting that you go, but that I do."

"You? Hmm—well—"

And in the end it was so decided.

A few days later, with a string of mules laden with merchandise, Claude set out into the countryside and was gone for two weeks. The trip was successful. He sold everything he had taken and acquired many bargains in return. And Mardik was delighted and urged him to go soon again. There had been only one difficulty—that mules and merchandise together were too much for one man to handle—and it was agreed that for subsequent trips Claude must have an assistant. He was not far to find. No farther than Hippolyte Lutz's. The priest, when Claude spoke to him, sighed and said, "Well, here is where the poor boy becomes a heathen again." But he offered only token resistance. Nothing could have resisted Vayu's excitement and pleadings. And from then on, when Claude went out on his rounds, it was as in the old days, with the boy at his side.

They moved from village to village. Across the fields, across the pastures, up and down through the hills. The long trail unrolled before them, over the spacious earth, under the spreading sky, and the sun shone, the land shone, and the lead mule's bell tinkled in enormous stillness. Sometimes they themselves were part of the stillness, moving silent and alone, each at one end of their small caravan. Sometimes they rode or walked together, and talked, and the talk was easy, it flowed and ranged, and Claude felt his own mind stirring to life again under stimulus of the boy's. Vayu was now eighteen years old—if Claude's original estimate of fourteen had been correct; a young man really, no longer a boy at all. ("At his age," Claude thought, "I had already lived most of my life as a poet; I had written *The Ravaged Heart, The Drunken Boat,* my *Illuminations;* I was in London with Druard, in the pit of hell.") But Vayu dwelt in no hell. His mind moved outward, not inward. And with Father Lutz, it was plain, he had become not only a Christian ("—but not a good one, sidi; truly not a good one—") but also, in his fashion, a thinker, a scholar—and a very good one indeed.

. . . Did Claude remember the books he had ordered from Aden before he had gone away? Well, they had arrived at last, and he, Vayu, had read them all; yes, the science, the history, the literature, even the ones in French (which Father Lutz had taught him). . . . He had liked the literature best: especially Voltaire and Victor Hugo. But the science, too; what made things the way they are; the inventions, old and new . . . like trains and steamboats. Claude had been on them, had he not? . . . Yes, he had. . . . And the telephone; had he heard of that? . . . No, he hadn't. . . . Well, it was a marvelous thing. Like the telegraph, with wires. But over the wires came not just clicking but real words, people's voices. . . . Yes, science was wonderful. And history. Modern history—politics. The American Revolution, and the French. *Liberté, égalité, fraternité.* And now it was spreading around the world—everywhere—even to Africa. Yes, he had been reading not only books, but newspapers too—the papers Father Lutz received from France—and they told how things were changing in Africa; how they would change more; with the slave trade gone and everyone free. . . . Why, soon even Harar might be free, with the Egyptians gone; it was said they might soon be leaving. . . .

"You read that in the papers?" Claude asked.

"Yes, sidi, in the papers."

"And you think it would be good?"

"But yes, of course it would be good. Should not a place belong to the people who live in it?"

They traveled on. Through the plains. Through the hills. One day, approaching a village, they came to a stream, and by the stream was a girl with a bucket, and Vayu smiled and said, "Remember, sidi? . . . Only this time I do not have to talk and make you angry, for now you have a woman of your own."

"Perhaps I should talk. You are old enough now to have one."

"Yes, sidi. Perhaps soon. But not this one. This one is not like the other. Not a sultana. . . ."

Then they came to the villages. They showed their wares and sold them, and bought coffee and hides and gums and durra. Later, beyond the village, they stopped and tethered the mules and pitched their tent and cooked their supper, and when supper was done they sat before the tent beside the fading fire, and Vayu strummed his *krar* (which he took with him always, strapped to a mule's back) and sang the sad sweet songs of Harar in the night of stillness and stars. As he sang, Claude watched him. He watched the brown young face, the supple hands, the slender smooth body. And that was all they were: the face, the hands, the body of a boy —a young man: of Vayu: and presently he looked away, he looked at the night and the stars, and when Vayu had finished singing they went into the tent and lay side by side and slept. No hyenas came. No Felix. No Druard. He slept, and when he woke it was morning, and they went on their way again, to the next village, and the next, across the broad land, under the wide sky—and eventually, in a long arc, back to Harar and home.

Home was Nagunda and her bed and her body. It was a room, silence, boredom, restlessness. Nagunda made no complaint at his absences; she had uttered no word of complaint in all their time together. But she uttered scarcely any other word, either. Not once did she ask a question as to where he had been or what he had done, and when he tried to tell her something of his journeys she seemed not to be listening, but went on with her household routine as if he had been gone for an hour instead of for two or three weeks. She cooked. She cleaned. When she had finished with these she tried on her various clothes or experimented with her hair and make-up, posing and preening at the mirror; or she lay on the divan (for she had long since accepted the divan as a happy substitute for the floor) and ate candy by the hour. She had developed a passion for candy —especially the rich sweet globs of paste known as Turkish delight—and it was putting weight on her; indeed making her fat. Her breasts, thighs, and stomach now bulged beneath the flimsy fabrics of her clothing. She moved slowly and lazily. She yawned and dozed. Watching her, Claude found it almost impossible to visualize her as she had once been: a savage —naked, lithe, strong-limbed; a dancer to jungle drums; wild, primitive, barbaric; a forest maenad, a Nigger Queen. . . .

Vayu came sometimes, and talked and laughed and played his *krar*, and when he had gone the empty boredom was all the worse. Egal came and talked, meanwhile eying Nagunda dourly, and on leaving said, "She is lazy, sidi. That is what is wrong—she is lazy. And for a lazy woman there is only one cure: a beating."

But he did not beat her.

He slept with her. He slept with her body, her flesh. They lay together on the rumpled divan, as once they had lain on the earth beside the Web Shebeli, and in the morning he rose and went to the store, and there he worked all day, and when day was done went to the coffeehouse, and, leaving there, walked the streets of night, alone. And again he thought: "It is my fault. I can give her nothing." She had been torn from her own world—from her people, her tribe, her customs, her gods—and there was nothing to replace them; nothing he could say or do to reach her mind and heart, for his own were too different, too remote, from anything she had ever known. Only Onuz, the Shankalla, another Negro and herself half a savage, could, apparently, understand, communicate, give to her—and through her, as his convert, as a Catholic, Father Lutz. . . . And in that too, of course, there was irony, deep and true. . . . He knew that Nagunda now went every few days with Onuz to Lutz's house, or to his church. On his return from one trip he found a rosary in their room, and, back from another, a tinted print of the Virgin tacked onto the wall. But he did not object; he made no comment whatever. For he knew they were all that she had—besides her clothes and her candy.

His trips for Mardik continued. Each time Vayu went with him. And each time, leaving Harar, leaving home, he was as if filled with the wine of air, space, and freedom. On successive trips they ranged more widely: to the spurs of the Chercher, to the edge of the desert, once on past Kondudo to Bubassa, and beyond that to the southern promontories where they could look out over the plains of the Ogaden.

"Oh sidi," said the boy, "can we not go on? The way you did before. Only this time together. Far, far, for many miles—to new places—through all of Africa—"

"No, Vayu," said Claude. "For such a trip one needs a great caravan. With much money and many men."

"And you and Sidi Mardik do not have them?"

"No."

"Some day you will, though—yes? You will have all you need and again take such a trip?"

"Perhaps."

"And this time I will go along, yes? Please, please—this time you will take me?"

Claude smiled as they turned away, back toward Harar. "Yes, Vayu," he said, "next time I shall take you."

What happened, happened.

Usually it was nothing—at least nothing that was not always happening. But sometimes it was something sudden and unforeseen.

No more than a week after their return from Bubassa a large caravan arrived in Harar from the Red Sea coast. It was not a caravan of Abou Dakir but of an explorer named Alberghetti, of the Italian Geographical Institute, and he proposed to move on from Harar to the southwest, through the unknown southern reaches of Abyssinia and the Sudan until he reached the White Nile and the great lakes at its source. Throughout the day the main square swarmed with his men and animals. In the evening the men crowded the coffeehouses. And at his table in one of them, as he drank and smoked slowly to defer the hour of home-going, Claude looked up to see the tall lean bearded figure of Alberghetti standing beside him.

The Italian introduced himself.

"And you are Claude Morel?" he asked in Arabic.

Claude nodded.

Alberghetti was appraising. In his face was uncertainty and indecision. "I—I had been told—" he began.

"That I was a European? A Frenchman? . . . Yes, I am," said Claude. "It is because I have been here so long that people are apt to be confused."

The Italian nodded, "Ah, I see—yes. Good. . . . May I sit down? Thank you. . . . I mean good," he said, "that you have been here long. That is what I had heard and why I sought you out. For if you would be kind enough you could be of much help to me."

"Help?" said Claude. "How?"

"With your experience, your knowledge of the country."

"I have not been to the country you are going to."

"No, perhaps not. But you have been many places, I am told—and not so different. You know the problems of African travel—the terrain, the climate, the tribes and languages—and I would greatly appreciate such information and advice as you could give me." Alberghetti glanced around him. "It is crowded here, and noisy," he said, "but if we could talk at my headquarters for a while—"

"No, I could not do that."

Claude's head was bent, his eyes fixed on his empty coffee cup. The Italian sat as he was for a moment, silent and rebuffed; then pushed back his chair to rise and leave.

"But I could do more than that," Claude said, looking up. "I could go with you."

"With me? On the expedition?"

"Yes."

Alberghetti was fully seated again. In his face there was first, surprise, and then, calculation. "Well—" he said. "Well. That is a thought—and most interesting." He paused. He studied Claude—considering. Then he said: "But I understood you were in business here. My expedition will take months, perhaps years."

"I could manage that," said Claude.

"And I could pay little."

"That does not matter."

For another several moments Alberghetti considered. He drummed on the table. . . . Then he rapped on the table. "Very well," he said, his voice brisk and businesslike. "I can use you. I will take you." He rose. "Come, we will go to my headquarters. We will discuss it further, draw up an agreement—"

"As I said," Claude told him, "I cannot come now."

"In an hour, then? It must be tonight. I plan to leave tomorrow morning."

Claude nodded. "In an hour," he said. Then, as Alberghetti turned to go, he added: "But there is one other thing—"

"Yes?"

"I must bring an assistant."

"An assistant?"

"Yes, a boy—a young man. He is my helper on all trips. If I go, he must go too."

"Hmm—" the Italian frowned.

"It would cost you nothing."

"Nothing?"

"Except food."

"He would get no wages?"

"I would pay him from mine."

"Hmm—well—" Alberghetti shrugged. "All right. With a hundred and fifty men to feed, one more or less doesn't matter."

He left.

Claude sat alone. He looked for a long time into his empty cup. He thought: "Tomorrow. Tomorrow morning. . . ." He thought of Mardik. Mardik did not matter. He owed him nothing. Even allowing for his three raises, he had given far more to Mardik than Mardik to him. . . . Then he thought of Nagunda. Much longer of Nagunda. For to her he did owe—but could not give. What of Nagunda? For months, perhaps years. He had no money to leave her, and from where he was going he could send none back. With him, perhaps, she was lonely and unhappy, but without him she would starve and die. What were the alternatives? He could take her to the house of the balcony, of the watching eyes; to the madam and say to her, "Here, take her. I present you with another whore." Or he could take her to the agents of Abou Dakir. He could sell her. Or, more appropriately, donate her. He could say, "With my compliments, gentlemen. She is really yours, you see; yours by right of an expensive commercial expedition, overlooked in the confusion and mine only by appropriation. Here—take her—I am through with her. Take my woman, my wife, and sell her as a slave."

Whore. . . . Slave. . . .

What else?

One thing else.

He rose and left the coffeehouse. But he went neither home nor to Alberghetti. Following the dark streets, he went to Father Lutz's and the priest was there alone and, as always, bade him a cordial welcome, saying, "Greetings, my son, greetings! See, I am all ready for you. The cards are on the table, and tonight, for a change, I am going to win."

"No, Father," Claude said. "I did not come to play cards."

"No? For what then? To talk, perhaps?"

"Yes, to talk. I am going away tomorrow."

"For another of your trips?"

"Yes, on a trip. But this will be a long one. Very long. Like the trip to the Web Shebeli."

The priest's broad face clouded. "I hope not again for—"

"No, not for Abou Dakir. Nor for Mardik either. You know of the Italian who is here—the explorer? It is with him I am going. To the Nile, the great lakes."

"So? That is really a trip. *Formidable!*" Lutz smiled. "But I should not be surprised, after all, at one like you—forever drunk with horizons and rainbows."

"And I should like to take Vayu with me," said Claude.

"Vayu? . . . Well, well. . . . But I should not be surprised at that either, of course. You are so attached to each other."

"It is all right with you, then? He will go with your blessing?"

"I am sure I could not stop him if I tried. . . . And since when, my son, are you interested in blessings?" Lutz smiled again; then the smile dissolved into a sigh. "I have tried hard to make him a Christian," he said, "and now, alas, it will all be undone. He will come back with you a thorough heathen, and I shall have to start all over again." He paused. The sigh, in turn, became a shrug. "But—as I say—what can I do? . . . Yes, he has my blessing. It should be a great adventure for him."

There was another pause. The priest watched Claude and waited.

"And Nagunda?" he said.

"Yes, Nagunda—"

"What of her?" said the priest.

"That is also why I have come. About her. To ask—if you would take her—"

"Take her?"

"I do not mean here. I know you have no room here. . . . I was thinking of other places. Your order has missions along the coast; in Obock, Djibouti—"

"Where she might stay until you return?"

"Where she might stay for good. And be happy."

Father Lutz did not answer.

"I cannot make her happy," said Claude. "Even when I am here I can give her nothing that she needs. Only Onuz has been able to give her anything—and through Onuz, you—the Church. She has a rosary at home; a holy picture. And they are all she has. If the church can take her, find a place for her, she will have a chance, I think, for a decent life."

Still the priest did not speak. His eyes, fixed on Claude, had somehow changed.

"You will not?" said Claude. "You think it wrong? . . . Truly, Father, I can tell you, she would be better off that way."

"She, perhaps—yes." Lutz spoke at last. "She alone. But as things are —with the child—"

There was a silence.

"Child—"

"Yes, with her pregnancy. Onuz says it is now four months along, and I do not see how such a thing would be justifiable. In fact," Lutz said, his voice hardening, "I am shocked, my son, that you suggest it."

Again there was silence . . . longer. . . .

Then the priest understood.

"You did not know?" he asked.

"No," said Claude.

"She has not told you?"

"No."

He turned away. The priest was speaking, but still he turned; he did not hear; he went to the door and into the street and through the streets of night to his home. Nagunda was in their room, on the divan, fingering her rosary with one hand and eating candy with the other, and he sat down beside her without speaking. She was wearing a cheap flimsy gown of gaudy colors, and beneath it her fatness showed—the fatness of breast and thigh and belly—and he put his hand on her belly and sat beside her for a long while, silently.

Then there was a knock on the door, and Vayu came in, and his eyes were bright, his face shining. "The Father has told me, sidi," he said. "That we are going—you and I—with the Italians. Oh, sidi, it is so good, so wonderful!"

Claude shook his head. "No, Vayu," he said. "There has been a change. We are not going."

"Not—" The boy's face fell; all but crumpled. "Oh sidi—why? What has happened? What is wrong?"

"Nothing is wrong. The plan is off, that is all." Claude rose and went to Vayu and put a hand on his shoulder. "Now do something for me, please," he said. "Go to the main square, and at its south side you will find the headquarters of the Italian caravan. Ask for the sidi, the chief—he will be waiting for me—and tell him I am sorry, I must stay here, I cannot go."

32

Africa: mid-1880's.

The African northeast in change, in turmoil. . . .

Through the Suez Canal, down the Red Sea, steamed the gunboats and freighters of Europe. Along the barren coasts stood forts, garrisons, trade posts, the flags of empire. The French were in Obock, Tajoura, Ambadu, Djibouti; the Italians in Assab and Massawa; the British moving across from Aden to Zeila and Berbera. Ten years before, with British support, Egypt had taken over this realm from Turkey. But now Egypt was no longer able to hold it. Weak and corrupt, its power was crumbling, as stronger hands moved in to pick up the fragments.

In his office on Steamer Point, beneath Aden's black ramparts, Monsieur Paul Colbert, consul of France, wrote dispatches, sent telegrams, and wiped his forehead in the furnace heat. "It is Djibouti that is important," he said to his friend, Emil Gorbeau. "Djibouti and the Bay of Tajoura, for they are the way to the interior."

"And Zeila too," said Gorbeau.

"Yes, of course—Zeila." The consul bit his lip. "That is also important, but there the British, alas, are ahead of us."

"With their eyes on Harar."

"Yes, with their eyes on Harar, I think. But that is a different matter. At least they cannot sail their damned ships to Harar—and besides, we are there first. . . . Thanks to you, *mon vieux*."

Gorbeau nodded his appreciation.

"And with you it goes well there, I gather. Your exports are large."

"Yes, they are satisfactory."

"That fellow worked out all right then?"

"Fellow?"

"You know—the one who was here, on my hands. You took him on and then sent him out there."

"Oh—Morel." Gorbeau shook his head. "No, he is no longer with me. For a time he was quite satisfactory, but basically—well—unstable. I have had to replace him."

"With a sound man, I trust."

"Yes, with my chief clerk. You know him—Rappe. He has been with me for years and is thoroughly reliable."

"Good. Good." The consul nodded. "That is essential: that we have a reliable man there. A man of experience and finesse. The way the situation is developing. . . ."

. . . *The way the situation is developing,* wrote the British Resident in Aden to the Foreign Office in London, *is that, as usual, the continental powers are refusing to honour the concept of fair play. Instead of adhering to the agreement of limited spheres of influence, both Italians and French are pushing as far and as fast as possible—the former to the north, the latter to the south—and there is reason to believe that the French have designs on the province and city of Harar. If, therefore, the Egyptian occupation force is soon to be withdrawn, I urge that as a protective measure. . . .*

The Foreign Office, however, had other things than Harar on its mind. For Egypt, which it had occupied and controlled for five years, was now losing its hold not only on its Red Sea outposts but on the far greater prize of the Sudan. There a stronger Moslem leader than the Emir Ismail had arisen—a desert imam, a new prophet, who called himself the Mahdi and whose followers were known as Dervishes. These had all but swept the country. They had taken its capital, Khartoum. They had killed one of the greatest of British generals, "Chinese" Gordon, who had been sent to defend it. The world of the Middle Nile was rampant, in ferment.

And, to the east, Abyssinia as well.

In 1869 the British had invaded Abyssinia, to effect the release of a mission that had been held captive, and the then emperor, Theodore, who resisted, had been defeated and killed himself. The victors had withdrawn quickly, leaving the country independent, as it had been through the centuries, and installing, as his successor, John, king of the northern province of Tigré. And since then John had ruled as Negus Negusti—King of Kings—in theory over all Abyssinia, but effectively only over the north; for in the central highlands, in Shoa, had risen a younger king, Menelik, who disputed his sovereignty. Menelik's forefathers had been, before Theodore, rulers of both north and south. He claimed direct descent from his ancient namesake, son of King Solomon and the Queen of Sheba. It was he, he avowed, who should be King of Kings, in his mountain capital of Ankober—not John, the British protégé, in Tigré's city of Axum—and to that end he was assembling his tribesmen, importing guns by the thousand, conducting raids and excursions against John's kingdom to the north.

It was these raids that spilled over into the Chercher hills, the lowlands beyond, the Moslem realm of Somalis and Arabs. And the Moslems watched the warring of the two Coptic Christian kings, to the west, with no less hostile eye than they watched the western Christians pushing in from the Red Sea. Even more hated than either infidel, however, were the Egyptians, now for ten years their masters, who, like themselves were caught between. The Egyptians, they now knew, would soon have to go. They waited. In his desert stronghold waited the Emir Ismail Abdullah. In his palace in Harar, Hajj Pasha wrote urgent messages to Cairo, received no answer, and gnawed nervously at the stumps of his cigars.

Africa seethed. Africa rumbled. . . .

Qu'importe?

In a room off a steep narrow street, some few hundred yards from Hajj Pasha's palace, Claude Morel sat on a divan beside his woman, Nagunda. His hand lay gently on her belly, beneath which, in fetal darkness, lay the hidden living thing that was his child.

He still worked for Mardik. But now he went only occasionally into the countryside, and his trips were short. Leaving the store, he stopped for, at the most, ten minutes at a coffeehouse, and went on home. He sat beside Nagunda. He did not talk to her, but simply sat, while she nibbled candy or fingered her beads, and watched the miracle that had taken visible form in her flesh.

For what had happened *was*, to him, a miracle. Through all his life, as boy and man, he had been a creature apart from other men: first as poet, prophet, seer, child of dream and fire, self-ignited and self-consumed; then as the relict of that consumption, that fiery hell, a man of ashes, fragments, hollow stone. For years he had scarcely believed his own self to be alive—yet now that self had proved capable of creating a new life beyond it. It was as if night had become day, the earth the sky, the desert the sea, the sea a mountaintop. He did not believe in miracles. Miracles were for the Church. For his mother, his sister; for Father Lacaze, Father Lutz, for the innocents and sophists of the world who lived their lives by cant and lies and self-delusion . . . yet now—now this had happened. This thing. This miracle. To *him*.

He sat beside Nagunda. Night came, and he lay beside her, and in the darkness, through the hours of the night, he thought of his son. For that was part of the miracle: that he *knew* this: that it was not a daughter but a son. It was a son, a boy, a man-child, and the child would be born in this room. There would be no doctor, for Harar had no doctor. There would be himself and Nagunda and a midwife—the Shankalla, Onuz, perhaps, or another woman sent by Onuz—and the woman would do as women did at such times, with water and towels and much moving and murmuring. But he would be there too. He would hold Nagunda's hand in her pain. He would see the moment of birth, the child emerging, the cord severed;

and the child would be there, no longer inside Nagunda, but a being apart, a child born and living, a new life in the world; and he, Claude Morel, its father, would bend over it; he would touch it, hold it, raise it, lift it high, he would hold high the miracle that was his child, his son.

His nigger son. . . .

For he would be a nigger. Not wholly black, perhaps; not as black as Nagunda—but surely not white; a blend of father and mother; perhaps brown, like Vayu; like himself, now, for that matter; perhaps darker, but with light hair, with blue eyes; with the skin of the south and the eyes of the north, half African, half European, half nigger and half Hun. . . . The image rose clear before him. And it was bright. It was good. . . . He would be what the world called a mulatto, a half-breed, and a bastard— and still it would be good. For that was what the man of the future must be: the world-man, the free-man: free of caste and clique and cult and race and nation, a man of many strains and many bloods, whose brother was everyman and whose home was the earth itself.

In those dark nights his thoughts ranged forward, multiplying. . . . His son must be strong, enduring, courageous. He must face the world without anger or fear. From his mother he would inherit the primitive power of the savage, from himself the mind and skills of civilized man. He himself would educate him—as he had Vayu—but earlier and better; he would give him the gift of tongues, the fruits of his travels, the grist of his own experience and knowledge. And when he could give no more, he would send him away—to Europe, to France. France had its faults, God knew (if not the French), but at least it was not fouled by racial hatreds, as were England and America, and a boy half-French and half-African would be accepted as any other. He would go to the heart of France, to Paris, the university; but not to the Sorbonne—no, not to the place of words —but to the other place, the place of facts, of science, the *Ecole Centrale*, to which he himself, his father, had once gone, and stopped, and turned away defeated. His son would become an engineer—like the Scotsman Mackenzie. No, not like Mackenzie; far more than Mackenzie; not a mere tender and custodian of machines, a puller of levers, a pusher of buttons, but an engineer-scientist, a builder, a creator, one of the chosen few who *made* machines, remade the earth with them, and to whom, in turn, the earth belonged. He would learn in France. He would learn all that France, that Europe, could give. But he would not stay there. He would return to Africa. For Europe was the past and Africa was the future, and this was a man of the future, not of the nineteenth but of the twentieth century; and he would return to the land of the future, to re-create it, to build it. He would build roads, railways, bridges, dams, canals. He would clear jungles, level mountains, water the deserts, bring light where there was darkness and wealth where there was poverty. It would be he, and such as he, who would change the face of Africa, and of the earth; who would be the *voyants*, the thieves of fire, the alchemists of the world to come. And for them, unlike the alchemist of words, there would be no day of reckoning, no pit of hell, for their vision, their dream, would be not inward but outward. They would deal not in illusion and hallucination, but in reality, the blood and bones of life; and reality would not consume them but make them free.

The free-men. The world-men. And among them his son. His son the Hun, his son the nigger. . . . As he sank toward sleep his thoughts moved on. And then he slept, and in his sleep he smiled.

Dear Mother, he wrote: *In my last letter I referred to "certain obligations" I had undertaken, and now I must report that these obligations have increased. Not to be cryptic about it any longer, I am now* . . . he paused and considered . . . *now a married man,* he wrote, *and in a few months' time I shall be a father. I am aware that this will come as a shock to you, and the more so when I add that my wife is not French, nor even European, but an African. But then, so am I, in many ways, now an African myself.*

At all events, it is a thing that has happened, and however displeased you may be, there are at least two aspects of which I know you will approve. One is that my wife, though not born a Catholic, seems well on her way to becoming one; and the other is that I am now faced with the necessity of making far more money than ever before. Much of what I earn—and I have definite plans on how to earn—will have to go toward the support of my family, and particularly of my son (for it will be a son), for whom I want the best training and education possible. But it will not be long, I hope, before my reserves are sufficient to send you considerable sums—enough even to raise the entire mortgage on the farm. . . . He paused again and smiled; then continued writing. . . . *At which, some day, perhaps,* he added, *my family and I will pay you a visit.*

Meanwhile I am sending the usual draft for one hundred francs, together with filial greetings.

He had thought long and carefully about his "definite plans." And now he set about putting them into action.

First he spoke to his employer, Mardik, but this was unimportant. Speaking to Mardik was a matter of protocol, of courtesy—and he expected nothing to come of it, and nothing did.

But then he went to Marcel Rappe, and this was different. For the first time since the day of his return to Harar he entered Maison Gorbeau, then the office that had once been his own, and Rappe, in his white linen and glinting spectacles, looked sharply up from his ledgers and said, "Well, so it is you. What can I do for you, Morel?"

"Let us put it rather," said Claude, "as what we can do for each other."

"You wish to be re-engaged, *hein?*"

"Re-engaged, no. A better word is reassociated. I have a proposition to make."

"What sort of proposition?"

Rappe had offered no chair, but Claude took one. "Let us begin," he said, "by being candid—both you and I.... For your part, the business of Maison Gorbeau has, of late, not been good. That is self-evident and generally known in Harar. One reason, perhaps, is your inexperience here; another, if I may say so, the competition of my own firm, Mardik's. I am saying this not as a boast but as a fact. Just as it is a fact that I, despite this, am not content with *my* present status. Mardik has done well, yes—for a small merchant. Local trade has been good, and we have even expanded a bit into the countryside. But now, I feel, the time has come for far greater expansion, and for such a thing, frankly, he has neither the imagination nor the capital. In fact I have already spoken to him of my idea, and he has said no. So I have come to you."

"And this idea of yours—?"

"Is to take out a caravan."

Rappe looked at him for a long moment, and when he spoke again his voice was dry and edged. "You have not, by now," he asked, "had enough of caravans?"

"This would not be like the other one," Claude said.

"No?"

"No. It would have nothing to do with slaves. Nor with Abou Dakir."

"Abou Dakir controls all the caravans."

"To the coast, yes. And to the south. But not to the west."

"The west?"

"To Abyssinia," said Claude. "Abou Dakir has never sent a caravan to Abyssinia; nor could he, because he is a Moslem. No caravan of *anyone's* has ever gone from here to Abyssinia. But one could, I tell you. It could go up through the Chercher into the highlands—not just to villages and savage tribes, but straight on to Tigré and Shoa, to the kingdoms of John and Menelik—and come back with a fortune."

Rappe stroked his chin slowly. His eyes, fixed on Claude, were still sharp, but the sharpness was different.

"Abyssinia," he said. "Hmm—"

"Have you ever considered it?"

"As a matter of fact, yes—I have. Monsieur Gorbeau has. We have corresponded about it."

"But done nothing."

"No."

"Why not?"

"There are many problems involved."

"Such as finding the proper man, perhaps, to lead the caravan? . . . You or Gorbeau could not do it. No Arab could do it. Who *could* then—is that it? . . . I shall give you the answer. I could. I know caravans; I know Africa; I know its people and tribes and languages. And that is what I am suggesting: that I go—that you send me."

"Then you *do* want to be re-employed?"

"Not re-employed. I want a partnership. You will supply the merchandise, the caravan, all material things that are necessary. I shall be the caravan leader—the trader—and for that I shall have one third of the profits."

"One third?"

"Yes, that is fair, and you know it. It will allow plenty for each of us."

"Or perhaps nothing for each of us," said Rappe, "—if history tends to repeat itself."

"It will not repeat itself. The circumstances would be wholly different. Still—" Claude shrugged, "—we would both have to take certain chances. If one is unwilling to do that he should not be trading in Africa."

Rappe said nothing, and after a moment Claude rose. "In any case," he said, "you will want to think it over. And no doubt write to Aden. . . . I shall wait to hear from you then? As it happens, I could not leave Harar for some two or three months, because of family matters. My *wife*—you remember her perhaps; you had the pleasure of meeting her on my return from the Ogaden—is pregnant, you see, and I must stay here until after the child is born."

He paused. Rappe still said nothing.

"But on the other hand I would suggest not delaying too long. For if the Egyptians leave—"

Rappe's eyes snapped up. "Hah—you have heard of that, then?"

"Yes. . . . And if the Emir Ismail comes—"

"The Emir Ismail? What are you talking about?" Rappe rose too, with a sudden jerk, and now his voice was as sharp as his eyes. "If the Egyptians leave it will be the British who come."

"I have heard that that too is possible."

"Not possible; it is certain. . . . The Emir Ismail? Absurd! Fantastic! It is the British who have been behind the Egyptians the whole time—and for their own interests. Do you think they are now going to turn Harar over to barbarians, to Moslem fanatics as bad as the Mahdi and his Dervishes? . . . No, Morel—that is the sort of idle talk you may hear in the coffeehouses, but I have my information from Aden—from the highest sources. . . . It is our own people, of course—the French—who *should* come. It is we who have pioneered here, done the work, earned our place. But no, that is too much to expect. It is never the French who get anything—always the

British. India, Aden, Zanzibar; now Harar. It is a scandal. . . . But at least not such a scandal as turning it over to desert Arabs. Nor such insanity. And at least they will be better than these Egyptians with their corruption and their *bakshish*."

"—And we would then be able," said Claude, "to sell Hajj Pasha's cigars and pâté to King Menelik of Shoa at a handsome profit."

"What?" Rappe's train of thought was broken. "*Hein?* What is that you say?"

"I said that, if the Egyptians leave, we should do even better with our caravan to Abyssinia."

"Oh. Oh yes—I see." Rappe became thoughtful again. "Well, there are many aspects to be considered—"

"And you will consider them?"

"Yes."

"I shall wait to hear from you?"

"Yes."

Claude nodded. Then he turned and left.

"He is interested," he thought, as he crossed the market square. "He is more than interested; his tongue is hanging out. He will do it. He will write to Aden, and Gorbeau will say do it."

He smiled.

"My son, you are on your way to the *Ecole Centrale*. . . ."

He waited.

He continued working for Mardik.

A few days later Egal appeared and said, "So it is good, sidi. I am happy. Soon now you will be again with Maison Gorbeau."

"Rappe has told you that?" Claude asked.

"No, he has not told me. Not that. But I know you have talked with him. Today he tells me we may soon have a big caravan; I should start sorting goods in the warehouse. And he has written a long letter to Aden."

Then he went on another round of the villages with Vayu. And he said to him, "Do not be too disappointed that we did not go off with the Italian. Soon, perhaps, we shall have a trip that is even better." The boy's face lit up, and the questions poured out. "To the Nile, sidi? To the lakes? With another explorer?" "No, not with an explorer," Claude told him. "On our own, with our pots and pans. I cannot tell you more; there is nothing certain." Then he smiled and added: "But you might ask Father Lutz to begin teaching you some Amharic."

Back in Harar, he spent each day in the store, each night at home. Nagunda was growing bigger quickly, and even he, the fool, the blind one, could now see that it was not with fat but with the life within her. The life had begun to stir. He could feel it beneath his hand. For hours he sat beside her in the dim lamplit evenings; and still they scarcely spoke; but now no words were needed. In the darkness, later, they lay together, and he felt her belly, round and swelling, against his own.

She no longer went out at all; but the woman Onuz came to her more often—and Father Lutz as well. And to them she talked, as she could not talk to him. Often, returning home from Mardik's, he would hear the murmur of voices as he approached the door, and then enter, to find the priest or the woman with her; but at his coming, invariably, she stopped speaking and almost visibly withdrew behind a wall of silence. It was not hostility toward him—that he knew—for in her own strange wordless fashion she was warm and tender; nor, after all their months together, was it shyness or fear. It was simply that she had nothing to say to him. . . . And to these other two she did. . . . Sometimes when she and Claude were alone she turned to the picture of the Virgin she had tacked to the wall, and then her lips moved silently, and he knew she was saying the prayers that Lutz had taught her. She had taken to wearing her rosary around her neck at all times, looped into strings of black beads and pendent crucifix, as she had once worn bright beads and blossoms and the teeth of wild beasts.

He made no protest. He was gentle and forbearing. And to Lutz he said one day, with a smile: "*Eh bien, mon père*, you are well satisfied, I hope, for we share her half and half. Her body is mine and her soul is yours."

"She has need of what I can give her," the priest answered. "Of what our Lord and our Lady can give her. And I am grateful that you have been understanding."

Claude shrugged. "What else is there for her?"

"What else is there for anyone, my son—in the end?" Now it was Lutz who smiled. "But each of us, of course, must learn that in his own good time."

"And some are fast as hares, and some as slow as tortoises?"

"Exactly. . . . And meanwhile I am glad that you seem at least to be gaining in tolerance, if not in faith. You do not, for example—or so I gather—object to her baptism?"

"Baptism?"

"She has not spoken to you—?"

"She speaks to me of nothing."

"She wishes to be baptized," said the priest. "To be taken into the Church."

There was a silence.

Then Claude said, "If it is important to her—"

"Yes, it is important. For herself—and for the child."

"The child—"

"Yes, of course: the child. It must be baptized too; that is even more important. Surely you will not deny it that? The first sacrament. The first blessing of God."

Claude did not answer. His face changed. He turned away.

"No, of course you won't," said Father Lutz. "You may not have thought of it before, but you will now, and when you have you will agree." He paused; and when he went on his eyes were bright, his voice was gentle. "I have known you now for some time, my son," he said, "and I shall tell you this. You are not so hard and lost and bitter as you may think; you have not turned so far from God or from God's love. I have seen this three times now. Once when you were sick, when you were dying, but would not die, because you were filled with the will to live. Again, when you returned from the south; alone, with only Nagunda, for you had left the slavers; you could not go on with what you had begun. And now again, once more, in what you have done; in your staying here with Nagunda and your child-to-be. These are not the acts of one who has rejected life, my son; who is dead to love and to the grace of God."

Lutz turned to go, and again he smiled. "Yes, they will be baptized," he said. "Nagunda. The child. Who knows?—perhaps even you, the shelled one, the tortoise, who has run his course at last. It would do you not a bit of harm, you know, to go back and start over at the beginning."

He chuckled. He left.

He came again. The woman Onuz came. Vayu and Egal came. Claude went to the store and returned from the store; he sat with Nagunda and lay with Nagunda; he waited—for the child that was coming, for word from Rappe; and the days passed, one after another, one the same as another . . . until the day came that, suddenly, was *not* the same . . . when, leaving home in the early morning, he felt at once that the city was different; the streets, as he walked them, were different, the crowds were different; and when he came to the main square the crowd was enormous. It was not, as usual, scattered about the market among the booths and stalls, but packed together before the wall of Hajj Pasha's palace; and it was milling and murmuring, pressing forward, craning, shouting, for on the wall by the palace gate was a posted notice. Claude could not get close enough, through the crowd, to read its message, but he did not need to. For the crowd knew, and its voices told him.

The Egyptians were leaving Harar. And its new ruler would be the Emir Ismail Abdullah.

Taklu Mardik did not come into the store, but sat through the hours in his adjoining office cubicle, his face slack, his eyes fixed unseeing on the wall. Twice Claude went in to him and spoke, but he did not answer. The third time he murmured dully: "Ten years. . . . Ten years I have been here. It has been my home, my life. And now—"

"Now what?" said Claude.

"Now it is all done—finished. I am without a business; without a home."

"You have decided, then—?"

"Decided?" The Syrian looked up at him. "What is there to decide? The decision has been made; it is there on the palace wall. The Egyptians go. The British do not come. The Emir Ismail comes with his desert bandits. We have been thrown to the hyenas. There is not a Christian, not a foreigner in Harar, who will be safe from these Moslem butchers."

From the living quarters across the courtyard came a woman's wailing, the voice of Mardik's wife. And suddenly his hands were trembling. "Decide? Decide what?" he asked shrilly. "To be slaughtered like goats? To be murdered? To see my wife and children murdered? . . . We have one choice, yes: we leave or we are dead. We are homeless or we are dead. After ten years, homeless; everything gone, thrown away—"

His agitation flickered out. Again staring at the wall, he relapsed into lethargy, and Claude went back to the store. It was quiet there. On the street outside, crowds flowed by, but for an hour no one came in. Then one man came, but it was not a customer; it was the Greek, Spiranthos, Mardik's bitter competitor, who had never during Claude's employment set foot in the store. Now he appeared, however, somber and distraught, and for another hour he and Mardik were closeted in conference, while the shop remained empty and still.

Then the Greek came out and left silently. And Mardik, following, shut the street door and locked it. "So we will close now," he said. "We will not open tomorrow. Tomorrow I will go to the Arab merchants and find a buyer for my stock, and then arrange with the Egyptians to leave with their caravan."

"Where will you go?" Claude asked.

"To the coast. Where else is there to go?" Mardik shrugged hopelessly. "Zeila, Djibouti, Aden—what does it matter? Anywhere I will be a stranger; with no business, no home."

"And Spiranthos—he is also going?"

"Yes, he is going."

. . . And so, too, Claude presently learned, was Marcel Rappe. He heard it first from Egal, who came running with the news; and then, going himself to Maison Gorbeau, found Rappe already clearing out his drawers and files.

"So your coffeehouse gossip was right, Morel," he said bitterly. "You should be well pleased with yourself."

"No, not pleased," said Claude. "But not panicked either."

"And who, may I ask, is panicked?"

"Mardik. Spiranthos. And, I gather, yourself."

"I am preparing to close the store and leave for Aden. That is not panic, my friend, but common sense."

"You have had orders from Gorbeau?"

"Orders, no. But I have had letters. Two, in fact. They came by yesterday's government caravan—the same that brought instructions for withdrawal to the Governor. It may interest you to know"—Rappe's voice became sardonic—"that the first, written some weeks ago, approves your scheme of a caravan to Abyssinia."

"And the second?"

"—concerns what has since happened politically. And instructs me to use my own judgment."

"Which is to leave—to run away?"

"Which is to act in the best interests of Maison Gorbeau—and incidentally, I might add, of myself."

"Meaning—"

"Meaning, Morel, that you may be a fool, but I am not. . . . Shall I tell you where I have just been? I have been for two hours with the Governor; with His Excellency in person. He is leaving Harar a week from today. He and all the Egyptians: his staff, the civil servants, the garrison, everyone. . . . Did you hear me clearly? I said *everyone*. . . . There will not be a soldier left; not a guard or policeman. What will be left will be a mob, a city of wild fanatic Moslems. And then worse—then the desert Moslems. The *shifta*, the bandits, this Emir Ismail and his cutthroat tribesmen; and what would happen to foreigners, to Europeans and Christians, I shall leave to your imagination."

"You will go with the Egyptian caravan?"

"With theirs or another; it is not yet arranged. But I shall go, I assure you—with all the stock of Maison Gorbeau. And unless you are an even greater fool than I think, you, my friend, will go too."

As at Mardik's, the front door of the shop was closed. From the warehouse at the rear came a sound of thumping and scraping, as Egal shifted crates and bales. The Harari clerk came in with sheaves of papers, and Rappe gave him further orders and turned to his littered desk.

"Now you must excuse me," he told Claude brusquely. "I am busy—very busy." . . . And as Claude left he heard a muttering behind him: "It is the British who are responsible. It is always they. The lying cheating *salopard* British. . . ."

Outside, the crowd in the square was even bigger than during the morning. It was no longer massed close around the notice on the palace wall—for everyone had long since learned its message—but flowed and eddied everywhere in aimless movement. The air was filled with the murmur of voices, with occasional shouts, with excitement and tension; yet the tension was controlled; it did not burst into stampede or violence.

Back and forth through the square, along its walls, among its booths and stalls and milling hundreds, paced Egyptian sentries in their khaki and fezzes, with shouldered rifles.

Claude, too, moved through the crowd. He tried to think. But his mind was numb. Numbly he crossed the square, and no one molested him. Now and then a voice greeted him—*"Salaam, sidi"* . . . *"Allah maak, sidi"* —and he spoke in return, and it was the same as always; yet not the same, never again to be the same, because now the doors of Mardik and Maison Gorbeau were closed behind him. Leaving the square, he entered a side street, and now for the first time, through his numbness, he was aware of disturbance, of the threat of violence; for the street was unpatrolled, and along it, suddenly, came a group of men and boys, racing raggedly by, waving sticks, shouting slogans. . . . "Harar will be free!" they cried. *"Allah akbar!* Down with *ferangi!* Down with infidels!" . . . But they, too, did not molest him. They raced on. They were almost past. . . . When suddenly, from among them, he heard one voice that he knew, saw one face that he knew; and then there was another voice, his own, and it called, "Vayu! Vayu!"

But the boy did not hear. He too rushed past and in a moment was gone, waving and shouting with the rest. . . . "With the *blouses blanches*," Claude thought. "Crying *vive la Commune!* Crying blood and the golden flame. . . ."

He moved on. He came to his own home, but did not stop there, going on instead, threading the steep narrow streets, until he came to the house of Father Hippolyte Lutz. The priest was there, but not alone. As he opened the door, there appeared beside him another priest, a tall black Abyssinian *kaess* of the Coptic Church, who bowed formally to both Lutz and Claude and then moved off down the street.

"And that is how it is," said Lutz, as he led Claude in. "Through all the years I have been here no Coptic priest would so much as look at me—*un sale catholique*. But now—now that there is trouble for us both—we are confreres, we are brothers."

"And the trouble," said Claude, "—do you think it will be bad?"

"I think it may be."

"What will you do?"

Lutz shrugged. "There is nothing to do at the moment—except to wait and hope for the best."

"You will not leave then?"

"Leave? Leave Harar?"

"Rappe is leaving. Mardik and Spiranthos are leaving."

"They are businessmen. I am a priest."

"But a priest, above all—"

"A priest, above all, must stay at his post. The others have produce and merchandise to think of; I have human beings, human souls." Lutz smiled wryly. "No great number, perhaps," he added. "There are more than three thousand Copts in Harar, and only some hundred Roman Catholics; but those hundred are here none the less. *They* cannot leave. There is nowhere, no way, for them to go. And my place is beside them."

His voice was quiet, his manner calm and gentle. With the Coptic priest he had been wearing his Capuchin robe, but now he took it off and scratched his broad chest and shoulders, and as he bent to lift an urn of coffee from the stove his crucifix thumped against the blackened bricks. "What the Lord wills will happen," he said. And then added, again smiling: "You see, I have been here so long I am talking like a Moslem myself."

He poured the coffee. They sat and drank. Over his cup he looked at Claude speculatively. And then he said:

"And you, my son?"

"I?"

"What will you do? Will you go or stay?"

"I shall stay," said Claude.

The priest nodded. "Yes, I thought so. It is not the same for you as for me, of course. But—"

"But this is my home," said Claude. "I am a Harari—an African. My wife is an African. My son is an African."

"Yes, I understand." Lutz paused, and his eyes grew thoughtful. "And yet, if Mardik is leaving—and Spiranthos—and Maison Gorbeau is closing—"

"I shall find work. This is my home, and my family's. I will find work and take care of them."

Lutz nodded again. They finished their coffee. When Claude rose to go the priest went with him to the door and said, "God bless you, my son." And that was all that was said. And Claude left and went home.

There, as usual, Nagunda was lying on the divan with her rosary and Turkish delight; and he sat down beside her.

"It is not yet dark. You are back early," she said.

"Yes," he answered.

"There has been noise in the street today. And many people."

"It is a holiday," he said. "A Moslem holiday. And they are celebrating."

Nagunda bit into a piece of candy and chewed it slowly with her strong white teeth; and he put his hand on her belly and felt the swelling mound that was their unborn child. "So it is not quite so straight a road to the *Ecole Centrale*," he thought. "But there are many roads, *mon petit*. And we shall find one. We shall build one."

That was the first day.

On those that followed, the crowds were again in street and square;

the murmuring rose in the city; the rumors flew. The Emir Ismail, it
was said, was in the northern Ogaden. He was in Bubassa. He had left
Bubassa and was approaching Harar. He was in a great encampment only
a few miles from the city, where the desert tribes were gathering from the
four corners of Somalia. There was still no general uprising, no riot or
violence. The crowds milled, aimless and leaderless, while the Egyptian
soldiery patrolled with shouldered guns. But each day the murmuring
grew louder, the shouts more frequent, the throngs denser and more
restless. From the minarets of the mosques the voices of the muezzins
rang shrilly above the rooftops, and within the mosques the men of Harar
stood closely packed, with heads raised, as the imams droned of freedom
and of surgent Islam.

The city hummed. The city waited. . . .

And the doors of the *ferangi* shops—Mardik's, Spiranthos', Maison
Gorbeau—remained closed and bolted.

In the office behind his store, Mardik paid out to Claude the wages that
were due him. "There is no need for you to come again," he said dully.
"There is nothing more to be done."

"The stock does not need moving?" Claude asked.

"No, it will stay here. I have been to see the Arab merchant, Kaid
Seif, and he is buying the business, both the stock and the store, and will
take them as they are. . . . At a criminal price, of course. But at least he is
buying. . . . And Spiranthos' business as well."

Claude took his money, and Mardik looked away. He looked blankly at
the wall before him and seemed again to be listening for a woman's wail
from across the courtyard. But today there was no wailing. Instead, after
a moment, there was another sound, a different sound, sudden and harsh:
the thump of a rock against the street door of the shop. The two men
turned. They waited. But that was all. There was no second thump, no
voices, no pounding on the door.

"Thank God there are the Egyptian guards," said Mardik. "And that in
four more days we will all be leaving."

"You have made your arrangements?" asked Claude.

"With their caravan? Yes. They will supply the camels, and of course
protection; but we must have our own food, tents, and I am seeing to
that."

Claude nodded and turned to go.

"For myself and my family, that is," Mardik added. "Not for you and
yours. That is understood, I hope?"

"Yes," said Claude, "that is understood."

"You are making your own arrangements?"

"Yes, I am making my own."

He left. In the street outside there was the usual crowd, but no mob, no stone-throwers, and, as before, he was unmolested as he walked through the streets and then the market square. Before the governors palace there was a deployment of troops and a barking of orders, and on the square's far side two languid sentries guarding Maison Gorbeau. The doors were shut, with Rappe presumably behind them, invisible; but in the rear courtyard, as he passed, Claude could see Egal and the Harari clerk busy with crates and bales under the jacaranda tree.

He did not stop. He went on to his home. Today, Nagunda was not on the divan, with candy and rosary, but standing before her mirror in her brightest clothing, and as he entered she turned, smiling, and said, "See—I have put on my best for the holiday."

"The holiday?" he repeated.

"It is still on, is it not? There are still the crowds and the noise."

"Oh, yes—yes, so it is. I had forgotten—"

"And you are again home early."

"Yes—"

She returned her attention to the mirror, and he sat on the divan and watched her. Then, reaching behind the divan, he pulled out a small Arab chest, and from the chest he took his money belt, and he counted its contents. From his pocket he took the money he had just received from Mardik, and he counted that too. And the sum total, in piasters and Maria Theresa thalers, was the equivalent of about ninety-three francs. As they lived now, it cost him two hundred francs a month to keep himself and Nagunda, not including his gifts to her of candy and clothes. Not including a child. Nor *Dear Mother, please find enclosed. . . .*

He put the money away.

"I will find work," he had said to Father Lutz. "I will find work and take care of my family."

He sat for a while, watching Nagunda, watching her black face and gold earrings reflected in the mirror and the great bulge of her belly beneath the bright cloth of her gown. Then he rose and went to the door —and she turned and spoke to him.

"You go out again?" she asked.

And he nodded.

"Take me with you," she said.

"With me?"

"Yes. It is a holiday. There are many people and I would like to see them. I would like them to see me in my nice dress, and with you I would not be afraid."

Claude shook his head. "No," he said. "No, I cannot."

"Why?"

"Because—it is a holiday only for Moslems."

"*You* are not a Moslem."

"But I am a man, and that is different. I must go now—"

And he went.

He went again through the streets and to the place of business of the Arab, Kaid Seif; and the Arab was there and he was courteous, saying, "*Salaam—salaam* and welcome, Sidi Morel; it is an honor that you come to my humble establishment." He bade Claude sit on soft cushions, and ordered coffee and hookahs to be brought, and listened quietly while Claude spoke. But when Claude had finished he shook his head. He said, "Alas, it is impossible."

"Impossible?"

"Yes. You are a most able merchant, Sidi Morel—that I know. And I have bought the stores of Mardik and Spiranthos and could indeed well use you. But alas—I say again, alas—I cannot. No. I have two sons, you see, for whom I have bought them. And four nephews who will work for my sons. And my wife, too, has many nephews, and so you see—I am sorry, truly sorry, honored sidi. . . ."

Claude rose and bowed and left. He went to another merchant, and a second, and a third. Through the rest of that day and all the next, he visited the merchants and traders of Harar, and all were courteous, all called for coffee and pipes—and all said, "I am sorry, sidi."

They said, "I have a brother, you see—"

"I cannot afford—"

"I am cutting down—"

"My business, alas, is poor—"

"—And will be poorer, I am afraid."

"—For if Harar will be free, it will now also have far less trade with the coast."

They said, "I am honored."

They said, "I am sorry."

(—"Which means *fous le camp*," he thought, "and I have heard it before. But then I could steal. Now I cannot.") And again he went home, and Nagunda cooked supper, and, supper over, he sat in the night, in the flickering lamplight, and, like Mardik, stared at the wall with dull unseeing eyes.

Then there was a knock, and he answered, and it was Vayu. And he said, "Well, it is the *blouse blanche*, the young Communard of the revolution—"

The boy looked at him blankly. "What, sidi—?"

"I thought you were too busy these days to come and see me."

"Oh . . . I am sorry, sidi. . . . I have been busy, yes—with Father Lutz. He has had much to do, because the Egyptians are going."

"And without Father Lutz—you have been too—have you not?"

"I—I do not understand—"

"Busy running in the streets, waving a stick, yelling 'down with *ferangi!*'"

Vayu's face became miserable. He said nothing.

"You have become quite the Harari patriot, eh, my boy?"

"I—I—" Vayu stammered. "That was only the first day," he murmured. "When the news came that the Egyptians were going; that Harar would be free."

"And so you celebrated."

"Yes, we celebrated. . . . But, for me, only then. Truly, sidi—only that once."

"And since then?"

"Since then I have been with Father Lutz, and he has told me much. That it will be not only freedom that comes, but trouble too. For himself and his people—for the Copts—for all Christians—"

"—And reminded you, perhaps, that you are a Christian too?"

Vayu hung his head. "I—I did not mean wrong," he murmured. "I was foolish; I did not know. . . . And then the Father told me: how it would be—how it is. That there is fear of the Emir Ismail. That Spiranthos and Mardik have closed—are leaving—and we will have no more trips to the villages. That Maison Gorbeau is closed, and we will not go for them to where I must speak Amharic—"

"No, we will have no more trips, Vayu," said Claude.

There was a pause. Then the boy raised his eyes, and into his sadness there came a hesitant smile. "But anyhow, you will stay. You and the Father, you will stay in Harar."

"The Father told you that?" said Claude.

"Yes, he told me, sidi. And I am glad. So glad."

There was again a pause—longer than before. Nagunda had been sitting on the divan, eating candy; but now the candy was gone, her head nodded, her eyes were closed, and, like a child, she lay back and was asleep.

"No, Vayu." Claude watched her for a moment, then turned back to the boy. "No," he said quietly. "I am not staying. I cannot stay. I must go."

"Go? Go, sidi? With the Egyptians?"

"Yes, with the Egyptians. With the others."

Vayu stared at him, stricken. "But—but the Father said—"

"Yes, I know. I told him I would stay. But that, too, was four days ago. And as with you, things have changed."

"Changed, sidi?"

"I cannot find work here. As a *ferangi* no one will now take me. And I must support my wife—and my child."

Vayu still stared. His lips moved, but soundlessly. And then the words burst out. "Then I will go too," he said. "If you go, I will go. To Zeila. To Aden. Anywhere—always—"

Claude shook his head. "No. It is no good. I could not take care of you. And this is your home."

"My home is where you are."

"No; now it is with Father Lutz. He is a good man. He will take care of you."

"He is good, yes, but it is only you that I want to be with. I have been waiting, sidi—waiting so long to come back—not just on the trips, but here, with you always." The boy's voice broke; his eyes brimmed with tears. "Please, sidi, please! If you go, take me with you—"

Now his voice had risen, become almost shrill. And Claude put a finger to his lips and pointed to Nagunda.

"Please, sidi. Please—"

"My wife is tired," Claude said, "and needs her rest. . . . Go now. Go. Quietly. We will talk about it again—tomorrow—"

"And you will do it, sidi? You will do it, yes? Yes? Oh, please—"

Claude put a hand on his shoulder and led him to the door. "We shall see," he murmured. "Tomorrow we shall see." Then he opened the door, and the boy was outside. . . . "Please," he said again, and then the door was closed, he was outside; and Claude stood for a while on its inner side, motionless, and then turned down the lamp and sat in the darkness beside his woman, Nagunda.

He sat there through the night, in the dark, with the sound of her breathing; and she did not wake. Once she turned and lay on her back, and he could see dimly the great mound that was the child within her; and later she turned again and lay against him, and he could feel the mound, feel the child and its stirring; and he thought, "It will not be long now. A month, perhaps, or less. Perhaps while we are with the caravan in the desert—and it will be hard. But she is a woman of the earth; she is strong; my son will be strong. They will survive. They will survive better there than here, with no work for me, no money, no food, nothing. We will reach Zeila. We will reach Aden. I will be again where I started, five years ago, but at least in Aden I will find work; I will start over again. . . ."

When the darkness thinned, he rose. Nagunda stirred and woke and, rising too, made their breakfast. From his chest he took his money belt and his money. He would go first to Egyptian headquarters and make arrangement for their camels. Then there was food—a tent. . . . "What else?" he thought. . . . And as he thought, there was a knock on the door.

"It is Vayu again," he told himself.

"—Or Father Lutz."

But it was not Vayu or Lutz. It was Marcel Rappe.

"I must speak to you, Morel," he said. And his voice, as always, was crisp and dry; his linen immaculate, his shoes shining. But behind his spectacles his eyes were distraught, and his face was drawn and tense, as if he too had spent a sleepless night.

"There is an emergency," he said. "A most serious affair—"

Claude let him in, and Nagunda stared at him. She had not seen him since the day she had arrived in Harar.

"This is my wife," said Claude. "Perhaps you remember."

"—and I have come to ask," Rappe continued, "if you will—"

"This is my wife," Claude said.

"Your wife?" Rappe bit his lip. "Oh yes, of course. *Bonjour, madame.*"

Nagunda still stared.

"—And I have come to ask," he said, turning quickly back to Claude, "if you will help in this most desperate situation."

"What situation?" said Claude.

"It concerns the caravan. As you know, it leaves the day after tomorrow. I had made all transportation arrangements with the Egyptians: for myself, for all the merchandise of Maison Gorbeau. Everything is sorted, checked, ready for loading. And now—now at almost the last moment —they tell me they cannot take it; that they have not enough camels. They have one for me. For my merchandise, none—not a single animal! I have been to the Governor himself, and he says he can do nothing. One camel can be assigned to each person, and no more. . . . And my goods must stay here."

He paused. Claude said nothing.

"So I have come to you," said Rappe.

"For what? What can I do?"

"You have been here far longer than I. You know the people. I do not mean the Egyptians—with them it is hopeless—but the Hararis, the Arabs. You know them well; you know the merchants, the traders. You know Abou Dakir, who has hundreds of camels."

"Abou Dakir is not here now. He is with the Emir Ismail."

"His agents, then. Or other traders. For me they will do nothing; but for you—"

Claude shook his head. "The only camels in Harar are the Egyptians'. The rest have all been sent to the Emir, for his march into the city."

"You are sure of that?"

"Yes, I am sure."

There was another pause. Rappe's hands opened and closed. He took a handkerchief from his pocket and wiped his forehead, and then his spectacles. When he replaced the spectacles the lenses glittered over his sharp febrile eyes.

"Nom de Dieu!" he said. "There must be some way—something. There must, I tell you!"

Claude considered.

"Could you not sell?" he said.

"Sell?"

"Like Mardik and Spiranthos. Sell your stock to Kaid Seif or one of the other Arabs."

"Like Mardik and Spiranthos? . . . Absurd! Impossible! . . . Their stock was worth—what? A few thousand francs at most. And do you know what mine is worth? *Eighty-five thousand*, by the last inventory. . . . Where is the Arab, please tell me, with that sort of money? Except Abou Dakir, and he is not here—and would not buy if he were."

Claude did not answer. He stood motionless. His eyes went from Rappe to the wall beyond, and along the wall to the corner where Nagunda stood watching. For a long moment he looked at her, and then back at Rappe. And then at last he said to him, "There is still one alternative: to sell on credit."

"On credit?" Rappe stared. "Are you mad? On credit to whom?"

"To me," said Claude.

The stare widened. "To you—?"

"Yes. Exactly."

"But—" For a moment Rappe was wordless. "But you are leaving too—" he said.

"No, I am staying. I wish to stay. This is my home, and my family's."

"But when the Egyptians leave—when Ismail comes—"

"It will still be my home. I am not a *ferangi*. I am an African. I shall stay and be accepted as an African."

Rappe was silent, studying him, and in his eyes was a blend of bewilderment and suspicion. "And what you propose—" he finally said.

"—is that I take over Maison Gorbeau. The store, the stock. That I run it again, as I once did, except this time not as manager but proprietor. I will sign a paper with you, as Gorbeau's agent. We will set a price, and I will pay it back in installments out of earnings. I will in effect be your partner—Gorbeau's partner—until it is all paid, and then the business will be mine."

"But how do I know—"

"That there will be earnings? That I will keep my part of the bargain? . . . You do not know; you will have to take your chance. . . . Or, if you prefer not to, simply leave your stock where it is, under the jacaranda tree, and let the thieves and scavengers take care of it."

Again Rappe was silent. He looked at Claude, and away, and back again, and once more his hands opened and closed.

"So you will think it over, *hein?*" said Claude. "You will go to the store and put out a sign: THIEVES WELCOME. Or you will go and make out a paper, and in an hour I will come and we will check the inventory together."

He went to the door and opened it. And Rappe hesitated, and then followed him slowly. "There will be much to discuss," he murmured. "Many points, many details—"

"Yes, many," Claude agreed. "But we have all day today, and tomorrow." He held the door as Rappe went out. And then added cheerfully: "First the inventory, then the signing, eh, *mon vieux?* And do not forget the ledgers. Ah yes, the ledgers. I have rather missed them, you know; I shall welcome them back like old friends."

Rappe said nothing. He crossed the courtyard to the street. "And their pouch too," Claude called after him. "Above all, you must leave the pouch. I would not want the ledgers spoiled by dust or dampness. . . ."

He closed the door. He leaned back against it. And then, suddenly, he laughed. He laughed as he had not laughed in years—from his chest, from his belly, from his very core—and then, still laughing, he crossed the room and put his arm around Nagunda and held her; and then the next moment, to his surprise, she was laughing too.

"And what do you find so funny, *ma jolie?*" he asked.

And she pointed to the door through which Rappe had gone, and then to her eyes, and with a finger she made circles around her eyes and said, "The sidi has four eyes. His own two, and two others." And she laughed again, and he laughed, and said, "Yes, it is funny—very funny"; and he held her close and felt the child within her; and he was still laughing, they were laughing together, when a while later there was a knock, and he called "Yes?" and Vayu entered.

He wrote to Gorbeau:

As of today I signed an agreement with M. Rappe, which he will of course present to you. But I wish also to assure you in person that I shall do my best to live up to it. . . .

And to his mother:

Because of a change of government, caravans will from now on be infrequent, and once again you may not hear from me for some time. Do not worry, however; I and my family are well. And my financial prospects, after a brief decline, are now better than ever. My first obligation, of course, will be to my wife and son (now soon to arrive), but you may safely assure Michel Favre and his Banque du Nord that you will not be paying them mortgage interest much longer. . . .

He gave the letters to Rappe. From Rappe, in return, he received a signed paper, the keys to Maison Gorbeau, and its ledgers—in their pouch. And the following day, in the main square, he watched the green flag of Egypt come down from above the palace; the troops assembling, deploying; the host of laden camels; the Governor emerging; the officials and clerks assembling, and their women and children; and Mardik with his family, and Spiranthos with his; and Rappe alone, in white linen and topee, his glasses glinting in the sunlight. And then the camels lurched up, the dust rose, a bugle sounded; the crowd became a procession, and the procession moved through the square, the Governor with staff and guards ahead, the others following, the troops with rifles along the line of march. And the line moved out of the square—slowly, swaying, while the dust rose higher—and into the street that led to the north gate of the city.

Then it was gone. The rear guard was gone. And the dust settled, and it was quiet. There were still crowds in the square—crowds of Hararis who had been silently watching—but they remained silent, there was scarcely a sound or a movement among them . . . until from the minaret of the mosque beyond the palace there rose the high reverberating cry of a muezzin, and the Hararis turned and knelt and prayed to Allah, while the muezzin chanted; and when the chant was done, and the prayer, they rose, and it was quiet again; the whole city was quiet—hushed and waiting in the sunlight, among its ancient stones.

The *ferangi* were gone. Egyptian, Syrian, Greek, French. He, Claude Morel, was left: the *ferangi-who-was-not-a-ferangi*, the changeling, the blue-eyed African, alone in the crowds, in the world of Islam. . . . And then, a moment later, not alone, for beside him was a brown robe, a broad beard, a broad and ruddy face that was no Arab's; and Father Hippolyte Lutz said, "Well, they have left, my son. Now it is you and I and *vive la France, hein?*"

"And the Emir Ismael," said Claude. "And *Allah akbar*."

"He will come soon now. He and his tribesmen."

"Yes, today, I think. They say he has been camped only a few miles off, near Mount Kondudo, waiting for the Egyptians to go."

"I shall call on him as soon as possible," said Lutz. "Tomorrow morning, perhaps. And I hope to find him not quite the ogre some of our friends have thought."

"How are your people? Are they frightened?"

"Some a little—yes. Some not. I have suggested that, until I have seen the Emir, they stay off the streets, to avoid possible incidents; and the Copts, I understand, are doing the same."

"Whereas you yourself—"

Lutz smiled, "—am like *your*self: an exception. As of the moment, one of Harar's two visible Christians."

"One of one, Father, if you please," said Claude.

"One? . . . Oh, yes, I had forgotten. Forgive me. One Christian, I should say, and one Zoroastrian—with a Christian wife." The priest's smile became a chuckle, and he put a hand on Claude's shoulder. Then he looked about him, across the market square. "In any case," he said, "I think we are in no great danger: neither we nor anyone. The crowds —look—how quiet they are. They have prayed, and now they are quiet, waiting. They did not want the Egyptians—no. They want their own ruler, and for that I cannot blame them. But they are not savages, not cruel and fanatic, and I do not think the Emir will be either."

He paused, glancing down at the crucifix at his waist. "They themselves, perhaps, have not found the true God, but they are God's children none the less. Catholics, Copts, Moslems—we are all his children." He looked up again, at Claude, and the smile returned. "Even Zoroastrians, my son," he said, "—however much they may resent it."

He moved on: out of the square, into the street that led to his house and church. And Claude crossed the square to Maison Gorbeau. The door was closed but not locked, and inside were Egal and Vayu—Vayu again, instead of the Harari clerk; and they rushed to him and seized his hands, excited, grinning, talking both at once. . . . "Ah, sidi! Welcome, sidi! . . . We three together again . . . Like in the old days. . . ."

Then they set to work.

Claude, with Rappe, had already acquainted himself with the current inventory, but much of the merchandise was still crated and baled for shipment, and through the hours they labored at unpacking it and stowing it back in bins and on shelves.

"Soon, of course, we shall be repacking again," said Claude, smiling. "But only selected items and for a different trip."

"You mean—" Vayu's eyes shone. "You mean I must again study Amharic?"

"Yes, you must study. You cannot get along in Abyssinia without Amharic."

"We will go, then! *Ayeee—ayaaa!* We will go! . . . But when, sidi? How soon? When?"

"When Nagunda is thinner," said Claude.

They talked on as they worked. The bales scraped. The crates thumped. Now and then they rested, and Claude raised his head, listening. But it was still quiet outside; there was only the dim murmur of the crowds; no shouts, no stamping feet, no rock against the door, as on that day at Mardik's. And Claude thought: "They accept me. They know I am here, and accept me. As an African, a Harari, a man who belongs; in his niche, his home." And again he smiled, but this time to himself, and they worked on into the afternoon.

When the change came, it was not he, but Vayu, who was first aware of it. Suddenly the boy straightened and stood still, and then he ran to the door and threw it open, and now Claude too could hear the change: in the square, in the crowds, in the whole city around them, as the murmur rose like the sound of a surging sea. . . . "They are coming—coming!" cried Vayu. "They are *here!*" . . . And he ran out and was swept up in the crowd, in the sea—and was gone.

"So, he is a boy—and a Harari. Why not?" Claude thought. And through the door, over the heads of the crowd, he saw horsemen and men on camelback entering the square, the men of the desert in white burnouses and kaffiyahs flowing up in a great tide to the gates of the palace.

Then he turned away. "You and I, Egal, let us get on with our business," he said. And closing the door, they returned to the bins and shelves, the hides and gums and cloth and hardware, while, outside, the din rose, and held, and then at last slowly faded, as the procession wound to its end in the palace courtyard; and now the Emir Ismail had entered the palace, and the city was his.

The sunlight faded at the windows, and it grew dark in the store. Egal brought out matches to light the lamps, but Claude said, "No, that's enough for today. I'm going home now to my wife, and we'll continue tomorrow." Heaving a final bolt of cloth onto a shelf, he turned; and as he tinned, the street door opened. "It is Vayu," he thought. "The scamp back from the excitement—"

But it was not Vayu.

It was an Arab. Behind him were other Arabs, perhaps a dozen in all: men of the desert—tall, lean, dark-faced, some with guns, some with broad-bladed tribal swords—and they entered silently and stood in a row, still silent, looking at Claude and Egal.

Claude's eyes moved along the row, but in the dim light the faces were indistinguishable. Then he addressed the one who had entered first—their leader?—saying, "*Salaam. Marhaba.* What do the sidis wish?"

"You are the *ferangi*, Morel?" the Arab asked.

"I am the Harari Morel."

"But Morel?"

"Yes."

"You will come with us, then."

"Come with you? Where?"

"That you will learn in due time."

"To the Emir, is that it? He has sent for me?"

"You will come—now."

There was a pause. Claude looked again at the row of dark featureless faces. "Very well, I shall come," he said. "But first I must close the store."

"There is no need for you to close it. It is no longer yours."

"No longer—"

"—or any other *ferangi's*. It is now the property of the Emirate of Harar."

Claude stood motionless, silent.

"Come!" The voice was harsher.

But Claude still did not move. The Arab waited a moment. The others waited. Then two of them sprang forward and seized Claude by the arms.

"No—no—"

The cry was from Egal, and he moved quickly to the leader. "It is his place, sidi. His lawful place. And he is a good man—a friend to all our people."

The Arab looked down at the dwarfish figure. Then he looked at his companions. "Who is this one?" he asked.

"I know him," a voice said. "He has been in this place for years. A servant, a creature of the *giaours*."

"Hah, a traitor dog—"

"No, no," Egal protested. "I am not. I am a good Harari, a good Moslem. And the sidi, he too is good. Truly, I swear to you—"

The leader's answer was a mere flick of a finger. And what happened then was so sudden, so quick, that it was no part of time at all, but a thing that was not, and then was, and was done—as in the instant timelessness of a dream. Out of the dimness of dream there was a glint, a blade. Claude had seen it before: the blade of laughing Felix, the green blade of absinthe in the Paris night. And it shone, it swung back, and forward. The curved Arab blade swung—huge, shining, then gone; too fast to be seen—and all Claude saw was Egal. He saw the small gnarled body, the goblin's face, the pointed beard, the small dark eyes; he saw them—he still saw them when the blade had passed—the eyes still open, the mouth open, as if trying to speak; and the head was still there, motionless, suspended, as the body fell away; and then the head, too, fell, it hit the floor, it rolled slightly and lay still; and the eyes and mouth were still open and in the tilted beard were flecks of sawdust from the packing crates.

Then Claude was plunging forward. He himself had not moved, yet he was plunging, being swept ahead, by hands, by arms, by thrusting bodies; and Egal was gone, the store was gone, and he was out of the store, he was in the square; around him were hundreds of bodies, hundreds of voices, a tide, a roar, sweeping him on; and out of the roar he heard a voice, a single voice, a boy's, crying, "Sidi—sidi—" And it was gone. The crowds and square were gone. There were only the hands thrusting him, dragging him, through doors, through halls, through growing darkness. And then the hands were gone, movement was gone, and he was alone. He was in darkness, in a place of stone, lying on a floor of stone . . . and it was quiet.

His knee hurt. He did not know why, for he did not remember falling or being struck, yet it hurt with a throbbing ache that seeped inward, spreading, through his bones and blood. He had lain still for a while. Then he had sat, stood, groped his way slowly, blindly, along the walls of the cell. For it was still dark. There was no light at all. Reaching a point where the stone gave way to the wood of a door, he pounded; but there was no answer. He shouted, and his voice was an echoing croak in the blackness. Then he sat again, on stone cobbles, and felt the aching of his knee.

He was in the palace—or in a cellar beneath it: that he knew. But how long he had been there he did not know; or whether it was day or night, or today or tomorrow. Often he listened—listened straining in black stillness—and sometimes heard faint sounds as of moving crowds, human voices; but whether they were faint because the city was quiet, or because of distance and the thickness of walls—this, too, he could not tell.

He sat. He waited. Perhaps, later, he dozed; he did not know. But in the darkness, whether of dream or waking, the head of Egal hung before him —the gnome's head, unmoving, watching . . . and then no longer hanging, then still motionless, but now supported; the head resting on a tray, a platter; and the platter was held by a woman, a Bible woman, Salome . . . except that this was not Salome; it was another woman, a woman he knew, black and gravid. It was Nagunda; and the head she held was not Egal's, but the head of a child; and Claude roused himself, trembling, and rose and found the door, and he beat on the door with his fists until they throbbed and ached like his knee.

No one came. There was no sound. He sat on the stones and waited, and the hours passed—three, perhaps, or five, or eight—and still he sat, still he waited . . . and then at last, in the waiting, in black stillness, there *was* a sound; not from the distant streets but from beyond the door; and the door opened and an Arab guard appeared, carrying a lamp, and behind him was another Arab, smaller and older . . . and, in the lamplight, Claude saw the bland face and pale eyes of Abou Dakir.

"*Salaam*, my friend," said the old man. "I am sorry your accommodations have been rather makeshift."

Claude rose, but said nothing.

"And I am sorry, too," said Abou Dakir, "that I have been so long in coming. But the last night and day have been busy ones in Harar."

"You arrived with the Emir?"

"Yes, I arrived with Emir Ismail. Indeed, I am happy to say I am very close to the Emir Ismail; in fact, his new Minister of Finance and Commerce." The old man paused and cleared his throat. "And you too, if I may say so, should be happy." He added, "for if I were not, we would not now be holding conversation together."

"What has happened?" Claude's voice was still a croak, low and rasping. "What has Ismail done?"

"The Emir Ismail has occupied Harar. As I believe I indicated at our last meeting, he is a Moslem patriot; he and his men do not take greatly to *ferangi*, to *giaours*, to infidels, and have found it necessary to purge the city."

"There has been a massacre—"

"There has been a purging, a cleansing. Last night, and through most of today. I think I am safe in saying that there are no longer many *giaours* in Harar. Nor any infidel churches, either Coptic or Catholic."

"And Father Lutz—?"

"The priest, Lutz, of course, was especially singled out," said Abou Dakir mildly. "It is unfortunate, perhaps, for he was said to be a worthy man—but inevitable, too, in view of his position. The reports, you may be glad to know, are that he died commendably, in the best French tradition."

The lamplight wavered on the walls. The walls themselves seemed to waver in shadowed stillness.

"And now—" Claude said quietly, "—now it is my turn?"

Abou Dakir shook his head. "No," he said. "No, with you it will be different. Different, if I may say so, thanks to me. You were originally, of course, high on the Emir's list—as high as the priest. But I dissuaded him. That is why you were merely escorted from Maison Gorbeau—which, incidentally, I shall try to run as efficiently as my predecessors.... My reasons?" The old man shrugged. "The same as before, I suppose. That I have a weakness, a sentiment; that you are not altogether a *ferangi*.... In any case—" His voice changed, became businesslike. "In any case, my friend the Emir agreed. You have not been killed, and you will not be. It is now night, and you will spend the rest of it here. It is not comfortable, I am aware, but at least it is perhaps better than a place on the street or the square; for there are, alas, many dead in the city, and tonight the gates will be opened for their traditional disposal. In the morning one of my caravans is leaving for the coast. And you will go with it. For the first few days, as a precautionary measure, you will be under guard. Then, when the desert is reached, you will be released and may travel freely."

There was a pause. Claude said nothing.

"This is clear to you?" said Abou Dakir.

Claude still said nothing.

"You have any questions?"

"Yes, one. What of my wife? She must be told."

"Your wife?"

"She is at home, and pregnant. She must be given time to prepare."

"There is no record of a wife," said Abou Dakir. "Nor was there anyone in your home when our men searched it."

"No one there?" Claude's voice seemed not his own.

"No. Inquiries were made of the neighbors, and they said there *had* been a woman there. A black woman—your servant; presumably the slave you brought back from the south. But when our occupation began, she became panicky, so it seems. She was alone and afraid, and ran off."

"Ran off—where?"

"To this Lutz, the priest, they thought. For she was a *giaour*, they said; always carried a rosary. . . . And such a woman was found at the priest's: black, fat, with a rosary. She did not die as well as he, my men reported, but that is of course to be expected of a woman."

In the stillness, the old man turned. The guard turned, and the lamp flickered.

"So I must go now; these are busy times," said Abou Dakir. And at the door he looked back and added: "We shall meet again, I imagine; we usually do. Perhaps in Zeila, Djibouti, Aden. And meanwhile be of good cheer: there are plenty of fat black women still in Africa. Indeed, I should be glad to sell you a new one myself, at a most reasonable price."

The pale eyes glinted in the lamplight. "If you are interested, speak to my caravan leader," he said. . . . "And so, *salaam*, my twentieth son. *Salaam aleikum*."

Then he was gone. The guard was gone. The door had closed. There was darkness, stillness. It was not until later that in the stillness, through the ancient stones, Claude could hear the hyenas howling in the streets of night.

33

February—

FROM: *British Resident, Zeila*
TO: *French Commissioner, Djibouti*

   Referring to your communication of 9/1, our records show no listing of the name Morel, for either arrival or departure at this port. No European of any nationality has been recorded as arriving from the interior since the Egyptian evacuation last September.

May—

FROM: *Italian Commissioner, Massawa*
TO: *Vice-Consul of France, Hodeida*

   No record of name Morel. Possible French national (or, more likely, French-Arab half-caste), calling self A. Bonhomme, listed as working on docks, February and March. Reported to have left 29/3 on coastal vessel Giovanna; next port of call, Jidda.

October—

FROM: *Préfecture of Police, Suez*
TO: *Vice-Consul of France, Jidda*

   No record Morel. French-speaking vagrant, giving name Alain Dakir,

arrested here 15/8, served two weeks hard labor, deported 2/9, on French packet,
Victoire, *bound for Djibouti.*

March—

FROM: *Vice-Consul of France, Djibouti*
TO: *Consul of France, Aden*

      All inquiries Morel fruitless. However, dispatch from authorities, Port Sudan, state possible French national, giving various names (all presumably fictitious), was recently detained and questioned as suspicious alien. Released 13/1, and believed to have found a berth or stowed away on southbound ship.

"And so," said the Consul of France, Monsieur Paul Colbert, to his friend Emil Gorbeau, "—so you may make your own guess, and it is as good as another."

Gorbeau shook his head. "Morel is dead," he said. "I am sure of it. Rappe is sure of it."

"And this other one—or ones—with the many names?"

Gorbeau shrugged, "—are other ones."

"Perhaps . . . Yes, perhaps." The consul put away the dispatch from Djibouti. "In any case, we have done all we could—I and the others," he said. "We cannot go on forever hunting a ghost. *Le dossier est clos.* The book is closed."

. . . The book was closed. The Book of Harar. The Book of Father Lutz, of Egal, of Vayu, of Nagunda. The book of the son that never was. It was closed, it was gone, dropped and lost in the flow of years, as another book once, long before, had been dropped and lost in the yellow coils of the River Meuse.

He was alone again. Now it was he again who walked the streets of night . . . the streets of day . . . the streets of Zeila, Djibouti, Massawa, Jidda, Hodeida, Suez, Port Sudan. He walked in the sun—again the child of the sun—through the glare of noons, through a world without shadow; of one shadow—himself. And he walked in the darkness, under the moon, the stars; out of the cities into the deserts, the wastes. He slept in the wastes, under thorn trees. He slept in the camps of nomads, on the Red Sea beaches, on the decks of dhows, on the floors of jails. And in the morning when his jailors questioned him, he answered nothing, or what came to mind, in Arabic or French or Turkish or any tongue; and when they let him go, he walked on through the city, through the wastes, to the next city, the next job, the next jail, the next boat—it did not matter which —whichever came first.

His body was bone and skin, and the skin was brown leather. His hair was the color of desert sand. His eyes were blue, depthless, unchanging: the eyes of a mask held up to an empty sky.

Now he drank again. When he worked it was for only one reason: to earn money for drink. What he wanted was absinthe. He wanted it with a clawing grinding hunger that filled his blood and bones. But there was absinthe only in French Djibouti and the big cities of Egypt, and he did not stay long there—or anywhere. And where there was no green magic he drank what magic there was—brown or yellow or amber or white; he bought his drinks, he cadged them, begged them, sometimes stole them; and he drank until the glass was empty, the bottle was empty, the bar was empty; until the bar was closed and dark, the streets were dark, his eyes and brain were dark, and in the darkness at last he would fall and lie still and sleep; *sleep on the pavements of unknown cities, uncared for and without a care.* . . .

He would sleep.

Then waken.

Why?

There was no answer. . . . There was the oven of the noonday desert and he moved through it, weak, hungry, skeletal; thinking, "This is the last desert, the end of the journey. Soon now I shall stop, lie down, and not get up again." . . . But he did get up. He went on. To the next city. The next bar. The next bottle. . . . There was the deck of a dhow at night, and he looked down into the dark water, thinking, "This is the time, the place. A step forward—one only—and it is done. . . ." But he did not step forward. He lay down and slept, and in the morning a wharf policeman found him and took him to jail.

"It is your will to live," Lutz had said.

But what had Lutz had? The will to die?

He tried hashish. But it made him sick. There were no dreams, no refuge, no comfort; only nausea and vomit. No blue caves, but sun-scorched streets and flies clustered on his lips and eyes.

He went south to Berbera and Mogadiscio as coaler on a freighter —but Mackenzie did not come to the stokehole. And in Mogadiscio he lived for a month in the hut of a Somali stevedore who had found him lying in the street. He went north again to Suez, then on to Port Said, and from a jetty in Port Said he threw an empty bottle into the sea. The bottle drifted north and west into the Mediterranean—toward the parapets of Europe—but the parapets were lost beyond the miles and the years. . . . *Dear Mother.* . . . He had written her last from Harar. Eight months before? Or twelve? Or twenty? He turned away. He moved south. . . . *Dear Mother: I am beyond the tomb, and no messages.* . .

He was in Suez again; in jail again. He was in Port Sudan, Jidda, Massawa. He was deck hand on a dhow bound for Hodeida, and then in Hodeida, in Obock—or at least he thought it was Obock—and then another town, and another, of which he did not know the names. He was in a third—bigger, louder, with streets of cobbles, not of dust—and he had awaked in an alley, and his bottle was empty, and his shoes were torn. He was examining a rotted sole, foot raised and turned inward, when suddenly memory came: the memory of words . . . *as if I played a lyre on my burst boots. . . .* The memory of place; and he knew where he was. He was in Paris. Turning, he looked at the wall behind him, to see the chalked word, MERDE. And it was no longer there, but it did not matter. He was still in Paris. He was in an alley in Montmartre, with the Grands Boulevards a few blocks away; and he rose and walked toward them; he reached them; he turned and walked down the broad avenue. He looked up at the chestnut trees. But there were no trees. There was rock. There was black rock rearing high and jagged into a burning sky; below were docks, warehouses, goats, flies, dust; and he walked down Queen's Way, in Aden, past the office of Gorbeau and Company.

"*Nom de Dieu! Nom de Dieu!*"

He saw the open window, the desk behind it, the face across the desk, and the face was white and startled, the eyes sharp behind glinting spectacles. He moved on, but not fast enough, for a door opened, and Rappe emerged and caught up with him, saying again, "*Nom de Dieu!*"

"*Salaam,*" said Claude. "*Salaam aleikum.*"

"You are back from the dead again—"

"Yes, from the dead. They send their greetings."

"And you—" Rappe stared at the rags of clothing, the sunken face, the dust-caked hair of head and beard. "You yourself are half dead. You are sick—"

"No, I am all right, thank you."

"And your leg—you were limping."

"Was I? I hadn't noticed."

Claude made as if to move on, but now another figure appeared. It was Gorbeau, markedly older than before, and fatter, but still he came hurrying from the door—all but running—and now he stood before Claude, staring too, saying, "*Nom de Dieu!*" And then, "Yes, I thought I heard—that I knew the voice—" And after a pause, wonderingly: "So, the prodigal returns. The man of mystery—"

The three stood still. Claude said nothing.

"You—" Gorbeau hesitated, looked around him. "You have just arrived?" he asked. "Like this? Alone? . . . I mean, you have no one—nothing—"

"No, monsieur," said Claude. "No profits—no installment on my debt."

"I am not speaking of—"

THE DAY ON FIRE

"No ledger," said Claude to Rappe. "Not even a rainproof dustproof pouch."

Gorbeau looked at Rappe, and Rappe looked at Claude's shoes. "We will talk of such things later, perhaps," said Gorbeau, putting a hand on Claude's shoulder. "For now it is enough that you are here—alive. . . . So come in, come in, man. You are tired, yes? You have been through much. Come in. Let us get off the street, into some coolness, and sit down."

As he spoke, he led Claude into his building, into his office. He made him sit and took a chair himself. "It is incredible," he said. "Amazing! You must tell me all." He paused and looked at Claude solicitously. "But first, is there something we can do for you? You look hungry, *mon vieux*. You would like some food, perhaps?"

"I would like a drink," said Claude.

"A drink? Yes, of course. Something cool and—"

"You have absinthe?"

"Absinthe? No, I am afraid—"

"Then cognac."

Gorbeau hesitated. Then he rose, went to a cabinet, and brought back a bottle and glass. He poured, and Claude drank, and the glass was empty.

"*Eh bien*," said Gorbeau. "Now tell me—"

Claude reached for the bottle. He refilled the glass. He drained it. He poured again.

"It has gone hard with you—yes?" said Gorbeau gently. "It has been —what?—*mon Dieu*, going on two years since we closed in Harar; since we were talking of an expedition to Abyssinia . . . and then the British fixed us; yes, always the British, you can count on that . . . and that desert bandit came with his barbarians . . ."

Claude's glass was raised again; and again, when he set it down, it was empty.

". . . and all this time you have been lost; we feared dead. But you got away . . . Where have you been, man? Doing what? And when did you reach Aden?"

Claude did not answer. He had risen. "I am sorry, monsieur," he said.

"Sorry?"

"That I cannot stay. That I must go."

"Go? Go where? You have just come. *Nom de Dieu*, sit down—rest—"

"I am very busy. I have—appointments."

He crossed to the door. Gorbeau rose and followed; Rappe followed; and both were talking, but he did not hear them. He was in the street, and they were beside him, still talking, trying to hold him; but he pulled away. He was walking quickly, and they followed. He was running and still they followed, calling; but the calls grew fainter, they receded, were gone; and he was around a corner, in another street, in an alley, alone, no longer running; and in his hand was the bottle of cognac, and he raised it and drank.

He was in the streets. But they were different streets. There were no wharves, no warehouses, no offices, no Europeans. Steamer Point was below him, invisible, and he was in Crater Town, Arab Town, in the pit of Aden's dead volcano, and around him its black walls rose into the burning sky.

He carried a broom and sack, and when he came to a pile of dung he swept it up. "Now the bulls will come back," he thought. "Now it is ready again for the bulls and matadors." And he went on to the next heap of dung, and the next, until his sack was full, and then he took it to the Arab Ibrahim, who dried the dung for fuel, and with the money he received from Ibrahim he bought araq. Araq was not green, like absinthe. It was not amber, like cognac. It was white and harsh and odorous and sold at a shilling for a liter gourd. But it sufficed. And he took it home with him. Home to the hut he had found in a Crater Town alley, and then he sat with it on the strip of burlap that was his chair and bed, and drank—each day the same; each night the same—until the night was total; and then the next day came, and with it, again, the broom, the sack, the shilling, the gourd.

It was dark in the hut, by day as well as by night, and on the morning when the visitor came, waking him from drunken sleep, he could see him only as a shadow against the light outside.

"You are Monsieur Claude Morel?" the shadow asked in French.

"And if I am," said Claude, "what do you want?"

"I have been looking for you for many days. I want to speak with you."

"And take me to jail?"

"No, not take you to jail."

"Then go away."

"Please—" said the shadow, and came in further. And now Claude had the impression of a young man in white linen, with a round boyish face and curly hair.

"Who are you?" he asked, trying to focus his aching eyes.

"I am Octave Gorbeau," the young man said.

"Who?"

"The son of Emil Gorbeau, for whom you used to work. We have not met before, but I think you have heard of me." He paused, seeming to wait for an answer, but got none. "When you were here before," he said, "I was in Paris, at the university. Now I am back in Aden, working for my father."

"And your father," said Claude, "has told you to find me, because I owe him money."

"No, it is not that—truly." Young Gorbeau's voice was earnest. "It is that he is concerned about you; would like to be of help. And he asked me too, if I found you, to give you these—"

From his pocket he took a bundle of letters, bound with a string, and handed them to Claude. On the topmost envelope, Claude, squinting, could see a Cambon postmark and tall angular lines of familiar script.

Putting the letters down, he groped for his bottle of araq, but could not find it. Then, after another pause, young Gorbeau said:

"Also, monsieur, there is one further reason why I have wanted to find you."

"So? What might that be?"

"Because," said Octave Gorbeau, "I know who you are."

"Who I am?"

"I know the name, Claude Morel."

"—late of Maison Gorbeau in Darkest Africa—"

"No, not from Africa—or here. From Paris."

"Paris?"

"I have read your poems," said Octave Gorbeau.

There was a silence. Gorbeau was still standing, Claude sitting on his strip of burlap on the hut's earthen floor. Claude again groped for the gourd of araq, and this time found it; but it was empty.

His visitor came a step closer.

"I have read *Selected Poems of Claude Morel*," he said. "Published by Boniface et Fils; edited by Albert and Germaine Chariol. . . . In fact, I have it with me here in Aden."

Claude put the gourd down, but his eyes did not leave it.

"I am only a merchant, an apprentice merchant," said young Gorbeau, "but still I am interested in literature—in poetry. At the university I read much poetry, and one day, in a shop near the Sorbonne, I found your book and bought it. I first read your poems then, monsieur; and I have read them often since."

Again he waited. Claude looked at the gourd.

"You have made a mistake," he murmured. "It was a different Morel."

"No, I think not. The book was published twelve years ago, when the author, the foreword said, was only twenty. That would make him about the age, monsieur, that you are now."

"What do you know of my age?"

"And also," said young Gorbeau, "there is what the poems are about. The poems of far places; of deserts and jungles; of Africa, black nations, the far, the lost—"

"It is someone else, I tell you." Claude's voice was stronger, harsher, and he looked up at last. "I—" he said, "—*I is another.*"

"No, you are he. I am sure. I can feel it—"

"Then feel it. Feel anything you want. Be a madman; but some other place—not here. . . . Mother of God, do I *look* like a poet?"

"You look, if I may say so, monsieur," said the young man gently, "like a man lost, a man sick with misery. . . . And we should like to help you. I—my father. If you will come to the office—"

"No. No, *mon petit*. No business conferences, thank you."

"Then to our home. For rest; for food. My mother, too, would like to see you—to help—"

"No thank you, either. No culture and tea cakes." Claude suddenly rose, jerking himself up, and seized his broom and sack. "And now, I am sorry," he said. "As I told your father, I am a busy man. I have many appointments."

He made for the door, but young Gorbeau interposed himself. "Please—" he said.

Claude tried to brush past.

"Please, I beg you—"

"I have work to do. Work! I am director general of *merde* for the Municipality of Aden."

Now he *had* brushed past and was in the alley, moving quickly away.

"I beg you—come," a voice called after him. "If not now, later. When you are through—tonight—to the house. We will wait for you—"

"Yes, wait," said Claude. "Wait."

Then he turned a corner. Another corner. The thousandth? The millionth? He turned the million-and-first, and moved through the streets plying his trade; and when his sack was full he took it to the Arab Ibrahim and received his shilling, and with the shilling he bought his araq. He took the gourd of araq to his hut and drank, and when the gourd was empty it was night; and then again he left the hut; he left the alley and streets of Crater Town; he came down to Steamer Point and walked down Queen's Way past the stores and warehouses. He came to the office of Gorbeau and Company, and then to the side street down which was the Gorbeau home; and still he walked on, the whole length of Queen's Way, until it ended, until all streets ended, and Steamer Point was behind him, Aden was behind him, and he walked on through sand and gravel, through the desert, through darkness, into the desert darkness, into the millionth mile. . . .

He was in the desert.

He was in a town.

In the town was araq, but no work, no money, and he had to steal the araq. As he sat drinking it in an alley he felt a lump in his clothing and brought out the packet of letters that young Gorbeau had given him. He held it for a while and put it down, and later, when he rose to move on, he left the packet in the alley.

In another town there was no araq. There was no food. Only rats. As once before, long ago, he became a ratcatcher. But now not to sell them. To eat them.

When there were no more rats he ate roaches, and the shells cracked between his teeth.

He came to many towns. Sun-scorched; full of dust and offal and crumbling walls. Full of roaches and flies—but the flies gave no nourishment. Full of children with swollen bellies and flies and pus on their eyelids. Full of old men on doorsteps, chewing khat, with eyes glazed and green foam on their lips.

He found khat, but, like hashish, it made him sick.

He came one day to a city, and it was called Shuqra. Later to another, and it was called Mukalla. Then one night he was entering a bigger city, an enormous city; and now he was no longer alone, but with Octave Gorbeau. They were walking through suburbs, past railways and factories, into long streets, into boulevards, and the boulevards shone under gas lamps like hanging moons. They were walking on the Boulevard Saint Michel, beneath the lights, past the shops and cafés; and all the shops were bookshops, and in their windows was one book. . . . *Selected Poems*, *Selected Poems*, *Selected Poems* . . . and in the cafés, at the sidewalk tables, were great crowds, and as he and Octave passed, the crowds knew him. They said, "Ah, he is here, he has returned. *Le Petit Sauvage des Ardennes.* The fierce invalid home from hot countries. The Boy Shakespeare. The Golden Alchemist." And then they came to a café—the biggest, the brightest—and at every table was a light, a green light, the green gleaming of absinthe; and he sat at a table and drank. Octave was gone now, but he was still not alone. He sat with Hugo the Olympian. With Zola, Villiers, Mallarmé, Druard: the great minds and spirits of the City of Light. And Druard, sitting beside him, put out his hand; but he turned away. He turned to the chair on his other side, the one chair that was empty. And he waited. He waited for the one who was still to come—who he knew was coming—and she came. The light was no longer green but blue, deep violet-blue; and she sat beside him, her eyes were on him, and she said, "Claude, Claude, we are so glad you are back." And he said, "We?" And she said, "Yes, we—Albert and I." And he saw that she was not alone; that two of them were there—she and Chariol. And Chariol smiled. He said, "Yes, welcome back, *mon vieux*, my dear friend." And now the light was green again, the green of absinthe; the green of knives; and Chariol held a knife; he raised it, he slashed, a hundred knives were slashing; and Claude was running down the boulevard, past cafés, past shops, past the end of the city—alone—out of the light, into darkness. . . . He was in the darkness of the desert, moving on, to the next town, the next city; and in the city he found araq, he found an alley, and there he drank, there he slept.

Then *the others* came—the ones who always came: the ghosts closer and more terrible than the ghosts of Paris, of long ago. Egal came: a head, trunkless, eyes open. And Vayu, beside him, calling, "Sidi—Sidi Claude" —but his voice made no sound. Then came Lutz, in brown robe with his crucifix; but now the crucifix was enormous, it was the cross of Golgotha; and he dragged it upon his back up a hill of stones, and there he raised it, he mounted it, he hung impaled, a murdered Christ. Beneath the cross knelt Nagunda: black, naked, pregnant. And she was praying. It was to Christ she prayed, to all Christs, to life eternal, for the life that was within her. But life did not heed her, the dead god did not hear; and when at last she rose and turned away and came toward Claude, she too was like the others, no longer woman but ghost; and the black ghost came nearer, naked, her arms outstretched, her belly swollen; and the flesh of the belly was now torn away, showing the womb beneath. And in the womb was death.

Only he, Claude, still lived.

He awoke.

He moved on.

He moved on to the next town, the next city, the next araq, the next alley. Through the nights alone. Through the days on fire.

Then came a night, in a city, when he was not alone. He was in the city of Mocha, on the Yemen coast, where he had earned a day's wages on the wharves, and that night, instead of gourd and araq in an alley, it was glass and brandy in a waterfront bar. The bar was crowded. A Portuguese tramp was in port, loading coffee, and its crew filled the place with brown faces, thumping glasses, and the chatter of voices. Claude, however, kept to himself, sitting alone at a table, in silence, the crowd unnoticed around him . . . until out of it, presently, came a voice that was different . . . he saw a face that was different . . . for the face was not brown, but pale, with red hair, a long jaw, a gold tooth; and the voice, now close beside him said in English, "Jesus, Mary, and Joseph, it's the loony frog!"

Neil Fitzsimmons grinned, and the gold tooth glittered. "Don't know me, eh?" he asked. "Don't know yer pal from the old days at Gorboo?"

Claude nodded. "Yes, I know you," he said.

"Good—good fer you, lad! On account of I know you too, and it makes us even . . . Oh, I grant ye it took me a minute or two. First thing I see ye, I says to meself, that ain't no Portugee, no sir. But then I asks, what *is* it? Maybe one of them E-gyptian mummies they been diggin' up rounda-bout. Then I says, no, no, it ain't that either. It's that frog, that's what—that loony Frenchy from Gorboo's."

The Irishman laughed; he thumped Claude's shoulder and sat down. "No offense, lad," he said. "But there been some changes, ye know. Like

yer hair, eh?—ye look like granddad himself ... And this—" He eyed
Claude's glass. "There's been a change there too, eh? Somethin' happened
to the pledge—"

He held a drink of his own, drank it down, and called for another.
"Well, more power to ye, lad. And more likker. Never was a man worth a
limey's fart who couldn't lift up his glass and pour down his likker."

His drink came and he drank. Claude drank. Fitzsimmons looked at
him quizzically.

"Still not talkin' though, eh?" he said. "Likker or no, still the bloody
sphinx."

"There's nothing—"

"Yeah, I know—nothin' to tell. Years gone by—five, six of 'em—and
not a fookin' thing's happened." The Irishman drank again. "All right, me
boy, have it yer own way—and I'll guess. . . . Yer the bloody King of Africa,
eh—that's what? The high cockalorum of Harar, of all the A-rabs—only
somethin' went a little wrong, eh, and the cockalorum's on his arse?"

He laughed again. "Like I say—no offense, lad." He called for another
drink. "—And one for me friend too," he added. "Me old friend the frog,
the ex-king of Africa. With the compliments of N. Fitz Esquire, of Jensen
and Fitzsimmons, Merchants and Entryprenoors, Limited."

Two drinks came. And they drank.

"Hear what I said, lad?" asked the Irishman. "Merchant and entry-
prenoor, limited—yessir—that's me. . . . Oh, I don't mind sayin' I had me
troubles fer a while—like you now, mebbe. Quit old Gorboo back three
four years ago; thought I had meself a good deal, runnin' a tradin' dhow
along the coast. Only it wasn't. The damn thing sunk. Fer a while nothin'
was no good; I had cruddy goin'. . . . Until at last, by God, I began gettin'
the breaks. First it was with an A-rab, up in Port Sudan, that's got a sort of
export business and needs a white man to help him out with the limeys;
and I take it on and it goes all right; in a year I got some money in me pants,
so I quit, I look around fer somethin' better—and by God, sure enough
I find it. Somethin' *big* at last—the rale thing—and I put me money in,
and I'm half of Jensen and Fitzsimmons, Merchants and Entryprenoors,
Limited."

He drank again, and his lean face smirked happily.

"Ever hear of Swede Jensen?" he said. "He's been around these parts
twenty years ... No? Well, ye will, I'm tellin' ye. . . . Swede's a Swede.
A smooth piece of goods if ye ever saw one, and he's been in and outer
everythin' ye can think of along these here coasts, includin' most of the
jails. In fact, between you and meself, he's a connivin' cheatin' bastard
—but a smart one, Christ yes, and when I meet him he's workin' on the
smartest thing ye ever heard of. . . Guns: that's what he's workin' on, by
God. . . . Two thousand of 'em he's got; or almost got. French guns, frog

guns—what d'ye think of that, Froggy?—two bloody thousand of 'em from back in some war that the frog army is through with; and he can have 'em fer two francs apiece, four thousand fer the lot of 'em; only they won't sell 'em except all together, and he's got only two thousand—until who shows up but me with the other two."

Fitzsimmons' smirk became a grin. "So be respectful, me friend," he said. "Yer talkin' with no slob of a navvy but a proper businessman, a bloody toff. Yessir ... And ye know where them guns are? Right here in Mocha, in what uster be a coffee warehouse: all two thousand of 'em —and all ours.... We ain't dumb, I'm tellin' ye. This Jensen, he's a smart one. We pick up the guns in Suez, and I say, where we take 'em—Aden? —and he says Aden hell, Aden's British, and them limeys go after contraband guns like they was slaves or opium; we take 'em to some straight A-rab place like Jidda or Mocha. So Mocha it is, and here they are, and me watchin' 'em, while Swede he's over in Tajoura makin' arrangements, and pretty soon they'll be made and we're on our way."

Their glasses were empty. "Hey," Fitzsimmons called. "Psst! *Isma!* Two more—" Then to Claude again, his face happily mysterious:

"Where? Yer askin' where, lad? Where we takin' 'em next?" He enjoyed a long moment's silence. "All right, I'll tell ye, by God. To Ab-y-ssinia, that's where. To the nigger king, Menelik. What d'ye think of that? ... That's what Swede's doin' in Tajoura now—fixin' it up fer a caravan —and when it's fixed I sail over with the guns and off we go. Off with two thousand guns, by God, to the bloody nigger king of Ab-y-ssinia!"

There was another pause. A pause of triumph. "What d'ye think of that?" he said. "Plenty, eh? Ye don't say nothin'—ye never say nothin', ye bloody sphinx—but ye think plenty; I c'n tell by yer eyes, them white loony eyes of yers ... But ye ain't heard half of it yet. D'ye know what we'll get fer them guns—what our friend Mr. Menelik'll pay fer 'em? ... He'll pay *fifty francs* apiece, that's what. Fifty sweet francs-worth in gold fer every single fookin' gun—a *hundred thousand* fer the lot that me and Swede picked up fer four...."

He talked on.

They drank.

The glasses were full, then empty—full, then empty—and Claude felt the liquor coiling in his eyes and brain. He saw Fitzsimmons' lips still moving, the gold tooth glinting. He heard his voice—but now the voice was blurring. The face blurred, receded; there was only a glint, a murmuring, and he searched for Fitzsimmons but could not find him. He reached for his glass, his drink, but could not find them. They were no longer there. Nothing was there. There was murmuring, blurring, darkness—thickening darkness; around him, within; there was only darkness ... and, through it, a long line moving—a caravan moving through the

THE DAY ON FIRE

wastes—and through the night he moved with it, toward the great hills in the west . . . until at last it was morning, and the sun rose on the hills: the sun rose on Abyssinia, gleaming, flaming; it rose on Mocha, on its streets and alleys, and he was lying in an alley, in mud, in the droppings of goats, and the sun shone on the droppings and they glittered like gold. . . .

He was in an alley, in a street, on a dock, on a beach.

He was in a desert.

In a town.

In the town there were Arabs, but there were also Hindus, and he stood before a Hindu temple and saw a holy man, a sadhu, seated on the temple steps: almost naked, his eyes closed, his body swaying. "He is seeking God," Claude thought. "In his cave of dreams he is seeking the God who is Brahma." And he moved on away from the sadhu and the odor of hashish, thinking: "Once I too sought God in the caves. But I could not find him."

Then he was in a mosque.

How he had got into the mosque he did not know. But he was there. Beneath his feet was carpeting, not stone nor dust, and his feet were bare, his head hooded, and around him were other figures, hooded, kneeling, and in the dim light a murmur rose and fell like the sound of the sea. And he thought: "They too are seeking God. Praying to their god, who is Allah. . . . I alone am not praying; because he is not my god. Not Allah, not Brahma, nor Yahveh nor Mithra nor Osiris nor Ra nor any of them; not the God of Christ nor the God of Antichrist. . . . Once, long ago, I had a god, but that was different. For my god was within me. He was myself. *I* was God. . . . But a false god. He raised me, then destroyed me. He cast me into the pit. I am still, and forever, in the pit, and I look up with blind eyes for God the Father.

"For that is what God is—the Father—and I have searched for Him. On my journey there have been many fathers. First my own, who begat me—whom I could never find. Then others: Father Lacaze, Father Mackenzie, Father Lutz, Father Abou Dakir of the twenty sons. But these fathers were men. And with men you live; you speak or act or love or hate; but you do not pray.

"Once, long ago, I prayed. I wrote a prayer. *The world is good*, I wrote. *I will bless life. I will love my brothers. God is my strength, and I praise God . . .* I wrote: *God of Judgment, I repent my sins but not my dreams. I have been damned by the rainbow, but still I will follow the rainbow—beyond the seas, beyond the deserts, beyond encompassing night. In the night always—always—my eyes will awake to the silver star, and I will walk in the night, I will walk with the Magi, toward the morning, toward the rainbow, toward the Christmas on earth that is to come. . . .*"

Then he was out of the mosque. It was later, it was night, and he walked in the night. But he did not walk with the Magi; he walked alone. And in the night there was no star, in the morning no rainbow, but only streets, alleys, dust, the dung of goats. There was araq, sleep, darkness, the ghosts of darkness.

And only with the ghosts was he not alone.

Once again on his journey of dreams he came to Paris. But only once. Thereafter the journey was different, it was across the wastes, and ahead, beyond the wastes, rose the high ramparts of Abyssinia. Yet it was the way to Paris, that he knew—the high way, the shining way—and he stopped and pointed for his companions—for Egal and Vayu and Lutz and Nagunda—and he said, "Yes, it is the way; we are almost there; at the *Ecole Centrale*, the school of science." And the child burst from Nagunda's belly and ran ahead of them, no longer dead but living, moving; and the rest moved after him, Claude moved after him; no longer in quest of the Father, but now himself the Father—the Father following the Son through the desert wastes.

He was in the wastes.

In a city.

In another city.

He was in hell.

He was in the very pit of hell, for again the city was Aden, and its black walls rose above him into the hell-fire of the sky. He was in the alleys of Crater Town, in its streets, with his sack and broom; he was in the place of araq, he had his gourd of araq, and sat with it on the stones against a crumbling wall; he drank, he drank deep, waiting—waiting for the ghosts —and they came . . . Except that this time there was a difference. For they came and went by. They did not remain. Only one remained . . . The ghost stopped, and it was not Egal, not Lutz, not Nagunda. It was a boy, his son; and yet not his son—no—for his son was a child, an infant, a fetus, he was dead, unborn, he had never been; and this one *was*. He existed. He was not a ghost. He was not a boy but a young man; and the young man stood before him in the street in Aden, and stared, and then moved closer. "Sidi, Sidi Claude—" he said. "I am Vayu. Do you not know me? It is Vayu."

And now he knelt beside Claude. He touched him, embraced him. "Oh sidi, sidi," cried Vayu, "it is I—yes, yes, it is truly I. . . . *And it is you!*"

34

He was in a hut again. But the hut was different from before. A rug covered the earthen floor; in a corner were a brazier and charcoal; beside them a shelf and a bin for food. There was a pallet for sleeping—two pallets—one for himself, one for Vayu. For Vayu was there. He was not a ghost, not a dream. He was there. He was Vayu.

True, he was not always there. When Claude slept, he vanished. When fever came, he vanished. And there were other times, too—long times, each day, as long as daylight lasted—when Claude lay alone on his pallet. "He *was* a dream, a ghost," he sometimes thought. But he was wrong. For each day, as the light faded, Vayu returned. He was there in the candle-light, in the glow of the brazier, cooking the evening meal, bringing it to Claude, sitting beside him until he slept; and in the morning he was still there, again cooking, bringing food, sitting beside him—until the sun rose and it grew bright in the hut, and then he too rose and said, "I must go now, sidi. I must go to work. But you will be all right, and I will be back in the evening."

Claude did not rise. He lay through the day. He had no work. He had no broom or sack. . . . And no araq. . . . One day, suddenly, the time came when he had to have araq, and he rose and moved to the door; but at the door he stumbled, he fell, and there he lay until evening, when Vayu came and helped him back to his pallet. Then the brazier glowed again, and Vayu knelt beside him with a bowl of liquid and made him drink. "But it is not araq," he protested. And Vayu said, "No, not araq, sidi. It is soup, and good for you." And he, Claude, said, "Ah yes, soup; oxtail soup; from the oxen of Alsace." . . . But that was wrong. That was somewhere else, sometime else. . . . And he drank the soup, and he slept.

Vayu knelt beside him often, and Claude watched him, and his face grew clearer. It was an older face than he had known; thinner; the boyish roundness gone, the bones visible beneath the flesh, and on cheek and chin the short stubble of a beard. But the skin itself was still brownly smooth, the eyes soft and dark, the voice deeper, but still soft and tender; and the body, when it moved, seemed harder, broader, but still with no grossness, with no gram of fat, still lithe and straight and young, as it had been in the old days.

And Claude said to him one night, "How old are you now, Vayu?"

And Vayu said, "When I came to you, sidi, you made me fourteen; and that is seven years ago, so I am now twenty-one."

"And how long is it since we were last together?"

"Two years now, sidi. A little more than two."

In the days that followed, as Claude's mind cleared, Vayu told him, bit by bit, of what those two years had brought him . . . He had—did sidi remember?—run out of Maison Gorbeau to see the entry of the Emir Ismail into Harar, and when he returned it was just as Claude was being dragged off by the desert tribesmen. He had been horrified and called out. Perhaps it was foolish, but still he had called out, "Sidi! Sidi!"—and other tribesmen had heard him; they had seized him too and asked, "Why are you calling out to this *ferangi*?"—and they had asked the Hararis, and the Hararis told them he had worked for Sidi Morel, for Father Lutz, that he was himself a *giaour*, an infidel; and then the tribesmen had taken him off and he had thought he was going to be killed.

But he had not been killed. He had been made a slave. He had been given to the men of Abou Dakir and put in the slave pen in the square, and he had stayed there many days, perhaps weeks—he did not know—and then was taken out and put in chains and sent, with many other slaves, from the south, from the west, from Harar itself, in a great caravan to the coast. To what town on the coast they came, he did not know, he could not find out; but there they were loaded into dhows and taken across the Red Sea to Jidda, in Arabia. Here was one of the great slave markets, where they would pass from the hands of Abou Dakir to their permanent owners. And it was said that most of the younger men, himself included, would go to a certain Sultan of Kalait, to be castrated and serve as eunuchs in his harem.

"But I was lucky, sidi," said Vayu. "In Jidda I escaped. And was not caught. And this I owe to you, and to Father Lutz, for I was not like the others; I could read and write, I could talk to men of different sorts; no one thought I was an escaped slave, and since then I have been free. But I did not stay in Jidda, of course. As soon as I could I came to Aden. I went to Gorbeau and Company—to see if you were there; if not, to ask about you. But the one I saw was Monsieur Rappe, who never liked me, and he said no, you were not there, they knew nothing about you, and then he chased me away. Since then, I have asked everywhere. I have looked everywhere. On the streets, in the stores, on the docks, on the dhows and ships coming from Africa. But there is nothing. It is like you are dead. I think at last, yes, he is dead, my sidi whom I love, he is gone and dead . . . Until last week when I walk through the street, when I see, I stop, I look, I cannot believe what I am seeing; but it is so, it is you—after two years it is you, Sidi Claude —and oh, I am so happy, so happy. . . ."

"Then you have been in Aden—?"

"For eighteen months," said Vayu.

"And are working."

"Yes, of course, working. For almost a year now, with Fitch and Sons; the big British company—even bigger than Gorbeau. At first it was just as a *walad*, a boy for errands and messages; but then they see I can read, I can write and do sums; and they make me a junior clerk. I do sums in a big book, like you used to do in Harar. And I speak English. Yes, English too, now. . . . 'Bloody well done, old chap. I say, it's a rum show, old chap.'"

Vayu laughed. It was the old laugh, the boy's laugh. Then he stopped, and there was a pause, and his eyes, fixed on Claude, were dark and gentle. "But I talk too much of myself," he said. "It is you now, we must talk of, sidi. For you are stronger—I can tell. You are better."

"Yes," said Claude, "I am better."

"You have been sick, sidi. Sick for long, I think. You—" Vayu hesitated. "You have had much trouble, sidi?"

"Yes, I have had trouble."

"Since you have left Harar?"

Claude nodded.

"And that was just now, sidi? A few weeks? A few months?"

"No, it was long ago. Before you left. The day after you last saw me."

There was another pause. Vayu looked down at the floor, and then back at him. "And—and the others—" he said at last. "They left too? They were with you?"

"No," Claude said, "they were not with me."

"They are—"

"They are dead. They were killed."

Vayu was silent.

"Father Lutz was killed," said Claude quietly. "Egal was killed. Nagunda was killed. Our child was killed before it was born."

It was the first time he had said it. And it was all he said. Presently Vayu rose and prepared their supper, and when it was ready they ate; and when they had finished they lay down to sleep. Claude slept, and in his sleep, too, there was a first: the first time in two years that there was neither dream nor ghost. One ghost was flesh and blood and slept beside him. And the others slept elsewhere and did not come.

A week passed.

And another.

Then one morning, with Vayu gone as always, Claude rose, and he too left the hut. He went to the Arab, Ibrahim, and was given a broom and sack, and through the day he plied his trade through Crater Town, and when it was done received his shilling. This time, however, he did not buy araq. He bought dates and goatmeat and a loaf of bread, and he brought them home; and when Vayu arrived he was cooking the meat and said,

"Today, for a change, I am marketer and cook. From now on we shall share all work and all expense."

Vayu protested. "But you are not yet strong enough."

"Yes, I am strong enough."

"But—" Vayu looked in puzzlement at the things Claude had brought. "But you had no money—"

"So I worked for the money."

"Worked? At what, sidi? What did you do?"

And when Claude told him he protested more than ever. "No, sidi, no —you cannot do such a thing. It is terrible, shameful, and I will not allow it."

"Not allow it?" said Claude.

"I mean—" Vayu was confused, unhappy. "I mean it is not right that you should do such work."

"What work do you suggest?"

"What you have always done—always been. A merchant, a trader. A big sidi, fine and important, that everyone respects."

"That was long ago, Vayu. And things were different."

"Different? How, sidi? Only that then you were in Harar and now in Aden. And Aden is bigger. There is more business, more chance. Even for me: a boy, a stranger, not a sidi—I found a chance, I found work. And for you . . ." Vayu paused; he had an idea. "For you, sidi—where I work, you too could work. At Fitch and Sons. They would take you, I am sure. . . . Or better yet—" A new idea came. His eyes lit up. "—Or better yet, you go to Gorbeau. Yes, that is it! To Gorbeau, sidi, and they will take you back. . . ."

Claude was shaking his head.

"Yes, yes, they would; I know it . . . You say no. Why, sidi? Because of the trouble in Harar with the caravan to the south? . . . But that was only with Monsieur Rappe, when you went to Mardik, and it was over before you left. Then you were going back to Maison Gorbeau, remember? You talked with Rappe; you were going back; we were going together for Gorbeau on a caravan to Abyssinia . . ." Vayu's excitement mounted. His hand pressed Claude's arm. . . . "And it can happen again, sidi," he said. "This time, *really* happen. Yes! There is no more Harar for Gorbeau. The trade with Africa is bad. They would want a caravan to Abyssinia more than ever, and who do they have who could do it like you . . . Oh yes, yes, sidi—they would take you, they would send you. And I would leave Fitch and come with you, and it would be like the old days again, you and I together. . . ."

He talked on. While their supper cooked. While they ate. While, later, they lay in the darkness and Claude sank into sleep. He talked on in the morning, begging Claude to come with him down to Steamer Point and Queen's Way. But Claude still shook his head. When Vayu left he remained behind. And then he took his broom and sack and did his day's work in the Crater Town streets.

It was the same that next night; the next morning; on all the nights and mornings of the week that followed. Vayu argued and pleaded. Claude shook his head, and at long intervals he answered.

"No," he said, "it is no good. It is too late."

"No," he said. "No projects. No changes. I have found my proper work at last."

Then, toward the week's end, in exasperation, he said: "Very well, you win; I shall make a change. I shall go down to Gorbeau's in my rags, with my broom and sack, and inquire if there is any goat dung in their court-yard."

He did not go. The next day, as before, he stayed in Crater Town, in its streets and alleys . . . But that evening there *was* a change . . . For when Vayu returned from work he was carrying a bundle; not the usual small bundle of food or charcoal, but a large one, wrapped in paper; and opening it, he brought out a shirt, a tie, and a linen suit. "They are for your visit to Gorbeau's, sidi," he said. "And please do not take them near the broom and sack, or they will get very dirty."

Claude held the clothes. He looked at Vayu. He looked at him for a long time, but did not speak. He did not speak all evening, nor in the morning; nor, in the morning did he put on the clothes, or leave with Vayu; but neither did he leave for his round of the streets—but sat, instead, unmoving on his pallet, unmoving through the hours, his eyes fixed on the clothing that Vayu had left neatly hanging from a nail on the wall.

It was midafternoon when he arose. First he went to the urn of water that stood in a corner and washed his hands and face. Then he put on the clothes. He had last worn a tie—when? In Paris? Cambon? His hands fumbled with it, but at last got it tied. And then he left the hut; he went along the alley, through the streets, down the long twisting street that led from Crater Town to Steamer Point; he came to the Point, to Queen's Way, and walked past the offices and shops, through the crowds of the busy port; and as he walked he put a hand in a pocket of his linen suit, and in the pocket was a piece of paper, and bringing it out, be saw it was a one-pound note. . . . One pound was what Vayu earned for each week's work as junior clerk at Fitch and Sons.

He passed Fitch and Sons. It was now late afternoon, and soon Vayu would be coining out. He would climb the long hill to Crater Town. He would enter their hut, and find it empty; but then he would see the bare nail where the new clothes had hung—and smile. He would smile again when, a while later, he, Claude, appeared; when he said, "Ah, good evening, my boy. I have been out in my finery, as you see. I have fulfilled your instructions." When, casually—oh so casually—he took from his pocket not one pound, but ten, saying, "Here is a little something, my boy, a small advance on my salary. Take it, please—it is yours. With my thanks. With my love. . . ."

He walked on. Ahead was Gorbeau and Company. . . . In a moment he would be there; he would enter; he would cross the office to a desk, and at the desk would be Rappe, and Rappe would look up from his pile of ledgers and say again, *"Nom de Dieu!"* . . . For an instant the image was clear. Then it blurred; it began to change. It was no longer Rappe who looked up at him—nor was it Gorbeau—but another, younger, gentler, with round face and curling hair. It was young Gorbeau—Octave; and the books piled on the desk were not ledgers but books of poetry. They were *Selected Poems, Selected Poems, Selected Poems, Selected Poems;* and from behind the great stacks young Gorbeau rose, and what he said was not *"Nom de Dieu";* what he said was *"I know who you are."*

Claude had stopped. He stood perfectly still. "Go on, go on," a voice said. But he could not go on. His feet were leaden. In the stone oven of Aden's streets his hands were suddenly cold and trembling.

He stood still. Then he moved. On the far side of the street, at the corner, was the Three Kings Tavern, to which he had sometimes gone in the old days with Neil Fitzsimmons; and he crossed to it and went in. It was crowded. Besides the usual freighters and coalers, there were two passenger ships in the harbor—a P. & O. packet bound west for Liverpool and a liner of the Messageries Maritimes bound east for French Indo-China—and the bar was full of transient drinkers, British and French. But he found a place. He ordered a drink. No araq here; he ordered brandy. It came and he drank it, and he drank another, and he paid the two shillings owed from the pound in his pocket. He felt better now. The trembling had passed, and his hands were warm. Leaving the bar, he recrossed the street, walked half a block, came to the Gorbeau office—and it had closed for the night.

He stood there a little while.

Then he walked up Queen's Way. He walked through the crowds going home and the crowds from the ships, and his hands were still all right, and the trembling, but now his feet were leaden again . . . or perhaps not his feet, but his knee . . . it was his knee that was leaden, that ached, and he was limping . . . and at the next bar he went in and had another brandy. "It will help," he thought. "It will help the knee and get me home, for with the aching knee I could not climb to Crater Town." With the next brandy he thought, "Yes, it helps—I can feel it. I shall get home, I shall sleep, and in the morning early I shall come down again and go to Gorbeau's, and it will happen."

Then he had left the bar. He was in the street. And he came to a third bar. This was the best bar in Aden—"where a drink costs *two* shillings," he thought. But the drinks would be better. And the price did not matter. He still had sixteen shillings in his pocket, and in the morning he would have his job, his advance of ten pounds. One good drink would get him up the hill with no ache at all ... He went in. . . . And here, too, it was crowded; but not so crowded as in the other places, and not so noisy; and the men were better dressed. "They are the first-class passengers from the ships," he thought. And he found a place and sat down and ordered a brandy; and as he drank, the man next to him jostled his arm and, turning, said, *"Pardon,"* and Claude said, *"Il n'y a pas de quoi."*

The man looked at him. "Oh, you are French," he said.

Claude hesitated. "Yes," he answered.

"But not from the boat?"

"The boat?"

"The *Provençal.* I have not seen you aboard."

"No," said Claude, "I am not a passenger."

He turned back to his glass. He drank. But he was conscious that the man was still watching him, and now the man spoke again. He said, "And yet, I am sure—"

Claude finished his drink, and the brandy coiled in his brain. In its coil, time wavered and changed; places changed; he was no longer in Aden but back in Mocha, at the bar in Mocha, and Fitzsimmons was watching, approaching; in a moment he would say again, "Jesus, Mary, and Joseph—"

He looked up, and he was wrong. It was not the Irishman, but a Frenchman. A Frenchman with a small smooth face, with a snubbed nose, with dark bright eyes—and the eyes were now staring. *"Nom de Dieu!"* he said suddenly. Just like Rappe. Just like Gorbeau.

But it was not Rappe, not Gorbeau.

It was Michel Favre.

". . . And so, *santé, mon vieux!"*

They drank.

"Garçon!—I mean, boy—another!"

And they drank again.

The old friends drank together. And Michel talked . . . and talked. . . .

His ship had come in at noon, for coaling. It would leave at ten: for Bombay, Colombo, Singapore, finally Saigon. That was where he, Michel, was going—Saigon. "Do you remember, *mon vieux?*—I told you you wouldn't be the only one to escape from Cambon; that I'd get out too. And I did. Six years ago. First the bank sent me to Reims, for two years. Then to Paris, for four. Yes, Paris! The main office. They took me out of real estate and put me in the foreign department—for training, you know —and now, *zut!* here I am, off to Indo-China. . . ."

From Indo-China he doubled back to Cambon. "Ho, was I glad to get out!" he said. "It's worse than ever now, believe me—dull, dead, *un vrai cimetière*. I'd have to go back sometimes, of course, to see my family. And it was awful. My wife hated it so, that after the first time she wouldn't come.... Yes, you don't know, of course: I'm married. For three years now. She's a nice girl—pretty—from Reims. And we've a baby." Michel brought out a wallet and produced a picture. "See, it's a girl. And she's pretty, *hein*? Both of them. They'll be joining me in Saigon in a while, when I get things established."

He put the picture away and ordered two more brandies.

"And you?" he asked. "You, you old scalawag? Have you got yourself a wife too? And little ones?"

Claude shook his head.

"Still the lone wolf, *hein*? The old bachelor?" Michel laughed. "Well, I'm a bachelor too, for a while—and between you and me, it's not so bad. Good for a fellow to get around a little—keeps him young." He looked at Claude and added awkwardly: "You—you know what I mean: keeps him *feeling* young." ... Then, cheerfully again, and leaning closer: "Say, I hear this Aden's quite a place for you-know-what. All kinds of girls: white, brown, black, everything. Maybe, you and I, we could—" He broke off, looked at his watch, shook his head. "*Merde!* It's too late. The lighter leaves the dock in half an hour ... Oh well—"

He drank his brandy and clapped a hand on Claude's shoulder. "At least I found *you, mon vieux*," he said. "And after I'd given up on it.... Haven't I told you? I've been looking for you—*mon Dieu*, yes. You didn't think I'd go through this part of the world without looking for *le beau gosse?* First thing off the boat this afternoon I went to Gorbeau and Company. Last month I was back in Cambon, saying goodbye to my family, and I saw your mother and asked about you; and she said you were here with this Gorbeau, or had been—or something—she didn't seem to be too up-to-date on things.... But anyhow, I go to Gorbeau's and see some dill pickle of a clerk, and I ask him about you, and he says yes, you used to work for them but not any more; and then I ask where are you, and he doesn't know. Are you in Aden? I ask, and he doesn't know, says he hasn't seen you for a year. Then I leave. I ask around at some other places—stores, offices, the French Consul—and nobody knows; nobody's seen you. So I give up. I say, well, that's that, and come in here for a couple of drinks before going back to the ship; and who comes in right after me but you—and by God, you don't look so invisible to me!"

He thumped his empty glass on the bar. "*Garçon!* Boy!" he called. "No, no, *mon vieux*, they're all on me. With the compliments of the Banque du Nord."

With the drinks bought and paid for, he turned back to Claude, and his manner became serious. "So I gather you're not much in Aden these days?" he said.

"Only on and off."

"Hmm—on and off. And you're in business for yourself?"

"Yes, for myself."

"Good. Good. It's better like that—the only way really to get ahead—unless of course you're with a great organization such as mine. . . . You're in general trade, I suppose? Import-export. And doing well, I hope?" Michel measured him with a shrewd eye.

"Yes, well," said Claude. "As well as can be expected."

"Not quite the Oriental potentate yet." Michel smiled. "Nor—if I may say so—exactly a *beau gosse* any longer. But doing all right—doing well enough. *Bien, bien, mon vieux.*"

His eyes moved from Claude's face to his clothing—the cheap but new linen suit. From there to his feet, his sandals, torn and rotting—

"I am much on the docks and in warehouses," Claude said. "It does not pay to wear one's good shoes."

"No, of course not. No new shoes in warehouses!" Michel laughed. "You old miser, you. A real Morel. Just like your mother."

He drank. Claude watched him.

"How is my mother?" he asked.

"How is she? *Mon Dieu*, man! She is amazing—incredible."

"She has enough—"

"Enough? *Deux fois mon Dieu!* Since she sold the farm—"

"Sold the farm?"

"But of course. You didn't know that? She didn't write you? . . . It's a year ago now—maybe more. I wasn't in Cambon myself at the time, but, believe me, I heard about it. From the bank. From everyone. They say such a deal hasn't been made since the Congress of Vienna."

"Such a deal—?"

"It was—as I say—incredible. One minute she seems in trouble, bad trouble. For a year she has not paid the mortgage interest, and the bank is ready to foreclose. Then—pouf!—the next minute she's sold it—*at three hundred per cent profit.* . . . Yes, that, exactly. Three hundred. To a crazy man from Paris, a millionaire—he's in textiles, I think—who wants a place in the country, near a woods and a river—and price is no object. So she sets the price. And she gets it. Enough to pay off the mortgage, the interest, and still have left twice what she put up in the first place."

Michel paused. "So now she's back in the store," he said. . . . "You don't know that either? . . . Oh yes, the farm's only part of it. No sooner does she sell it than the fellow she sold the store to goes bankrupt, and she gets it back for almost nothing; so there she is, where she was before—only a lot better off, and the store a lot bigger—a regular *grand magasin*, with three clerks, no less, and a stock boy. . . . Know who the stock boy is? One guess. Your brother Felix . . . He was married; I suppose you knew that. But his wife left him or something, and the old woman took him back. Guess she figured she could get him for just room and board and save two francs a week."

Michel shook his head in admiration. "What a woman!" he said. "*Quelle femme d'affaires!*" Then he laughed. "If you were half the businessman she is, *mon vieux*, by now you'd own the Suez Canal."

He drank again. Claude's glass was empty.

"*Garçon!* Boy! . . ." Michel looked at his watch. "One more, *hein*—for old time's sake—"

And Claude's glass was full again. He looked at its glinting amber. He drank. Then he looked at Michel.

"And Yvette?" he said.

"Yvette?"

"My sister. Have you heard of her?"

"Oh. Oh yes—the little one . . . No, I haven't. She became a nun, didn't she? Went to a convent. You don't hear much from convents, I'm afraid. . . ." Michel brightened. "But I can tell you about some of the others," he said. "You know, the old crowd. . . . Like Mimi Vuiton: used to be Rouger. You were pretty sweet on her once, even if you wouldn't admit it. Well, you wouldn't be so sweet any more. She's as big as the Bourse and has eight children; she and poor old Georges . . . And Louise Croz: not so good there either. Married a fellow from Antimes—a drunk; she supports him doing laundry. . . . And from the lycée—let's see . . . Pierre Berthoud —he was the tall one, remember?—he's a policeman. Jacques Bran's in Foyot's grocery. Louis Carnot's on his father's farm. . . . And then there's Henri Clauson—yes, by God, old Henri: the one we used to say washed in cowflop. D'you know what's happened to him? You won't believe it. He's a *lawyer*. An honest-to-God lawyer, diploma and all, and back in the lycée he was the school idiot. Used to drive poor Chariol out of his mind. . . . And now a lawyer, no less . . . If Chariol knew about it he'd be spinning in his grave."

Michel chuckled. He raised his glass and drank.

Then Claude said: "His grave—?"

"Yes, he's gone, poor fellow. About—let's see—a year ago, I guess. I hadn't seen him for years, of course—since he left Cambon. Hadn't thought of him either. And then one day in a Paris paper I see a notice: *Professeur Albert Chariol, of the Sorbonne; after a short illness*—they never tell you what it is—and then his age and what he'd done and *his widow survives*. That was it. As I say, it had been a long time since I'd seen him—maybe fifteen years—but I was sorry just the same. He's the one teacher we ever had that was almost halfway a human being."

He shrugged. "Well, so it goes—"

And then a whistle sounded: the deep-throated toot of a steamer from out in the harbor. Michel again looked at his watch and said, "So, the lighter goes in ten minutes." And he rose; most of the others in the bar were rising; they were leaving; but Michel remained for a moment, still speaking, and now his hand was again on Claude's shoulder. He was saying, *"Mon vieux."* He was saying, *"Bonne chance."* He was saying, "I'm so glad . . . again, maybe . . . take good care . . . when you buy that canal." (Here again he laughed.) . . . And then a last *"mon vieux."* . . . And he was gone.

Claude sat alone.

"Boy!" he said.

And again, later, "Boy!"

Still later, there was more tooting from the harbor. And still he sat. He sat until the last of his pound was gone, and then he rose and left the bar; and in the street, outside, he fell. He fell again, once or twice, on Queen's Way, and several times climbing up the hill, and once more in a street in Crater Town, and then in an alley; and it was the right alley, that he knew; but this time he could not get up. He did not try to get up. He lay still and slept until morning, when he was awakened by the flies crawling on his face.

"You did not go to Gorbeau's, sidi?"

"Yes, Vayu, I went. But they were closed."

"So you will go back today?"

"No, not today."

"Why, sidi?"

"Because my new suit is dirty."

"I will clean it for you."

"No, don't clean it. I am not going anyhow."

"Not going?"

"No."

"But, sidi—"

"I am leaving Aden."

"Leaving—"

"Yes."

"Why, sidi?"

"Because Aden is too big. There are too many people."

Vayu looked at him uncomprehendingly. He started to speak again, but Claude had risen.

"Anyhow, I am going," he said.

"Going where, sidi?"

"I don't know. Just going."

"You mean—now?"

"Yes, now."

Claude went to the door of the hut, and there he turned. "You have been good to me, Vayu," he said. "You have been better to me than anyone ever in my life. I cannot repay you now, but perhaps some day I can. I hope that some day I can."

He went out and down the alley. But Vayu followed and caught up with him.

"Then I will go too," Vayu said.

"No, you must stay here."

"I will not stay without you."

"You must. You have work. You are doing well."

"It is not well without you. I will find other work where we go."

"No Vayu, you must stay."

"No, sidi. Where you go, I go too."

They were on a dhow.

"*Ayeee, ayaaa—*"

They trimmed the sails, cleaned the decks, shifted crates and bales with the changing winds. The dhow moved along the low bleak coasts, put into this port, that port, another, and they removed the crates and bales and brought on others. The dhow came to its last port, and they left it, each with fifty piasters in his pocket. With the piasters they bought shelter, they bought food. And Claude bought araq.

They were on a beach, and the piasters were gone. The food and araq were gone. They went to the nearest port and moved up and down the docks. But there was no work on the docks. No berths on the dhows.

They were in the town, and there was no work there either; and they slept in alleys by day and hunted rats at night. Vayu was the better hunter of the two (—"you'd have been the champion," Claude told him, "at the Hôtel de Babylone"). So good, indeed, that they seldom had to eat roaches.

They were in the desert ... walking ... walking ... and Vayu said, "Now it is like the old days on our trips, sidi. Except that we have no mules and no merchandise." He smiled and looked at Claude, and his face was thin, the bones protruded; and Claude knew he was hungry; and he himself was hungry too.

But then they had luck. They found an oasis. It was a tiny oasis, lost in sand and gravel, with no inhabitants, no caravan encamped; but it had a spring and palm trees, and in the palms were dates, in the spring were frogs, and for three days they stayed there and ate and slept.

"You dream much when you sleep, sidi," said Vayu, as Claude wakened one morning.

"I do not remember any dreams," Claude said.

"You dream of your home. And Paris. You talk much about Paris. You are walking in Paris and say the names of many streets."

Claude said nothing.

"And you dream of a woman," said Vayu.

Claude glanced at him, then away. "Yes," he said, "I sometimes dream of Nagunda."

"It is not Nagunda you dream of now, sidi. It is a woman in Paris, and you look for her through the streets."

They came to other towns—to cities. And Claude had come to them before. They came to them under the sun, under the moon and the stars; and one night under the stars, but with no moon, he seemed to be coming again into the enormous city. But he did not reach it. The street did not become a boulevard, but branched off, twisting, darkening, and led through a forest, along a river, and he came to Cambon, to the house of his mother. It was the house, now, that was enormous. The store was enormous. He entered, and at its far end stood his mother, waiting, beside the cash drawer; and he approached, and it was the same as always . . . only not the same, because the drawer was different . . . it, too, was enormous; it was open, with streams of gold spilling out. And his mother—she also was different; still, as always, in black, but the black was not cloth, it was flesh; still, as always, with ribbon and cross, but they were not of silk and of wood, they were of gold and of jewels: and that was all she wore—the jewels, the shining splendors—on her blackness, her nakedness, her huge black belly bursting with child. . . .

They were in a city. They found work. They had piasters. And they ate.

When they had eaten, Vayu said, "We still have money, sidi. They say there is a good house in this city. Let us go there."

But Claude shook his head.

"Yes, come. You need a woman, sidi. Like before—remember?—when you were first in Harar. Come, let us go. It will be good for you."

"No," Claude said.

"Then I will go myself," said Vayu, leaving.

And with the piasters he had left Claude bought araq. And Vayu found him in the morning.

They were in Mukalla.
They were in Shuqra.
They were in Mocha.

In Mocha, too, they found work—sorting coffee. They worked for three days, and on the night of the third Claude bought araq, and the next morning was not able to get up. Vayu went to work alone, and Claude lay until noon; and then he rose and walked alone through the streets, and to the docks, and along the docks past the line of dhows.

And on the deck of a dhow was Neil Fitzsimmons.

The Irishman was lying on the deck, staring vacantly into space; but as Claude approached, his head turned a little, his eyes focused, then stared. And then, rising, he climbed up onto the wharf beside him. "By God, it's the Wanderin' Jew again," he said. "Beg yer pardon, lad—the Wanderin' Frog. . . . Don't tell me ye been hidin' out here in Mocha all this time?"

"No," said Claude.

"Been here and there, eh? Travelin' businessman. Big deals all over."

"That's right."

Fitzsimmons laughed, but not pleasantly. "That's the way, lad," he said. "Big deals fer us all." He seemed about to go on, but changed his mind and was silent. His eyes again wandered off into distance, and his long bony face was slack.

"And you?" said Claude. How is yours?"

"Mine?"

"Your deal. With the guns."

"Oh. Oh, yeah." Fitzsimmons' glance drifted back to him. "It's fine, lad—fine," he said. "Everythin' comin' along, gradual-like—" His voice trailed away.

"But you're still here in Mocha," said Claude.

Fitzsimmons didn't answer.

"And the guns—where are they? Still here too?"

"Yeah, still here. In the warehouse. . . ." The Irishman's voice was dull, almost inaudible. Then, suddenly, a change came over him. His voice grew harsh and savage. "Two thousand guns," he rasped, "sittin' nine months in that bloody warehouse. A hundred thousand francs just sittin' there on its arse—"

"You can't get them to Abyssinia?"

"To Ab-y-ssinia—hah! We can't even get 'em to Tajoura. Not even across the fookin' Red Sea . . . Nine months they been sittin' here. Nine months I been sittin' here. We got the guns, we got a dhow, we're all set. And on account of them bloody frogs over there. . . ." He broke off; he was silent; he was staring straight at Claude. Then there was a second change —in his eyes, his face, his whole body—and he had grasped Claude's arm with one hand, and his other hand was pointing, and in the next instant he was shouting: "Yer the answer! Yes, by Jesus, Mary, and Joseph, yer the bloody goddamn answer!" He was shaking Claude in his excitement. His eyes were shining, his mouth grinning, and the gold tooth glinted. Then abruptly he turned to the dhow and called, "Hey Swede—Swede! Come up here! Come up here fast!"

Still calling, he leaped down to the deck, and after a moment a second man appeared from below. He was an older man than Fitzsimmons—perhaps fifty, perhaps more—with a square red face, a bald head, and the cold blue eyes of the north; and Fitzsimmons seized him and pulled him up onto the wharf, saying, "We got it beat at last—we got the answer," and then brought him to Claude and said, "this is Swede Jensen, my partner . . . Swede, this is an old friend of mine, Morel. And he's a frog. . . ."

Jensen looked Claude over: slowly, coolly. 'Yes?" he said.

"Yes. Yes. And don't ye see what it means? A frog for Tajoura, and we're set—we're on our way—"

Jensen nodded slightly, but his face was impassive. "You would like to go to Abyssinia?" he asked, speaking in stiff precise English, with only a shade of accent. "You are interested in our venture?"

"Of course he's interested," Fitzsimmons broke in. "Look at him. He's dead beat—starvin'."

"And my partner has told you—?"

"He knows about the guns. And the money."

"But of how you can be of use to us? . . . No?" Fitzsimmons started to speak again, but Jensen continued blandly. "Then I shall tell you," he said. "We have these guns. We have a letter from Menelik, king of Shoa, who will pay much for them. Several months ago we were ready to go. But then there were difficulties. The only practical way to Shoa is by way of Tajoura, on the Somali coast, which is held by the French. And knowing that there are always certain problems about the transportation of arms, I first went over myself, alone, to make the necessary arrangements."

"—Which was when ye was here last," said Fitzsimmons to Claude.

"As it turned out," Jensen went on, "the problems were worse than expected. In fact, insurmountable. The French in Tajoura said, yes, we could pass the guns through, but only at a tax of a hundred per cent of their value—and *they* would set the value. 'That is robbery,' I told them. 'No,' they said, 'that is the tax. The tax for all foreigners.' 'And for Frenchmen?' I asked. 'For Frenchmen,' they said, 'there is no tax. But you are not Frenchmen.'"

"So we try everything," said Fitzsimmons.

"Yes, we tried many things. First I looked for a Frenchman to come in with us. Not in Tajoura—there are none there except a few officials—but in Djibouti, even in Aden. No one is interested, however. They say the risks are too great. From the desert; from the Danakil tribes; from Menelik himself—that even when he gets the guns, he will as likely as not refuse to pay. The French businessman, if I may say so, is not a gambler. He is cautious, conservative, bourgeois. Anyhow, we found no one . . ."

"And we figger what else can we do."

"But there is not much. It is of course impossible to do business with the British; they consider all arms contraband—except their own. The Italians? I try them next. I go to Assab and Massawa, and they say no, no chance: they have their own guns to sell. So what then? There are, to be sure, hundreds of miles on the Somali coast with no French, no British, no Italians; and we could land the guns on a beach, in a cove. But there would also be no camels, no drivers, nothing at all for a caravan. . . . No good. . . . So we are back again to Tajoura—and a Frenchman. I go up to Suez and look around, and at last I find one; a trader in spices, and he says he is interested. He says he will join us here in Mocha in a month. But he doesn't come. It it now more than two months—"

"—And *you* come," said Fitzsimmons.

Claude said nothing. He looked at neither of them. His eyes were on the line of dhows and the harbor beyond.

"—And he's a better bet than any of 'em," said the Irishman to Jensen. "Been in Africa fer years, this one. Knows the desert, the tribes, the A-rab lingoes. Bet he even knows the stuff they talk up there in Ab-y-ssinia."

Jensen's cold blue gaze was again fixed on Claude: measuring—appraising. "Of course, you are not a merchant," he said bluntly. "Not a man of means. With you we would have to make a rather different deal than with the others we had had in mind. The guns would, of necessity, have to pass through Tajoura in your name. But it would be distinctly understood, and in writing between us. . . . You can read and write?" he said.

"Yeah, he can read and write," said Fitzsimmons.

" . . . distinctly understood that you would be in no real sense a partner. On the other hand, we would of course make the venture worthwhile for you. That we can discuss. And if you can be useful, not only for Tajoura, but in other ways, as Fitzsimmons suggests. . . ."

He talked on.

Fitzsimmons spoke.

Then Jensen spoke again.

But Claude heard only their voices, not the words. His eyes had moved out from the harbor to the sea beyond; and now they moved across the sea, to the shores beyond, the shores invisible but shining. They moved from the shores of Africa into the wastes of Africa, across the deserts, across the miles of sunlit stillness, toward the purple ramparts rising in the west. . .

And, later, in their hut, he said to Vayu: "Once, back in Harar, you studied Amharic. How much of it do you remember?"

"Amharic?" Vayu stared at him. "Why, sidi?" he asked. "Why? What do you mean?"

"I am not sure. What do you think I mean?"

"I think—I think—" Vayu stopped. His stare grew wider. His eyes were shining. "Oh, sidi, sidi," he cried, "you are smiling! I am so happy. In all the while we have been back together it is the first time that I have seen you smile!"

35

"Ayeee, ayaaa—"

The camels swayed. Dust rose in sunlight.

Three months had passed since he had met Fitzsimmons for the second time in Mocha; seven years since he had last moved inward from the sea across the wastes of Africa.

Of the three months, the first week had been spent in Mocha, loading the guns, readying the dhow, and preparing a contract. Or, rather, two contracts; one (for public use) transferring all assets to Claude Morel, Citizen of France; the other (private) canceling the first. And the drawing of them had taken longer than guns and dhow together, for Jensen had proved as meticulous as a Palais de Justice lawyer and had written the agreements over and over, until every word was to his—if not Claude's —exact satisfaction.

Then they had been four days in the dhow: on the Red Sea, the Bab-el-Mendeb Straits, the Gulf of Aden, the Bay of Tajoura. And Jensen's contracts (at least the public one) had been worth the labor, for at Tajoura's dockside the *chef de porte* had read and reread it, frowning, pulling his beard; had looked with jaundiced eye at the familiar face of the Swede; but in the end had had to shrug, resignedly, and let them through tax free.

On the night of the day on which the guns were unloaded, Jensen carefully destroyed the document.

They were still, however, to spend eleven long weeks in Tajoura; for the transport of the guns required an enormous caravan, and its assembling was no easy matter. Until a few years before, Tajoura had been simply a primitive Danakil village of mud and thatch. Even now, with the French in possession, it was not a great deal more; in comparison Zeila had been a metropolis. And there was a dearth of camels, drivers, food, everything. They succeeded in selling the dhow to an Arab merchant for ready cash; and from him too, finally, for the return of most of it, they got their needed provisions. The camels they acquired, lot by lot, partly from local tribal chieftains, partly from small incoming caravans. And most of the men they acquired, too, from these caravans: Arabs and Somalis and Issas, of the sort Claude knew well from his earlier journeys. Of the Danakils themselves they hired few. For though, at first sight, impressive—tall, lean, bushy-haired, carrying great curved swords and leather shields—they were, for the most part, diseased and lethargic, with scarcely the vigor to drag themselves through Tajoura's streets, let alone across the long desert miles to Abyssinia.

"If them's the horrendous savages I've heard tell about," Fitzsimmons said, "I sure ain't goin' to waste much time at worryin'."

"These are coast Danakils, tame Danakils," Claude told him, who have"—he smiled—"had the benefits of civilization. Inland, I think we may find them different."

They foraged, bargained, haggled. They sold a hundred guns (at coastal rates) to raise more money. Each camel, they had found, could carry roughly twenty-four guns, which meant that, with extra ones for carrying men and supplies, a total of a hundred were needed. Thirty men, they had agreed, was the minimum for effective transport and protection. And the weeks dragged by, as they slowly approached these figures. Fitzsimmons fumed with impatience. "Fer Christ's sweet sake," he said, "let's get goin'. At this rate half the bloody traders on the Red Sea Coast'll be in Ab-y-ssinia before us." But Jensen was thorough, patient, imperturbable. "I have been twenty years, my friend," he said, "on this Red Sea coast. Now at last I have the chance I have been waiting for, and I am not throwing it away with any foolishness."

So Fitzsimmons fumed. The days came and went. The sun beat down on the squalid streets of Tajoura.

. . . And at last they were ready.

At last, now, the camels swayed, the dust rose, the long file moved out of the town toward the west, toward Abyssinia. It was a file five times as long as that with which Claude had once set out from Zeila; longer, even, than the caravan of Abou Dakir, leaving Harar for the Web Shebeli. The camels were heavy-laden. They moved slowly. But they moved. They were on the way.

"Ayeee, ayaaa—"

Like Zeila, Tajoura lay on a strip of land between the sea and a range of hills, and behind it was a sweep of glaring sand and salt flats. But the hills here were closer—and higher—and by midday they were winding up steep defiles between crumbling brown rocks. Jensen rode at the head of the caravan with the chief of the drivers, an Arab called Rashi. Fitzsimmons was roughly at its mid-point, and Claude, with Vayu, at the rear, to keep a watch for stragglers. As always on a caravan—and now even with Vayu—Claude rode a little apart, and in silence. Indeed, he had talked little during the weeks in Tajoura; he had drunk nothing; he had done the work assigned him, made a few suggestions—and waited. When Vayu, like Fitzsimmons, had grown restless and impatient, he had smiled and said, "Be calm, be easy; it is better. What happens, happens." . . . And now, too, he thought, "What will happen, will happen," as he looked ahead at the great file slowly plodding into Africa.

Forward: the march, the burden and the desert.
"I returned," said the Preacher, *"and saw under the sun that the race is not to the swift. . . ."*

The sun blazed. Then it sank and set. That night they camped on a plateau high in the hills, and the next morning descended the western side —even farther than they had climbed—for the valley beyond was below the level of the sea. Here was a salt lake, called Assal: still, lifeless, a dark stagnant green. But the salt flats around it glared so blindingly in the sun that the men had to ride veiled as they moved across them. Beyond were more hills, but lower than the others, and at first these too were white, with gleaming limestone. Then brown returned, the endless dun brown of sand and dust and crumbled lava rock, and they came down from the hills into flat miles of wasteland. When dark came, they camped in the waste, pitching their tents close together, with sentries posted. They were still too close to the coast to be in wild Danakil country; and even when they reached it, it was unlikely that so large a caravan would be attacked. But Jensen was taking no chances. He ran the caravan with methodical efficiency—less like a footless adventurer than a commander of troops.

He had estimated two months for their journey. Or, rather, two months to the River Ahwash, at the western end of the desert. Beyond the river rose the great escarpment of Abyssinia, on the summit of which was Ankober, King Menelik's fortress-capital; and how long it would take to climb the escarpment it was impossible to tell. But Jensen was resolved that they would at least reach the Ahwash on schedule. And though he still showed no impatience, no nervous urgency, as did Fitzsimmons, he was nevertheless insistent on a rigid quota of miles for each day.

The ancient trail led west-southwest. And it was empty. No caravan approached them from the interior, nor were there any signs of one moving ahead of them—nor of Danakil villages or encampments. But, as they posted armed guards at night, so too did they ride armed during the day: not only the three white men and Vayu, but the drivers as well, along the length of the caravan—Arab and Somali and Issa: all of them, indeed, except the six Tajoura Danakils who were with them, for these Jensen, from the outset, had refused to trust with firearms. And he was proved right; for on the fourth night out the Danakils rebelled. While the cook fires burned they came to Jensen, sullen and scowling, and, with Claude interpreting, listed their grievances. The marches were too long, they said; the work too hard, the pay too small. That was too bad, said Jensen; but nothing could be done about it. Then they would quit, said the Danakils. Very well, they could quit. They could have one camel and four days' rations and go back to Tajoura. And to Fitzsimmons and Claude Jensen added, "It is better to have six less men and one less camel than such as these, to be forever watching." . . . The Danakils protested further. They needed two camels, they said. They needed a gun. They demanded their four days' pay. But Jensen said no. He said it a second time. Then he rose slowly, holding his gun . . . and the Danakils left.

He had not been bluffing, and they knew it. And Claude knew it. He still had almost no personal knowledge of Olaf—called "Swede"—Jensen: of his life, his past, of what lay behind the square bland face and cold blue eyes. But that much he knew: that he would have shot, and shot to kill. A year before, in the bar in Mocha, Fitzsimmons had called him "a connivin' cheatin' bastard." And since then, on and off, he had dropped other vague hints: that he had been in prison, several prisons—and not for vagrancy or petty theft; that he had killed men, more than a few men—and for less reason than if he had killed the Danakils. Jensen himself gave no hint. He spoke of the past no more than did Claude. There seemed, for him, to be no past, but only the present—and his present purpose: to get his guns to Menelik, king of Shoa. Whatever had gone before was hidden and lost, transfused into what was obviously the great gamble, the great enterprise, of his life. And to that enterprise he brought a quiet but fierce determination, and an iron will.

On the fifth day, with the Danakils gone, some of the camels strayed. It took two hours to find and bring them back into line, and when night fell they were a few miles behind schedule.

On the sixth day, Jensen started them off earlier, set a faster pace, and they made up the deficit.

On the sixth night, while the others slept, he went ahead alone, in the moonlight, to reconnoiter their next day's route through a maze of low hillocks.

And on the seventh morning, as he prepared to mount his camel, an adder, rearing from its burrow, struck at his leg; and in an hour he was dead.

Once, in another place, in another year, there had been a slave girl to be buried. Now there was Jensen. The ground was hard and stony, and it was almost noon before it was done. From their general supplies Claude took two staves of wood, nailed them into a cross, and set the cross on the grave. And on the cross, with his knife, he carved the name OLAF JENSEN.

They did not move on at once. Claude glanced at Fitzsimmons, but the Irishman was staring at the ground. Then he moved away a little, sat down on a rock, and stared out across the waste, occasionally turning to look at Claude, at Vayu, at the waiting men, the waiting camels. He was their leader now: the sole proprietor of the caravan—and the guns. And, in the realization his face was slack and empty; then, for a moment, tense, with eyes narrowed, as he looked quickly, guardedly, at Claude; and then slack again, as he sat motionless, silent . . . and then suddenly, once more, changed, suddenly hard and tough and angry, as he leaped to his feet and shouted: "All right, come on—come on, all of ye! We're wastin' time. Christ Jesus, let's get goin'!"

And they mounted and rode on, and what had happened had happened. The dust rose. The sun flamed. The cross receded behind them.

"*I returned*," said the Preacher, "*and saw under the sun that the race is not to the swift . . . nor the battle to the strong. . . .*"

Their order of march was now changed. Fitzsimmons rode in the van with the chief driver, Rashi. Claude remained in the rear. But Vayu moved up to take Fitzsimmons' place in the middle. He was younger than all but two or three of the drivers, yet he had no trouble with them. His section of the file kept up the pace, with no dissension and no mishaps.

The days passed: monotonous, identical. At night they pitched their tents between the sand and stars. Fitzsimmons was quieter than he had used to be. Only occasionally, in the evenings, did he burst out in jerky spurts of talk, and he spent much time hunched close to the cook fires with pencil and paper, setting down columns of figures and making slow calculations. "What you need is not paper but a nice ledger, Monsieur Rappe," Claude told him one evening. But Fitzsimmons merely grunted and went on with his figuring. And Claude thought, "No, it is not like Rappe, really." For Rappe's figures added up to Emil Gorbeau's profit, and Fitzsimmons' to his own.

The ramshackle feckless Irishman would return from Abyssinia a rich man—rich beyond dreams for one such as himself. It was amazing. More than amazing: fantastic. "All right," thought Claude, "let him enjoy his arithmetic."

Leaving the fires, he sat before his own tent in the starlight. . . . And he himself, Claude Morel: how would he return? . . . Quite differently, to be sure; not rich beyond the dreams of anyone. In his pocket was the contract he had signed in Mocha—the "private" contract—and by its terms he was to receive 2.5 per cent of the net profits. Allowing for expenses, that would probably come out to some two thousand francs—exactly what Jensen and Fitzsimmons had each had to his name before the expedition began. . . . "So—" He shrugged inwardly. "All right, again." There had been a time when he cared about money—when he had thought and planned and dreamed about money. The time of *Dear Mother, please find enclosed....* The time of an engineer son and the *Ecole Centrale....* But those times were gone. He had not come for money ... For what, then? Why *had* he come? Why was he again in the desert, on the trail, on the long hard bitter trail through the wastes, through the dust, under the burning sun, to still another far horizon of savage Africa, to still another remote and savage Nigger King?

He sat alone a while, and then Vayu came and sat beside him. "The others are asleep, sidi," he said. "It is as if we were alone, as we used to be on our trips from Harar, and I wish that now, too, I had my *krar.*"

"Even without a *krar* you can sing," said Claude.

So Vayu sang. And Claude listened. And the voice was no longer a boy's but a man's—yet still soft and sweet and true; and Vayu sang a while and then rose and went to his tent, and Claude looked after him and smiled a little; for at least he now knew one of the reasons he had come on this journey. It was the light that had shone in Vayu's eyes on a night in Mocha when he had said to him—oh so casually, "Once, back in Harar, you studied Amharic. How much of it do you remember?"

The days passed. They became weeks. They had been traveling two weeks ... then three ... then four. If their maps and measurements were correct, they were now about halfway to the River Ahwash.

And through each day, from dawn to dusk, Claude rode alone at the end of the caravan. His camel swayed beneath his rump; his gun rested across his knees; ahead, the dust of the long column rose like a plume in the windless air. Through all the miles since the white salt flats of Lake Assal the country had not changed. It still unrolled before them in a brown monotony of waste and distance, of low hills and hollows and the ancient trail. Words passed through his mind. Words remembered ... *The path is rough. The hills are covered with scrub. The air is motionless. How far the birds and the springs are!* ... And then? What then? ... *This can only be the end of the world—going forward ...*

Perhaps it had been over this same path, more than two thousand years before, that the first Menelik had come—the son of Solomon and Sheba —to claim his kingdom in the heart of Africa.

The stillness was immense—but not absolute. At long intervals he would see a movement, a stirring, in the distance: a spout of dust, a cloud of locusts, a darting antelope. When dark came there were the eyes of jackals and hyenas. And one day, toward evening and the march's end, he reined in suddenly and stopped and looked behind him, for he had become conscious of a movement, a presence, that he had not seen or felt before. They had just crossed a low ridge in the waste, and at the time it had seemed level and bare; but now, as he peered back in the fading light, its crest seemed humped and notched, as if by a row of jagged rocks ... or of crouched and watching men. He did not call to the nearest driver, but waited alone. And nothing moved. He waited, eyes straining, gun ready, and still nothing moved—or seemed to move; but still, again, there was a change, for presently, against the darkening sky, the humps and notches were gone, and the ridge once more was level and bare.

When he caught up with the others they had stopped and were making camp. But he said nothing. That night he stayed awake until dawn with the sentries. But all that moved in the darkness were the jackals and hyenas.

No Danakils came.

What came, a few days later, was wind.

As the land had remained the same throughout their journey, so too had the sky. But now at last it changed, it stirred and darkened, and out of the north, fierce and howling, a storm descended. It was not a storm like those of the south, beyond the Web Shebeli. It brought no thunder, no rain. It was wind only—wind and sand; but the sand swept in a vast tide across the wastelands, denser than rain, more impenetrable than cloud, enveloping the caravan, hiding one man from the next, each camel from the camel directly ahead; and presently they could make headway no longer and had to stop. For three days they stopped. For three days the sand blew, while the camels crouched motionless, rumps to the wind, and the men crouched beside them, wrapped in burnouses and veils. No tent could be pitched, and they slept in burrows in the sand. No fires could be lighted, and they took only such food as could be eaten uncooked; and even this was scarcely edible in its thick coating of sand and dust. Worst of all was the problem of the guns. For the wind ripped their coverings open, the sand poured in, and for the full three days—and nights—while Fitzsimmons fumed and shouted, they floundered back and forth in the drifts, struggling with ropes and wires and wildly flapping canvas.

On the fourth morning, at last, the storm slackened. By noon it was gone; the world again was still. It took them the rest of the day, however, to dig themselves out; to clear at least some of the sand from their clothing and bodies, from the camels, from their food and equipment, and from the guns. The guns that they carried themselves they cleaned and oiled carefully. But the rest they simply rewrapped and reloaded, for they could not clean and oil nineteen hundred.

The next day they moved on. Through space. Through stillness. And now the sky was as before—bare, empty, glazed, burning with sunlight —but the earth itself, for the first time, began to change. It was not a change of structure or contour; they were still in wasteland, still alternately among low hills and hollows and then on great flatlands stretching endlessly to the horizon. It was the earth's color that changed, that grew darker—as air and sky had darkened during the storm; and each day now its darkness deepened; from tan to brown, from brown to brownish black;

until at last it was wholly black—and they moved through a world of black sand, black rock, black twisted hills of basalt and obsidian. The waste, before, had been a thing of degrees. Now it was absolute. Not only was there no movement, no animal life, but no life at all, no growth; not a blade of grass, not a shrub, not a thornbush. It was a mineral world— rigid, lunar—an arctic world of the tropics, frozen not white but black, not in ice but in flaming sunlight; frozen at night, transfixed and spectral, under the barren stars.

Here at last, Claude thought, *was* the end of the world. The Omega World. The place of endings. It was as if the winds of a few days past had ripped away the earth's covering, the last tattered remnants of its living sheath—and what was left was black bones. What was left was death.

Through the long day, under the sun, alone, he thought of death. And of the dead. He thought of Jensen, now far behind them, his journey over, lying quiet forever in his shroud of earth. He thought of the slave girl—nameless, traceless—in her desert grave. He thought of others, and these had names—their names were Lutz, Egal, Nagunda—and then of another, nameless, too, who had never been ... They were all dead. And one more as well. Chariol was dead. ... And he thought of Chariol. Chariol in the lycée classroom, in his book-lined lodgings, in the home of his sister in St. Quentin. Chariol in his bachelor rooms near the Sorbonne; in other rooms—larger, brighter—on the Rue Martine. Chariol opening the door, and first staring, then smiling, embracing him, drawing him into the room, calling "Darling, darling!" ... and then another door opening, *the other* appearing, her face at first smiling too—and then no longer smiling—the face white and bloodless, with eyes of dark violet ... and Chariol speaking again, his hand on Claude's shoulder, saying "Darling, may I present an old friend of mine? Old friend, may I present my wife?"

He tore his mind away. That was past—gone. Chariol was gone and dead. As dead as the others. They had each made their journey—some long, some short—and they had come to its end, to their world's end, Omega ... as he at last, now, had come too: to the place of endings, the place of death.

He looked up. And he saw death. Death black and frozen across the miles of the waste ... But it was not all he saw. He saw the caravan too. The caravan still plodding, still moving—through the place of death, the place of endings—still going forward, still a thing that lived. Through the end of the world—going *forward*. ... And above it the sun, too, went forward; it lived and shone; it moved past them, beyond them, to the west, and then it sank in the west. It sank beyond the earth, the black wastes, the place of endings; and behind it the sky still lived, still shone in the silent evening, first in a fiery blaze of red and orange, then in a vast gleaming of deep violet-blue.

Soon the caravan stopped and made its camp. A camel broke away and had to be caught. Two drivers were wrangling. Fitzsimmons was swearing. The smell of roasting mutton filled the air, and the cook fires burned in the night.

In the night, later, he awoke and could not sleep again. For a while he lay in darkness, then lighted his lamp. And then, with an old forgotten movement he felt in his pockets for pencil and paper. There were none there, of course. There had been none there for years.

He lay back again. He reached to turn off the lamp. But he did not turn it off. Instead, he held it and rose and left the tent; he moved among the dim piles of their baggage until he found the crate that held their small stock of clerical supplies; and from it he took what he needed and returned to his tent.

He sat by the lamp with the paper on his knees, and the pencil felt strange and awkward in his hand. *"Dear Mother—"* he thought. But he did not write it. Instead, he sat for a long time, motionless, looking down at the blank page before him.

Then at last the pencil moved. But he wrote no salutation. He wrote: *I have only recently heard of your loss. Once—more than once—long ago, you reached out your hand to me, and I could not take it. May I now reach out mine to you, over the miles and the years, with my sympathy . . .* He paused. The pencil hung motionless. Then he added . . . *and my love. C.M.*

He had brought an envelope too. And on this he wrote:
Mme. Germaine Chariol
18 rue Martine
Paris, France
(Please forward if necessary)

Then he put out the lamp and slept. And when he awoke in the morning the sealed envelope was beside him, and he held it in his hand as if he had not seen it before . . . "So I shall take it down the block to the post office," he thought. "And they will send it off to the moon. To the moon of the planet of Fomalhaut. . . ."

He crumpled the letter and dropped it and left the tent. And soon after they were again on their way.

The fifth week passed. And the sixth. They were out of the black lands; the earth was brown again. But it was still wasteland, still bare and parched and empty, and there was as yet no hint of the great mountains to the west.

Apart from Jensen's death, the caravan had had good fortune. No other men had died, or been seriously sick. They had lost only six camels out of a hundred. And thanks to Jensen's planning they had enough food, enough water, and even emergency camel fodder for the periods when they passed through regions that were wholly barren. Now, however, the sheer length of the journey was beginning to tell. Several of the camels went lame. A few of the drivers were ailing. Their food was so saturated with sand that, however they treated it, it still gritted between their teeth, and the liquid in their goatskin bags tasted less like water than stale urine. Many of the men, indeed, preferred the actual urine of the camels, and drinking it, became sick; so that for several days there were only half the usual number of effective drivers, while the rest rode limp and strengthless, strapped to their camels' backs like the bales of guns.

They came to a range of volcanic hills, and on their far side to a great basin that had once, obviously, been a lake. Even now, there remained scattered pools and puddles—the first water they had seen since the salt lake of Assal; but it was yellow with sulphur and burned their mouths like fire. Beyond the basin were more hills, a wilderness of hills, brown and crumpled, and their progress was slower, plodding this way and that way, now up and now down.

It was at this stage that they became aware that they were not alone in the waste; that they were being watched and followed. It was not merely the sort of intimation—or perhaps even illusion—that Claude had had earlier, before the storm and the black lands, but a certain knowledge, the evidence of their eyes: once a column of smoke in the distance; once a silhouette of man and camel appearing suddenly on a ridge on their flank, and as suddenly vanishing; once, closest of all, a file of moving figures on a hillside—near enough for them to see the swords and shields and bushy heads of the Danakils. But a volley of shots into the air had set them running, and they did not see them again.

"We're safe from the buggers all right," said Fitzsimmons. "They know what guns are, I'm bettin'—and if they don't we'll soon show 'em."

There was no need to show them. No Danakils reappeared. What appeared, three days later, was a caravan heading toward them, heading eastward, and they stared at it as if at an apparition from the world of spirits.

It was a small caravan—not a quarter the size of their own—and at its head was a wizened whiskered Swiss called Koerner ... Where was he coming from—Ankober?—Fitzsimmons asked, eyeing him with uneasy suspicion. And what had he brought in with him? Guns? ... No, not guns, the Swiss said. He had brought the usual trade goods: cloth, knives, utensils, hardware. And he had been, not to Ankober, but farther north—to the lands of King John of Tigré ... Fitzsimmons showed obvious relief, but he was still not wholly satisfied. "If it's to Tigré ye've been," he said, "why're ye comin' back this way? Why not the shorter way up north, to Massawa?" ... He had come in from Massawa, Koerner said. But going out that way, now, there might be trouble.

"Trouble? Why trouble?"

"Because," said Koerner, "they say an expedition is on the way from Massawa. A military expedition—Italian troops."

"Goin' to Tigré."

"No, not to Tigré. To Shoa. To Menelik. The Italians and Menelik have been having trouble, and they are going after him. I heard it everywhere in Tigré. They are coming from the north, of course; Menelik, they say, will not run, but go out to fight them; and I have enough trouble, thank you, without finding myself in the middle of a battle."

There was some more talk. Fitzsimmons checked his maps against the Swiss's reports. The two waiting files were strung out for more than a mile through a shallow ravine, and Claude rode back to the end of their own to make sure the guards were staying alert. In a short while both columns began to move: first past each other . . . then away . . . finally out of sight: one east, one west.

That evening, when they camped, Vayu came quickly to Claude, and he was smiling.

"I sent your letter, sidi," he said.

"My letter?"

"Yes—that you wrote many days ago. One morning I was taking down your tent and I found it; and it was all crumpled, but not torn, and so I smoothed it and put it in my pack. I would give it to you that night, I thought. But I was stupid. I forgot. I did not think of it again until today, when, just as he is leaving, the Swiss sidi asks Sidi Fitz does he have any messages to send. And he says no—but then at last I remember. I say yes, *I* have a letter, and I reach in my pack, and he takes it."

Vayu smiled again. Then, watching Claude, his expression changed. "It is not all right, sidi?" he asked anxiously. "It was for sending, no?"

Claude didn't answer.

"I thought it was for sending and you had lost it. I hope I have not done wrong . . . I had still two piasters, and I gave them to the Swiss sidi, and I think he is honest and will mail it."

Claude was silent for another moment. Then it was he who smiled. "From the post office down the block," he said. "To the moon of the planet of Fomalhaut."

"What, sidi?" Vayu was confused. "I do not understand."

"Never mind. It is all right," Claude told him.

"You are not angry, sidi?"

"No, I am not angry."

That night, Fitzsimmons was moody and abstracted, prowling restlessly about among the tents and baggage. And, later, he sat hunched and brooding in front of his own tent, staring silently out at the wasteland.

Suddenly he jumped to his feet and came over to Claude. "It's no good!" he said vehemently. "It's no bloody fookin' good!"

"What isn't?" Claude asked.

"This fookin' bloody business with Menelik and the Eyetalians."

"Wars seldom are," said Claude.

"The hell with that. They can fight all they want, fer all I care. They can chop 'emselves up into bloody mincemeat. . . But not before we get there, that's the thing. *By God, not before we get there!*"

The Irishman leaned forward. His voice was tense and rasping. "Don't ye see what happens if they do?" he said. "The Eyeties come. Menelik goes out and fights 'em. And whoever wins we're sunk. The Eyeties win, and they kill him—or chase him halfway across Africa. Or *he* wins, and what's the first thing he does? He grabs their guns. New guns—not old ones, like ours. And when we show up later he laughs at us."

Claude shrugged. "Perhaps," he said. "But those are chances we have to take. There's nothing we can do."

"The hell there ain't!"

"*What* can we do?"

"We can go faster, that's what. Get to Ankober before he leaves."

Claude shook his head. "The caravan can't go any faster."

"The whole caravan, no. With all the guns, no. But I'll tell ye what we can do, and we're goin' to do it." Fitzsimmons pointed a bony finger. "You'll take over the caravan—the main part," he said, "and keep goin' just like always. Me, I'll go ahead. Startin' tomorrow. I'll take a few men, a few camels—that's all. We'll travel light. We'll get to Ankober in half, mebbe a third of the time it'll take the rest of ye; and I'll see Menelik; I'll tell him the guns are comin'—nineteen hundred of 'em—and he'll wait. The Eyeties can't fight on no mountaintop, no matter what they got. They'll have to cool their arses till he comes down, and he won't come till he's got our guns—he'll wait fer 'em, by God—and by then he'll be so hungry fer 'em he'll pay me in bloody diamonds instead of gold."

His eyes glinted in the darkness. He began pacing again. "Yes—yes, by Jesus—that's it!" he said. "Tomorrow I'm leavin' ye, hell bent fer Ankober."

Claude watched him for a moment. Then he said, "Are you sure you think it is worth the danger?"

"Danger?" Fitzsimmons wheeled back to him. "What danger?"

"Before you get there. From the Danakils."

"The Danakils—hah!" The Irishman spat. "All this mallarkey about the fee-rocious Danakils . . . We been in their country fer weeks, and what's happened? Nothin'. They take a look at us now and then, we go boo at 'em, and they run like rabbits."

"That's because we're a big caravan, and they're afraid of us. With a small one it might be different."

"That Swiss had a small one. He was doin' all right."

"But—"

"But nothin'. Tomorrow I'm goin'. And if there's a risk or two I'll take 'em." Fitzsimmons scowled out into the darkness. "Jesus Christ, man, d'ye think I'm just goin' to sit back and lose out on the biggest thing in me life, on account of I'm scared of some naked niggers—?"

He stalked off to his tent. A while later, Claude followed and tried to speak to him, but he wouldn't listen. "I'm runnin' this show, Froggy," he said, "and that's the way it's goin' to be."

And in the morning he started off. With him he took five men, seven camels, and only the guns that they themselves were carrying. As they left, his mood changed, and he grinned, shouting, "See ye in Ankober!" And then they moved ahead swiftly, lightly laden, and soon were lost to sight in the brown distance ahead.

The rest of the caravan plodded on. Through the miles. Through the days. And now the order of march was again changed, with Claude moving up to the front, Vayu remaining at the center, and Rashi dropping back to watch over the rear. It was still a long procession. With only five camels dead, one given to the Tajoura Danakils, and now seven gone with Fitzsimmons, there were still eighty-seven left of the original hundred, and they moved on with their loads of guns as they had moved from the beginning—as they might well move on through eternity. Of the drivers, eleven were gone—the six Danakils, the five with Fitz—leaving nineteen; or twenty-one, with Claude and Vayu. The ratio of men to beasts was low. But they managed. There were no mishaps, no incidents. Each day was the same as the last—and the next.

Out ahead, Claude set the same pace they had now used for hundreds of miles. Most of the time he rode, like the others, but now and then his legs grew cramped, his right knee began to ache, and then, dismounting, he would walk for a while, and though more often than not it was with a slight limp, legs and knee soon felt better. The trail was easy to follow; easier now than before, because of the tracks and droppings of the Swiss's caravan and Fitzsimmons'. He saw no sign of Danakils. Nor, yet, of the great escarpment that should soon be rising out of the west.

He was riding ... riding ... Through the wastes, toward Abyssinia. Through the Somali Desert. Among the hills of Harar. Across the plains of the Ogaden. Through the land of whirlwinds and darkness. . . .

He was walking ... walking ... Across the wastes toward the Web Shebeli. In the streets of Harar, the streets of Aden. Along the coasts of Arabia, through the miles of Arabia. Through the miles of Egypt, of Tripoli, of Cyprus, of Greece; then of Italy, Switzerland, Germany, France. He was walking through a forest, through a town, through a city, the enormous city, and in his pocket was a poem . . . no, not a poem: it was a letter . . . and above his head were trees, beyond the trees was the sky, and the sky was blue, violet-blue; it swept in a great arch over the earth, bright and gleaming above, darker and deeper as it curved toward the earth ahead, and the earth seemed to rise to meet it . . . it *did* rise; and it, too, was blue-and-violet, high and gleaming . . . and he walked on, staring, out of the wasteland, toward the mountains of Abyssinia.

The caravan was unseen behind him. He was alone. And then, after a time, not alone; for Vayu rode up with a message and dismounted, and for a while they walked together. In silence, walking, they looked at the mountains, and then Vayu said, softly, "It is strange, sidi."

"What is strange?" Claude asked him.

"To see the mountains now. After so long in the deserts, one almost forgets that there are mountains. That there are forests and lakes and rivers and fields and cities. One thinks there is nothing else in all the world, but only deserts."

Claude nodded. "Yes, one forgets," he said. "That the world is many things; has many faces." And then, a little later: "That God Himself, who made the world, has many faces."

Vayu was silent. Claude looked at the mountains. Then he said:

"You and I, we have talked of many things—but never of God. What face of God do *you* see?"

"I—I do not understand, sidi."

"Are you now really a Christian?"

Vayu hesitated. "No, I do not think so," he said.

"We are coming to a Christian country." Claude smiled. "It will be healthier for you if you are. Underneath, if you want, of course, you can still be a Moslem."

"No, I am not a Moslem either."

"What then?"

"I think—" Vayu paused. "I think I am like you, Sidi Claude."

"Like *me?*"

"Yes. One who is of no church. But who believes in God, who seeks him."

"And you think that I—"

"Yes, I think it, sidi. Father Lutz has told me. And I have seen it myself. I do not think there could be anyone in the world who has searched so long, so far, after God. . . ."

They walked on.

The sun was setting. Then it was down.

"We will camp soon," Claude thought. But his eyes had returned to the mountains, now black and looming, with the sun behind them; and he watched them, walking in silence, until Vayu spoke again.

Then, "Sidi—" Vayu said. "Sidi!" And his voice was different. With one hand he had grasped Claude's arm and with the other was pointing to the trail ahead. "Oh, sidi!" he said once more. And, looking, Claude saw what he saw, and they moved forward and stopped and looked down.

They looked at the six bodies: five brown and one white. There was nothing else to be seen—no camels, no tents, no guns, no clothing—but only the bodies, naked and bloody. Their noses and ears were gone. Their genitals were gone. But the Danakils apparently did not know the value of gold, for in Fitzsimmons' open mouth was still the familiar yellow glint. And in his eyes, open too, was the same blank stare with which he had used to lounge on the docks at Aden, looking out toward the sea.

"And now, sidi?"

It was the next day. The graves had been dug and filled and closed.

"And now, sidi?" Vayu repeated. "What do we do now?"

Claude had been sitting on a rock—as Neil Fitzsimmons had once sat beside the grave of Olaf Jensen. But, as Vayu spoke, he rose and moved toward his waiting camel.

"Now we go on," he said.

"To Ankober?"

"Yes, to Ankober."

"We will still take the guns there?"

Claude did not answer. Turning, he gestured to the chief driver, Rashi, and Rashi called out an order, and the men mounted their camels. Between them, shuffling slowly into marching order, were the other camels with their bulging loads.

"The guns, sidi—" said Vayu. "I have been wondering—whom do they belong to?"

"Soon they will belong to Menelik," Claude said.

"Yes, soon. But I mean now. Whose are they *now*, sidi?"

"Now they are ours," Claude said. "Yours and mine."

The mountains grew nearer and clearer. They were a rampart filling the horizon ahead. And each day, too, the land around them changed, as it sloped away gently into the valley of the River Ahwash. On one day they came to patches of grass, on the next to scattered trees; and toward evening of the next, just as the sun was setting behind the purple mountains, they reached the Ahwash.

The stream did not descend from the mountains—at least not here—but flowed from south to north along their eastern base. Nor was its flow a free full current, but a mere trickling of small rivulets through sand and stones. Yet the trickling was of water—sweet water; it did not taste of salt or sulphur or urine or rotting goatskin; and men and camels alike bent to it, bent motionless, and drank and drank.

Through the next day they still drank. They rested. They looked across the river to the mountains beyond. The mountains did not have foothills, building slowly up to the heights; indeed, they were not properly mountains at all, but a vast escarpment, a wall, a battlement—the buttress of the eastern end of the Abyssinian plateau. The base, it appeared to Claude, was some eight to ten miles beyond the Ahwash, and leading up from the base he could see the outlines of steep gorges and ravines. Still higher, the outlines blurred in distance and in trailing scarves of cloud and mist; but at the very top the knobs and domes and promontories of the plateau's rim could, at most times, be seen dark and looming against the sky. Among them, atop them, Claude knew, was Ankober, the fortress of Menelik, his mountain eyrie above the wastelands. But of this he could see no signs in the skyline stillness of rock and space.

Also he knew that the trail continued on, up the escarpment—the trail of centuries—to Abyssinia; but that it would be difficult if not wholly impossible, for the camels. And therefore now, as Jensen had originally planned, they set about the procedure of looking for mules. They had reached the Ahwash at an uninhabited point. And none of its valley, to be sure, could have been described as a center of civilization. But along the river were many villages and encampments; their inhabitants, though largely Danakil, were of a quieter breed than those of the desert, and living close to the highlands, they had mules as well as camels. For more than a week the caravan moved up- and downstream. As in Tajoura, weeks before, there was bartering and haggling. And at last all eighty-seven camels were gone, with eighty-seven mules in their place (for the mule, though smaller, was stronger, and could carry an equal weight) and by the end of the tenth day on the Ahwash Claude was ready to go on.

Not so all the men, however. Of the nineteen remaining drivers, nine refused to go farther. They were camel-men, they said—not mule-men. They had come far enough, they knew nothing of mountains; they were Moslems and would not enter a country of infidels; and they would stay by the Ahwash until Claude returned, or join another caravan bound out for the coast. In the desert, their defection would have been a disaster. Here it was, luckily, no more than an inconvenience. For the end of the journey was near; it would take a mere three days to ascend the escarpment; and mules were well known to be more tractable than camels. In three days with ten men—or five, or none—they would be in Ankober, he and Vayu. They would deliver the guns to Menelik.

. . . If Menelik was there, that is. And that he did not know. . . . He had asked in every village of the Ahwash, but no one knew. No, they had heard of no *ferangi* coming; of no battle or march to battle. They shook their heads. They did not know. . . . In three days he would learn for himself.

On the eleventh morning they crossed the river and that night camped at the base of the escarpment. The next day they climbed, all day: first up bare shale and gravel, then through a belt of stunted forest, finally into a gray tumbled world of brush and rock. As they ascended, the sun lost its warmth, the air grew cool and damp, and then the sun receded and was gone, and they moved through clammy veils of drifting mist. That next night, in camp, they huddled close around their fires, wearing all the few clothes they had, and with burlap bags over backs and shoulders. But still they were cold, with a cold that pierced to their bones. Far below, in the valley, they could see the pinprick glint of other fires, from the Ahwash villages. Above, on the barren slopes, there was only darkness.

Vayu looked upward, and then away again, and he was shivering. And Claude put a hand on his shoulder.

"Don't be afraid," he said gently.

"I am not afraid, sidi," said Vayu. "With you I am never afraid."

In the morning four more drivers left them. There were now six, including the headman Rashi—plus themselves—plus eighty-seven mules. As before, Claude led the train, with Vayu at its middle, Rashi at the end, and the others spread out widely between. It was still colder now. The mist was thicker. Claude picked his way half-blindly up a twisting ravine, between bushes and rocks and boulders; and as the hours passed the way grew steeper, the twists were sharper, the boulders loomed darker and taller in the mist. At one point, indeed, in the dimness ahead, they appeared to him not to be boulders at all, but, rather, the figures of men, waiting and watching; and as he drew closer the impression persisted, and grew stronger; in a moment they would move, become men . . . And they did. . . . In the mist, they stirred. They came closer. They stopped. And he stopped too. And tall cloaked men with shields and spears stood all around him.

He spoke, in Amharic, but they did not answer. And then he dismounted and stood beside them. They let the mules go past, up the trail —his own first and the others after it—and at intervals a figure detached itself from the group and went along to lead them. But each time a rider appeared they made him dismount and stand among them—until they were all there: three drivers, then Vayu, then two more drivers, and finally Rashi—and now the last mule had gone by and they started up after them.

They did not climb long. Perhaps an hour—no more. And now and then Claude spoke again, but again received no answer. As they climbed, the mist thinned. The slope lessened. It was gone. They were on the escarpment's summit, moving between bleak knobs and domes and jutting headlands. Ahead were huts and tents and walls, the walls of a city;

572   JAMES RAMSEY ULLMAN

and now the mist too, at last, was gone; it lay below them; and in the clear quiet light of evening they came to Ankober.

He thought of another coming, another pilgrimage. Of a riverbank clearing, of naked savages, of dancing black files in the jungle night. But this had been far away, long ago. Now he stood in a high-beamed hall, gleaming with torches, on the highest dome of the escarpment, and the hall was the court of a Nigger King who was one of the lords of Africa.

Vayu was not with him. The drivers were not with him. Ranged on either side, along the walls, were tall cloaked warriors with spears and shields, and before him, on a dais, sat Menelik of Shoa. He was a man in his prime: tall, even though seated, and broad and powerful both in body and limb. Over a white robe he wore a black silk cloak with a scarlet lion embroidered on the chest; and on his head was a black bead-trimmed hat, over a white tight kerchief that bound his face like a nun's. It was no nun's face, however—nor any priest's, for that matter. Like the rest of him, it was broad and strong. It was the color and texture of rhinoceros hide, and pock-marked besides, and it was framed below by a thick black beard and, above, by black eyebrows, almost as heavy. He was an outsized man —a giant, a titan, of a man. Of the whole of him, frame and face, there was only one thing small—and this was his eyes; and now that Claude had inclined his head and said, "Your Majesty," the small eyes looked at him, shrewdly, steadily, and a long moment passed before Menelik spoke.

Then he said, in a deep rough-edged voice, "In this court, *ferangi*, it is customary to make a deeper bow."

Claude inclined his head a little farther.

"That is still not very good," said Menelik.

"I am sorry," Claude said. "But my back is stiff."

"From your long journey, no doubt? Well, that will pass as an excuse. But if your rump is the same, be careful where you sit down."

He laughed and looked at his warriors. And the warriors laughed too, so that the sound of it filled the hall.

"I have brought you guns," said Claude, when the noise had subsided.

"Yes, I know," said the king. "We are already unpacking and sorting them. We are very efficient here. And, at the moment, quite in a hurry; for our own country is being invaded, and that of course we must stop at once."

"You mean the Italians—"

"Yes. They are apt to be rash, the Italians. And I am sure your guns will be most useful in our coming victory."

Menelik rose. And now his height was tremendous.

"If it please Your Majesty," said Claude, "I should like to say—"

"It will please me to hear what you have to say when I return to

Ankober. As I have said, we are very busy. I lead my troops to the north tomorrow."

Claude spoke again, but his words were lost as the king thumped down the steps from the dais. As he crossed the long hall, his men fell in behind him; outside a drum rolled, a trumpet sounded; and then the hall was empty except for Claude and four spearmen. They approached and formed a square around him, and walked with him from the hall, and outside it was night. They descended a slope, came to another building, entered and moved down a corridor. At the end of the corridor was a small square room, and they led him in and withdrew, and he heard the bolt slide on the door. Except for a small barred window and a pile of hides on the floor, the room was much like the cell in the Governor's Palace in Harar.

36

In this room, this cell, he lived eighteen days. Three times each day the door was opened and food brought in; and twice—once in the morning and once in the afternoon—he was taken into a small compound behind it, where he could either sit or walk about. But the compound was enclosed by a high timbered wall, and he could see neither above nor through it. All he could learn about the world beyond was the approximate time of day.

He had three guards, who appeared in rotation, and during the first days he tried persistently to talk with them. "Where are my drivers?" he asked. "And the young man, my assistant? . . . I demand to speak to someone in authority . . . If the king is gone, then to his deputy . . ." But though he spoke in what he knew was clear Amharic, he received no answers; and by the fourth or fifth day he stopped trying.

He counted the days. He counted the timbers in the wall of the compound and the roaches he found in his room. He counted the prisons and jails he had been in . . . In Paris, first. In Italy, Germany, Greece, half the countries of Europe. In Tripoli (as inmate, clerk—then liberator). In Aden and many Red Sea ports. And in Harar. . . . All his imprisonments had been brief, and his memory of most of them were dim. But he remembered Harar. And he remembered Paris. . . .

He did not want to. He thought of other things. He resolved that on the twentieth day he would make a break; how or to where, he did not know, but he would do *something*. . . . The twentieth day, however, did not come, for on the morning of the eighteenth he was awakened by an astonishing sound: the sound of firing cannon. And he thought, "So the Italians have come. Menelik is beaten: a prisoner, a fugitive—or dead. And if nothing else, I shall at least have my freedom."

But the next day it was again his Abyssinian guards who appeared. And this time they took him out and through the streets and up the hill to the king's palace, or *gibbhi*, and on the terrace before the *gibbhi*, flanking its wooden steps, were two black iron cannons. Here his old guards left him and others took their place, and after a wait of some minutes in an anteroom he was again led into the central beamed hall, and down its full length to where Menelik sat on his dais. This time there were no lines of warriors. There was only the king—and the guards. And the king was dressed differently: no longer in robes of black and white, but in brown tunic and tight trousers, such as his soldiers wore, except that over his shoulders, as a cape, was the enormous skin of a lion.

He looked at Claude for a moment in silence, his broad pock-marked face impassive, his small eyes shrewd and unmoving. Then he said:

"Your back, I gather, is still stiff."

Claude bowed slightly.

"And your knee, that is stiff too? You were limping."

"Yes," said Claude, "it is a little stiff."

"Hmm—the dampness perhaps. But otherwise I trust you have been comfortable?"

"No," said Claude.

"No? . . . I am sorry. We have done the best we could, in our humble African fashion."

"Why," said Claude, "have I been kept a prisoner?"

"A prisoner? That is a strong word, I think. Let us say, rather, in protective custody. My people here, you see, are not used to *ferangi*. They might well have thought you an enemy—an Italian. I thought you would be safer if they did not see you."

"And *my* people—?" said Claude.

"Your people?"

"Those who came with me. What have you done with them?"

"There were, I believe, seven," said Menelik. "The six who were Moslems were sent back down to the Ahwash; we do not welcome Moslems here. The other—a rather young man—appeared to be a Christian. A rather peculiar Christian, I gather; certainly not of the true Coptic faith. But he was permitted to stay."

"And where is he?" Claude demanded.

"He is safe and well. You will see him presently. And he will leave Ankober when you leave—which I assume you plan to do in the near future."

Claude nodded. "When I have received my money."

"Money?"

"For the guns, Your Majesty."

"Ah—ah yes, the guns."

"They were satisfactory, I trust. And useful in your defeat of the Italians."

"Yes, of some use, I suppose. Of course, we were well armed to begin with, and as it turned out, we could, I think, have done quite well with clubs and spears. The Italians are not very good fighters, I am afraid. They had two cannons with them—perhaps you noticed them outside—which they had dragged all the way from Massawa. And they seemed to think that was all they needed. No strategy, tactics, discipline; no knowledge of desert warfare. Only two cannons—which they could not even turn around in the sand."

Menelik laughed. "Well, they can think about it on their way back to the coast," he said. "Those that are left of them. . . . Think about what they learned from the poor niggers of Africa."

He laughed again—then stopped. His small eyes fixed on Claude. He said:

"Most Europeans, of course, think that is what we are: niggers. That I, Menelik, am a Nigger King. But we are not, you know. *I* am not. Our skins are dark—yes—because we have lived long in the sun of Africa, but our ancestors lived in the land of Christ in the days before Christ was born." He leaned forward a little, and at the same time seemed to draw himself up. "Do you know who I am, *ferangi?*" he said. "I am the Lion of Judah. My royal blood is older than that of all the kings of Europe together. My ancestors were kings in Israel, when yours were savages in the northern woods."

"I am aware of your lineage, Your Majesty," said Claude. "But if I may say so, you make one mistake about mine. My forebears did not live in the woods."

"France was full of woods in the time of Israel. You are a Frenchman, aren't you?"

"I am called a Frenchman today. But my ancestors were not French— nor woodsmen. They lived on plains, in open country. Very much, I think, like the country of Abyssinia."

Menelik's broad face grew puzzled. He frowned. "And who were these?" he asked.

"They were called Huns, Your Majesty."

"Huns?"

The king's frown deepened. Claude smiled. "But it is not important," he said. "And I do not wish to waste your important time. If it pleases Your Majesty, I suggest that we conclude our business."

"Business?"

"The matter of the guns. The guns that I brought you."

"We have already spoken of the guns. As I said, they were of some use. But they would have been of more, had they not been full of sand and dust."

"I regret that. But there was not time—"

"And there were only nineteen hundred of them, whereas I had expected two thousand."

"I am aware of that, and will of course make an adjustment."

"What do you mean, an adjustment?"

"In the price, Your Majesty."

Menelik looked at him blankly. "Price?" he said. "Price?"

"Of one hundred thousand francs," said Claude. "Or the equivalent, of course, in other currency."

"I am afraid I do not know what you are talking about."

"I am talking of the amount you agreed to pay for the guns. And with the proper deduction for—"

"That I agreed to pay?" the king broke in. He shook his head. "You are confused, my friend. Perhaps your long journey has unnerved you."

"You have just said that you expected—"

"Yes, I expected the guns. As a gift. A most generous gift, I may say; and I am most grateful—indeed touched." Now it was Menelik who smiled. "It seems to me most—fraternal, shall we say: a gift of guns from *ferangi* to a Nigger King, to protect his kingdom—and kill other *ferangi*."

Claude's body was rigid, his jaw was tight. But he kept his voice low and controlled. "Your Majesty," he said, "you know quite well—"

"Yes? What do I know?"

"That you wrote a letter, a document, agreeing to pay for these guns."

"I see . . . And you, of course have this document?"

"Yes, I have it."

"May I see it, please."

"I do not have it with me. It is with my baggage, from which I was separated when I arrived here."

"Ah, with your baggage. And it is from me, you say, and addressed to you."

"No, not to me. To my partners."

"Hmm—your partners. And who might they happen to be?"

"Their names were Jensen and Fitzsimmons."

"And where are these partners, may I ask?"

"They are dead," said Claude.

"Hmm—that is unfortunate. Or perhaps, you had thought, *not* unfortunate. Because you of course have a second document showing that you are the surviving partner."

Claude did not answer.

"Do you?" said Menelik.

"No."

"It, too, is with your baggage?"

"No."

"In other words, there is no such document." Menelik's small eyes grew smaller. His face was no longer either blank or smiling. "You should have thought of that, my friend," he said, "before you killed your friends in the desert."

"Killed them—?"

The king's face changed again; became relaxed, almost pleasant. "Why not?" he asked. "It would be a fine stroke of business. The only item, alas, that you failed to consider is that I might be a businessman too."

Claude tried to speak, but he waved him into silence. "Do not ruffle your feathers. Perhaps you did—perhaps you did not. Frankly, it is no concern of mine. . . . But it also is no concern of mine when you babble about payments. . . . So all is even, eh, my friend? Our business is concluded. And I shall not keep you any longer."

He half turned away, but Claude did not move. And Menelik looked at him.

"I had thought you were anxious to leave Ankober," he said.

"I shall leave when—"

"Ah, I see—when your caravan is ready. And that has been dispersed and must be reassembled. . . . Well, we are not the simpletons you took us for, perhaps, but we are not inhospitable either. I shall have a place assigned to you and your young assistant and you may stay there while you make your arrangements. It will be more comfortable than the last place, I hope, and better for your stiff back and knee."

"If you will please listen, Your Majesty—" Claude said quietly.

But the audience was over.

Menelik nodded to the guards, and they led him out.

The "more comfortable place" was merely a *tukul*, a circular spike-topped hut of mud and thatch. But, other than the palace, a few lesser official buildings, and the churches, there were only *tukuls* in Ankober, and this *was* larger and better furnished than the room of his confinement. Indeed, it was the best of all the uncountable shelters he had had in the more than two years since he had left Harar.

Also, as the king had promised, Vayu appeared. Claude had scarcely entered his new quarters when a guard brought him in; and Vayu gave a shout and embraced him, and in his joy was close to tears. Claude's guards were gone. Now Vayu's left. And they talked and talked. . . . No, Vayu said, he had not been harmed. On the first day he had been questioned, together with Rashi and the other drivers. "And I remembered what you had said, sidi," he smiled, "and was very Christian, and they did not make me go." But, like Claude he had been locked up. And he had been worried, terribly worried. About you, sidi. And what they had done to you."

Then, suddenly, he was smiling. His eyes shone. "But now—now that

is over," he said. "We are together. You are all right. . . . And you have seen
the king?"

"Yes," said Claude, "I have seen him twice."

"And he gave you the money?"

"No, he did not give me the money."

Vayu's smile faded. "You mean—there is trouble?"

"Yes, there is trouble."

"And what will happen? What will you do?"

"What will happen," Claude said, "I do not know. What I will do is wait
and be patient."

Their guards did not return. What came was a servant, bringing food,
and he came each day thereafter, to cook and keep house for them. They
were allowed to come and go as they pleased, and though Claude knew
they were carefully watched, they were not interfered with. On the streets
they drew small attention, for in clothing and coloring, they were almost
indistinguishable from any other lowland visitors. Only occasionally, at
close quarters, as among the market stalls, did someone pause to stare
suddenly, curiously, at Claude's eyes.

There had, he knew, been other Europeans in Ankober before him—
among them Father Hippolyte Lutz. But how many, he did not know. And
there seemed to be no others there now.

The town was far smaller and more primitive than Harar. And, at the
same time, beautiful and hideous: beautiful in its majestic site on the great
rim of the escarpment, in its cedared hills and thrusting headlands, in
its high clear sky and wide horizons, and the white ocean of cloud that
often covered the wastes below; hideous in its filth and squalor, in its close-
packed fetid huts, in its streets, deep in offal and garbage and the carrion
of animals, that made those of Harar and Aden seem, in comparison, like
the boulevards of Paris. In the sunshine, in the clean highland wind, it was
bad enough. When, as happened every fourth or fifth day, the cloud-ocean
arose, spilling over the escarpment—and fog and rain pressed in—the
stench was all but unbearable.

Still, they bore it. The Shoans bore it—indeed, were not even aware of
it—and were, in all aspects of their lives, more active and vigorous than
the peoples of the deserts and the coasts. For several days after Menelik's
victorious return there was almost continuous celebration. From the
palace, on its hilltop, sounded the boom of the captured cannons, the blare
of horns, the thud of drums; and in the town below there was dancing,
singing, shouting-and drinking. For the Shoans, unlike the Moslems, were
drinkers, heavy drinkers, and the cloacal streets were now all but awash
with the yellow of *tej*, their potent spirit of fermented honey, and the
brown of *tala*, their thick sweet beer.

Vayu tried them both and was later sick, and the next morning pale and rueful. Claude drank only one mug of *tala*, and it was the first liquor he had touched since the days—the two years—of the gourds of araq.

Together they walked the streets, and Claude's limp was now better. They moved past the huddled *tukuls*, the market sheds, the squat octagonal Coptic churches, picking their way through the offal and carcasses, between laden mules, among goats and sheep and chickens and the swarming crowds. The people were dark-skinned, ranging from coffee brown to black, as black as Negroes, mostly with full lips and thick bushy hair. But as Menelik had said, and Claude knew, they were not Negroes. Their heads were long and fine-boned, their noses aquiline; watching them, one did not think of tropical Africa but of figures from Biblical stories, from the pages of the Old Testament, and the days when Israel had been a raw and young, yet age-old, nation of warriors and priests. In the cool high air, they dressed as warmly as their poverty permitted: the women usually in shapeless sacklike robes that fell from neck to ankles; the men in blouses and tight trousers, with, on their shoulders, invariably, the cloaks of wool or hide that they called *shammas*. In the wind or the cold of evening, they drew the shammas up high over throat and face, leaving only their dark eyes visible as they moved through the streets.

It was still a nation of warriors and priests. And they were everywhere: the warriors loud and proud and tall, with their long spears—or guns— wearing leather breastplates and headgear trimmed with pelt of lion or leopard; the priests with long staffs, with torn robes, dirty and beggarly, like the Coptic priests of Harar—but at the same time different, here not humble in their rags, but proud and arrogant with the knowledge of their power. . . . "Priest—warrior—" Claude thought. "The saver of souls and the killer of bodies. The Unholy Two. In Israel, in Abyssinia—the same. The same as anywhere. . . ."

And another thing, too, was the same as anywhere. . . . *Les fonctionnaires. Les assis*. . . . He had waited for a week after his second audience with Menelik to see if the king would again summon him. But no summons had come; and thereafter, each day, with Vayu, he climbed the hill to the palace. Sometimes the guards stopped them; sometimes they were allowed to pass. But even when past they did not get to the king. They came to corridors and anterooms, to clerks and chamberlains, to Officials A and B and C; and the officials said, "His Majesty is busy. He is away. You must have an appointment. . . . Yes, tomorrow, perhaps. Next week, perhaps. You will fill out this form. And sign here. . . . No, it is not yet in order. It must be stamped and counterstamped. . . ." A large supply of rubber stamps and ink pads (made in France) had, Claude learned, arrived by recent caravan, and the palace halls resounded with a steady and rhythmic thumping.

Now and then they saw the king at a distance. Once it was on a high platform in the palace courtyard, on which he was hearing petitioners and dispensing justice; but the crowd around him was so dense that they could not penetrate even its outmost ranks. And every few days, on his way to here or there, he would pass through the streets of the town. These, too, were impressive occasions, for he came always with a full cortege of his nobles—called *rases*—mounted not on mules but on prancing caparisoned horses, preceded by drummers and trumpeters, followed by troops in full panoply and the priests of the court with ceremonial umbrellas. Soon, a few of his retinue were known to them by name and figure: Ras Abbata, his senior general, as tall and powerful as the king himself; Ras Makonnen, a royal nephew, younger and slighter, with the face of a scholar; Tai Haimanot, the high priest, an old man, white-haired and bearded, and seeming as frail as a specter. And once, among them, seated on a litter borne by eight servants, they saw Menelik's queen, Taitu, an enormous billowing woman covered with beads and brocades. As the procession passed, the people of Ankober bowed low, touching their foreheads to the muck of the streets. And Claude and Vayu watched, and then, if the king was going up to his palace, followed and tried again—and again—to gain an audience.

They could not. It was hopeless.

And then, suddenly, they did.

A stamp thumped. A door opened. An attendant led them down a hall and through a second door into the great beamed hall, and they were standing alone before Menelik.

"Yes? State your business," said the king.

"I am sure," Claude said, "that Your Majesty remembers—"

"Remembers? Remembers what?" Menelik's small eyes examined him.... "Oh, it is you," he said. "Morel—the Frenchman. I beg your pardon—the Hun. I had thought you had left here long ago."

"No, Your Majesty, I have not left."

"So, you like it here, eh? Good. Excellent. If enough *ferangi* come, and like it, we shall have a fine tourist business. Though most, I trust, will be more solvent than you."

"That is what I wish to speak—"

But Menelik was not listening. He was looking at Vayu. "This, I suppose, is the young Christian," he said. "Your accomplice."

"My partner," said Claude.

"Hmm, partner ... You have quite a turnover in partners, do you not? They go—and they come."

"If it please Your Majesty"—and this time Claude spoke on until he was finished—"we have been appreciative of your hospitality. And I am aware of the truth of what you say about my solvency. But may I point out that the reason is that I have not been paid."

"Paid?" said Menelik. "Paid for what?"

"For the guns that I brought you."

"Oh—we are back to that."

"Yes, we are back to that. And if you will be good enough to pay me, we shall be glad to remove ourselves as a burden—to leave Ankober—"

"You have no money now?"

"No, none. As you know, we have been living on your bounty."

"Hmm—" The king studied him. He rubbed his beard and considered. Then he said: "Very well, I tell you what I shall do. I shall continue to be bountiful. These guns of yours were in bad condition. There were not the stipulated number. And they were probably not yours anyhow. But I shall forget all that and be generous. I shall pay you the equivalent of two thousand francs, and you can be on your way."

"Two thousand—"

"Yes."

"But that is fantastic, Your Majesty. You agreed in your letter—"

"Ah, that letter again. The mysterious document."

"There is nothing mysterious about it. You wrote it. As I told you, it is in my caravan baggage, which has not been returned to me, and—"

"—and which might be lost, eh?" said Menelik. "Or strayed. Strayed to the most unlikely sort of place—such as, even, a king's palace."

He smiled pleasantly and turned to a low table beside him. "Such as here," he said, holding up a sheet of embossed parchmentlike paper. "*From Menelik, King of Shoa,*" he read, "*to the Messrs. Jensen and Fitzsimmons. . . .*"

He paused, still smiling, enjoying the game of cat and mouse. "You may be talented otherwise, my friend," he said, "—such as at lying or even murder. But you are not, I must say, a very good businessman, allowing such valuable items to be mislaid."

The cat's-paw held the paper . . . The lion's paw. . . . Then the paw struck; the paper crumpled; the paper ripped. "Well, now there is no longer any letter—just as there is no longer any Jensen or Fitzsimmons." The lion dropped the shreds of paper. The lion laughed. Then he roared. "And you, my friend the Frenchman—my friend the Hun—can now get out," he said. "Out of here. Out of Ankober. And do not bother me any more!"

Claude stood unmoving. "I cannot go, Your Majesty," he said quietly. "I have no caravan. I have no money."

"Walk then. Or crawl. Eat thornbush, like the camels. And be grateful that I have not had you killed, for your fraud and insolence."

"I am grateful for nothing," said Claude. "And I shall go only if I am forced to."

"Forced? You do not think I can? You are challenging me?"

"No, not challenging."

"But you will not go of your own accord?"

"No."

"You prefer to stay here?"

"Yes."

"And do what? Go on forever living off my charity?"

"No."

"What then? Go into business, eh? To cheat my people. Take over their land. Bring your fine white civilization to Darkest Africa."

Claude tried to speak, but the king overrode him. "What else could you do, eh?" he demanded. "What else do you know, you trader and peddler, except cheating and conniving?"

He paused, waited—and then was answered. But it was not by Claude. It was by Vayu.

"We know how to teach," Vayu said.

The king stared at him. He had forgotten his existence.

"Teach?" he repeated. "Teach *what*, for the love of God?"

"Many things, Your Majesty," said Vayu. "How to read and write, and languages and figures. The sidi and I have both taught, when we lived in Harar. And I have seen there are no schools at all in Ankober—"

The king still stared—as if at a strange species of beast that had been brought before him for inspection. He started to speak, changed his mind —and then laughed. "Teach! By God, that is a good one!" he said at last. "A Hun trader and a Harari servant to teach the people of the Lion of Judah—"

He went on laughing, and the sound of it filled the hall. Then he gestured to his guards, and Claude and Vayu were led out. They were taken from the palace and down the hill and through the streets and to their hut. And this time the guards did not leave, but remained outside with their newly issued guns.

"And now, sidi?"

Claude shrugged.

"He will send us away—without even the two thousand francs?"

Claude shrugged again. The rest of the day passed. And the night. And the next day. And after dark of the next day their guards came in and they were marched again through the streets.

"They will make us leave at night, sidi?" Vayu whispered. "With no caravan—nothing?"

But they were not made to leave. They were taken up the hill to the palace, where Menelik sat in his torchlit hall. Beside him, on the table where the letter had been the day before, there was now a bowl of yellow *tej* and a silver goblet. And as Claude and Vayu stood before him he drank from the goblet, and then, for what seemed a long while, sat looking at them in silence.

Suddenly he said to Claude: "How do you know Amharic?"

"I have studied it," Claude answered.

"Why have you studied it?"

"Because I was interested. And because I thought that some day it might be useful."

"Such as now?"

"Yes, such as now."

"You know many languages?" asked Menelik.

"I know fairly many, yes," said Claude.

"Name them."

"I know most of the European languages. And Arabic, and Amharic and Somali—"

"And the language of the Huns, of course."

"There is no longer a language of the Huns, Your Majesty. But there is Hungarian, which derives from it, and I know some of that."

The king drank again from his goblet. And again looked at Claude in silent appraisal.

"I shall tell you something," he said. "You are different from most *ferangi* I have met."

"I am perhaps better educated," said Claude.

"Educated? Yes, perhaps that is part of it. But there is something else too. Something deeper. Perhaps it is that you are—better disciplined."

"Disciplined?"

"Yes. I have not made it easy for you here, I am aware of that. And why should I? If I made it easy for *ferangi*—for every conniving thieving European in Africa—how long do you think I would hold my throne and my country?"

He expected no answer and received none. "No, I have not made it easy," he repeated. "In certain ways I have made it hard. But you have shown neither fear nor anger. You have shown discipline. My guess would be that you had good training when you were young."

He paused. "In any case, I shall tell you this, too. I am impressed. In Europe, I am thought of as a Nigger King; my people as barbarians, savages. But we are not, my friend. We are a proud and ancient race, and among our prides is our discipline." With a quick catlike move he reached under his robe, and now in his hand there was a dagger. "Look. I shall show you something," he said. "A small exercise in discipline." And holding the dagger in one hand, he drew its point slowly, strongly across the palm of the other, making a line of blood in the dark tough flesh.

When he had finished he smiled slightly. Then he held out the knife toward Claude. "Now let us see, he said, how a *ferangi's* discipline compares to an African savage's."

Claude did not take the knife. He shook his head.

"You will not do it?" said the king.

"No."

"Why will you not?"

"Perhaps because I *am* a *ferangi*," Claude said. "And though we each have our disciplines they are different."

Menelik was no longer smiling. He looked at Claude, then at the knife. Then with another quick sudden movement he drew back his arm and flung the knife, spinning, across the hall. It struck a cedar beam, hung half-imbedded for an instant, and fell with a clatter to the floor.

And now Menelik laughed. "I am glad my troops are not here to see how badly I am out of practice," he said. Then, clapping his bloody hand against the other one, he summoned a servant from behind the dais and pointed at the bowl of *tej* and the goblet. And in a moment the servant had brought two more goblets.

"So, let us drink to better marksmanship—and to discipline," said the king, raising his own.

The servant filled the other two and gave them to Claude and Vayu, and they sipped the sweet strong liquor. But Menelik drank his down, and refilled his goblet and drank again, and from the hand holding the goblet the blood dripped down, unheeded, onto his silken robe.

"So—" he said again. "After discipline it is good to relax. Even for a king ... And you may relax too, my friend the Hun, and tell me some things I would like to know about you."

Claude met his gaze and waited.

"Such as," said Menelik, "*why* you are as you are."

"Do any of us know that, Your Majesty?"

"You have not always been a trader, a gunrunner?"

"No."

"What were you before?"

"I have been—many things."

"In France? In Europe?"

"Yes, in Europe."

"You have a wife? A family?"

"No," said Claude.

Menelik paused. He drank again. Then he looked at his bloody hand, as if aware of it for the first time. "I have a wife," he said. "A great deal of wife. Perhaps you have seen her. I am a Christian, of course, not a Moslem, and so can have only one; but she is equal, I assure you, to any four of a sultan's."

He paused again. "I am her fifth husband," he said. "The previous four are—dispersed. And she has children by three of them. But none by me. No. I am the king, the Lion of Judah, the heir of Solomon—and I have no son."

He stared broodingly into his goblet, noticed that it was empty, and refilled it with *tej*. Then he brightened.

"But I have a nephew," he said. "A fine nephew, Ras Makonnen. He is brave, loyal, dependable, intelligent. He has been of much help to me in the ruling of my country, and soon now he will be Governor of Harar."

"Harar?" Claude repeated.

"Yes, Harar. The city, the province, all of it. That is my next campaign, and it will start at once. I am sick and tired of these outsiders—first the Egyptians, now some desert bandit called Ismail—in what should properly be a part of my own kingdom."

Menelik drank again. Then he warmed to his subject. "Yes, first I shall take Harar," he said, "and install my nephew as governor. Then there is work to be done in the south—with the Gallas and Shankallas ... And finally, of course"—here his broad face smiled, his small eyes shone brightly—"finally there is the north; there is Tigré."

Claude said nothing, but the king raised a hand as if to stop him. "Do not misunderstand me," he said. "I am not going to attack Tigré—nor King John, my royal cousin.... There has been enough of that sort of thing in the past.... But John is old. He has many troubles. The Egyptians press on him from the north, the Italians from the east, the Sudan Dervishes from the west. Only I, in the south, do not press. And I shall not. I shall go about my business at Harar and with the Gallas and Shankallas, and when the time comes—only then—I shall move north. Then, at last, Tigré and Shoa will be one. All Abyssinia will be one. And I, Menelik, shall no longer be merely a *negus*, king of Shoa, but *Negus Negusti*, King of Kings —yes, the Emperor of Abyssinia, the one free and sovereign empire in all of Africa!"

As he spoke, his voice had grown stronger. It was harsh and fierce. His eyes, and even the dark flesh of his face, were as if lighted by a flame from within.... Then, suddenly, the flame faded. His face changed, and his manner.... He drank his *tej* again, and belched, and said mildly, "But we were speaking, not of me, but of you, my friend. Of what you have done—and what you will do now."

He paused. Then he had a thought. "You—or the young one here— said you had lived in Harar. Perhaps you would like to return there. You can come with me and my army."

He looked at Claude questioningly and waited. But Claude slowly shook his head. "No," he said. "No, Your Majesty—I do not want to return to Harar."

"You do not want to go to Harar. You do not want to go back to the coast.... What *do* you want then? Will you tell me, please?"

"I would like—"

"Yes, I know: you would like a hundred thousand francs. But you are not going to get them. At the most you will get the two thousand I have already offered; and I may say that, with my campaigns to Harar and south, I can ill afford even that. Unfortunately, along with my ancestry, I did not inherit King Solomon's famous mines."

Menelik enjoyed this. He laughed. He poured another goblet of *tej*. "Of course the easiest thing," he said, "is simply to pack you off, as I intended. Or better yet, to have you executed for murder. . . . But, as I have said, I find you interesting. I have a feeling you could be useful."

He drank and belched again.

"But at what? . . . You said you have done many things: what does that mean?" . . . He had another thought. "What was that about teaching? You —or the young one here—said you can teach."

"Yes, we can—we have—Your Majesty," said Vayu, speaking for the first time.

But Menelik did not look at him. He still looked at Claude, and his small eyes squinted. "And what is it you could teach, eh?" he demanded. "How to be a successful trader, maybe? How to get a hundred thousand francs from a Nigger King? . . . Or maybe it would be something even better for my people. Like how to leave the true Coptic Church and become Catholics. Or how to turn against the king that God has given them."

"No," said Vayu, "It would be things that would help your people. As I said before: how to read—to write—"

"Ha, yes—that is just what they all need: to write. As it is, I get so many petitions each day that I go blind from looking at them . . . And the priests: what about them, eh? What will they say? Where would they be if anyone but themselves and a few *rases* could read and write."

"The priests, Your Majesty, are—"

"Stop!" The king raised his hand, and his voice was again harsh and imperious. "I will hear no word against the priesthood. They are the pillars of the state, of my kingdom, and of the Kingdom of God."

His eyes flashed. Then they went to the *tej*. He drank again, poured again, and now the bowl was empty. "Still," he said. "Still—" And now, once more, he was smiling; he was almost grinning.

"Hmm—well—"

He sat silent for a few moments, his thoughts turned inward, and when he next looked at Claude and Vayu it was as if he had forgotten their presence.

"So, you are still here?" he said. "You have been here long enough. The audience is over."

Again he clapped his bloody hand against the other, and this time guards appeared and he gestured, and Claude and Vayu were led away. Behind them, the king gave a final belch, and this one, thought Claude, was as loud as the best of his brother Felix's.

This time, as once before, the guards left them at their hut. The servant came with food and cooked. And they were free. But Menelik did not summon them again—nor did they see him—until one day, some time later, when the cannons boomed, the trumpets blared, and they watched him ride out of Ankober toward the south, at the head of his army.

"And now, sidi?" asked Vayu.

But again there was no answer.

There was only the hut, the streets; walking, eating, sleeping . . . until one morning they awoke from sleep to find a figure standing in the doorway of their hut. And it was not the servant, not a guard, but one of the chamberlains of the palace; and he told them to come with him and waited while they made ready; and then he led them through the town and up the hill and to a smaller building near the palace. In the building was a large room, and in the room, faces turned to the door, wide-eyed and silent, were some thirty boys, ranging in age from perhaps ten to fifteen. The chamberlain drew himself up. The boys stood at attention. "This is Ato Morel," he told them. "This is his assistant, Ato Vayu. You will at all times obey them."

Then he turned to Claude and Vayu.

"These are your students," he said. "Teach."

They taught.

For a month—and then two—and then three.

They divided the boys into two groups, Claude taking the older, Vayu the younger, but what they taught was the same; the curriculum of Grade Number One. It was not easy at first, for though they spoke Amharic— and now fluently—they knew little of its reading and writing, and it was only by studying, along with their pupils, that they succeeded in keeping safely ahead. Also, the boys were not *always* wide-eyed, silent, and at attention. They were—boys. There were the wild ones, the sullen ones, the timid ones, the dumb ones. There were Georges Vuiton, Pierre Berthoud, Henri Clauson, Michel Favre. . . . And there was also Albert Chariol, the ghost of Chariol. "And that is *you, Professeur Morel*," Claude thought. "Late of the Academy of Harar, of the Academy of Basel."

All the pupils were of the dominant families of Ankober: the sons of *rases*, commanders, landowners, officials. And he soon learned that among the fathers—or at least those of them who had not gone off with Menelik —there was little enthusiasm for the project. Among the priests, from whose monasteries they had to draw their small supplies of books, there was, as the king had foretold, even less; indeed, an abiding and pervasive hostility. But the king's order had been given. The king's warrant had been issued. And the hostility remained passive; the books were provided; the pupils appeared; the teaching went on. When trouble threatened in class,

Claude rapped sharply on the table, in the best tradition of the Lycée de Cambon, and said, "Silence! Order! You are Shoans—Abyssinians—have you forgotten? And the mark of an Abyssinian is his discipline."

He looked around, and there was silence.

"Very well, now: we will drill in the cardinal numbers. Follow me please: *and, hulet, sost, arat, amist, sidist, sabat, simint. . . .* Good. Again. . . . And inwardly he smiled and murmured, *"Et voilà la plume de ma tante."*

Late in the fourth month, however, on an afternoon when he was expounding the mysteries of Amharic spelling, the moment came which no discipline could have mastered. It came first as a sound, the sound of cannons firing; and then, beneath it, distant but clear, came the braying of trumpets, the rumbling of drums; and in the next instant the classroom was empty, every room and house and hut in Ankober was empty, as its people poured out to welcome their king . . . Harar had been taken! It was now part of the kingdom! . . . The news reached the town even before the army. And then the army came, proud and victorious, with its prancing horses, its spears and guns, its breastplates and plumes and banners and booty; and at its head rode the generals, and, before the generals, Menelik; and he led them up the hill to the palace, and the cannons boomed again; and they boomed all night, until sunrise, while the *tej* and *tala* flowed in the streets of Ankober.

Then another month had passed. And Claude stood again before the Lion of Judah.

"I have been busy," the king told him. "Very busy. There is no end, my friend, to a king's labor for his people."

"It was a fine victory, Your Majesty," said Claude.

"Yes, it was fine. It was most gratifying. The resistance was slight, almost nothing. Almost the only ones to fight and not run were the Emir Ismail Abdullah and his personal guard. And that, too, was good—that was excellent." Menelik grinned. "You have seen the Emir?" he asked, "—when you lived in Harar?"

"No," said Claude, "I have not seen him."

"Well, he is not very pretty. He is even uglier than I. And his head looks much better on a pole than on his shoulders."

The grin became a laugh. Then Menelik grew thoughtful. "Indeed, there was only a single disappointment," he said. "Do you know of one Abou Dakir, the Arab trader and slaver?"

"Yes, I know of him," Claude said.

"I had hoped that he would be in Harar with the Emir. It was he, you know, who has been behind the Emir—who financed him, brought him to power—with his money from slaves, from plundered caravans; and half the caravans have been mine . . . Yes, I should very much have liked to see his head, too, on the top of a pole . . . But, alas, he was not there. Do you know where he was? He was in Zanzibar, they said. And why was he in Zanzibar? It is fantastic. He was in Zanzibar to see one of his wives, who had just given birth to his twentieth son . . . The old goat, the old bandit. He at his age with a twentieth son—and I Menelik, in my prime, cannot even have *one*. . . ."

The king glared. Then he subsided.

"Well, there is at least my nephew," he said. "Ras Makonnen. I left him in Harar, and he will be a good governor. He will turn the mosques into churches, collect taxes efficiently, and it will be the good Abyssinian city that God intended it to be."

His attention focused on Claude.

"And you?" he said. "How is it with my friend the Hun, the wealthy gunrunner? . . . I beg your pardon, I mean the schoolteacher."

"It is well enough, Your Majesty."

"I gather that the parents of your pupils are not altogether happy. And the priests—hah! The chief priest, Tai Haimanot, has spoken to me, and his enthusiasm is, let us say, restrained. . . . But I have seen some of the boys as well. The son of Ras Abbata; two or three others. And I was impressed. I asked them to write their names, and they wrote them. I asked how much is four and three, and they said seven. I asked where is Rome, and they said Italy . . . Yes, I was impressed, astounded." Menelik laughed. "At this rate, soon, we shall be a nation of scholars and pundits."

"I am pleased that *you* are pleased," said Claude.

"Yes, I am pleased. And what the others say I do not care. 'Do you want to live forever in the Dark Ages?' I ask them. 'Do you want the *ferangi* to be right: that we are only savages, barbarians?' . . . Anyhow, you will go on with it. They will learn if it kills them . . . And in Entoto I shall see that you have better facilities."

"Entoto, Your Majesty?"

"I am moving my capital—have you not heard? Within a month now; a few weeks. This Ankober, I have outgrown it. It is a place for a bandit chief, not a king. Entoto is four days' journey to the west: in better country: richer, more civilized. And also it is more central—better located for administration; and also for my coming expedition against the Gallas and Shankallas. For centuries it has been only a village, but it will not be a village much longer. Already my workmen are there, building a palace and all else that is needed, and soon it will be a fitting capital, a true city."

The king paused briefly, allowing himself to enjoy the vision. "Yes, it will be much better there," he said. "For me and my people . . . And for you . . . Yes, there I shall see that you have all you need. Not just a room, but a proper school. It will be called the Royal Academy. And you, as head, will have a title too. You will be Minister of Education. Or, perhaps, Chancellor of Pedagogy." He laughed again. "Yes, Chancellor of Pedagogy," he said, "—that is very good. How do you like such a vocabulary, my friend, from a Nigger King of the Barbarians?"

Again he paused—still enjoying his thoughts.

"And I shall be generous too," he said. "I shall raise your salary."

"My salary?" said Claude.

"Yes. What do you receive now?"

"I receive nothing, Your Majesty. Only food and shelter."

"Hmm—an oversight. But it shall be rectified." The king considered briefly. "My exchequer, as you no doubt know, is based—for most complicated reasons—on Maria Theresa thalers. As Chancellor of Pedagogy you will be paid—hmm—four hundred thalers a year, starting in Entoto; and I hope you are appreciative of my munificence." His small eyes studied Claude for a moment, and his broad pock-marked face was grinning. "At the present rate of exchange," he said, "—and if my calculations are right—you will have to serve in the post only fifty years to make your one hundred thousand francs."

The caravan was enormous, stretching from horizon to horizon across the plains. It was early in the rainy season on the high plateau, the land was turning from yellow to green, and the chains of hills, ranged around them, stood sometimes brilliant in sunshine, sometimes hidden in cloud.

At the head of the procession rode troops of cavalry. Then came Menelik and his court: nobles, generals, ranking priests, high officials, all of them mounted too, all sheltered from sun and rain by great long-poled tasseled umbrellas held up from behind by walking attendants. And next were their women and children: first the queen, Taitu, in her litter; then the others, in order of rank—the older also in litters (though smaller) and the younger on horseback. Then followed more troops, some mounted, some afoot, with the two Italian cannons among them, bumping and jerking over the rough terrain. Then a miscellany of lesser officials and their families. And finally, stretched out for miles behind, there flowed the river of the people: a vast undulating stream of men, women, and children, farmers and laborers, soldiers and priests, mules and cattle and sheep and goats, and baskets and barrows and food and furniture. It was said that, besides the court and the army, more than half the population of Ankober was also moving to Entoto, and that so long was the procession that its van was two of the four days' journey ahead of the rear.

As government officials, Claude and Vayu rode well forward in the march; not, to be sure, among the *rases* and generals, but among the minor bureaucracy, behind the troops and the cannons. Claude had been issued a horse, Vayu a mule, and as they rode Claude smiled and said to him, "So here we are, Sancho Panza. But where is the windmill?"

Vayu looked at him blankly.

"You do not know *Don Quixote*?"

"No, sidi. What is that?"

"That is us," Claude said. "No—I mean it is a book. I thought I had told you about it."

"No, you have not told me," said Vayu.

The first day's march lasted for some eight hours, and as had often happened before, Claude's knee stiffened from the protracted riding, and now and then he dismounted and walked. When it was late afternoon they halted and camped, and, up ahead, the king's scarlet tent blazed in the sunset. The others, before and around them, had smaller tents of varying size, depending on wealth and station; but in the long stream behind, the marchers simply sat where they stopped and wrapped themselves in their shammas against the evening cold. Brush was collected by the women, and cook fires lighted. And when night came the fires glittered like a terrestrial Milky Way across the black miles of the plain.

Claude and Vayu had a tent, and in the night they sat out before it.

"This book with the funny name, sidi," said Vayu. "*Don Quixote*. It is about schoolteachers?"

"No," said Claude.

"You said it was like us."

"Yes, it is, in a way. But not that way."

He did not go on. Vayu waited. Then he asked a question, but it was not the question Claude expected.

"With our teaching, sidi," he said, "are you pleased? Is it all right?"

"Yes, it's all right, I suppose."

"I like it much, sidi. It is interesting. And I think that perhaps we do much good."

"I hope so," said Claude.

"The king, too, he must think we do good. He has made you a minister and will pay you a salary."

Claude nodded.

"How much? You have not told me, sidi. How much will he pay you."

"Four hundred thalers a year. That is two hundred each for you and me."

"Two hundred each? ... No, that is not fair. You are a minister, and the headmaster, and I am only the assistant. It is right that you take three hundred, sidi, and that I take one."

"No," Claude said, "we will take two and two."

Vayu still argued. "For me a hundred is very much," he said. "But for you even three hundred is little. What is three hundred thalers compared to one hundred thousand francs?"

"The guns were yours as much as mine," said Claude. "And not mine either, really, by any law."

"Mine, no, sidi. But whose then, if not yours?"

"I don't know. Anyhow, now they are Menelik's."

"And he has said nothing more about them—since he came back from Harar?"

"He makes jokes, but that is all."

"And you? You have said nothing to him?"

Claude shook his head.

"Why? Why not, sidi—now that he likes you? . . . Do you not care any more?"

"No, Vayu," said Claude, "I don't care any more."

They crept into the tent. They slept. And in the morning they went on. Through a second day and a third and into the fourth, the vast tide flowed on across the Abyssinian plateau. At intervals the tide constricted and passed through villages, and in each of them the inhabitants lined the way, touching their heads to the ground as the king passed, and then quickly bringing out produce and livestock and trying to sell it to the passing travelers. Then, for the travelers, the spike-roofed huts would recede. They would be in the open plain, in the seas of grass; and each day the grass was greener, each day they came to more shrubs, more trees—to cedar, juniper, wild olive, standing green and brown on the hillsides; and the hills grew larger, they became mountains, shone in sunshine, loomed in rain. On the third evening they saw, to the southwest, a mountain higher than all the others, its peak purple in the distance. But during the night, again, it rained, and in the morning, with the sun beaming, the peak was no longer purple, but white—white with snow. Vayu pointed and shouted, for he had never seen snow before. And Claude had not seen it since his last winter in France.

The mountain remained visible all day. But from noon on it was not at the mountain that they looked; it was at a gentle hill, broad and green, that rose directly ahead into the clear highland air. It was the hill of Entoto. On its flat summit could be seen the outlines of a great building, the royal palace-to-be, and around it and spilling down the hillside were the other buildings and churches and huts of the new capital of Shoa. In another hour they were at the base of the hill. Indeed, the advance troops were already near its top, and their horns blared the king's coming. Claude's eyes were raised; he scarcely noticed the last village, at the hill's base, through which they now were passing . . . until, suddenly, he was aware that Vayu, riding beside him, had reined in, and that Vayu again was pointing.

This time, however, it was not at snow—not at Entoto. They had passed beyond the village and were riding beside a stream that came down from the hill; and it was at the stream that Vayu pointed—at a woman, a girl, who stood beside the stream; and he said, "Sidi—sidi, look! We are in

Harar again. We are riding with our goods to the villages. . . . Yes, yes, sidi, don't you remember? She is like the one we saw then, with her bucket. The proud beautiful one. The sultana—"

Claude looked and he nodded. For he saw what Vayu meant. This girl was not dark-skinned as the other had been, but light, lighter even than himself or Vayu. She was not bare to the waist, but wearing the usual long robe of the women of Shoa. Yet as she knelt to the stream, as she rose and put her bucket atop her head, she had, unmistakably, the same grace of movement, the same tall and slender and molded beauty as the Somali girl by the stream, years before. And Claude smiled and said, "Yes, the sultana." And then rode on; and Vayu rode on too; but now not quite beside him, as usual, but a little behind.

Then Vayu said, "Sidi—"

"Yes?" said Claude, without turning.

"I am thirsty, sidi. I am going to stop and drink from the stream."

"I shall wait for you," Claude said.

"No, do not wait. Go on. I shall catch up with you."

So Claude rode on: up the gentle hill, in the midst of the great caravan, into the new city of Entoto. And in the city there was great confusion and searching and milling about; but in the end he found the hut—almost a house—that had been assigned to them; and a servant was already there with food and firewood (a new servant, for their old one had stayed in Ankober); and he cooked the food and Claude ate, and when he had eaten it was dark.

It was perhaps an hour later that Vayu came, and Claude said, "There is your supper on the table. But by now it is cold."

"That is all right," said Vayu. "I am not hungry."

"Nor thirsty?"

"No, sidi."

"The stream water was good?"

"Yes, very good."

"And the girl?"

"The girl?"

"The sultana," said Claude. "How was she?"

Vayu hesitated. Then he said, "She was beautiful, sidi."

"She lives in the village?"

"Yes."

"What is her name?"

"Her name is Biri."

They established their home. They established their school. As Menelik had promised, the new school was not merely a single room, but a building—or at least the wing of a building, one of the government offices—and they had space to separate their pupils according to age and aptitude. They were still the only teachers. The number of pupils had increased. And they worked hard: from seven to two each day in the school itself, and later around the town, in the new monasteries, among the hostile priests, searching for books, pens, pencils, paper, to add to their meager supply. They worked together from almost dawn until after dusk —closely, happily, as they had always been one with the other. But when night came, now, it was not as it always had been; they were not together. For as soon as their evening meal was over, or sometimes even before the meal, Vayu would leave the hut and walk down the street and usually not return until after Claude was asleep.

Now and then Claude too went out: for a walk, or to a shop for a mug of *tej* or *tala*. But more often he stayed in the hut, still working by lamplight; correcting his pupils' sums and spelling, preparing the next day's program, carefully reading the Amharic texts, with which he still had certain difficulties. The students were strictly forbidden to write in the books (which they loved to do, once they knew how); and one night, turning a page, he was annoyed to find many penciled words covering the margins of the text. Looking closer, however, he saw that the writing was not a student's. Nor were there many words, but only one word, written over and over, down the length of the page; and the word was

> *Biri*
> *Biri*
> *Biri*
> *Biri*
> *Biri*
> *Biri*
> *Biri*

On another night a week later, he went out for a walk and a drink, and on the way home he passed a shop that was still open, and on its counter were flutes and horns and lyres and *krars*. Entering, he bought a *krar* and took it with him, and in the morning, before they left for school, he gave it to Vayu.

Vayu's eyes shone, as they always did when he was happy, and he said, "Oh sidi, sidi, thank you! You are so good, so kind—and I am so glad again to have a *krar*. Now I can play and sing for you again, as I used to long ago in Harar."

Claude shook his head, and then he smiled a little. "No," he said. "No, this is not Harar any more, but Entoto. And you will not play and sing for me, but for Biri."

37

"I am a *fonctionnaire*," he thought. "*Un assis*. . . . Perhaps a hard-working one. But still *un assis*."

He smiled at the thought, and in the classroom stood up and walked about more than before. When the day's work was over, he walked up and down the hillside of Entoto, and along its broad summit, through the muddy streets of the raw growing town. The more he walked, the less his knee tended to stiffen. And walking at night, he felt less alone than when he stayed in the hut.

It was about a month after their arrival that he was next summoned by Menelik; and leaving Vayu in charge of the school, he climbed to the highest rim of the hilltop and the doors of the new royal *gibbhi*. Most of the city was on the northern slope of the hill, but the palace faced south, looking out over a wide green valley, and, beyond it, to the great snow-topped peak they had seen on their journey—the extinct volcano called Zoquala. Then, as he entered, the long vista was behind him. He was led down corridors and through courtyards far larger than those in Ankober, and then into the great hall, the audience chamber; and this, too, was larger than the old one—a room of barbaric splendor, high and vaulted, its beams hung with arms and shields and helmets, its walls with the hides of boar and zebra, lion and leopard.

The king, as before, was on a dais at the far end of the hall, wearing his robes and headdress of black and white. But now his throne was no longer a thing of mere wood and leather; it was made of the tusks of elephants, joined and banded with gold; and at its top, made all of gold and gleaming fiercely, was a huge and rampant Lion of Judah.

Below it, the Lion King watched as Claude approached and bowed, and then he nodded and said pleasantly, "Well, how goes it with the Chancellor of Pedagogy and the Royal Academy? You are content here in Entoto? You are pleased with your new quarters?"

"Yes, Your Majesty," said Claude. "I am, on the whole, content and pleased."

"You have any complaints? Any requests?"

"No, Your Majesty. But I have—if I may make it—a suggestion."

"What suggestion?"

"I think that the school should have more students."

"More students. But there are already—"

"There are already all the sons of the *rases* and high officials. But no others."

"What others could there be?"

"There could be the sons of some lesser officials. Of clerks and tradesmen. Even a few, well chosen, from the people themselves."

Menelik stared at him. "The people?" he repeated. "You mean the—people? The mass—the herd?"

"Yes, that is what I mean," said Claude.

The king still stared. He seemed undecided whether to laugh or be angry. "And what, may I ask," he said, "would be the sense of that? What need have such as they for any schooling?"

"I believe it would help—"

"Help whom? Help what? For a mule driver to know the multiplication table. A farmer behind his plow to know the list of Roman emperors."

"I was not thinking so much of that sort of knowledge—"

"No? Of what, then?"

"Of more practical things. Say, of how to plow better. How to make better tools. How to keep cleaner and healthier. . . . Entoto has been occupied for barely a month now, and its streets are already filthy and full of disease."

"So—I see." Menelik scowled. "You do not like my capital? You would like to change it? . . . And you are not only a teacher, eh?—but a doctor too. My Minister of Health, of Tools, of Everything."

"I am only suggesting, that if at least some were less ignorant—"

"Suggesting—suggesting—"

"—that if you want a healthier country, a stronger country—if, as you say, you want to be part of the modern world—"

"The modern world is so good eh? Europe is so good. France is so good . . . Why did you run away from them—tell me that, my friend—if they are so damned good? Why did you come to a country of dirty ignorant niggers?"

Menelik jerked up from his throne and paced up and down across the dais. "Dirty—ignorant—" he muttered. "And *why* are they that way? Because God made them that way—that is why. . . . He wants them that way. The priests want them that way . . . I have had enough trouble with the priests and this school of yours, as it is. That's all the high priest Haimanot ever talks about—that the school should be closed; that any teaching not by priests is the work of the devil. And how do you think it will be if you start taking *more* students? The peasants—the rabble—the ones the priests really have by the throat? . . . Hah. . . . Well, at least I shan't be here for it. I have more important things on my mind. In a few days I am off to the south: to the Gallas and Shankallas. You stay with your books, teacher—with your dirty streets and snot-nosed children and sniveling priests. And leave me to carve my empire. . . ."

He sat again on his throne and glared at Claude.

Then he smiled.

"The audience is over," he said. "We shall have a glass of *tej* and you may go."

Again the cannons boomed, the trumpets blared, the drums rolled, the horses pranced. For the better part of a day, from the crest of Entoto, a long column could be seen cutting across the southern valley. Then it vanished beyond the flanks of the volcano, Zoquala.

In the capital the king had left behind him, everything continued as before. In the streets, the piles of garbage mounted higher. In the school, the bright students remained bright, and the stupid ones stupid. In the hut, Claude sat alone at night, when he returned from a walk or mug of *tala*, and sometimes awoke when Vayu came in, much later.

The first day in a month distinguishable from any other was the day of Vayu's wedding.

It came as no surprise to Claude. Almost from the beginning it had been obvious that what Vayu felt for the "new sultana" was no mere carnal attraction; and as his nightly absences continued, and occasionally he spoke of them, it had been with the eager voice, the shining eyes, that by now, to Claude, were so long familiar. Then, presently, as one day they walked home from the school, Vayu had swallowed and stammered and at last had come out with it. He wanted to marry Biri. And Claude had nodded and smiled and said, "Good. Now at last, perhaps, you will get some sleep at night."

"Then—then I have your permission?" asked Vayu happily.

"Permission? What permission do you need? You are twenty-two now —a grown man."

"But still, sidi, it is right that I ask. In your country, does not a son, in such a matter, always ask permission of his father?"

Claude looked at him for a moment, and then away, along the hillside street. "For one thing," he said, "I am not old enough to be your father."

"Not old enough?" Vayu's voice held surprise. "How old are you, sidi? You have never told me."

"I am thirty-four."

"Oh."

"You thought I was older?"

"Yes, I thought—" Vayu broke off. "But anyhow," he said, "you are my father. My friend and father. And I have asked you, as I should—and oh, I am so happy that you say yes."

Claude had made but one comment—raised but one question—and that was about religion. "You are partly Moslem," he said, "and partly Christian, and mostly not anything at all. If she is a strict Copt, going always to church and seeing priests, there will be problems."

But Vayu had reassured him. "No, no, sidi, Biri is not like that at all
—truly—and when you know her you will see. She is not just beautiful;
she is intelligent. Oh, she loves so much to think, to learn.... Yes, her
family, it is old-fashioned. They are simple people on a small farm. But she
is different. She is wonderful.... And besides, we will not see much of her
family. We will not live with them, down below, but here with you."

"With me?" Claude shook his head. "No, Vayu."

"But of course, sidi. There is room here—two rooms; we could make
three—and she will come and keep house for us." Vayu smiled. "And in the
evenings I will play the *krar* for you both."

But Claude still shook his head. "No," he said. "No, it will not be that
way. You and Biri must have a place of your own."

And on that he insisted. And it was the way it was done. On the day
of the wedding, with the school closed early, they put on the new clothes
they had bought and rode on rented mules down the hill to the village;
and there Vayu and Biri were married in the Coptic church. But when the
wedding and the feast were over, they rode back up again—with Biri on
the rump of the larger mule, behind Vayu—and when they came to the
new hut that he and Claude had found, the bride and groom dismounted
and waved and entered, and Claude rode on to the old hut, and from then
on lived alone.

But it was no more alone than it had used to be, when Vayu went down
the hill every evening. Indeed, he now saw a good deal more of him than
he had before.

Entoto was growing. Although the army, and many camp followers,
were away with the king, newcomers arrived, day by day, week by week:
merchants and traders and villagers and nomadic tribesmen, who had
heard of the new and greater capital and had come to see—and in many
cases to stay. Tents filled the open spaces of the sprawling hillside, and
among them there sprang up huts and sheds and stalls and even houses.
From the woods on the nearby slopes came the steady sound of axes
chopping at cedar.

The town grew. And with it—though more slowly—the school grew
too. At first it was only by the occasional addition of a younger son from
one of the ruling families (for these, however reluctant, did not dare to
disobey Menelik's orders); but then, carefully, Claude began to broaden
the base by taking in a few others. None of them, to be sure, were from
"the people," the primitive and half-savage poor. They were the sons of
lesser officials, of clerks, of traders and shopkeepers, and soon there were
a dozen or more of these among the original higher-born students. To
Claude's surprise, there was less parental opposition in this class than
among the wealthy and powerful. And to his relief, no protest from the

boys already there. Or at least not to him or to Vayu. What they told their families when they went home in the evening he of course did not know.

Presently there were almost fifty pupils of assorted ages. And one day Vayu said, "With so many, sidi, we need not two rooms, but three. And there is a good place—I will show you—where we can build a wooden partition."

But for three rooms they needed a third teacher. So for several weeks they searched. And finally they found one. He was a young man named Rahanit, roughly midway in age between Claude and Vayu, and he was short, thickset, and hairy, looking more like a muleteer than a schoolmaster. But here, if ever, was an outer shell that belied the man, for Rahanit was both lettered and intelligent, gentle and determined. He had come from a town in northern Shoa, where his family had destined him for the priesthood; and it was from the priests, in a monastery, that he had learned to read and write. Once this was accomplished, however, he had left. The Coptic Church and its laws and rituals were not for him. He had gone to Ankober and found work as a government clerk, and then on to Entoto, where he was still a clerk when Claude met him. But when Claude broached the possibility of teaching, his eyes had lighted up, almost like Vayu's, and he had come with them at once—first to help build the new partition, then to take charge of a class. And though his education was limited, he proved a natural, able teacher. The question of his payment was a problem, for Claude well knew that, with the king away, they could squeeze no extra salary from the government. And he solved it by paying it out of his own. To Vayu, however, he lied, saying that the government *was* paying; for otherwise Vayu would have insisted on paying his share —and he already had a wife to support.

Then the day came, a few weeks after Rahanit had joined them, when Vayu made an astonishing statement. "There is another one I know, Sidi Claude," he said, "who would like some day, too, to be a teacher."

"And who is that?" asked Claude.

"It is Biri."

"Biri?"

"Yes." Vayu smiled. "Do not look at me as if I am crazy. I have told you —Biri is not only beautiful; she is very smart. She wants always to learn, to understand, and has already learned much. . . . Yes, I have taught her, sidi. She can now read, and write a little, and count. . . . And I am joking, of course; she could not teach now. But some day, when she has learned more, yes, she could—like you, and I and Rahanit. Only of course it would be for girls."

Vayu paused for breath. "Yes, for girls," he said. "And why not, sidi? In Europe there are schools for girls, are there not? In all civilized countries? And the king wants so much to be civilized . . . Yes, sidi. . . . And so some day you will go to him and say, 'Your Majesty, we wish to open a school for girls.' And he will look at you and say, 'Why? Why a school for girls?' And you will say, 'Because that is civilized.' Then he will say, 'But who will run such a school? There are no women in my country who can do such a thing.' And you will say, 'Yes—yes, Your Majesty, there is one such woman.' And he will say 'Who?' And you will say, 'Biri, the wife of Vayu, my assistant.' "

He stopped, triumphantly, and smiled. "I see you do not look at me the same, sidi," he said. "And you have listened."

"Yes," Claude conceded. "I have listened."

"And you no longer think I am so crazy?"

"No, only a little crazy." Claude smiled back at him. "Which is the way it should be with a man in love."

He himself, of course, saw Biri frequently, for the hut where she and Vayu lived was only a short distance from his own, and at least once or twice a week he was there for supper and the evening. He did not yet, perhaps, quite see her as a potential schoolteacher, but he saw clearly enough—and approvingly—why Vayu had married her, and had, besides, grown very fond of her himself. For she was not only lovely to look at, with the fine features, smooth skin, and dark eyes of a Biblical princess —and as lithe and graceful in the cramped hut as she had been with her bucket by the flowing stream. She was also gentle and tender. She laughed easily and softly. She was a good cook, a good companion. A good wife.

The favorite Abyssinian dish was a stew called *wot*, made of mutton or goat or fowl, or whatever was at hand, and then soaked and covered in a red, and red-hot, sauce known as *berberi;* and of this concoction Biri was a mistress, preparing it each time Claude came, with pride and care, and then solicitously bringing *tala* for the two men, whose mouths were not yet of Shoan toughness. Dinner over, Claude and Vayu would talk—of the school and its problems and the events of the day—and sometimes Rahanit would appear. But Biri did not then, like most African wives, vanish from sight, but remained with them, listening, and sometimes even speaking herself; and when she spoke it was not foolishness.

One night, at Vayu's urging, she read aloud, hesitantly but accurately, a few pages of one of the simpler school texts. On another, she recited the multiplication tables, up to five times five; and on a third listed the Roman emperors—as far as Nero—while the men applauded and laughed. Toward evening's end Vayu often brought out his *krar* and played and sang: both the old songs of Harar and the new ones—for him—of Abyssinia, which Biri had taught him. And now and then, when he played, Biri danced for them; and when she danced she was no longer cook and housewife, nor earnest student, but again the sultana of Vayu's rapture —a princess dancing, slim and radiant in the lamplight.

It was not, however, the image of Biri the princess that Claude took with him to his own hut. Nor of Biri the housewife or Biri the student; nor indeed of Biri alone, at all. It was the image not of *one*, but of *two*, of Biri and Vayu together: the pair of them in their hut, their home: singing and dancing, cooking and eating, talking and laughing—or even, sometimes, arguing—but always the two of them, together, in the closeness, the communication, of husband and wife. And in his own hut, alone, he thought of husbands and wives, of men and women and their pairing, that was the way of the world everywhere, the way of nature, the way of God. He too had once—only once—had a woman. He had had Nagunda. But that had been different—and less—for with them there had been no true communication, but only the two bonds of mutual gratitude and of the flesh. Never in his life had he known what Vayu now had: the closeness, the sharing, the easy and natural give-and-take of man and woman's cohabitation.

He rarely thought of Nagunda now. Or of the child, their child, that had never been. Indeed, he rarely thought of anyone, or anything, beyond the circle of the high plateau, the hill and town of Entoto, and the new life that he had found there. Once or twice he had considered writing his mother, as he had used to, but had not done so. Now, sharing his small salary with both Vayu and Rahanit, he could not have afforded to send her money (which she no longer needed); nor could he imagine, either, what he would say. It was now three years since he had written. She must think him dead. And it was better to remain so.

In the nights, alone, before sleep, he sometimes thought of death. Of its meaning. And nonmeaning. He thought of Neil Fitzsimmons, and for his death there had been a reason, bare and obvious. But what of Jensen and *his* death? If there was reason there, it was too obscure for his understanding. And what of Lutz, of Egal, of Nagunda, and their child? ... *What of Albert Chariol?* ... They were all dead. Why? He was still alive. Why? He was alive; he was breathing, thinking; he slept and woke and ate and talked and walked and worked; he worked hard and long, with will and purpose.... And yet he too, alive, was also dead; as dead as they; self-exiled, self-buried—himself, no less than his past, buried deep and dead in his belly—the self that remained, *another*—a ghost, an exile—another from the one he had once been, who had dreamed and aspired, molded and created; and yet, at the same time, not another, but still the same; still as he had always been, alone, apart—alive and yet dead, dead and yet still alive—moving on through the desert, the waste, the death-in-life of a man alone, without a woman....

He slept, and in his sleep a woman came. But it was not Nagunda. Nor was it Bertha, the barmaid-whore, the wife of Felix. It was his mother, tall and black, with white bony face, and she stood now beside his bed and in her harsh voice said, "No self-pity, son. Never that. Be strong. Be proud." And then she left. And he awoke. And he went about the day's work . . . and the next day's, and the next week's, and the next . . . he taught his pupils, he worked with Vayu and Rahanit, he went in the evenings to the house of Vayu and Biri. He listened to Vayu play the *krar* and sing, and watched Biri dance. . . until a time came when she no longer danced; when, watching her move about the hut, he saw that she had changed, that she was no longer slim and lithe, but heavier, and that she moved more slowly . . . and he was not, this time, as stupid as he had been with Nagunda, but knew at once that she was pregnant.

And on the night he knew it he did a thing such as he had never done in his life; that was wholly strange to him—and yet wholly natural. He arose and went to where Biri sat, and bent and kissed her. And then he smiled and shook Vayu's hand and left, and for a while walked the streets, limping only a little, and then went home and to bed, alone: one soul and one body.

Menelik was still in the south. Then in the southwest. And the west. Now and then messengers appeared: at first bringing news of battles and victories; later with the word that battles were no longer necessary—that the Galla and Shankalla chieftains were flocking to the king with petitions and tribute, asking to become vassals of the realm of Shoa. Soon, it was said, the kingdom would extend, in the south, almost to the Web Shebeli, and in the west to the far borders of the Sudan.

In Entoto, the axes rang, the huts and houses sprang up; the town still grew. And although the school did not expand much further in number of students (for that would have required both more space and more teachers), it, too, now grew in an even more significant way: by the enrollment of two pupils from the out-and-out poor. One was a young cousin of Biri's, whose father, like her own, was a small farmer and herdsman; the other the son of the servant who cooked Claude's meals and cleaned his hut. And both were boys of about ten, bright and eager to learn. Aware of the importance of the step, Claude took it with care and forethought, buying them suitable clothes with his money and coaching them in the manners and customs of the upper classes. And, as in the earlier experiment with the middle-class boys, it seemed to come off; there was no friction or protest. . . .

At least at first. For a week. For a month. . . . Until a summons came to him one day by messenger from Tai Haimanot, high Coptic priest of Shoa.

Claude waited a day. And a second. Then he climbed to Entoto's crest, to the main church of the city, close by the royal palace, and was led into a sort of annex at the rear, which comprised the private domain of the topmost level of the Coptic hierarchy. "His Eminence is at prayer," he was told. And now it was he who was kept waiting—for almost an hour. But at last an attendant appeared and led him into the presence of Haimanot.

The high priest's chamber was not large, but it was high and vaulted and richly adorned: its walls covered with old paintings of the lives of the saints, its tables laden with chalices and missals, censers and miters and candelabra, gleaming golden and silver in the filtered light. Claude approached the dais. For here, too, there was a dais—not so high or broad as the king's, but still a platform raised above the floor—and upon it a large carved chair that was not wholly unlike a throne. And on the chair sat the aged prelate, wearing a white skullcap and a white robe encrusted with silver. He did not, however, look at Claude as he stepped before him, but sat with eyes half-closed and lips moving; and around and behind him stood six priests, their lips moving too, intoning a liturgy. The words of the liturgy were not Amharic. They were Geez—the ancient sacerdotal language of the Coptic Church. And for another few minutes Claude waited, while the chant continued, the priests swayed and murmured; and he thought wryly, "No, it is not quite like my last visits to a holy man; to Lutz's bare cell in Harar for a mug of wine and game of bezique. . . ."

Then the chanting ended. The high priest looked up. His face, between white cap and white beard, was the brown-gray of parchment, withered and skeletal—as frail, Claude thought again, as a specter's. But the eyes that looked out from it were no specter's. They were as black and sharp and shrewd as the eyes of Menelik.

"You have been long in coming," said Haimanot evenly. "It is now three days since I summoned you here."

"I am sorry, Your Eminence," Claude said. "I have been busy."

"Yes, so I gather. Busy. And how long, may I ask, is this busyness of yours to continue?"

"I do not understand, Your Eminence."

"You understand," said Haimanot. "And I recommend that you answer . . . Just what are your plans for this school of yours?"

"For the school? The same as the plans of the head of any school. To make it the best that I can."

"The best—I see. And the biggest too, perhaps."

"I shall make it as big as my funds and staff allow." Claude paused. "And if I may say so, Your Eminence," he continued, "I fail to see how it is a concern of yours—any more than your conduct of your church is one of mine."

"That is perhaps *your* opinion," said the prelate.

"I am the Minister of Education. I have a warrant from the king."

"You have a warrant from the king to run a small school for the sons of his courtiers. That in itself may or may not be advisable, but at the

moment it is beside the point. What is not beside the point is that you
have been expanding this school: first to take in the sons of clerks and
tradesmen, and now to accept even those of the common people."

"And there is objection to this?"

"Yes."

"From whom? The nobles? They are afraid their sons will be contami-
nated?"

"There have been protests, yes; from several parents. But that is not
why I have called you. There is a matter of far more importance involved,
and that is the danger to these new ones themselves."

Claude smiled slightly. "You mean," he said, "that *they* may be contam-
inated by the nobles."

"Your humor," said Haimanot, "might be appreciated in Europe. But
not here.... Here," he said—and now his voice rose and the black eyes
blazed in the spectral face—"here we do not think it a joke to corrupt our
people; to fly in the face of God and God's will."

"And what, if you please," asked Claude, "has God to do with it?"

The high priest did not answer at once. He watched Claude for a few
moments in silence, and the other priests watched him too, silent and
hostile. Then the old man said, his voice again slow and even:

"I shall tell you, *ferangi*, what He has to do with it. He is the One
God, the True God, and we are His true church on earth. We have been
ordained by Him to guard His kingdom, to be the instrument of His
will, and we do not intend to let our stewardship fall negligently into the
hands of others... This profane and godless so-called education that you
are trying to impose: it is one thing for the rulers and nobles. Perhaps not
a good thing—no—yet useful, even necessary, for those whom God has
appointed to govern others... But for the people themselves it is wholly
different. They do not need such things. Such things are poison to their
minds and souls. They are God's children, simple and pious, and all they
need is God's wisdom, God's guidance and blessing; and as long as I am
His vicar on earth, the High Priest of the Abyssinian Coptic Church, I shall
strive to preserve their goodness, their innocence—"

"—and quite incidentally, of course," said Claude, "the power that the
church now has over them."

There was a silence. Then Haimanot rose.

"I do not intend to sit here in this holy place," he said, "and argue with
an atheist and blasphemer. I shall ask you one question—only one—and
then the interview is over."

"And the question, Your Eminence—?"

"—is what do you propose to do?"

"To do? About what?"

"About this school of yours."

"I have already told you. I propose to make it the best that I can."

"And these new students—from the poor, the people. What will you do about them?"

"I will do my best for them too."

"You will not dismiss them?"

"No, Your Eminence."

"If it is my order—?"

"I take my orders only from His Majesty."

The high priest stood motionless on his dais. The others stood ringed about him, watching.

"You are an evil man, *ferangi*," said Haimanot. "An evil man, and godless."

"Many people have thought that," said Claude mildly. "And you are free to think so if you wish."

It was the season of sunlight. Then the season of rain. Again, with the rain, the land turned from burnt yellow to green, and the flat top of Zoquala gleamed white among the scudding clouds.

There was no further summons from the high priest. There was no trouble at the school. Through the days, at the school, Claude taught his classes and did such administrative work as was necessary, and in the evenings he was either home alone or at Vayu and Biri's. The meals there were still good; and after the meals, the talk and laughter. Vayu still played the *krar* and sang. And Biri sat and listened, and week by week grew bigger.

Then came a night when Rahanit, too, had been there, and he and Claude left together. When they reached Claude's hut they were in the midst of a discussion about some matter of teaching; and they went in together and a while later were still talking, when there was a sudden movement at the door and three men burst in. They carried knives and clubs, and seeing Claude, they rushed at him. And he was barely able to leap to his feet in time to fend them off for a moment with his stool. A moment, however, was all that was needed. For then Rahanit, whom they had not seen, leaped on them from the side with his own stool, his powerful muleteer's arms flailing and battering; and in an instant the tide was turned, a knife clattered to the floor, an intruder staggered, another yelled in pain; and then Rahanit was at the door, his stool now splintered but still held high, and the three were gone and vanished in the night, as quickly and suddenly as they had come.

"You are all right, Ato Claude?" Rahanit asked, turning.

"Yes, all right—thanks to you. And you?"

"I am fine." Rahanit grinned. "But I do not think our visitors are so fine. Next time, perhaps they will try robbing the rich, instead of poor and defenseless schoolteachers."

He remained for a while. They resumed talking, pausing now and then to listen or to glance out the door; but there was only stillness and darkness in the night around them. It was not until Rahanit had gone and he was alone in the hut that Claude realized that one of the intruders' clubs had found a mark. For his right knee was now swollen and throbbing.

In a week both swelling and pain were gone. The knee was still stiff, and he limped when he walked—but only a little more than was usual during the season of rains.

He himself got a knife and club and kept them handy at night. But there was no second attack. The weeks passed. Nothing happened.

It was other things that happened. . . .

First, Biri had her baby. It was a girl: brown, round, and great-eyed. And they named her Claudette. "And what sort of Abyssinian name is that?" said Claude to Vayu, protesting. "No, it is not Abyssinian," Vayu conceded. "But neither is it Harari. Biri and I could not agree on which of them it should be; so we decided on—how do you say?—a compromise." Vayu was smirking. "And it was just by accident that we found one that I think is French."

Then, when Claudette was one month old, a messenger appeared in Entoto. But this one was not from Menelik. He was from the north. And the message he brought was that King John of Tigré had been killed in battle with the Dervishes of the Sudan.

And two weeks after that, Menelik himself, at the head of his army, returned to Entoto.

Claude stood again before the king. He inclined his head. He said, "Your Majesty."

"Your Imperial Majesty," Menelik corrected him. "With the death of John, I am now not only King of Shoa, Ruler of Harar and the South and the West. I am King of Tigré too. I am Negus Negusti, King of Kings, and Emperor of all Abyssinia."

"Your Imperial Majesty," said Claude.

The king nodded. "Yes, that is better. You have never learned to bow properly, and I have let it pass. But at least you can learn to use my correct title."

His small eyes looked down at Claude from the throne of ivory and gold. During his months in the field his beard had grown longer and fiercer, and the flesh of his broad face was more than ever like the hide of rhinoceros. "I am afraid I must make this audience brief," he said. "As an emperor is greater than a king, so he is also busier; and I have many affairs of state and only a few days in which to deal with them."

"A few days, Your Imperial Majesty?"

"Yes, at week's end I leave again. For the north. For Tigré. I am now, as I say, King of Tigré, Emperor of all Abyssinia, but I wish to make sure that the Tigrean *rases* and chieftains are well aware of it. First I shall have myself crowned in their capital, and then tour my new province to make sure all is peaceful."

"You are a great traveler," said Claude.

"Yes, I must travel much. It is my duty—to my land and my people. Sometimes, I confess, I find it wearisome. But then of course—as I believe they say in Europe—it is at the same time *broadening*."

The rhino-face grinned. Then it stopped grinning. It frowned. "And while I travel about," said Menelik, "wearing myself out, bringing peace to the country, you sit here at your ease, causing trouble."

"Trouble, Your Imper—?"

"I would call it trouble. The priest Haimanot calls it trouble. My God, that's all he's done since I've been back here: gabble on about that damned school of yours."

"If I may explain—"

"No, you may not explain. I am sick of the subject, and I said this also to Haimanot. I said, 'You are a priest. Run your church.' And to you I say, 'You are a teacher. Run your school.' And that is all I say. Stop your squabbling."

"Then it is with your permission—"

"You are Minister of Education, Chancellor of Pedagogy. I repeat; run your school. If you run it unsatisfactorily to me, I assure you that you will soon enough find out."

For a few moments Menelik was silent. His eyes brooded. Then he said: "My country needs a church, and it needs a school. Both. The trouble is that it has now had the church for almost two thousand years and the school for ten months. But we shall have them both. Yes. Yes, by God! On the campaigns I have been on—to Harar, to the south and west—I have seen more than ever what it takes to be a great modern nation. . . . Shall I tell you why we were always victorious? Because we were braver than the others? No. Because God was with us? Perhaps, a little. But mostly it was because we were stronger, we had guns and cannons, the tools of power. . . . And schools, too, and education; they are tools, they are power. And we shall have them as well. Your one school now, but soon more. Yes, more. In the new capital, when we move to it, there will be, to start, at least four, and—"

"The new capital?" said Claude.

"Yes. You have not heard of it? When I return from Tigré I shall begin the planning, and in a year or two we shall move."

"But you have only just built Entoto."

"So I have built it. And I shall leave it. It is better than Ankober, yes;

for a small savage kingdom. But for an empire's capital—no, it will not do. How many of Europe's capitals are on hilltops, tell me that? Hilltops are for barbarians, for savage chiefs and their fortresses. But I am now an emperor, of what one day will be a great and modern nation, and I shall move down from the hilltop to the valley."

"And where is this valley?" asked Claude. "Is it far?"

"No it is not far." Menelik rose and came down from his dais. Beckoning Claude to follow, he crossed the audience hall, went out through a door flanked by rigid guards, and now they were on the terrace above the southern slopes of Entoto. "It is there," he said, pointing to the valley below—the broad green gentle valley sweeping on toward the slopes of Mount Zoquala. "No farther than that. There I shall build my city, the capital of all Abyssinia, and it will be called Addis Ababa—the New Flower."

"The New Flower—"

"Yes." Menelik laughed. "A silly name, is it not? It is the fancy of Taitu, my queen—I mean my empress—and now and then it does no harm to humor a woman. . . . Anyhow, that is what it will be: Addis Ababa. And I will *make* it a flower, a jewel, a place of beauty in the wastes of Africa, and at the same time a city as modern as those of Europe."

They turned back to the palace. "Yes, of *Europe*," he said. "Do you know what I am going to do? I am going to send to Europe, to Switzerland, for an engineer and an architect—the best available—and they will come and help me build my city. They will lay out avenues and squares and parks and markets. They will build me a palace like your palace at Versailles, and a church like St. Peter's, and great buildings for my government. . . . And do you know what else, my friend, my Chancellor of Pedagogy? What else—for *you?* . . . For you and the Royal Academy they will build, not one school, but four—one north, one south, one east, one west—so that my capitol will be ringed by schools and by the light of learning."

The emperor smiled. His face shone with the pride of his vision. Then they re-entered the great hall and crossed it, and as they walked he glanced sidewise at Claude and said, "Your limp is worse since I last saw you."

"Yes, a little," Claude conceded.

"This is the rainy season, and it must be the dampness."

"No, it is only partly the dampness," Claude said. And he told of the attack of a few weeks before.

"And you do not know the reason for this attack?" asked Menelik, when he had finished.

Claude hesitated. Then he answered, "No. It came—and luckily ended —so quickly that I know nothing; saw almost nothing. It was an attempt at robbery, I suppose. The same as could happen in any city."

Menelik had remounted his dais. He sat on the throne and frowned.

"In Addis Ababa," he said, "we shall also have police for such things. Meanwhile, I suggest that you take care and go armed."

"Yes, I had thought of that. And I wished to ask Your Imperial Majesty—"

"Ask me what?"

"If I might be issued a gun. They are unprocurable in Entoto except from the army."

The emperor considered. Then he nodded. "Yes," he said, "you may have a gun. I will give you an order to the Imperial Armory. It might prove useful against thieves or thugs, or even who can tell?—against others, high placed, who might be foolish enough to break my laws, or hire others to do so."

He looked at Claude shrewdly, half-smiling, but did not follow the thought farther. Instead he said, the smile broadening: "And as a token of esteem to my valued Chancellor of Pedagogy, I shall order that the gun be issued free of charge."

Menelik marched off to the north. The school enrollment remained the same. Claude slept with his gun beside him: one of two thousand that had once lain in a warehouse in Mocha.

But no more attackers came.

Nor any further summons from Haimanot.

What came instead, one evening, was a messenger he had not seen before, and what the messenger brought was a letter. "It arrived today," he said, "with a caravan from the coast." Then he left, and Claude sat alone in his hut holding the letter in his hand. It was the first he had received since young Octave Gorbeau had come to his shack in Aden's Crater Town carrying the packet of letters from his mother.

And these he had not read.

The envelope was soiled and battered, and whatever stamp had once been on it had fallen, or been torn, off. Holding it to the light, he saw that it was covered with postmarks—one from Mocha, two from Djibouti, one from Zeila, three from Aden—with dates ranging from three to six months before. The original mark, whatever it may have been, was obliterated beneath them; as was the original script of the address, over which had been roughly printed (when and by whom he could not tell) simply

C. MOREL

COMMERÇANT FRANÇAIS

ABYSSINIE(?)

The envelope crumbled in his hands as he opened it. But the paper within was intact, the writing clear. And the writing was not his mother's.

He read:

My dearest Claude—

It was a miracle. I mean receiving your letter. First, that you remembered the Rue Martine address (where I still live); second, and far greater, that you should write me after all these years. It is the first time, you know, that you have ever written me.

Now, as I answer, I hope for another miracle: that this will reach you. For you gave no address. There was only a postmark from Aden. Upon receiving it, I wrote to your mother, in Cambon, asking for your exact whereabouts; but I have heard nothing in return, and hope this does not mean that she is ill or has passed away. . . . In any case, though, I cannot allow your letter to go unanswered, and so here, now, is my answer, and tomorrow I shall send it off. I shall address it in care of the General Post Office at Aden, in the hope that you will be known there or that they will be able to find you. It is a little like putting a note in a bottle and setting it adrift on the sea. But it is at least better than doing nothing at all.

I wonder, of course, how you came to hear of Albert's death. It was almost two years ago now—very sudden, of a heart attack—and he was buried in Saint Quentin, which is the home of his family. Now I must tell you something else, Claude. I was not with him when he died, for we had been separated for two years before that. He had moved to another flat, several blocks away, and I remained here—alone—for we had no children.

In fact, we had had no marriage, really. And I can say this to you, and to no one else in the world, in the thought that after these many years you will understand. Albert was a good man, a kind and decent and honorable man, and I was very fond of him. But I did not love him. I could not love him —because I loved another. I tried to be a good wife, to make him happy; but it was hard, very hard, for there was nothing to build on. You, you alone, had been our bond, and I knew it, and he knew it. And at last we faced it, we parted—not in anger and recrimination, but quietly, almost fondly—and now he has gone altogether and I hope is at peace.

As for myself, I am now—let us face it—a middle-aged woman. Or almost. But I get along. Sometimes I see the de Bercys (remember?), with my aunt still playing la grande duchesse and my cousin bursting into tears if anyone says boo to her; but her son, now seventeen, is most charming and, attractive. Maurice I see too, and rather more often; for he still lives here in the Quartier, and I go over every week or two to clean up a bit and try to straighten out his papers. It is amazing, and pathetic too, for when he sets his mind to it he can still write like an angel. But as a man, I am afraid, there is nothing that can be done for him. He lives in squalor and long bouts of drunkenness (during which he sometimes speaks of you), and I do not think there could be a man more terribly and utterly alone.

As a professor, Albert, of course, did not leave much money—nor would I have expected him to leave it to me, if he had. So I have been earning my

THE DAY ON FIRE

own living; and you will laugh (or maybe swear) when I tell you how. I am a teacher, Claude. Yes, I too, am now a teacher—of French literature and composition in a school for girls near St. Germain des Prés. My parents, who are still living, were properly shocked at it and have been urging me to come back with them, but I prefer to work and have my independence. On the side I do some reading for publishers, as a sort of part-time editor, and have had the satisfaction of finding a few young writers of promise. But there have been no Claude Morels among them. No flame to light up the mind and heart, as if the day itself were on fire.

—Which brings me, at last, from me to you. *You know, I suppose, that you are no longer the unknown rejected young writer you were when you left Paris, but a name known to everyone—to conjure with—one of the pantheon of "new" French poets. Part of this, perhaps, is because of your disappearance—what many, myself included, thought might have been your death —which has made you into a sort of legend. But there is also a more valid and important reason: that writers, and readers, are at last following where you led and can now understand you, where before they could not. Two years ago Boniface brought out a second edition of your* Selected Poems—*but now using your own old title,* Illuminations—*and it was a tremendous success. And last year, finally, came the publication of* A Season in Hell, *which was even more of a sensation. Now still another book is being planned, with an introduction by one of the leading critics, in which your principal works will appear along with those of Maurice—and Baudelaire. I am so happy for you, Claude. And for poor Maurice, of course, as well. And not a little proud, I admit, that of France's two greatest living poets, I was once cousin to one and—shall we say—friend to the other.*

And you yourself? Do you know of all this, there in faraway Africa? And if you do, what do you think and feel? . . . Do write me again—please—and tell me something of yourself and your life. Are you married? Do you have children? Are you happy? Above all, are you still the Claude I knew?—following your rainbow and your golden birds, sailing the seas, proud, wild, in your Drunken Boat? *I shall answer my question: of course you are. How could you be otherwise, and still be you? . . . If you are again writing poetry, it would be wonderful to hear. But if not, I can understand—after all that it cost you. And while, for the world, it would be a pity, to me you are less important as a poet—however great—than as a man, a human being. For this you must know, Claude: that to me it was never what you did, or had done, or would do, that truly mattered, but what you inwardly, eternally,* are.

It is late now here in Paris, and not a sound comes up from the Rue Martine. Perhaps it is late where you are too. So good night. You sent me your sympathy, and for that I thank you. You sent me your love. And I send you mine—always.

G.

It was late. It was later. The lamp had gone out. But still Claude sat in the darkness with the sheets of paper in his hand.

Then the darkness was grayness. It was light. It was morning. Vayu came by for him, and together they walked up the hill to the school.

Claudette smiled. She bawled. She began to crawl. One day she crawled into the stand supporting the brazier on which her mother was cooking, all but knocking it over. On another, she crawled into the street and was almost stepped on by a mule. "If you cannot manage a single baby," Vayu said to Biri in exasperation, "how do you expect, some day, to manage a whole class-full of girls?"

"And if you are so superior," she asked in return, "why do you want a wife who can do *anything?*"

Claudette bawled—but more often she smiled. Her parents argued —but more often they were loving. In the evenings now, when Claude arrived, the baby was usually being fed, at Biri's breast, and when the nursing was over she was put to bed, and Vayu played his *krar* softly and sang a lullaby. Then, with the baby asleep, the three of them ate—or sometimes the four, if Rahanit was also there—and later they talked, and the men drank *tala;* and more often than not, before the evening was over, Vayu strummed and sang again—but now no lullaby—and Biri danced, again as slim and lithe and lovely as before the baby was born.

As she danced, Claude watched in silence, with half-closed eyes. He watched the grace of her body, the smile on her face, the smile on Vayu's face, the baby asleep in the corner, the lamplight warm and gleaming in the little room. He heard the strumming, the voice, the voice of Vayu . . . and yet not of Vayu . . . not, presently, the voice of a man at all, but the voice of a woman, a girl . . . and the girl sang, not in Harari, not in Amharic, but in French . . . very softly, faintly . . . but he knew the tune, he knew the words. The words. . . . *Au clair de la lu-ne, mon—cousin—Pierrot* . . . And then the words were gone, the song had gone; Vayu had stopped playing. Biri had stopped dancing, and they were looking at him; and Vayu said:

"Is there something wrong, Sidi Claude?"

And Claude said, "No—no. What makes you think so?"

"It is your face, sidi. It is different, strange—. Is it your knee, perhaps? Is it hurting you?"

"No, it is all right. I am all right. Truly."

On some nights there was no music. Only talk. Talk of the school. The coming move down to the valley and the four schools they would have there had fired them all with excitement, and the discussion of plans went on late into the nights. Four schools would of course mean many more students—and from all groups of the population (priests and thugs to the contrary notwithstanding)—and one of them, the emperor willing, might even be the school for girls they had half-seriously, half-jokingly envisioned. Not only the student body but the curriculum too, Claude was determined, must be broadened. But, for both, more books would be needed, and more teachers as well, and neither were to be found in Abyssinia. "If Menelik can import engineers and architects—" said Claude.

"Not to mention guns," said Vayu.

"Yes, not to mention guns ... then he can import some books and teachers too."

And it was agreed that Claude would speak of this to the emperor when he returned from the north.

One day, a holiday with school closed, they went down into the valley that was soon to be Addis Ababa. There were the four of them—Claude and Vayu and Biri and Rahanit (with a neighbor coming in to watch out for Claudette)—and they brought along lunch and a jug of *tala* and a notebook in which to mark down preferred locations for the new schools. It was now again the dry season, and the sun was brilliant, with Zoquala standing clear and snowless in the highland sky; but though the plateaus around it were dry and yellow, the valley itself was green with flowing streams. They moved down from Entoto through tall stands of cedar and clumps of juniper and for hours crisscrossed the wide basin of grove and meadow, through the streets and squares of the still imaginary city. They drew maps in the notebook and argued about school sites; and each time they agreed on one someone would say, "No Menelik will want this one for his palace.... And this one for his law court ... And this for his stable ... And this for the Empress Taitu; the trees are so thick she would not be able to squeeze out between them." And then they laughed and walked on and came to a flowered meadow, and Vayu said, looking about him: "Yes, Taitu may be fat, but I do not think she is stupid; for the New Flower will be a good name after all."

Through the heart of the meadow ran a stream. Sitting beside it, they ate their lunch, and Vayu made Biri stand beside it, holding the *tala* jug, in the identical pose in which he had first seen her on the day he and Claude reached Entoto. And when they had finished eating they did not move on, but remained through the afternoon, talking—of the new schools, the new city, the future; and when they were tired of talking still sat there, resting, looking about them, in the mellowing sunlight. Claude looked at Zoquala, at the hill of Entoto, at the stream descending from the hill, flowing beside them. And he thought of other streams he had sat beside —and of the rivers. Of the Ahwash, beyond the wastes: that was most recent, yet now almost two years ago. Of the Web Shebeli, before that. Of others long, long before: of the Seine and the Meuse. And then idly he tore a blank page from the notebook beside him, and, folding it several times, set it adrift in the swift stream.

Vayu was watching him.

"It is a boat, sidi," he said.

"Yes, a boat. A Drunken Boat."

"Drunken? I do not understand. How can a boat be drunk?"

Claude pointed. "Look at it. How it wobbles and lurches. Is that not drunken?"

"The stream is fast, sidi, and it is frail."

"Yes, frail. Frail, too." Claude watched the boat drift out of sight. "A Drunken Boat," he said, "as frail as a May butterfly. . . ."

When at last they bestirred themselves it was late afternoon and the sun was sinking. As they climbed back up the hill toward Entoto, the sky above them was deep violet-blue.

The rains returned.

Claudette had colic.

Claude's knee grew stiffer.

He walked more—even in the heaviest rains—before school, and after, and often, too, at night, if he did not go to Vayu and Biri's. When he walked at night he carried his gun, and when he went to bed he still kept it close at hand. But no one followed him in the streets; no one came to his hut. He walked alone, and he slept alone. On some nights he did not sleep, but lay through the hours with eyes open, looking up into darkness.

Menelik returned from the north—from Tigré—and his army was larger, the celebration greater, than ever before. But he did not soon send for Claude, as was his custom. A week, and then two, went by, and he did not send for him; and it was Claude, on his own, who at last went up to the palace and requested an audience. And a few days later he stood once more in the great hall of the palace before the Negus Negusti, the Lion of Judah.

The emperor looked at him, and he looked at the emperor. And he was still the lion—or the rhino—tall, broad, and powerful, dressed in the robes of empire, his face filled with the pride of empire . . . and he was the same as before; yet not quite the same; there was a difference in his face . . . and at last Claude realized what it was.

"Yes," Menelik said, "that is right. I have shaved my beard. They say that beards are becoming less fashionable in the capitals of Europe, and I would not wish it said that I am behind the times in the capital of Abyssinia."

He laughed. Claude smiled.

"Then you are not displeased, Your Imperial Majesty?" he said.

"Displeased? Displeased at what? My naked chin?"

"No, at me. At the school. You have not sent for me, and I thought perhaps that—"

Menelik waved a hand. "No, I have been busy, that is all. Immensely busy. I am emperor now, not only in name but in fact, and it is harder work, if you will pardon me, than being a schoolteacher. Tigré is mine —yes—and well under control; I have left Ras Abbata there to see to that. But still there are things one must keep an eye on. All over the country there are things, and people, I must keep an eye on—and beyond the country, on the Dervishes, the Italians. Then there are the plans for the new capital, the New Flower, I am working on those. Soon I shall send to Switzerland for the engineer and the architect. But there is more to it than that. Much more. The Swiss will handle the details, yes, but they will not tell me what sort of city I shall have. I shall decide that myself. I am deciding now. Everything. Where the palace will be, and how it will look. About the cathedral, the churches, the law courts, the barracks, the roads and streets and squares and markets. Yes, all of this—I am deciding. *I* am planning. And more, too. I am thinking not only of the present but the future; and in the future do you know what my capital will have besides all this?" Menelik paused, and his eyes flashed with the pride of his vision. "It will have a *railway*," he said. "That is what. A railway from the coast to Addis Ababa. A railway into the heart of Africa, built by the emperor who was once a savage Nigger King. . . ."

His voice had risen. He himself had all but risen from his throne. Now, abruptly, however, he stopped; he sat back; he looked at Claude, and when he spoke again it was quietly.

"And you, my Chancellor of Pedagogy," he said, "need not be worried, for I have not forgotten your schools, either."

"I am glad, Your Imperial Majesty," said Claude.

"You have been making plans for them?"

"Yes, we have been planning."

"And you know your needs?" The emperor chuckled. "Other than guns, I mean, to protect yourself from the priests."

"We shall need, most of all, more books and more teachers. And these are not available in Abyssinia."

"We shall send for them then, to Europe. As for the engineer and architect. Submit to me a list of your requirements, and I shall have the letters sent off as soon as possible."

"That is kind of Your Imperial Majesty, but the letters are not necessary."

"Not necessary? What do you mean, not necessary?"

"I mean," said Claude, "that I shall go to Europe myself."

There was a silence.

Menelik stared at him.

"That is why you wanted to see me," he said.

"Yes," said Claude.

"You have come to ask my permission to go?"

"No."

"No?"

"I do not—if I may say so, Your Imperial Majesty—require your permission. I am in charge of the school, yes; your Minister of Education—and I hope a loyal one. But I am not an Abyssinian. Not one of your subjects."

The emperor still stared. His eyes were small and black. In the next instant, it seemed, the lion would roar.

But he did not roar. He said quietly, "I see. Yes, I see. An interesting point; you should be a lawyer instead of a teacher . . . And what, my friend, will happen to the school *while* you are gone?"

"I have two competent assistants," said Claude. "They will be able to manage during the short time I am away."

"Short time?"

"Yes, short. I shall go and return as quickly as possible."

"How do I know that? How do I know you will come back at all?"

"You will have to take my word for it. I have been happy here. I *want* to come back."

Menelik was silent again, studying him.

"You will go—and return—eh? You will get the books, the teachers, and that is all?"

"Not quite all, Your Imperial Majesty. There is one other thing too."

"And what is that?"

"I intend also," Claude said, "to bring back a wife."

"A wife?" said Menelik.

"Yes. Does that seem so strange to you?"

"It—it seems—" For the first time since Claude had known him the Lion of Judah was at a loss for words. "It is unexpected," he said. "It is surprising . . . To put a point to it, I thought you had more sense."

Claude smiled. "It is I who will have to be the judge of that, Your Imperial Majesty."

"There has never been a *ferangi* woman in Abyssinia. What will she do here? How will she get along?"

"I think she will get along all right. She is not the usual sort of woman, you see. She is strong, brave, willing to try and dare . . . And also, she is a teacher."

"A teacher?"

"Yes. In a school for girls in Paris. And we had been hoping—I and my associates—that one of the four new schools in Addis Ababa could be a school for girls."

Menelik opened his mouth and shut it. He said nothing.

"My wife," Claude said, "would be capable of running such a school.

Also, there is the wife of my assistant, Vayu, who soon could qualify as *her* assistant." He paused, but the emperor still said nothing. "I hope that the idea does not entirely offend you," he said. "I know it is a sudden thought —a new one—"

"No," said Menelik, "it is not new."

Claude looked at him questioningly.

"My empress, Taitu—she has had the idea for a long time. Ever since you began teaching in Ankober. Just as the high priest talks against a school, so does she talk *for* one—a school for girls as well as boys—gabble, gabble, gabble, until I am out of my mind."

Claude smiled again. "Then it is not impossible—"

The emperor brooded. "I am not promising anything. I must think about it; talk again to the empress." He made a sound that was half laugh, half grunt. "Talk *to* her—hah! I will say three words, and then *she* will talk and I will listen, and I will end up doing anything at all, simply to keep her quiet."

For another moment he brooded. Then he pulled himself up. His face hardened. "So, that is enough of this," he said. "I am the Emperor of Abyssinia. I have a thousand things to think of. My country, my people, my army, my conquests, Tigré, Harar, Gallas, Shankallas, the Dervishes, the Italians, guns, cannons, money, my new capital, my new palace, my railway, everything—and I am sitting here wasting my time on a *school for girls*." He waved an imperious hand. "All right, go now. Go! . . . You will pay your respects to me before you leave. . . . But now go. I am busy."

Claude bowed and took his leave. As he walked across the great hall, Menelik muttered behind him: "Girls. Mother of God—girls! Like everything else in the world, soon even my empire will be run by women. . . ."

Vayu listened. His eyes shone.

"Oh sidi, Sidi Claude," he said, "it is so fine, so wonderful—"

"Yes," said Claude, "there will be schools now that are really schools."

"And the other—that is wonderful too. That you will have a wife and a home. That you will have a baby too, a son—yes, I am sure, sidi, you will have a son—and he will play with Claudette."

"And together," said Claude, "they can push over the brazier."

He assembled his caravan. And it was not difficult, for he had a warrant from Menelik: for men and mules, for food and guns. The men and mules would go only as far as the Ahwash, and from there on he would have, instead, the desert Arabs and Somalis with their camels. It would be not nearly so large a caravan as that with which he had come, for it would have no heavy cargo to carry; but at the same large enough, at least from the Ahwash on, to be safe from attack by the Danakils.

"Across the desert," Claude said to Vayu, "I plan on twenty camels and fifteen men. With myself, that is sixteen and should be enough."

"And with seventeen," said Vayu, "it is even better."

"Seventeen?"

"With me, Sidi Claude. You have forgotten me."

"You? You are not coming."

"Yes. Yes, I am. To the coast with you—to Tajoura. And then I will come back with another caravan."

Claude shook his head. "No, it is no good. Impossible. There is the school—"

"I have thought all about the school, and it is all right, it works. First —have you forgotten?—there is the long vacation that is coming soon. Then, for when there is not vacation, it is also all right. Rahanit and I have talked about it. We have looked around. And we have found the answer. There is a man we have met, a clerk in the court, and he is very bright, very eager—like Rahanit—and Rahanit says that with the two of them together. . . ."

Vayu continued arguing. And Claude to shake his head. "And also there is Biri," Claude said. "And the baby. You cannot desert them like that."

"Who is deserting? I am going on a trip, that is all—like any man of affairs. Sometimes it is good that a man get away for a little."

"But—"

"The baby has no more colic. She is well. And Biri is well too. I have saved some money and she will have enough, and there is her mother and family who will help if there is any trouble."

Claude again said no. And again, and again. But still, through each day that remained, Vayu persisted.

"But *why?*" Claude demanded. "Why must you come? What sense does it make?"

And at last Vayu answered, quietly, "Very well, Sidi Claude, I will tell you why. It is your knee."

"My knee?"

"Yes. I do not like the way it has been. The way you limp."

"My knee is all right."

"No, it is not. I can see."

"It is only the rains, the dampness."

"I hope it is only that, sidi; but still I am coming. I will not let you be alone in the desert with strangers. And if you do not let me come with you, then I will get a mule and camel of my own and follow you. . . ."

So, on the day of departure, it was Claude and Vayu together who rode up to the palace to pay their respects to Menelik.

And the emperor looked at them and scowled and said, "So the school system of Abyssinia collapses. And my teachers vanish."

"No, it will not collapse," Claude told him. "And we are not vanishing; we shall be back. Vayu in three months, or so, and I in no more than six."

Menelik grunted. "If your wife lets you," he said.

"She will let me. She will want to come herself. She is that sort of woman."

"Hmm—" said Menelik. And again, "Hmm—"

Then, after a pause:

"You are ready to leave?"

"Yes, Your Imperial Majesty."

"You have all you need?"

"Yes."

"My treasurer has issued you the funds for travel and the purchase of books?"

"Yes."

"Then," said Menelik, "there is nothing further. You may go." Turning, he reached down to the side of his throne. "And I hope," he added, "that this does not add too much to the burden of your caravan."

In his hand he held a sack, made of leopard skin, and for a moment he held it, then let it fall on the dais before him. The sack was heavy. The dais trembled. "In Addis Ababa," said Menelik, "I shall have a better dais, made of marble."

Claude looked at the sack.

"The young one is strong," the emperor said, nodding at Vayu. "He can carry it out to your mules."

Claude looked up from the sack. He looked at Menelik.

"Another thing we will have here too, when we are more civilized," said Menelik, "is paper money. Meanwhile we must use what we have —silver thalers, gold, gems, and such. Rather a nuisance. But a nuisance that you will find redeemable, I think, for roughly two hundred thousand French francs."

He consulted a slip of paper. "One hundred thousand francs," he said, "is a fifty-year advance on salary, so I will no longer have to be bothered with monthly payments. Ninety-five thousand is in settlement of an old bill for nineteen hundred guns, which seems to have been overlooked by my accountants. The remaining five thousand is an imperial wedding gift to my Chancellor of Pedagogy."

The Lion of Judah put the paper aside, and his broad pock-marked face spread into a white-toothed grin. "No, do not thank me, my professorial Hun," he said. "Thank the late King John of Tigré, for whose estate I am now the humble administrator."

The sky was clear, the sun shone, as they rode down the hill through Entoto. They came to Vayu's hut, and Biri appeared and kissed them both, and then stood looking after them, holding Claudette in her arms. A few minutes later they passed the school, and all the students were in a line outside, waving and shouting, with Rahanit at one end and the new teacher, the ex-clerk of court, at the other. Then they came to the base of the hill, and the village of Biri's family, and the broad plain beyond.

Here the sun receded; the clouds came; it began to rain. And when, after a while, Claude looked back, both Entoto and Zoquala were invisible behind them.

It rained for the rest of the day. Toward midafternoon Claude's knee began to stiffen, and dismounting, he walked on the muddy trail behind the rump of his mule.

38

It took them less than three days to reach Ankober.

And Vayu said, "If we can go so well the whole way, sidi, we will be in Tajoura within a month."

The old capital was nothing like what it had been when they left it. Indeed, it had shrunk to little more than a village, with hundreds of its huts pulled down for firewood and the skeleton of the old royal palace standing gaunt and lonely against the sky. During the half-day and night they spent there the sky was clear; but, below, the familiar sea of cloud buttressed the walls of the great escarpment, and the next morning, as they began the descent, they were soon wrapped in a pall of fog and rain.

It was cold, too. They kept their shammas tightly drawn across shoulders and throat. And underfoot the earth was so steep a maze of muck and rock that even the mules floundered, and sometimes fell, as they groped their way cautiously downward. At one point Claude's fell and rolled on him. And thereafter he went again on foot, hobbling and stumbling through the gray wet hours.

"It will not be for long, though, sidi," Vayu cheered him. "Soon we will be on flat land in the sun, and your knee will be better."

And on the next day the rain *did* stop. The sun reappeared, at first wan behind the mist, then full and bright, and the slope eased and leveled off into the plain of the Ahwash. Like Ankober, however, the river, when they reached it, was not what it had been before; no longer a trickling current in the sands and mud flats, but a torrent fed by the swollen streams of the escarpment; and it took them the better part of a day before they were across it, soaked and battered on its eastern bank.

Then again there were the visits to the villages, up- and downstream, in search of camels and drivers—until at last they had their fifteen men and twenty beasts. And then the Shoans, with their mules, recrossed the Ahwash and filed back toward the highlands, while their new hands made ready for the trip across the wastes. These, as they had planned, were all Arabs and Somalis—for, though there were plenty of "tame" Danakils available, they took none—and they seemed a competent lot, old professionals of the trade routes, most of whom had come in from the coast with one of Menelik's caravans only a week or two before. It was not long, however, before some were staring curiously at the bulging leopard-skin sack. And Vayu said to Claude, "I think it is better, sidi, if you carry the treasure yourself. In a sort of belt, maybe, such as you used to have in Harar."

So in one of the villages they bought a length of heavy cloth, and Vayu folded and sewed it into a makeshift belt. And in their tent, on the night before departure, they transferred the riches from sack to belt, and Claude bound it about himself under his clothing.

They left the Ahwash on the tenth day after leaving Entoto. Behind them, the vast escarpment of Abyssinia rose skyward, its crest lost in cloud and rain. Ahead, in bright sunlight, was the desert. And from escarpment to desert, as the camels plodded eastward, soared the arch of a rainbow.

Ayeee—ayaaa—

Dust rose. The camels swayed. Now the Ahwash was gone. Clouds and rainbow were gone. There was only the sun and the waste.

They were unused to the heat of the waste. It was enormous, encompassing. At first the sweat poured from Claude's flesh, soaking him as thoroughly as rain or river. Then the sweat dried, there was no more left in the flesh, and his body was dust-dry and burning.

"The knee is better now, is it not, sidi?" said Vayu.

And Claude nodded.

But the burning in the knee was worst of all.

With a smaller caravan, their order of march was more elastic and variable than on the way in. Sometimes Claude led, with Vayu in the rear; sometimes their positions were reversed; and often they both rode together ahead, with the chief driver, Hassan, at the procession's end. As before, guns were carried by all, at all times, and a careful watch kept on the ridges and hillsides. But there was no sign of Danakils. On its forays both against the Italians and to Harar, wings of Menelik's army had passed through this section of the desert, and it was said that most of the tribesmen had fled far to the north. At night the usual watches were kept, but only of two men at a time on four-hour shifts, and all that was seen were the eyes of jackals and hyenas.

With the camels lightly laden, they averaged, at Claude's estimate, some eighteen miles a day. At intervals they passed the sites of old caravan camps, occasionally using them themselves; but whether any had been their own Claude could not tell, for there was little or nothing in the waste to distinguish one place from any other. During the fourth and fifth days he peered ahead through the glare, searching out one landmark he *would* know: the six upright staves, one with a nailed crosspiece, with which they had marked the graves of Fitzsimmons and his five drivers. But they did not appear. The waste rolled on, empty. They had been taken by man or beast, or lay buried in wind-blown sand.

There was no wind now. There was only the flaming sun. In the sun, under his burnous, the belt, tight and bulging, was a smothering weight around his waist.

Only the nights brought relief, calm and cool under the stars, and when supper was over he and Vayu lay in their tent, with the belt and his gun lying beside him. His fingers touched the gun, and its feel was familiar, for it was one of those they had brought in from Mocha. Then they touched the belt, felt the coins and treasure within the belt; and looking up in the darkness with half-open eyes, he saw the broad pock-marked grin of the Lion of Judah. He thought of Menelik and the school and the two years just past. And then his thoughts moved ahead: across the waste, to the end of the waste, to the sea, across the seas—to France, to Paris. He was going back at last, after more than ten years; and that in itself was inconceivable enough. He was going back, not in poverty, not a tramp, a vagrant, as he had always been, but a man of means, of wealth; and that, even a few weeks past, had been more than inconceivable.... He was going back to claim a wife. To claim Germaine. Who loved him. Who had loved him since they were both sixteen years old.... He was going as a man who could support her; who could be a husband, a father; not a piece of flotsam drifting by on a stormy sea.

He was going to claim a wife. But would she consent to be claimed? Would she have him? There were times when the thought rose and hovered above him like a specter.... But then he felt inside his burnous. He felt the letter that he had carried with him every day since its arrival. And the specter faded, for he knew then: yes, she would have him.... He did not need to bring the letter out. He remembered all of it. He remembered: *I could not love him, because I loved another*. He remembered: *You sent me your love. And I send you mine—always*.

He would go, he would claim her, he would return. For that he knew too: that he must return to Abyssinia. In part, perhaps, it was because of what he now owed Menelik; but only in small part; he would have returned anyhow, if he had not been paid a franc. For the true reason was deeper, and inward, and was that there, in the high heart of Africa, he had, for the first time in his life, been content and at peace. Once before, at certain periods in Harar, he had perhaps come close to it. But only close, never all the way. For he had not been at heart a trader, a *commerçant;* he had hated Rappe's ledgers; he had built his wall of ledgers and tried to hide in the garden within. . . . Whereas now, as a teacher . . . It was strange, as inconceivable as the rest; a few years before he could not have imagined it. But as a teacher he had been happy.

In the desert night he remembered words long since forgotten; the words of Heine he had spoken to himself in the days of the Commune and the Golden Flame: ". . . I am a soldier in the war for the liberation of man. . . ." And he thought now: "As a teacher, perhaps, I can do more toward that liberation than emperors and generals, governments and armies."

When he returned to Abyssinia he would be both teacher and husband. His wife, too, would be a teacher. . . . For that he knew, along with the rest. That Germaine would come. That she would *want* to come. That the girl who had twice followed him to the *Quartier Latin*, who would have gone with him anywhere, penniless and starving, could not have changed that much in eighteen years—or a hundred. . . . She would come with him to Abyssinia. To be with him; to share his life, his work. And of all the things that would happen, that thing, that one, would be the most important— the sharing. For, with men, over the years, he had sometimes shared: first with Chariol; then strangely, terribly, with Druard; later with Mackenzie, with Father Lutz, and most of all with Vayu. But with a woman, never. Not with Nagunda, except in the flesh. Not, certainly, with any of the other women he had known—and fled. Not with his sister, except when she was very young. Not with his mother—ever—and that, of course, had been the beginning of everything, the dark thread that ran through everything. . . . Until now. . . . Until he took Germaine as wife. Until they came, the two of them, to Abyssinia; to live together, work together, love together—*sharing*—the two as one, yet each whole and complete. . . .

The days passed. And the nights. The mornings followed the nights.

And one morning, when they rose, Vayu smiled and said, "It is a nice name, sidi—Germaine."

"I have been dreaming, eh?"

"Yes, you have been dreaming, every night. And if it were not for the dreams I would still know nothing about your lady."

"Be a little patient," said Claude, "and you will meet her."

"Yes. But meanwhile I am curious. You have told me nothing, sidi. What is she like? Is she beautiful?"

"Yes," Claude said, "she is beautiful."

"The same as Biri?"

"No, not the same. Biri is beautiful too. But they are not the same. They are different."

"I hope she will like me," said Vayu.

"Do not worry. She will like you."

"Because I know already how much I will like her. It is strange: that I know, though you have told me nothing. . . . Do you know that, sidi? In all the years we have been together you have never spoken of her."

"No," said Claude, "perhaps not."

"But you have thought of her much? And written to her too?"

"Yes, we have written each other."

"If she is beautiful, sidi, she must love you very much. For she has waited for you a long time."

"Yes," said Claude, "we have both waited a long time."

Out of the stillness rose the wind. It blew for two days and two nights, while they plodded on, shoulders hunched, faces covered against the streaming sand, and through the darkness lay wakeful in their flapping tents.

Then the wind died. It was stiller than ever. And hotter. They came to the black lands, to the end of the earth, but still the earth spread on before them, unending, cinder-black, beneath the flaming sun. The sun seemed not only in the sky but in the earth itself, as well. They were moving, not under, but *through* it; it was around them, within them; it was in Claude's eyes and his brain and his body; in the flesh of his waist, where his belt chafed and galled until the skin was raw. It was in his knee—most of all in his knee—becoming each day hotter, larger, more painful, until the knee itself was like the sun, swollen and burning. Each day he set off from camp mounted, like the others. When the pain became too much he got down and walked. But, for the first time in his memory, the walking did not help.

In their tent at night Vayu looked at the knee. "I will bind it, sidi," he said. "With a binding it will be cooler; there will not be the friction." And with strips of cloth from their extra clothing he fashioned a bandage, and tied it carefully about Claude's leg.

Then he said, "When you are in France, sidi—or even, first, in Aden —you should see a doctor. It is now a long time that the knee has been a trouble."

Claude nodded and said, "Yes, I shall see a doctor."

"It is now—what?—six years that that it has been trouble; since you went south from Harar with the men of Abou Dakir. . . . That was when you first hurt it, was it not, sidi?"

"I hurt it then—yes. But it was not the first time. The first time was long ago, when I was a boy."

"What did you do, sidi?"

"I jumped from a train and fell." Claude was silent a moment. Then he added, "And later it was hurt again. I was shot."

"Shot? You have never told me that, sidi. How were you shot? You were a soldier once? It was in a war?"

"Yes," said Claude. "Yes, it was in a war."

He tried walking with the bandage. He tried riding. And it was better, a little better—for one day, and a second—and then the same as before. He rode and walked and rode again, and they made the day's journey, and at dusk pitched their camp; and in their tent, each night after supper, Vayu dampened the bandage and rewound it, and then Claude lay in the darkness and tried to sleep. Sometimes he did not sleep; sometimes he did; and when he did, he dreamed. But the dreams were no longer of Germaine. They were of a train plunging through darkness; of steel rails beneath it, and ties and cinders—cinders black as those of the cinder desert; and he jumped, he fell, he lay in their blackness, and a whistle screeched in the night. . . . They were of Druard—the first dream in years he had had of Druard—and the skull-like face hung before him, the revolver pointed, glinted, fired; and his knee seemed to burst in a blaze of pain, and the pain woke him . . . and he lay in the night, his hands clutching his gun, sweating and trembling as he had used to when a boy. . . .

He dreamed during the day, too. He let himself dream, for it took his mind off the pain. And in the day, too, he could control his dreams; they were not of the past but of the future; of the desert gone at last, of the pain gone, of the sea, a ship, a shore, of France, of Paris—of Germaine.

Dreaming, he walked and rode and walked again, through the hours and days; and now the black lands were behind them, they were again in the brown lands, the lands of dust and thorn and low eroded hills. It was late afternoon, and he was on foot, limping, at the end of the caravan.

He had been walking a long time. His bandage had loosened. He stopped and retied it. Then, as he moved on again, a wind sprang up, the dust blew, and for perhaps an hour he groped through a brown streaming veil, with everything around him blotted wholly from sight. When the wind dropped, and the dust, it was as suddenly as they had risen. But now there was no caravan ahead. There was no trail. He had strayed from the trail. There was nothing but brown miles, brown hills, an empty sky; and the sky was darkening, for the sun had set. Far ahead, there was a notch in the hills—a likely passage, he thought, for the trail—and he moved toward it. But it was miles away; as he moved, it seemed to come no closer. And finally he could move no more. His leg buckled and he fell; he rose—and fell again—and sat in the dust and stones in the thickening dusk. He would fire his gun, he decided. The others would already be looking for him; they would hear the shot and find him. And only then did he realize that he had left the gun strapped to the pack on his camel.

He tried to crawl, but it was worse than walking. He shouted, but when the sound died there was only stillness. . . . And then, as he looked up, as he listened, something besides stillness. Something that moved, that watched him. . . . "It is the Danakils," he thought. "The Danakils, who have been following and waiting." And now *he* waited; the movements came closer, they became shapes. But they were not Danakils. Danakils did not have four legs or sloping backs or yellow eyes. And now it was night, and the eyes shone. They shone in a ring around him, and moved closer—as they had moved once, long ago, in a crumbled garden. And he could smell the hyenas; he could hear their breathing, the sound of their pads on the gravel. . . . And then beyond them, suddenly—at last— another sound, the sound of voices. He saw lights, the flare of torches, the shapes of camels, of riders. He saw Vayu, heard Vayu's voice, shouting, "Sidi! Sidi! It is you! We have found you!"

Vayu made him ride.

"But it is harder than walking," Claude said.

"We will make it so it is not harder," said Vayu. And with the help of the drivers he fashioned a sort of truss which they attached to the back of Claude's camel, so that his leg was held out rigid away from the friction of its flanks.

But this, too, was worse than walking. The projecting leg seemed to catch every molecule of heat in the furnace of sunlight, and the swelling and pain, instead of lessening, increased. Claude dismounted. Again he walked. Now Vayu made sure that either he himself or one of the drivers rode behind him. But he did not lag again. He kept the pace. He moved on through the hours; through the furnace, in the blinding shattering sun. And it was like—what? He remembered. Like Italy. He was *in* Italy, in the dust of Tuscany, in its fierce sunlight, stumbling on toward the sea. He was in the deserts of Egypt, of Tripoli, of Yemen, of Somalia. He was on the plains of the Worombu country, stumbling on with Nagunda toward the Web Shebeli. He moved through dream, through hallucination. Only one thing was not hallucination, and that was pain, monstrous and searing. . . . What would stop the pain? Araq, he thought. He must have araq, gourds of araq. Or absinthe. Or hashish. . . . No, there was something better than those; far better. Nagunda's herbs. He must apply her herbs again, and he turned to her—but she was not there. A young man was there, and he knew the young man. He was making an important trip with him—a trip to the sea. And now the young man spoke and said, "You are all right, sidi? We are not going too fast?" And he answered, "No, we must go faster, faster. Or the *Ecole Centrale* will be closed for the night. . . ."

"We will stop, sidi," said Vayu, "and rest for a day."

"No," he said. "No."

But whether they stopped or not, he could not later remember.

Nor did it make any difference, he thought. What happened now did not matter—but only the future—and he thrust his mind into the future. He thought of the sea and a ship, and of France. He thought of Germaine. And this was *not* hallucination. She existed. She was real. Under his burnous was her letter, and he felt it, and it was real. He thought of her writing the letter, in the room on the Rue Martine; and he remembered the room, he remembered her entering it, and what she had worn and how she had looked, her white face, her violet eyes; except that then he could not look, he could not bear to see them, for they had been the eyes of Chariol's wife. He thought of the times they had met before. Of the night she had found him in the café on the Boul' Mich; the night of Herz and absinthe and the green knives. Of the day she had come to his room and cleaned it, and then spoken her love, and he had lashed out at her in his terror and shame. Of her sitting at table, descending the stairs, in the house of the de Bercys. Most of all—most clearly—of her walking beside him, in her prim school uniform, through the autumn streets of Passy. Of the dusk and the early moon and her watching it, her smiling, singing: *"Au clair de la lu-ne. . . ."*

And it was not until then that he realized he had been wrong. That he was not thinking of the future but of the past. That the girl he had known was long since gone; was a woman of, now, thirty-six; a widow, a schoolteacher.

And she too, Germaine, in her letter: was she too not thinking of the past? Of the boy she had once known; not the present man. Surely not of a skeletal, leather-skinned, cold-eyed ghost of a man lurching on a throbbing misshapen leg through the dust of Africa. "Are you still the Claude I knew?" she had asked. And had answered herself: "Of course you are." And even if the outward did not matter—and no, to her it would not—what of the inward? Of what he once *had been* and what he now *was*? He might be a vagabond, a trader, a teacher—whatever—and she would accept it. But beneath it, deep within, she would expect at least some remnant of the past. Her letter had been full of talk of his poetry: of *The Drunken Boat*, *Illuminations*, *A Season in Hell*. And what was left of it—of all the dreams, all the words, so long buried in his belly?

. . . once if I remember well if I remember well if I remember my life was a feast and I strung garlands on the Three Magi and Christmas and had been damned by the rainbow . . . and yes, there had been a rainbow over the escarpment of Abyssinia . . . *and boulevards too boulevards of raised platforms and the polar night skies fabulous and false and false and false with being of beauty with golden birds oh host of golden birds of scarlet birds of white cities of black tribes and black is A and A is black and E is white and I is red I is another and*

U is green and O is blue yes blue blue blue O is omega—Ω—blue deep violet-blue. . . .

And the words subsided. They lay dead again in his belly, in the burning flesh, the burning knee. And it was morning again—some morning—and Vayu was bending over him adjusting the bandage, and now his mind was clear and he smiled, and Vayu smiled back at him.

"You have been dreaming again, Sidi Claude," he said.

"Of Germaine?"

"No, this time not of Germaine. It was of—" Vayu groped. "As you dreamed once in Harar," he said, "after you had the fever. Full of words and pictures, like a sort of song. And Father Lutz and I listened, and he said he thought you had once been a poet."

Claude said nothing. Vayu had loosened the bandage, so that the knee lay bare.

"*Were* you once a poet, sidi?" he asked.

It was another moment before Claude answered.

"Yes—once," he said.

"Then why no longer? . . . It is so wonderful, I think, to be a poet. To make beauty in an ugly world."

"I did not make beauty, Vayu. I made more ugliness. I made evil."

"Evil? Evil from poetry, sidi?—No, how could that be?"

Claude looked at Vayu, kneeling beside him. Then, raising himself, he looked at his bare leg; at the flesh, white and red and purple, at the monstrous bloating, the skin stretched tight and hard as a drumhead, seeming ready to burst from the poison within.

He pointed. He said, "There is my poetry, boy—all that is left of my poetry. That is evil, is it not? That is ugliness and evil and corruption and death. . . ."

Death moved slowly toward them out of the waste ahead. It was two staves, one upright, one nailed across it. Jensen's cross was still standing.

Then they came to other crosses. First, Fitzsimmons'. . . . But why was that here? . . . Then to a row of others: Lutz's, Egal's, Nagunda's—except that Egal's was no cross but only a single stave—and beside Nagunda's, a smaller cross with no name. Beyond them, apart, was another—Chariol's —and beyond that still another, alone in the waste; and Claude rushed at it—to rip it out, to throw it down—but he could not reach it, it receded before him; and running, he stumbled and fell and lay prone on the ground, until Vayu and the drivers came and lifted him up again.

Then he was riding again. But not the same as before. He was no longer upright, with his leg projecting in a splint, but lying in a sort of harness, strapped to the camel's back, in the way sick men had been carried on the caravan through the Ogaden. His leg was braced and covered, and at intervals Vayu or one of the drivers appeared and poured water on the covering. But the water was as hot as the sunlight; it rose in steam from the cloth, leaving it, in a few minutes, as dry as before. . . . And, in his lying position, his face was turned up toward the sun. . . . Pulling the hood of his burnous over his face, he shut the sun out. But now he could not breathe, he stifled; and soon he pushed it back again, he faced the sun; and the sun beat down, shattering, splintering, through his closed lids, into his eyes, into his brain, his blood, his bones; into the great burning swelling mass that was his crippled leg. And its flame was yellow, it was blue, then fiery red, then white—and now everything was white, a blinding glare of whiteness—and Vayu was beside him, saying, "We are at Lake Assal, sidi. The lake of salt. It is not much farther now. We are almost there."

He lay. He rode. The camel swayed. The earth swayed—and the sun. Then he was plucking at the straps that held him. He pulled, strained, loosened them, slid down from the camel to the swaying earth. And he fell—but rose—and he walked again. He walked on the trail behind the camel—as he had walked so many miles, so many years. And Vayu was beside him, protesting, but he did not listen, he did not hear. He heard only another voice, a distant voice, and it said *"Be strong. Be proud. . . ."* And he walked on. He would walk into Tajoura; not be carried in; and if strength would not take him, pride would. And it did. He walked in pride, as in the old days—as Attila, as Lucifer—defying the miles, defying the pain, defying defeat and death, defying God Himself. . . .

No.

Not that last, he thought. Not Him. Not God.

Out of the dead, out of the grave of the past, words rose again, and he spoke the words. *"God is my strength, and I praise God. . . ."*

He lay still and looked up, but it was not at the sun. It was not at the walls of a tent, but at a ceiling. He was in a room. In Tajoura.

He was on a dhow, on the deck of a dhow, propped on a sort of couch of cushions under an awning, and all around him was the sea. He saw the sea, heard it, felt it; but he could not smell it. What he smelled was something else, with sloping backs, yellow eyes, and the loathsome stench filled his nostrils.

"The hyenas," he said to Vayu. "The hyenas—drive them away."

"I have driven them, sidi," Vayu told him. "They are gone now." And he sat looking down at the couch of cushions—at the thing that had once been a leg.

He was in a place that was both a room and a boat. But it was no longer a dhow; it was a great ship, he was in a cabin; and between dhow and cabin there were shifting images. There were the black walls of a dead volcano. There were docks, godowns, a harbor crowded with ships. There were faces—known faces. Of the Gorbeaus: father, mother, son. Of Marcel Rappe, the glasses glinting. And something else had glinted too. A syringe. A needle. And a doctor had talked, and he had not heard him. But the needle had glinted, and the pain had gone.

It was gone now, as he lay in the cabin and looked at Vayu. An enormous clarity seemed to fill the cabin, and his mind.

Reaching beneath his pillow, he drew out his money belt. Or, rather, two belts, two halves of the belt, for he had cut it in two; and he handed one half to Vayu.

Vayu stared at it. "No," he murmured. "No, sidi—"

"Yes," said Claude, putting the other half back under the pillow. "This is mine. That is yours."

"No, sidi, not so much. It is a fortune. . . . And not now. When you come back—when we are again together—then maybe you will give me something, something small, and I will take it—"

"You will take this."

"But—but it is—"

"It is yours," Claude said. "And we will not argue."

There was a silence. Then, above them, the ship's horn sounded—humming, echoing, in the little room.

"So, go now," said Claude.

For a moment Vayu stood motionless. Then he dropped the belt. He flung himself on his knees beside the berth. "No—no—" he cried. "Do not make me go. Take me with you, sidi! Please, please, Sidi Claude, take me with you!"

Claude shook his head gently. "No, I cannot. And you cannot go. You must get back to Biri and Claudette."

"They can get along—till we come back together . . . Please! please!" Vayu embraced him—held him. He was no longer a young man, but a boy again; a boy pleading and sobbing. "I will not leave you, sidi. I will go with you anywhere—stay with you always. Oh please, Sidi Claude, take me—take me—"

Claude still shook his head. "No," he said. "Go, *fous le camp!*" He pointed to the floor. "And take your half of the belt, or I will throw it after you."

He tried to smile. Perhaps he did smile. And Vayu took the belt and slowly rose and stood before him.

"And now, *salaam, mon vieux,*" said Claude. "*Salaam aleikum.*"

Again the ship's horn hooted. In the corridor there was the sound of a gong and a steward's voice.

"*Salaam,*" said Vayu, his voice a whisper. "*Salaam, my sidi—*"

Then he turned. He ran. He was gone.

The brief clearness was gone.

Where there had been clearness, there was now dimness. In Claude's eyes was a blurring, a tingling, a sensation strange and uncontrollable, that he had never known before in all the years of his life.

Turning to the wall, he covered his face with his hands, and wept.

39

"Vayu," he said. "Vayu—"

And a voice answered.

But it was not Vayu's voice. It was a woman's. It spoke in French. Then he opened his eyes. And everything was white. As white as the salt flats of Lake Assal. The ceiling was white, and the walls, and the bed. The figure beside him, beside the bed, was white: the figure of a nun. And he remembered where he was. He was in Marseilles. In a hospital.

He remembered other things.

But not all things.

He did not remember the sea. For he had not seen the sea. Nor fellow passengers, for he had not seen them either. He remembered a steward with a red face and a doctor with a sallow face; and the doctor's needles. Later, a blurred, confusing hour on a stretcher, with voices and faces around him. And then a bed. This bed. He remembered nuns—many nuns—and gentle hands, gentle faces.

He remembered questions.

"How old are you?"

"Thirty-six."

"Your residence?"

"Entoto, Abyssinia."

"No, in France, monsieur."

He had thought.

"In Paris," he had said. "Number 18 Rue Martine."

"Your next of kin?"

He had thought longer.

"Madame Natalie Morel."

"Relationship: wife?"

"No, mother."

"Of Number 18 Rue—?"

"No. Of Cambon. Département des Ardennes."

He remembered the nuns—and the doctor. Not the one in Aden, nor the one on the ship, but another, a third one. And then a fourth. And the third and fourth talking at the far side of his room. He remembered pain. And more needles. And a sort of pulley hanging from the ceiling, with his leg hoisted high into the air. Then there had been needles (again). There had been doctors and nuns and voices. And a paper. He had signed the paper. He had made some joke about signing—about the problems of penmanship while writing on one's chest. And then he had smiled, and slept; slept long and deeply, as if in a cave far beneath the earth.

Now he was rising from the cave. Into light. Into whiteness. And into pain. He looked up, and the pulley was gone; his leg was no longer suspended above him. But the leg hurt. His knee burned with a pain even more intense than under the desert sun. He looked down along his body, along the sheet; at the contour of the sheet; and suddenly he pulled the sheet away. The nun beside him tried to stop him, but he got it down, got it off, and saw the bandages on the stump of his leg. The stump did not extend very far in the bed, for the leg was off at the thigh.

Then he slept again—the sleep of needles. At intervals he awoke, and someone was speaking or holding a spoon to his mouth; but he remained awake only briefly before slipping back into darkness. How long this went on he did not know. But one day he awoke and it was different, for he did not sleep again for a while; and the next time he was conscious longer, and the next time still longer; and now there was only a dull distant aching in the leg that was not there. The doctor came and went, and the nuns, and he knew all the nuns now, by face and name . . . or thought he did . . . until one day a nurse stood at the door (one of those he knew), and said, "This way, please, Sister Annamarie," and a strange nun entered the room. Those of the hospital wore white, but this one was in dark brown, with only a white coif framing her face, and she came quickly in and knelt by his bedside, with bowed head.

"Do not waste your time, or God's, praying for me, Sister," he told her gently.

And then she raised her head, and he saw her face. And she was not very young—many of the hospital nuns were younger—but her face was smooth and delicate, almost childlike; her eyes were as blue and clear as the eyes of a child; and when he saw the eyes he knew her, and he said, "But the sister who brought you called you Annamarie."

"That is my name in Christ," said his own sister. "But to you I am always Yvette." And rising, she kissed him on the cheek and forehead, while the clear eyes blurred with moisture; and then she sat beside him holding his hand.

"Mother could not come," she said. "There is the spring sale in the store, and she said she could not trust the clerks without her. But I was able to get leave. The Mother Superior was very kind. And I have come, Claude dear, to take you home."

She came each day thereafter—twice a day, each time for an hour. "And when I am not here," she told him, smiling, "I am praying for you. To Our Lord and Our Lady and the Saints, and they will hear my prayer, and soon you will be strong enough to travel."

The doctors came too. They examined him and consulted. There were fewer needles now, but still the pain had ebbed—it was scarcely notice-able—and one day they told him to sit up in bed, the day after, on its edge. Then came the time when he stood, holding onto the bed, and though he swayed he did not fall. And then crutches were brought, and precariously he crossed the room to a chair.

"I shall have to get used to the crutches," he told them.

But they shook their heads cheerfully and said, "No, that will not be necessary. Today there are great modern improvements, and you will have a fine artificial leg, with a joint at the knee, and made of the lightest metal."

And soon after, a man appeared and took measurements, and he was told the leg would be made and shipped to arrive in Cambon by the time he was well and strong enough to use it.

Then the day came when he was discharged. A new suit was brought, and the nuns helped him into it, and into one shoe, and neatly pinned up the right leg of the trousers. A clerk brought a bill, and he paid for it out of the francs which Vayu had got for him in Aden. Then a wheelchair was brought, and he was rolled down a ramp to the street and helped into a fiacre; and in the station was another chair, and he was wheeled to the train, and then he and Yvette were alone in a private compartment. Presently the train started. It moved out of the station, through the city, through suburbs, into the countryside of France. For a while a stranger, Sister Annamarie of the Carmelite order, sat beside him counting the beads of her rosary, just as Nagunda had used to do in the room in Harar. Then the stranger looked up, her clear blue eyes smiling shyly, and became again his sister Yvette.

His dream in the Arabian desert had not been false. For the store seemed enormous. It had spread out on both sides into the next-door buildings, and several clerks, some men, some women, looked at him curi-ously as he was carried through. But upstairs it was the same as always. His room was the same. There was the cot (one only, not two). There was the bureau, the table, the chair, the window, and, beyond the window, the walled yard. The plane tree beside the wall was green, for it was late spring; the privy again—or still—needed a coat of paint.

He looked at the yard and then back around the room, and this time saw that something *had* been added. Under the cot there was a chamber pot. The men who had carried him up had set him down on the chair, and he remained there for a while, simply looking. Then he took his temporary crutches, which had been left within reach, and moved back and forth for the short distances that the walls permitted. When he was tired he sat down again. Forgetfully, he tried to cross his legs and fell to the floor.

His mother came and went.

He and Yvette had arrived in the late afternoon, the busiest time in the store, and she herself had been behind a counter with the clerks, waiting on customers. But when she saw him she had done something he had never known her to do before; she left a customer. She came to the door. Once there, however, she had not known what to say or do—nor had he; for he was sitting on the linked hands of two men, with his arms on their shoulders; and she had merely stood looking at him for a long moment—at his face, his body, but *not* at his legs—and had then brusquely instructed the men how to take him upstairs.

Thereafter, her visits to his room were the same as they had always been. And she too was the same: almost identically. Though she was nearly sixty now, her black tight-pulled hair held no trace of gray. Her face was white, bony; and thin—but no thinner than before; her figure tall and thin, but still straight, as if braced with iron; and it was still clad in long black bombazine, with collar high at the throat, and from the throat, as always, hung the black ribbon and its cross.

Her eyes, too, were the same: as sharp as ever. And the sharpness was heightened by annoyance, as, one morning, she appeared holding an opened envelope. "It is from that hospital in Marseilles," she said. "A bill for extras. And the amounts are outrageous."

"Wasn't it addressed to me?" Claude asked.

"Yes, of course to you."

"Why did you open it then?"

"I wanted to see if they had been cheating you—and they surely did." She looked at the bill. "For instance, what is this business about a private room, may I ask?"

"They felt a private room was desirable."

"Desirable? Humph. Yes for *them*, I should say so."

He took the bill from her. "It is for me, Mother, not you," he said quietly. "And I shall take care of it."

"Do as you like—if you want to be swindled." She looked at him for a moment in silence. Then she said, "At least you have money, *hein?* I am glad to know that."

"Yes," he said, "I have some money. And I have been meaning to say to you: I want to pay for my keep while I am here."

"Humph. We will see. We will talk about it another time."

She wanted, Claude could see, to ask more questions; but he did not give her the chance. "And you, Mother," he said. "You, I gather, are doing all right."

"With the store, you mean? . . . Fairly. Fairly. . . . It is bigger now, of course, since I sold the farm and took it back. But there are problems, many problems. The expenses are terrible. And the clerks: utterly incompetent, for fantastic wages—"

"And Felix?" said Claude. He had from the first, of course, been aware of his brother's absence; but his mother had not spoken of him—nor, until now, had he. "Where is Felix?" he asked. "The last I heard he was back working for you."

His mother's face became, if possible, more rigid than before. "I took him back for a while," she said. "A few years ago. But it was hopeless. I will tell you what happened, but you are not to repeat it to anyone—even to your sister." She paused. "He stole," she said. "From the store. From me. And I put him out for the last time. I believe he is now in Lille or Rouen, or some such place, driving a cart again, when he is not drunk in bars. . . . But I do not know, and I do not care. I am through with him. He no longer exists to me. He is dead."

She turned away, as if to leave. But at the door she stopped, she turned back, she looked at Claude. And then she said—and her voice was different: "As you, too, were dead. I thought you dead—for a long time—"

Claude said nothing.

"I wrote to you so often. To Harar—Aden. Then at last to your company. And they said you were no longer with them. That they did not know where you were. You had disappeared."

"I am sorry, Mother. I should have written. I—I moved about a great deal."

"And things were not always good with you?"

"No, not always good."

There was a pause. His mother watched him. Then she said: "In your last letter, many years ago, you said that you were married. That you expected a child."

"Yes," said Claude.

His mother waited.

"They died," he said. "Not I, but they." He was silent for a moment. "There was—an epidemic."

He was sitting on the chair, by the table, and now he turned to the table, away from her. A few moments passed, and he thought she had gone. But then he heard her footsteps. He felt her hands. Standing behind him, she put her hands on his shoulders, and he felt them there, strong and bony, through the cloth of his shirt. She said nothing, and he said nothing, and after another moment she turned again and left the room.

His mother came.

Yvette came.

Then the day arrived when it was time for Yvette to return to her convent in Amiens, and she kissed him on the forehead and cheek and said, *"Au revoir, mon frère, mon cher frère."*

"When will I see you again?" he asked.

"It won't be long," she told him. "Amiens isn't so far . . . And you—" She smiled. "At least now we have you back, and I shall know where you are."

Then she was gone.

And he saw only his mother.

In spite of the size of her business, and the fact that she worked at it as long and hard as ever, she would have no part of the notion of hiring a cook, and herself prepared all meals, which she and Claude ate together in his room. Also, two or three times a day, she would come up from the store to see him. And the rest of the time he was alone. He lay on the cot and looked at the ceiling. He sat at the table and looked from the window. Occasionally, with his crutches, he walked about for a few minutes, and then sat or lay down again.

"You are too much by yourself," his mother told him. "Wouldn't you like to see someone?"

"See whom?" he asked.

"Some of your old friends. They are still about, I imagine."

He shook his head. "It has been too long. We would be strangers."

"Well, the priest then. He would be glad to come."

"Father Lacaze?"

"No. Father Lacaze has been dead for many years. This is Father Mercerau, a very fine young man, and—"

He shook his head again. "No, Mother, no young priest. I am all right this way, and it will not be much longer. Soon the artificial leg will come, and I will be busy learning to walk. And then when I have learned I must go to Paris."

"To Paris?"

"Yes, I have things to do there. Things I have promised the Emperor of Abyssinia." He stopped, seeing his mother's expression, and smiled a little. "That sounds strange, doesn't it, here in Cambon?" he said. "'For the Emperor of Abyssinia.' But it is true: there are things I must do for him. . . . And another thing too. Someone I must see. . . ."

He did not speak of Germaine. But he thought of her. That was all he did, day and night—instead of seeing visitors, instead of reading, instead of everything, even of sleeping. He thought of Germaine. . . . In the first shock of losing his leg he had tried to shut her out of his mind, in despair and renunciation; but that had ended even before he left Marseilles. The doctor had told him, "The metal leg will not be like an old-fashioned wooden one. Or a crutch. When you have practiced a little you will scarcely limp at all." . . . But even that was not the important thing. What was important was Germaine herself, and what he knew of her. She was not the woman to reject a man because he was crippled. She would love him no less with one leg than with two.

His stump ached rarely now, and then not badly. The only real pain came occasionally at night—in the knee that was not there—and in the morning it would be gone and forgotten. Sometimes his impatience to get to Paris became so great that he could scarcely bear it . . . and then he would pull himself up; he would move off and watch himself and smile inwardly, thinking . . . that for so many years he had lived alone, within himself, with scarcely a thought of Germaine; but that now, since her letter had come to Entoto—no, even longer, since he had met Michel Favre in that long-gone night in the bar in Aden—his whole life, first unconsciously, then consciously, had been—and was—the need to reach her, to claim her.

The hours dragged. And the days. But he contained himself. He waited. Once he sat down at the table and began writing a letter; but he quickly tore it up. . . . No, that was no good. No letters. No *Dear Germaines*. He did not want her coming to Cambon, to find him sitting helpless in his room. . . . It was *going* to her that counted. He himself. Under his own power. The leg would come, and he would practice, and he would go.

Then the leg came.

It arrived one morning, and one of the men clerks brought it upstairs, and when it was unpacked it gleamed like silver in the spring sunlight that streamed through the window. A page of instructions came with it, and Claude read them carefully. And for the rest of the morning, closing and locking his door, he experimented with it, adjusting the straps that went around his waist and over his shoulders and studying the workings of the hinged knee. It did not go easily. For the straps bit into him, the knee wavered, and, worst of all, the cup at the top of the leg seemed too small for his stump. But he persevered. "I shall get used to it," he thought. And at last he had it on, and kept it on. Sitting on the cot, he removed the pins from his trousers, pulled the trousers on, and when he looked down he had two legs. He pulled a shoe onto the metal foot, and it fitted. When he stood up, the pain in the stump made him wince; but he kept standing. Then he began moving about the room, supporting himself on cot, chair, and table, and at noon, when his mother appeared with their lunch, he was soaked in sweat, but smiling.

That afternoon he moved about the room, for short periods, without support. The next day he made his way down the hall to the kitchen and parlor. And the day after, he stood at the top of the stairs, took a tentative step, and plunged tumbling down the flight into the store.

He broke no bones. But he broke the leg. It had to be sent away, to a prosthetic appliance company in Paris; and while his leg went to Paris he remained in his room. A doctor came: a man he had not seen before, named Jardine. "No, I do not need a doctor," he had told his mother. "I am all right. When the leg comes back I will walk as well as you." But she called the doctor anyhow. He undid the wrappings, examined the stump, and prescribed a salve and a medicine.

And Claude waited.

Using the crutches again, he prowled the room restlessly. Sitting at the table by the window, he watched the late spring pass into summer and the dust thicken on the leaves of the plane tree. But increasingly, now, he lay on his cot, looking up at the ceiling; for his stump, in spite of the salve and medicine, had begun to swell; and with the swelling came pain—no longer the vague psychic pain in the knee that was gone, but gnawing physical pain in the flesh that was there.

He waited. For the pain to go. For the leg to come.

"The rest is good for you," his mother said. "You must rest and have patience."

"Yes, patience," he said.

"You would perhaps like some books to read? To pass the time?"

"No, I do not want to read."

"Have you thought of writing, then?"

"Writing?"

"Yes—as you used to. With all your travels, you must have seen some interesting things, and you could perhaps—"

"—sell something to the *Journal des Ardennes?*"

"Yes, why not? Now that you are a grown man, I am sure you could do much better than when you were a boy. You could write while you rest. Writing is not work. But it would keep you occupied." His mother paused, then added: "And also you might make some money. I should think some money would be very useful, after all the expenses you have had."

Claude shook his head. "I still have enough," he said.

"So? Hmm—I see. You *have* done all right then, *hein?* And you have saved?" She studied him with her sharp black eyes, and finally could no longer hold back the question burning inside her. "How much have you saved?" she asked. "Five thousand francs? Ten thousand?"

"Enough," he said. "Enough for my needs." And, as before, he would say nothing further, but turned the conversation to her and the store. . . . "And you," he said, "—with enough for yours: why are you still working so hard? It is not good for you, at your age."

"At my age—hah! What has age to do with it, when one must work for a living? At a hundred, I shall still be working: ten, twelve, fourteen hours a day—"

And with a snort she drew her angular body up, and rose, and went down to the store. And Claude sat alone in the room, and looked at the ceiling, and at the chamber pot, and at the yard, and waited . . . until she came again; with his lunch, with his supper, with a medicine or fresh dressing that the doctor had prescribed . . . and he thought, "Ah yes, of course—I remember. *I shall enter the Kingdom of Savages, the Kingdom of Ham. I shall return with limbs of iron* (well, *one* limb of iron), *dark skin and furious eye. I shall have gold* (well, gold, silver, jewels—since Aden, paper). *Women nurse these fierce invalids, home from hot countries. . . .*

And what then?

Then—*I shall be mixed up in politics.* (With Hajj Pasha? The Emir Ismail? Menelik?)

And then?

Then—*saved.* Yes, *saved.* I SHALL BE SAVED. . . . ("How much have you saved? Five thousand francs?")

The words flickered, receded, were gone. What was left was the room, the yard; above the yard, the summer sun; and the sun grew hotter. His stump was hot, and his body, and his forehead. As he lay on the cot the sweat soaked his clothing; when he sat up it ran from his forehead into his eyes. And then he closed his eyes. And when he closed them, the room, too, receded and was gone; the yard was gone; all that remained was the sun; and he was no longer in Cambon, he was back again in Africa, in the dust and heat and glare of Africa, on a swaying camel, in the desert, under the desert sun. . . .

Then his mother was there again. And she said, "While you were sleeping, a couple came into the store and asked for you."

"A couple?"

"Yes. Their name was Vuiton."

"Vuiton?"

"A tall man and a fat woman. I think you used to know them when you were at school."

Claude shook his head. The sun's flaming seemed to fill his head. "I don't remember," he murmured.

"They are coming back. You don't want to see them?"

"No."

His mother turned to leave. Then she changed her mind and stopped and watched him for a moment. "I have said before and I say again," she said, "—you are too much alone. You should sometimes see someone, talk with someone."

He did not answer.

"If you will let me speak to the priest—"

"No. No Father Lacaze."

"I have told you: it is no longer Father Lacaze. It is Father Mercerau. He is young and strong, with deep faith, and I am sure that to talk with him would be of help to you."

He shook his head again. "No thank you, Mother. I do not need his help. My faith is all right—my own kind of faith—and when the leg comes back, I too shall be all right."

His mother hesitated. Then, once more, she turned to go.

"But if you could send word," Claude said, "to Michel Favre—"

She looked back at him. "To whom?"

"To my friend Michel Favre, at the Banque du Nord. I should like to see him. . . . And Albert, too. You know, Monsieur Chariol. If you could send a message . . ."

He broke off. He closed his eyes and put his hand to them. "I—I am confused," he said. "It is from sleeping. I am sorry. . . . No. No, I am all right, Mother. I need no one. I will be all right."

Then his mother went. And he was again alone. He lay on the cot, his eyes still closed, listening to the dim sounds from the store below. And then through these, presently, he heard another sound, a different sound—the sound of music—and he lay listening to Vayu softly singing and playing the *krar*. He opened his eyes, and Vayu was there. He raised his head, and Vayu moved. Rising and holding his crutches, he went across the room toward Vayu—toward the movement—to the mirror above the bureau, in which his own reflection moved slowly toward him, and now stood still. He stood and looked at himself—as he had once looked in the same mirror, years before, when he had come home to this room, sick and broken, from London.

Then his face had been white—as white as his mother's. Now it was dark; even after the weeks indoors it was dark as an Arab's, a mask of leather and bone. Then it had been a boy's face. Though sunken and ravaged, it had still had the contours of youth, youth's smoothness of flesh, the cheeks covered with soft down, the head a tangle of wild yellow hair; and with a scissors he had cut the hair away until his head was bare as a skull. Now the face was an old man's—of a man of thirty-six, yet old and withered—the sparse hair and stubble the color of desert sand; and he needed to cut nothing to make it into a skull. For a long time he looked at the skull, at the mask of leather and bone. He looked beyond the mask, to the eyes that watched him. And the eyes, too, were old; they were cold, they were a skull's eyes. Yet not wholly a skull's, not dead, not empty—but still alive, still watchful, looking back at him steadily, burningly, with the bright burning cold fire of fever.

The leg came back from Paris. And again he struggled patiently with the recalcitrant metal and the harness of straps. The cup that fitted over his stump had been enlarged and repadded, but it still seemed too small; it pinched and chafed; and in spite of the layers of felt, each step, at first, struck against his flesh like the blow of a hammer. He kept trying, however; kept practicing, with tight lips and gritted teeth; first up and down, up and down, in his room, and then, again, out into the hall, and down the hall to kitchen and parlor (but avoiding the stairs); and gradually, as he moved, the pain diminished. In the parlor he sat at the walnut table and saw the long line of scratches, the carved keyboard, that he made as a small boy; and he thought, "No, it is not a *krar* I have been hearing, but a piano. The sound of a ghost piano in the room of ghosts."

When his mother appeared he pointed and said, "You still have not had it refinished. How is that? Does it no longer upset you?"

"It is not a question of upsetting," she answered, "but of what the cabinetmaker would charge for the work. When I moved back from the farm I had him look at it, and his price was outrageous—fantastic."

He walked back to his room. Again to the parlor. Around the table. Back and forth through the hall. When, after a few days, he had made a dozen consecutive excursions without support from wall or furniture, he asked that two of the men clerks in the store be sent to carry him downstairs, and he walked, on his own, through the store and into the street. This first time he went only half a block and then returned. But the next day he went farther, the day after still farther: to the Place du Sépulcre and the beginning of the Rue Gauchet. Later in the week, in the *place* he passed a group of boys walking together, swinging bags and kicking stones, and knew they were coming home from the lycée. But he did not go out toward the school—that was still too far—but in the other direction, along the Rue Gauchet, toward the center of town. He passed the library, and it was the same as ever, with its warped steps leading up to the dingy foyer, and *les assis* reading, hunched and motionless, at the window tables. Farther on, however, there were changes, with old buildings gone and new ones in their places; and the buildings were larger than before, the town larger, the crowds greater. Moving carefully, he threaded his way through the crowds without mishap. Among the passing faces he saw none that he knew, and no one, insofar as he could tell, knew him.

He came to the Banque du Nord, and this was a new building, broad and imposing. And it was here, as he passed it, that things suddenly went wrong. Until now the pain in his stump had been merely the usual dull ache that he was coming to accept as inevitable; but all at once, without warning, a sensation like a jet of flame shot through him, not only in the stump itself, but streaming outward from it, up his side, into his groin; and he had to lean against the wall of the bank to keep himself from falling to

JAMES RAMSEY ULLMAN

the street. Presently the spasm passed, but only briefly. And then it came again—and again—as he clung to the wall, lathered with sweat, struggling with all his might neither to fall nor cry out. In the next respite he looked around for some conveyance that could take him home; but Cambon, though larger, was still no town for public fiacres, and he had to stay where he was until he could master the pain enough to walk. Then, down the block a little, he saw an awning, a café awning, and on the green canvas the words CAFÉ DU PRINTEMPS. And struggling to it, he found a seat, and the waiter came, and he ordered a cognac. It went to his head. It went to his eyes, his brain, his blood stream, so that in a few moments café and street were revolving around him. But at the same time, mercifully, it went to all his body—to his pain—and the pain lessened, it dissolved. And he ordered a second cognac, and a third, and he thought, "Yes, the *Printemps;* it was always the place for magic." And again he called the waiter and said, "I would like to send a drink to the fat gentleman in the corner: my old friend the magician, Monsieur Archambault. . . ."

Then, later, he had left the café. He was on his way home. The cognac was still potent within him, and the pain no more than the usual dull ache; but he had to walk slowly and close to the walls, to make sure he did not stumble or sway. He came to the end of the Rue Gauchet. He was in the Place du Sépulcre. He was moving around it. And it was not until he was halfway around that he realized he had made a mistake; that he was not in the Place du Sépulcre but in the Place de la Gare. Across the square was the station, and there was a train in the station. As he turned to retrace his steps, a bell clanged, a whistle shrilled, the train pulled out. It was going in the direction of Paris.

The stump was bigger—there was no question about it—much bigger. Apart from pain, as a sheer matter of size, he could scarcely force it into the padded cup. And the flesh above the binding was no longer white but a purplish blue. One afternoon in his room he was sitting on the cot examining the flesh, probing it carefully with his fingers, when there was a knock on the door; and pulling on his trousers, he opened it and found one of the clerks from the store.

It was the youngest of the clerks, a tall thin boy of perhaps eighteen, who, on Claude's sorties to the street had helped carry him down and up the stairs. And as Claude looked at him he said nervously, "Excuse me that I disturb you, monsieur. I am Roland Didier, who works for your mother."

Claude nodded. "What can I do for you?" he asked.

"You—you—I mean, Madame Morel has gone out for a while. And I thought if I came up—if I asked you—you would be good enough—" The boy swallowed. In his hand, Claude saw, he had a book, and now, with an awkward jerky movement he held it out. "—good enough perhaps, monsieur," he said, "to sign this for me."

"Sign it?"

"Yes, your new book. I would be so grateful—"

Claude took the book from him and moved back a little into the room. Looking at its cover, he read:

LES POETES MAUDITS
Choix de poésies de
C. BAUDELAIRE
M. DRUARD
C. MOREL

He looked at the boy; then back at the book. He smiled slightly. *"Les Poètes Maudits,"* he said. *"The Damned Poets.* Rather a nice title, don't you think?"

The boy started to speak, stopped, and stood silent and embarrassed.

Claude turned a page.

"Introduction," he read aloud. *"The works of Charles Baudelaire are now part of our literary heritage. Those of Maurice Druard have become widely known. And now, in the last few years, it has been recognized that, along with these two, forming a triumvirate of supreme 'new' French poets, should stand the name of the late Claude Morel. . . ."*

He put the book down. "The *late—"* he said, still smiling. "And that, too, is rather nice."

"Monsieur, I am sure—" young Didier fumbled in confusion. "I mean —that is—if it were known—"

"That this Morel had a namesake?"

"You are no namesake, monsieur. I know that. You are he."

"Know it? *How* do you know it."

"Because this is not the first book of yours I have seen, monsieur. I have read your *Drunken Boat,* your *Illuminations,* your *Season in Hell.* And I had known that the author was from here in Cambon—that he had gone to Africa—and since you have come back I have wanted so much to speak to you, to see you. Really see you, I mean. But there was your illness—and your mother—"

He broke off again. Claude looked at him for a moment in silence.

"All right—so now you have seen me," he said. *"Ecce homo. . . . Ecce homunculus."*

Didier shifted uncomfortably.

"Or perhaps you are unfamiliar with Latin?" Claude said.

"No, monsieur. I know Latin. I studied it for many years at the lycée." The boy paused; then took courage and plunged forward. "And that was when I first read your poems—while at the lycée. Not in the classes themselves, no; it is an old-fashioned school, and we went only as far as Lamartine and Hugo. But when school was out I used always to go to the library and read all I could that was new and alive. The poems of Baudelaire, Mallarmé, Druard—and yours—yours most of all: not only because you too were from Cambon and I felt close to you, but because I felt that you, you above all the others, were the purest, the freest—the true leader of the *avant-garde*."

"Of the what?" said Claude.

"The *avant-garde*, monsieur."

"In the caravans of Africa we used to have an *avant-garde*. Now and then I would lead them; but more often, I am afraid, I brought up the rear."

The boy's mind did not make the leap. "And as the founder of the Symbolist Movement—" he went on.

"The Symbolist Movement?"

"Yes, of course—it is you, monsieur. Mallarmé is the chief theorist, perhaps; and the others of course have contributed. But it is you who have done the most in your actual poems: to break the old dead forms, to point the way ahead. In *The Drunken Boat*, *The Sonnet of the Vowels*, *The Ravaged Heart*. . . ."

The boy had lost his diffidence. The words poured out. His eyes shone—as Vayu's had used to shine when Claude talked of great journeys and far horizons. . . . But then, once more, he broke off. Diffidence returned, and shy embarrassment. . . . "You—you will forgive me, please, monsieur," he murmured. "I did not mean to talk so much—to interrupt you. It is only that—that I am so proud to meet you—so happy. And if—if you would do me the honor to sign your name for me—" He picked up the volume from where Claude had laid it. "—I would be even more so."

Claude stood for a moment without moving. Then he took the book and, going to the table, wrote his name with pen and ink on the flyleaf.

"Oh thank you, thank you," said young Didier.

Claude waved his gratitude off. He had been standing now since the boy had entered, and his stump was gnawing and burning.

"Now you had better get back to work," he said, "before my mother returns. You will never get very far as a merchant, I am afraid, if you spend your time on such stuff as poetry."

Didier took the book and held it lovingly. "Yes, I know—that is true, monsieur," he said. Then he smiled shyly. "But also, I shall not get far as a poet if I spend all my time selling merchandise."

"As a poet?" Claude looked at him sharply. "You mean *you* are a poet?"

"Yes, monsieur. I am trying to be. It is the hope of my life."

"If you are a poet, what are you doing in Cambon? What are you doing in this store?"

"I was born in Cambon. Last year, when I left the lycée, I had hoped to go to a university, but my parents did not have the money. So I have found work to earn my living."

The pain in Claude's stump was growing worse.

"Earn your living?" he demanded. "Why?"

"So that—"

"A poet does not earn a living, boy. The world *gives* him a living—out of admiration and gratitude." Claude's voice was harsh and rasping. He wheeled around on the boy and now his cold eyes glittered. "If you are a poet," he said, "get out of here. Get out! Go downstairs now and walk out of that store. Go to the church steps with a piece of chalk and write, *merde à Dieu*. Go to the priest, your teachers, your parents, and tell them, '*Va te faire foutre!*' If you are a poet, be a poet, a *voyou—a voyant*. Get out on the road, in the alleys, in the ditches, under the bridges. Steal your food, go to jail, leave jail, steal more. Get drunk, boy. That above all—get drunk. On absinthe. On hashish. Go to the blue-green caves, the deep caves. Become a pervert. Roll in the filth of the streets, in the filth of life, shouting, '*va te faire foutre*'—to life, to man, to God—yes, above all to God, the Creator—because He is the enemy. He is the lie—for you are a poet, a seer, a prophet—you, not He, who is the creator—yes, you *you* YOU, the poet, who is truly God Himself. . . ."

The glitter of his eyes had become a burning. The burning, outward and visible, of his flesh and brain. His voice rasped and broke and was silent, and he stared at the boy, who had backed to the door and stood rigid and afraid. In one hand he held his book, and with the other, now, he reached out a little, frightenedly—or pleadingly?—and seemed about to turn, to vanish. . . . And then Claude said—and the burning died, his voice was different, it was low and gentle: "Yes. Yes, I remember. That, too, I remember. *Hold out your hand to me . . . please . . . I beg you. . . .*"

The boy stood motionless, and there was silence.

"Have you written much?" said Claude at last.

"Yes, monsieur," the boy said faintly.

"And you think it is good?"

"I think that some is good."

"What have you done with it?"

"Done?"

"Have you sent it to editors?"

"I have sent a few poems, yes."

"But they were not accepted?"

"No, monsieur."

"Would you like me to read them?"

"*You?* Would I like—?" Young Didier's face came alight again. "Oh monsieur, Monsieur Morel—" He could scarcely speak. "It would be so wonderful! I would not have dared—"

"When you have time," said Claude, "bring them to me. Leave them here and I shall read them. In a while now I shall be going to Paris, and if they have promise I shall take them with me and see if something can perhaps be done."

Didier stood transfixed—in ecstasy. "Oh monsieur—" he said, and tried to speak again.

But Claude raised a hand. "That is enough now," he told him. "I am tired."

The boy opened his mouth once more. But all that came out was, again, "Oh monsieur—"

Then he was gone. The door had closed. Claude sat at last, on the cot, and he *was* tired. His stump ached. His stump burned. His groin burned, and his side—and all his flesh and his blood and his brain.

He lay down and closed his eyes. After a while he reopened them and, looking at the door, called "Vayu—Vayu—"

But there was no answer.

The next day the boy had brought his poems, and now they lay in a neat sheaf on the table. But Claude did not sit at the table. He lay on the cot. He lay in the stifling heat, in the grinding pain, and waited for the pain to pass. But it did not pass. It grew worse. He could neither bestir himself nor could he sleep. The doctor had prescribed a sedative powder, which his mother had brought him, and he began to take it, but with no effect. Then he took it in larger quantities, and the pain ebbed slightly, and with a great jerk of his will and body he rose from the cot and went to the table. He picked up the poems and began reading. But he could not read. The words blurred, the lines wavered, and presently he rose to go back to the cot. As he reached it he tripped over the chamber pot, which he had neglected to push under the cot, and fell, tipping it over. He tried to rise, but could not, and was still lying on the floor, in his spilled excrement, when his mother came, bringing his supper.

He had not broken the metal leg. But he did not use it again. The doctor came and examined him and pulled thoughtfully at his beard. And then he said, "It is better that you do not use it for a while; that you use the crutches again. But best of all that you lie still and rest."

So he rested. He took the sedative powders. But soon, even with larger doses, their effect was negligible, and pain tore at him like a clawed beast. The doctor came again, and this time, instead of powders, there was a needle. He came often now—with more needles.

And, with the needles, Claude slept. And in his sleep he journeyed.

He no longer had to be carried downstairs; nor were his travels merely down the street, to the Place du Sépulcre, to the Rue Gauchet. They were great journeys, the journeys of old—across the miles, across the deserts, to far oases, white cities, blue horizons—and sometimes he was alone; but more often not; more often he was with Vayu, with Fitzsimmons and Jensen, with Egal or Lutz or Nagunda; and the camels swayed; they passed through the black lands, the brown lands, the wastes; and beyond the wastes ran a great escarpment looming purple in the sunset. He was going to Abyssinia, returning to Menelik, with his caravan behind him; and he turned to view the caravan . . . but something was wrong . . . for it was not there. He had lost the caravan; forgotten it. He had forgotten the books and the teachers. And he rose on his camel's back, searching. . . . He rose in his bed and looked around. And it was night . . . yet not altogether night. The darkness was not blackness; it was thinning, day was coming. In the room he could see the familiar outlines of bureau, chair, and table; and on the table was a sheaf of papers (for he had forgotten this too); and beyond the table was the window, beyond the window the sky; and the sky, too, was not black, but deep gleaming violet-blue.

In the distance a whistle shrilled. A train whistle. He listened.

Then he rose.

He groped for his metal leg, but the leg was not there. . . . All right, it would be the crutches. . . . He pulled on shirt and trousers, and the right trouser leg hung limply, for it was unpinned; and he had no pins. . . . But that was all right too. . . . He finished dressing, went to the table, put the sheaf of papers in a pocket, and left the room. In the hall it was dark and quiet, and he moved carefully toward the head of the stairs. Reaching it, he sat on the topmost level, and then eased himself slowly down the steps on his rump, pulling the crutches behind him. The store, too, was dark and empty; and, now using the crutches, he moved swiftly across it and then out the door into the street.

The town still slept. The street was silent in faint dawnlight. And he too made no sound as he moved on his rubber-tipped crutches. He crossed the Place du Sépulcre, entered another street, and then another, threading his way through the town, until he came to . . . where? . . . For now suddenly he had stopped; he was looking around him. And he saw again, as in the dream, that something had gone wrong. He had come to an open place, but it was not the Place de la Gare. Before him was not the railway station, but a park—a park with grass and trees—the trees of the Bois d'Amour. He looked down and saw that something was wrong there too. He had no valise, no bag. How could he go to Paris without a bag? And how could he have carried a bag, with his two hands holding the crossbars of his crutches? . . . Despair filled him. "All—*all*—has gone wrong," he thought . . . But the despair did not last. He looked up: at the park, the trees, the brightening sky beyond; and despair faded—as pain faded when the needles, cool and blessed, entered his flesh. And he thought, "No, it is not wrong, after all. It is as it has always been—except for the crutches." And he moved on through the flaming sunrise into the Bois d'Amour.

He came out of the park and stood beside the River Meuse. He sat on the bank, watching its thick yellow coils, and then rose and moved on again: first along the river, then across a field, then into a forest. *He moved through the forest of the Ardennes—the forest of wolves*, of Huns; the forest of dreams—and sometimes a crutch caught on a root or bramble, and he stumbled; but he did not fall. He moved on steadily, untiringly, toward the heart of the forest, and then at last he stopped, he sat again, at the foot of a tall oak; and a bird appeared on a branch above, and sang and watched him, and then flew away.

He sat in stillness. He heard the stillness. He watched the branches, the leaves, the sky and sunlight above the leaves. Then he thought again. He thought, "Why am I here?" But even as he asked, he knew the answer. He had come for the same reason he had always come. . . . To write. . . . With the old familiar movement he reached into his pocket and found paper. Then he searched for a pencil, but could not find one—and for a moment was upset—until he looked down at the paper and saw that it had already been used. In his hand were many papers, a whole sheaf of papers, and they were all written on, all filled with poems; he had already done his day's work. And he smiled and slept.

In his sleep, though, the smile faded. It grew gradually darker. And in the dark he was no longer alone. There was movement around him; there were shapes; there were eyes, eyes like yellow lanterns, and the eyes moved closer—the wolves, the hyenas, moved closer—and they were around him, then upon him. Their fangs tore at his flesh, rending, devouring. They had eaten his leg. Now they ate his flanks, his back, his groin, his belly. And he screamed in pain. He awoke, and still he screamed, for the pain was devouring him. Frantically he reached in his pockets for a syringe, a needle—a magic needle; but there was none; the doctor would not let him keep them. There was only the paper, the sheaf of poems, and he pressed the papers to his mouth to stifle the sound of his voice.

He seized his crutches. He tried to walk, and fell. He tried again, and fell again, and abandoning the crutches, crawled on his hands and one knee. Toward evening he reached a road and lay motionless at its edge, and presently a farmer came by in a cart and picked him up and took him home.

The sun set earlier—always earlier. There had been days when it was light until almost nine; then until eight, and seven; and now it was dark before six. As spring had passed into summer, so now summer passed into autumn, and when night came it was cold. Often it was cold in the daytime too, with the sun lost behind rain or fog, and the branches of the plane tree stood black and bare against the heavy sky.

The fog seemed to enter the room, to weave in gray veils about the cot. "It is the fog of the escarpment," he thought. "Soon, now, I shall rise above it into the bright sunlight of Abyssinia." But no sunlight came. When the fog lifted it was night, and when night ended it was gray again, and cold. Before, he had lain on the cot sweating and burning. Now he was chilled in his blood and his bones.

The stump of his leg had grown enormous. The swelling and discoloration had spread farther up his trunk, and the glands in his armpits were so enlarged that he could no longer use his new crutches. But at least the pain was now less than it had been, for the doctor came regularly with his needles. One day he came, not alone as usual, but with another doctor, who made an examination, and when they left Claude could hear him talking softly with his mother in the hall.

His mother was working harder than ever; for she was planning a new section of the store—a department for gifts and novelties, such as were sold in the best stores of Paris—and wanted it open in time for the holiday season. Through the days there was the sound of hammering from below, as carpenters put up new racks and counters; and his mother moved about giving orders, inspecting merchandise, interviewing applicants for the new clerking positions that would soon be open.

"Clerk, clerk," he thought, lying on his cot. There was something about *clerk* that he was trying to remember; something, perhaps, about Marcel Rappe. . . . But then at last he had it, and it was not about Rappe. It was about the boy downstairs, the sheaf of papers on the table. And when his mother next appeared he said, "I should like to see young Didier —Roland Didier."

"Who?" she said.

"The young clerk. The tall thin one."

"Oh." She remembered. "That one. . . . He is not here any more. I discharged him, it must be two months ago. He was hopeless, useless: always mooning around. And almost as stupid as your brother Felix."

A voice called from downstairs: *"Madame! Madame Morel, s'il vous plaît!"* And she left.

When she returned later with his supper, he said, "Clerk—clerk" to himself, but again he could think only of Rappe.

When the meal was over she went out, but returned in a few moments carrying a cake topped by a lighted candle. "Had you forgotten?" she said. "It is your thirty-seventh birthday."

One morning, perhaps a week later, he awoke and he was cold. But this time it was not only his body. His mind was cold too. Cold and clear.

When his mother brought his breakfast, he was not lying in bed but sitting on the chair. And he said to her, "Mother, I must leave."

"Leave?" She stared at him. "What are you talking about?"

"I must go south, where it is warm."

"Go south? Fantastic! How can you travel? You cannot even—"

"Yes, I know: I cannot walk. Or use my crutches. But I came from the south without walking, and I can return the same way." He looked away from her toward the window and the cold October fog beyond it. Then he added, "It is the only thing that will help me, Mother. The warmth of the south, the light, the sun."

"But during the summer here—"

"Yes, I know. In the summer I complained of the heat. Now I complain of the cold. I am a difficult invalid. . . . But of the two, the cold is worse. I am more used to heat. I shall go south: first back to Marseilles, then somewhere on the coast nearby. I shall spend the winter there, and I think maybe it will help me. By spring I should be able to use the crutches again —or even the metal leg—and then I shall return north. I shall go to Paris, where I have affairs to attend to."

His mother argued.

She left, and returned, and argued.

Then the doctor came, on his regular visit, and Claude told him his decision, and still she argued. But the doctor listened to Claude attentively; he pulled at his beard; now and then he nodded. And later, when she had seen the doctor out, his mother returned and said reluctantly, "Well, he thinks it is not a bad idea. That it may do you some good. Or at least no harm."

". . . But you cannot go alone," she said. "That is out of the question."

". . . And I cannot go with you. There is the store—the new department. I must keep a watch on everything: ten, twelve, fourteen hours a day."

". . . But there is your sister. Yes, your sister. Her Mother Superior is an understanding woman. She will give her leave again, and Yvette will take you south, as she brought you north, and stay with you until you are settled."

Then Yvette was there again. Sister Annamarie was there. She stood beside him in her dark brown robe and white coif, her smooth child's face gently smiling, and she bent and kissed him on cheek and forehead, and packed the one small valise that, with his crutches, was the sum total of his baggage.

The train was due to leave at three fifteen in the afternoon, and a carriage had been ordered for two thirty, to get them to the station in ample time. By two o'clock, he was fully dressed and waiting. He had left the cot and hopped to the chair by the table (for he could not manage the crutches), and now he sat there, in unfamiliar collar and jacket, with trouser leg neatly pinned (by Yvette); and he felt scarcely any pain, in his stump or elsewhere, for the doctor had paid his final visit at noon, bringing syringe and needle. Yvette sat across the room, on another chair that had been brought in, her head bent to her rosary. But whenever he looked at her she was instantly aware of it, and looked back at him and smiled.

Downstairs there was some sort of trouble. He heard his mother's voice raised in anger; then a man's voice, and his mother's again; and when presently she came upstairs her lips were tightly drawn and her eyes were flashing. "It was a man with ladies' handbags," she said, "who called himself a salesman, but I called him a thief. Because my store is not in Paris, on the Grands Boulevards, they think I am some sort of country imbecile."

She looked sharply about the room: at the valise, the bound-together crutches, the new overcoat and hat that lay on the cot. "You have forgotten nothing?" she asked.

"No, Mother," said Claude.

"You have your watch, your medicines, your handkerchief?"

"Yes, Mother."

"And your money?"

"I have what I shall need," Claude said. Opening the table drawer, he brought out a thick paper-wrapped packet. "The rest I shall leave with you."

He gave her the packet, and she held it in both hands, looking down at it.

"I would suggest putting it in the bank," he said. "Or at least in the safe. And there is no need to count it. It is exactly one hundred thousand francs."

She looked up. Her black eyes fixed on his face.

"You want me to keep it for you?" she said at last.

"No, not for me. It is yours." He smiled a little. "You are the family treasurer."

Her lips moved again, but made no sound.

"Perhaps after a while," he said, "I shall apply for a loan. If I need to. That will depend on my—plans."

"But—"

"But now it is yours. For the store, for the house, for what you want."

Claude's smile returned. "Perhaps, as a start," he said, "you could have those scratches removed from the parlor table."

There were steps on the stairs; a knock on the door. "The carriage is here, madame," a voice said.

Then the door was open. Three of the men clerks came in. One helped Claude on with his overcoat and gave him his hat, and then, with a second, carried him downstairs, while the third followed with Claude's valise and Yvette's and the crutches. They moved through the store and into the street, and Claude was lifted into the carriage, and Yvette sat beside him.

"So goodbye, Mother," he said.

"Goodbye—son."

The Widow Morel stood in the street: tall, gaunt, and black: black except for her white bony face and white bony hands. And now, suddenly —almost, it seemed, inadvertently—she raised a hand and touched it for an instant to Claude's cheek.

Then she said, "I have made arrangements for the carriage; it is two francs, no more. And there is no need to tip the driver."

40

Forward:
the march, the burden and the desert.
From the same desert, in the same night,
always my tired eyes awake:
always....
And in the dawn we shall enter fabulous cities.

But the dawn was far off. It was dusk. Then night. The countryside of France slid by in darkness and rain, and he closed his eyes and shifted in his seat.

"It is only another hour now to Paris," said Yvette.

He reopened his eyes. "To Paris? We are going to Paris?"

"Of course, dear. We must change trains there, remember? The same as when we came north."

"Oh."

But he did not remember. Of the trip north, he remembered leaving Marseilles and reaching Cambon, and that was all. The rest was a blur of movement, of dream; of the narcotics from the needle of the doctor in Marseilles.

"The doctor in Cambon is not so good," he said.

"What, dear?" said Yvette.

"His needle is not so good. It is starting to hurt. Do you have the powders?"

Yvette opened her small traveling purse and took out a folded paper. Then she left the compartment and returned with a glass of water, and he swallowed the powders and closed his eyes again.

"So the little *mioche* comes again to Paris," he said.

"What, dear?" said Yvette.

"We must be careful when we get out at the station, or the ticket taker will catch us."

"I have the tickets, dear. Do not worry about anything."

He must have slept then. He did not see the suburbs or the stone walls or the cinders or the jumping place. When he awoke, the train had stopped, Yvette was touching his arm, and beyond the window was the face of a porter.

"One more, please," he said.

"What, dear?"

"One more powder. Please. Now."

"When we are on the other train," said Yvette gently. "The doctor said you should not take them too often."

Then he was being carried again. He was in a wheelchair. He was riding through the high cavern of the Gare de l'Est, with Yvette beside him and a porter behind; and then they were out of the cavern, at a line of fiacres; he was lifted once more, and they were in the fiacre, and he said to the driver, *"Numero dix-huit rue Martine."*

Yvette looked at him in astonishment. Then she said in her gentle voice, "No. No, dear. We are going to the Gare de Lyon."

"The Gare de Lyon?"

"Yes. For the train to Marseilles. It leaves at ten o'clock."

"At ten? Oh—yes. . . . And it is now—what? Only eight. There is plenty of time, and I have affairs to attend to."

"But, Claude dear—"

"There is time, I tell you." And to the driver he repeated brusquely, *"La rue Martine. Vous savez où ça se trouve?"*

"Oui, monsieur," said the driver.

It was still raining. The rain pattered on the windows of the fiacre and gleamed blackly on the asphalt streets. Above the streets the gas lamps flared like yellow moons. But in the rain there were no crowds. Even on the Grands Boulevards there were few people, little traffic, and their horse's hoofs clopped loudly in stone stillness.

They went south on the Boulevard de Strasbourg, then on the Boulevard de Sebastopol. Once Yvette started to speak, but changed her mind, and they rode on in silence. Off to the right now were Les Halles, dark and sprawling; to the left, already behind them, the squat stone mass of the *Ecole Centrale*.

Then they came to the Seine, the Ile de la Cité, and Notre Dame. Claude looked for a moment at the church, and then away, in the other direction; at the river flowing black toward the west; and on the river's bank, in the middle distance, he could see through the rain a huge shape thrusting skyward.

"You have heard of the Eiffel Tower?" asked Yvette. "It was built two years ago, for the Great Exposition."

He nodded. But he was no longer looking at the tower. They were crossing a bridge, and he looked down and to one side, at the embankment beneath the bridge. A figure was moving there, toward the shelter of the bridge, under a gas lamp; and as they passed it raised a whiskered face and peered up at them with small bleared eyes.

"What is it, dear? What is the matter?" his sister asked him.

"Nothing," he said, turning away. "Nothing." And now they were off the bridge, on the Left Bank. They were in the Place St. Michel. On the Boulevard St. Michel. . . .

And he said, "Let me have a powder, please."

"When we are on the train, dear," said Yvette.

"No, now. Please. Please, now."

"The pain is bad again?" she asked.

"Yes, it is bad."

"But there is no water."

"I can take it without water."

She opened her purse, gave him a powder, and he swallowed it. Then, sitting back, he watched through the spattered window as they moved away from the Seine down the blocks of the Boul' Mich. Here too the streets were almost empty in the rain and cold. In the cafés, the crowds were far back under the awnings or in snug yellow-lighted rooms behind glass partitions. But now and then a figure passed, alone, on the black pavement. And he saw them. He knew them. . . . A man, white-faced, in a long cape: that was Dar Misheram. . . . A small man: that was Herz. . . . A tall broad man: that was Hugo (back from the dead). . . . An old one; withered, drunk, swaying; swaying and falling to the street, and looking up from the street with the dead eyes of a skull.

The fiacre had driven on. It was gone. Lost. He stood beside the old one and pulled him up, and said "*Merde!* Get up—control yourself!" And then he and Druard walked on in the rain, under the gas lamps. They did not go to a café. They had just left a café. They passed the dark gray walls of the Sorbonne, came to a side street, and in the lamplight he saw a sign, and the sign said RUE DE LACQUE; and they walked down the street and into a house and up three flights of stairs into a room. The room was small and snug, like a lighted cave, a blue-green cave. In one corner was a desk. And he sat at the desk. And now Druard was gone; he was alone at the desk; alone with pencil and paper, and he took them and wrote. He wrote: *Autumn. Risen through fog and rain, our boat turns toward the port of misery, the enormous city with fire-and-mudstained sky.*

... And he tried to write on. But now he was no longer alone. There was a knocking, a voice—a woman's voice, saying, "Claude, dearest—" And he looked up toward Germaine. But it was not Germaine. It was Yvette, his sister; it was Sister Annamarie, the nun. The nun said, "Claude dear, we are there, at the Gare de Lyon." And he was in another wheelchair, in another cavern—not a cave—and not blue-green, but black and sooty—and he was carried again onto a train.

Yvette had reserved a compartment in the new type of coach called *lit-coupé*, and he lay on a sort of couch with his head on a cushion. Sitting opposite him, Yvette opened her valise, took out a brown package, and said, "You should have something to eat now. And then you can sleep through the night." ... But he shook his head. He was not hungry.... There was something on his mind. Something he had forgotten. And he could not remember what it was.

The train started. It was out of the station, in the night and the rain. He lay for a while with his eyes closed, and then opened them and asked, "Where's Mother?"

"She had to stay at home, dear," said Yvette. "With the store."

He was silent again, listening to the click of the wheels, watching the rain on the black window.

Then he said: "We are children of the sun."

"What, dear?"

He looked up, and there was Druard again.

"We are children of the sun," he repeated. "We are going to the sun. Except that we got on the wrong train and are going to London. In the morning we will be in sunny London—"

And he laughed.

He laughed louder. The sound of laughter—or perhaps, now it was not laughter—filled the compartment, drowning out the click of the wheels. From far away he heard, again, a woman's voice calling his name. But he could not find the woman anywhere.

Then he *was* in London.

But not in fog and rain. In whiteness. In the hospital. Druard's revolver had fired, and his knee was shattered. He was in the hospital bed, wrapped in bandages, wrapped in pain, and soon now they would come to question him.

When he heard a voice, however, it spoke in French, not English. When his eyes focused he saw a nun—and the nurses in London had not been nuns. There were two nuns in the room: one in white, who stood beside the bed, and one in dark brown, who sat on a chair against the wall. The brown nun was Yvette, and as their eyes met she rose and came to him.

"We are in Marseilles?" he murmured.

"Yes, dear—in Marseilles."

"And—"

"And you had a hard time on the train. It is best that you rest a few days."

He rested.

He lay resting in the bed. In a sea of pain. The nuns came with medicines and compresses; the doctor came with his blessed needle. But the needle was no longer blessed. It no longer worked. Or if it worked it was only for an hour, a few minutes. Then pain returned, monstrous and consuming.

"Where is Nagunda?" he asked. "Where is Nagunda with her herbs?"

"Who, dear?" said Yvette.

He didn't know who.

"I mean, where is Mother?" he asked.

"Mother could not come," said Yvette gently.

There were more needles. He slept. He woke. His body, beneath the pain, beneath the sheet, felt bloated and enormous, and he tried to push back the sheet to look down at it. But something was wrong: he could not move the sheet. He could not move his arm. He tried the other arm, and that too would not move; nor would his left leg when he tried to bend it.

"Yes, the infection has spread a bit," the doctor told him, "and there is slight paralysis." Then he added cheerfully: "But it is nothing to worry about, *mon brave*. Soon we will have you back as fit as ever."

Then he slept again, and dreamed, and in his dream he was no longer motionless in a bed, but moving across seas, across deserts, across mountains, toward a white city; and the sky above the city was not fire-and-mudstained, but a luminous violet-blue.

When he awoke he said to Yvette, "I was talking, wasn't I?"

"Yes, dear," she said. "You were on one of your trips, I think."

"I have been on so many trips. So many." He was silent for a bit. Then he asked: "And you—you haven't traveled yet, have you? I remember when I visited you in Cambrai, you said you wanted to."

"Yes, I would still like to. So far I have been only in Cambrai and Amiens—and on these two trips with you. But I think in time, if I am really worthy, the Order will send me somewhere. To China, perhaps. Or India, or Africa."

"Yes, there are nuns in Africa," he said, "—though I didn't see any. But I knew a priest, a Capuchin. And he was a good priest. A good man."

"I am glad to hear you say that, dear," said Yvette.

Another time he awoke and said, "Come closer, Sister."
And she came and stood beside the bed.
"I want to pull your pigtails," he said.
Yvette said nothing.
"But there's no need for you to get angry. After I've pulled them I'll give you a rubber ball. And on my next trip I'll send you a scarf and a locket."

The next time, she was already close. She was kneeling, head bowed, by his bedside.
"No, none of that," he told her. "Please. None of that."
She looked up at him earnestly with her clear blue eyes. "To pray is good, brother," she said. "For all of us. It would do you good, truly, if you tried yourself."
"What would do me good," he said, "is a gourd of araq."
"You said you thought so much of the priest you knew in Africa. There are some fine ones here too, some wonderful Fathers. Don't you think you might like to—"
"No," he said. "No." And he shook his head.
That was the only part of him he could move: his head.

Then:
"Where's Mother?" he asked.
"You will be back with your mother soon," said the doctor. "We are all very pleased with your progress."
"What you should be pleased with," said Claude, "is your lying. Now go away, please. For the love of God, go away."
But the doctor did not go. So he went away himself. He went on another journey, a long journey. To Paris (when had he last been in Paris?) —to London, Basel, the Alps, then Italy. Then he came to the sea. (From his bed he could not see it, but he could smell it, taste it, feel its reflection in the blue southern sky.) And he crossed it. He crossed many seas. He crossed the jungles of Java, the wastes of Tripoli. He crossed the wastes of Egypt, of Arabia, of Somalia, of the Ogaden; through the dust, the wide horizons, the arches of rainbows; he moved on into Africa, to the far lands, the hidden lands, to what he was seeking, what he must find; the far ones, the savage hidden ones . . . the Nigger Queen, the Nigger King . . . and he had found them. Yes. Yes. He had found them both. And then left them. . . . Then lost them. . . .
And now the doctor was gone. There was only Yvette. And raising his head a little, he said to her in a low voice, but clearly, "Is my valise still there in the corner?"

"Yes, dear," said Yvette, "it is still there."

"At the bottom, in the blue trousers, you will find my wallet, and in the wallet about ten thousand francs. It is not mine, it is expense money, and what I do not use should be returned. When you have paid the hospital and all other bills, send what is left to. . . . Do you have something to write with?

"Yes, dear," said Yvette.

". . . to His Imperial Majesty, Menelik, Negus Negusti, Entoto, Abyssinia." He spelled out the strange words for her; then added, "You had better also write *via Aden-Tajoura;* the post office can be very stupid. And in a note say it is from me and I am sorry."

He was silent for a while.

Then he said:

"I have already taken care of Vayu and his family. . . . And to Nagunda I can send nothing."

There was something else in his valise, too. And later, again waking, he remembered what it was.

"You will find a sheaf of papers in an envelope," he told Yvette. "On the envelope is the name Roland Didier and an address in Cambon. But do not send it to him. . . . Do you have something to write with? . . . Send it to Madame Germaine Chariol, 18 Rue Martine, Paris."

Again he was silent for a time.

Then he said:

"With this it is not necessary to send a note; only the boy's name and address. When she sees what is in the envelope she will know what to do."

Now Yvette receded. The doctor, the nurses, the room receded. He lay alone: one soul and one body.

I shall be free to possess the truth, he had said, *in one soul and one body*.

And he had been free: yes: no man had ever been freer. . . . But what truth he had possessed he did not know. . . . Truth, like the world, like God, had many faces, and the faces rose and flickered and dissolved, like the images in a dream.

He was watching faces now—many faces—as they passed before him. A face whiskered, leering, with bloodshot eyes. A face like a weasel's. A face like a skull's. And the skull's mouth was a black hole, with broken teeth, and from the hole came a whisper, "Dear boy, dear boy. . . ." There was another face, not a skull's, but dead as a skull's, dead and white; it was Chariol's. And behind it, beyond it, another face that he could not see. There was the face of Egal, hanging bloody in darkness; the face of Nagunda, black in darkness; and in her swollen belly another face, lost in darkness—a face unborn, that had never been. There were the faces

of Father Lutz and Vayu, and these were close above him; and Lutz was
smiling, but Vayu was weeping; and Claude asked, "Why does he weep?"
And Lutz answered, "Because he loves you, and you are going to live. I
have never seen a man with such a will to live. . . ." And then he put out
his hand to Claude, and Claude tried to take it. But he could not reach it,
could not find it; it was another hand that was there, a long hand, with
yellow eyes behind it; and Lutz had receded now, he was far away, and
Claude called after him, "Father! Father!" . . . And the father turned; but
it was not Lutz. It was Abou Dakir and his pale eyes watered, and he said,
"Yes, my twenty-first son?" It was Menelik, King of Kings, his face broad
and pocked and leonine. It was Mackenzie, the Scotsman, his face broad
and red and streaked with coal dust. It was one without a face—like his
own son; one in uniform, blue, with the striped sleeves of a general, and
he was riding—riding fast and far, far away, receding, vanishing—and
Claude ran after him, calling; calling again and again, "Father, Father!"

"Yes, my son?" said a voice. (Not Abou Dakir's.)

And he opened his eyes and saw Lutz.

No, not Lutz. There was no beard, no Capuchin robe.

It was another priest who stood beside him, beside the bed in the
hospital room. And he said, "You wished to see me, my son?"

"No," said Claude. "No, I do not wish to see you."

"Sister Annamarie said you had called."

"Sister Annamarie was wrong."

He closed his eyes again. It was easier to keep them closed. The priest
was farther away now, but he was still speaking. Claude could hear his
voice. He could hear words. He heard the word *faith*. He heard *sin* and
repentance and *grace* and *salvation*. He heard *prayer*. He heard *soul*. He
heard *redemption*. And he thought, "Yes, once I knew a prayer, a prayer of
redemption, the soul's redemption: *My eternal soul . . . redeem your promise
. . . in spite of the night alone . . . and the day on fire. . . .*"

Then the priest's voice was gone. There was another voice: Yvette's.
And she was pleading. "Please, please dear, please Claude. Come back to
us. To those who love you. To the Church. To God. . . . Speak to the Father.
Confess to him. Give him your heart, your soul, and he will absolve you,
he will bless you. Give your heart and soul to God—oh please, my dearest
—and He will embrace and hold you in His love forever. . . ."

Then her voice, too, was gone. The words were gone.

"Words—words—" he thought. Was that all that Life and Love and
God were made of: words?

No, not for him!

For him, to hell with words. *Merde* to words. *I have buried the dead in my
belly*.

. . . But out of his belly, now, the dead rose. It was the belly itself that was dead: a swollen sac, a carcass. His stump was dead, and his other leg, and his loins and his trunk and his arms and his hands. The body, the flesh was dead, all of it. But out of the flesh, from the putrescence of death, there rose that which was not death; there came that which had never come from Nagunda's belly; there came Life, Life itself. His own belly had burst, and from it poured word and image, dream and vision, rising, soaring, shining, like golden birds; and again he saw the birds, he saw the jungles, the seas, the rainbows, the star-archipelagoes, the silver star burning in the southern sky; he saw the *being of beauty*, clothed in words, robed in vision, but beyond cloth and robe was the core, the essence, the truth itself; and this he saw too, again—as he had once seen it—only now clearer than before, brighter than before, bright in newborn life, in birth, in resurrection. . . .

And he heard a voice, a voice intoning: *I am the resurrection and the life: he that believeth in me, though he were dead, yet shall he live: and whosoever liveth and believeth in me shall never die.*

And then Yvette was there, Yvette kneeling beside him. And she said:

"Oh Claude, it is so beautiful—"

"What is beautiful?" he said.

"What you have been saying. In your sleep, your dreams. The pictures —the colors: all you have seen. And the words you use to tell it."

She was holding his hand. He could not see it. He could not feel it. But still he knew that his hand was in hers.

"Mother told me that you had once been a poet," she said. "It had been long ago, she told me, but she was wrong. You are still a poet. What you dream, what you say, are full of wonder and beauty."

She was silent a while. Faintly he felt her hand.

Then she said, "There is another wonder, dear. Another beauty. The most wonderful and beautiful of all. There is Our Lord and Christ His Son. . . ."

He lay motionless, with eyes closed.

"Oh please, Claude, please!" she said again. "Turn to Them. Come to Them. It will bring you such joy, such peace. It will fill your soul with light. . . ."

He still lay silent, unmoving.

"The Father is coming again soon. When he comes . . . please . . . he wants so much to help you. God Himself wants to. If only—only—"

The words faded. Where words had been there was now another sound: the soft sound of sobbing. And now at last Claude moved. He opened his eyes and turned his head and saw the face of his sister close beside him. He saw the child's face, the blue child's eyes, the eyes welling with tears; and he wanted to raise his hand, the hand held in hers, to touch her, to comfort her. But the hand would not move.

It was his lips that moved.

"It would make you happy?" he said.

And she could not answer. She could only look at him. And then, her eyes streaming, she bowed her head and pressed her lips against his hand.

Now the priest was there again. He seemed always to be there. He was talking... talking... and then Claude was talking. He heard the dim croak of his own voice. He was confessing. But what he confessed he did not know.

Then it was the priest talking again. He held a cross. He was giving absolution. He spoke in French and in Latin, both with a Marseillais accent, and Claude thought, "No silver wreath for him on Prize Day." And he murmured to the priest, "You should watch your diphthongs."

Then there were candles burning. There was lace and white cloth all around him. There was more Latin—with no improvement; the priest touched his eyes, his ears, his nose and lips; and Claude thought, "With Nagunda it was different. She put the oil on herself."

The priest talked on. Words... words... Not from his own belly, but from another; the bottomless belly of ritual. Beyond the words, beyond Latin and oil and lace and candles, were golden birds and the shining sky.

There were white nuns around him, murmuring *Ave Marias*. Murmuring, "Lord, have mercy. Christ, have mercy. Lord, have mercy...." Then the white ones were gone, and there was only the brown one. Only Yvette. And now she was weeping again, but this time differently, for her face, close to his, was transfigured with happiness.

He smiled at her.

He said, "Hello, princess."

In his life he had not made many people happy. Vayu, perhaps. Now Yvette. That was all.

He had matters of his own to attend to. He raised his head and said clearly:

"Do you have something to write with?"

"Yes, dear," said Yvette.

"Then take a letter please.... *To the Messageries Maritimes, Port of Marseilles.... Gentlemen: Enclosed find my draft covering first-class passage* ... no, that's a waste; make it second ... *for your next scheduled sailing to Port Said, Suez, and the Red Sea Ports. I will appreciate your informing me of the embarkation time. Very truly yours, et cetera....* Do you have it?"

"Yes, dear," said Yvette, "I have it."

Then he slept.

And he awoke. And it was morning.

Always my tired eyes awake, he thought. *Always....*

But now they were not tired. They were clear and strong. His body was strong. And he rose from bed. On a chair were his clothes, and he put them on: white shirt, starched collar, black tie, his blue serge suit. When he had dressed his mother came in and said, "Don't forget your umbrella." But he said, "No, Mother, no umbrella; the sun is shining"; and she did not argue. Then Yvette was there, and Felix too, in their Sunday clothes, and they began the march to the church; but before they reached the church there was a change—the others dropped behind and were gone—and he walked on alone, past the church, out of the town, through the park, and along the river into the forest. He walked as he had used to walk, without lameness, without tiredness, strongly, steadily; and he came out of the forest into fields, into towns and cities; and beyond the cities were mountains, beyond the mountains was desert, and he walked on through the desert wastes. In the wastes, he knew, were the ones who waited: the ones with sloping backs, with great jaws, with yellow eyes. But they came only in the darkness, and it was not dark now. The sun poured its light on him, bright but not burning. The day shone in its brightness, but was not on fire.

He saw the end of the wastes. He saw a glint, a gleam. And it was water. It was a tiny patch of water—a pool, a puddle—and in the puddle was a boat, a child's boat, a toy: a thing of paper and thread and the twigs of bushes, as small and frail as a May butterfly. . . . Or so it seemed at first. . . . But as he approached it, it grew. The puddle grew. It spread out before him, to each side of him, becoming a pond, a lake, a bay, a sea; it became a great harbor, with the sea beyond; and in the harbor, at dock, was the boat—the ship—and it too was larger now; it was tall, immense, with masts soaring skyward and sails set full. But there was no wind. It did not move. It was waiting. It waited, ready and tall and still; not swaying, not heeling—not a drunken boat but calm, majestic—and its sails shone like gold, in sunlit radiance, between the sea and sky.

He was on the shore. On the dock. Then he boarded the ship. He stood on the deck, at the wheel, and looked out at the harbor; and the harbor was clear. He looked at the sky, and the sky was clear; it was cloudless, stainless; deep violet-blue, omega-blue. Then he looked at the shore, but the shore was not clear. It was hidden; a mist had covered it, a mist stirred now by the faint movement of a wind; and he knew that behind the mist, hidden, lost, was the one thing he had forgotten.

He reached out his arms. "Germaine—Germaine—" he tried to say. But what he said was "Mother—Mother—"

Then the wind rose. The ship put out to sea.

Lightning Source UK Ltd.
Milton Keynes UK
UKHW04f0618221018
330961UK00002B/633/P

9 781943 910441